THE INNER COMPASS
TRILOGY

BOOK ONE

AWAKENING

A NOVEL BY
ABBY WYNNE

PRAXIS
PUBLISHING

First published in 2022 by Praxis Publishing
www.praxispublishing.ie

Edited by Elizabeth Henry and Niamh Deveraux

Source ISBN 978-1-9163627-2-7
Ebook Edition 978-1-9163627-3-4

Dedicated to all the magical children in the world,
no matter how old they may be.

DISCLAIMER

This is a work of fiction. None of the techniques in this book are designed to be utilised by any reader. In other words, you are not encouraged to use any of the techniques in this book with others or on upon yourself.

The information provided in this book is designed to provide an insight into the subjects discussed. Not all opinions offered here are those of the author. Conflicting information may have been delivered from time to time at the author's discretion for the purposes of the story, delivered from the point of view of a character.

This book is not a training manual. If you wish to become a fully trained psychotherapist, Reiki practitioner or shamanic practitioner you are encouraged to find a teacher or school in your location that is appropriate for your training needs.

This book is not intended as a substitute for the medical advice of physicians. For diagnosis or treatment of any medical problem please consult your doctor. The author is not responsible for your or any specific health needs and is not liable for any damages or negative consequences from any treatment, action, application or preparation to any person reading or following the information in this book.

If you are interested in learning more about the techniques or want advice on your healing process, you are invited to read the author's non-fiction books, listen to her podcast or find her via social media, or her websites www.abby-wynne.com and www. abbysonlineacademy.com

BOOK ONE

AWAKENING

A NOVEL BY

ABBY WYNNE

'The exercise of true magic does not require any ceremonies or conjurations, or the making of circles or signs; it requires neither benedictions nor maledictions in words, neither verbal blessings nor curses; it only requires a strong faith in the omnipotent power of all good, that can accomplish everything if it acts through a human mind who is in harmony with it, and without which nothing useful can be accomplished.'

— Paracelsus

PREFACE

When it comes to solving a problem, sometimes the obvious answer is the best answer. But perhaps the answer you're looking for is more elusive, the type of answer that's complicated, elegant, and only appears when you're not thinking directly about the problem.

You're engrossed in something else – a daily activity perhaps, or contemplating the workings of the universe. Then, when you least expect it, the answer reveals itself to you. Of course, it doesn't simply creep in of its own accord, like a cat stalking its prey, or be so brazen as to explode into your mind like an atom bomb. No, there must be some sort of trigger for you to take notice of it.

Inspiration could come in the shape of a blade of grass curling up in a certain way, or the swoop of an eagle's wings as it flies past, if you're lucky enough to live somewhere where eagles do that type of thing. Your brilliant idea could spawn from a conversation you overheard in a café, the specific combination of words coming out of strangers' mouths unlocking a chamber of secrets in your mind. Perhaps you bent down one summer's afternoon and picked up a coin that glittered in the grass, and when you held it up between thumb and index finger, it sparkled in the sunlight in a certain way. The sky was bright blue and a white cloud passed by at that exact moment, the sparkle and the blue and the exact shape of the cloud throwing you back into a dream that you had when you were five years old. And in that dream is where you found what you were looking for.

Clearly there's a reason for the way that solutions come, but we human beings never look for reasons; we live more in the dramas of our problems and our entanglements. We seem to thrive when we are stressed or worried; we love to fret, we chase our tails, run around in circles and go over and over the tiniest and finest details, making smaller and tighter spirals of thought. Only by loosening these spirals, by changing their frequency, can we create a space for the solution to appear. This requires an expansion and an unfoldment, which is the exact opposite of the thing we want to do when we are distressed.

So where do the best solutions come from? Do they really come from our dreams? And how do our dreams merge and blend into everyday reality?

Dreamscapes are landscapes where we run free, a theatre where anything can happen, the place where our magic resides. Our dreams are access points into the field of our astral existence where we live in our immensity, where we forget that we are small, because we are actually not small. Our bodies are small, but our souls reside in vast planes; we span dimensions that contain worlds, universes and galaxies holding the entirety of our essence, holding everything we have ever done or seen, everything that goes beyond our physical bodies and our material reality.

We incarnate into bodies, are given an ego, character and personality, and sign a contract with lessons to learn. We live our material lives, we dream, we age, and at some point our body dies, but our soul lives on. We are the ultimate paradox, being human, we live forever and we also do not. And echoes of all of the aspects of our soul that have ever existed, and all of the learnings through all of our incarnations, reside in the planes of our astral dimensions.

So how do we access this learning? These hidden treasures and gifts that lie buried in our astral field from our previous incarnations? They are imprinted in holographic form, embedded in our energetic field – proverbial diamonds and sapphires in the mud, waiting to be discovered by our latest incarnation.

Remember that glittering coin which lay in the grass waiting for the perfect blue sky and white fluffy cloud to trigger a remembering? What about the eagle, or the conversation in a café? In our more vulnerable dream state these images, which are laden with meaning, trickle into our consciousness and tuck themselves away somewhere safe and warm to wait patiently until they are needed.

As new incarnates begin to build their life for what seems to be the first time, they may stumble over something they recognise, which doesn't make sense. What if, during moments of disconnection from material reality, the hidden gifts from past experiences appear? What if humans need to tear themselves away from the illusion of what is 'real', to notice the magical stones glistening in their field?

Perhaps these gifts stay there, hidden in the psyche, glistening with promise, holding the exact potential that is required to push through whatever difficulty has arisen in the here-and-now, in the reality of the mind of the human, waiting to be discovered. Perhaps these gifts are the source of inspiration. If the incarnates accept what is offered to them and make sense of it, they might embody that gift and enlighten their incarnated self. But if they cannot, perhaps they become overwhelmed and the gift goes back into the mud, unused, unappreciated, and the challenge goes unanswered.

But let's make this about you, since you are here, reading this. You are navigating this life, thinking you have nothing to support you, thinking you're a beginner at most things, believing you know nothing more than what you have experienced in this lifetime alone. Yet all you need to do is remember who you are in your immensity, plough your field, so to speak, seek your gifts, find the creations you made in previous lifetimes and allow them space and time to expand.

If you ignore this calling and keep going through life ignoring the diamonds, stepping on top of sapphires and sinking them even deeper into the mud of your field, perhaps some sort of conspiracy between the Universe and your soul is designed to stop you in your tracks. What if ignoring your calling causes an incident so grand it makes you fall into the mud so deeply, so that you become completely covered in it? While you seem to have no choice but to drown in it, you are actually being offered the opportunity to find the gifts within.

But it is not all love and light, dear one. Realising that many gifts lie in the darkness as well as in the light is one of the biggest lessons of many lifetimes. Know that this darkness is within all of us. We do not become whole until we accept all of it – darkness and light. We have created so many elaborate and complicated ways of hiding dark parts of ourselves, and we are especially successful at doing this as we have a busy field with many places to bury our secrets, and plenty of mud to cover them up with.

But they weigh heavily, these dark secrets that we bury. We place them deeply in the planes of our dimensions, so deeply that we hide them even from ourselves. They may look small, like rocks and stones, yet some are, in fact, as large as planets. Remember, we are immense. The fields of our existence go beyond the scope of what our minds can imagine. And this is what makes some people seem heavier than others.

Yes, indeed, perhaps you have noticed this: heavy people and light people, expansive people and contracted people. People who have spent the time clearing their fields and embodying their gifts are not afraid of their secrets, have faced their demons; these people are lighter than those who have not.

But there is one more thing you must know, dear one. The darkest of dark secrets have an energy and a life of their own. You can try to ignore them, but even while neglected, they attract in to themselves more darkness, which makes them stronger. The longer they are left to lie dormant, the more powerful they become and determined not to be ignored. They may, one day, spring into form. Call them demons, if you will. These demons from deep within can come out to play and disrupt and destroy our lives if we don't befriend them over a cup of Irish Breakfast Tea and address them directly, saying, 'I see you, I'm not running from you, what do you want? Let's talk.'

Shocking, isn't it? Having tea and discussion with a demon. Who would have thought? Yet, we must. For they are part of us, truth and lies, light and dark. The dark recognises the light, and just as diamonds can hide in the mud, darkness can hide in plain sight. It becomes dangerous though, when dark masquerades as light. Don't kid yourself. The darkness knows exactly what it's doing.

So how do we know what is dark and what is light, what is a lie and what is truth? And to make it even more confusing, who says we incarnate in chronological time? Who says that we only reside in one incarnation at a time?

Is there some sort of internal compass that can point us in the right direction? Perhaps. But before we can see our own darkness for what it is – a part of us that needs to be seen, heard, understood, embraced, embodied – we have to be strong enough to face it. Collective darkness, well, that's for another day.

Darkness is a space where love, of itself, cannot penetrate. And hidden deep within us are gifts that we haven't realised are there. These gifts make us stronger, they can give us the strength we need to face the darkness. Through our dreams we have the doorway in, we can access all of it. Once you open that door and step through it and into the planes of your dimensions, magical things begin to happen.

2002

Marissa Tori Rosenthal hated her last name almost as much as she hated her curly dark brown hair. She had hated both her first and last names for a long time, but since she turned seventeen she felt like she had almost grown into becoming an actual 'Marissa'. She had always loved the Tori part, but the Rosenthal still felt alien to her, as if it didn't belong to her at all. It was something that she wanted to pull out of herself, as if she could take out from the middle of her stomach and cut it away.

Marissa never felt like she belonged. She always felt there must have been a Great Mistake when she was placed into her family. When she was younger she often sat at her window looking out into the night sky waiting for her real parents to come and get her. Either they would land in the garden in a spaceship, or call to the door in the Royal Carriage, either would be fine, as long as they would come, and take her back home. To her *real* family. But that never happened. She had to resign herself to the possibility that she was indeed her mother and father's daughter, and, by seventeen years of age, she was beginning to reluctantly believe that she was in fact, her parent's child.

She decided in a rebellious moment that she did not need to be a carbon copy of her parents or play by their rules, or, indeed, by anyone's rules. However, she did it anyway, stick to the rules that is. Yet the things that she would rather be doing often played in the back of her mind.

Marissa walked to school every day with her heavy backpack on her back. Her school was twenty minutes' walk from where she lived and her mother always handed her her coat and pushed her out the door without fail, well before school was due to begin. The slower she walked the longer it took to get there, she didn't rush to be early, but managed to be exactly on time so she didn't have to speak to anyone. She wasn't particularly outgoing and didn't have many friends; looking back on her life she thought perhaps her sense of not-belonging was exacerbated by her lack of effort to belong. But she gave herself the benefit of the doubt as we do our best with what we know at the time.

Growing up as an Orthodox Jew in Catholic Ireland was a predicament that a specific few were presented with. Marissa's dark brown curls and sallow skin didn't give away her religious background so she would have managed to hide it pretty well except for the fact that she went to a Protestant school where morning prayers in the assembly hall were a daily occurrence. She was not supposed to attend such prayers, and by school policy, anyone not Protestant was required to wait outside the assembly hall during the prayers.

It was humiliating to be forced to wait around in a group of 'outcasts' while the rest of the student body were inside the assembly hall in prayer. Far worse than that, the 'outcasts' were summoned into the hall once the prayers were finished so they could hear the school announcements, which were for everyone. This was what Marissa dubbed 'the parade of the outcasts', where they had to walk down the centre of the assembly hall with the entire student body watching them stumble through, until they reached their classmates and could duck inside their familiar groups and breathe a sigh of relief. But by then it was too late, they had been seen, and were recognised as outliers, reinforcing Marissa's inner sense of 'not belonging' and unfortunately, creating an outer sense of the same thing. Not good. By the time she was sixteen, Marissa was sneaking into assembly as she much preferred hiding among her classmates and reciting the Lord's Prayer to being paraded alongside the 'outcasts'. However, hide as she would, her sense of not-belonging, remained long into her adulthood.

Marissa didn't actually consider herself religious, or orthodox, so going to prayers whether they be protestant or otherwise didn't create any internal moral conundrum, and of course she never told her parents she was doing it. She figured that the religious traditions in her family were more of a reason to get together and eat, rather than for celebrating God. In fact, she couldn't remember the last time anyone in her family had a conversation about, or even mentioned God, bar of course the occasional swear word. Marissa had stopped going to Temple a long time ago, as had her brother Eli, once their grandparents had died her parents only went on high holidays, probably because it was so ingrained and felt wrong not to.

It was no surprise to discover that Marissa really didn't really enjoy school, although her grades were above average. School was more of an endurance test for her, the school day seemed to go on forever. There weren't many subjects that she liked, but her favourite was chemistry. She loved how the teacher came alive, his eyes lit up when he spoke about his experiences working as a researcher in laboratories across the world. The students seemed to come alive too in response to him, asking him lots of questions that they genuinely wanted to know the answers for. As far as Marissa was concerned, it wasn't so much his experiences that fascinated her, but the chemistry itself. She loved thinking about the possibilities that existed when mixing different chemicals together. There was something magical about the process of taking one thing and transforming it into something else. When she was four she loved mixing ingredients that she found in the kitchen, making her own chemistry experiments, which had to stop once her parents caught her with bleach, chocolate powder and vinegar. She never liked baking and she wasn't good at mathematics, she loved reading but couldn't express herself well enough in English. For some reason chemistry made sense to her; when oftentimes her classmates were befuddled with some problem she would find herself explaining difficult concepts to them after classroom hours. When Marissa wore her lab coat and lit her Bunsen burner she felt more alive than any other time during the week.

'You're weird,' said Joanne, after Marissa explained some aspect of chemistry that was once obscure and suddenly made perfect only after coming out of Marissa's mouth. Joanne was her best friend from primary school, they met in junior infants and had always been close. Marissa loved playing wizard and witch with Joanne, she was always the wizard and Joanne the witch. Joanne wasn't sure if being a witch was good, or if a girl could actually be a wizard, but Marissa didn't care. She would stand at the glass door in the kitchen holding her arms outstretched, directing raindrops down the window using her magical powers.

'You're weird too!' said Marissa and they laughed. Joanne lived close by the school too. Since being in Secondary they stopped playing wizards and witches, instead they would go to the shops to buy ice cream or chips, reminisce about things that haven't happened yet, invent secret codes so they could pass notes to each other in class and discuss how time slowed down when they did things they didn't like, and how it speeded up when they were doing things they enjoyed. But as she got older, Marissa stopped believing in magic.

On this particular day in September it had just been raining. Marissa walked reluctantly to school kicking at the fallen leaves at her feet. She was always nervous of slipping on wet leaves, it had happened to her a few times and she ended up flat on her backside, soaked and feeling sorry for herself, so she was all the more cautious around where she stepped. There was an especially large puddle ahead and as Marissa slowed to approach it she noticed a strange sort of glistening on the surface of the water. She stopped walking and peered into the puddle and saw an old woman looking back up at her. Her heart leapt into her mouth, she looked away and shook her head in a double take, then looked into the puddle again, but *she really was there.* The old woman had long white hair and a shrivelled face like a prune, she wore many necklaces. Marissa froze for a moment, ice cold sweat trickling down her back. She looked away once more and caught her breath and decided she was seeing things. She felt tingles down her spine, the hairs at the back of her neck had risen, her whole body was shaking. When she caught her breath she noticed her heart was beating in a double palpitation. *That's very odd. I must be making this whole thing up. Mum always says I have an overactive imagination. Yes, that's it.* Bracing herself, holding her breath, she looked back into the puddle, the woman wasn't there. Instead it was her own face with her woolly hat, school scarf wrapped around her neck and her school coat half unfastened, her uniform showing through.

I knew I was making that up, I must have been making it up. How odd, why would I do that? She hoisted her backpack up onto her back and continued on her way, mulling over in her mind what might have happened. Was it an old woman in another dimension reaching out to me for help? Maybe she was on another planet? Yes! The puddle was a portal to another Universe? Or she was me, all grown up, Ha ha! That's funny. No, it's didn't really happen, it's just me, making stuff up again as usual.

Later that night as Marissa searched for a fresh shirt for school for the following morning, the full length mirror which hung on the back of the wardrobe door in her bedroom caught her eye. She was feeling playful so she crept up towards it slowly, seeing if she could approach it without appearing in it. *I wonder if that old woman is behind my mirror too? Ah that's silly, it was just the sunshine, the rain and my imagination – I didn't see any old woman in the puddle at all. I must be bored, it's the end of the summer and I really don't like going-back-to-school time. I guess I need to preoccupy myself with something a little more interesting than school.* Marissa turned and looked at herself square in the face in the mirror. Nothing unusual here; a new pimple coming up, curly hair dishevelled and slightly flatter than usual from being stuffed into a woolly hat, but it was her own face staring back at her, the one that she didn't love so well. *Nothing to see here folks, move along, move along.* She had a sense of a shadow hovering behind her out of the corner of her eye, she moved back to the mirror and looked at her reflection again, but it was gone. She shrugged her shoulders, put her pyjamas on and carried out her usual bedtime ritual. However, she couldn't get that niggling feeling out of her system that maybe the old woman *was* real, after all.

2012

CHAPTER ONE

It was a Sunday in early September, and a sunny Sunday at that. Marissa lazed in bed with her covers strewn about her, morning sun seeping in behind the curtains. Tobermory meowed insistently wanting to go outside.

'Okay, Tobermory, okay. I'm getting up.'

She reluctantly shoved the last of the covers off of her legs, they fell onto the floor in a heap as she stood up and got her bearings. Marissa opened the back door of her garden flat, the cat mewed appreciatively and slunk out to do its business. Opening the fridge to see what she had, Marissa grabbed the carton of milk, swigged a mouthful, then spat it out and shuddered. Looking at the date, she lamented not drinking it fast enough, as usual. *Into the bin with that.* She dropped the carton into the grey swing bin then plodded out the back door with the cat to sit in her favourite morning spot in the garden.

Marissa's one-bedroom flat was where she called home. It was small but comfortable, her bedroom had a double bed, bedside locker and wardrobe, and she had fitted a small desk just under the window up against the wall. She had just enough room for a collapsible chair which fit snugly underneath the desk. The ensuite was painted white and had a small marbled window to let light in, a sink with a small mirror on the wall, and a bath with an electric shower attachment. The living room had a fireplace at the back wall with a stone hearth, there was a small kitchenette and a door out to the garden on one side, and a large bookshelf filled with books on the other. She had fitted a small TV over the fireplace and had kept the comfortable blue two-seater sofa which came with the flat. She bought a coffee table with a shelf underneath and had 'procured' a large old armchair from her parents, which just happened to have been her favourite chair when she was growing up. The old worn cream covering now had a cream throw lovingly placed over it which was less cream and more brown from Tobermory's black cat hairs. She had long given up trying to extract them; it was Tobermory's favourite chair now.

Her kitchenette was white, well stocked with condiments and not so well stocked with groceries. There was a small gas hob and oven, the sink faced the window which looked out into the garden. She accessed it via a heavy wooden back-door with a lockable cat-flap that she had painted sky blue to match the sofa. She often left the door wide open to let the air and sunlight into the flat.

The flat got cold in the winter. Marissa loved lighting fires and cuddling up on the sofa with blankets to read a book, but there still was a chill in the air. She loved it in the summer, especially when the light streamed in through the windows and the open back door. Stepping outside there was a small sunken courtyard filled with garden pots, a round garden table and two deck chairs which were collapsed up against the wall of the house to give the illusion of having more space. A small wall beyond the courtyard cordoned off the rest of the garden which was mostly grass and a few hedges. The original garden had been very long, but the landlord had sold it to a neighbour who wanted to build an extension to their house. Marissa's garden was less than half of the size of the original garden but she didn't mind. It was a sun-trap in the morning, which she loved. Her very favourite thing to do was to bring her morning cup of tea outside and sit with it on the wall beside an old magnolia tree, savouring the morning air, the singing birds and the heat of the cup in her hands. She loved these quiet moments where she could disconnect from the world outside and sit with the flowers, feeling the heat of the sun on her skin. This particular morning was still warm, her summer flower pots were coming to the end of their flowering season, the weather would be colder soon so she was making the most of it.

Sitting outside listening to the noises around her, Marissa was drawn back into the dream that she had been having earlier. She didn't usually remember her dreams but this one was vivid, emotional, very real, and familiar. She had dreamed this particular one before – many times before. And always the same thing, she was in a barren place, there was a body of water and she was in the middle of it, on a single stepping stone. There were many other stepping stones around her, all slightly out of reach. It was like a puzzle, she needed to get to the shore but she didn't know how. All around her was stillness. It felt like she was inside someone's painting, the textures were otherworldly, they had a translucence about them. Marissa seemed to spend most of the dream looking at her feet on the large stepping stone, unable to move in any direction. She was wearing her old yellow tennis sneakers, the ones she had when she was seventeen. They were frayed at the edges from overuse, and her oversized shoelaces were dirty and tied in big bows. *I loved those shoes.* As she sat in the garden, she thought about how glassy the lake's surface was and how the sky's reflection on the water's edge made it impossible to peer into the waters beneath.

What really puzzled her, more than what was beneath the still waters or why she was there at all, was that she was always anxious in real life, but in the dream, she wasn't anxious at all. In fact, she was certain that if her dream was real, she'd be worrying about man-eating fish, giant water snakes or some other monster that she could conjure up in her mind, rising to the surface, opening its big mouth and swallowing her whole. But the Marissa in the dream was contained, cool of mind, clear-headed. She didn't recognise herself like that. It didn't feel like it was her at all. Ever since James had left she felt lost in the world, as if some part of her had left with him and hadn't returned, even now, three years later. Marissa had low-level anxiety most of the time, even with simple things like going to work on the bus or going out for her coffee. Therefore feeling strong and certain in her dream was unexpected and unusual and difficult to make sense of, and when the dream felt so real, as it often did, it took some time for her to return to herself.

Marissa played back the dream's images in her mind, ignoring her stomach as it started growling for breakfast. It was definitely her own face she saw reflected in the lake, those were her feet, her old tennis shoes. She saw her hands and arms too, as she had held them out to help balance herself. Dream Marissa was decisive, took calculated (and not so calculated) risks. Real Marissa felt the hunger pains growing stronger. She reluctantly padded back into the kitchen and opened up the fridge, one egg, a small bowl of leftover spaghetti, an old carrot and some lettuce. She grabbed the spaghetti, swung around and closed the fridge with her hip, and switched on the kettle for a second cup. It made a hissing noise, the kind of noise a kettle makes when there is no water in it.

'Oh shit,' she exclaimed and quickly removed it from its dock, opened the lid and was hit by a bout of steam in her face. She turned on the tap. The loud hiss of cold water on hot metal brought her fully back to reality and completely away from her dream world. Once she filled the kettle to a reasonable level for making tea, she switched it on again, went back into her room and opened her wardrobe to choose something to wear for the day. Most of Marissa's clothing was black. Black slacks for work, black vest T-shirts, black cardigans, her underwear were black, and most of her socks were bought in the same shop. *For convenience.* She had a few skirts but didn't wear them very often, usually if she had a meeting and wanted to make an impression. She pushed through the rack to find her favourite jeans, grabbed a black vest top (she had at least ten of these, each one the same, she liked continuity) and dropped them onto the bed. She went back to the kitchen and made her tea and brought it, and the spaghetti, back out to the garden, still wearing her pyjamas.

Tobermory was lying in the sunshine under the magnolia tree. He stretched out his claws and seemed to sigh with pleasure. At least, she reflected, James had left Tobermory behind. Completely black with green eyes, he was a handsome cat. He had a slight crook in his tail where he must have broken it when he was small, but in Marissa's eyes, he was perfect. She and James had inherited him when they moved into the flat as the previous tenant was offered a job in America and couldn't bring him. Never having had a cat before Marissa had let Tobermory teach her what he needed, and now she was very grateful for his company.

Once the spaghetti was in her stomach and the tea had been drunk, she went inside to get dressed to go out and meet Joanne. Checking her reflection in the mirror she decided didn't look too old today. She felt old most days, even though she was only twenty-seven. Some days she felt like she was eighty-one. She thought she wasn't beautiful, but she wasn't ugly either. She could walk into a room and not be noticed, which suited her just fine. Marissa liked people, as long as they were at a distance. She put on some black eyeliner, grabbed her pink scarf, locked up the flat and went outside.

It was only a five-minute walk to the bus stop. There was a line of people there, all of them gazing into their phones. Not to be left out, Marissa pulled her phone out of her bag then saw that the battery was at 20%. She felt a pull to go back to her flat and get a charger but the bus came into sight so she decided to keep going.

Marissa tapped her travel card off the ticket machine and went straight up the stairs, looking for a window seat. She enjoyed people-watching and could certainly see them better from the top deck. She used to love wondering what they were doing or thinking and making up stories about their lives. Marissa never classified herself as one of 'them', there was always a 'me' and a 'them'. Until James, of course, then it was an 'us' and a 'them', for a time anyway. Since James had left, Marissa was back to being 'me', and at times, she felt very alone. Familiar feelings of loneliness swept over her on the bus as she looked around at the people on the top deck with her. Only two of them weren't engrossed in something coming through a screen, and one of those was a baby. The other was the man holding the baby. He was looking into its eyes and smiling, and it was smiling back at him. Marissa was entranced by their invisible dialogue, she thought it was beautiful. Marissa loved seeing men with babies, it showed their sensitive side. Sinking back into her seat she wondered if she would ever feel able to let a man back into her life again, or ever have a baby of her own.

James had filled Marissa with the magical feeling that maybe someone could actually love her for who she was on her own merits, and not for any other reason. Perhaps she belonged somewhere after all. She had met him in college, he was a year ahead of her and had been studying engineering. It was love at first sight – well, she'd thought it was, anyway. They moved in together when she was in her second year and after two years together, they got engaged to be married.

There was uproar of course, from both families. He was Catholic and she Jewish. But they persevered as a couple and set a date, organised the registry office and found a venue for a party. They even sent out the invitations. It was tough going. There were many arguments with both families which took their toll on the relationship, and James even fell out with his own mother for a while. Everything seemed to brighten about a month or two before the wedding, as if the sun was coming out from behind a cloud after a heavy storm. So it came as a total shock to Marissa when James disappeared the week before their big day. He had left the note on the kitchen table. Marissa could remember the words even now:

Hi, love,

I'm so sorry to have to do this to you, but it's all too much for me. Your family, my family, the whole family thing, and you. Well, it's mostly you. Wedding is off. I can't do it. I can't do us anymore. Going to stay with my cousin in America. He has a job for me on his site. Sorry, love. It's for the best for both of us. Hope you can forgive me,

James xx

To be rejected by the only person in the world who she believed had ever loved her for herself was hard. Three years on and the wound still cut deep. Many of her friends and family didn't understand why she still didn't feel ready for a new man. But what was the point of even looking?

Her phone beeped in her handbag. It was Joanne.

Sorry, can't make lunch today, baby has tummy bug, vomit everywhere. Got 2 stay & mind him. Maybe next weekend? J x

Marissa's heart sank. Joanne was married with three children now and her world was quite different to Marissa's. Even though they didn't see each other often, they were still tangled together by the strong bonds of friendship and it never took them long to reconnect. *Maybe it's just as well, me getting all sentimental, I really don't want to hear about Joanne's children today. I might as well keep going into town.*

I could go for a walk, it's still sunny out. Stephen's Green and then a doughnut and coffee after sounds good...

Doughnuts. Who invented doughnuts? Who thought of taking dough and frying it, then stuffing it with jam, or cream, or covering it in chocolate? Mmm ... food of the devil. Guilty pleasure. A new doughnut shop had opened at the top of Grafton Street, Marissa imagined herself biting into thick, creamy, chewy deliciousness. She could definitely go there. She felt a little more cheerful already.

She texted back: OK, hope he feels better soon. Chat soon xM.

Marissa looked up as the man and baby stood to leave the bus. He held his baby tightly to his chest as he walked past, grabbing hold of the handrail and swinging himself gently as he manoeuvred down the tight spiral staircase. They got off at the next stop and Marissa watched from the window as they walked down the street, the man had shifted the baby to a jockey back position and both of them were laughing. As the bus pulled away she shook her head to shift the heavy feeling that had descended. *I'm on a doughnut mission.*

The sun was shining when Marissa got off at George's Street a few stops later. Dublin was a hive of activity as it always was on a Saturday around lunchtime. Marissa shouldered her bag and walked away from the crowd spilling off the bus. She felt slightly lightheaded suddenly, surrounded by so many people. *Feet on the ground. Breathe.* She took a moment and felt her feet inside her shoes, her shoes on the pavement, the ground beneath her. Her therapist had been very helpful by teaching her this grounding technique. It wasn't as beneficial when her anxiety was high, but there were just little waves of anxiety passing through her right now. She took her time focusing, with each step feeling her feet on the ground, until she felt better.

When she got to Stephen's Green she was much more settled, then the sun went behind a cloud, and it became a little darker and more chilly. Marissa shivered, then walked through the large gates into the park. *But look, it's lovely here.* The flowers were still in bloom even though it was so late in the season, the grass was perfectly manicured, and people were strolling around, enjoying the freedom

Marissa headed to the pond at the centre of the park. Passing the bandstand she decided to go onto the balcony. Standing there, looking down at the sun reflected off the water, Marissa couldn't help but remember the times when she'd been here with James. She shook her head. *Feet on the ground. Breathe. I'm really having a feeling-sorry-for-myself day today, amn't I?* She sighed.

Overwhelmed by anxiety and despair when James had left, Marissa had tried a suite of therapists but only really benefitted from a few techniques, like this one. She had actually received so little practical help from the therapists that she'd decided to become one herself – a better one. *That couldn't be too difficult, could it?* And, to her surprise, it wasn't. She'd started out doing an intensive course that had a high dropout rate and had found it quite enjoyable. The work came naturally, and some techniques were handy to use on herself too. Now, for instance, she could banish the unwanted memories by bringing her awareness away from them, and focusing on what was going on around her in the present moment instead.

What *was* going on? Ducks were squabbling over crusts of bread that a girl about three or four years old was throwing at them. Most of the bread was landing at her feet. The girl had fuzzy blonde hair which blew about her face in the wind. She was wearing a cute black raincoat with red cherries peppered on it in a pattern, and matching red wellington boots, perfect for splashing in puddles. *A raincoat? Isn't it a little warm for that? But yeah, it'll probably rain at some point.*

Walking down from the bandstand, Marissa moved to stand at the water's edge. She looked in but couldn't see her reflection. It was precarious to look any further, not wanting to lose balance she decided to try a mindfulness meditation with the other reflections on the water. But just as she began to concentrate on the reflections dancing on the pond's surface, loud quacking sounds interrupted her focus. She looked around for the duck and then realised the noise was coming from her handbag. She had chosen a quacking ringtone for her mother, she laughed and fished out the phone and answered it.

'Marissa? It's me, your mother.'

Marissa smiled wryly. Her mother always forgot that 'these new-fangled mobile phones' had a contact list. 'Hi, Mum, yes I knew it was you. How are you? What's up?'

Her mother sounded hassled. 'Can you make it to dinner tonight at your Uncle Lou's? I know it's short notice, but he wants to make an announcement and he wants us all together for it.'

'That's fine,' said Marissa, wishing she had enough of a life to be able to say that she couldn't make it. 'I was just going to have a pizza and watch TV,' she confessed. 'What time?'

'6.30-ish, but your father and I will be there at six. No need to come any earlier, though.'

'Okay.'

'See you later, baby.'

She hung up the phone then it died in her hands. *Nevermind. I'll enjoy the quiet time before the chaos later tonight.*

Marissa's family weren't a typical Irish family. They were possibly a typical Irish Jewish family, but there were so few of those it was difficult to make an accurate comparison. Her great-grandparents had come to Ireland from different parts of Russia, not speaking any English or Irish for that matter. Her grandparents, and her parents, had been born in Ireland. Marissa didn't think her family fit into any niche at all, however, at times, they might resemble a New York Jewish family, particularly at get-togethers where there was lots of food. She once saw a Woody Allen movie and realised they'd all be right at home there, it sent shivers down her spine. One thing could always be guaranteed, any family get-together would be chaotic.

The sun emerged from behind a cloud and Marissa suddenly noticed the stagnant algae, crumpled crisp packets, rusting drinks cans and glistening coins in the pond. Then the rain came down.

Marissa walked back to the main gate noticing the little girl's mother raising the hood on her little girl's coat. The doughnuts were calling. Which one was she going to have?

CHAPTER TWO

The house was full. Full of people, full of noise, full of smells, cooking and cologne. The familiar feeling of anxiety had come about five minutes earlier when she knocked on the door of her uncle's house. *Feet on the ground, breathe.* She heard someone make a joke through the door and the noise got noisier. *I can do this.* Marissa's mother opened the door and ushered her to come into the hallway.

'It's good to see you, baby. I'm so glad you could come. Did you have to cancel any of your plans to be here?'

For a moment, Marissa thought about making up some wild night out that she had to sacrifice for the family, then she thought the better of it. 'No, Mum, like I said on the phone, I was just going to have a pizza and watch TV.'

Marissa wasn't sure if it was a look of approval or disappointment that crossed her mother's features, it left as swiftly as it came, but some part of it hung in the air for just a moment longer than it should have, leaving the air tasting slightly sour.

'I'm a little nervous, I wonder what your Uncle wants to tell us. I hope it's good news.'

'Yeah, Mum, me too.'

Louis' house was spacious and bright, but tonight, with the whole family present, it didn't feel spacious at all to Marissa, even in the hallway. She loved her family, but it became quite claustrophobic when they were all together. So many strong personalities in one place could be overbearing. Marissa sometimes felt like she was in a chapter of *Alice in Wonderland,* she was not so much wanting to join the Mad Hatter's Tea Party as wanting to shrink down and hide under the table.

A waft of expensive perfume filled the air as Marissa's Aunty Naomi glided over to say hello. Her shoulder-length brown hair was swept off of her face and freshly coated in layers of hairspray. She wore a stripy apron over her floral print dress and she looked too perfect to have been standing by the oven all afternoon. Marissa suspected that she had been heating the food rather than cooking something from scratch. But it always tasted great, so she didn't mind.

'Marissa, darling, great to see you! It's been such a long time. How are you?' Naomi held out her perfectly manicured red-finger-nailed hands and clasped Marissa's hands in her own.

'I'm fine, Aunty Naomi. Dinner smells great – you must have been cooking all day.' Marissa said with a smile, pulling her hands back and putting them deep into her coat pockets, trying to deflect the attention.

'Oh, thank you. Yes, slaving over a hot stove, me! But I must admit I got some help from that little deli in the village – their food is just divine. I'd better check the potatoes. Glad you could make it.' She drifted off again in the direction of the kitchen.

'Let the girl come in and take off her coat at least,' said a familiar, comforting voice from behind.

'Dad!' Her heart warming, Marissa turned to see the big, friendly face beaming at her. 'Hi, Dad!' Marissa went to him and her body softened immediately as his arms wrapped around her.

He whispered in her ear. 'You can escape in a couple of hours if it's too much for you love. Just wait long enough to hear Uncle Lou's announcement, whatever it is about.'

'Thanks, Dad. I'm okay, really I am. I've been doing better these days.'

'Good girl,' he said, pulling back from her but still holding her and looking her up and down. 'You look tired. How's the job going?'

'Good, thanks Dad. Pays the bills for Tobermory and me.' Marissa usually couldn't hide anything from her dad, but tonight he seemed a little preoccupied.

'Good girl. We can catch up properly later.'

He went into the living room. Marissa was alone for a moment, so she took the opportunity to catch her breath. She hung her coat up under the stairs and looked at the wall for a few seconds, pressing her feet into the soles of her shoes and slowing her breathing down. Then she meandered into the dining room where her cousin Amanda was playing a game on her father's phone.

'No! It's my turn!' shouted Marcus and stood up, stamping his foot. He was eight, Amanda was twelve, but she seemed much older for her age. She was straight-laced, there was no joking around with her unless she was the one making the joke. Amanda had her long brown hair scooped back into a loose ponytail and tied with a ribbon. She wore a blue plaid dress and shiny black school shoes with white socks. Marcus was in his Saturday trousers with a blue shirt which had a stain on it, probably from a food item that he had stuffed into his mouth, and missed. Marissa was glad she ditched her jeans at the last minute and put on a blue pencil skirt, a cream blouse and a black cardigan from her work wardrobe. And flat shoes for comfort. She always dressed for comfort, it was much more practical, and who was she trying to impress anyway? Amanda and Marcus were technically Marissa's cousins as their mother Helena was Marissa's first cousin, but it was easier for them to call her Aunty because of their age difference. Helena encouraged it, and Marissa kind of liked being an aunty, so she didn't mind.

'Hello, Amanda. Hi, Marcus.'

'Hi, Aunty Marissa!' said Marcus, and knowing he would get no sympathy from Marissa, he ran from the room searching for someone else to bemoan his grievances to.

Amanda looked up sheepishly. 'Hi Aunty M.,' she said with a grin.

Marissa pursed her lips together trying to keep a straight face with their running joke. 'You know I don't like that. I'm not *that* old. And, anyway, I don't know anyone called Henry.' She raised an eyebrow.

'And her little dog too!' Amanda couldn't help but giggle out loud.

Marissa sighed then laughed, finding patience in her heart for this girl that she loved, which wasn't that hard to do, especially as she hadn't seen her in a few weeks. She gave the girl a hug.

'How's Tobermory?'

'He's just fine, thanks. He loved the sun today – he was outside for most of it.'

'Ahh, he is such a lovely cat-person. He is so black, he reminds me of a witch's cat. But not a wicked witch, a good witch, maybe. I bet Tobermory is just as clever as a witches' cat would be. I think I'd rather be a good witch myself, than a good fairy.' Amanda thought about it then nodded her head in confirmation, then added, 'If I actually was a witch, I would want Tobermory to be my familiar.'

'Familiar?' asked Marissa curiously.

'Yes, that's what you call a helper or a pet for a witch or a wizard. Like Harry Potter had Hedwig, and Lyra had Pan. Of course, Pan wasn't actually a familiar...' Amanda's train of thought was suddenly disturbed by Marcus running back into the room.

He ran around the dining table in circles, chanting 'Told ya so, told ya so, told ya so!' as he ran.

Marissa and Amanda both put their eyes up to heaven, then caught each other doing it and laughed again.

'That boy acts like he's four and not eight years old. What a baby,' said Amanda, adding, 'Do you have any news for me?'

'No, not really.' Marissa caught herself wringing her hands and stopped, tucking a stray hair behind her ear instead.

'Oh, okay then. I'm going to wash my hands before dinner.' Amanda said, getting up and hugging Marissa around the waist. 'You should look up more about familiars, it's really interesting,' she added, before leaving the room.

Leo walked in with two glasses of lemonade for his children and put them on the sideboard. 'Hi Marissa, or should I call you stranger?' Leo was Helena's husband, tall, taller than both Uncle Lou and Marissa's Dad. He had fair hair, which Marcus had inherited. Helena and Marissa used to joke that he was a blow-in because he looked like a stick of wheat. He was also wearing slacks and a blue shirt, with black polished shoes.

'Hi, stranger!' said Marissa, and gave Leo a brief polite hug. 'Did Marcus dress you up this evening, or did you dress him?'

'Ha, ha, yes, he wouldn't change out of his dirty play clothes until Helena suggested we wore matching outfits. If it works, it works. Anything for some peace. How's life with you?'

'Okay. I'm enjoying college, but the assignments are a little difficult. What is Uncle Lou up to tonight? I hope everything's okay?'

'I'm not sure. You know Louis, he loves drama, and he particularly loves being the centre of it all. But he's a good guy, with a good heart. And anyway, it's a good excuse to get together, I've not seen you in ages.'

'Yes, true,' said Marisa, wondering how life can go by so quickly, yet in that house, with her family, it didn't seem to pass by at all.

'You'd better ask Helena what's going on if you want insider information, she *is* closer to her father than I am.' Leo raised an eyebrow and put his index finger across his lips as if to say, 'Shh.'

'All intrigue tonight,' said Marissa with a smile, 'I've not seen her yet, I'll go find her and say hello. Lovely to see you!'

Marissa wandered into the kitchen, Helena was standing with her back against the kitchen counter with a glass of white wine in her hand in conversation with Naomi. She wore a purple printed dress and had perfectly manicured fingernails and coiffured hair, purple high-heel shoes and costume jewellery were perfect finishing touches. *She looks more and more like her mother every time I see her. I guess we don't have that much in common anymore.*

'Marissa! Hey! Great to see you!' As warmly as it came out Marissa felt Helena's voice waver slightly as she put her drink down and gave Marissa a hug. It wasn't the close, warm hug of their childhood days but a more tempered, 'grown-up' hug. Marissa hugged her back, feeling like their relationship really had moved on from what it used to be. Helena extracted herself from Marissa and went back to her place at the counter to continue the conversation with her mother.

'Yes, I totally agree, he should fire that tennis tutor and find another one. I'm sure there are plenty of other people out there who would be very happy to work for her instead.'

Feeling excluded, Marissa smiled weakly and made for the door.

They ate a hearty dinner of roast chicken, roast potatoes, overcooked broccoli and peas, and a delicious gravy which Naomi said came from the deli in the village ('Yes, I admit it. But I promise I cooked everything else myself!'). When they had finished, Louis, sitting at the top of the table, tapped his wine glass twice with his fork to get everybody's attention. Louis was a big man, twice as large as Marissa's father, Bernie. He had a deep, commanding voice and magnetism you couldn't ignore. When he wanted your attention, he got it, plain and simple. Louis began to speak.

'As you know, and have been wondering about, yes it's true. I have gathered you all here to make an announcement. Louis looked around the table with a serious expression. 'And it's a good one.' He raised one eyebrow and smiled.

There were audible sighs of relief from around the table. Marcus started rolling a leftover potato on the table cloth, squashing and smearing it into the fabric and giggling in delight. Helena tapped him lightly on the hand, snatched away the remaining offensive potato and put it on her plate. Marcus's face fell. Amanda mouthed at Marissa, 'four years old', and Marissa shook her head and lifted three fingers in response. Amanda laughed so much her eyes started to water.

Louis went on regardless of their shenanigans which he was well used to. 'The company did incredibly well this last quarter, we made our first million in clear profit. My first million in clear profit.' He paused for effect, holding eye contact with everyone in the room as he slowed down to emphasise each word. 'I am now a millionaire.'

Eli made wide eyes at Marissa across the table, and she made wide eyes back. Her brother had arrived in the middle of the main course, hastily making his excuses and taking his place at the table, heaping large helpings of potatoes and chicken (pass on the vegetables), while entertaining everyone with a story about his latest escapade at work. His girlfriend Carol was working that night so she couldn't make it. *Probably better that way, there's enough going on without having a row between Eli and Mum.*

Marissa really liked Carol but the rest of the family weren't as accepting. It took them a while to get used to new additions to the family. They had all been through the drama when Marissa had brought James home, too much drama to mention. Marissa had thought all the fuss was because James wasn't Jewish, but there was drama yet again when Helena brought Leo home for the first time. 'At least he's Jewish,' her mother, Rose, had said, as if that made any difference. It seemed that anyone disrupting their tight-knit 'pack' was a cause for upset. Marissa always felt that comment was a derogatory reference towards James, but even though Leo *was* Jewish, it still took the Rosenthal's a very long time to accept him. Paradoxically they only seemed to accept how she felt about James once he had left and they saw how upset she was. After the horse had bolted her family was happy to make him into the bad guy, taking her side in imaginary arguments. She had left them to it, not having enough energy to argue with them. *Sometimes they really are too much to handle. Even for me. No wonder James had trouble with them.* She had genuinely hoped they'd take to Carol a little quicker, but it was still rocky, even though it was over a year and Eli was so happy. It was the longest relationship he had ever been in. Maybe it was happiness that they couldn't handle.

The announcement of Louis's new wealth caused quite a ripple across the table. Marissa could see from the looks on their faces that neither Leo nor Helena had any inkling this was coming. Naomi was looking down at the table with a smile on her face, but of course he had to have told her before anyone else. Marcus looked around to see if anyone was looking at him, no they weren't, so he quietly took the potato back from his mother's plate and continued his game of squashing it into the tablecloth. Louis tapped his fork on his wineglass again to get their attention.

'Now,' he said, with the biggest smile that could possibly fit on his face, 'the reason I wanted to get you all together is to tell you,' Uncle Lou stopped speaking and cleared his throat, then continued, 'is because I want to give some of my exceedingly hard-earned money…' he raised his eyebrow and waited for a suitable reaction, which he got from Helena and Naomi as they sat up straighter and nodded in agreement. '…towards helping the family. Celtic Tiger or not, I see how hard you're all working too,' and with another raised eyebrow and a smile, he added, 'and I want to show you that I love you all. But you know that already! I just happened to be in the right place at the right time, and in the right industry. I appreciate that, and I appreciate you all, yes, even you, Bernie!'

Louis looked at his brother, Bernie, who was looking back at him. He raised both of his eyebrows and grinned, Bernie mimicked him, and everyone laughed. Their mock-rivalry over the years had been the butt of many jokes which had become edgy enough at times for Eli and Marissa to wonder if they really were joking with each other, or if there was actual animosity there.

Louis said 'Hopefully, this will be the first round of gifts, as I expect much more profit to come in the next few years.'

The excitement in the room rose by several degrees, rippling across the table in hopeful expectation by everyone else bar Marcus who was now making a sculpture with his potato. He scanned Leo's plate to see if there was anything he could swipe to add to his creation.

'Of course, I don't want to jinx myself, so I will keep things on the Q.T. for now, and you will know in time if, and when, they go the way I expect them to.' He tapped his nose, then cleared his throat, took a swig from his wine, and continued. 'Now, back to the business of tonight. I love giving presents! Firstly,' said Uncle Louis, 'I have a gift for my beautiful wife.' Louis stood up and opened the cabinet behind him. He took out a long jewellery box from the top drawer, turned around and handed it across the table to Naomi, who was beaming. 'If you don't like it, love, you can always change it,' he said with a wink.

Naomi opened the box and a sparkle escaped as she lifted the lid. She gasped and looked up at her husband. 'Ooh, Louis! This is crazy! So expensive!!' She turned to the table and breathed out audibly, then said, 'I love it. It's so beautiful. I've never had anything like this, never held anything like this in my life, actually!' Everyone was intrigued and craned in to see what the gift actually was.

'Here, let me help you put it on,' said Louis, walking around the table to his wife. He gently extracted a sparkling diamond and emerald necklace from the box, placed it around Naomi's neck, and after a short struggle with the clasp, it was on. He stood back from her admiring it, and her. He looked proud of himself too, in his ability to bring home something so extravagant.

Naomi's hands fluttered as she touched the diamonds at her throat, she looked almost as radiant as they did. 'You kept that from me well,' she said, trying to calm herself in front of everyone. 'How did you manage to hide this without me knowing?'

'Ahh, we all have our ways, I know you pretty well by now, my darling, and your hiding places are not the same as mine.' He winked, then kissed her. 'Of course now you know that one, I'll have to find another!'

Everyone laughed as Louis returned to his place at the top of the table. Naomi sat down, still touching and stroking her new necklace. Louis turned to his daughter and son-in-law. 'Helena and Leo, you're both doing amazing, I want to take the pressure off. I'm making a substantial contribution to your mortgage payments, and I will put you both on my health insurance. Maybe then Helena love, you'll think about going back to college. Only if you want to! Study something you're interested in, like Marissa is doing.'

'Louis, thank you! I knew you were up to something,' said Leo, standing up to make a toast. Louis gestured for him to sit down, which he did.

'Dad, wow, I don't know what to say.' Helena blushed, then looked at Marissa, who also didn't know what to say.

'I'm not done yet, sit down, sit down. Now. I have set up a trust fund for Amanda and Marcus, which I will continue to add to until they are old enough to spend the money when they are eighteen.'

'Aww,' said both children out loud, looking down at the table in disappointment. Marcus knocked over his tower of potato mush and a pea tumbled its way across the table and lodged itself underneath Marissa's almost empty dinner plate.

Louis turned to his grandchildren 'Hey, can't you guys wait 'til you're eighteen for a present?'

'No!' they both said, in unison.

'I thought as much. So I got you a small-ish present for today, one for each of you. Go, hunt around in the kitchen and see if you can find them.'

The children immediately brightened up and got up, pushing each other out of the way as they ran into the kitchen. Everyone laughed.

'Nick and Deb of course are also getting some money. Obviously, they can't be here tonight. I'll skype them tomorrow.

David and Rebecca get a trust fund too.' Louis and Naomi had two other children who were working abroad, Nicolas worked in Seattle in a large IT firm and Deborah was a nurse in Sydney, Australia, she was married with baby twins, David and Rebecca. It was rare that they were all together.

Bernie had been very quiet during this time. His business was not doing as well as Louis's, in fact, Louis had left him far behind. He tried not to let it upset him, but there were times he wished he could buy diamond necklaces and other similar gifts for his family.

'And now,' said Louis, 'for the rest of you.'

Silence ensued.

'I'm going to give a lump sum to Marissa to help pay for her education so she can finish her counselling degree without being stressed.' He looked at her directly. 'It will more than cover your fees, Marissa, so if you need to take some time off of work to study, well, now you can.'

Marissa blushed and sat up straighter, not sure if she could believe what she was hearing. She addressed her Uncle, 'I don't know what to say… Thank you so much, Uncle Lou. Thank you.'

'My pleasure, girl, we've never had a therapist in the family, so I feel somehow that this is me doing my part for the world too. Keep going, it's important work, almost more important than mine.'

Everyone laughed at that and she flushed, feeling the heat she emitted radiating across the room. She took off her cardigan for the first time that night, trying to dissolve into the chair so she could hide from being the centre of attention.

Louis went on, 'Next. I'm giving a lump sum to Bernie and Rose to go towards paying off their business loans.'

Marissa was relieved to no longer be the focus. She looked at her Dad and could see that her father's smile of gratitude hid his disappointment at being bailed out yet again, and his flush of embarrassment made Marissa's heart go out to him. Thankfully, at that moment Amanda and Marcus rushed back in, faces beaming, waving around new PlayStations and squealing with delight. Both of them ran over to Louis.

'Thank you, Grandpa Lou,' said Amanda. 'None of our friends have these! I can't wait to show them. Thank you, thank you so much.'

'What do you say, Marcus?' Helena prompted her son.

'A PlayStation, just what I always wanted.' Marcus stood there, waving it in the air.

'Thank you Grandpa Lou,' said Helena with a raised eyebrow and pursed lips.

'Thank you, Grandpa Lou,' said Marcus not bothered a bit by his mother, looking delighted to find something more interesting than a smushy potato.

'You're very welcome, my loves,' said Louis. 'Tell your friends they are a gift from the Celtic Tiger.'

The children sat down in their places, examining their new toys and wiggling around in their chairs with excitement.

'Is that tiger guy like the tooth fairy?' asked Marcus, looking puzzled but only half interested in the answer.

'Kind of,' said Louis with a smile.

'And me?' asked Eli, expectantly, never one to hold back.

'Yes, I was coming to you,' said Uncle Lou, smiling and taking an envelope out of his pocket. He held it out in Eli's general direction. 'This, my boy, is for you.'

Marissa noticed her father shiver as Eli reached across the table and took the envelope. He shook it a little (always the joker), and then his eyes widened. He opened it quickly and pulled out a set of car keys.

'The Merc?'

'Yes, the Merc, she's all yours. You can come by the office and get a ticket for a valet and service from my man so that she will be as good as new.'

Marissa knew there couldn't be a better gift for Eli. He'd had his eyes on that car ever since his uncle had got it.

'Wow,' he said, wondering what car his uncle got to replace the Mercedes.

'Thank you, Uncle Louis,' said Bernie, trying not to mimic Helena from earlier.

'Yes, thank you, Uncle Lou,' said Eli with an embarrassed smile.

Bernie pushed his pride to one side, cleared his throat and stood up, raising his glass. 'To Louis!'

Everyone else got up, even Amanda and Marcus managed to put down the consoles and lift their glasses of celebratory lemonade.

Everyone said in unison, 'To Louis/Daddy/Grandpa. L'chiam!' They toasted and drank.

+++

Uncle Lou is so thoughtful, thought Marissa as she walked the long way home, still trying to get her head around the news. Eli had offered her a lift back to his house for a nightcap but she had hugged him close and said she'd see him the following week. 'Give my love to Carol, tell her I missed her tonight.' Dinner had finished early enough, it was a school night, but Marissa needed space to make sense of what had just happened. Juggling work and her diploma had been a struggle for the last year or so, even though it had been worth it. But now, as she walked towards her flat in the darkening evening, the idea of paying off the rest of her college fees, having some money in the bank and possibly paying off her credit card too became more real to her, and she felt her body relaxing as she walked. *I guess I've been stressed about money without even realising it. It's nice to be stressed about something normal for a change.*

She reached her flat, put her key in the door, opened it and went in. Tobermory was waiting for her on the bed, loyal as always. She put the kettle on and brought her duvet out to the sofa to settle in for the night. The dinner had finished early as the children were back to school the next day. Marissa had an assignment due but she didn't feel like working, she was still buzzing from the events of the evening. Some mindless television show and a cuppa was called for. It was time to rest.

CHAPTER THREE

It was dark. The only light came from the bright full moon above which was reflected upon the water's surface. The water seemed to be still, but she could hear the soft lapping of water against the stepping stones. Looking down, she saw her feet inside her tennis shoes once more.

'I'm here again.' *She got her bearings. Looking ahead she could see the next stone on the path, but it seemed so far away. If she jumped, she would probably miss it.* 'What am I afraid of? It's just a little water. The worst thing that could happen would be that I would get wet.'

It wasn't as if she hadn't walked across stepping stones before. Suddenly she heard a rushing noise and turned to her left. A snake-like body rose high above the water and then sank back down into it, disappearing completely. Marissa shivered. Then another rush and again, a thick round shape covered in glistening silvery scales, with the occasional fin, rose and fell, this time a few feet further away from where it had been, its scales shimmering in the moonlight. The sight of its body rising and falling made Marissa cold. It continued to rise and fall, it seemed to take forever for this creature to pass by. 'How long is it?'

Finally, the tail rose up and shone resplendently under the moonlight, the fan of its scales throwing rainbow sparkles under the moonlight. It hovered for a moment, then flicked upwards and sank back down into the water, to finally disappear.

'Okay then.' Looking back at the stepping stone she was standing on and back at the point in the water where the creature had disappeared. 'Getting wet is obviously not an option.'

Marissa woke in a cold sweat. The sea serpent had taken her by surprise, and if that's what it was, she didn't remember seeing it before. Cool, collected, dream Marissa *might* have handled it, but 'real'

Marissa wasn't so sure. She pressed the light button on her clock radio, the green glow showed that it was 3:33am. The fullness of her bladder suddenly made itself known, she got up as deftly as she could, trying not to disturb Tobermory, and went to the bathroom. As she sat on the toilet she felt like she was still in her dream. Where was she? It felt like an in-between place, like she was really there, yet it felt like she wasn't completely here, either. She finished and flushed, and a thought entered her head. *I feel stuck there... But I kind of feel stuck here, too. Maybe the two are connected? How do I move out of this place?*

Suddenly she remembered Uncle Lou's gift. She was awake now, her eyes opened wider like someone flipped a switch in her from off to on. *That money, he said it would more than cover my college fees... Maybe I'm not stuck here like I think I am.* She washed her hands and went back to bed.

Tobermory had shifted on the bed so it was a little trickier to get into it, the place where she had been lying previously was still warm, and that, of course, was where he now was. She felt the coldness of the sheets beneath her as she sank back into the pillows, trying to connect back into the dreamtime, back to the lake with the stepping stones, but to no avail.

Her alarm went off for work what seemed like a few minutes later. Marissa opened her eyes to find Tobermory looking straight back at her, only his face was upside down. She jolted, and he mewed and leapt off the bed, circled around once and then went into the kitchen. She could hear him scratching at the back door.

'Coming,' she said, switching off the alarm. She pulled herself out of bed. She felt like she had a hangover, but she hadn't been drinking. 'Shite,' she said, almost tripping over her slippers to let the cat out.

Kettle on, leaning up against the kitchen worktop, she felt different. Like she had a direction, an angle, finally, after drifting for so long. She had time and space now, she could figure this out, and she had the money to help if she needed it. She was going to get off of those damn stepping stones and onto the other side, sea serpent or no sea serpent. *It's just a dream, for God's sake! Why am I becoming obsessed with this?* It seemed the more determined she was to discover an answer, the more elusive the answer became.

Marissa got the bus to work, made it to her desk on time and settled into her routine. Around 11.30 in the morning, she opened her newsfeed on Facebook when she thought nobody was looking (nobody was ever looking). An inspirational quote caught her eye.

"What you are seeking is seeking you." Rumi

She stopped scrolling. *What does this mean, exactly?* This is fun, I like feeling free to be able to think about stuff like this. But I don't even know what I'm looking for... I'll keep looking. Another quote came up on her feed:

"People who write down their goals are more likely to succeed." Brian Tracy

Writing stuff down is a great idea. That would help me at least figure out what I'm trying to figure out and make my head feel a little less muddled. Marissa found a small hardback notebook in the office supplies cupboard and made it her own. She sat back at her desk, wrote her name on the inside cover, turned to a fresh page and started a list. She wrote *'My Goals'* on the top of the page and underlined it twice. Then she crossed it out and changed it to *'What do I need to know?'* She sighed, pulled the page out, ripped it up and put it in the bin. She started again, writing, *'Questions I need the answers to.'*

Sarah walked past her desk and peeked in behind the dividers. She was slim with long blonde hair tied back in a ponytail, blue eyes, long pink nails and matching lipstick. Today she wore black tights, high heels and a short black skirt.

'Whatcha up to?'

'Hi, Sarah! Erm, I'm trying to organise my thoughts. I feel a bit muddled at the moment. Not work stuff, though, personal stuff.'

'Ahh, okay,' said Sarah. 'Do you need to make a mind map? We made one in night-school, it was really fun – you can use lots of different colour markers and do doodles and stuff.'

'Oh! A mind-map, I didn't think of that. Yes, that could be a great idea – thanks. I'll have a go at that when I go home.'

Sarah leaned in closer and lowered her voice, 'Have you heard that I'm booking tickets to Peru?'

'Peru? No, I didn't know you were going there. Why?'

'It's calling me,' Sarah said mysteriously and waved as she turned, flicking her ponytail so it almost hit Marissa, but Marissa was used to this, and ducked out of the way just in time. She watched as Sarah drifted back to her own desk at the other side of the open-plan office, ponytail swinging from side to side with every step.

After a moment, Marissa's email pinged. There in her inbox was a new email from Sarah with *'Coffee after work?'* as the subject line. Marissa replied with *'Usual place?'* Sarah replied with a smiley face.

Marissa had taken a part-time job as a personal administrative assistant in a small software company owned by Noreen Brennan, a friend of her mother's, three years earlier, after the whole James thing. Working there helped her get back on her feet, and she met Sarah, who was becoming a real friend. She was able to keep their flat while she stayed with her parents, James had been the one paying rent, so her father had covered it for the couple of months it took her to get organised. Before she moved back in, Marissa found herself spending her free time there, she loved the light and, of course, the garden. Eli helped her get rid of all of James's things, and then she really felt like it was her own flat, a place she could call home. Tobermory stayed, trying to get a cat to move out temporarily just wasn't worth the effort. She needed to visit the flat and feed him, but she found she was using him as an excuse to keep going back to what she began to feel was *her* flat. When Marissa knew she was ready to move back in, she asked Noreen if she could work full time. Noreen was delighted. When she paid the rent for the first time herself, she felt such freedom and independence, like nothing she ever felt before.

Marissa always intended to go back to college and get her Master's degree, but three years later, she was still working for Noreen. Although she had little or no interest in the work or the product, she was very loyal to Noreen. Noreen was very organised, so she wasn't often overloaded with work, Marissa usually had time to spare. She had found the part-time 'Introduction to Psychotherapy' course while browsing the internet at work and it tickled her fancy. She went to the open evening because, why not? That lead to her signing up for the course, which lead to her showing up for the first class, and the next, and the next. It felt like she drifted into it without really planning to. But she really enjoyed it, the study was much more interesting than her primary degree had been, she seemed to have a flair for it, for some reason it seemed to come easy to her. This was starting at the beginning again, a diploma course, not even a degree, but she had lost the desire to do the masters she had planned to do and became focused on completing this instead.

Noreen's company sold accounting software, it paid well and they never asked her for anything outside of working hours, so it suited her just fine. There were busy periods and not so busy periods. Sarah knew more about office work than she did, and always gave her a helping hand if she needed one. Marissa was quite comfortable there, she liked her routine, especially with the anxiety she often felt. She wanted to keep her life as simple as possible.

Her email pinged again, from Sarah, again with a photograph of Peru attached. *Peru? Is Sarah serious? What the heck is this all about out of the blue?*

In between pretending to juggle pages of paperwork on her desk and actually typing up a report on her computer, Marissa looked Peru up on Google. The first thing that came up in the search results was an article about Machu Picchu. She flipped to Google Images to take a look and was suddenly captivated, scrolling from one image to the next, her eyes and her full attention became drawn into the photographs, each one seeming more vivid, more dream-like than the next. And then up popped a photo of a mountain by a lake that looked very familiar.

'Oh. My. God,' she said out loud. She suddenly felt as if she'd been hit in her stomach by a football. It was practically identical to the one in her dream. She looked again, mesmerised by the photo, feeling queasy. *It isn't exactly the same, okay? It can't be. Breathe. Take a step back. It has the same feel to it though, the same power. But it couldn't be the same, could it? No way. No, I'm imagining things.* Once again, the emotions of her dream coursed through her body and she felt stronger flickers of anxiety stirring deep within her stomach.

At that moment, Noreen came over to her desk and broke her focus. She looked tired but was dressed immaculately in a red and black plaid A-line skirt and a cream blouse. Her short brown hair was swept back by a gold comb, she wore her red glasses – Noreen loved wearing different frames to match her outfits. Marissa quickly flipped the screen back to Excel and turned to look up at her, hoping she hadn't noticed and that she didn't seem more flustered than normal.

'Have you got that spreadsheet ready for me?' Noreen asked with a smile. 'And I'll need that PowerPoint too. Can you put it on a USB key as well as emailing it to me just in case?'

'Sure.' said Marissa finding her efficient assistant voice. 'Yes, of course, I'll get that sorted for you right away.'

+++

After work, the café was buzzing. Marissa had already had three cups of coffee that day, so she ordered a hot chocolate. Sarah ordered a mocha latte and they sat at their usual table. They often went for coffee and lunch together, though they were more like work colleagues than close friends. Sarah had worked for Noreen since leaving school, she had helped Marissa settle in, showed her where the coffee and tea was and how to set up a profile on the computer. Sarah looked and acted like she was always having a 'blonde moment,' but she really was rather clever. She was taking a night course in accounting and enjoying it, although she pretended at times that it was too difficult for her. Marissa knew better, and she knew that Marissa knew. She was a ray of sunshine in Marissa's working day, and Marissa had become Sarah's confidante.

Marissa decided to face this head-on. 'So what are you talking about – how is Peru calling you? What do you mean?' Marissa stirred her hot chocolate and kept her eyes on Sarah, waiting for an explanation and pushing any flickers of anxiety into the ground beneath her feet.

Sarah smiled, batted her eyelids and flicked her ponytail over her shoulder. 'Well, I always need something to look forward to this time of year. I don't like the winter, and it's great weather over there, in South America, I mean. There's lots to do too, Lima is one of the hot spots for dancing, you know.'

'No, I didn't know.'

'It's very spiritual there,' Sarah continued, cocking her head to one side. 'I heard that the people there walk around naked!' She giggled like a schoolgirl. 'Can you imagine?'

'I was looking at pictures on Google after you told me,' said Marissa, doubtfully, 'and it looks very cold for naked walking.'

'Well, every girl needs an adventure,' winked Sarah, reaching into her handbag and pulling out a brochure from the travel agent across the road from the office. 'Look at this. What do you think?'

They both pored over the pictures and hotel listings.

'Wow, look at that swimming pool…'

'The colours are fantastic, aren't they?'

'Oh, I love that.'

'Is that an alpaca?'

'Do you want to come with me?'

Marissa was taken aback for a moment, she felt another flash of anxiety. 'I'll think about it,' she replied, thinking, *It's just another one of Sarah's flights of fancy.*

That night Marissa did her laundry, brushed Tobermory and swept and hoovered her flat. Thoughts of Peru, of sea serpents, of having money in her account drifted in and out of her mind until she felt the anxiety coming back in. *I'm too tired for this right now. And I'm very tired of the anxiety, it never seems to let up. Maybe I need to book another session with Olive.* Olive was her psychotherapist, and as she was about to start practising with 'real' clients at college, she really needed to be seeing a therapist on a regular basis. She didn't feel like disclosing anything to anyone right now, not to a therapist or to her classmates. It had been six months since she had last been to therapy, she had to do at least one hundred and fifty hours for her diploma, the thoughts of going back were exhausting. *My personal therapy hours are the only thing that is holding me back...* Client practice sessions meant that not only would she get to practice being a therapist, but she would have to be a client too.

Marissa didn't want to talk about her dream or her seeming obsession with the dream. It seemed silly to ask for help with a dream, but it did seem so real, and it had happened more than once so it must mean something. Perhaps going would be useful as it would clock up some of the requirement for college. *How could I go to therapy and get away without doing any therapy?* Once she was settled into her bed, she grabbed her laptop from her desk and looked up Peru on Google Images again, taking her time and scrolling through, wanting to find her mountain, but it didn't appear. She felt the need to see it becoming stronger in her, turning into an urgency. It was getting late, she had to get up for work the next day. She shut down the laptop and put it back on the desk, switched on her alarm for the morning and decided she really wasn't quite ready for the excitement all of this seemed to be bringing her. She lay in her bed, counting her breaths until she calmed down and fell asleep.

+++

Tuesday was college day. On Tuesdays, Marissa tried to get off about a half-hour earlier than the rest of the week so she had time to grab a bite to eat and take the two busses across town to her class which started at 6. However, today was a day off. The sounds of the photocopier filled the open-plan office as Marissa helped herself to yet another cup of coffee.

She really didn't want another cup, but it was 3pm and she had two more hours until hometime. There was something soporific about the office environment. She would have opened a window for a breath of fresh air, if they had had a window that opened. The flickering fluorescent lights didn't help much either. As it was, the coffee would have to do. At least she could go home leisurely tonight. Racing around to get to college was tiring, too. She made herself a cup of proper coffee in the office kitchenette, they had instant too, but she didn't like it much, although her stomach wasn't sure if it could hold another cup of the strong stuff. *I wonder if coffee makes me more anxious?* She took a couple of digestives from the office stock and walked back to her desk. The autumn colours were coming in, she liked to see the colour behind each leaf, but like Sarah, she wasn't a real fan of winter either. *Something to look forward to would be nice alright...* She sat down and looked around, nobody was about, so she opened her web browser and clicked the 'Facebook' button. *I'm really misbehaving these days, I hope the IT guys don't send a record of my browsing history to Noreen...*

She scrolled through her newsfeed, not paying attention to it until up popped a photo of the most beautiful mountain range she had ever seen, so many colours, it was like it was made from a rainbow. It wasn't the same photo she stumbled across on Google, it didn't look anything like *her* mountain, but she felt a hit in her stomach anyway, slightly lighter than the last time, and then came with it a rush of emotion. This time it felt wet, like water dripping down her arms, trickling down her face, rather like being suddenly thrown into a lake. *There's that lake again...*

Marissa put down her coffee and gathered herself then looked at the Facebook post in more detail. A friend of a friend was sharing a post from someone in Peru, wearing bright colours and smiling. 'Could be anything,' she said out loud, shaking it off.

She scrolled down a little further and read a few inspirational quotes, saw some cat videos (making sure the sound was off) and then an article about the indigenous people of South America showed up. *Why is all this South American stuff showing up on my newsfeed? Is Facebook playing games with me?*

She heard footsteps, so she quickly shut the browser and pulled out her Excel spreadsheet. It was Tim, the IT guy. He smiled at her as she caught his eye, she smiled back and turned back to her screen. The numbers on the spreadsheet seemed to dance before her eyes, she could not focus at all on her work.

That night the dream returned, this time in more detail.

All around her was stillness. Leaning on one foot, with her other slightly raised, she recognised where she was and caught her breath. She still didn't know what to do. She looked up and saw massive mountains, so tall they seemed to be scraping against the sky. In the moonlight they still appeared green and lush, filled with life. Looking down past her feet, she saw the next stepping stone, but it seemed wrong, somehow. She looked at it with a purpose, knowing that she needed to put her foot down somewhere, and soon. Her leg was getting tired. She felt the rustle of the water around her and she remembered the serpent.

'Come to me,' she said to the nearest stepping stone, and it felt like the stone was laughing at her. 'I mean it,' she said, more determinedly this time. 'I want you to come to me. Now!' She felt something open in her chest, something large and powerful. She imagined she was a magnet, and she was pulling the stepping stone closer to her. And then the stone seemed to drift, just a little bit, in her direction. It was exhausting, but it was possible. She had not thought of this before – using her will, she could call the stepping stone to her.

She looked at the greenery around her, that which felt so familiar and yet she didn't remember seeing it so colourful before. It had always been grey, all the other times. And then the stone... She looked at it again, giving it her full focus and attention, and suddenly it lifted up from the lake surface and flew towards her, so fast, it hit her in the chest and knocked the breath out of her and she fell...

Marissa woke with a start to find Tobermory sitting on her chest, mewing to get outside. It was only 4am, her head felt groggy and heavy, but the abrupt end of her dream and the weight on her chest suddenly made sense. She pushed him off of her and breathed with relief, then stretched, and her mind drifted back to the mountains. They did seem familiar but from where?

'Damnit, Tobermory!'

On the bus into work that morning she looked on YouTube for a decent video to watch later. The third one in the list of suggestions was called 'What to do if you have five days in Peru'. *Is this what they mean when they say the universe is speaking to you? It's all a bit too fast for my liking. Peru, Peru, Peru, what do you want from me? Are you calling me as well as Sarah?*

Marissa thought what Sarah had said was funny, the idea of a place calling a person to it, yet it seems as if Peru had left a lingering taste in her mouth, as if it had crawled under her skin. After seeing that photograph she was certain it was the lake in her dreams, a real place, not just made up. It felt deeply emotional. Peru seemed to be everywhere.

Marissa sighed with the heaviness of it all. Maybe she should go there with Sarah, if Sarah *was* serious, that is. She had the money to do it now, or she will have, soon... Maybe she deserved to have some fun for a change. Maybe it would be just the thing to help her find her enthusiasm for life again, instead of this plodding from day to day with no real urge or desire for anything other than study and rest and hibernation. Or maybe she was just being silly.

+++

This internal push and pull went on for Marissa for just over a week. Fighting it was beginning to be exhausting. It really did feel like Peru was 'seeking her'. It was Thursday, and on Thursdays there was a lunchtime food market at the park. Marissa looked around for Sarah to see if she wanted to go with her, but she had already left. Marissa grabbed her coat and stepped out of the office, making her way to the park where the buzz of the people laughing, the lightness of it almost being the weekend, and the smells of the different foods being prepared filled the air. The leaves were on the ground now, autumn had taken away summer's watch, and there was a colder nip in the air. The market always lifted her. *So why am I feeling so miserable? Is it because summer is really over?* She walked past the muffin stall, the paella stall, the sausages, all the while wondering why she was feeling so down. *I have no reason to feel upset today. Look – is it this Peru thing? Why don't I want to go? Why do I want to go? What's going on with me?*

Marissa sighed and settled for a burrito and a can of coke – well, it *was* Thursday, and she had a whole afternoon of work to look forward to. Taking her burrito (and chips and Diet Coke, you know, Thursday...) to a quiet spot under a tree, she sat and ate and watched the people passing by. After a time she started feeling a little calmer. Then her phone buzzed in her bag, so she picked it up.

Check your bank. Love you lots. It was from Uncle Lou.

Thanks! she wrote back.

It's the first of 3 for your 'education'. It's prob more than you're expecting. I know you'll know what to do with it. Love Lou xx

Marissa felt a huge wave of something come over her – was it excitement? Anxiety? She didn't know what it was, only that she was relieved she was sitting down. She looked at her burrito and chips and suddenly didn't want them anymore. She sipped her drink until the feeling passed. She wiped her forehead, yes there were drops of sweat there. *What is wrong with me? It's a gift, it's money, I get to choose what to do with it. Calm down.*

Marissa came back to her desk, still a little shaky, and discovered a brochure for Peru had been shoved under her keyboard. As she pulled it out she saw the colours and the mountains and her heart leapt as if she had discovered contraband. She held her hands out in front of her and saw that they were shaking. *What is this about?* She felt hopeless, whatever this was, she needed to surrender to it. She shoved the brochure quickly into the top drawer of her desk and sat down, catching her breath and bringing her focus back to the moment. She woke up her computer and there was an email in her inbox from Sarah with just three words in the subject line: *Come with me.* She deleted the email immediately and, still shaking, slowly opened up her spreadsheet.

Everything seemed to be happening in slow motion. Her stomach was nauseous. As she looked at the numbers she started to feel a little more settled, the shaking subsided, then another email popped in from Sarah. '*Well?*' it said. *Jeezuz it's as if she knows what's going on inside me. But I have money now, I actually could go... How much money did he give me?* Marissa opened a tab on her web browser and logged into her bank account, not really knowing what to expect. There was a deposit of €8,000 with a note '*from Uncle Louis – first instalment*'. Suddenly, a wave of calmness swept over her and something inside solidified. *That's enough to pay off my loan and cover my college fees, with some left over. I really could go to Peru with Sarah.*

The texture of this thought felt very different from the ungrounded, anxious thinking she had been doing the past few days. *I could ask Michelle from the upstairs flat to mind Tobermory for me. Half term is coming up, so I'd not miss too much college. This would be a great adventure and it would also be educational – What am I afraid of? I've got the money.*

She emailed Sarah back: *'When are you going and how much will this cost me?'*

Like magic, Sarah was there at her desk with a big beaming smile.

'Are you serious?'

Marissa nodded her head as the butterflies flew in droves in her stomach against the calmness, it felt like she had swallowed one of those majestic mountains.

'Look. At. Me.' said Sarah. 'Are you serious?'

Marissa turned to Sarah and looked her in the eye. 'Yes. Yes, I am serious.' Marissa was suddenly calmer than she had been for a whole week.

'OHMYGOD!! That's fantastic!' Sarah jumped for joy, then turned around quickly to make sure nobody had seen her. 'I was so worried about going on my own and I really, really want to go there with you. Jesus Christ, let's do it! Let's meet up after work and plan it.'

'You mean you haven't booked it already?'

'Shite, no! I was waiting for you to say you'd come with me... *Ha*! I just knew you would if I kept working on you.'

The last of the fight drained out of Marissa as she decided that she was definitely going to go to Peru with Sarah, and she had nothing to be afraid of, it was going to be a very fun adventure. They both laughed. Marissa didn't realise Sarah thought so highly of her. Perhaps the friend she was looking for was right here in front of her. Marissa's face softened as she finally stopped struggling with herself.

'Okay then. Let's have dinner together, bring your brochures, and we can figure it all out.'

'Yay!!' giggled Sarah and disappeared, leaving Marissa with thoughts of her lake, alpacas and snow-covered mountains.

CHAPTER FOUR

Only a couple of weeks later, they were on their way to Peru. October was a great month to travel, Sarah got a special deal on the flights and accommodation and they both still had holidays from work available, so it all came together rather quickly.

It had been a very long flight to Miami from London. Marissa and Sarah were excited but also exhausted, and they had four hours to kill before their flight to Lima. They were on the train between terminals C and E. Marissa felt like she was in a dream. The sun was going down and spread gold and orange light across the sky. On the train up so high surrounded by golden light, Marissa wondered why the sunset colours never really struck her this strongly at home. Perhaps it was because here she wasn't in her comfort zone and was hyper-aware? She was feeling nervous but happy, managing to keep her anxiety under control so far. Even Sarah's excitement hadn't knocked her off-side, well, not yet anyway. She was surprised, actually, at how calm she was. Sometimes the mixture of emotions in her stomach was verging on nausea, but she repeated her mantra quietly to herself – *Breathe in, breathe out* – and it seemed to be working. And Sarah *was* very funny.

Marissa was looking forward to the tour, the relief of not having to figure out which train or bus to get seeped into her bones. Good old Uncle Lou giving her that money, she decided to pay that little bit extra on top of the standard to get the comfort she felt would take the edge off her nervousness. Was 'comfort' the word? Or was it 'safety'? She wasn't sure, her confusion added to the mixture of different coloured butterflies in her stomach. Either way, she deserved it. Yes, definitely she did. Marissa reminded herself of how difficult it had been for her the last few years since the whole James thing.

Yes, the James thing again, but it feels better thinking about it like that, a thing that happened, and now it is over. I need to feel alive again. I want to move on from it. I have the rest of my life to be getting on with. This trip will be good for me, an adventure could really help me get back to myself. Ignoring that her thoughts were veering into sounding like something her mother may have said, Marissa continued to breathe in and out and distracted herself by focusing on the colours in the sky. She jolted when the train finally came to a stop.

'We're here!' said Sarah, jumping up and putting her backpack over her shoulder. She was very summery, wearing short denim shorts and a pink zipped up hoodie with a matching tennis style visor hat. Her usual ponytail was now in plaits, one on either side of her bright and hopeful face. Marissa had gone for her usual jeans and a sweatshirt, but she had invested in new walking shoes in anticipation of the hikes that were to come. *Nothing seems to shake that girl!* The further they got from home, the more it seemed that Sarah unwound, as if she was melting off a stiffness that she had within her. Marissa thought it was a little bit like seeing a fan opening slowly.

'We're in America!! We're bloody here! I'm going to get some cinnamon rolls from that famous chain shop, I've seen them on YouTube, they look amazing,' said Sarah. 'Do you want some?'

'Okay,' replied Marissa, wanting a coffee to help her stay awake. They walked down the concourse, looking at the shops with their backpacks slung on their backs. Sarah had a reusable bottle which she had filled with water once they got past security. Marissa had been looking at it on the plane and decided she wanted to buy one too, it would be useful on the trip. They kept themselves relatively busy buying a few trinkets and looking at all of the different merchandise while they waited for the next flight to board. Marissa was playing with her new water bottle and Sarah was turning her new bracelet around in her hand when they announced the flight to Lima.

About five and a half very squashed hours later, they landed in Peru. It was a relief to get off the airplane and stretch. The airport was bustling, the smell of food and the busyness of so many people in one place was the first thing that Marissa noticed. *It feels like a dream, but I couldn't be imagining this awful smell! We're really here in Peru.*

It seemed that now Sarah was the one who was dopey and disjointed.

'Let's get our bags and go exploring!' Marissa whispered.

Little did she know they'd be at least an hour, if not longer, in customs. Finally waiting at the carousel, there must have been about 100 people at the same one. Marissa's tired heart leapt with joy to finally see her bag, and once they got through the red tape, they were in the main concourse, free, and in a country neither of them thought they would ever have a chance of visiting. They looked at each other and smiled, Sarah seemed more awake and relaxed now, and as they walked into the throng of people and the humidity, Marissa felt some anxiety, but nothing overwhelming. *Feet on the ground, breathe. I can do this.*

'Oooh the heat! I love it here already. Ha, ha, they're all in the cold at home, and here we are in the flippin heat – it's fantastic,' said Sarah, taking off her hoodie to reveal a yellow strappy tank top, which was almost the same colour as her white Irish skin.

They flagged down a taxi as they both wanted a shower and to change. It took almost an hour to get to the hotel, the traffic was very slow. They were surprised that Lima seemed just like another American city, it had all the familiar restaurant chains and some not so familiar. The hotel they had chosen was clean and bright, and their twin room was facing the sea.

'Not a bad choice from a few photos online,' said Sarah. 'I had a good feeling about this place.' She unapologetically jumped onto the bed beside the window, stretched out her legs and kicked off her runners.

'I'm so glad we are not going on to Cusco just yet,' said Marissa. 'I need some time to recover from all the plane rides. I feel so dehydrated.'

Sarah was yawning, but she couldn't sit still. She got up and threw her suitcase on the bed and opened it. She rummaged around and pulled out and held up dresses to her body to decide which one she would wear that evening. 'Well I, my dear, am going to hit the dance clubs tonight. I want to see some of the local talent.'

'Don't let me stop you,' replied Marissa.

'Aww, come on Mari, it will be great gas, sure you never know who you may meet...' Sarah cocked her head to one side, trying to look cute.

'You know I'm not looking for love just now, I just need to drink some water and sleep. I don't fancy going dancing tonight.

'Aww, but we are on holidays now, Marissa. Maybe love is looking for you?' Sarah smiled and threw down the pink dress and picked up another one. 'What do you think, the pink or the green?'

'Definitely the green. Right now all I'm looking for is my toothbrush! My mouth has a forest growing in it!' said Marissa dismissing the idea of going dancing and looking for love completely. Having an adventure was one thing, meeting a man was a whole other thing altogether. 'Go without me, have some fun, don't let me stop you' Marissa opened her suitcase and rooted around it for her wash-bag. 'Do you mind which side of the sink I take?'

'Not at all. But you're coming with me tonight girl, you can't get away that easy.' Sarah was still rummaging through her clothes. She held up a black dress and a yellow skirt and admired herself in the full-length mirror. 'Aha! This is it!' Her enthusiasm was sparkling, Marissa had to laugh.

'Welcome to Peru!'

Later that night, Marissa sat at a table in the hotel bar and watched Sarah dance. After all the travelling, they felt safer staying close to home, and Marissa wasn't up to navigating a brand new city just yet. Thankfully the tiredness had hit Sarah too, so she was less argumentative but still wanted to bop to the local beat.

+++

Lima was a large busy city. Marissa was surprised as she had half expected somewhere that seemed lost in space and time. Instead, Lima had many restaurants and bars, food chains, market places and tourists. Many of the locals spoke English and seemed very friendly, but Marissa kept her bag clutched tightly to her body just in case.

It had been a long time since she travelled, she admitted to herself that it was good to get away. She loved the heat of the sun on her face, she could relax a little, they had four whole days to acclimatise before their tour.

Lima reminded Marissa of a holiday she took to Spain with her parents and Eli about five years previously. She hoped that she and Sarah could get into an easy routine, but sharing a room with Sarah sounded better in theory than in practice. Marissa was so used to having her own space she hadn't thought about how it would affect her. And as few days passed, Sarah seemed to be more and more focused on a mission to find a man. This was not what Marissa had signed up for. After the third day, she decided she didn't want to care so much, she wasn't Sarah's keeper, and she wanted to have a little bit of fun too, albeit not the same type of fun as Sarah. After this, she started to relax a little more and began to enjoy watching Sarah watching the local talent, but Sarah's taste certainly had a lot to answer for.

They were having a drink at the hotel bar, it was their last night in Lima.

'We go to Cusco tomorrow', reminded Marissa, 'so don't stay up too late. I'm going to the room to pack and try to sleep, I'm really excited.'

'Okay, I'll be upstairs in a bit,' said Sarah, chewing her lower lip and peering at a suntanned twenty something year old through her sunglasses as she took a sip of her Margarita.

'You're impossible!' said Marissa, leaving the table and laughing. 'Sunglasses indoors, at night.'

'Yes, of course! So they don't see me looking,' whispered Sarah.

'Okay then! But I don't think it works that well. Can you see anything through them at all?'

'Let me have my fun!' Sarah pulled down her sunglasses, revealing intensely blue eye-shadowed eyes. She glared at Marissa and then giggled.

'Sure we are on holidays,' said Marissa 'anything goes.'

They looked at each other and said at the same time, 'What happens in Peru stays in Peru!!' And they laughed.

When the alarm went off as promised at 3am, Marissa was packed and ready to check out of the hotel, but Sarah was not that organised and threw her clothes into her suitcase right up until the last minute.

'I couldn't eat breakfast right now,' said Marissa looking at the time on her phone, 'My body has no clue what time it is anymore.'

'We can get something at the airport,' said Sarah 'you ready?'

Marissa chuckled. 'I was ready 10 minutes ago. Let's go.'

They got a charter bus from their hotel to the airport and it seemed to take forever as it stopped in so many hotels on the way, but they were not too late. The flight to Cusco from Lima was fully booked. It reminded Marissa of a scene in one of her favourite old movies, *Romancing the Stone*, when the bus was overfull, all her airplane lacked was some chickens. Thankfully it was a quick flight and they arrived in Cusco with no incidents.

When they got into the small airport and retrieved their bags, Marissa tuned into the smells and sights of Cusco, which were quite different to Lima. After the smells, the next thing she noticed was the chatter, so many different languages, it seemed even busier than Lima. It was spicier, if that was possible. Marissa felt relatively calm, she focused on staying at an even keel.

Then Sarah was pointing and shouting, 'Over there, over there!' Marissa looked towards where she was pointing and saw a rather old looking small man with short sticky-out hair wearing a yellow Hawaiian shirt, blue shorts and worn-out sandals (he was actually only thirty-four, as they found out later). He held up a sign with many people's names on it, theirs was on it too.

'You've got brilliant eyesight, I wouldn't have seen that. Is it our tour?' asked Marissa, who had left most of the finer details of the booking to Sarah.

'Yes!', she replied, 'But don't worry, we get to rest in the hotel now.'

'I like that idea,' nodded Marissa, still tired from the very early start.

They walked over to the man who would be their tour guide for the next five days.

'Welcome, welcome, welcome,' he said in a thick local accent. 'And you are?'

'Sarah Davies and Marissa Rosenthal,' said Sarah.

He looked at his list and ticked their names off. 'Welcome!' His beaming smile revealed broken teeth, some of them blackened. His thin lips pushed his cheeks back and revealed many more wrinkles in his brown leathery skin. He had beautiful dark brown eyes with a twinkle in them. He seemed gentle and kind, Marissa liked him immediately.

'I am Miguel, and I am delighted to meet you. We will have great fun, no? Please wait here until others come. Shouldn't be too long.'

'Your English is very good,' commented Sarah. She bent to whisper into Marissa's ear, 'Do we need to give him a tip?'

'Yes, I imagine so, but we can probably wait until the tour has finished.'

The other people in their group arrived within the next twenty minutes. Miguel led them all outside the terminal to the van park. He walked towards a rickety white van which looked about twelve years old and very well used. It had 'Peru Tours' spray-painted on its side along with a picture of a mountain. It lifted Marissa's heart and made her smile. She couldn't wait to see the mountains, she remembered that was why she was here. Miguel opened the back of the van to reveal coach style seats with seatbelts which were probably more for show than for safety. 'Come on in!'

Miguel managed to pack all of their suitcases into a box and then strapped the box to the roof of the van. Marissa noted how the Americans in the group seemed to have twice as much luggage as everybody else.

'We go to hotel now, I give you two hours for resting, then we meet in lobby for walk-around tour of Cusco in this afternoon. You need one day to get used to altitude, so no go to Machu Picchu today. Cusco is highest point of our journey, some of you may feel sick, this is normal. Tomorrow morning we meet at four in morning for first real trip.'

'What time is it now?' Marissa asked Sarah as they took their seats.

'I think it's about noon so we can get a late breakfast if you like, or you could get a nap. 4am tomorrow is a very early start!'

'It's all about beating the crowds here,' chipped in a very tall man from behind them. He had a broad American accent, Sarah and Marissa turned around to see him. He offered his hand to them through the seats. 'Hi! I'm Ralph. What's your name?'

Ralph was tall and had shoulders as broad as his accent, beach blond hair and a California tan. His smile showed sparkling white teeth, Marissa recoiled slightly. He was looking at both of them as if wondering which one he would choose for himself. *Well, he might keep Sarah quiet for a while, but he can stay the heck away from me.*

'Hi, I'm Sarah, and this is my friend Marissa,' replied Sarah a little bit too enthusiastically, taking Ralph's hand and shaking it. Marissa smiled tiredly and nodded in his direction, then shifted back around in her seat so he couldn't engage with her any further. She put on her earphones to make sure she gave a clear message and left them to it. After the four days in Lima, Marissa was getting more comfortable in her own skin and less interested in Sarah's antics. Both of which were probably a good thing.

The hotel was smaller than the one they stayed at in Lima, but it was very clean and had everything they needed. Marissa took the bed by the window this time. She enjoyed stretching out for a couple of hours to catch up with herself. The restaurant in the front afforded them a lovely view of the city. There was a large reception area with sofas and plants, filled with information leaflets and very helpful staff. It seemed that most of the tour group was staying here, although there were a few people in the hotel across the road. Miguel held counsel at 2pm as promised. He handed each of them a map of the town.

'Cusco is not big city like Lima, but still there is lots to see here. Plenty of local people, markets, food is beautiful. Lots of crafts, and of course we have our Centro Históico, museums and many historical sites. You choose today what to see, remember after we see Machu Picchu we will also visit Sacsayhuaman and Coricancha, so save those for another day.'

'Will they take dollars?' came a voice from the back, another American. *Well, this is South America. I suppose it's a popular place for North Americans to visit.*

'Yes, is good,' said Miguel. 'Dollars, sterling and euro they take, but they prefer soles and is better for you, soles, as they may give you wrong change. Many people may not change you properly. There are many cash machines for soles. Use them if you can.'

Marissa made a mental note to check how much cash she had on her when they were back in her hotel room.

'So yes, have fun, explore city and I see you right here this place tomorrow morning at 4am for Machu Picchu. Exciting, yes?'

'Yes!' shouted some members of the group.

'Remember – important – please clothes for hiking, you will need good strong shoes. And please also bring passport, it may be required for identification. See you tomorrow.'

There were about twenty people in their group, everyone seemed tired and indeed, excited. They broke up into smaller groups and left the hotel, Sarah was hanging back to look for Ralph, but he had already disappeared.

Marissa looked at her map. She thought she would just walk around the local area and get the feel of the place. She wasn't in the mood for museums, it was too hot and she was still tired.

Sarah cocked her head to one side. 'Can we check out the market?'

'Yes, of course. Sounds like fun.'

Sarah had been doing some research and wanted to see the San Pedro market, they looked at the map and got their bearings. Marissa put her hat and sunglasses on, Sarah fixed her visor, then they stepped out into the hot air outside. Suddenly Marissa felt alive. *This place is amazing. So many colours, so much life... This is the most interesting place I've ever been to.*

Marissa took in the cobblestone streets, the white buildings and the fabulous architecture. Somewhere in the back of her mind, she thought Cusco would be more primitive, but no, it was a mixture of old and new. The main square was immense, busy with tourists and locals, buzzing with business, laughter, song and dance, and oh – so beautiful.

She looked in admiration at the church, its twin bell towers towering over all of the other buildings, and the backdrop of the mountains stopped Marissa's heart. It was stunning. She knew these were not *her* mountains, the mountains from her dream, she didn't get *that* feeling in her stomach, but she did feel a connection to these mountains, too.

They approached the market, eyes wide, taking everything in. 'I hope you're hungry,' Sarah said as they walked in through the tall and somewhat imposing gates.

Marissa hadn't eaten in quite a few hours. 'Yes, very!' she replied, realising she was ravenous once she brought her awareness to her stomach.

The colours were overwhelming, the smell of spices and food hit them as soon as they were inside. It was like nothing they had experienced before, they stood there, taking it all in.

'Thursday market has a lot to learn from this place!' said Sarah, laughing.

'Ha ha yes, totally.' agreed Marissa. 'Let's eat something first, yes? My mum always says you shouldn't shop on an empty stomach.'

'Great idea,' agreed Sarah. 'Fancy a smoothie?'

'Maybe,' Marissa replied, checking in with her stomach, which had started to feel queasy with all the smells. She wasn't sure if she was anxious or finally feeling the effects of the altitude.

Well, they were not short on choice – neither of them had ever seen so much food in one place. After some serious consideration, they went for burritos and noodle soup, which was very spicy. They found somewhere to sit to eat. Once Marissa decided that she didn't *need* to buy anything, she took her time with the food and felt better soon after.

Sarah spent hours looking at all the different textiles and silver jewellery and wasn't able to choose anything, she was hovering back and forth over the same three stalls for what seemed like ages. While waiting for Sarah to decide what she wanted, Marissa bought herself an alpaca hat and scarf and a little pouch to carry her wallet and phone. She found a keyring of an alpaca for Amanda and a tiny Peruvian boy made out of wool for Marcus.

By the time they went back to the hotel it was dark. Marissa was still feeling a little nauseous, but she put it down to altitude. They showered and went to bed early in anticipation of the big trip ahead.

'I wonder if Ralph is thinking about me?' said Sarah as she tucked herself into her bed.

'Ha, ha! Night, night.' said Marissa turning to face the wall and closing her eyes, pretending to be asleep before Sarah could ask again.

The alarm seemed to go off two minutes later.

'Wakey Wakey!! Come on lazy bones, today's the day!!' Sarah was already out of bed multitasking, brushing her teeth and tying her hair back into a ponytail at the same time.

'Yes, so it is,' replied Marissa, trying to wake up. They had both thrown together what they needed for the trip the night before. Marissa dressed quickly, threw some water on her face and grabbed her bag. 'I think it might be cold there, it's very high up.' Marissa said, quickly stuffing her new hat and scarf into it. 'Did you bring something warm? Hey, you're the one who did all the research. What do you think?'

'Yes, you're probably right,' agreed Sarah, and she grabbed her fleece and packed it into her own backpack, just in case.

They went downstairs to reception where the group was assembling. People were excited, the buzz was contagious. Marissa was smiling, she couldn't help herself. Sarah was looking out for Ralph. She saw him and waved. He came over and brought his friend with him.

'Hi!' said Sarah brightly.

'Morning,' said Ralph. 'This is Andrew. He's my travel buddy.' Andrew was also tall, tanned with blonde hair, but not as well built as Ralph.

'Hi, Andrew!' said Sarah with a smile, looking at Ralph. Marissa felt resistance in her body straight away. *They had better not try to set me up with Andrew...*

Miguel walked into the reception area checking his watch, holding an old phone and a map sticking out of his pocket. He was wearing a different Hawaiian shirt with the same shorts and sandals. His hair looked messy like he had just gotten out of bed himself. 'Everyone ready? All got passports, yes? Good. We leave now, please follow me.'

It was still dark outside. As the group filed out behind Miguel, Sarah pulled Marissa along with her as she tried to keep up with Ralph and Andrew to get seats beside them. They walked past the rickety white van from the day before and over to a larger bus. Miguel stood at the bus door and checked off everybody's name as they got on board. Sarah was happy with their seats beside the boys.

The bus pulled out onto the road, and they were off. It didn't move quickly, but just quick enough that Marissa had her heart in her mouth for most of the trip. Only when the sun came up did she realise she was holding her breath. After a time, Marissa realised the bus driver knew what he was doing, even if she didn't. *He must have made this trip a thousand times before.* She relaxed a little bit and allowed herself to enjoy the nature, the colours and the beauty, which was all around her. The roads were so narrow at times it seemed like the bus wouldn't make it past the busses going in the opposite direction. At these junctures she would close her eyes until they were through. She looked to see if Sarah was as worried as she was, but Sarah and Ralph were chatting together, heads nudging inwards towards each other. There was no doubt that the chemistry was there. Marissa brought herself back to the view out of her window. At times it felt like she was floating out of her body, the colours were so vibrant, the morning sun was bright, it felt like she wasn't really there. But she was there, in Peru, on her way to Machu Picchu.

After a short time they pulled into a small busy village called Aguas Calientes, where Miguel suggested they have a toilet break. He told them to make sure they had enough food and water for the rest of the journey. There was a bus station buzzing with queues of tourists buying tickets trying to get on a bus.

Sarah turned to Marissa 'Thank you for paying for this tour,' she said. 'I really appreciate not having to queue like that.' She nodded in the general direction of the sweating, tired tourists.

It took forty more minutes to get to Machu Picchu. The bus zig-zagged up incredibly steep and winding roads to get to the top of the mountain. Marissa's stomach wasn't enjoying the trip one bit. The bus finally arrived, and the driver parked it in the coach park. When the driver turned off the engine, Marissa felt her head spinning as well as nausea. Miguel hopped out to organise their tickets. While Marissa waited she put her backpack on, she was still lightheaded, whether it was from the trip, from her anticipation, or the altitude, she wasn't sure.

Miguel boarded the bus with a bunch of tickets in his hand. Standing at the front beside the driver, he addressed the group.

'Hello! We have made it! Exciting trip, no? This driver, he is good, yes? Expert driver!' One of the Americans started clapping, and they all joined in. Marissa clasped the back of the seat in front of her and tried to focus on her breathing. The driver stood, faced them and bowed, nodding his head in thanks. Miguel shushed them, and the clapping died down.

'Our day is here, yes? But we only have three hours before the turnover – many people come so you must make most of this time. There is no food allowed, you cannot eat or drink in this place so keep food in your bag or leave it on the bus for later. There is no toilet after this gate so if you need toilet you come back outside, and back to here. You expressly cannot smoke. Please keep to rules, it helps me if you do it good. Now go! Have fun, explore. If you need me, I will be near the central place. Meet back at the bus in three hours. Then we find food and toilet stop on way back to hotel.'

Everyone stood up and the bus swayed slightly with the shift in the weight. Marissa's stomach lurched, she kept a hold of the seat until it passed, but she felt the anxiety kicking off and combined with her light-headedness, it wasn't a pleasant experience. One by one, they went to Miguel and got their ticket.

Sarah turned to Marissa. 'The golden ticket!' Her smile was bright. Marissa smiled back in return, doing her best to hide how she was feeling.

They made their way up to the top of the bus, Marissa clutching each seat as she passed by to keep herself steady. When she got to Miguel, he handed her a ticket and she delicately stepped off the bus. The others were already through the gate. As soon as Marissa felt her feet on solid ground, she felt dizzy. She needed a moment before she could continue, she kept one hand on the bus for support. Sarah seemed a little annoyed, but she hung back with Marissa. She offered her arm, and Marissa took it gratefully. Walking slowly together, they eventually made it through the ticket barrier. The vibrancy of what lay before her surpassed everything she had seen on the bus journey.

'I guess we didn't need our passports after all!' said Sarah, but Marissa hardly heard a word as she stood there, torn between the awe of the beauty that surrounded her, and the swelling nausea in her stomach, combined with light-headedness. She managed to look up and saw a cloud just hanging there, right in front of her, just a few feet away from the gate where they came in.

'Jeez, we are so high up here!' said Sarah, depositing Marissa where she was and skipping over to investigate the cloud. She disappeared into it as she became completely enveloped. Now Marissa couldn't see her at all. Realising how high up they were made her feel incredibly dizzy, her breath became short and shallow, and she thought she would fall over. She found a short wall nearby where she was standing, she placed both of her hands onto it, holding on, feeling the world spinning beneath her. *Oh God, I hope this passes. I really want to explore.*

Marissa managed to navigate herself to a break in the wall and sat down on the stones. She breathed, trying to get her bearings. Long slow breaths seemed to ease it a little. Sarah was still running about, happy and oblivious, looking for Ralph.

The tourists looked like insects crawling around the landscape. There was a constant hum or buzz from their chatter and a whistling from the wind as it blew through the stones. Marissa pulled her new hat out of her backpack and put it on. It was tight around her forehead and gave her a sense of being held. After a few minutes she found her stomach relaxing slightly, and the cloud passed by. Marissa could see a few llamas walking around, nibbling on the grass, people were sitting or lying on the ground, some were petting the llamas. She saw Sarah in the distance, skipping around the ruins, enjoying the experience. *It's now, or never, I have to get up and take a look around.*

Marissa gathered herself and stood up. It took all of her resources, but she was determined she was going to continue. She walked slowly down a pathway, arm outstretched, fingers tracing lightly on the wall just to feel it there beside her. She got cold and put the scarf on. After a few steps it became easier to move than she had anticipated, but when she looked up, she felt nauseous again. As long as she kept her head down and watched where her feet were going, her body seemed to behave itself.

Marissa followed the water channels and went up and down steps, moving further and further from the gate. As she settled into it, she extended her senses outwards to try and tap into the sacredness of Machu Picchu and find out what it was that drew so many people here. But all she felt was rising anxiety. *Peru, you were calling me, drawing me to you, and here I am... Is this where you wanted me to be? I don't know...*

Marissa had come to a ledge and was afraid to look down. She pulled herself back and sat down again for another minute or two. An American couple from their tour bus looked at her compassionately but said nothing. She nodded to them and moved to sit directly on the grass instead until she got her breath back. She immediately felt better on the ground. She lay down and stretched out, feeling the world slowing down, the grass beneath her, supporting her whole body. This wasn't what she had expected at all, she had thought it would be life-changing, that she would be awe-struck. She didn't know what she expected, she certainly didn't expect to be incapacitated. She opened her eyes and pushed aside her expectations. Out of the corner of her eye she could see the ruins around her in the sun, with the clouds and the brightness of the sky. Just as it was, it *was* beautiful; the architecture was very special and unique. She decided to just enjoy it for what it was, right here in this moment, rather than force herself to find a greater, deeper meaning. She let go and felt relief surge inside her body. Her shoulders softened, she relaxed, then realised that she had been holding her breath. She stretched out her legs and felt more at ease. *This is what it is, and I am how I am, and it's all okay.*

After a few minutes she felt able to sit up, and then, after a few more minutes, she was able to stand up. Marissa managed to walk about for a little bit, even to take some photographs. The light and the colours were beautiful, the contrast between the bricks and the green grass, the blue of the sky – her little camera could not do it justice. She stayed away from the outer walls and ledges, particularly the ones that had a sheer drop on the other side, and was even able to stand on her own two feet without the support from a wall.

That pull that she had felt in her dream, the pull from the mountain she had seen on her computer, she thought that it was pulling her here, to Machu Picchu. But now she was actually here, she didn't feel like this was the place that was calling to her. It was strange. Now she was more contained in herself, acclimatised, it was as if she was just a tourist looking at a beautiful ruin. *What were my expectations coming here? What did I think I would feel? Did I make myself dizzy back then with all the worry?*

She sat back down on the grass for a while and watched the tourists around her. A couple were filming a video, others had sneaked in sandwiches and chocolate bars and were eating them, leaving crumbs on the grass for the llamas. A llama came up to her and started to nibble on her shoelaces. She giggled and stroked its fur. It didn't seem to mind. She got up and walked around a little more, slowing herself down, taking in all the beauty around her.

Miguel was nearby, herding everyone back to the bus. He walked past her and whispered, 'It's time to come back now.'

As she traced her steps back to the main gate, Marissa realised how deep into the ruins she had gone. *Three hours already?? That was so fast. It only felt like a few minutes.* But she still felt that she'd missed something really big and important.

'Wasn't that amazing?' said Sarah, taking her seat on the bus. She looked radiant. She leaned into Marissa and whispered, 'I kissed him! I *s* I had to come to Peru for a reason – it was to meet Ralph!'

Still trying to make sense of her own experience Marissa didn't quite know what to say to that. She closed her eyes and slept for most of the bus ride back to the hotel

CHAPTER FIVE

Back in Cusco later that evening, Marissa found herself out for dinner with Sarah, Andrew and Ralph. Ralph and Sarah were deep in conversation. *It's a little too much, guys – just get a room, please – and preferably not our room!* Andrew looked just as awkward as Marissa felt, and when they spoke to each other, they were equally relieved to find out that neither of them was interested in the other.

Tired and still slightly nauseous, Marissa would rather have been back in her hotel room alone with her thoughts. But she had to eat something, so she ordered soup, hoping it wouldn't be too spicy. She sipped and made polite conversation with Andrew and excused herself as quickly as she could. She went back up to her room, showered, put on her last pair of clean pyjamas and clambered into bed. Scrolling through the photos she had taken that day, she felt they didn't quite capture the majesty of the place, although there were a few really good ones. She sent her favourite one to Amanda: I made it! It was amazing xxAunty M

As she pressed 'send' she wondered if it really was amazing or if she was just saying it because it was expected. Her phone buzzed with a text back almost straight away: Wow! BSF TLK2UL8R xxA

Marissa smiled. OK U got me, no clue what that means!

She waited for a few minutes for a reply, didn't get one, so she switched off the phone and breathed for a little bit.

I guess it was what it was. That's okay then. If I was in therapy, Olive would tell me to just be with how I feel. Guess that's the best thing to do. Marissa could breathe easier then. Once she decided it was okay to not be in awe even though everyone said it's the done thing, some tiny part of her, deep, deep inside, finally felt at ease, and soon she fell fast asleep.

When she woke at 3am Sarah's bed was still empty. She switched on her phone and got a single emoji response from Amanda with its eyes to heaven. She smiled and closed her eyes again, thinking that they had two more days in Cusco, and then it was time to go home. *Yes, I think I'm ready to get back to my flat now.*

The next day Miguel brought the group to Sacsayhuaman. It was much more open here, less exposed, and Marissa, not feeling under any obligation to enjoy this place specifically, felt much happier than she had done at Machu Picchu. She wasn't feeling ill either, thankfully, and was able to take in the scenery and the energy of the mountains. She didn't mind that Sarah was walking around arm in arm with Ralph, sure they were both grown-ups and could do what they liked. Andrew was there, he nodded at Marissa but didn't come over, instead he was chatting with some of the other single men in the group.

Marissa preferred to watch the locals rather than the tourists. Their colourful clothing, the busy way they moved around, looking so happy to see everyone appreciating their country was a joy to be around. She didn't even mind when they tried to sell her things, she didn't have any room in her suitcase for more stuff so she just smiled and shook her head no in response. She was finally feeling more relaxed, and the sunshine on her face was a real blessing. It felt good to be there.

Miguel took them on a short walking tour and explained the history and the mystery of the site. There had been no trees when it was built, so the Inca could not have pulled the stones up from Cusco using rope and wooden rollers, as they would not have had the wood to do it. It was fascinating – the stones and the walls were so large, how did they build it?

The last official part of the tour was the Temple of the Sun in Coricancha. Miguel had them all up early and they spent most of the morning there. It reminded Marissa of Roman ruins, it was the least interesting part of the trip so far, but the view from the top of the hill was stunning.

Then, they were done! It came as a surprise, although they had been expecting it. Miguel dropped them back to the hotel and said his goodbyes, then they were free to do what they pleased for the rest of the day. Sarah had booked a transfer for the following morning to take them to Cusco airport, and then home.

Marissa didn't feel like she had gotten what she came for. She was disheartened and felt like she wanted to get away by herself so she went back to the markets, leaving Sarah and Ralph to their own devices. She still didn't fancy a museum, it was just too hot. She got herself a juice and sat in the main square taking in the sunshine and the sights. It was good to walk around Cusco, she felt very independent.

Sarah had asked if they could go for dinner with Ralph and Andrew as they would all be going on their separate ways the following day. Marissa figured that Sarah was in denial that she probably wouldn't see Ralph again, but she let her chatter on and on, making plans for a future that wouldn't come to pass. She chose a restaurant a few blocks away from the hotel and was fussing and preening about what to wear. The busy market square had been blissful in comparison to being around Sarah for the last few hours.

+++

The night was hot and dusty, the restaurant was dark and loud, Marissa wasn't sure what was on her dinner plate, but at this stage, she didn't care. She had a small appetite at last; when she lifted her fork to her mouth and ate the meat (she thought that it was fish), it was quite spicy and seemed to lift her a little bit. The altitude sickness had taken its toll on her and she didn't want to eat too much in case it came back.

Sarah and Ralph were all over each other at the table, nuzzling, holding hands, kissing... Andrew was as awkward as the first time they had sat together, but Marissa didn't mind. She had come to terms with what was, let go of her expectations, felt happier in herself, and was beginning to look forward to going home to her own familiar space.

Looking around, she saw Miguel at the bar. He was looking around as if he had lost something. She went over to say goodbye to him again – his face brightened to see her.

'Ahh, Marissa, I thought I might find you here. I am so glad to see you. A few friends and me, we are going out to see a shaman.

Tonight. This is not for everybody, but I think you will like it. Will you come? I think you need to come with me. I was looking for you. I don't know why, but yes, you must come.'

Marissa felt safe with Miguel, he had been lovely to the group, but the butterflies suddenly hit her stomach and she suddenly wanted to vomit. Speechless, she looked at Miguel. *Why me? Why was he looking for me in particular?* This didn't feel the same as altitude nausea, it was more visceral. This went deeper.

'Is perfectly safe,' he reassured her. 'I think is important for you.'

Important for me? Maybe it is... Her stomach settled almost instantly. 'Okay,' she said hesitantly.

Miguel smiled. 'You will not regret this. I know is supposed to be for you. Meet me at back of this restaurant in ten minutes. Do not bring anyone else.' Then he was gone.

Marissa went back to her table and watched Sarah giggling as Ralph fed her from his plate. *It's not as if Sarah would miss me if I was gone for a couple of hours...* Andrew was staring off into the distance. She pushed the rest of her food around on her plate, trying to eat some more, but she wasn't hungry now. *I'm happy for her, I truly am. This holiday wasn't what I expected at all, I don't know what I expected. Or why I had such a pull to come here. But it was lovely all the same. What's a shaman anyway?*

She cleared her throat and faced the lovebirds. 'Sarah, here's some money for my dinner. I'm going back to the hotel. Ralph and Andrew, it was lovely to meet you.' She left some cash on the table and stood up to leave.

'Lovely to meet you too,' said Ralph, beaming as if he'd won the lotto. Andrew nodded at her. It had been as trying for him as it had been for her. She smiled back, took her handbag and cardigan and went to the bathroom at the back of the restaurant. She looked in the mirror and adjusted her hair, then went outside through the staff entrance.

Miguel and two of his friends were outside leaning up against the wall, smoking cigarettes, laughing and speaking in Spanish. He nodded at her and beckoned her over. He spoke quietly so only she could hear.

'I say this, so we are clear. I do not want to make sex with you. You are totally safe with me.' He looked around and added 'This experience is not for tourists, I never asked anyone from group before.'

'Why me, now?' asked Marissa.

'I don't know.' Miguel shrugged his shoulders and put both hands up in the air. 'I just have feeling, it is right thing. I feel push. Just wait, and you will see.'

Miguel looked at his watch, nodded to his friends, put his cigarette out with the bottom of his shoe and beckoned to Marissa to follow him to his car. His friends were laughing, and for once, Marissa wasn't feeling like they were laughing at her.

Miguel opened the back door and she got in. His friend sat in the front with Miguel. The car had torn leather seats, it smelled of sweat, cigarette smoke and heat, but there was something oddly comforting about the combination.

Miguel drove them out of the city and away from the lights. Marissa put her cardigan around her shoulders and felt herself relaxing the further they got from the city. She didn't understand it, surrounded by strangers in a strange country, why would she be feeling calmer than she usually does at home? The men in the front were speaking Quechuan; she liked how musical it was, it was almost soothing. It felt like she was getting a real experience of Peru instead of the tourist experience. She had heard Quechuan at the marketplace but not in day-to-day conversation. Calmness entered her body completely and she felt like she was, indeed, supposed to be there. She heard a voice speak in her mind, 'Don't worry child, this is what you have come for.'

Miguel drove for what seemed like an hour and a half, but nobody was keeping track of time. There was condensation on the window where Marissa had laid her head down, she felt completely lulled, there was no sign of any butterflies anywhere. It was very dark, there were only a few streetlights when they drove through several small villages. Mostly they were on a dirt track which wound up tracks steeply and down hills sharply. She sat up as the car changed gear and slowed down. Something inside Marissa's heart opened, it seemed to be in anticipation. *Of what, though?* Her body became taught, she felt adrenaline flowing through her veins. *Is this fight or flight? Or just excitement? It's like my body knows what is happening, and my mind doesn't...* Her eyes took in even more light from the surroundings, she was wide awake now. There was a strong presence beside her, one that was familiar, but never this strong. Right now it felt like it was right on top of her. *None of this makes any sense at all.*

When Miguel finally stopped the car there were no street lights, just the light from the moon, which was almost full. They were on a street in a small village with only a few houses. Marissa was alert, her senses were widened and took in more than usual, but she couldn't put her finger on what she was feeling.

'Come,' Miguel said gently, opening the door for Marissa and holding his hand out to her.

She hesitated.

'Totally safe, again, I promise you.'

She nodded and unfolded herself out of the car. She stood, then stretched herself out to her full height. She felt taller, if that was possible, her whole body was pulsing. There was nobody else there, not that she could see, but that presence was so strong... Standing there in the moonlight, she looked around but could not poinpoint what it was that affected her heart so strongly.

'Is beautiful, yes?'

'Yes.'

Miguel pointed towards the East. 'There, you see, snow-capped mountain? Is Ausangate. Much clearer to see from here, especially in daytime. Is so beautiful, my favourite place in all the world.'

Marissa felt a cold sweat drench her body. She turned around to where he had been pointing. *A snow-capped mountain.* She craned her neck to see beyond the village as her mind put the pieces together. That was what this was all about, the whole trip, the pulling, the struggle. She felt a deep knowingness enter her, it was difficult to describe the feeling of it, but suddenly, she knew. This was her mountain. At last. She was here. She breathed a massive sigh of relief. Yes, she was really here.

I had totally given up, I thought... But yes, it makes sense now. The last night, when I give up hope and accept, then there she is. Her face broke into a smile, and she nodded to the mountain. She felt 10 ft taller, then suddenly, acknowledgement from the mountain rippled deep within her. *The mountain sees me, too!* It didn't matter what happened next, this felt like where she was supposed to be.

Miguel led them all into a small, heavily decorated, cottage-like house off of the main track. Miguel's friend had already gone inside. There were candles lit outside making a pathway to the front door, there were woven baskets with flowers hanging on the walls beside the house, and in the flickering light, Marissa could also make out a mural, but she couldn't tell what it was. The front door was ajar. Miguel stopped for a moment at the threshold and said something under his breath before entering. Marissa followed him in and was suddenly hit with thick hot air, many smells and sounds. She suddenly had a sense that she had been to this place before. *Déjà vu?* Her heart was pulsing, she could reach out beyond the four walls of the cottage and sense the mountain there, close by. She didn't need to see it to know it was there. It felt comforting, and she was calm.

The house was packed, there were so many different types of people, all seemed local. Marissa was the only tourist there. Most of them were talking Quechuan in low, hushed tones, it seemed quite serious, although there was some laughter, too. She had difficulty for a moment, separating out everything that impacted upon her.

Miguel picked his way through the crowd and led her to the back room. The air was cloudy with smoke. A woman in traditional costume was waving around a thick and heavy burning stick with a pungent aroma. The woman was chanting, Marissa thought, in Quechuan, but it seemed different in some way. Candles were burning down to the quick in glass jars, Marissa could see people drinking a greenish coloured liquid, others were curled up in blankets lying down on the floor.

It was like nothing Marissa had ever seen, yet it felt familiar, she knew she was safe. She felt the presence of the mountain nearby, the whole scene, it was like she was acting out a designated role in a movie.

Marissa looked at the faces of the people in the cottage. The woman with the stick at the top of the room looked back at Marissa, as if to study her, then looked at Miguel, then nodded her head in approval. She walked over to a small table draped in a colourful cloth. Marissa craned her neck to see what was on it – bits of bones, candles, a rattle and some carvings. The woman rearranged something, put her burning stick down in a dish and then left the room. The talking stopped suddenly, and the energy in the room changed, it became electric.

Miguel found a space on the floor towards the back and motioned for Marissa to sit beside him. There were cushions and blankets strewn around, she chose a red cushion and lowered herself onto it, finding it quite comfortable. The people in the room began to chant. It started as a low murmur but grew louder when the shaman appeared. She looked like she was 200 years old, her wrinkled face lifted when she looked at the group in front of her and she smiled, showing black, broken teeth. She wore a square, richly decorated hat patterned with colourful beads and a black cloak that had a similar pattern running through it. She also wore many beaded necklaces, some made of bones. The woman closed her eyes and swayed back and forward for a few moments, chanting to herself, and after a few minutes, she seemed to be in a trance. She held a rattle in her hand, suddenly raising her voice in a louder chant and started shaking her rattle at the crowd. Suddenly, with three loud shakes of the rattle, all the chanting stopped, and the room fell silent.

Dried leaves were burning in a dish, all Marissa could hear in the silence was the hiss and crackle as they succumbed to the flame. The shaking of the rattle began again, softer this time, and the shaman started to sing. With closed eyes she sang and turned in circles, it was hypnotic.

'She's calling the directions,' Miguel whispered. 'She asks healing spirits and ancestors to come, also asking spirits of the land to come for the healing tonight.'

'It's a healing?'

'Oh yes! Shaman Healing, very powerful. You will love. Very special.'

The shaman spun around in circles and rattled up to the sky, then turned to everyone, opened her eyes and gave the biggest smile Marissa had ever seen. She was so very beautiful in that moment, there was a great feeling of love coming from her, it washed over everyone, including Marissa, and Marissa felt warm rushing sensations filling her body, all the tightness and worry left her, and her heart softened in its new, expansive state. She was glowing, she felt vibrant, alive, better than she had ever felt in her whole life.

'Who is first?', said the shaman very slowly in English, pointing at Marissa with her rattle. Marissa suddenly felt hot, and another wave of sweat poured over her body. The shaman looked around the whole room and smiled and winked, and everyone laughed.

'Welcome, welcome to my home,' said the shaman to Marissa, lowering her rattle and smiling directly at her. 'We talk later, you and me. Do not worry.' She turned back to the group and added, 'First, ceremony.' Marissa felt relieved as the attention shifted, but she didn't get her usual sense of needing to shrink, instead, she continued to feel the presence of the mountain beside her. It gave her more confidence than she usually would have. *I don't mind them seeing me here, I feel the mountain wants me to be here. It's okay.*

The shaman winked at Miguel and he suddenly sat up taller, he seemed very pleased and relieved with her reaction. Marissa thought if he had a tail, he would be wagging it. She laughed and relaxed, and Miguel beamed again, and the love, well, the love seemed to soften everything.

When she finished her ceremony, the shaman sat her bulky body down on the mat and faced the room. She gestured to the group, and people began to line up to see her. Marissa stayed sitting and watched with Miguel, smiling all the while, her heart filled with love. She looked at Miguel, and he smiled back at her. *I feel so comfortable here, even though these are total strangers to me. Even Miguel is a stranger.* They stayed together, watching the shaman speak to and heal the people in the room as they came up to her one by one.

Marissa had been watching her work but was not able to discern any particular technique or pattern. Each time the woman interacted with someone it was different, the movements were different, the parts of the body that she touched, the tools that she used. Sometimes she motioned for the person to lie down on the floor on a pile of blankets and cushions, and she would raise her rattle and shake it over the person, spinning around and making hand movements over them. Sometimes she drank from a little bottle and then spat the contents out from her mouth and into that person's face, or onto their body, or both. The noise when she spat was loud and strong, the first few times Marissa heard it she jumped with fright. Everyone she paid attention to seemed grateful, everyone asked for blessings, everyone returned to their place without argument when the shaman said she was finished with them.

'And now, my child, it is your turn,' said the shaman in broken English, turning to Marissa once more. 'What is it that you want to learn from me?'

Marissa was taken aback by the question. She wasn't expecting it, and with the shaman looking directly at her in front of the crowded room, she didn't want to make a mistake. Marissa had been working on her list of questions in her little notebook back home, and the most important one of all jumped into her mind.

'Who am I?' she asked.

The shaman's laughter was loud, like crows cackling in cacophony. Everyone else in the room laughed too, it was contagious. Marissa found herself laughing as well. She felt confident that that was the correct question.

The shaman seemed to agree. 'Very good,' she said slowly, emphasising each word as if it was a sentence in itself. 'Very good. Yes indeed, very good.'

She pulled a snakeskin out of her medicine bag, threw it up in the air and watched how it fell onto the bed of blankets. She seemed pleased and grunted in approval.

Marissa was still sitting on her red cushion on the floor.

'Come, come,' said the shaman, gesturing for her to come and join her at the top of the room.

Marissa stood hesitantly, then carefully picked out her way through the other people to the front of the room. 'Sit', said the medicine woman as she pointed to a colourful blanket where some of the others had been sitting or lying for their healings. Marissa acquiesced and sat facing the shaman, cross-legged, with the snakeskin on the colourful blankets in front of her. The shaman chose a small bottle from the altar behind her and opened it, pouring a single drop of a black sticky liquid onto her index finger. Placing the bottle back on the table, she reached over towards Marissa and drew a cross on her forehead, marking her skin with the black substance. She then lightly tapped Marissa's heart and blew on Marissa's face.

Standing on the stepping stone, surrounded by water, Marissa found herself back in her dream. Or was it a dream? The snake-like body of the silvery scaled creature below the water seemed to be getting closer to her. It took her a few moments to orient herself to her surroundings. She saw the mountain and felt its presence in her heart, strong, large and loving, telling her, 'You've got this.'

She wasn't afraid. The creature raised its head out of the water and looked at her. It was a sea serpent, it had bright blue scales underneath its eyes and on the crown of its head. It was actually quite beautiful. Marissa held her precarious position on the stepping stone and didn't waver. The moonlight glinted off of the silver scales on the sea serpent's face. It cocked its head as if examining her, once, then twice, then it plunged back into the water, swimming over to her. As it got closer, Marissa realised how huge it was, a single scale below its left eye was almost as large as she was. But she wasn't scared. The sea serpent opened its mouth and swallowed her whole. She felt darkness engulf her, and then her eyes fogged up, she felt her heartbeat, it seemed like she had completely dissolved in the darkness of the maw of this beast and was nothing now but the beating of her own heart. Then suddenly, the fog cleared, and she was looking out through the eyes of the serpent. She had become the serpent! Oh, the freedom!

She flew and dove in the water, she felt the full length of her serpent's body, the strength of her tail propelling her through the dark waters. She swam down towards the bottom of the lake and saw lights, a hidden city, and her heart leapt. Fish moved quickly out of her path, the light was faint down here, yet she could see the seaweed fronds swaying in the current. It was amazing. She felt the beast that she was moving swiftly, and she went up this time, up and up until she crashed through the barrier between water and sky. Feeling the cold air on her scales, she rose up into the crisp air, night sky and the moon. She flipped in honour of the high mountains, the feeling of freedom surging in her blood. Why had she been so afraid of this majestic creature? It felt like she had wings, she could go anywhere, do anything, she was invincible.

She splashed back down into the water and suddenly found herself on a forest floor, belly to the ground, tongue out, tasting and smelling humid air, feeling the moist earth beneath her. She was still moving, undulating past the base of tall trees, smooth vines and dark, green leaves. She wove her way towards one of the trees and wrapped her long, limbless body around it. With large muscles rippling, her snake-like body worked its way swiftly upwards into the branches until she wound herself around a limb and stopped. She looked down at all the lush richness below. She felt something stroke her cheek.

'Lady, lady, are you okay?'

The concern in Miguel's voice was clear, but Marissa couldn't make sense of where she was. Wasn't she in the forest? Or was she in the water? Was she a snake or a serpent? She felt someone holding her hand, stroking the skin on her arm. She wasn't limbless anymore.

'Are you here? Come back to me, is time to go, you must get back to catch your flight.'

Marissa's eyes fluttered. She felt the heavy weight of her body as she crash-landed back into it, aching and slow. She opened her eyes to see Miguel's bright eyes smiling with relief.

'I knew you were there! I am glad you come back to us. Come, it is time to go.'

'But the ceremony? The shaman?'

'Is long over, she has gone. Is time to go back to hotel, you leave for airport soon. You do not want to miss your connection.'

Marissa tried to shake herself fully awake. *What happened? Where was I? What time is it?* Her heart leapt with worry. She looked around, she was still in the room where she had been with the shaman, she had blankets over her, she must have been sleeping. But the room was empty, there was nobody else present except for the woman wearing the traditional costume earlier, only now she was wearing jeans and a dirty white tee-shirt. The sun was starting to come up, light trickled in through the windows, there was a different quality to the room, it wasn't as magical as it had seemed the night before.

'Drink this,' said Miguel, handing her a bottle of water. 'We need to drive now.'

As Marissa walked slowly to the car she felt like something was unfinished, she badly wanted to talk to the medicine woman to ask her what happened. Had she passed out? Why had she been back in her dream again? But the shaman was nowhere to be found. She glanced over towards the mountain, her mountain, but she felt foggy and unsure which direction she was facing. Marissa could see the mural on the side of the cottage now, it was a large green snake wrapped around itself in a circle, its tail inside its mouth.

Miguel opened the passenger side door and helped Marissa in, as she was still a little doddery on her feet. His friend had left earlier, so it was just the two of them heading back to the city.

As Miguel drove away from the mountain, Marissa felt a deep sadness come onto her. This expedition seemed to create more questions than answers. She remembered the smiling face of the shaman, her colourful beads, her broken teeth, the love that poured out from her, and as she thought about that love, it was as if she could feel it again, and she felt a little better. Marissa noticed her surroundings as they drove in the early morning light. She was able to see things she had not noticed on the way there in the dark, lizards running across the road, cactus flowers, the colours of the rooftops of the shack-like houses as they passed them by. When they finally entered the outskirts of Cusco she noticed how sleepy the streets seemed to be. The city was waking up, people were setting out the fruit and vegetable stalls, the stall owners chatting happily to one another. The colours were strong in the warm waking sunlight, and everything seemed like it was in high definition.

He parked the car across the road from the hotel, then Miguel turned to Marissa with a concerned look on his face. 'How are you feel? I was worried,' he said.

'I understand,' said Marissa. 'I don't know what happened. Did I pass out? I'm okay, I guess.'

'It seemed that way to me,' he said, 'but you fell on blanket, so I knew you were not hurt.' He scratched his head and then looked at his watch. 'It's already almost time for your transfer. I will see you in reception in thirty minutes, I bring you to airport. I hope you can be ready for your journey in that time.'

He smiled, and Marissa smiled back. They got out of the car.

'Miguel?' said Marissa. 'Thank you. I don't know what that was last night, but I feel different today. In a good way.' She smiled. 'I saw some incredible things in the shaman's house, to see those healings, yes, it was very special. That will be something I will never forget.'

'Good,' said Miguel returning the smile. 'Now go, I see you soon, in reception. With your suitcase and your friend, too.'

Marissa found her key-card and went into the hotel and back up to her room. Sarah was there, crying and packing, her mascara running down her face.

'What's wrong? Why are you crying?'

'I can't believe it. Of all the things... I just found out that Ralph is feckin married!'

'Oh dear,' said Marissa, figuring that Sarah didn't notice that she had been missing all night. She pulled out her suitcase and started to throw things into it. *It's going to be a long journey home.*

CHAPTER SIX

Well, at least I still have my hat and scarf. Marissa picked them up and held them to her face, drinking in the smells from the marketplace that still clung to the fibres of the wool. She hung them up on the back of her front door, alongside her coats and a few older scarves.

It was lovely not having anywhere to go that day. 'What day is it today anyway?' she asked out loud, and finding her phone, she looked at the date. 'Shit, shit, shit, my assignment is due tomorrow.' She felt herself on the edge of a spiral of anxiety, she pulled herself back and caught it before it tipped her over. She pushed the soles of her feet into the ground and let out a deep breath. *Okay, it will be late, I have a good excuse. Or ... maybe it won't be late. Let's see...*

Marissa pushed the clutter that had accumulated on her desk over to one side and switched on her laptop. As it thrummed into life she switched the kettle on, brushed her teeth, and put warmer socks on. She entered her password, got her alpaca scarf back off the door and wrapped it around her shoulders. A fresh cup of tea from her favourite mug in her hand, she sat down at her desk and searched for, and found, what she had already written.

She was studying a module on the work of Carl Rogers. He was the founder of person-centred counselling. His work was based on the idea that the client should control the conversation completely, talking about anything they wanted, with the full support of the therapist. Marissa wasn't sure if this was such a good idea, she knew that in her own experience of therapy she would have happily talked about the roads and weather for sessions at a time. She looked at the screen.

> *Emphasis is placed on the three core conditions: empathy, congruence and unconditional positive regard. Using*

these conditions helps the therapist try and understand the client's experiences and feelings, allowing the client to feel heard and understood, accepted and valued, enabling the relationship to grow mutually.

It seemed like a lifetime ago Marissa had been in class discussing the pros and cons of the person-centred method.

'I've got to focus,' she said to herself, getting up to let Tobermory out. She sat back down again. Her scarf was certainly warm, and she held it in her hand, gazing into the pattern and remembering the green grass in Manchu Picchu, the alpacas nibbling at her shoelaces, and the sunshine on her face. She looked out the window at the rain, then pulled herself back to her computer screen. *What am I trying to say here?*

She started typing:

Where the person-centred method is focused completely on the needs and wants of the client, it is possible that the client may not want to confront the issue that brought them to counselling in the first place. In order for the counselling sessions to be both effective and economical for the client, some gentle direction may be required. For this reason, I do not feel that leaving the pace of the work completely up to the client is warranted in every case. I feel that Person-Centred Counselling in combination with some other methods of working would be more of an ideal situation for both client and therapist.

She nodded her head as she re-read and agreed with what she just wrote. *I'm back!*

Just as she was finishing off her assignment a few hours later, the doorbell rang. It was her mother, excited to see her and wanting to see all the photographs from Peru. She had brought groceries with her, for which Marissa was very grateful as she had not left her flat all day. Her mother made some light supper for them both as Marissa described the hotels, Sarah's need for male attention, and how much she enjoyed the tour. She deliberately left out her evening with the medicine woman, she didn't think her mother would understand, and she still didn't fully understand it either.

'So this Miguel person,' her mother said, as she washed and dried the dinner dishes, 'was he the driver too? How many people were on your tour?'

'Yes, he drove too some of the time. We had a different driver for Machu Picchu. But he did everything else. About twenty-two of us, a mixed group, mostly Americans, but there were some Germans and a few French people.'

'Any nice single men?'

Marissa sighed. 'Mum...'

Rose dried her hands with the towel and came and sat down beside her daughter. 'Marissa, it's been three years now since James left you.' She reached over and gently pushed a strand of hair away from Marissa's face. 'You're beautiful, you're intelligent, and time is ticking by. Why aren't you looking for someone to love? And to love you? Me and your father – by the time we were your age, we were already married.'

Marissa sighed and pulled back a little, out of her mother's reach. She hated feeling pressurised, but instead of getting irritated, she was becoming emotional. 'I don't know, Mum, my heart still isn't ready. I thought I was doing better until I saw that photograph last year on Facebook, the one of James with his new wife and their baby. Why would he marry her so quickly after running away from me? He hardly knew her, and we had been together for four years...'

Marissa could feel tears starting to pool behind her eyes as she remembered how happy James and his new family looked in that photo. Without her. She had dreamed about having a family with James, she even had a name ready for their baby when the time was right. That baby that would never exist now. She was grieving as much for it, as for the loss of the relationship. She still really didn't know why he had left. They never had that conversation.

Marissa's mother passed her a tissue and moved towards her, starting to rub her back. Marissa waved in the air and sat forward in the chair to avoid the contact. She blew her nose.

'Anyway, I have my course now, and my job, I'm busy and I love learning about psychology and how to help people.'

'I'm just trying to help you,' said Marissa's mother, looking down and fingering the silver broach Marissa had got for her in Peru.

'I don't want any help.'

Her mother made eye contact. 'Well, why would someone want *your* help, if you can't accept help yourself?'

Marissa was quiet, her face still wet with tears.

'It's time to move on, love, time to make plans for yourself now. You're twenty-seven and your life is waiting for you. I'm sure there are many men out there that would love to be a part of it.'

Marissa blew her nose again and tried to push her anger, frustration and feelings of hopelessness to one side. She didn't know why she wasn't over James yet, either. Three years was a long time, and it was only in the last few months that she hadn't been thinking about him every day. Well, not every moment of every day, anyway. It didn't seem normal. Or maybe it was normal. One of the things she was learning in her psychotherapy diploma was that normal didn't exist.

'I'll think about it,' she said to her mother with a sigh.

'Well, I suppose I will have to be happy with that.'

'Now, can we change the subject?'

'I brought cake... '

'Perfect.'

+++

At work the next day, Sarah seemed in much better form than she had been on the plane and almost already completely over Ralph.

'I swear I could kill him,' she said, in between bites of her egg sandwich at lunch. 'I'm going to start over and try online dating.' She looked determined, but the sigh that escaped her gave away her sadness. Looking at Marissa, she lifted her shoulders again and added, 'Hey! Why don't you do it too? With me? I know you said you're not interested in a man, but you have a lonely look about you, I know it would cheer you right up.' Sarah was beaming once more, as if she had just found the answer to life, the universe, and everything.

Marissa shook her head, she couldn't believe it, it was like the world was conspiring to fix her up.

'Come on,' said Sarah enthusiastically, 'at least it would get you out of the flat, meeting new people, it would be a bit of fun.'

'I've met some nice people on my diploma course,' said Marissa defensively, putting half of her sandwich back into the wrapper.

'But they're all miserable there, moaning about their lives. Anyone studying psychology must have something wrong with them. Except for you, of course!'

'It's psychotherapy, not psychology, and no, they're not any more miserable than anyone else that I've met,' said Marissa.

'Anyway, you told me there were only three men in your class, and two of them were married?'

'Yes, that's true.'

'Well, just make an online profile, and you can always say no if you don't like the look of them.' Sarah looked at her watch. 'It's time to go back, we can talk about this later – hey, think about it at least? I'll email you with a website that I'm thinking about joining up with.'

Sarah had a habit of wearing Marissa down with her enthusiasm and persistence. 'Okay, I'll think about it,' Marissa said with a tired smile, dropping the last bit of her sandwich and its wrapping into the bin and going back to her desk.

That night Marissa had class. They were split up into groups of three, one was the observer, one the client and one the therapist. It was Marissa's turn to be the client and she had butterflies in her stomach, she didn't want to talk about what was going on for her right now. It wasn't that she didn't like the people she was paired with, it was more that she wasn't sure about how she was feeling about dating, not quite ready to put it into words. So she thought she'd talk about Peru instead.

'Whenever you're ready, Marissa,' said Emmet, her designated therapist (and the unmarried man in the group).

Marissa cleared her throat and began. 'I'm finding it difficult to settle back into a routine after my holiday.' She thought this would be a nice and easy topic to discuss, rather than the pain she was still feeling around James.

'Okay,' said Emmet. 'So what you're saying is that you had a great holiday, but you're not feeling the benefit of it right now. What is difficult for you around, as you say, 'settling back'?'

'Well, I don't know if I'm not feeling the benefit of it. Peru was so sunny and warm, I felt free there, no responsibilities. I do feel like I had a break, but coming back to my everyday routine, I am feeling a reluctance to do things that I have to do, like get up and go to work.' Marissa wondered where this was going, it wasn't going in the direction she wanted it to, that's for sure.

'Ahh, okay. So tell me, what was it like to have no responsibilities?' asked Emmet, while Barbara, the observer, scribbled a few notes.

Marissa thought about the question. 'Well, I felt free, lighter. I didn't have much anxiety at all while I was in Peru, that was surprising to me.'

'Surprising how?' Emmet coughed. 'I mean, you're saying you felt surprised, what exactly was it that surprised you?'

'I thought a strange place, a different country, well aren't they good reasons to be anxious? I would be anxious here about anything really, small things like remembering to turn off the immersion, locking the door of my flat, those types of things. Or just standing waiting for the bus, sometimes I just seem to feel anxious for no reason. Most of the time in Peru, I felt happy to be there, for the opportunity to see somewhere amazing.'

Marissa could feel the butterflies swarming in her stomach, it was getting on the verge of becoming intense. She kept her feet pressed into the ground. *I'm okay, it's just therapy practice, and it's only Emmet and Barbara.* Practice never felt like real therapy anyway, especially with the observer present. And nobody else was really watching them.

Emmet nodded. 'So, what is the actual problem you're experiencing, now that you're back?'

Marissa thought about it for a moment. It felt like the problem was tangled in something bigger, she couldn't see exactly what was going on. It was as if someone had jumbled together lots of different coloured balls of wool and only one of them was important. She was a mess of feelings, so she decided to be abstract.

'Colours,' she said. 'There were lots of colours in Peru, and not so many colours back here.'

'Please continue,' said Emmet.

'We have three minutes left,' noted Barbara.

Both Emmet and Marissa nodded.

'I know it's coming into winter here, no that's not it. There are fewer colours and the days get shorter, but you can still see colours in the winter. No, this is more like a television, the quality of the image. Peru was full colour, high definition. Dublin is black and white, routine is boring maybe, or my job, well, I don't actually dislike what I do. Not that I do very much... No, that's not it either. It's not boring, there's just something missing. I didn't notice it so much until I went to Peru, and now I have something to compare it to.'

'When you say Dublin, do you mean the city?' asked Emmet.

'I think I mean my life.'

'Time's up,' said Barbara. 'I thought you were really good,' she said, turning towards Emmet. 'I liked how you reflected back in your own words to clarify the client's problem.' She looked at Marissa. 'Was that useful to you as the client?'

Marissa was sitting with what she had just blurted out. Her life – colourless, black and white, missing something. She had felt this for the longest time but never voiced it before, never told anyone before either. It was quite unsettling to have done both so quickly. 'Oh, sorry – you're talking to me?' she asked, looking up.

'Yes,' said Barbara matter-of-factly. 'Did you think the way Emmet handed you back your issue was useful?'

'I don't know. I suppose you could say that.'

The tutor's bell rang, getting everyone's attention.

'Okay, everyone, back to the main circle. Let's share how we got on,' said Ms Greene.

There was more chatter and sounds of chairs scraping off of the floor as everyone moved their chairs back into a larger circle, so all of the students present were facing Ms Greene.

'I want to hear from the observers first. Who wants to share what they learned?'

Marissa sank deeper into her chair. It was as if this feeling of dullness that she had just unearthed was sitting right there beside her. Once she recognised it was there, it started growing. She felt heavy. Images of the night with Miguel and the shaman appeared in her mind, people on the floor looking for healing, the shaman waving her rattle over them and chanting. Why? Did she need healing too? She hadn't had her dream since before she went to Peru, she wondered what that meant. And more importantly, she wondered what had happened to her between the shaman tapping on her heart and Miguel waking her up. What had she missed? She remembered that those moments of full colour came right after the healing, and they seemed to have dissolved away somewhere between Peru and Ireland. *Was it full colour the whole time? Or just after the healing?*

'Marissa? What was it like for you to be Emmet's client?' Ms Greene's question snapped her out of her thoughts and back into the group.

'Actually,' said Marissa, 'he was very good. He really made me think. I have to think some more about what I discovered while talking to him.'

Over the course of the year, Marissa had realised that it wasn't so much about the content of the issues that the tutor wanted to know about, it was more about the process.

'Good to hear. Well done, Emmet,' said Ms Greene. 'That's it for tonight. Don't forget to hand in your assignments on the way out, well done everyone, see you next week.'

Marissa was troubled. Emmet had given her a lift to the end of her road. It had been raining, so she was grateful. She looked at his face as he concentrated on the drive, she knew there would never be an attraction between them. Perhaps she *would* try the website. She turned the key, opened her door, took off her wet coat, and switched on the kettle. Straight into pyjamas and her alpaca hat, she turned the heating on for an hour and made herself a hot chocolate. As she settled into bed with her drink and her laptop, she couldn't stop thinking about the colours, the sharpness and the brightness around her after she had been healed (had she been healed?) and then thinking about life in Dublin, the greyness, how dull everything seemed. What exactly was it that was dull? She was very aware of the heaviness, now that her attention had been brought to it.

She opened her laptop to distract herself, and there was the email from Sarah, as promised, with the name of the dating website she had chosen.

'I wonder if that's what the missing piece is?' Marissa said out loud. But first she opened Facebook in a browser window and searched James Smythe. It had been a good few months since she did this, she felt like she just needed to check on him, see what he was doing. His face popped up in the search results and she clicked his name. Photos of him and his new (blonde) wife appeared, they were on the beach with their baby. She scrolled through a few of them and noticed how his wife appeared to be putting on weight. Or else she was pregnant again. But strangely, she didn't feel upset at the thought of a second baby. She flicked back to an older picture of James, one that she would torture herself with when he had just left her. One she would gaze at for hours. But now, she felt more settled. She could look at him and not feel like crying, the devastation was not as bad as it was. She zoomed in on it so his face filled the screen.

'Goodbye, sweet James,' she said to the photograph, 'I will never understand why you left like that. What was about me that wasn't good enough for you? Why is this new woman (she refused to learn her name even though it was there on Facebook) the one? Yes, I wonder what life would have been like if we did get married and that baby was ours. But it isn't ours. And I'm here, and you're there, and you seem to be happy.' Marissa sighed. 'Yes, you do seem happy as much as it hurts me to admit it.' She stroked his cheek on the laptop screen. 'I suppose I still love you, and I do want you to be happy. And if you're happy now, then maybe it's time for me to be happy, too.'

She felt something leave her body, a tension she was holding somewhere deep down that she wasn't aware of. Something inside her felt more settled, calmer. She typed the address of the dating website into the browser and closed the Facebook window. Up came the dating site with its friendlier than friendly introduction and promise of romance, love, and possibly more. She had a look through some of the profiles, they didn't seem so bad, and a couple of the men there looked like they could be a bit of a laugh.

I could do with a bit of a laugh. Okay, here goes. She clicked 'Sign up.'

It was quite straightforward: name, age, photograph. Photograph – which one would she use?

Marissa didn't like how she looked, and since James had left – okay, maybe she would have to stop punctuating her life by 'before James left' and 'after James left', but her life had felt that way. Maybe today it was time for a new chapter. She reached up and touched her straggly curls. *I'll get my hair done and buy some new makeup, then I'll get a good photo and make a profile. I'm not sure if I want to do this right now.*

Marissa searched instead for Ausangate, the mountain. She recognised it right away from the pictures and felt a familiar burst of love in her heart. *Ahh, there you are. Now I know your name, I can always find you.* She saved one of the photographs to her computer and turned it into her desktop wallpaper. She closed the applications and stared at the photograph for a while, until her eyes began to blur.

She shut down the laptop, got up and put it on her desk, switched off the heating and lights, and got back into bed with her phone. She looked at Facebook on her mobile phone in the dark under her bed covers for a while. Up popped a post from Joanne. *I'll contact Joanne. It would be great to see her, it's been too long.*

Marissa clicked the message button and sent: *'Fancy a catchup?'*

It had been a long, emotional day. She turned off her phone, turned on her alarm, turned over in bed and closed her eyes. Thank goodness tomorrow was Friday.

CHAPTER SEVEN

They met at their favourite restaurant for lunch that Sunday. After the laughter, looking through the latest photographs of Joanne's three children and the catchup of the day to day, Joanne took a long look at Marissa.

'Okay what's going on?' Joanne asked. 'I've not seen you since ages, you didn't even tell me you were going to Peru, I saw that on Facebook. I really should be angry at you over that... But I'm not. 'Cos I never am.' She smiled. 'So tell me?'

'I'm thinking of joining a dating website.'

Joanne smiled and sat back in her chair, looking relieved. 'About time! Get back in the game! Susanna met her fiancé on a dating website, so there must be some good people out there. I'm delighted for you.'

'No, I don't think that's the problem,' said Marissa, 'besides my needing a complete make-up overhaul and a new wardrobe for going out.' Marissa touched her hair, feeling the springiness of the curls. She'd got it cut the previous day and still wasn't sure about it.

'Your hair is lovely, by the way,' said Joanna.

'I think it's too short, I'm not used to it like this. It'll grow back. Nobody can ever cut curly hair well. I hate getting it done, but I needed to cut the split ends away. Thank you, though. No, there's something else going on, something I've not talked about with anyone else.'

Joanne sat forward in her chair again, looking concerned. 'What is it? Did something happen?'

'No, I mean yes, I mean... well, I don't actually know what happened. That's the problem.'

'I don't understand...'

'Okay, well, yeah. Sorry for not telling you about Peru, it was all kind of last minute. I guess I was caught up in work, and college, and stuff. Anyway, thanks for not being upset with me.'

'That's okay, we do our own things, we don't always have to know everything about each other. Sure you don't want to know half the stuff that preoccupies me, I'm sure!'

Marissa smiled, and was genuinely relieved.

'So?' Joanne raised her eyebrows in impatience.

'Oh yeah. Well, I went with Sarah, from work. She's becoming a friend. It was our last night, me and Sarah, Sarah met this fecker called Ralph there. Anyway. She was going to spend the night with him, you know, saying goodbye.' Marissa rolled her eyes. 'Miguel, our tour guide, he just happened to be in our restaurant,'

Joanna sat on the edge of her chair, moving further forward at the mention of a man.

'He took me and one of his friends to this little house outside the city.'

'Oh my God! Are you okay?'

Marissa laughed. 'Yes, I'm okay, it's nothing like that at all. The house was full of people. There was a medicine woman there. He called her a shaman. She was doing healings and he'd brought me to see her.'

Joanne fell back into the chair with relief once more. 'Oh dear, I was worried there for a moment.'

The waitress came to take away the empty plates. 'Would you like to see the dessert menu?'

'Just coffee for me, please,' said Joanne.

'Yes, coffee for me too, thanks,' said Marissa.

'Well?' said Joanne, once the waitress had gone.

'It was such a strange place, but I felt very safe there. There were only local people there. Miguel said it wasn't for tourists.'

'Did they want any money?'

'No – no money. I really believe he thought I should be there. And the medicine woman was really happy to see me. She called me up to the front of the room. Look, this is a little weird. I've been having this dream, lots of times over the past few years. It's like a puzzle, I get stuck, can't move forward or backwards, it's been preoccupying me.'

Marissa looked at Joanne to see if she was still with her, and she seemed to be, so she continued, 'When I saw the medicine woman, whatever she did, helped me get unstuck in the dream. I've not had the dream since. It was amazing and strange. I wish I knew what it was, what she did, and what it meant. Afterwards, well, until I got back to Ireland anyway – everything was like *The Wizard of Oz* – you know, how Dorothy steps into Kansas and its full colour from black and white?'

Joanne nodded.

'Well, for me, the colours came back. For a little while anyway. But I hadn't even realised they'd gone. There's more going on here than I understand. I'm excited and nervous about it. I want them to come back again, I don't know what I should do to get them back, but at least now I know that it's possible.'

'I thought there was something different about you, now I can see it – there you are, you've come back,' said Joanne. 'You were missing for so long, like you were missing in action or something. Your sparkle, the old Marissa, magical, funny, silly, clever Marissa is back. I've missed you so much.'

Joanne got up off the chair, moved over to Marissa and embraced her. Marissa froze for a moment, then softened and hugged Joanne in return. Joanne sat down again.

'I'd forgotten how beautiful you are when you sparkle,' said Joanne.

'What do you mean?' asked Marissa, who was now confused.

'I don't quite know. When we were at school, you always sparkled for me when you got excited about something. When you had a strange idea – like that story you wrote for English about interdimensional portals. I didn't understand it, but I loved how you sparkled when you spoke about it.'

Marissa smiled.

'All through college, it was like your sparkle, well, got lost somewhere. Dimmed away over time. Until you met James, but even then, it wasn't quite the same.'

The coffees arrived. Joanne stirred sugar and milk into hers and then poured a dollop of milk into Marissa's. 'You still take milk, don't you?'

'Yes,' said Marissa.

'Anyway, looking back on all of that, and seeing you now, I don't think your sparkle is man-related.'

Marissa stirred her coffee and took a sip. It was a little too hot and a little too bitter. 'Not man-related,' she repeated, leaving the coffee aside to cool down. Marissa looked thoughtful, and then her face relaxed a little bit. 'Yes, I had a feeling that you'd be able to help me with this.'

'Aha! I knew it. You only contact me when you need something.'

Marisa blushed.

'Hey, it's okay, we will always be friends, friends forever no matter what, remember? I'm the same, life gets very busy with three children, especially as Tom has to travel so often for work. I'm glad he's home this weekend so I could come see you and see your sparkle.'

There was a pause in the conversation for a moment. Marissa tried her coffee again, it wasn't as bitter as she had originally thought, or perhaps she had gotten used to the taste.

'I saw a Facebook picture that said 'Never dull your sparkle' and another one that said 'Leave a little sparkle behind' but I never thought of it as being a real thing,' said Marissa.

'You definitely sparkle when you're excited about something.' Joanne sipped her coffee and grimaced at the bitterness. 'Well, I'm certainly not excited about this coffee,' she said.

Marissa laughed. She wondered if she sparkled during the healings in Peru. Or was the sparkle something the medicine woman gave her? *How do I get my sparkle back? I wish I could have seen what she did to me, what actually happened that night. I don't feel like I'm sparkling now, but I'll take Joanne's word for it. Perhaps anything is an improvement on what I've been like over the last few years.*

'You do look much happier than I've seen you in a very long time, even if you don't know it yourself,' said Joanne. She raised her coffee cup 'To sparkle and joy, and a happy life for us both. God knows we work hard enough. We both deserve it.'

Marissa raised her cup and they clinked them together.

'Next time with champagne!' suggested Joanne. 'Or with your new date. Speaking of dates, do you need some help with your make-up?'

'I thought you'd never ask!'

That afternoon Marissa went walking. She had a lot of thinking to do, and walking was her favourite way to organise her thoughts. If her sparkle wasn't man-related, what was it related to? She thought back about what Joanna had said: 'The old magical, silly, funny, clever Marissa is back.' *Where had that Marissa gone? I never thought I was magical or clever. Silly? Yes. Funny? Perhaps. I certainly used to have more magical ideas. The most magical thing for me in the last while was that dream. Ahh, maybe that's why it was in my thoughts so much and becoming so important to me.*

She thought about when she was small, when she believed magic was real. Like Peter Pan, she did believe in fairies. *When did that stop for me?* Was it when she was nine and discovered her mother was The Tooth Fairy? She remembered pretending to be asleep when her mother came into the room and gently felt under her pillow for the tiny tooth that she had wrapped in a swatch of bloodstained toilet paper. She left a fifty-pence-piece in its place. Marissa was so disappointed that day, yet she knew not to ask her mother about it. Instead, she pretended to be delighted with her prize.

As for Santa, he never came to their house. She always felt left out at Christmas time, when she was younger she always wondered why Santa would bring presents for her friends and leave herself and Eli out. Getting seven little presents for the seven days of Chanukah was nice, but she still envied her friends with their Christmas trees, the sparkly lights and their presents from Santa. She enjoyed putting up decorations and a Christmas tree in her flat that first time she moved in with James. It was so much fun, and realising that she *could* have Christmas herself if she wanted to did feel magical. It was like a coming of age, of sorts. But that was a kind of magic sparkle coming into her life, rather than out of it. So when did the magic leave her life? She really didn't know. But perhaps just asking the question was enough for now.

She found herself walking to Eli's house. She hadn't seen him since the dinner at Uncle Lou's. His new Mercedes was parked in the driveway. She rang the doorbell and Carol opened it, wearing her dressing gown with her hair wrapped in a towel on top of her head.

'Oh! Sorry. Am I disturbing you? I was just passing by. I thought I'd call in to say hello.'

'Hi Marissa, no, not at all. I was just in the shower. I was painting the spare bedroom and I felt grimy, so I needed to get changed. Come on in, Eli's out in the back garden, I'll call him.'

Carol was a little older than Marissa, whereas Eli was three years younger. Eli used to liaise with many younger women on frequent nights out, relationships and Eli didn't mix, until he met Carol. They had been together for almost two years and Eli was much happier, settled and seemed much more sure of himself. She stabilised him, if there was such a thing. Marissa liked Carol and always took her side if the family carried on about her not being Jewish.

'Most people in Ireland are not Jewish,' Marissa argued, 'and the community of Jews is so small, it would be like dating your cousin if you found a nice Jewish girl or boy.' Every so often, they needed to be reminded.

Carol led Marissa into their sitting room and gestured to the two-seater sofa for her to sit. It was a small house and a small sitting room, but there was just the two of them, and it was in a great location in Phibsboro. Carol had bought it before the property boom, and when Eli had moved in, they had redecorated it so he felt like it was his place too. And they had a parking space and a back garden, which added value.

'Hang on and I'll get him.'

'Carol, no, it's okay, I'll get him – you go get dressed.'

'Thanks, okay. See you in a few.'

As Carol left the room, Marissa stood and looked at the framed photographs on the mantelpiece. One of Carol as a small girl, daisies in her hair, holding her parents' hands. Beside that was a photo of Eli and Marissa, also small, with chocolate ice cream all over their faces. Marissa chuckled, she remembered the photograph, if not the details of the day itself. Next to it was a photo of her parents, much younger, probably in their early twenties, before either of them were born. She always loved that photo. She picked it up and looked at it, it was black and white. *Mum's dress will be coming back into fashion soon.* It was taken outside her grandfather's shop, they looked so happy. And they still were happy.

That's magic, right there. She put the photo back, went into the kitchen and out the back door. 'Eli, are you there?'

'Mar! Hey, great to see you. To what do I owe the honour?' Eli was wearing a brown sweater, beige trousers and had a mustard coloured scarf around his neck and a rake in his hand.

'I was just passing by, thought I'd drop in on the off-chance. Can I make us some tea?'

'Good timing, I'm just finishing up here. You go ahead, you know where everything is. I'll be there in a minute, I just want to finish raking up these leaves.'

'Grand.'

Marissa went back into the kitchen and filled the kettle up from the sink. By the time she had turned it on and got three cups down from the cupboard, Carol was coming down, rubbing her long brown hair with a small green towel.

'So, how was your trip?' she asked. 'Sounds like the trip of a lifetime.'

'It was fantastic, really fun. I've heaps of photos on my phone. I'll show you both when Eli comes back in.'

'I was delighted you went, I'd love to go to Peru,' said Carol, draping her towel over the radiator and smoothing her hair out of her eyes. She opened a cupboard door. 'Chocolate digestives?'

'Lovely,' said Marissa.

Eli came in, closing the door behind him. He went to the sink and washed his hands. 'Tea is perfect. You timed this well, Sis,' he said to Marissa. As he dried his hands, he leaned over and kissed Carol on the cheek. 'You smell great, love.'

More magic. Marissa smiled. 'You're looking suitably autumnal, Eli. It's great to see you both so happy,' she said. 'I hope you're not putting that on for me!' She laughed.

'No, not at all,' said Eli, smiling at Carol, who was smiling right back at him. 'We are very happy. And, we have some news. Can I tell her, Carol?'

'Why not? Sure.'

'We're going to have a baby!' The couple beamed smiles and joy, happiness was spilling off both of them, and it seemed to fill the room with light.

'Oh my god! That's wonderful! Congratulations! Wow!' said Marissa, genuinely delighted. She hugged them both. And then reality hit. 'Mum will have a field day – about you not being married, I mean!'

'Who cares?' said Eli, standing behind Carol as she poured the hot water from the freshly boiled kettle into a bright red teapot. He wrapped his arms around her stomach and kissed the back of her neck.

'Stop it, you're giving me shivers,' Carol said happily.

'She'll get over it quickly enough,' said Eli, looking back to Marissa. 'One look at this baby and she won't care either. Her first grandbaby – how could she be angry for long? And you're going to be an aunty, a real one this time.'

Marissa smiled, 'I'm going to be a real Aunty M! I think Amanda and Marcus would be delighted to have a new cousin, especially one younger than them, in the same country too. This is so great! I'm genuinely happy for you both.'

They took the tea and biscuits into the living room and placed them on the coffee table. Eli and Carol sat beside each other on the couch while Marissa took the armchair.

'Have you told anyone else? When is the baby due?'

'Well, we haven't actually told anyone yet. You're supposed to wait three months, and that's not for another two weeks. It's so difficult to keep this a secret. Here, look,' Eli rummaged in his trouser pocket and pulled out his wallet, and out from his wallet he took a small piece of paper. He opened it up and handed it to Marissa. It was a print-out of a scan.

'Look, there's the head, the hands, the tiny baby feet.' He pointed to each one.

'Oh wow! Yes, I can see it. It's so tiny.'

'Yes, it's exciting.'

Marissa looked at Carol's stomach. It didn't look big at all, you'd never know there was a human being growing in there.

'Have you had any cravings for anything?'

Carol shook her head. 'Not yet, anyway. I read in a book somewhere that cravings happen when the baby gets a little bigger, so poor Eli is on guard in case I need to send him to the chipper at 3am.'

Eli smiled, his happiness was contagious.

'Are you sick?'

She nodded. 'I have trouble in the afternoons more than the mornings, though.'

'Oh dear, sick isn't fun. I hope it's not too awful,' said Marissa.

'It will be worth it,' said Carol, taking Eli's hand. 'And so far, it's not been horrendously awful.'

'I'm really excited for you. So the baby's due in June?' Marissa asked, counting on her fingers.

'Yes, the middle of June.'

'A summer baby. How fun! I finish my diploma in June too! That's going to be a great month for celebrating. I won't mention it to anyone else until you tell me you've told them,' said Marissa, dunking her digestive into her tea, 'particularly the parents.'

'Yes, I knew you'd be happy for us,' said Eli. 'But it won't be too long before we tell the others – we're having trouble keeping it in as it is.'

Marissa turned to Carol, laughing, 'You'd better keep that baby in until it's ready to come out!'

'Ha ha! Now show us your photographs of Peru. What was the best bit?'

'Before that, which I will tell you about, I have something I wanted to ask you.'

Eli and Carol focused on Marissa expectantly.

'Do you remember, Eli, when we were smaller, how life seemed more magical?'

'It feels very magical to me right now,' Eli said, putting his arm around Carol's shoulder and grabbing a chocolate biscuit with his free hand.

'Yes, I suppose it would,' said Marissa. 'But I feel that somewhere along the way, I've lost my magic.'

'What do you mean by "magic"?' asked Carol, placing one hand on her stomach and snuggling deeper into Eli.

'Well, I don't really know. Sparkle? Colour? Joanne said that my sparkle had come back since Peru. But I didn't even know that it had gone.'

'Hmmm, maybe she meant 'enthusiasm for life'?' suggested Carol.

'Maybe she meant that you've been a dry shite for a long time and you weren't so boring today?' said Eli laughing. 'Face it, Marissa, you've been quite caught up in your own world since that whole James thing, and it is a little boring. I'm glad he left you before you married him – it would have been much worse if you had got married and then he'd left. Or even if he had stayed and strayed... Which was also possible. It's time to move on. Get a new man, have some fun. Some more fun. Peru is the first fun thing you've done for yourself in ages.'

'Thanks for the vote of confidence, Eli. Yes, I admit I've been preoccupied with my own stuff, but I think I'm coming out of it now. And Peru was good for me in many ways. It's great to see you be the wise one for once. I suppose some questions have many answers, and magic can be many things to many people.'

'The difference between someone who is interesting and someone who is not so interesting?' asked Carol.

'I guess there's more to think about here than I first imagined.'

'Ahh, I think I have it,' said Eli with a knowing smile. 'It's about your imagination. You used to be very creative, dreaming up strange and wonderful things, spaceships in the back garden and the like. But not so much now. You're all work and study and bills. That's your magic. And that's you sorted. Now, where are those photographs?'

+++

Marissa was glad of the quiet in her flat later that evening. She wanted the space to think and sort this out. She had many answers but none of them felt like the right ones. Marissa sat on the sofa with a college textbook in her hands, fully intending to read it. The next thing she knew, Tobermory was scratching at the door to get out. Marissa looked at the clock, 23:44. *I guess I must still be jet-lagged.* She rose to her feet, stretched and wrapped her alpaca scarf around her shoulders. She opened the back door. 'Come on lovely cat, let's go outside,' she said. The full moon was waning, it hadn't rained for two days, and the grass was dry enough for her to walk on without worrying about getting mud on the kitchen floor. She had her slippers on and felt snug under the scarf, it wasn't frosty yet, but she could see her breath turning to condensation under the glow of the neighbours' lights. It never really got dark in Marissa's garden because she lived in the city. There was always a street light on somewhere or a bright security light set off by a cat or a fox.

Marissa went to her favourite spot beside the tree and placed a hand on the bough. 'Hello Tree,' she said. 'Are there fairies living around you?'

Of course, there was no answer, but Marissa noticed how her heart felt lighter than it had done in a while. It seemed as though things were going well for her for a change. She was looking forward to the week ahead. It was lovely to see Joanne, Carol and Eli so happy, and of course to look forward to a new arrival. *I need to catch up on my sleep though and shift this jet lag.* More than that, Marissa felt like she was on a quest. She had a purpose and a new understanding of herself and a direction to move towards. *Finding the magic. That's what I need to do, I don't know how, but I will open my mind to it. What makes life magical for me?* The dating site could wait for a while. Magic was not man-related as Joanne said, it might be for Sarah, but it wasn't for her.

'Magic *is* real, isn't it, Tree?' she asked. 'Will you help me find what makes my life feel magical?' She didn't really expect an answer, sure it was just a tree. But for a moment, just a sliver of a moment, she thought she could hear a voice from somewhere deep inside her whisper, 'Yes.'

It was quiet, achingly quiet. Marissa looked around. She was standing by the water's edge, her lake and the familiar mountain in front of her. The moon was half full, its light reflected on the surface of the water. There was a stirring, the sea serpent rose its large head out of the water and looked at Marissa directly.

'Hello again,' said Marissa, quietly, unafraid.

The sea serpent stayed looking at her for a moment longer, then disappeared back into the stillness underneath.

Marissa stayed, enjoying the silence, the stillness around her. She noticed a presence behind her. She turned around.

'Hello Marissa, we meet again. It is very nice to see you.'

It was the medicine woman from Peru, looking slightly younger than she had done in person. She wore full ceremonial dress, her many necklaces glittering under the moonlight. Marissa's heart leapt with joy to see her. She had so many questions, but all she could say was: 'Hello, it's you?'

'Yes. It is me. I have many things to show you, to teach you. But not for tonight. Tonight just hello. Again! Your lessons are only beginning. You have come a long way, but you have a long way to go. Do you want to learn?'

'Yes,' said Marissa without hesitation.

'Good,' said the medicine woman.

'What do I have to do? Where do I begin?' asked Marissa.

'You will know when you see it. You will know. Trust your instincts. Trust your inner voice. Your training comes from in here.' She reached out her hand and tapped Marissa on the heart, just as she had in Peru.

Marissa awakened. When she realised she was in her bed, she noticed how she felt – different, stronger. As if dream Marissa and real-life Marissa were more similar than before. She had a sense that the medicine woman was going to help her in some way, and her life was not going to be boring anymore. She turned in her bed, pulled the covers up and went back to sleep.

CHAPTER EIGHT

She was in college and they were doing practice sessions. It was Marissa's turn to be the therapist, her client was Yvonne, and Kate was the observer. Yvonne had ongoing family problems and repeatedly mentioned them to everyone, whether it was practice time or not. Marissa wondered if she did it because she enjoyed being the focus of attention or if the retelling was her way of figuring out what was going on for her. Sitting there in practice time listening to yet another rendition of the story she'd heard during tea break last week, though, she found her patience running low. She loved being the therapist, but found that she could only do it well when the client was, as they said in class, 'being real'.

At practice a few weeks previously, a student from one of the other groups was her client. Marissa struggled with the short session, she found no 'way in' to help with the issue. Her client spoke at length about her situation until the observer, also from the other group, clapped her hands together and fell back into the chair laughing. Marissa was shocked – 'What's going on?'

'It's *Brokeback Mountain*, the plot! She's playing the part of the wife.'

There was a cohort of people who constantly brought made-up things to the class practice sessions. It seemed that they were still afraid to reveal themselves, even in their second year.

Marissa snapped back into the moment and realised that although Yvonne was talking about real problems she was having, she was disconnected from what she was saying, as if it was the seventh time she said the same thing. *Is she bored of hearing the same story over and over herself?* Marissa had had enough and wanted to put a stop to it and do some actual work.

'Can we stop a minute?' asked Marissa, 'I'm not clear about what you are saying to me, and I really want to understand it.'

Yvonne stopped talking and looked puzzled. Kate wrote something down in her notebook.

'Okay,' said Yvonne, a worried look coming into her eyes.

'I can't find *you* in all of this. You're telling me about all these things that have happened to you, but you're not telling me how you feel about them and how they have impacted *you*. How do *you* feel, right now?' Marissa held eye contact.

Yvonne looked away and looked back at her again briefly, and then looked down at her feet. 'Oh. Well, right now, I feel jittery and uncomfortable.'

'What else?'

'Short of breath, anxious... Yes, anxious.' Yvonne looked up once more.

'Okay. Good. What exactly is making you anxious?'

Kate wrote something else in her notebook, and Yvonne looked at her. 'Kate, making notes about me. What is she saying?'

'Never mind about Kate. She's not here, it's just you and me here,' said Marissa. 'You can tell me. What is making you feel anxious?'

Yvonne looked at the ground and then back up again once more. She took a breath. 'You know I think I feel anxious all the time. I think I do. I've never realised this before. It's not a nice feeling.' Her face coloured, she looked down again, Marissa could see the emotions starting to show on her face.

'I'm sorry you're feeling that way,' Marissa said, 'but it's good to know this, so you can do something about it.' She uncrossed her legs and turned her body to face Yvonne directly. She rested her hands in her lap, palms outwards, hands open, feet flat on the ground.

'Can you sit to match the way I am sitting?'

'Okay,' said Yvonne, shifting in her chair and copying Marissa's body.

'Let's forget about all the stuff that is going on, and forget about the other people in the room, and Kate, and be here, in this moment, just you and me, with how we are feeling. Together.'

Yvonne smiled a little bit. 'Okay I can do that.'

A moment passed then Marissa said, 'Here's something that always helps me when I feel anxious – I press my feet into the ground and slow down my breath. Then I imagine that the anxiety is like butterflies in my stomach. I can almost see how many of them there are. Then I breathe into them, and as I breathe out, sometimes I imagine that they fly up and out of my stomach with my breath. Do you want to try it?'

'Three minutes left,' said Kate, looking at her phone.

'Okay, I'll try it,' said Yvonne.

They breathed together for a few breaths. Yvonne looked more relaxed.

'I think we're getting somewhere now,' said Marissa.

'I do feel better,' remarked Yvonne.

'So what is actually going on for you? What are you really worried about?'

'I'm worried about what people think of me. I want them to like me.' Yvonne's hand went to her mouth, she seemed surprised by her admission.

'You do know that this is a perfectly normal thing to worry about?' Marissa told her.

Yvonne nodded.

'You don't need to impress anyone, or prove anything, just be who you are. What do you think?'

'Sounds good.'

The bell rang.

'Come back to the circle now, please, everyone,' said Ms Pearson. She was a well-established psychotherapist who had been in practice for fifteen years. She was teaching a module on Cognitive Behavioural Therapy, which is all about understanding and changing thought patterns to create different behaviour.

'So who would like to share tonight?' she asked.

Emmet put up his hand.

'Emmet?'

'I found tonight more difficult than usual,' said Emmet.

'Were you a client or a therapist?'

'Therapist. I have to admit that I couldn't concentrate on what my client was telling me. I kept thinking about what I should ask them next and wanting to have my notes in my hand.'

'That is a common complaint with therapists in training,' said Ms Pearson, 'and it's very brave of you to tell us about it. The client just wants you to listen to them, and they want to feel heard. If you're thinking about what to say next, you're not available to listen to them fully. It's not about what you say or the next question, it's about being available and present. The techniques we teach you here are tools, but the relationship between the client and the therapist is the most important thing. You certainly don't want to have your notes in your hand when working with someone. You will grow more confident with time. Thanks, Emmet.' She looked around the room. 'Anyone else want to share?'

Kate put up her hand. Marissa's heart jumped as Ms Pearson nodded at her.

'I thought our session was really good,' said Kate. 'Yvonne was the client, she seemed to be stuck telling her story, and Marissa-as-therapist brought her back to her feelings. I didn't know where the session was going until she did this – I must remember to always bring the client back to their feelings.'

Ms Pearson turned to Marissa. 'Sounds good, Marissa. How was it for you?'

'Erm... Yes, it was good, I learned from it, I think. I didn't want to use the CBT technique as I felt the client was going around in circles with her story, and it wouldn't have worked until she broke free of it so she could see what she was doing. By bringing her back to her feelings I think I made some progress.' Marissa looked at Yvonne, who smiled at her. 'With all due respect, honestly, sometimes I think the story of what happened is a great distraction from what is really going on, or how a person is feeling.'

Ms Pearson nodded. 'It is true, telling and retelling the story can be used as a distraction, a way of avoiding going deeper. But it can also be a protection mechanism if the person isn't ready to talk about their feelings just yet. Yvonne, what was it like, for you as the client?'

Yvonne was quiet for a moment.

'Do you want to talk about it?' Ms Pearson prompted.

'Yes, I can talk about it,' said Yvonne, sitting up more. 'I did feel surprised and shut down, but then I realised that I *had* gone off on a loop. Marissa brought me back to the moment and made me feel safe by telling me that she felt anxious sometimes too. I was very uncomfortable at first, and almost angry at Marissa, but she normalised what I was feeling, and then I felt better. I liked the butterfly thing she talked about. I will use that.'

Everyone in the group was looking at her expectantly.

She went on, 'We learn in theory how to do counselling and I know we did a lot of work over the past year. Experiencing it and being here is totally different from reading about it. Once Marissa guided me to connect to my feelings, what I was telling her, the story, I guess you could call it that, well, it didn't seem as important anymore.'

'Great work, everyone, ' said Ms Pearson. 'I'm fascinated with the butterflies! It sounds delightful. Maybe you could share the technique with anyone interested over the break?'

Marissa nodded. 'Sure.'

'Okay, now we will look at the next model, Motivational Interviewing. But please remember that the client is more important than the technique, and, as we saw, the feelings are more important than the story. Ronan, yes?'

Ronan never really spoke in front of the group, everyone turned to look at him, and he blushed. 'When you say "story", it feels as though you're putting down the client when what happened to them is real and important.' He looked at Ms Pearson expectantly.

'Yes, it is real and important. We must tell the story of what happened to us to make sense of it. But it changes with the telling, like every story. And we don't remember everything that happened objectively, because we are subjective beings. How you feel in the moment can dictate how you interpret what happened to you.'

She went on. 'When the story of what happened to us defines who we are, we can lose a sense of who we truly are. We are not what happened to us, we experience what happened to us. The more we tell the story, the more power it can have over us. That's where CBT comes in, to catch hold of the language we use when retelling the story, to see clearly what we are telling ourselves, so we can refine it. This way, it can help us grow, rather than hold us back.'

'According to Freud, all of our memories are not what actually happened but a fantasy of what we think happened. And over time, what we believe happened to us can become more important to us than what actually happened. We become invested in the story we tell ourselves. Of course, as therapists, we need words to describe how we think and talk, so we use the word "story" where it can be, as you say, Ronan, something very real and important to someone, it is not in any way belittling what might have happened, or their perception of what might have happened. A story has a beginning, a middle and an end. If the client is still in their story of what happened, it usually hasn't ended yet. Or they didn't like the ending, so they replay it over and over to try to get some closure. We talk about story in session so clients can process their feelings around what happened to them, get closure from it, and move on. That's the job of a psychotherapist – to make the story more objective. This way, the client can see the bigger picture, which helps them process their part in it. We cannot change what happened, but we hope that by discussing it and making more sense of it, the client's feelings around what happened, will change.'

Marissa remembered that her father always said to her that there were three sides to every story: your side, their side and the truth. And from Yvonne's story, the feeling that Marissa got was that there was nothing solid there that she could hold onto and work with. It was hard to describe that feeling, but once she felt the solidness of something true, she felt an 'Ahh, there it is,' in herself, then she was able to go into it and unravel it and help that person see what was at the core of their issue. She was thrown when clients used movie plots or made things up because the client wasn't emotionally connected to it. Perhaps it was real emotion that she was tracking down, the story might just be the words around the emotion? She decided not to solidify how she worked just yet. Although it was empowering to realise the difference between what was real and what was not, what was story and what was emotion, it could also be so confusing sometimes. She knew you could never make an assumption. Marissa was glad she had done well tonight. She felt she was finding her feet as a therapist, and she liked the solid knowing that she was good at something. She hadn't felt that way since chemistry class at school.

When she had woken up, Marissa had wanted to spend time thinking about the medicine woman from her dream and what saying 'yes' to her meant. But the day had flown past, and now she was home from college having a light meal, and it was already almost time for bed. She had an early meeting the next morning, she didn't want to stay up too late, but she also didn't want to let the day end without acknowledging her dream, and the agreement.

What did I actually agree to? She found an old notebook in one of her desk drawers. It was pink and slightly dog-eared, it only had a few used pages. She ripped them out and tore them up into smaller pieces, not wanting to see what words she had inscribed upon them in case they were laments about the loss of James. She wrote a lot of laments around that time when she had fallen into a pit of despair. *Talk about story…* She felt good now and was practically certain that reading scrappy old bad poetry written from pangs of grief would destroy the moment. She threw the shreds of paper into the bin, then changed her mind, fished them out and tore them even smaller and placed them in the fireplace as kindling for the next fire. Then she went back and rummaged in the drawer a little longer and fished out a biro, one she knew would still have ink in it.

She opened to the first clean page and wrote:

> *Medicine woman training. What does this mean? What is the training? Is she really the medicine woman from Peru, or is she a figment of my imagination? How can I tell the difference?*

She sat for a while, reading and re-reading her thoughts. Then she dated the top of the page and wrote:

> *I am a good therapist. Feelings are more important than story. Story is what we tell ourselves and it can change the more we tell it.'*

She felt she was getting somewhere now. A word formed in her mind, she wrote that down too: *Distortion.* She looked at the word, wondering where it came from, but yes, distortion was what we did to our stories when we tell and retell them. *Is this my training? Delving deeper into myself to find what I've been distorting? But how do I know?*

Marissa looked out the window at the moonlight. It was half a moon and seemed to glisten through the tree branches. The leaves were falling, the days were getting darker earlier and earlier. A single star blinked in the pale sky, but the sky was too bright with light pollution to see anything more. She looked at the cloud as it crawled towards the moon, shifting and changing its shape. She could see a dragon in it for a moment, then it turned into puffs of smoke, and then the moon was hidden.

She put the notebook down beside her laptop and climbed into bed, leaving the curtains open. She liked moonlight. Her room in the half-light felt like an in-between place, her breathing slowing down, her body relaxing. Tobermory jumped up beside her, looking straight into her eyes. She stroked his back.

'My familiar, my friend, my cat,' she said, 'what do you think? Do you have an answer for me?'

As usual, Tobermory was silent, but he held eye contact for a moment longer than Marissa expected him to. Perhaps he understood her? He mewed, then curled himself into a black circle on the bed beside her and began to purr.

Training, she thought to herself as she settled under the covers. *But who is going to teach me?'*

+++

Marissa had to visit her therapist, Olive, as part of the requirement for her degree. Even though she had spent six months and many hours with her three years earlier, those sessions didn't count as far as her college course was concerned. She had 10 hours left to do, and since coming back from Peru, she had managed to avoid talking to Olive about the medicine woman. She wasn't sure why she was avoiding it, she had felt relief after telling Joanne, but it still seemed a little weird. And it was also nice to have a secret, well, 'nice' wasn't the word, it was as if talking about it might make it less interesting, more normal, less magical. But was she telling and re-telling a story in her mind? The previous night's discussion about what a story is, was also on her mind. She didn't want to be too invested in a fantasy. *No, my dream is important to me, so that makes it important. But it might still be a good thing to check in with Olive, see what she thinks.*

She took an early lunch and caught a taxi to her session which was across town. It did seem a little extravagant, but she wouldn't be able to make it there and get back to work on time otherwise. The traffic was light and quick and the taxi left her right outside Olive's house. Still deep in thought, she rang the small bell for Olive's therapy room which was underneath the main house bell.

After a moment or two the gate latch lifted open, and Olive greeted her with a smile. 'Hello, Marissa, come in, come in.' Olive was in her mid sixties. She wore her silver hair back in a bun, she wore a colourful green and gold shawl over a darker green cashmere jumper, with a forest green skirt.

Marissa followed Olive through the gate, past the small courtyard filled with summer pots, under a small trellis with a rose bush which crept over it, pink and red blossoms bright under the lunchtime sun, and into the purpose-built counselling room. The smell of a lavender candle hung in the air, the room was comfortable and warm from the sun. She took off her raincoat and hung it on the back of an ageing red armchair.

'Just a moment, I need some water – would you like some?' Olive was a wise woman, she took her time to think things through, and when she spoke, it was sensible and, well, solid, Marissa thought. *Solid and no-nonsense. Perhaps I'm a little bit afraid of her... I'm full of nonsense at times. It's like she can see through me.*

'Yes, please,' said Marissa breathing out the butterflies as she rearranged the cushions and sat down in the red armchair. 'You're all in green today. It's nice.'

Olive brought two small glasses of water over and handed one of them to Marissa, who placed it on a small table beside the chair. 'Thank you dear, yes it's in homage to the change in seasons.'

Marissa couldn't help feeling slightly anxious as Olive settled into the armchair opposite her. The room was beautifully kept, it had lots of windows and light coming in, and it was filled with greenery. There was a large cheese plant in a pot in the corner which took up a large portion of the room, and many smaller plants hanging from the ceiling in containers. There was a small sink at the back corner of the room, a floor to ceiling bookshelf overflowing with books, and a small bathroom. Marissa wanted to have plants like that, but her flat wasn't as bright as this room, she had failed with them many times. Ferns just needed more sunshine than she could give them, and it was simply too cold to leave them outside.

Olive waited patiently for Marissa to begin. But she didn't, so Olive opened the session. 'You're anxious, I can see it in your face,' she said, settling herself more deeply into her chair and loosening her shawl.

After a moment, Marissa replied, 'Yes, I am, a little. I can't hide it from you. I don't know why I want to. You know me so well.' Marissa shrugged her shoulders.

'What do you want to talk about today?'

Olive's kind voice helped Marissa relax, but she had to admit, 'It feels difficult to talk today. I have some things I've not told you before. I want to tell you, though.'

The room was silent as Marissa gathered her thoughts. Olive smiled and folded her hands in her lap.

Marissa took a breath. 'Ahh, okay then, here goes. Something strange happened in Peru. I had an experience there. I saw some things, met a medicine woman, it was amazing and magical, and mysterious. It's as if a door has opened and I'm afraid to walk through it. I want to, but I'm scared.'

Marissa told Olive about the night with the medicine woman, her dream of the lake and the sea serpent, and how the medicine woman appeared to her in her dream asking her if she wanted training. She hesitated, and then told her about the mountain, how it felt to be standing there beside it, how she felt the presence of the mountain before she even realised that she was close to it. Olive stayed silent the whole time, nodding her head and making eye contact. Marissa felt less anxious once it was all out in the open.

'Oh dear, my hands have gone asleep,' Olive exclaimed and stood up, rubbing her hands together to bring them back to life. 'I don't believe you are really afraid. Sometimes we tell ourselves we are afraid, when in fact we are excited.'

She went over to her bookshelf, still rubbing her hands together, looking for a book. 'Ahh yes, here it is,' she said, selecting a book and coming back to the chair again. 'Why didn't you tell me about this in our last session? What was so problematic about it all?'

'I'm not sure. The whole thing was like a dream, I could have dreamed it all. It's so strange. But fascinating. And I reluctantly admit that I'm not really afraid.'

Olive smiled with a twinkle in her eye. 'Well, there is more to this world than meets the eye. And there is great power in keeping it to yourself until you are ready to share it. I'm pleased you feel able to share it with me. I have read about this, shamanism, I have studied some. It is not for everyone, and you need to be ready, and brave, and strong of heart.' Olive handed the book to Marissa. The cover was old and battered, the title in big letters said: *Shamanic Journeys, Shamanic Wisdom: The Way of the Truth Keeper.*

'This book may have some answers for you. I'm not in a rush to have it back – you can hold onto it for as long as you like. Consider it a gift from me to you. It seems like your path is taking an interesting turn.'

Olive looked as if she wanted to continue speaking, but instead glanced at the clock on the mantlepiece. She picked her diary up from the coffee table, which was her way of signalling that the session was over. She opened it and turned to a page.

'Same time next week?'

'Yes, please,' said Marissa. She put the book in her handbag and clutched it to her chest. 'Thank you, thank you so much.'

'My pleasure, dear,' said Olive, making a note in her diary. 'Let me show you out. Have a good week, and enjoy the book.'

Marissa walked out the door, then turned around.

'Oh! I forgot to tell you, I used the butterfly technique you gave to me in class and it worked well with my client, in our practice session. She told everyone about it during the share, so I had to teach it to everyone at tea break.'

Olive looked puzzled. 'I don't know a butterfly technique? Are you sure you got it from me?'

Marissa looked equally as puzzled.

Olive smiled. 'It would seem that you're further through your door than you know.'

Marissa didn't think of Olive as a person with a life outside of the therapy room, she had even simply labelled her as 'my therapist' in her head. *Olive studied shamanism? I would never have guessed it.* She found it difficult to concentrate on her work (as usual), and today she had work to do that required focus. *I'd rather be drinking coffee and getting stuck into that book.* She counted the hours until it was time to go home. Marissa usually had difficulty focusing after therapy anyway, it seemed to bring up something in her that would take the rest of the afternoon to settle. She would have preferred to see Olive in the evening after work (she would have saved money on taxi fares, too) but Olive only had Thursday evenings available and that was the same day as college. So she was restless while she wrestled with whatever it was that had come up in her. On her way home, she wondered about Olive, the person, as opposed to Olive, the therapist. *Shamanism and Olive! I'd imagine there is a story there, alright.* The thought 'we only see what we are presented with,' popped into her head as if someone had said it to her, she remembered it was from her first-year, person-centred counselling class. *Of course, we don't see what we're not shown.* Marissa felt grateful that Olive could show her some part of herself that she never had before, even after all this time.

As soon as Marissa got home she took the book out of her bag and poured over its pages. It was a large dusty book, written in the 1960s; the language was thick and academic and not as easy to understand as she would have liked it to be. Her stomach growled and she looked at the time, it was dinnertime and she was hungry. She put the book down and heated some leftovers she found in the fridge. She tried to continue to read while she ate, but it was clumsy with fork bowl and book, and she didn't want to get food on Olive's book. Not just because it was Olive's, Marissa was very careful with books, she always treated books with respect. She only ever wrote her name in them, and was always upset when someone folded the top corner of a page of one of her books to keep their place. If someone did that to one of her own books, she would never lend them a book again. *Notebooks are for keeping notes, books are for reading.* That was her excuse for buying many notebooks, and it was still a good one.

Once dinner was over, she washed the dishes, dried her hands and picked up the book once more. It opened on her lap on a random page: *In some of the workshops we discovered that a small percentage of people were able to use the exercises of core shamanism, in particular the shamanic journey, for healing purposes, with almost instantaneous results.*

Shamanic journey, what's that? She got her phone as it was handy and looked it up. The first result was a reference from Wikipedia with an image of people from Russia in traditional dress, the second was an Australian website with Aboriginal artwork on it, the third was in German.

Shamanic Journey Ireland, she wrote into the search box, just to see what would appear. Her heart leapt into her mouth when she pressed the search button, she didn't know why. After the Google definition and the Wikipedia entry, the next entry was: *Shamanic introductory workshop, training in the skill of journeying.* Marissa's heart leapt again as she clicked the link.

> *Seamus O'Driscoll will run "Introduction to the Shamanic Journey" in Glasnevin, November 13th. Entry Fee €50, lunch not included.*

The 13th was the following weekend. Marissa's heart leapt – she could go. *How could that be? Is it the right year?* Websites were renowned for not being kept up to date. Best to check it – she looked again, yes, the date was correct. *Should I go?* She pulled out her diary, she had a lunch date with her mother planned for that day – well, she could postpone that. *Mum won't mind...* The workshop felt important, scary, but she had a feeling that she should go. But who was Séamus O'Driscoll? She looked him up and found a YouTube video where an art student interviewed him for a college project. They were outside in Stephen's Green, in the bandstand in the rain. *Interesting choice of venue...* Séamus had a strong face, chiselled features, and he wore a cowboy hat with a coloured braid tied around the brim. It looked like a cold day, rain was dripping off the roof of the bandstand, making it difficult to hear what he was saying. She turned up the volume.

'And that is why I believe that we all have the power to heal ourselves, but not everyone has the power to heal others. It takes a certain make-up. Healers wake up to it, they already have the power inside of them. Of course, many healers in the making don't want to heal themselves for this very reason. They are terrified of what it means to be a healer, and they are very used to the comfort of their pain. Pain can become comfortable when you're faced with the unknown, even preferable.'

Marissa got shivers. *What he says makes sense, it might explain why I'm so nervous. But I like him.* She watched a few more of his videos then flicked back to the workshop page, and without thinking about it too much more, clicked the 'Pay a deposit' link and paid €20 from her PayPal account.

There. Done. She sat, feeling her emotions which flowed in many different directions. Then the confirmation email came in, and something within her stilled. She felt excited and a little nervous. *I'm not usually so spontaneous. But the timing was just exactly right... I'm going to a shamanic workshop, on my own, and it's in just a few days time. Who would have thought?*

CHAPTER NINE

Séamus O'Driscoll was a big man with a big personality. He seemed to fill the room with his smile. His voice was warm and melodic as he welcomed Marissa to the workshop, took the balance of payment, ticked her name off his list and invited her in.

He wasn't wearing his cowboy hat today. He wore a green buttoned shirt, with the top three buttons open, black jeans and a thick brown leather belt with a silver buckle. His long silvering hair was tied back in a medium-length ponytail. His face didn't give away his age, but she guessed he was in his late forties, possibly early 50's.

She was early. Grabbing a blanket and a large cushion she found a spot on the floor beside several other early arrivals. She looked around the room, it was one of the upstairs workshop rooms in a community centre; bright, not cold but not warm either, with windows that looked across the rooftops of the city and three wall hangings which brought in a little more colour and warmth. Marissa spotted the cowboy hat hanging on the wall behind the door. Seeing it made her feel a little more at ease. Her nerves had started when she woke up that morning but that was normal for her when she was trying anything new. She was grateful for Google Maps helping her find the centre, this part of Dublin was unfamiliar to her. Yet, when she looked down she recognised the carpet – dark brown, cheap and easy to clean – just like the carpets her father had sold for a while. *Can't get away from my family!* She laughed and relaxed as soon as she recognised it.

In the middle of the floor was small a circular rug with colourful patterns on it, and in the centre of that rug was a black square cloth with a white pillar candle in a square holder, a rattle, some fresh flowers and a large, freeform, quartz crystal. There was a fold-out chair beside the rug with a pillow and a large drum leaning against the leg.

It wasn't as strange a place as the medicine woman's house in Peru, yet she felt less at home here and significantly more anxious. She couldn't make sense of it. *I'm in Ireland, I'm at home, so why is this more uncomfortable than a strange place in a strange country?* She looked around, the room was filling up, she could hide amongst the other participants if required.

She noticed the woman beside her who was wearing a colourful tunic and yoga pants. There were many bangles around her wrist, and dangling from her ears were long earrings that looked like dream catchers. She smiled and got a nervous smile back. *I'm not the only one who is a little nervous. That's good, isn't it?* Marissa's stomach rumbled audibly, and the other woman laughed. Marissa laughed too, and it broke the tension, if only for a moment.

Marissa's anxiety grew as they waited, and soon it became very strong. She tried to breathe out her butterflies. *I didn't feel this worried before I came here. Why do I feel worse now?* Marissa's anxiety seemed to have doubled, hot prickles of agitation ran up and down her arms as well as the butterflies which refused to leave her stomach, preferring to multiply instead. It was hard to sit still, she looked out the window across the rooftops and chimneys, trying to coax the butterflies out of her mouth with the lure of so many interesting places they could be exploring instead of the dark recesses of her stomach. That seemed to help a little bit. She closed her eyes and softened her body, felt the floor beneath her. It was beginning to get unbearable, her head was almost swimming, and she started to feel nauseous.

The woman beside her was shifting around as if she couldn't get comfortable. Marissa wondered if she was feeling the same way.

Séamus closed the door and walked over to the group. Marissa counted around 18 people in total sitting together in the circle.

Séamus bowed, then raised his head, put his two hands together, looked at the group, then said, 'Welcome, welcome, one and all. Make yourselves at home. My home is your home, and today, we are all going home! Well, to a home of a sorts, perhaps a home you will remember for the first time in this lifetime. Now, before we begin, how many of you have done shamanic work before? Don't be shy, raise your hands.'

Two people raised their hands hesitantly. Marissa wasn't sure if she had done any, so she kept hers firmly by her side.

'All righty then, this is the "Introduction to the Shamanic Journey" workshop, starring yours truly,' he took another bow, 'so we need to understand what the journey is, and what shamanism also is.' He raised an eyebrow and added, 'Although that is a little more difficult to explain in simply one day. So let's start with a discussion, yes? What is shamanism? Anyone?'

Séamus looked around the room expectantly, everyone seemed to be extremely shy. Eventually, he took his seat facing the others and enthusiastically picked up his drum. Marissa noticed it was painted with a buffalo in the centre and had symbols all around. Something in Séamus's face changed, he became soft, and quiet. It was quite entrancing to watch him, he knew all eyes were on him, he drew them all in with his charisma.

'Shamanism,' he said, starting to drum softly with his fingers on the hide of the drum and declaiming as if reciting poetry of great importance, 'shamanism is a word that encapsulates many things. It has many myths, and many people fear it.' He picked up his beater, stood up and started to walk around the people, weaving in and out and around them, drum in one hand and beater in the other. He crouched down low and said almost at a whisper, 'But obviously not you... Because you are here!' He jumped back and smiled. Some of the group laughed and seemed to relax a little bit. He continued his walk, everyone's eyes were on him, following his every move.

'Shamanism is everything and nothing. It is consciousness and imagination, it is the veils between the worlds, the land of the spirit, of the dead, of the many things that we cannot see with human eyes alone. Shamanism is the pathway to your soul.'

He put the beater to the drum and banged the drum softly for a while, his rhythm increasing in speed and tone, mirroring how he was walking. And then he stopped.

Marissa felt tingles running down her back, the hot prickles had dissolved away and her butterflies were easing out. She noticed people had taken out notebooks and started to write in them, she didn't think of bringing one. *Dammit! Well, never mind.*

Séamus turned centre once more. 'And what is the soul? Many things to many people. The drop in the ocean, the ocean in the drop. Many people write about the soul, yet many people never experience their own. Soul songs, Soul Lines, soul-full, the quest to fill your soul. But to fill it with what?' He banged the drum loudly and a few people jumped. 'With drugs? Money? Power?' He turned back to the group. 'If this is your desire, then you are in the wrong workshop.' Bang!

Marissa couldn't help but join in with the laughter.

'What again then is shamanism? Many things to many peoples. Peoples, plural. Communities, people in communion with each other. Connected – not communion from the Church, no, this is community in action. We cannot live without each other. And we have lost that sense of belonging in the way that we are living.'

The word 'belonging' hit Marissa in the stomach. How did he know she felt lost and alone? Never belonging anywhere? Was it a community that she was looking for? But she had a community, hadn't she? What about her family? Did they not count?

Séamus continued to walk while he spoke. The drum went BANG! 'There are many ways to walk this path.' Bang! 'The shamanic path has too many ways for us to count. Ways known and ways still unknown. The path of the medicine plant – you have heard of it I am sure – ayahuasca, peyote, cacao, and the humble mushroom, just like *Alice in Wonderland* – remember that story?'

He started walking around the room in the opposite direction to before, still weaving in between the people on the floor, drumming intermittently.

'Drink this!' BANG!

Marissa jumped.

He turned sharply and said, 'Eat me!' BANG! There was laughter.

'There is a fine line between drugs and plant medicine,' he said, crouching down to meet the group at eye level, softly beating his drum. 'Can you tell the difference?'

He put the drum down on the rug, took a lighter out from his pocket and lit the candle. He was captivating, all eyes were on him.

'Shamanism appears in all of your myths and legends, magical portals to other worlds, you remember *The Lion, The Witch and the*

Wardrobe? The Wizard of Oz? The Neverending Story? All of them had portals to other worlds. Wardrobes, tornadoes and a book.'

Marissa felt the nausea leaving her. She was on more familiar territory now.

'Any other portals that I have forgotten?'

'Harry Potter and the platform on the train station?' someone said.

'Yes! Anyone else?'

'*Dr Who?*' questioned a male voice.

'Yes, even the humble Doctor had a portal in the TARDIS. You get the picture now.' He winked. 'Today, we will experience shamanism, explore shamanic wisdom, through the shamanic journey. And we need a portal, and a guide. The pathway we will take is the path of the drum. She is all-powerful, and she will hold us and guide us, and guide you, if you let her.'

He picked the drum up again and made his way back to his chair, and sat down.

'For on the wings of her music we will travel to the great worlds of the healers and find answers to the questions that you seek.'

The room was silent. He held the tension for a moment and then continued.

'Our portal will be our heart. We go inwards through the body, into the landscape of the heart, and outwards and down. And then we shall go up. But up is for later, after lunch. Trust my voice, trust the drum and you shall all travel freely. 'So I ask you now – what are your questions?'

There was a murmur then some people tentatively put up their hands.

Another bang. 'Your questions are not for me.'

The hands reluctantly went down.

'That is the beauty of the path of the shaman. For I am not here to answer your questions, only to lead you to the path, where all questions may be answered.'

He smiled at the group and held out the drum.

'Isn't she a beauty?' He winked, and the mood instantly changed, it was less intense, the room breathed an audible sigh.

'I have a question,' said a male voice from the back of the room. Marissa had noticed that there were just as many men there as women. *Perhaps men think shamanism is cool, so they aren't as hesitant to come as they are for psychotherapy.*

'Yes?' asked Séamus. 'And is it a good question? For the quality of the question determines the quality of the answer.'

'I don't know...'

'Good. Now I know I have your attention. Hold that question for now. Because before we begin, we have to open a sacred space. For it is only in a sacred space that we can do our sacred work. Everybody stand and face North.'

There was shuffling as everyone stood, but nobody seemed to know which way was North. They looked at Séamus as he pointed and turned to the wall with a hanging that depicted a snow-peaked mountain. Everyone shifted around to face it. He drummed loudly three times and chanted:

> *Great Spirit of the North, we come to you and ask for the strength and power to bear what is cold and harsh in life. We honour our ancestors who have also received the winds that truly can be overwhelming at times. Support us and warm us as we do our work, hold us as we release the patterns that are holding us back and place them into the fire.*

He banged the drum three times and turned. Everyone turned with him.

> *Great Spirit of the East, direction of birth, of the sunrise, of hope and faith. We turn to you to help us fly above our problems, to bring in light to the darkest places, to show us the direction of the next mountain that we need to climb. Support us and lighten our way as we choose to walk on this pathway of healing, so we may rise to be the best that we can be.*

Again he banged his drum three times and turned, this time to face south. And they followed him. Marissa found herself becoming greatly moved by what he was saying.

> *Great Spirit of the South, spirit of growth and compassion, of fertility and warmth. We come to you to you to support*

us as we shed our skins and leave the old controlling ways behind. Unwind from us what is no longer needed and teach us the way of compassion and beauty, so we can walk softly and leave no footprints behind.

As he turned to the West, Marissa noticed her anxiety had diminished to almost nothing. Séamus continued his opening prayer:

Great Spirit of the West, direction of death, of the sunset, of powerful medicine that goes beyond this lifetime. Teach us to live better lives, to be unafraid of death, to lift off the heavy chains that hold us back, support us as we transform our darkness into light, and help us bring that light to others.

Nobody ever talks about death that way, I wonder why. Isn't it a part of life, too?

Séamus crouched down to the floor and drummed softly.

Mother Earth, you are our true mother for you have given birth to all of the creatures in our world, the finned and the feathered, the two-legged, four-legged and many-legged. The trees and the oceans, the mountains and the valleys. We honour you and all of your children, all of our relations. Teach us how to treat you better and remind us that we all share the same blood.

Tears were forming in Marissa's eyes and her heart seemed to have doubled in size. She felt a huge pressure wanting to release itself. Séamus stood up tall and drummed up towards the ceiling.

Father Sky, you look down upon us and see our true potential. You know the things that we do not know. We ask you to come and hold this space as we remember the truth of who we are. For we are not alone, we are all connected in this great universal family. Thank you for the chance to sing this song of life for one more day.

He put the drum down.

Marissa looked at all the faces, some people were smiling but nobody else seemed as emotional as she was. *He could have been reading a menu from the local takeaway as far as they're concerned. I wonder if I can get what he just said written down to read again later?* Marissa still felt the reverberations of his words ringing in her body, they were lighting her up, her blood was flowing and she was hungry for more. She felt her heart, it had expanded and was so big in her chest, like a bird that wanted to fly out of her mouth. Birds and butterflies today. She gathered her cushion and blanket and sat back down on the floor.

Séamus banged his drum again. He had sat back in his chair. He looked at everyone to see if they were settling down and ready for him to continue. 'Let us go then, you and I, to a mystical land called the Lower World. This world lies beneath our feet, deep in the belly of Mother Earth. Otherwise known as Hell, for the Church did not like the independence of the tribal peoples and needed some way to scare them and keep them hostage in Church law. Ha!' He scanned the room again. 'Are yis with me? Say aye if yis are.'

'Aye!'

'A little louder please.'

'AYE!'

'Aye indeed. Know this, my fellow travellers, if any of you are fearful of shamanism, or if indeed, any beloved member of your family is anxious about you coming here, to this workshop, it's because of the old scripts. Because of spite and fearmongering by people who do not want you to walk this path and have direct communion with God. Did I say God? Yes, for the Great Spirit we speak of is another name for God. Read the first verse of the Tao. This is not the discussion for today. Be empowered, seek the answers, and if you are righteous and persistent, then you may find them.'

He paused for dramatic effect. There were a few sniggers from the crowd.

'I will take you there right now. Are you ready?'

'Yes!'

Ooh, my mother is gonna kill me, Marissa laughed to herself and knew that this was exactly the right place for her to be.

+++

Lunch was a quick sandwich and a packet of crisps from the local shop. Time was passing quickly, there was only one more journey to do before they closed for the day.

'And so lovely people, it is time once more to travel. Grab an extra blanket and a pillow if you need them, for you may find it cold or warm, depending on your process. Lie down on the floor if you want to, or sit on a chair, and let the drum carry you. Follow my voice and the rhythm of the drum and relax. Remember from earlier, here is the call-back signal once more.' He banged it out on his drum. 'I'll give you another minute to get settled.'

The group settled and got ready, this time Marissa was sitting up in a chair. She had fallen asleep the last two times as she chose to lay down, now she was determined to stay awake so she could remember what she was seeing.

Bang bang. Bang bang. It was more like a lub dub, lub dub. Lub dub, lub dub. Séamus's drum was echoing the heartbeat of the world. 'Listen to the drum, lub dub. Lub dub. Listen to your breath, in and out. Breathe in lub dub, breathe out lub dub. Let the drum breathe you. Lub dub. Lub dub.' Marissa's eyes closed.

'We are going on a journey now, into our bodies, feeling our foreheads and our eyes, lub dub lub dub, moving down to our cheeks and the insides of our mouths lub dub lub dub, down through our throats and into the tops of our chests, breathe in lub dub breathe out lub dub and now down into our heart. Breathe and expand and into the heart and down and we walk into a corridor, a long white corridor with the photographs of your life hanging on its walls. Don't stop and look at them, keep walking... There's a door at the end of the corridor – open it.'

Marissa felt herself shifting in her body. She still felt the chair beneath her, but she allowed herself to relax a little more deeply this time. She felt her eyelids soften.

'You go down a flight of white concrete stairs, and another, and another, and the stairs start to change, they are more living, breathing, made from living breathing material. You go down another flight, and another, and the stairs are alive, they are carved from a tree, another and another. And our bodies are melting away. The skin off of our flesh and our bone. Dissolving away. Nothing but light. The light of our souls, the light of who we are. We are but light and we are moving deeper now, into the centre of the world. And here is another door and you step out into the jungle.'

Marissa was drifting now. The images of what that rich land may have looked like started to fill Marissa's imagination. Lub dub. Lub dub. She saw hanging vines and rich grasses, luscious, colourful creepers and large orange flowers that looked like little birds' heads.

'You are now in the belly of the Mother. Mother Earth, the lushness and heat, the richness and love for all things. Tropical rainforest. Lub dub. Lub dub. She is the mother of us all, she holds us and she is beautiful and alive. Lub dub. Lub dub.'

She was there, walking in the tall wet grasses, the sun was shining, the sky was a bright blue through the greenery around her.

Lub dub lub dub the drum carried her and she couldn't hear Séamus's voice anymore. A monkey swung past her on a vine, she laughed and continued walking.

Lub dub lub dub surrounding her and holding her. She came to a clearing and in front of her was a tall, wizened, old oak tree. She looked up, the tree was so tall she couldn't see the top of the uppermost branches. She felt in awe of this tree, as if this tree was the king or queen of all the trees. It had a thick trunk and long deep roots which snaked and coiled outwards so Marissa had to walk around them deftly as she approached it.

Lub dub lub dub let the drum carry you. Marissa stood in front of the tree, she felt once more that heavy weight in her chest that hadn't left her since the morning. The air around her was still, and the tree seemed to stir. Marissa bowed deeply to the tree, it felt like the right thing to do. The tree acknowledged her somehow, she felt a fluttering in the lower branches.

'Get up, child,' the tree said to her. 'It is good to see you here. I was waiting for you.'

Marissa stood back up again and looked at the tree. Features had formed on the trunk, there was a wise face looking back at her, smiling gently. Marissa smiled back. This tree, this whole place, it was all so very familiar, yet she knew she had never been here before.

'Ahh, but you have been here before, and many times,' said the tree. 'What is it that you actually know, compared to what it is you think you know?'

'I don't know?' said Marissa, suddenly confused.

'Indeed, none of us knows as much as we think we do,' said the tree, in a very patient and loving tone. 'I have a message for you. What you think you know is only one part of who you are. And you cannot heal who you are in your wholeness, when you work with the mind alone.'

The tree reached out its branch to her, she reached out her arms in return and touched it. A little bird landed on the branch, it was smaller than a robin, golden in colour with a bright orange beak. It hopped down her arm, reached its beak into her chest and leaned in. Marissa wasn't afraid. Even though this was very strange, she felt safe with the tree beside her. The bird dug around inside her for a moment, then grabbed hold of something that was deeply buried with its beak. The bird pulled it out and Marissa could see it looked like a thick, sticky cobweb. As the cobweb released from her body the pressure around her heart eased. The bird pulled out the last piece, and suddenly, her heart felt light and free.

Lub dub lub dub The bird flew away, taking the cobweb with it. The tree gently pulled its branch back in and Marissa felt a glowing light surrounding her.

Marissa heard a bang. It startled her. Then another bang. Then the lub dub changed from Lub dub lub dub into dub dub dub dub – oh yes, the call-back signal, she remembered. It was time to go back.

'Come visit me again,' said the tree. 'I will always be here.'

Dub dub dub Marissa found herself being pulled away from the tree and back to the forest. 'Thank you, I would love that,' she said, wanting to stay longer, but it was as if strings were attached to her heart and her stomach and she had no choice but to follow the drum. Back to the forest, to the tall grasses. Back to the colourful creepers, the orange flowers. Back to the door, the stairs...

'And we climb up and up and up, dub dub dub dub, flesh appears upon bone. You are the light within and now your body envelops you. You feel your skin, fingers and toes. Your face, hair and skin. You are coming back to yourself as you climb up to the concrete stairs, through the door, close it behind you, move through the corridor, past the photographs, and back up into your body here, into the room right here.' Bang bang. Bang bang. The drum stopped. 'And into your body now. Feet on the floor, legs, hands, arms, eyes and face. Open your eyes, stretch your fingers and toes. You are awake. You are back.'

Marissa felt groggy. She rubbed her eyes and saw that many others were doing the same.

Séamus put the drum down on the carpet by the altar. 'No talking just yet,' he said. 'Keep it all to yourself for now. Walk. Stretch. Get a glass of water or a cup of tea. Breathe in deep – get some fresh air. Then come back to the circle in ten minutes.'

Séamus got up, walked over to reach for his wide-brimmed hat. He put it on and went out the door, leaving the others to sort themselves out.

The images were so real, so vibrant, so strong in Marissa's mind. She felt like she really had gone somewhere, unlike the journeys they had done earlier that day. It was difficult to orient herself in the room but she managed to get up and walk to the kitchen. She joined a group of people who were making tea. She was offered a cup – it was comforting to feel the heat of the cup in her hands.

'How was it for you?' asked the woman next to Marissa. She was dark-skinned with long thick black hair woven into many plaits, slightly overweight and wore a long purple skirt and a fringed tunic. She smiled at Marissa, looking expectantly. Marissa liked her immediately.

'It was so real, really real this time, I felt like I was actually there.'

The woman smiled. 'Yes, for me also. The first time I didn't seem to get in, but this time was amazing. What did *you* see?'

'I met a tree, a very wise old tree. There was a lot of love, I felt the love around me. It was beautiful.'

'I met a fish – and it talked to me!' the woman said, shaking her head and smiling widely. 'I thought for a moment I was crazy, but then I remembered it looked like a fish I had when I was a little girl. It called me by my name and told me that I took really good care of it, it thanked me for singing to it every night before I went to bed. I really *had* done that – I must have been five or six at the time. I'd totally forgotten about Sammy, my fish. I was so happy to see him, and I asked, 'Are you Sammy?' and it did a little flip up into the air, making me laugh! I wonder how much of this I am making up... I would love to think that it really was my Sammy and that he was happy and recognised me, and would say thank you for the singing.'

Marissa smiled. As the woman was talking, she had felt a feeling of 'Yes' deep in her body, right in the pit of her stomach. Yes.

She wasn't sure what that was. *Is this true?* And the 'Yes' was there again. It felt like a rush, a lightness, hairs on the back of her neck standing to attention, prickles down her arms. Yes. It felt good, that 'Yes'. She recognised the feeling from before when she knew that something was true.

She looked at the woman and said, 'I do believe that was your Sammy. I was getting shivers when you were speaking, shivers that usually mean 'yes' to me. So yes, your Sammy remembers you. How wonderful!'

They walked back into the room and stood at the door, the woman beaming with delight. 'I didn't know what to expect at this workshop, this has been more than I ever imagined!'

Marissa took her seat just as Séamus came back into the room. He hung his hat back up on its hook on the wall and sat down on his chair at the top of the room.

'We have just enough time left before we finish for questions and closing. How was that journey for you?'

A few stories were offered from people in the room, each with a deep emotional connection to what they had seen. One of the men said he met his aunt who had died the year before. Another person said they met their favourite dog from their childhood. Marissa seemed to be the only one who had met somebody new.

'Yggdrasil,' said Séamus, after she had described the tree to the group. 'An extraordinary tree. The Tree of Life. The tree of death and birth. From this tree comes the Seed of Life and The Flower of Life. The Fruit of Life. This tree spoke to you and sent a bird to heal you, then, it is here for you. It is significant.' He nodded his head at her.

Marissa felt another 'Yes' rushing through her body at his words. She was a little lightheaded now, but not from anxiety.

Séamus looked at his watch. 'And now it is time to close our circle. We must first close the sacred space that we have opened. Stand with me once more, and turn to each direction with me as before.' Everyone pushed the chairs out of the way and stood and followed his movements.

> *Great Spirit of the North, we thank you for offering us your strength, your power. We honour you, we honour those*

that came before us and those that will come after us. We release you now, with great gratitude. Ho!

Great Spirit of the East, we thank you for lending us your wings, for showing us the way. We are humbled in your presence, we see how far we have come, but we acknowledge we have much further to travel. We release you now with great gratitude. Ho!

Great Spirit of the South, we thank you for helping us shed our skins and transform into the beings that we are becoming. We endeavour to continue with the process of healing and growth. We release you now with great gratitude. Ho!

Great Spirit of the West, we are humbled to have been in your presence, reminding us to have great appreciation for each moment of every day of our lives. We see life everlasting in everything around us. We release you now with great gratitude. Ho!

Oh magical Mother, oh mystical Father, thank you for holding us as we do our healing work. We peel the illusion from our eyes and see the world as it really is, to know and experience the interconnectedness of all things. With majesty and grace we offer ourselves in service, to follow the beauty way, the path of light. And to walk gently upon you and leave no footprints, only light. And so it is.

Marissa felt a sweet sadness at the close of the circle. She was tired and ready to go home to rest but not ready for the magic to end. Not yet anyway. Séamus, standing with his back to the door, turned to the group with a beaming smile on his face.

'Thank you, ladies and gentlemen, for spending this beautiful day with me. It is a day that you will never get back, therefore it is a day that I hope will change something in how you see the world. Remember, there is more to this reality than that which you see with your eyes. There is so much more than that which you can touch with your fingers or hear with your ears. Be of open mind, of silent brain, sit with the flower and watch it grow. That flower has wisdom to show you. Perhaps we will meet again. You know where to find me.'

He opened the main door and stood beside it with a big smile to say goodbye as people made their way outside.

Something that was opened now felt closed. Marissa felt very present and lighter in herself. *I'm so glad I came.* She put on her coat and moved to the throng at the doorway to leave.

When it was her turn to exit, she turned to thank him. 'Wait,' he said to her in a low voice, and he gestured back into the room.

Marissa felt compelled to do as he bid her, so she went back inside and absently leafed through a booklet on the countertop while she waited for the others to leave.

When it was just the two of them, Séamus stretched, turned towards her and looked her up and down. She suddenly felt naked and very small.

'You are a medicine woman in the waiting,' he said. 'You have a choice: to lie dormant, or to grow. But you are here, and as I see you listening to me, I know that you are already awakening. Your Inner Compass has activated. You have a long way to go, Marissa, kin of the Mother Spirits. Your lineage is long, and you have been here many times before. It is not the easy path, but you know this already. I would be honoured to have you at my fire to join me as my apprentice. I can teach you many things. You are already a good healer, but with my help, you could become a great one. Think about it.'

'I will think about it,' she said, feeling her power gradually returning to her as she absorbed his words.

'I will see you again,' he said with a knowing look.

'Thank you,' whispered Marissa and she left quickly, going out the door and down the steps. With every step she felt her energy returning to her. She went out the main door and turned in the direction of home. With the fresh air on her face, she felt free and light. As she walked, she saw the colours around her, felt the love from the tree inside of her and knew that a door had opened.

My training has truly begun. It felt like the way was prepared for her, and all she had to do was follow the pathway, wherever it was to lead.

Yes, she thought. Yes, yes, yes, yes, YES!

CHAPTER TEN

It was the Monday after the workshop and Marissa had a lunch date with Sarah at their usual café. They had eaten quickly and still had twenty minutes before they had to go back to work. The subject for discussion, as usual, was Sarah's love life. Sarah flicked her long loose hair out of her eyes and took her phone out from her handbag. It was in a turquoise phone case, the exact same shade of her painted turquoise nails. And, coming to think of it, the same colour as her shoes, too. Sarah scrolled to a photograph of a blonde, blue-eyed man and handed her phone to Marissa who raised an eyebrow.

'That's him – what do you think?'

'Honestly, Sarah, is this the third or the fourth guy you've been crushing on since you signed up for that dating website?'

Sarah blushed. 'Fourth? I think fourth. Maybe fifth…'

'What's different about this one?' Marissa stirred some sugar into her hot chocolate, trying not to giggle. She looked at Sarah, who seemed a little flustered.

'Oh Jesus, I don't know.' Sarah slammed her phone down on the table. She was exasperated. She looked at her perfectly manicured nails, then looked up at Marissa. 'I'm tired Mari, I keep trying, and it just doesn't seem to work for me. They're boring, or they're secretly married, or they're on the rebound.' She sighed. 'Maybe it's just as well you didn't go through with registering on that dating site. It's like going on a never-ending wild goose chase, and the geese knew you were coming, so they scarpered, leaving only ducks pretending to be geese.'

Marissa smiled. 'That's funny, but a little sad too. And I think that's the most honest you've been with me.'

Marissa put her hand on Sarah's. Sarah pulled hers in quickly and looked around to see if anyone noticed.

'Shite Marissa, That's the last thing I need, them thinking I'm a lesbian!' The girls looked at each other and cracked up.

'Well, at least you know *I'm* not married,' said Marissa, and they laughed even harder.

When they'd collected themselves Sarah finally asked, 'So, what are you up to these days?'

'I've been busy with class. It's going really well. And family news – Eli and Carol are having a baby.'

'Wow, brilliant!'

'They've not told anyone yet, so don't say anything.'

'Of course not!'

'And,' Marissa hesitated and then went on, 'I went on a shamanic workshop. Just to try it, you know, after Peru and all.'

'Wow! When? What was that like?' Sarah's eyes were wide in expectation.

'It was only the day before yesterday. I'm still figuring it out. It *was* good though, I liked it. I wasn't sure what to expect, I was nervous.' She sipped her hot chocolate. 'He said I was a medicine woman in the making, the teacher I mean, he said I should do more training with him. I don't think he said it to anyone else, which was a bit strange. I don't know what's involved, or even if I have time to do it...'

'Ah, come on, Marissa, you're more interested in training than in men, and I always have time for men. Sure I've not had much luck lately, but I'm not going to give up, so I'm sure you can figure it all out. Is he nice? The teacher?'

'He's very charismatic! He has a way with words. I admit that some of the things he said felt true to me, and I think he has more things he can teach me.'

'Go on, go on, go on! You medicine woman you – Ha! Then when you're qualified, you can fix my man problem. I'll have men coming out of my ears... Ooh, not a pretty picture that!'

As soon as they came back from lunch Marissa opened a browser window (firstly making sure nobody was lurking around her desk to catch her) and looked up Séamus O'Driscoll's website. *Why didn't I do this yesterday?* She typed his name into the search box. She definitely felt happier having Sarah know. She hadn't told anyone else yet, it was reassuring not doing this in secret. She wasn't able to tell her mother, she had just told her it was a workshop, so it could have been anything. She wasn't able for the onslaught of questions that her mother was sure to have, and the fear and drama that usually comes when someone does something out of the ordinary. She was still getting used to it herself, so she didn't have the energy to look after her family as well. Sarah was so much more easy-going, it wasn't an effort talking to her, and if she did end up disappearing down a rabbit hole, at least Sarah would know where the hole began. She might even tell Olive, too, at their next session.

Marissa scrolled through Séamus's website twice, but she couldn't find any apprenticeship training programme. Maybe she was looking for the wrong thing? She clicked the 'Contact Me' page and started to fill out the form. *Hi it's Marissa, I was at your workshop yesterday and you mentioned that I could be an apprentice...* No. She deleted it. She wasn't quite ready yet.

+++

As part of her psychotherapy diploma course Marissa had to volunteer as a psychotherapist in a placement position. Marissa secured such a placement in a priory in the Northside of Dublin. That Wednesday after work, she was going to see the place and meet her new supervisor. She was nervous about it, she really didn't know what would be involved, and she wasn't that familiar with North Dublin so she had no image of where she was going to be. She hoped she wouldn't feel like a fish out of water as a Jew in a Catholic priory. *Or an ex-Jew. Can you be an ex, when you don't practice a religion? Or are you always connected to it? But I managed to find Séamus's place all right, and that worked out really well. I know I'm probably making things worse in my head than they are.*

The priory was a separate building in the grounds of a church. One of her classmates was already working there and gave her directions so she was able to find The Priory. It wasn't as tall and imposing as the church, yet it was just as old, built around the same time with the same stone. There was an added extension made of wood and aluminium, the combination of marble and stone for the church with the curved wooden beams for the roof of the extension was interesting on the eye. The ceilings were tall so it was very spacey on the inside, draughty and decorated to the minimum. Mr Blakemore, her assigned supervisor, met her at the door. He seemed very nice, late sixties average build, he had glasses and his hair was slightly balding in places, most of it was swept over to one side. He wore slacks, a white shirt and a green blazer. They walked together down the echoing corridor as he showed her around.

'Here's the kitchen area, you can make yourself a cup of tea in between your sessions if you like.' Marissa looked at the chipped cups and the sink, which only had a cold water tap.

'The boiler is here,' said Mr Blakemore, pointing to a BERKO on the worktop behind him, 'tea here, coffee here, and biscuits here. We only have instant coffee, in these big tins.' He picked up a shortbread, 'They're always very generous with the biscuits. Would you like one?'

'No, thank you,' said Marissa, managing the butterflies in her stomach and paying attention to the layout was about all she was able to do. Her phone, buried inside her handbag, started to ring, making her heart leap.

'Would you like to get that?' Mr Blakemore asked.

'Thanks, it's okay.' Marissa reached into her bag and found the silent button, and switched it off.

'I'll bring you to the room that you're going to be using for your sessions.'

'That would be great, thanks.'

Mr Blakemore led her down another corridor to a narrow spiral stairway made of wood and steel. They climbed up two flights to a refurbished attic space which felt very different to the building below. It was well insulated, much quieter, and the ceiling was not as high. It felt much cosier up here. They stood in a carpeted corridor, the quality of light was different here too. Marissa looked up and saw a Velux window in the celling.

'We have five therapy rooms up here, and a small bathroom.' Mr Blakemore opened out the basic bathroom door. 'You can use this, and so can your clients.' He brought Marissa to Room Three. 'This will be your room.' He opened the door and invited her in. The pale green carpet was springy and new, but the furniture was old, two brown armchairs, a small coffee table and a place for hanging coats. A darkened painting hung on the wall depicting a ship out at sea, and a small window looking out over the church grounds. There was a small clock on the table with an audible tick-tock sound, and a buzzer on the wall by the door. It was altogether quite a pleasant room, a little stuffy and smelling of damp, but Marissa wasn't going to be living in it, just seeing clients there for three hours each week until the end of her college term.

'Can I light a candle in here?' she asked.

'Of course! As long as you don't leave it lit when you leave the room. The window doesn't open, and we have smoke detectors in all the rooms. The buzzer lets your clients in, but it's better for you to meet them at the front door the first time they come. The receptionist lets them in, if she's here. Now, let me show you the bathroom.'

Back in Mr Blakemore's office, Marissa sat in the chair opposite his to finalise their arrangements.

'We have a waiting list of clients for you, so you won't have to worry about finding people to see. And for every ten sessions you do, you will need to see me for one supervision session. The supervision is free, and your client work is voluntary. They did mention that to you, didn't they?'

'Yes, they did. This is great, thank you!' Marissa said brightly.

'Good. You can arrange your hours with the secretary, as far as I know, the room is yours on Thursday evenings 6–9pm. I'll give you a key so you can access the front door and your room for the duration of your stay with us. You can park your car in the church car park, the latest session we allow for is 9–10pm, but we prefer not to go that late. The church gate will be locked at 11 sharp every night. So we will see you here for your first session next week, yes? Good. I am happy to have you here, Marissa. I hope you enjoy it, and I look forward to our first supervision session soon.'

They shook hands, and Marissa left the main building. Standing outside the main door she fished her phone out of her bag to see who had phoned. It was Carol. She pressed 'redial' as she walked through the church grounds in the darkening evening, walking towards the bus stop.

'Hi Carol, what's up?'

'Ahh, Marissa, thank God you've called back. It's Eli, he's not good, he told your parents about the baby this afternoon and there was a big fight. He stormed out and now he's locked himself in his room with a bottle of whiskey. He's been in there for two hours. I can't get through to him – I hate to ask you, but can you come over?'

'Sure. I'm in Cabra, so it will take me a while to get there, I'll have to take two buses. Be there as fast as I can.'

'Thanks, Marissa, I owe you one.'

She hung up the phone and looked up their address on Google Maps. The next bus was in twenty minutes, and it would take fifteen minutes just to get to the second bus. She flagged down a taxi. As she gave directions to the driver, her stomach growled, she hadn't eaten yet. The driver wanted to chat as they drove. Marissa answered in mutters and grunts, wondering what had gotten into Eli.

Twenty-five minutes later, she was outside Eli and Carol's house, it had gotten dark by the time she arrived, and all the lights were on. She paid the driver and stood on the porch steps, taking a moment to gather herself and to check the temperature inside. She couldn't hear any shouting, so that was a good sign. She rang the doorbell and immediately heard Carol's footsteps as she came downstairs to the front door.

'You made it. Thanks so much for coming. You didn't take that long to get here? He's a little calmer now, but he still won't come out of his room.'

Marissa followed Carol upstairs. Carol pointed to where Eli had locked himself in. Marissa knocked on the door 'Eli? It's Marissa. Do you want to talk?'

She waited there for a few minutes, then Eli opened the door just a crack. Marissa could smell the drink on his breath, he looked very dishevelled and his voice sounded defeated.

'Hi, Sis. What is it about our family? They never want us to be happy. I'm sick of it.'

'Hey. I'm your family. And I'm happy that you're happy. You know they need some time, that's all.'

'They choose to stay in Ireland. If we were in Israel then I might even find a nice Jewish girl. What are the chances in Ireland? You'd think they'd have figured that out by now. Heck, I'm not even religious. I wouldn't be looking for someone based on religion anyway. "You're not Jewish? Next!" That'd be a lot of nexts...' He shook his head.

'I don't know why they haven't figured this out yet either. I do remember that Louis and Naomi made a huge deal when Debby got engaged to Charlie. Remember? And Mum and Dad weren't happy about me and... well, you know, *him*.'

Eli softened and opened the door a little more. 'Yeah I remember. Hey, you're better off without him.' He opened the door fully and went and sat on the bed, holding his bottle of whiskey by the neck.

Marissa went into the room and sat on the bed beside him. She put her head on his shoulder. 'I remember how happy everyone was when the twins were born, especially Louis and Naomi. Always with the hypocrisy and the double standards, but that's what they do.'

'Yeah,' agreed Eli, reluctantly.

'Exactly. They got over it. They even tolerate Charlie now, although Debby did have to move to America to get some space from them... You're doing it differently, Carol's pregnant, so this is when they have their canary with you guys. Look, I'll talk to Mum and Dad for you. I won't try to make them see sense because they probably won't. But I will remind them about how they eventually accepted James and me, and how Louis and Naomi adore the twins, and hopefully, they'll back off. You guys don't need the stress.'

'Thanks, Sis.' Eli took a swig of whiskey, offered some to Marissa. She shook her head. He closed the bottle and put it down on his bedside cabinet.

'I wonder if this baby will look like you or like Carol,' said Marissa after a few minutes.

'Well, I hope for its sake it looks like Carol. All I wanted was for them to be happy for us.'

'When Mum holds her grandbaby in her arms for the first time, she will forget all of this crap. I know she will. Maybe they feel like they have to do this, express themselves in this way, because their parents would have done it to them if it was them. They didn't have it easy, so I guess they don't think we should have it easy either. When you take a step back from the situation, look at the people in it and wonder why they may be reacting the way they are, you see more of a picture. It helps you make sense of it.'

'I think I know why you're becoming a therapist, it's certainly useful to have you around. You're very calming. Thanks for coming.' Eli smiled.

'It didn't take very much to calm you,' said Marissa.

'Well, it was the thought that counts. Actually, it was more than that, it was what you said. About you being my family too.'

'Hey, always. And Carol's family.' She raised her voice. 'Carol?'

Carol peeked in. She had been hiding outside in the hall.

'Hi. Eli, I'm glad you're feeling better.'

Eli opened his free arm up and gestured for Carol to sit on the bed beside him. Marissa shuffled over to make more room. Carol snuggled into Eli, and discretely put the whiskey bottle on the floor, out of view.

After a lovely dinner Eli promised not to drink any more whiskey. Marissa declined the offer of a lift home and got the bus back to her apartment. It was 10pm by the time she got home. The air outside was crisp, she made a cup of camomile tea and sat on her deckchair out in the garden with her alpaca scarf and her pyjamas. It was quiet, the first moments of quiet she had had all day. The steam from her mug and the smell of camomile was relaxing. She sniffed the scarf deeply and noticed how it was losing the smells from Peru. She could still feel Eli's emotions as if they were right there with her, almost like it was wrapped around her like her scarf.

'I know he felt better when I left, but he's still sad,' she said out loud, thinking of how his face looked when he let her into his bedroom. She breathed out and imagined she was gently pushing his upset away from her, as if she was making more space for herself. After two more similar breaths, she felt noticeably better. She could feel his upset still, but it was further away, not right in on top of her.

Interesting. I wonder if that was my upset at seeing him upset, or if it was actually his upset?

She took a moment and asked herself if she still felt upset. She registered a no, she wasn't deeply upset, she expected her parents to act out, in fact, she was surprised it took this long.

Her phone beeped a text inside, but she stayed outside with her tea. She closed her eyes and softened her body. She wanted to go back and visit the tree from her journey, but her head was swimming in and out, between imagining herself seeing clients in the priory, wondering who she would be working with, then the idea of work brought in images of work and of Sarah, and then she came back to Eli. She finished the last drain of tea from her cup. She couldn't be still.

'Well, Spirit Tree, I will try to connect to you tomorrow. Maybe I need some help to do that.'

She went inside and put her cup in the sink and checked her phone. There was a text from Eli waiting for her.

Thanks, sis, appreciate it, appreciate you xx

She smiled, closed the back door and locked up for the night.

As she held her phone to put on the alarm for the next day, she opened her email and hit Compose.

Dear Séamus,

I really enjoyed the workshop with you on Saturday, thank you. I think I would like to do more training but I don't know what I should do next. Can you help? Looking forward to hearing back, Marissa Rosenthal.

She typed Séamus's email address at the top of the email and typed *further training* as the 'Subject'. Her thumb hovered over the 'Send' button, and then she clicked it. She breathed out. *Done. I'll wait and see what he says.*

She turned off the phone and put it on her bedside locker, switched off the lights and rolled over onto her side, tucked into her duvet. Tobermory sensed her there and leapt up onto the bed, then curled around at her feet. She didn't feel upset or nervous, and for once she didn't second guess sending that email. She felt still, like the lake from her dream, as if she had total stillness inside of her.

The images of the lake came into her mind, she imagined herself there. She imagined diving into the waters without breaking them, without making a sound. Going down into the water until she was totally submerged. Not cold, not hot, feeling the water all around her, holding her, supporting her weight. She didn't feel the need to look for the serpent or to ask herself what she needed to do next. She could see the surface, but she hung there, not needing to breathe, or to move, or do anything. It felt like going into a womb. A safe place.

She fell asleep.

CHAPTER ELEVEN

It had been almost a week and Séamus still had not replied to Marissa's email. She wasn't fretting, but she kept wondering if she should write to him again and ask if he received it. She had been doing some research on shamanic training and had found several more teachers in Ireland, but none that were close by, or that she thought she liked the look of better. Olive's book was still lying where she had left it, unopened, its frayed edges beckoning her to open it, even to a random page. But still, she resisted. This was normal for Marissa – any time a big decision or a change was imminent she went back and forth with it for days, weeks even.

She was still in bed. She wasn't in any rush to get to work, even though it was close to 9am and she was supposed to be at her desk in ten minutes. 'Will I won't I email Séamus?' thoughts rolled into 'Will I won't I go to work today?' until Marissa couldn't stand being alone with herself. She had already read the morning headlines and looked up all her three hundred and fifty-four friends on Facebook (she didn't know she knew so many people). *If I do call in sick, what would I do all day? If I can come up with a better plan than work, I'll do that, as long as I can still make it to class afterwards.*

She rolled over and looked out the window. Marissa was currently working on a new project for Noreen who was hoping to do business over in Canada, but typically, Noreen had already done all of the research herself. All Marissa had to do, was put it all together into a reasonable looking document so that Noreen could present it to the shareholders, and that would only take her 5 minutes.

She plodded to the bathroom, brushed the grime off her teeth and looked at herself in the mirror. She didn't look too tired today, her skin was mostly clear, her slight tan from Peru had faded. *I could go to the cinema. When was the last time I took a sick day?*

That decided it. She called the office and asked for Ashley, head of HR.

'Hi, Ashley, it's Marissa. I've got some sort of bug. I was up all night with it, and I'm still in the throes... Yes, I know it's awful, hopefully it will be just one of those twenty-four hour things. Yes, I will, thanks so much. Can you tell Noreen? I can email her the file we were working on from my laptop here at home – I'll send it on now. Cheers. Thanks, yes, I'm sure I'll be in tomorrow. Bye.'

Marissa felt relieved as she switched on her laptop and the kettle. She let Tobermory into the garden to do his business and breathed a sigh of relief. She joined him outside and stood in the fresh air. A whole day free, well, almost. Class was at 6pm, and she *was* looking forward to it. It was the last of six Cognitive Behavioural Therapy classes with Ms Pearson. Next, they were going to start Transpersonal Therapy, she was very interested in that, too. She had never been this interested in her undergraduate degree course. She had found the lectures tedious and dreaded the assignments and exams, but with the psychotherapy diploma, it was different. The work came naturally to her, she didn't have to learn facts and figures, she just got a hold of the concept, then somehow, it seemed to be inside her. She discovered that she had opinions, too, of what worked and what didn't work. She found herself trying things that she hadn't read about anywhere, like the butterfly technique, which was very effective (and her classmates were using it now and sharing it with their clients). She didn't think it extraordinary, it was just an extension of herself.

The kettle switched itself off. Marissa went back in and made tea, sat at her desk, found the file Noreen wanted and emailed it. That was her work done for the day. What would she do now? It was clear out, a brisk day and not raining. She didn't want to spend the day inside, so she showered and dressed, got her bag together, put on a raincoat just in case, and locked the back door. Just before she left the house, her eye caught Olive's book, so she threw it into her bag, too. *Why not?*

She walked into town and found herself outside the DART station. *It's been ages since I've been to Dun Laoghaire. That could be fun!* She got a ticket and wasn't waiting long for a train. Marissa enjoyed getting out of the city, she had not done it in a long time, it was like having a treat. She had the carriage almost all to herself for the whole twenty-five minute journey. The station wasn't that busy, she bought herself a can of Diet Coke, shouldered her bag and made her way to the main pier for a walk by the sea.

Dun Laoghaire had been getting a facelift. There was scaffolding over some of the buildings, builders were sawing wood and pouring concrete, laughing and joking with each other as they worked on the new Ferry Port building. The wind and salty air whipped against Marissa's face, she smiled with pleasure and continued walking. She always found it peaceful by the sea, and with only one 'What if?' going around in her mind, she felt much more settled. She thought of whistling at one of the builders as she went past but couldn't bring herself to do it. Finally, she reached the pier and turned to walk down it, towards the sea.

The pier was always busy, people were strolling along, some with dogs on long extendable leads, some with push-chairs or prams, and a few people walking together using frames for support. Marissa and Eli would regularly come to the pier on Sundays when they were growing up. Their Dad would bring them, sometimes their Mum would come too. Walking the pier and back, then getting a 99 in Teddies afterwards as a reward made it a good weekend. Although Teddies was closed today, Marissa didn't mind. One of the advantages of being a grown-up was that you could have ice cream anytime you wanted, so she didn't feel like she was missing out.

She sat on a wooden bench right at the bottom of the pier, looking out to sea. *So magic in my life isn't man-related. Yes, I think Joanne is right. And I don't want a man, I've still not signed up for the dating site. So I'm much happier without one. Then, am I truly over James?* She watched the waves coming in and out. *Do I have complete closure? That sounds like a question I'd ask a client – I guess I could be my own client today – ha ha! A therapy session, for me, from me. Why not?* She asked her brain out loud, 'Well, brain, are you still holding onto James? Is there some part of you wishing that he would leave his new wife and baby and come back on begging knee asking for my hand? Would I take him back?'

She laughed at the absurdity of the image, and her body got tight at the thought of James being there on the bench beside her. *No bloody way, no. I'd not take him back, not now, not ever.* 'It's time to move on, so.'

She looked down at her feet and saw a stone about half the size of her fist, she picked it up, examining its black, wet, irregular features. *All my hopes and dreams out the window, but now I have new hopes and dreams – at least I think I do. Psychotherapy, shamanic training, seeing clients. I do, in a way, find that magical, especially when I help someone feel better. I wonder what else will come my way.* Marissa turned the stone around in her hand, her fingers tracing the soft and hard edges of it.

She suddenly had a strong image in her mind of her Grandfather Abraham. She hadn't thought about him in a long time, she quietened her mind and felt his presence beside her as if he was right there. It could have been out of context, but she remembered he used to bring her here to the pier when she was really little, herself and Eli. If it really was him, what would he say to her?

She heard a voice outside of her, and to the right, it didn't feel like her inner dialogue, the texture was different, it seemed wiser, stronger somehow. 'Good Girl,' it said. 'It's time to move on. I'm proud of you, and I'm here for you, watching and helping from behind the scenes.' At least that's what Marissa thought it said, she could have been mistaken, it seemed a little fuzzy.

She spoke out loud. 'Okay, Grandpa, if you *are* here, I ask you to be my witness. I throw this stone into the sea to signify my letting go of everything to do with James, with the life that will never be. And I promise myself that I will follow my dreams and follow this path, wherever it will take me. I can live a happy and good life if I keep going the way I am going. And who knows, I may even be able to help a few people along the way.'

She took in a breath, lifted the stone and held it for a moment, along with her breath. Then she threw it, breathing out at the same time. The stone flew true and hit the sea with a splash, then went down. She felt a sense of satisfaction. A raindrop fell on her nose, then another, and then another. She felt a release too, from her chest, as if she had taken off a coat that was too small for her. *Strange. But good. I didn't know I was holding it in my chest.* Another raindrop fell, and then it was a rain shower. *I think it's time for a coffee.* She pulled up her hood, shouldered her bag once more, turned back and walked towards the town.

It had gotten darker, but the rain was still light. Marissa walked briskly up the hill and into Dun Laoghaire main street and went into the shopping centre. It was warm inside. She took off her damp coat, shook it out then hung it over her bag. Strolling along, she passed several shops that didn't interest her. She was focused on getting a coffee, preferably in a place with comfortable seating. She ended up on the top floor of the centre and found herself standing in front of an angel shop, which was called, funnily enough, The Angel Shop. *Why am I up here? There's no café here.* The windows of The Angel Shop were crammed with books and crystals, card decks and dream catchers. The window seemed to be glowing and calling her in. Marissa's eyes were immediately drawn to a card deck with a Native American medicine woman on the cover. *Well, a little look inside won't hurt.*

The shop smelled of sage and lavender, there was gentle music playing in the background, and the shelves were crammed full of angel statues, candles, books and crystals. Sunlight came in from the small windows on the opposite side of the store and threw rainbows onto the wall through crystal carvings hanging from a display. As she looked from shelf to shelf, Marissa felt herself getting anxious. Before long, her heart was racing and she started to get upset. There were too many things, she didn't know what she wanted or where to start.

The woman behind the counter was talking to a customer, they were laughing together. As the person paid for her goods, the shop owner took small price stickers off the items, wrapped them in pink paper, and put them into a bag. She was in her sixties, had a gentle face and was wearing a beautiful dark pink scarf, her hair was perfectly coiffured. She looked over at Marissa and smiled.

'I'll be with you in a minute, dear. Don't fret, it can be difficult coming into a place like this for the first time.'

Marissa felt instantly better. The woman finished helping the customer, and once she was free, she came out from behind the counter and smiled.

'I'm Mairead,' she said. 'Lovely to meet you. Welcome to my shop. Have a look around, let me know if you need me to help you with anything.'

'Hi, I'm Marissa. Thanks for saying that earlier, yes I was getting a bit upset. I've never seen a place like this before.'

'It's an Aladdin's cave, isn't it? So, what are you after today? A crystal to help you sleep, a card deck for reassurance, maybe some sage to help clear an energy space?'

'Actually, I did see a card deck in the window with a medicine woman on it. Can I have a look at that?'

'Certainly.' Mairead went to the back wall and found a similar deck for Marissa. She brought it and three others over to the shop counter and placed them upon it.

'Here are a few decks. Which one do you feel is for you?'

Marissa went over and looked at the other two decks first. They were both angel cards. The images on the first one looked very religious. The second one was prettier but still felt strange to her. She had never met an angel and she didn't know anything about them. Her eyes were drawn back to the first pack.

'I do like this one,' she said, pointing to the medicine woman.

'Ahh, a medicine woman for a medicine woman in the making,' Mairead said knowingly.

Marissa felt a flash of heat run through her body. 'Someone else has said that to me too recently,' she said, looking up at Mairead.

'Well, no surprise there then. Did you know that it's a tradition that your first deck of cards, whether they be oracle or tarot, be gifted to you?' Mairead looked into Marissa's eyes for a moment, and then she nodded her head to herself, picked up the pack and held it out to Marissa. 'Please consider these a gift from me to you.'

Marissa looked up at Mairead and saw only kindness in her eyes.

'This is no accident, the angels want you to have this, really, from my heart to yours.'

'I really don't know what to say,' said Marissa, breathless and suddenly emotional with the kindness of a stranger. 'Are you sure you don't want me to pay?'

'Absolutely. But if it makes you feel any better, you can pick something else to go with it and pay for that.'

Marissa blushed and smiled. 'Thank you so much, this means a lot to me. This type of thing never happens...'

'Well, open your heart to it happening quite a lot from now on. The angels told me to tell you that your path has turned, and your destination has been revealed. You are a medicine woman in the making. The world needs more people like you, it is my absolute pleasure to give this pack to you, with my blessings. Now, why not choose a crystal to help support you on your path? That, my girl, you can pay me for!'

Marissa asked Mairead to help her choose and she offered her a clear quartz, double-terminated crystal, which was chunky and about as long as her thumb. It glistened rainbows in the light, Marissa was delighted with it and it was a lot less expensive than it looked. She also got a couple of white pillar candles, similar to the one Séamus used in the workshop, and a small dish with a mosaic in greens and blues for the candle to sit into. Marissa gladly handed the money over to Mairead who wrapped everything up for her and put it all into a colourful paper bag. Then Mairead pulled out some angel confetti from under the counter, closed her eyes and added a handful into the bag, closed the bag and handed it to Marissa.

'Now then. When you have a nice quiet space to yourself, sit and hold the card deck in your hands. Before you start to use it, you must open it up and separate out each card, spend time with it, look at it, so that you make this pack your own. If you like, you can ask if it will work with you, but I can see already that it will. It called you in here! Then, when you've seen all of the cards, you can put them together and shuffle them, hold them again for a moment, then ask a question.'

'What type of question?'

'Well, a really good question is: "What do I need to know now?" If you ask that type of question, you can cut the pack wherever it falls, pull out one card, and that is your answer. You can also do a three-card spread, which is my favourite. Ask the question, then shuffle and cut, and pull out three cards – one for the past, one for the present and one for the future. There are lots of other ways of doing it, but these are my personal favourites. There's a booklet in the pack to help you understand each card better. I know you're really going to enjoy these.'

'Thank you so much again,' said Marissa, turning to leave.

'Come back and see me anytime girl, you're welcome here. I'd love to see you and hear about how you're getting on.'

'I will,' said Marissa, putting the paper bag into her book bag. She smiled at Mairead with genuine thanks and enjoyed the smile she received in return.

Back down on the ground floor, she left the shopping centre and walked outside for a while along the road, feeling lighter than she did earlier that day. She spotted an interesting looking café on the main street and remembered she still hadn't had her coffee. She was hungry now, too. She opened the door and went in, the clink and clatter of cutlery and plates from the kitchen and steamy windows from the warmth were reassuring. Marissa found a table with her back to the wall and ordered a tuna roll and coffee. The food came quickly. She was tempted to open the card deck, but she felt she should wait until she got home and spend some quiet time doing it properly.

Sitting at the table she relaxed, once she ate her sandwich and finished her coffee she realised she wasn't in a rush to get home. If she stayed on for an hour or two, she could go directly from Dun Laoghaire to her class. That felt like the best plan. She ordered a pot of tea and settled into the chair to stay a while longer. She pulled out Olive's book from her bag and opened it to a random page.

> *The journey activates the primal archetype deep within, the jungles of the lower world may be represented by sparse desert or rocky outcrops depending on the circumstances of the original trauma. Ramakrishna says 'How to get rid of the lower self? The blossom vanishes of itself as the fruit grows, so will your lower-self vanish as the divine grows in you.'*

She wasn't sure what the book was getting at, maybe she had missed something. She flicked back to an earlier chapter and read:

> *The Shamanic Journey is not a journey outside of oneself to an actual land per se, but a journey inwards into both the individual and collective psyche. By travelling*

inside of oneself, one can see the current state of the anima and animus, and challenge it using the power of the imagination.

Okay, so landscapes are the places you travel to when on a journey, and they are inside you, but what are archetypes? She flicked back to the table of contents to see if there was a chapter about archetypes, which there wasn't. *I guess I'll have to read the whole thing from the beginning. No shortcuts here.* She sighed and poured out her tea.

She was only a few pages into the first chapter when she felt the presence of someone standing at her table, hovering over her. She looked up, it was Séamus. He was clutching a book bag, he had his hat on and had just paid at the counter, looking like he was about to leave.

'Well hello there, fancy meeting you here!' he said to her with a smile, pocketing his change.

'Hi! Yes indeed! Thanks again for the great workshop. I really enjoyed it.' Marissa put the book upside-down on the table.

'You're very welcome. Did you give any further thought to my invitation? Hmm, what are you reading here?' He flipped the book around so he could read the cover. 'Good choice! Well?'

'Yes, please. I emailed you last week – did you not get it?'

'Nope, but what is for you will not pass you by. One door is beckoning, so it pulls you in! Do you usually come to this café?'

'I've never been here before!'

'Well there you go. Neither do I! The Universe works in mysterious ways.'

'Would you like to join me for a coffee?' asked Marissa.

'Got to run, but hey, I'll get in touch, I'm working on something with a few other people, and I think you'll like it. It'll be in a week or two, for a half a day or so, to start with. We can talk then and make some plans for your training, yes?'

'Yes, great!'

They swapped phone numbers. He tipped his hat to her and left the café. Marissa remembered what Mairead had just said to her in the shop earlier, about the angels wanting her to have the cards, that she was a medicine woman in the making (whatever that was), that she should be open to her path taking her to new places. *I have so much to learn.* She looked at the time. 'Oh shit, I have to get to class!'

Marissa got a window seat on the DART back into the city and kept her eyes on the sea until the train went through the tunnel and veered away from the coast. She felt emotion rising in her and tears coming into her eyes, but they were tears of happiness, of gratitude. She whispered under her breath to the sea, 'Thank you thank you thank you thank you thank you,' mirroring the sound of the train and the wheels on the tracks as they made their way back to the big smoke. She grabbed a sandwich and a bag of crisps at the train station for later and caught the bus to college. It was rush hour now, and the bus was packed full of people, the air was humid from lack of ventilation.

Marissa got to college in plenty of time. She went into the kitchenette to make tea, then sat at a table and waited for her friends to arrive. Yvonne walked in first and smiled.

'Tea?' asked Marissa

'Oh yes, indeed.' Tea was a ritual before class. It wasn't long before Yvonne was seated beside Marissa with her tea cradled in her hands.

'What a fast week that was. It's lovely to hold a mug of hot tea, it's getting so cold outside.'

'Yes, isn't it! Sure it will be Christmas soon!'

'Ha ha. No.' They smiled at each other.

'So, how are you getting on with your clients?' Yvonne asked Marissa.

'I've not started yet, I just met my new supervisor and saw my new room. He seems nice, it's in The Priory, in Cabra. I start Thursday.'

'Ahh, Kate is going there I think, or is it Linda? I can't remember. I've got my placement in St Marys, it's the women's refuge, about twenty mins drive from where I live. It's handy enough and they seem very organised there, but I'm still a little nervous about it. I've given a few sessions there already.'

Marissa was impressed. 'I guess this is all becoming quite real now,' she said.

'Very real, my first client was in buckets of tears, I didn't know what to do. I was quite uncomfortable with it.'

Marissa wondered what she would do if one of her clients was to cry uncontrollably. 'What did you do?'

'I just gave her tissues and waited for her to stop. I didn't know what else to do.'

'Maybe she needed to cry, I know that I have trouble sometimes with crying, so maybe it's really good she felt able to cry in front of you.'

'Oh, I didn't think of that. Yes, that makes sense.'

Kate and Ronan had joined them at their table, and Barbara had arrived and was making tea for herself. Marissa noticed how the conversation started with what one of their teachers called 'roads and weather' and then moved onto something a little deeper, and then went back to 'roads and weather' when someone new joined the table. *'Roads and weather' is a warm-up act,* she thought and laughed.

They went into the classroom and found seats.

The class went by quickly, their new teacher was Mr Crowley, and the subject was Transpersonal Therapy. Marissa felt a twinge in her body when he mentioned archetypes and became excited when he explained what they were. She couldn't believe how many coincidences were happening for her that day. She became very sleepy on the bus home.

Later that night, she was already in her pyjamas when she remembered the visit to The Angel Shop. Marissa found the paper bag she got from Mairead in her bag and put it on the coffee table. She opened it and golden angel confetti spilt over the sofa and floor. Marissa thought it was very funny. She normally would be angry with something like that happening, but she couldn't possibly be today. It had been a very good day for a "sick day". She carefully unwrapped the dish and candle and put the candle into the holder. It looked great right at the centre of the table, the blues and greens reminded her of the sea, it was nice to have something to mark the occasion of her finally letting go of the past. Next, Marissa pulled her crystal out from the bottom of the bag, unwrapped it and held it for a few moments. It felt nice to hold, she was going to put it down on the table too, but she didn't want to let go of it. So she kept a hold of it and finally pulled the deck of cards out of the bag.

The medicine woman on the cover of the box seemed to look at her, and suddenly there was an electric charge between Marissa and the cards. She used her fingernail to slit the plastic open at the edge of the box, it ripped easily enough. She pulled it off with an urgency that wasn't there before and put it into the paper bag with the rest of the wrapping. Clearing a space on the table, she took off the lid and placed it on the chair beside her. There was a little booklet sitting neatly on top of the deck which fit snugly in the box. Marissa took a glance at it, it was filled with information written in very small print. She put it down beside the lid and turned over the box so that the card deck fell into her hands. It felt substantial to hold. The edges of the cards were leafed in gold. Marissa held the pack in both of her hands the way that Mairead had suggested.

Hello cards, nice to meet you. Thank you for being my pack of cards. As she thought the words, she imagined she sent them into the pack. The cards were slightly stuck to each other, so she carefully separated out each card, turned it over to look at the image and words written there, placing each one face up onto the table as she moved through the whole pack. The artwork was beautiful. There were symbols and animals on each card as well as written words. Some of the cards were of people, and some were of animals. A particular card with a brown bear and the word 'Courage' stood out, almost as if the colours were brighter and stronger than those of the other cards. She picked it up and studied it in more detail. The bear was standing to his full height, he had very friendly eyes but would be quite terrifying if you were to meet him in real life. He was standing in a forest with strong trees all around him and yellow flowers by his feet. Marissa looked through the whole pack, gathered the cards together again and shuffled them for a few minutes. She cut the pack and drew a card. She turned it, and it was the bear. Her heart fluttered, but she wasn't surprised. 'I never asked a question,' she realised. She looked up Bear in her little booklet.

> *It is a time of change for you, a time of awakening.*
> *Sometimes you will feel like a fish out of water, other times,*
> *you will feel stronger and more capable. Bear wants you to*
> *know that it is standing beside you as you grow and will*
> *protect you and give you the courage you need if you feel you*
> *are lacking. Ask Bear for help in moments of uncertainty.*

She put the bear card on the top of the pack and put them back into the box. She was exhausted now, and it was all too much for her to process. 'Time for bed, Zebedee,' she said out loud, 'for tomorrow is another day.'

CHAPTER TWELVE

Marissa lit the candle in Room Three. It took three tries to get it to burn as the wick was so small and had curled in under itself, surrounded by wax. She had brought a new one with her, but when she got into the little room there was one already in the holder, so she thought she should use that one instead. She had her quartz in her pocket, she believed she was ready for her first client. Underlying everything was the familiar thrum of anxiety in her stomach.

She rearranged the chairs then sat in both of them, trying to decide which one would be better for her and which for her client. *I'll let the client choose which one they want.* She looked at the clock, it said ten minutes to 6pm, her first client was due at 6. She knew that after the first client, it would get easier.

These sessions were free, she didn't get paid, and the client didn't have to pay. At ten minutes past six she went downstairs to reception to see if someone was waiting there for her. There wasn't, and the receptionist had gone for the day.

She went into the little kitchen, resigned to feeling anxious a little longer, and made herself a cup of tea to try and calm her nerves. She had someone else scheduled for 7, so she didn't have much choice but to wait around. She looked at the notices on the noticeboard trying not to get upset at being stood up. She remembered that Kate had mentioned this happening to her quite often, and it seemed quite frustrating. Marissa wondered if she could claim it in her school hours as a session because she was there, even though the client was not.

She took her tea back upstairs to the room. When she opened the door the candle was flickering and she remembered Mr Blakemore asking her not to leave the room with the candle still lit. *Oh well.* She put her tea down on the table and went over to look at the painting on the wall, a ship out to sea. It was quite dark, the ship was in stormy waters yet appeared to be holding its own. There were no people on deck, nobody below. The clouds were swirling, tempestuous, and it did have an eerie feel to it as if the storm was going to get worse. *I suppose it could be suitable for a counselling room but wouldn't something more joyful be preferable?*

Marissa sat in the counselling chair, imagining how she would redecorate if the room was hers. She felt antsy after a while, so she got up and wandered down the corridor to stretch her legs. The door to room number two was open so she peeked inside, it was empty. She entered to take a look, it was exactly the same as room number three, except the painting was different. This one was of a lighthouse on jagged lonely rocks. It was painted in the same style as the ship out at sea. *Perhaps they're part of a set?* The chairs in this room were also similar. *They must have bought everything around the same time, from the same shop. What a pity. I'm sure Dad could have given them much nicer paintings.*

She went back to room number three and was surprised to discover a woman standing inside the door.

'Hi, I'm Mandy,' said the woman, smiling at Marissa.

'Hi, I didn't see you come in.' Marissa became quite flustered and pulled out her list of clients for the evening. Scanning down through the names on it she saw that Mandy was her second client, but they weren't supposed to start until 7pm.

'I know, I'm quite early,' said Mandy. 'Sorry.'

'Yes, you are half an hour early, it's only 6:30. But my first client didn't show up, so I suppose we *could* start our session now, if it suited you.'

'That would be great, thanks. I thought I'd have to wait around 'til 7...'

'Well, if the first client *had* shown up, then you would have had to wait...' said Marissa, feeling a little irritated at Mandy's lack of boundaries.

'Oh dear, well, the door was open and nobody was here, so I thought I could just come in.'

She sighed. 'It's okay this time, yes, as there *was* nobody here, they didn't turn up, but maybe next time they will.'

'That happens here a lot,' said Mandy, taking off her coat and hanging it on the hook behind the door. She chose a chair and sat down in it, putting her handbag on the floor beside her. She was about twenty, not much younger than Marissa. Her hair was dyed dark red, (some of the dye was on her scalp) and she had dark eye make-up. She had a tattoo of a rose on her left wrist, which took up most of her forearm, and she had three earrings in one ear and none in the other.

'Have you been here before?' asked Marissa, taking the cushion from her own chair onto her lap as she sat into it.

'Yeah, I came before, a few times last year, and then last Christmas when my father died. And then before that too, when I was 19 when my brother killed himself.'

Marissa steered herself into the session, so she could consciously let go of the irritation she was feeling and focus completely on Mandy. *Yes, that's better.* 'It sounds like you've had a very difficult time.'

'Yeah. My life is always difficult, there's always something going on either with me, or with Mammy, or with my sister. Or her baby. Thank God I don't have a baby of my own. I don't think I could handle that.'

Marissa waited for her to continue, but she didn't. Instead, she looked at her nails and started picking at one of them.

'What would you like to talk about tonight, Mandy?'

She looked up. 'Erm... Well, I've not told anyone about this, but it's been on my mind for a while. I thought it would be good to tell someone so I could, you know, move on from it like.'

'Okay, in your own time.'

'Hey, do you have a boyfriend?'

Marissa smiled. 'This session is about you, Mandy. It doesn't matter about my life. We can't share here like friends, I'm your therapist, and I'm here to listen to you talk about anything you want me to help you with.'

'Oh yeah, right, sorry, I forgot. I just thought it would be nice to get to know ya first.'

'Yes, I understand that it can be difficult to trust someone when you've only just met them, especially if you want to tell them something important. You don't know anything about me at all. So I totally understand.'

Mandy cocked her head to one side. 'So, tell me, *do* you have a boyfriend?'

Marissa laughed. 'No, I don't have a boyfriend, not at the moment anyway. We don't have to talk about the difficult thing tonight. We could talk about other things first, and then maybe next week or the week after you could tell me if you want to.'

'Yeah, that sounds good. How many times can I come to you?'

'Six times in this cycle, then if we need more, I can apply for you, and we can do another six times.'

Mandy relaxed in the chair. 'Great! That's good.' She looked around the room. 'What a bloody awful painting!'

Marissa's 8pm client was also a no-show. After waiting the extra half hour, she was particularly disheartened. She waited until 8:15pm, then packed up her things and left. Going home on the bus, she was quite frustrated, she had only gained one client hour for three hours of volunteered client time. How was she ever going to do 100 hours? *I'll give it a couple of weeks, and if it continues like this, then I'll have to do something about it.* She didn't want to let Mandy down, they had had a nice session, and Mandy seemed a lot more comfortable with her when she was leaving. *I'll have to stay for six weeks either way, I guess.*

Marissa was committed to her supervisor, she didn't really have much choice in the matter. From what the others said, they were having plenty of difficulties securing placements so she knew she was fortunate to have found that one. *Maybe my expectations were too high. It is what it is, and it will take as long as it takes.*

+++

Time seemed to slow down as the days shortened and the nights got longer. Marissa visited her parents on Eli's behalf and tried to smooth things over for them. She didn't feel like she got anywhere, but her father hugged her as she was leaving and thanked her for coming. He insinuated that they had to dance the dance, it was just a thing they felt they had to do, and the situation would probably change closer to the babies arrival.

There was a birthday party for Marcus, Eli and Carol didn't go. Marissa popped in with a present and gave hugs to everyone.

Sarah was still pushing Marissa to go on a double date. Her newest crush had a friend who had a friend, but Marissa was more focused on her college assignment. The sessions with Mandy and Theresa, a second client, were proving to be very interesting. She managed to reschedule Mandy for 6pm and Theresa for 7pm, so she felt two for two was a good deal, and Mandy was beginning to open up to her. There was still no word from Séamus.

It was coming into early December. Marissa had her first supervision session with Mr Blakemore.

'Thanks for coming in on a Monday, Marissa, normally we would have supervision before your sessions to save you having to come in two times in a week, it's just the way it worked out this time.'

Marissa nodded and followed him into his office.

'So how are you finding things here at the Priory?' asked Mr Blakemore, inviting her in. His office was much larger than the cosy rooms upstairs, its high ceilings reminded Marissa of a church yet it wasn't imposing due to the amount of clutter. Mr Blakemore's large oak desk was covered with papers and paperweights, stacks of books and pens, and there were piles of files and A4 notepads, the kind Marissa used when she was at school, beside it on the floor. A big dirty window looked out upon a green, a shaft of light shone through and Marissa could see dust particles hanging in the air. The room overall was quite dark and musty. It seemed as if there was a layer of dust over everything, including Mr Blakemore. Two battered leather armchairs stood in the corner of the room, Mr Blakemore invited her to sit on one of them, and he sat down on the other. He crossed his legs and his trousers rode up, exposing the pale flesh of his calf, and creme socks where his feet poured into his brown leather shoes. He waited for her to answer with a pleasant smile on his face.

'Good, thank you, I'm settling in now, I think. Although I still am quite disappointed that my hours are cut down to two instead of three.'

Mr Blakemore nodded. 'It is possible we will have another client for you. I have someone in mind, this person is quite difficult, though. He has been with more than six of our other therapists, he never stays with anyone for long. I wanted to wait until you were more confident before suggesting him to you.'

Marissa was immediately interested, yet she didn't think she could ask why this person was so problematic. She decided to hold back and wait to see how much she would be told.

Mr Blakemore continued, 'I also wanted to wait until we had at least one supervision session together so I could get a sense of you. As you may need me outside of hours, it's good for us to get to know each other, just in case things get serious.' He laughed. 'Don't worry, we take everything seriously at the Priory, but we do have a duty of care to our clients, and I have a duty of care to you. What are your thoughts?'

Marissa wasn't sure what she thought. She was willing, but was she able? 'I think I may need to have more information before I can answer that.'

'Good. Good. You're not put off then?'

'No, not at all!' She wanted to add 'unless he's a murderer', but she decided quickly against it and held her tongue.

'Well, he's not a murderer,' said Mr Blakemore, surprisingly, 'he's just a disturbed young man. It can be difficult to handle a case like this. Unfortunately, the system isn't designed for his kind. We would obviously prefer that he went to an established professional, but the choice for him at the moment is a therapist in training or nobody at all. And as you probably know, an ear to listen is better than no ear.'

'Sure,' said Marissa, wondering if he could read her mind.

'So, if you feel you could manage it?'

'Well, is it possible to know the cause of his disturbance?'

'Bipolar disorder, with schizophrenia.'

Marissa didn't know anything about bipolar disorder, and she shuddered at the word schizophrenia. 'May I ask why he has quit so many of your therapists?'

'Each time it's something different. Usually after three or four sessions, he decides they cannot help him. He did stay with someone for longer, but then there was an argument between them, and the therapist was the one who quit. Have a think about it, it will certainly help your client hours. Don't get me wrong, he's a lovely man, just troubled, he needs help. I have an obligation to inform you beforehand. Let me know in the next couple of days?'

'Actually, Mr Blakemore, I think I could let you know now. I'll give it a try. Like you said, if he just wants an ear to listen, I can do that. I don't need to cure him, just be there to reflect back to him what is going on in his mind.'

'Perhaps you could look up schizophrenia in the meantime, do a little research? Sometimes reflecting back is not helpful. But it will, all in all, be a good learning experience for you.' He made a note on a scrap of paper he took from out of his pocket. 'That's great Marissa, I'll let our secretary know, and you can start seeing him as soon as we can get him in. Now. Tell me, how are you getting on with Mandy?'

Marissa smiled. 'Mandy's great. She shows up for the sessions, is enthusiastic, and very chatty. She told me she has something she wants to tell me, but she's managing to tell me everything else that's going on in her life but the core issue. I'm not sure if I should push her. I think I'd prefer to leave it up to her. There could be a trust issue with relationships, she wants to feel like she knows me better before telling me. We are at four sessions out of six now, I think we may need another six, would that be okay?'

'In an ideal world, yes, it would be, but I have a list of people waiting. I don't want you to push her, no indeed don't push, but do gently remind her in your next session that you only have two sessions left, including that one, of course, and if she wants to tell you something that she needs to do it now. Otherwise, you might not have a chance. But leave it up to her.'

Marissa was surprised and disappointed at this.

'I can see by your face you do care, it's nobody's fault. It's lovely to have a chat with your client and make friends, however, there are other people who are in despair who could be making better use of your time. Remember the difference between therapy and a chat with a friend.'

Marissa felt like she was being told off and didn't like it. 'Of course. I just assumed we could get another six sessions if we needed them?'

'Oh yes, in severe cases, yes, but I do not hear anything severe, or is there something I'm missing?'

'No. It's more than roads and weather so far. There is no big trauma or event that I'm aware of, it's just that it's been insinuated.'

'Ahh. Well, sometimes people come to counselling because they are lonely. There may not actually be anything there at all. Or there may be something quite extraordinary and traumatic that they indeed cannot talk about.' He paused. 'On reflection, Marissa, I think you have chosen the right way to go with Mandy. It's always best to give the benefit of the doubt. But please keep what I have said in mind. Let me know after the next session if you believe there is a genuine trauma in the background, and I could organise another six sessions for you both.'

Marissa was relieved. 'Thank you, I will.'

It wasn't that she didn't like to be told off, but she felt like she had an instinct for this work. Sometimes she couldn't put it into words, she was more often right than wrong. The more time she had spent with Mandy, the more she felt Mandy *was* skirting around something big. It was like a game of cat and mouse, Marissa could be the cat for as long as was needed until the mouse was tired and gave in. She hadn't factored in the time limitation, that was the problem here. So the mouse needed a smaller field to run in, so it would get caught more easily. She could do that.

'I understand better how the system works now, Mr Blakemore. Thank you for explaining. This will help me in how I work in the future.'

'Ahh, Marissa, I wasn't upset with you, it's all learning, and so far, you seem to be doing grand. I look forward to our next session. Now, before we close, make sure you have my phone number in case you have to contact me outside of hours. I'll put Martin on the call sheet for you.'

Marissa finally got word from Séamus that evening in the form of a text message inviting her to come to his centre for a few hours the following Saturday to meet with some other people also looking to begin training with him. There was no mention of money or commitment but she decided to go along and find out more regardless.

As she'd been getting used to working with her oracle cards, she thought she'd ask them about this, just to see what they would say.

She waited until after she had eaten, lit the candle and sat for a few minutes at her table holding the pack of cards in her hand. They felt more familiar now, like friends. She wasn't referring to them every day, but she had started to do so every few days as it helped her feel like she was going in the right direction. She thought she'd try a three-card spread: past, present and future, asking if doing the training with Séamus was the right thing. She shuffled and cut the cards and laid down the first three.

Past card: Bear. Well, that was no surprise, she didn't know why she needed courage, but she did feel that the bear was a nice support, and clarification that the cards were listening to her. *Cards listening to me, how silly is that!*

Present card: Bison – Will Power. *Hmm, never saw that one before.* She looked it up in the card booklet.

> *Bison radiates depths of inner power, rising up in a will to survive. Bison holds the power to overcome adversity, but it will do it in its own way, it will not bend to rules and will never become domesticated. Call on your inner bison when you feel that you need to push through a block in your path.*

Not really sure what that means. Will I be feeling controlled, pushed into something that I don't like? Needing to assert myself to get out of it? I wonder.

She turned the card for the future: Swan – Lovers. Her heart jumped. *Lovers?* Totally not what she was expecting. She picked up the booklet and leafed through the pages to find the entry:

> *Swans mate for life, they are loyal and true to each other. When you get the Lovers card, it could be a sign that a new love is coming into your life or you are healing some aspect of the relationship you have with yourself.*

She looked at all three cards for a moment, really not sure if they had helped her at all or if they made things even more confusing. She studied the swan card, noticing the detail in the background with children in the distance, holding hands. The swans in the foreground had their necks entangled in the shape of a love heart, and the sun was shining.

It feels like a nice card, so maybe it's not a bad thing. Healing the relationship I have with myself, yes, that could be it. She looked again at the Bison. It was standing in a cold place, very white and snowy, almost harsh. She realised that this was the present moment card, and she did actually feel stuck, or frozen. Perhaps it meant she had to use her willpower to make a decision, but it had to be her decision and not somebody else's. *I thought oracle cards would be more straightforward than this. Okay. I'll go and meet with Séamus and see what he has in mind, I don't have to make any decisions right now.*

She put the cards away and then changed her mind and took them out again. *What if I'm wrong? What if I'm missing something? Oh, why am I fretting about this?* She held the pack in her hands again. *Okay, what do I need to know now?* She pulled out one card, a new one that she hadn't seen before. Owl – Wisdom.

The owl was sitting in the branches of a very large, very old tree. It felt good to see the tree, even if it wasn't the main subject of the card. Marissa felt that wisdom went well with the tree. 'Thank you,' she said out loud, not needing to read the booklet entry. She took a photograph of the card with her phone and then put the card back into the pack. She felt she wanted to carry that card around with her for a bit, so the photograph in her phone would do well instead. She blew out the candle but felt strange doing that, it didn't feel right to blow it out. *I'm still learning, there is so much to learn...*

She sighed and stretched. Opening the text from Séamus, she saw it wasn't too late to send a text, so she wrote back:

> Hi Séamus yes that sounds great, I'll see you there, just let me know what time.

She wasn't sure how to sign it. So she didn't, and just pressed send. *What if the lovers card meant...?* Well, that didn't bear thinking about. She would keep her bear close to her for protection.

CHAPTER THIRTEEN

'So then I said, "Yeah, go on, I'll have another pint!"'

Marissa was beginning to get irritated, it was twenty minutes into their fifth session, and Mandy was still avoiding the issue. Was there an issue after all?

'Mandy, I have to stop you for a moment. I was talking with my supervisor, he told me that we can't extend to another six sessions unless there is an issue that you need to talk about. I think we've had plenty of time to get to know each other now, so I have to ask you, is there something that you *want* to talk about with me?'

Mandy went pale. She stayed silent for a while, then she twisted her hair in her fingers, looking up at Marissa. Her face had changed.

'Yeah. Yeah, there is.'

'Okay. Can you give me a hint of what it might be?'

Mandy looked down at her feet. 'I'm actually embarrassed about this. It's difficult to talk about. I never talk about this stuff with anyone.'

'That's okay. There are many things that people don't talk about that are actually normal things.'

'This isn't a normal thing. I just find it hard to say the words. Because, you know, like, once you say the words, it makes it real. I don't want this to be real, but it *is* real – you know what I mean, like?'

'It can be hard to admit to something or to hear yourself say something for the first time, yes, totally,' Marissa agreed. 'But whatever happened, if it really happened, then it did happen and pretending it didn't can be worse for you. It's better to get it out, so tell me, and we can figure it out together.'

'Okay.' Mandy went from totally pale to completely red-faced. She took a breath and blurted out, 'I was raped. There. I said it.' She sank back into her chair and dropped her eyes to the ground to avoid seeing Marissa's reaction.

Marissa felt her whole body jolt at the word 'raped', but she held her ground, stayed steady. She wasn't supposed to react or sympathise. Knowing Mandy, it was difficult not to be sympathetic, but she was a therapist here, not a friend. She was about to ask 'When did it happen?', but then she remembered one of the tutors at college saying, 'You're not a detective, you don't need to know the where, why, what and how.' *So what do I ask next?*

Mandy continued speaking in a low voice, keeping her eyes down. 'It was last summer, in my house. There was nobody else there. I've told nobody. You're the first one.'

Marissa had her way in. 'How does it feel to tell someone?'

'My head is spinning.'

'Would you like some water?'

'Yeah. Yes, please.'

Marissa poured a fresh glass of water from a jug into a small tumbler and handed it to Mandy, who drank it all in one gulp.

Marissa poured out some more. 'We can sit for a while until your head stops spinning if you want.'

'Yeah, that would be great, thanks.'

The room had changed, the energy between them had become very heavy, almost sticky. It wasn't tension, it was something else. Marissa wasn't sure what had happened, but she certainly felt something there that wasn't there before. They only had ten minutes left. Marissa decided that instead of asking Mandy to go deeper into what happened, she would make sure Mandy was okay to leave, perhaps next week they could talk more about it.

'Thank you for telling me. I will talk to my supervisor about getting further sessions with you. Would that be okay?'

Mandy nodded her head.

'We only have 10 minutes left now. I want to make sure you're okay when you leave me so you don't feel like you have opened a can of worms that are wriggling around and eating into you for a week, until we can talk again.' *Interesting image, yes, I suppose it fits well enough.*

Mandy looked up and caught Marissa's eye for a moment, then looked away again. But she laughed, and at the sound of it,

Marissa relaxed a little. 'Well, I guess I have opened a can of worms. It's a real can of worms, alright – lots of horrible squiggly worms.' She shuddered.

Marissa had an idea. 'Can you try something with me?'

'Yeah, why not.'

'Can you see the can and the worms in your head? Like a picture in your mind?'

'Yeah. It's a mess.'

'Okay. I want you to imagine that I'm there with you, and we are pushing them all back into the can and closing it up.'

Mandy closed her eyes. She looked as though she was concentrating really hard. 'It's not working – it keeps opening up again when we close it.'

Marissa thought for a moment. 'How about I take out a safe, like the ones in the movies when they're going to rob a bank. This safe has a big door and an iron handle. Can you see that?'

Mandy nodded.

'Okay. You and I are picking up the can of worms.'

'Ugh, I don't want to touch it.'

'Right, I'm here, we have all the worms in the can, and I'm picking it up for you, okay? And I'm putting it in the safe and locking the door. They are all inside the safe now. How does that feel?'

Mandy was quiet for a moment. 'Yeah, it feels better.'

'It will be safe in there for the week, and when you come back next time we can open it up again, but only if you want to. Is that good?'

'Yeah.' Mandy was beginning to look more relaxed. Her face was returning to its normal colour.

'Let's try one more thing before you go – a breathing exercise. Can you do that with me?'

'Okay.'

'Let's breathe in together, and out together, in together, out together, in, out.'

With each breath, Mandy seemed to be stronger. 'Yeah, that's good.'

'So here's the thing,' Marissa said, standing up, 'that can is safe in the safe,' Mandy giggled, 'and it will stay there. If you imagine those worms are escaping, they're still inside a can, behind the iron door, and we will deal with them together later. If you think they're going to escape from the safe, you can squash them back inside again. Or maybe it will only be one or two worms that escape, and that's a lot better than a whole can of them. Is that good?'

Mandy stood up to leave. There were tears in her eyes. She hugged Marissa, then jumped back. 'Is it okay to hug you? I do feel better knowing that you know, and that you don't hate me.'

'Of course I don't hate you, and yes, a hug is fine if you want one. But please ask me first next time.' Marissa smiled.

'Can I have another one?'

Mandy hugged Marissa again. Her face was much brighter, but the room still felt, well, heavy was the best way to put it. Mandy put on her coat and said goodbye, and then she left.

Martin was coming in ten minutes and Marissa felt nervous. She went out to the little bathroom and splashed some cold water on her face. After that, she felt a bit better. Mandy's issue wasn't what she had expected, she wasn't really prepared for it. *I've never handled something quite that serious before. I hope I did okay. Mandy definitely seemed happier when she left... I guess I'll find out next week.*

When she came back into the room it was as if she walked into treacle. The room was stifling, yet it wasn't hot. It was the strangest thing, it seemed as if Mandy's emotions were still there, that Mandy had left them behind. Marissa's anxiety went up another notch.

Just then, there was a knock on the open door. Marissa jumped.

'Hello, I'm Martin. You must be Marissa?'

She turned to look at the man who stood outside the door. He was wrapped in a heavy winter coat even though it wasn't that cold just yet. He was about thirty, of average height, with short hair and a nice face. Marissa seemed relieved. *What was I expecting? A monster? He seems fine to me.*

'Hi! Yes, I'm Marissa. Come in. You can hang up your coat here. Which chair would you like to sit on?'

'This one, please.' Martin had on a grey v-neck jumper with a white tee-shirt under it, jeans and dirty white runners. He had picked the chair Marissa had just been sitting in. She sat in the opposite chair where Mandy had just been. She liked the change in perspective, and the room didn't feel as heavy anymore, although it still felt unpleasant.

They sat there for a moment. Marissa collected herself, she was still feeling uncomfortable and not really focused, as if everything was happening too quickly. She then remembered to call on her bear. *Bear, can you come and support me?* In her mind's eye, she saw the bear from the oracle card step into the room and move to stand behind her. She felt a strong, calming energy, and something inside her eased. She sat up in her chair, having a sense that the session would be okay.

'Hello properly, Martin. It's lovely to meet you.'

'You've probably heard about me, hey?' Martin asked, raising an eyebrow.

He has lovely blue eyes. 'Well, I've heard you like to swap around your therapists quite a bit.'

Martin grimaced. 'I've not found someone that can help me. I mean, *actually* help me. They're all very nice, but nice isn't really helpful, is it?'

'No, and you can get nice from a friend. You want a therapist who will be able to support you and give you some tools that you can use, so you can eventually help yourself. I hope I will be able to do that.'

'I hope so too, hey.'

'Let's start together by being completely honest with each other.' Marissa heard herself say the words, but she didn't know where they'd come from. She certainly hadn't prepared this, however, she liked what she was hearing, so she let herself continue to see where she was going. 'If you think that I'm just being nice or not being helpful to you, will you let me know straightaway?'

'Okay,' said Martin, sitting up a little in the chair and looking curious. 'But I don't know if you *can* help me – nobody really has been able to.'

'Try me.'

'Okay.' He shifted in his seat. 'Well, I'm bipolar, I feel very sad, or I feel okay, I never get hyper. I have episodes, but I've not had one for a while. The doctors say I'm schizophrenic too, but I don't know if that's really true. The medicine I'm on, it's strong, I have to take it all the time, so they say anyway, and, well, I don't do well on it. Or off it.'

'I see things, like I go into a room and I see things that other people don't see. Even on the medicine, that hasn't stopped. Sometimes the things that I see scare me, a lot. And then they won't go away, they follow me home, and I see them in my bedroom late at night, in the dark, like monsters from a horror film. I think some of the stuff I see is real. I've seen some horrible things.'

Marissa listened with an open mind, conscious of keeping her breathing on an even keel. 'You seem very aware of what your problem is,' she said. 'That's good – that means that we have something to work with.'

'Oh! I like that. Nobody has said that to me before. Thank you.'

'Thank you for telling me, and being honest with me, I do think that is the best way for us to work together. We have to get to know each other, so it may take a few sessions for you to feel comfortable enough to tell me things. And I might not be able to help you right away, but if you tell me what you want help with, I can do some research in between sessions and come back to you with some ideas, so you might need to be patient with me. Will that be okay with you?'

'Very much okay with me,' said Martin, smiling for the first time.

'Good,' said Marissa. 'So, is there anything I can help you with tonight? Something small to start with, perhaps?' She smiled, and he laughed.

'Yes, okay, something small to start with.'

Marissa taught Martin the butterfly technique and he seemed happy when he was leaving. Marissa felt like she passed some sort of test. *We shall see.* Theresa had once again been a no-show. She had seen her twice out of five sessions, which was very disappointing. After waiting for 15 minutes Marissa closed up the room, finished for the night. Two very interesting sessions out of three, she was getting the hang of this, but she was still disheartened by the missing client hours.

As she walked in the fresh night air, though, she still felt the heaviness from the emotions of the room around her. The minute she got home, she took off all of her clothes and jumped into a hot shower. She didn't usually wash her hair at night, but tonight she felt she needed to. She lit a fire and sat on the sofa in her pyjamas, her wet hair wrapped in a towel, Tobermory curled up beside her. She looked up Facebook to see what her friends were doing, and a picture came up on her feed of a bundle of leaves that had smoke coming from them. The text read: *Sage cleans heavy energy.*

Oh, I wish I'd known that earlier. There's another serendipity. I must get some sage. That could really help me in the room in Cabra.

+++

It was Saturday afternoon on a cold crisp December day in Glasnevin, and Marissa was waiting for Séamus to begin. He looked a little tired today, he was wearing black jeans and a white shirt with a shiny silver waistcoat. His long hair was tied back in a ponytail, a few strands were loose around his face. There were four people there already, all sitting on chairs in a circle with Marissa. Once the last person arrived, Séamus closed the door, sat down at the top of the circle and smiled. This time there was no altar and no drum.

Marissa looked around at the others, sizing them up, wondering if any of them were medicine men or women in the making too, whatever that meant. She had felt a little nervous going there alone and not knowing anyone, but at least this time, she knew where the place was and how to get there. When she took her seat she called her bear to come and be with her. She felt better almost immediately.

Séamus began. 'Well, lads, it's great to have yis all here. Welcome, welcome. This is a discussion group, as you know, I'm planning to run an apprenticeship programme, and I think yis would all be a good fit for it, for me and for each other. Some of ye know each other, some of ye are strangers, but you know what they say, strangers are friends you haven't met yet.' He got up and walked around the outside of the circle, and continued speaking.

'So this is what I have in mind. Today is a "getting to know you" afternoon, so we can get that out of the way. I'll also be telling you how the training will look, what I have in mind. If yis want in, then yis have a week to think about it, and our first training weekend will be on the Solstice, a powerful time to do some shamanic work.'

He took a dark brown walking stick with a feather attached to the top of it out of the umbrella stand, held it in his hands as if weighing it, and took his seat again.

'So let's get to know each other. This is a talking stick.' He presented the stick to the group. On a closer look, Marissa noticed that it was carved, a snake was winding around it, and what seemed to be a tree fashioned into it. It was quite beautiful.

'When you hold the stick it's your turn to talk, everyone listens. Then when you're finished, put the stick down, and someone else has a turn. Usually I leave it in the middle, but I can tell yis are all shy today,' the room giggled nervously, 'so we'll pass the stick around the circle.'

Marissa was sitting in the middle so she knew that whichever direction they went, she'd not be first or last, which was good.

'I'll start. I'm Séamus.' Another giggle. 'I've been walking the shamanic pathway for over thirty years. I was like you once, in a dead-end job running in the rat race, not really knowing what I was doing, or why. I was in IT, computers, which were better than people, but still not the reason for my existence.' He raised an eyebrow and leaned in for effect, then pulled back and went on.

'I drank a few beers, tried a little Aya, had an awakening, met some new friends, went to Peru, it sounds like the usual story, but there is never anything usual about an awakening. Trust me. I can see from some of yis that yis know what I'm talking about. I won't give the rest of yis any spoilers.' He smiled, and they laughed. 'This will be the fourth year I've had an apprentice programme. I have twenty-four graduates out there in the world doing healings, helping other people, and I'm finally feeling I've found my role, teaching and passing on the knowledge.'

'All of ye have done one or more workshops with me already, so ye know something about shamanism, but I want you to start clean, clear and have what I call a beginner's mind. You know nothing, you are but an empty casket to be filled with the fruits of your labour. For I am only showing the way, you are the ones who are on the journey.

Separately, but together. Now, time to hear from you all. Tell me your name, what brings you here, and what you'd like to get out of training with me.'

Marissa noticed that Séamus's accent once again seemed to fade as he spoke more beautifully, more eloquently. It was almost as if the man stepped out of the way and something else stepped in. *Teacher? Is it like Bear stepping in?* She remembered back to the opening prayer during the Introductory day, how it caught at something in her chest, invoking deep emotions. *Whatever it is, I like it.*

Séamus handed the stick to the woman who was sitting next to him. 'In your own time,' he said with a smile.

She smiled back, first to him and then to the circle. 'Hello, I'm Jennifer. My friends call me Jenny. I'm a Reiki Master. I love energy work, I'm excited to learn more to add to what I have to offer my clients.'

A Reiki Master? Marissa looked at Jenny a little more closely. She had long tangled curly brown hair and glasses and wore a traditionally knitted Aran tunic with faded blue jeans. Jenny had taken her shoes off and was sitting cross-legged in her chair. The crystal pendant around her neck had caught Marissa's eye earlier. *Is that Quartz?* She also had a silver ring with a large pink stone in it. Other than the unusual jewellery, she looked like an ordinary person you'd see on the street, yet a Reiki Master sounded so unusual and strange. Marissa made a mental note to ask her more about it.

Jennifer shrugged her shoulders. 'I hope that's enough?'

Séamus nodded. Jenny passed the stick to the man beside her. He had short, almost-white blond hair and striking blue eyes. He wore tight blue jeans with rips over the knee and a bulky, multi-coloured wool jumper with ribbons through it and a white cuff at the end of each sleeve. It looked very unusual, Marissa hadn't seen anything like it before, except maybe in a fashion show. He was slim in stature, and when he spoke, he had a soft lilting accent and a gentle manner.

'Hi, I'm Terence. My friends call me Terry.' He looked at Jenny and nodded, Jenny smiled and nodded back. He continued, 'I'm from Cork. You'd never have guessed, would you?' He waited, and there was a collective giggle. He relaxed a little bit. 'I'm a model, and I'm also gay, another thing you'd never have guessed.' He held out his arms and turned them, the light from the window making the ribbons quite shiny. He smiled.

'It's one of the perks, not that there's many of those... Anyway. My family don't understand me at all, not one bit, so I moved to Dublin so I could get away from them. I like dressing up, and make-up, all of those things.' He shifted in his chair, enjoying the attention. 'I'm here because I think shamanism could really help me. I'm very drawn to Native American culture. I was told once that I have a Native American as a spirit guide, so I hope I can get to know them a little better. God knows I could do with some extra support! Especially when I go home to see the family. It's nice to meet you all. I'll definitely be signing up, Séamus. You can put my name down for the Solstice training. I can't wait!'

It felt like the ice had broken in the group. Terry seemed to have a way about him that made everyone feel more relaxed, and he seemed very comfortable in himself. He passed the stick to the next person in line.

'Hello, I'm Stephanie. I work in a job that I hate, an office job like Séamus said. It's not my life. I liked the idea of magic and miracles. I think there's more to life than meets the eye, so I went to Séamus's introductory workshop – I think I saw you there?' She looked at Marissa quizzically, and she recognised Stephanie as the woman who had met her childhood pet fish and nodded back to her with a smile. Stephanie's dark, thick plaited hair was tied back into a pony tail sweeping it off her face. Today she wore a long dark green skirt with a pattern on it and a teal tunic with yellow fringes.

'I love mermaids,' she went on, 'and angels. Like Séamus said, I just want to feel like my life isn't all about work.' She shuddered. 'So, yes, I'll be coming too on the Solstice, for sure. What a magical time it's going to be! And it's very nice to meet you all too.' She smiled at them all, then handed the stick to Marissa.

She cleared her throat and looked around the room, surprised to find she wasn't as anxious as she'd thought she'd be. 'Hi, I'm Marissa. I'm training to be a psychotherapist. I'm interested in learning more about healing. I think that it's great to talk about what is wrong, but

I also want to learn how to heal it, and I don't think talking about it heals it.' She took a breath, then decided to tell them what was on her mind. It seemed appropriate.

'I don't know much about shamanism, but it seems to be drawing me in, I went to Peru about a month ago and met a medicine woman there, I don't really understand what happened but I've felt different ever since. It just feels like the right time for me to learn more.' Marissa looked at the group again, but they were all still smiling. It felt like they all really heard what she said and accepted it, and her, as she was. It was a nice feeling, so she continued, 'I've also never felt like I belonged anywhere, so it would be nice to find a group of people where I can feel safe to be myself. Thanks.'

Marissa saw people nodding, and she smiled, then handed the stick to the woman beside her. She was small and slender with a short pixie cut. Even though it was cold in the room she was wearing a vest top and blue jeans, and she had thrown her woollen cardigan over the back of her chair. Marissa noticed that she had tight, muscular arms, even though she was quite slim, almost bony. Her face had a troubled look.

'Hi. Excuse me, I'm a little nervous. I'm Elizabeth, you can call me Liz, everybody does.' More giggles. 'I'm a massage therapist. I like yoga, I'm training to be a yoga teacher. I think it would be interesting to do some shamanic work, too. I'm not good with groups, and I want to talk more in front of them, like this. I've had a few traumas in my past, and I know that shamanism has helped me. I want to go deeper and heal some more, to feel happier and have more to offer my students. It's lovely to meet you all.'

She smiled, and her eyes lit up as she handed the talking stick to the man beside her, the last person in the group. He was sallow-skinned, had short jet black hair with a long fringe and brown eyes. He wore a sky blue long sleeve tee-shirt with a picture of a rock band on it and brown cords. He had been very quiet up to now. He spoke with a soft voice and a strong accent, which sounded like a mixture of something foreign and Dublinese.

'I'm Zaad. You spell it zee ay ay dee, but you say it like zee-ad. I'm Irish. It's great to be here in this group, and it's very nice to meet you all. Someone said earlier they never felt like they belonged anywhere, well, I feel like that too. I'm Muslim, so it was hard to grow up in Ireland, very difficult at times. I did what the family told me to do, and now I am grown and I want something for myself. I did not tell my family I was coming today, they are very traditional. They'd be afraid for me, afraid of this. I am a little afraid too!' The group nodded in support.

'We are originally from Lebanon, my father brought us to Ireland when I was two, and one of my sisters was four. My little sister was born here. People treat me like I'm not Irish, not part of the culture. But I am. Ireland is all I know. I want something that feels like it's mine, not what my family tell me to do or think or my community. I'm not very good at talking. Maybe shamanism will help me with that, too.'

He looked at Liz, nodded to her, smiled, then handed the talking stick back to Séamus.

Séamus looked around the group approvingly, thoughtfully. He closed his eyes for a moment and then opened them again. 'We're missing some people, I think two more. I'm sure they will show up before the Solstice. Sure nothing is guaranteed just yet, not at this stage anyway. Let's take a short break, and then when we come back, I'll tell you what I expect from you as individuals and as a group. There's coffee and tea and some biccies in the kitchen next door.'

The group broke up. Stretching and chattering they made their way into the kitchenette. The boiler was on a rolling boil so the hot water was ready, and they helped themselves to whatever they could find. Marissa wanted to speak with Jenny, the Reiki Master, but she was deep in conversation with Zaad. He was laughing, his fringe got into his eyes, and he kept pushing it away. His skin was sallow, like Marissa's, he reminded her of one of Eli's friends, but she couldn't remember his name.

'So what's it like to study psychotherapy?' It was Terry, dipping his digestive into his tea and just managing to get it into his mouth before it fell apart.

Marissa turned to face him. 'It's great actually, I really like it. First time I studied something that I enjoy.'

'I've a friend who is thinking about doing it too, it sounds like a lot of work. Is it true? One year of introduction, then three years of diploma, then another year for a degree?'

'Yeah, though you can do the introduction as a one or two-week intensive now. It's faster. You also have to put in 100 client hours, 100 hours of personal therapy and thirty hours of supervision. And that's even before you become accredited!'

'Jeez, that *is* a lot of work.' He took another dunk and a bite, and then asked with his mouth full, 'What's accredited mean?'

'It means you're approved by a regulating body. They keep an eye on you to make sure you don't misbehave.'

'I'll bet you don't misbehave much, Marissa! You seem pretty straight-laced to me. Do you have any gay friends?'

'Actually, no. I don't really have many friends at all.'

'Oh, how sad for you! Well, maybe you'll make some more here! Look, I think it's time to go back.'

Marissa went back into the room, not knowing how she felt about Terry being sad for her. She decided to hold off and not decide anything just yet.

+++

Back at home Marissa went over the handouts they got from Séamus. The training was to be split over several weekend sessions, most of it would be residential in Galway, but there would be other venues to be decided in due course. There would be additional training if Séamus thought it was needed. The entire course would take about a year and a half to two years, depending on how they went as a group. But it was starting at the end of the year, on the Winter Solstice, which was only a few weeks away.

They would learn healing techniques they could use with clients, they'd be working on each other to start with, and then they would have to find a few 'guinea pigs', plus write a report on how they were getting on. It seemed very informal compared to her psychotherapy training. She could pay in instalments too. If she wanted to do it, she needed to buy a drum and a rattle for herself before the Solstice event, which was to be in Galway. Séamus gave them a list of places where they could buy some of the items they needed. Marissa noticed that the Angel Shop wasn't listed and wondered if Mairead could help her. She was coming closer to deciding to commit to the workshops, it seemed like the natural next step. *And the group were all so nice, and I have some money still leftover...*

She decided to sleep on it, it had been a long and tiring day. Marissa remembered a saying about making decisions in haste, that they may not be a good thing. Then she remembered Terry feeling sad for her. 'Feck him!' she said out loud.

Then she remembered Zaad laughing, looking bright and happy. *What would my parents say if I brought home a Muslim? Well, Eli and Carol would definitely be off the hook that's for sure!*

CHAPTER FOURTEEN

Marissa brought a bunch of sage to Cabra that she found in a health food shop she usually passed by on the way home from work. She arrived ten minutes before the session with Mandy and thought she'd try the sage before they started. Marissa lit the candle first, then held the thickly tied bunch of leaves over the flame. It took a moment to light up, then it started to burn. Marissa pulled the sage quickly out of the candle and blew out the flame, and the leaves began to smoke. *There, that's it.* She had never done this before, she worried a little whether it was too smoky for the fire alarm, but she couldn't see a smoke detector when she looked around the room. Marissa waved the smoking sage around, not really noticing any difference to how she, or the room, was feeling. The room had a stale smell to it. It felt stale, too, as if Marissa was the only person using it, which couldn't be the case. She had seen other volunteers coming and going but hadn't met any of them bar a nod and a hello in the kitchen. Everyone at Cabra seemed to keep themselves to themselves.

Marissa walked around the room with the sage. She made sure the smoke licked up the walls and into each of the four corners like it did in the video she watched on YouTube, which taught how to do it. After a minute or two, the room was becoming a little too smoky for comfort. She wanted to put the sage out but couldn't see anything she could use to do it. She walked to the bathroom across the hall, ran the tap, and put the smoky sage under it. It stopped burning immediately, but the water made the bunch of dried leaves very wet. Now they were dripping into the sink, she shook the bundle off and looked in the mirror at herself. Marissa usually just glanced at her hair to make sure it was tidy or to make sure she didn't have anything in her teeth, but this time she actually looked at her reflection. She saw a woman who was working hard, doing her best, trying to do better, who was also a little tired. She liked that. It felt right. She smiled at herself and left.

When she got back to Room Three Mandy was already waiting for her, sitting in her preferred chair.

'Hiya!' she said. 'Smells nice in here! Have you been smoking something?'

'Ha, ha, no, it's sage. I'm trying something out. Hi, how are you, Mandy? How was your week?'

'Really good, actually.'

Marissa sat down. 'Tell me.'

'Everything seemed to go really well. I felt great when I left here. Oh, wait till I tell you – those worms, remember them? They stayed in the safe. All week! That was brilliant. You're a genius!'

Marissa laughed. 'I don't know about being a genius, but I'm very glad you had a good week, and the worms stayed locked up. What do you want to do with them tonight?'

'Oh!' Mandy looked suddenly sunk, deflated. 'I don't know. I didn't think that far ahead. It was really about me just getting on with things.'

Marissa stayed silent for a moment or two. She didn't know how to approach the suggestion of talking about the rape, and Mandy seemed to be doing everything to avoid the issue. Maybe all she needed was for someone else to know. It had already been several months since it happened, and Mandy did seem to be navigating everything else in her life... What should she do? *When in doubt, go back to the feelings.*

'Okay then, what is it like for you to be walking around with a safe full of worms in the background?'

'It was grand. It's only been a week, though. I don't know. Maybe in another week, it won't be so grand.'

'Does it feel heavy? Like a real safe?' The word 'heavy' reminded Marissa of how heavy the room had felt the week before. *Is emotion heavy?*

'No, it doesn't feel heavy at all. I feel much lighter than I did before we – well, 'built' isn't really the word, is it? Imagined it? Created it. Yes. We created it together. I've definitely felt much happier since last week. Even my ma told me she loved hearing me laugh. She said she hadn't heard me laughing like that in a long time. So it was great, a great thing you did for me. Thank you.'

Okay, they must be related, the heaviness and the safe, and the emotions, but possibly not in the way that I had anticipated. I suppose I should stick to how she is feeling now, because now is where we are.

'So what do you want to talk about this week then?' asked Marissa.

'Well, there's this guy that I fancy...'

Mandy practically skipped out the door when her session was over. They didn't talk about the rape, and the safe full of worms didn't come up in conversation again, either. While Mandy described Dessie from up the road in great detail, what he liked and how he dressed, Marissa wondered why she felt the need to pull Mandy back into a dark place when she seemed so good. But was she really good? How long would this last? And even if it wasn't going to last, what right does a psychotherapist have to decide what is more important to talk about? Mandy obviously was working through things in her own way, and right now, Dessie was on her mind, not the rape. So if Marissa *had* dragged her back there, who is she doing it for? For Mandy? Or for herself? Certainly, the session on Dessie was, okay, a little boring and probably not really necessary. Certainly not as challenging as a rape. But Marissa knew that the sessions were for her client and not for her. *I guess I'll be dealing with all sorts of issues over time... I don't think I want to force anyone to talk about things if it's not the right time for them. I need to learn patience.*

Marissa looked at her watch, Martin was due shortly. She wanted to be completely focused this time for him, not like last week, so she decided to mull over the Mandy thing later. She took a breath and cleared her mind as best as she could. She started a mindfulness technique: *There's the chair (breath), there's the painting (breath), there's the wall (breath).*

As soon as her mind had settled, the buzzer by the door rang. 'It's Martin,' said the far-away voice. She buzzed him in. A few moments later, there was a tentative knock on the door. Marissa stood up and opened it, and there he was, wrapped in his heavy coat again.

'Martin. Lovely to see you. Come in. Which chair would you like?'

Martin seemed more sedate today. He was also very pale. He moved to the chair he had sat in the previous week and sat down, keeping his coat on. Marissa sat down in the opposite chair and gave him a minute to begin the session, but he didn't say anything.

Marissa sat with him in silence. She didn't mind, it wasn't uncomfortable, and after a few minutes, the colour began to come back into his cheeks. It was as if he had gone far away someplace inside himself and was returning, slowly. He turned and looked at Marissa. She saw wolf-like fangs growing out from his mouth, a dark fire in his eyes, he rose as if about to jump out of his chair to attack her. But when she blinked and looked again, he was just sitting there.

Weird. It must be my mind playing tricks on me. She quietly asked Bear to come and stand behind her, but she couldn't feel the connection this time. That had never happened before. She saw herself in her mind's eye running frantically through a forest, alone, looking for her bear, but she couldn't find him. She started to get anxious.

'Your bear isn't here today,' Martin said.

Marissa froze.

'Did you lose him someplace?' He smiled at her, his clear blue eyes looking menacing all of a sudden.

'How do you know about Bear?' said Marissa, keeping her feet firmly on the ground and ignoring her body which started to shake slightly.

'I told you, I see things. Do you want to know what I can see right now?'

Marissa didn't think she did. This was beginning to really freak her out. As the therapist, she knew she had to take back control of the room. That was her role, her job, so she decided she had to do it, as that was what she signed up for. She wanted to win this, to show her strength, so she set an intention to be in control. She pushed aside her anxiety, stayed silent and focused and went back to the forest in her mind, and there she was once more. She saw herself rummaging in a pile of leaves on the forest floor. She didn't want to control the images or orchestrate them so she pulled back and allowed the images to appear naturally and unfold in her mind, just as they would in a dream or a shamanic journey. From the leaves, she saw herself pull out a large crystal, similar to the one she had at home, but this one was much bigger and glowing from the centre. Holding the crystal in her hand she felt its energy reassuring her, and she felt it in her body, too, in the therapy room. There. That was better. She brought her awareness back into the room with Martin. Then he spoke.

'Sorry if I freaked you out,' he said. 'I guess I'm testing you a little. But I did see a bear last week. It was standing behind you.'

Marissa cleared her throat. 'Did I pass your test?'

Marissa looked at him with a cold stare, feet firmly on the ground. It was as if she was in two places at once, Marissa in the forest standing strong, holding the crystal in both hands, absorbing the power it emanated, and Marissa in the therapy room, becoming stronger and more present.

Martin was becoming warmer. He stood up and took off his coat, hung it on the back of the door, rubbed his hands together and sat down again. Facing Marissa, he smiled and said, 'So, how was your week?'

Marissa wasn't sure how to react. He was trying to take the reins of the session, but she decided to take the question at face value and be nice to him. She said in a warm tone, 'My week was just fine, thanks. How was your week? Did you find occasion to use the butterfly technique we discussed?'

Martin seemed to shrink back a little. 'Oh yes, that was you, wasn't it? I forgot. So sorry. Yes, I like you, I just remembered. I'll try harder next time. The butterflies, breathing them out, I had a room full of butterflies about two nights ago. I made them all myself,' he laughed. 'I do like you. I won't do that again. Sorry.'

'Okay.' Marissa was still shaken and not sure if she should take his word for it. He did seem unpredictable. She also wasn't sure of exactly what it was that he did, either. It still felt very strange between them, there was a tension now in the room that wasn't there before. She had to go on, so she put the spotlight back onto him.

'Now then. Let's talk about you. This is your session, it's for you. What can I help you with this evening?'

'Hmm. Not sure. You can see I'm a little off-balance right now. I have had a change in my medication, it makes me irritable. Only a slight change.'

He did a full-body shiver, Marissa held her ground. She felt a calming presence come in behind her. *Bear?* she thought, and got a full body 'Yes'. She relaxed, feeling immediately safer. Her bear *would* come if she asked him.

They talked about Martin's medication, about how his mother always took the side of the doctors, and he told her about the time he had been in hospital, and they had tied him to the bed for a night and a day.

'That must have been awful for you.'

'I was completely drugged out of it. They totally don't know how to deal with this, or with me. Not when I'm like that anyway. Hey, I'm really sorry for freaking you out earlier. I like your bear. He's cool. I had a wolf once, I don't know where he went. I'd like to get him back. You said you could help me? Maybe you can help me with that.'

'I'd like to help you, very much.' Martin seemed more human now, and Marissa did forgive him, this time. She continued, wanting to help, 'I'll have a think about your wolf for you, for next time.'

Marissa had a strong image suddenly reveal itself in her mind. Back in the forest, this time it was as if they were all sitting down on a long table having tea. It was straight out of *Alice in Wonderland*. Herself and her bear, Martin and his wolf, and a few other animals too. All of them seemed happy and jolly, passing cups of tea and eating little pink muffins. It was a very colourful scene, it felt strange but pleasant.

'Is it time up?'

Marissa looked at the clock. 'We have about five minutes left. Is there anything else I can do to help you today?'

Martin's eyes slowly glazed over, and he retreated back inside himself. He seemed similar to how he appeared when first he came into the room, as if he was gone away somewhere. He shook his head no and got up and put on his coat.

As he turned to leave, he spoke in a neutral tone. 'I like pink muffins. And I like your bear, too.'

Cold chills ran through Marissa.

Martin nodded to Marissa and then to where Marissa felt her bear was standing behind her. 'See you both next week.'

He smiled and left the room.

Shaken to her core, Maria stayed in her chair, feeling the reverberations of all she had just experienced. She had prickles down her arms and cold chills from when he said pink muffins. *How did he know about the pink muffins? Or my bear?* The room felt like he was still in it. If she closed her eyes, Martin could still be in the chair opposite her.

She closed them briefly and the image of him with fangs and fire in his eyes came back strongly, only this time it felt much more threatening. Her heart flipped and she opened her eyes quickly, heart still racing. The room was still empty, but it didn't feel safe there. Marissa remembered the sage. She tried to light it from the candle once more, but the candle was down to the end of the wick and the sage was still wet from before. She shivered. She really didn't want to leave, but she couldn't stay in that room any longer. She slowly got her coat and put it on, it was so heavy it felt like it was made of lead. She thought of the forest scene, she wanted to know what was going on with Marissa-of-the-forest, but she couldn't summon up the connection to see the images again.

There is way too much going on here, I haven't a clue about any of this. Maybe Séamus will be able to help me. The apprenticeship – that will help me learn how to handle this. I've got no choice now. I really need to sign up.

Her body was going through the motions as if it was on autopilot. Turn off light, close door, leave corridor, go downstairs, sign out, leave transcript for Mr Blakemore, check nobody else here, switch off hall light, close main door.

She was standing in the cold car park in the dark December night. The light pollution from the city's street lamps bounced off the sky and obscured everything but the northern star. She started to walk, trying to shake off the feelings from her session. She didn't want to bring this home. How could she get rid of them? She got to the bus stop, but standing there waiting didn't feel right, she didn't want to stop moving, she realised she didn't want to get on a bus, either. So she kept walking. She knew the way back into town from taking the bus so often.

She walked past streets where houses were derelict and dark, streets where families were putting their children to bed, where people were opening bottles of wine and settling down for a night of television. She walked past closed offices and shops, closed cafés and restaurants that were open. She could see the people at their tables eating, talking, laughing. She walked past pubs where people were standing outside drinking pints and smoking. The closer she got to the city centre, the more people and life she passed by, and she began to feel reassured by ordinary things, ordinary life; it *was* an ordinary night. But something extraordinary had happened, and this time she couldn't play it down. Martin really saw Bear. He saw the pink muffins. And what had she seen? Some sort of devil in him? Or a demon? Were demons real? She had heard of them, too, but she never asked herself about them before.

As she walked she remembered the angel card packs that Mairead had shown her in the shop. She hadn't wanted them because she had never met an angel. She didn't know if they were real either, but if she had to make a choice between meeting an angel or a demon, she would much rather meet an angel. Perhaps she had better meet one soon. *Oh God, what way is my mind going at all?*

Her feet kept walking until she got into her local area. More familiar scenes helped her to feel more relaxed. She found her shoulders dropping, she realised her legs and feet were getting tired from the walking. She also realised she was hungry, and there, right in front of her, was the chipper. She went in and felt the steamy hotness of the air from deep-fried cooking. It was nice to be enveloped by heat after being out in the fresh, cold night. She ordered a large chips with lots of salt and vinegar. She wasn't waiting long. Marissa took the hot parcel to a table and sat on the white plastic stool, placed it on the white plastic table and felt the heat of the freshly cooked chips and the sting of vinegar on her face as she opened the brown paper bag. They were too hot to eat, but she licked the salt off of one of them and looked around her.

People were laughing, oblivious to the possibility of the existence of angels or demons, wolf spirits and bears. *What if they could see them too? What would the place look like then?* She imagined the chipper full of spirit animals, angels and demons as well as the people. It reminded her of college when they put an acetate sheet under the projector then placed another one on top, which had more detail. Here's what you see, here's what you don't see. Except some people *could* see. See spirits. *If Martin could see them, there must be other people that can see them too. What exactly are they? Oh dear.* She felt like she was going around in circles. *No wonder he ended up tied to a bed for a day and a night.*

She put a hot chip into her mouth. The heat and the salt with the sharp vinegar flavour brought her back to herself, back into the moment. She crunched her teeth into it, feeling the hot soft potato on her tongue, in her mouth, and she swallowed. She delicately chose another and ate that, then another, and another. Soon, the whole bag was gone. She thought about ordering a second bag, but they had given her a good large helping and she wasn't hungry anymore. She felt much better with the bag of chips inside her, the salt seemed to really help. She remembered a scene in Harry Potter where they ate chocolate to recover from being attacked by Dementors. Maybe she needed the chips to help her recover too? Or was it the salt? She had so many questions.

She smiled. *Look at me, opening a can of worms, a real big one. Okay, I admit I like this, though. Having so many questions is much better than not having any at all. Life has just taken a very interesting turn. I'm not a Muggle anymore... I'm finding magic right here.*

She walked slowly the rest of the way home, licking the salt off of her vinegar-tainted fingers and smiling. *I need to slow down or I'm going to miss something important.*

When she got back to her flat, the first thing she did after washing her hands and taking off her coat was to send Séamus a €100 non-refundable deposit for the training. Once she quit PayPal and turned off her laptop, she felt calm. She did the mindfulness technique again. *There's my computer (breath), there's my bed (breath), there's my desk (breath). Yes.* She was out of it. She felt ready to settle down for the night.

She was in the forest again, running, running for dear life. It felt like a pack of wolves were at her heels, she couldn't slow down, she couldn't turn around to see them, didn't know where she was going, she kept running through the darkness under the canopy of leaves. There, a stone house –

look! The door was open. She ran through the gate posts, up the drive, past the rose bushes which climbed around a trellis, went straight inside and closed the door firmly behind her.

She pressed her back to the door and caught her breath. She was panting from the running, it was dark inside the house, but it felt safer here. She took a moment to get her bearings and recognised this house as a place she had been to before. On the hall table was a candle and lighter, she lit it and walked confidently through the hallway to the back room. She noticed a spiral staircase going down.

'This is new.' She climbed down the stairs. The staircase was similar to the one in Cabra. She held the candle deftly in her hands as she went down three twists of the spiral. When she came to the bottom rung, she stepped off and was in a small, stone corridor. The first room was a laboratory, fully stocked with glass jars of many sizes, all had various amounts of liquids in them, some had objects floating inside. There was a worktop filled with objects as there was an experiment in progress – beakers, pipettes, Petri dishes, swabs, tongs, a crucible... A large triangular beaker was held in place by an iron clamp and stand, positioned over a Bunsen burner. The burner was on low, and the purple and gold liquid in the jar was swirling and moving upwards through a series of complicated glass rods. Marissa followed the rods with her eyes and saw the liquid was going into another jar on a high shelf which looked like it should be overfull, but there was hardly any liquid in it at all. As the liquid dropped into the beaker, the meniscus went down, as if it was subtracting itself from the beaker instead of adding itself to it. 'Strange.' She looked around the room to try to understand what was happening.

Marissa recognised her lab coat from school hanging on a hook behind the door. She half-expected to see it there. It was definitely hers as it still had that stain from when Joanne accidentally knocked over a beaker of chromium chloride in second year. Marissa went over to her coat and put it on, it was a little small across the shoulders, but then it seemed to grow and change to fit her better. The purple stain became darker and richer, then started to spread across the material of the lab coat until the entire coat became a deep shade of purple. The material changed too, it became more velvety, softer, some of the threads turned to gold, and small and *large golden stars appeared and peppered themselves throughout the entire cloak. Yes, it was more like a cloak now and less like a lab coat.*

She wasn't scared, things shifting and changing shape felt natural to her, she was in a dream, after all. This type of thing happened in her dreams all the time. Marissa went over to the laboratory bench and swapped out one of the bottles from the experiment for another. Dream-Marissa knew exactly what she was doing. The liquid in the glass tube changed colour, the almost empty beaker started to fill up slowly. She nodded her head, yes, that was what she wanted. How did the worktop get so cluttered? She decided she needed to reorganise it so she started rearranging everything. But the bottles... They weren't cooperating. She moved a few of them and then, while her back was turned, they moved back. This was frustrating, even Dream-Marissa got very agitated and decided to rearrange the whole room. Then she heard a loud CRASH!!!

Marissa woke with a jump, she was disoriented. She heard a scraping and someone whistling outside her front door, ah yes, the bin man, it was bin day, and she had forgotten to leave hers at the gate. He sometimes came up to take it if he wasn't too busy. She flopped back down in her warm bed and checked her clock, 7:15am. She still had time to have a shower and breakfast and get to work for 9am.

As she stretched out under the duvet, she brought her mind back to her dream. *I really enjoyed seeing my old lab coat. It was as if I was working something out in that lab... The direction of the liquid in the jar, wait, yes, there were bubbles in it, it must mean something.* She was sure she had been there before, had that dream before, but she didn't remember the details. The cloak was excellent, she had never seen anything like it. *If I ever had to go to a fancy dress party...* The alarm went off 10 minutes later, and it was time to get up. Then she remembered what happened the night before, with Martin. She shivered. She decided she needed to meet an angel, not really sure what that would look like, but if things were going to proceed in the direction they were already moving in, she would certainly need a little bit of help.

CHAPTER FIFTEEN

It was the last class of term. They had most of December and half of January off to catch up on client hours, assignments, and personal therapy. Marissa was looking forward to getting all her assignments over with, but she was sorry to finish up, too. Mr Crowley packed his books up at the end of the evening. His module with them was finished and they wouldn't be seeing him again that year. His classes were so animated and interesting, a line was forming from the group as people wanted to ask him final questions. Marissa watched them, it was as if he was a celebrity author, and they all wanted his autograph. She didn't feel the need, although she wasn't completely confident with the material she felt that if she took some time to read the textbook over the holidays she'd have a better handle on it. She observed her classmates from her desk. They were filled with Christmas cheer and just as delighted as she was that the term ended tonight. They all needed a break, some time to catch up with themselves.

Marissa had grown fond of them all. Each of them were different in their own way, some more annoying than others, but all of them enthusiastic about helping other people. She hadn't told anyone about starting the Shamanic training, she wanted to keep it to herself for a while. She hadn't told her parents about it either, not even Eli. He had his hands full with Carol's pregnancy, her morning sickness had gotten so bad that she had missed several days of work and had been in bed for a week. Marissa's mum, Rose, relented her crusade against her and called over one evening with a pot of chicken soup to try to get something into her stomach. When it came down to the crunch, her families' hearts were in the right place.

'Coming for a Christmas drink?' Emmet interrupted her train of thought with a smile. He was wearing a Christmas jumper that had lights sewn into it. He had switched them off during class but they were back on again, they were quite funny to look at.

'Why not.' Marissa said, not really able to find an excuse. She packed up her things, grabbed her bag and went with the others to the pub, feeling like a student again.

Sitting at the table surrounded by people with drinks and chatter, Marissa was hit by a wave of grief, just for a moment. Remembering nights out with James and his friends, how much she loved being with him, it all flooded back. And she felt an echo of how much she still missed him, the life they had planned together had fallen apart completely. Her heart still hurt, ached in a private place that was so deep it was easy to ignore most of the time, pretend that it didn't exist. But it did, and at times like these, the pain rose up and demanded to be seen, to be felt. She immersed herself completely in the sweetness of it, almost addictive, then realised what she was doing. She decided to stop feeling sorry for herself. Here were some new lovely friends of her own, right in front of her. As difficult as it was, she deliberately pulled herself out of the memories and brought herself back into the present. She was drenched in emotion, it really was like getting out of the sea fully clothed, with wet, heavy garments dragging her down with the weight of water. She watched her new friends from the side-lines until she got her bearings again. Realising she felt better, she noticed she was still holding back from the group's banter. After some moments had passed, the heavy feeling dissipated, and she was able to gradually join in the fun.

Learning that you need to do this and actually doing it is so different. I have to really make an effort here. She consciously replaced the images of James that had flooded her mind with a memory of the moment when she threw the stone into the Irish Sea, the rain about to pour, she in her raincoat defiant and determined to move on. But even in her determined state, her heart still felt like a piece of it was missing.

Marissa got the bus home from the pub once the group started to break up around 11pm, not exactly wild like a college Christmas get-together, but she was tired. It had been a long day and the emotions from earlier still trickled over her. Sat upstairs, she looked out the steamed-up window of the bus at the flashing Christmas lights outside. The sun had set very early that day, around 4:30pm. It was coming up to the shortest day of the year, and the sparkling cheery white and coloured lights adorned the shop windows and some of the houses near where Marissa lived.

Her phone beeped a text. Knowing that it was late, she figured it could only be someone from her family, or Sarah. It was the latter, once again asking when they were going to go shopping for clothes for the work Christmas party. For the past week Sarah had been bugging Marissa about dressing up, so in the spirit of her new determination, she wrote back and agreed to go clothes shopping, said they could figure it all out at work the next day.

When she got home, after having some tea she pulled out the small artificial Christmas tree that she and James had bought together. It was hers now, like the flat, and Tobermory. *Of course, Tobermory doesn't belong to anyone. Sorry, cat.* She looked at the tree. 'Why not?' She put the pieces of greenery together on the metal frame until it looked tree-shaped. Then she strung the lights around it. Switching them on added a sparkle to the room that she had been missing for a long time. It felt nice. *I do want to bring the magic back. Maybe this will help. You're my Christmas tree now.*

She looked at the decorations that were left in the box, but they seemed wrong to her. She and James had chosen them, she didn't want them anymore. But one of the decorations seemed brighter than the others as if it was calling out at her. She picked it out of the box and looked at it. It was an angel. It was silver with white feathers on the wings. It didn't look religious, it was quite attractive, she liked it.

I'll keep you and get rid of the rest of it. She hung the angel up close to the top of the tree; it was only a small 4 ft tall tree, just perfect for her apartment. *Yes, I like this. It makes me happy. I choose more happy now.*

She was tired at work the next day. Yawning, Marissa checked the time. She had a session booked with Olive at lunchtime. Her heart sank. She wasn't up for it today, but she knew that she had to do it. In the taxi on the way over, they became caught in traffic in the rain. Christmas shoppers clogged the streets and they were held up at traffic lights for what seemed like ages. Marissa needed something to occupy her mind so she checked her diary to audit how many sessions she had done and how many were left for her college requirement. She kept losing track, counting up the sessions wrong. Maths wasn't her best subject at school. She was convinced she had done fifteen sessions already, she needed thirty therapy hours by the time she finished her diploma, which would be the following June. She had started therapy late, this meant she needed another fifteen hours by the time she finished her diploma. Her heart sank even further. *Now I feel pressurised. I don't like this...*

And now she was late for therapy. The taxi had pulled up on the curb and switched on its flashing lights as the driver waited patiently to be paid. Marissa jolted out of her thoughts and handed him the €10 note she had ready in her hand.

'Keep the change.'

'Thanks love!'

She hopped out and grabbed her bags, rushed to Olive's side entrance and rang the bell hurriedly – she never liked being late. Olive came to the door with a smile and gently invited her inside. She was wearing red today – shawl, jumper and skirt, red suited her.

'Sorry Olive, there was traffic... Christmas and all.' Marissa took off her coat and arranged her chair, and then sat down.

'I can tell you don't want to be here today,' said Olive with a raised eyebrow.

Marissa's eyes widened. 'How can you tell?'

'You never like coming to therapy, Marissa. How do you expect to be a therapist when you don't enjoy being here yourself?'

'I didn't think therapy was something you were supposed to enjoy...'

Olive sat back and clasped both hands to her stomach. 'Well, some people *can* enjoy it if they open their mind to it.'

'But most people only come to therapy when they are upset if something bad has happened...' She sighed. 'And now we need to do fifteen sessions before next June...'

Olive picked up her notebook, turned to her notes on Marissa and silently counted the dates she had kept track of. She looked up with kind eyes. 'Sorry, dear, we need to do eighteen more, you must have counted them up wrong. And yes, most people only come when something bad has happened. But you child, you are not most people. Use me. Share things. Tell me things. You don't do that. Perhaps if you did, you'd learn something.'

+++

It was Friday and Marissa was feeling overwhelmed. The Winter Solstice, the shortest day of the year, was in two weeks. Séamus's first training workshop would be residential, a weekend in Galway, starting on the Friday at lunchtime and incorporating a solstice celebration. Marissa juggled, trying to figure out her holidays, client evenings and work, wanting to fit everything in. Christmas was always hectic. The work Christmas party was the Thursday before, but she wasn't in Cabra that week, so she *could* make it to both. If she caught the morning train that Friday, she would be in Galway town around lunchtime. Marissa had a few holiday-day's leftover from her work allocation. They had to be spent before January anyway, so she booked the Friday and the following Monday and Tuesday off. Christmas was on Wednesday so work was closed for the rest of that week. *Sorted! Phew. That gives me a good chunk of time to recover from the training AND get my college assignments done.*

She still needed to get organised before the workshop, including sourcing and purchasing either a drum or a rattle. *Two weeks and one weekend to get it all done. I can do this.* She put the box of Christmas ornaments by the door of her apartment to bring to the charity shop tomorrow. That felt right, too, better than throwing them out. A new start. Remembering she needed to meet an angel and still wracking her brain about where to get a shamanic drum and rattle, she decided that she had to pay Mairead in The Angel Shop another visit. *I could go tomorrow...* She had a Chanukah dinner with her parents tomorrow too, it was going to be a busy day. She set her alarm for 9am.

Marissa woke to the sound of rain thrashing down on her window. It was still dark, nearly 9am, and the thoughts of going outside were not appealing. But then she remembered her plans to visit The Angel Shop, and her energy and enthusiasm returned. Switching off her alarm just before it went off, she got herself ready to go out.

The DART platform was crowded. Everyone seemed to be out doing last-minute shopping for the holidays. With a week to go, everyone was manically running around looking for everything they needed. Dublin got so excited about Christmas, it was as if the whole country closed down for two weeks. People believed they had to buy everything well in advance, things they needed and things they didn't. If you didn't have everything in stock at home before Christmas Eve, tough luck to you! However, nowadays, the shops were open over the holiday period, but Marissa did remember a time when they were not, yet the mentality seemed to have lasted.

The train arrived, she got on and managed to find a seat at the back. The carriage was crammed full of people. She realised she could either hate it or love it, so she decided to love it, and soon she enjoyed the chatter and the laughter. The train went dark then came out of the tunnel and there was the sea. Always at that moment her heart lifted, she felt at home. She looked out at the waves, she felt a strong connection there. *Maybe I used to be a mermaid.*

It was still raining when she hopped off the train at Dun Laoghaire. Marissa made her way up the hill to the town pulling the hood of her raincoat down over her forehead. She gratefully arrived at the shopping centre and took some time to shake the rain off of herself. She then went straight up to the third floor. The Angel Shop was closed. Her heart fell. *Oh no! What will I do now?* She had no idea where to get a drum in time for her workshop. She bought a pastry and a coffee and walked around the centre feeling deflated and damp.

Her phone beeped. It was a text from her mum: Don't forget Chanukah dinner tonight at our place.

Oy vey, why am I so disorganised? Marissa wasn't prepared at all, it *had* slipped her mind, so she was grateful for the nudge, and she was in the right place. She found some trinkets to bring with her and some wrapping paper and Sellotape. She got home by late afternoon, wrapped the presents, showered and changed. Even though she had offerings for the Chanukah table, she had no drum and felt like it had been a wasted day.

The blinking lights on her Christmas tree were cheerful. She hung up some new baubles she had picked up at the shopping centre. They were like small mirror balls, colourful and bright, further set off by the coloured lights. Maybe she could make a drum? *Never mind, it will all work out some way or other.* She decided that with or without a drum, being there was more important.

She sat on her sofa and admired the tree lights, the new baubles, the angel, and dozed off. Her body relaxed into the chair, the noises of her neighbours and the sounds of the street outside surrounded her. Then her heart leapt – *Tobermory!* She hadn't asked anyone to feed him when she was going to be away. She'd have to ask Michelle from upstairs, hopefully, she wasn't going away that weekend too. She texted her immediately and got a No problem text back almost straight away. *Great. Sorted.* She settled back to her dozing, it felt good to rest after the day walking around outside in the blustery rain and wind. She could almost see her Christmas tree through her closed eyelids.

She half-opened them and focused on the angel she had placed on the top. It had a radiance about it that felt good, it seemed to be brighter than anything else in the room. She closed her eyes and could see the light from the angel still, thinking it was strange, she opened her eyes quickly again. *No, nothing strange to see here.* She hoped her mind wasn't playing tricks on her again like it did the other night. Yes, it was a trick of her mind, that was all that it was.

It had stopped raining so she walked to her parent's house, focusing her mind on the present moment. *A cat, a car, a house, a streetlight, a rose bush. Ooh roses, isn't it a little late for roses?'*

'Hello, love, it's so good to see you. You're looking well! How are you doing?'

'Hi Dad, I'm well, thanks. Work is so busy at the moment, too busy, we have the Christmas party next week and I just finished college for the holidays. It's great to have some time to catch up. How are you?'

Marissa came inside, hung her raincoat on the rail behind the door and walked down the narrow corridor into the main part of the house.

'Hi, Mum! What's for dinner?'

'Hello, baby, great to see you! I've chicken, roast potatoes, peas, stuffing, with chicken soup to start and chocolate cake for dessert.'

'Ah, lovely. How's the shop doing, Dad?'

'Good, business is ticking away. Your uncle is doing very well. He sends his regards to you.'

'Is Eli coming?'

'Yes,' then he added with a hushed voice, 'Would you believe it your mother invited Carol too? She seems to have settled down with the idea of the baby. Wonders never cease.'

'That's fantastic, long may it last.'

'I can hear you...' Rose chimed in from the kitchen, which was practically in the same room, it was a small house.

The doorbell rang. 'I'll get it,' Marissa said.

'Can you set the table, Bernie?' asked Rose.

'Of course, love.'

Marissa went to the front door and opened it. The first thing she noticed was that Carol seemed to have lost quite a bit of weight since the last time Marissa had seen her.

'Are you okay?' asked Marissa, quite concerned, as they came into the house.

'Getting there. I'm almost into the middle of the second trimester, it's not supposed to be so sick-making, but it's still making me sick. But I can keep food down now, which is good.'

The three of them stood at the threshold, with the door slightly open, wanting to catch up before they made an entrance.

'Hi Sis,' Eli reached over and hugged Marissa, whispering into her ear, 'It seems okay now. What did you say to Mum? You worked some magic there for sure!'

'I don't know that I did anything... Maybe she realised that she'd be cutting her nose off to spite her face. If she excludes Carol, she's excluding the baby too. Anyway, you've been very sick. Mum's always good when there's a crisis, she must have put her feelings aside to help get you through it. Hopefully her feelings won't come back into the foreground once things have settled down. '

Eli pulled back and looked at Marissa, 'You know, I think it's because of James.' Carol gave Eli a look which Marissa took to mean

"Don't mention the war". Eli shrugged his shoulders. 'Seriously, Mum knew that you and James were going to get married whether she was in or out. I think she had given in and accepted that and tried to make the best of it, remember?'

'And then he left me,' Marissa said, but in hearing herself say it she noticed that it didn't hurt as much as it used to.

'Yes, he did, bastard thing to do. But Mum came back to you before he left, which was ironic. His loss anyway, and it would be Mum's loss if she wasn't around for Carol and me. And baby!'

'Can I sit down? I'm so tired.' asked Carol.

'Oh shit, yes, of course, let's find somewhere for you to sit down.'

They all came in and shut the door, Eli hung his and Carol's coat and they went into the back room. Marissa's parents' house was much smaller than their Uncles, it was always a bit of a squash and a squeeze.

'It's great to see you, come in! Come in!' Rose was wearing an apron and the house was filled with aromas of cooking. Carol slumped down on the sofa, Marissa took a chair out from the dining table and sat, and Eli found an armchair. The menorah was out on the mantlepiece with four candles for the third night of Chanukah, ready to be lit before dinner, as was their family tradition.

'How are you feeling, pet?' Rose asked Carol, tea towel in hand, putting cutlery down onto the table.

'Much better, Mrs Rosenthal. Thank you so much for the soup the other day. I'm pretty sure it helped settle my stomach.'

'Call me Rose, dear. There's nothing like chicken soup when you're not feeling well. Morning sickness isn't any different. And it's our secret family recipe,' she winked, 'which I *might* share with you, at some stage, depending on himself,' she nodded over towards Eli, who pretended he didn't hear the not-so-subtle hint. 'Now, would you like something to drink? Bernie? Can you sort the children out with drinks?'

'Of course, love.' said Marissa's Dad. Marissa watched him get a beer for Eli and one for himself, and sparkling water for Carol and for her. She looked at his face, really looked at it, and she noticed how the ache in her heart had lifted. Even with Eli's mentioning James, she felt filled with the love that she had for her family. Trouble as all as they were, they meant the world to her, and nothing could change that. Even with their silly eccentricities, they were her home.

'Dinner's ready in five. Shall we light the candles?' said Rose.

Eli motioned to Carol to stand up. They all stood, and Rose lit the Shamesh using a box of matches and spoke the Hebrew prayer for Chanukah. 'Amen,' they all said. Carol kept her head down. She had been to the house for prayers before but not for Chanukah as it was only for family. So this really was a declaration of peace on behalf of Rose, and Bernie too. Rose used the Shamesh to light the other three candles. 'Happy Chanukah,' she said, turning to the family. 'Happy Chanukah!'

As the dinner progressed, Carol looked a lot more at ease. There were small gifts for everyone, Marissa was glad she had something to give in return. It was a lovely night, everyone was avoiding any potent subject matter. When they were ready to leave, Eli offered Marissa a lift home, which she gladly accepted. She was looking forward to a day to rest before the craziness of the coming week ahead.

'Do you want to come in? I'll make us some tea…'

'I've not been in your flat for a long time, yes why not!' said Eli. 'Carol, are you up for it? We'll only stay for a few minutes.'

'Yes, that would be lovely.'

Marissa welcomed them in through her front door.

'Ooh, you have a tree!' said Carol, a big smile on her face.

'Yes! Only small, but I love it!' said Marissa, 'The magic of Christmas, it really cheers me up.'

Eli looked at the tree, then looked Marissa up and down. 'You're different. There's something going on with you, isn't there? What are you not telling me? First, you don't flinch when I mention you-know-who, and now you have a tree, which you've not had since you-know-who left...'

Marissa filled the kettle. got out some mugs, and took out a packet of chocolate biscuits from the back of the cupboard while Eli took their coats and he and Carol squished down together on her sofa.

Marissa sighed and said, 'I just decided it was time to get on with my life. I'm tired of being anxious all the time. I even said I'd go dress shopping with Sarah for the work Christmas party next week.'

'I'm so happy you're starting to enjoy life again.' said Carol approvingly.

'About time too,' Eli said with a nod. He noticed the candle and its holder on the coffee table, 'Is this new, too?' he asked. Then he found and pulled out the pack of cards from the shelf underneath. 'And what are these? Are you turning into a witch?'

Marissa felt a cold shiver down her back. She wasn't quite ready to explain herself yet. The kettle had boiled so she poured out the tea and brought it over to the coffee table. Eli opened the pack and was fingering through the cards.

'Interesting'

The cold feeling had left, but Marissa still felt edgy. She looked at Eli, she didn't like him touching the cards, he never asked her if he could. He smiled back at her, and then she warmed a little. She sat down on the armchair.

'So how do these work then?'

'Well, you hold them in your hand, ask a question and then pull a card out.'

'Can I try?' asked Carol.

'Me first!' said Eli.

'You're such a kid!'

Eli closed his eyes, held the cards in his hand, then cut the pack and pulled out a card. It was a crow. It looked a little menacing, it was standing on the ground, with other crows flying in the sky behind it. 'What does Crow mean?'

'I'm not sure.' said Marissa, 'There's a book with the cards, did you see it? Yes, that's it, here give it to me, and I'll look it up.' She took the booklet from Eli.

> *Crow wants you to know that you have magical abilities within you that you might not be aware of. Everything you have been working towards is now coming into fruition. Call on Crow to support and help you find new opportunities for growth.*

'What was your question?'

'Never you mind.' said Eli, sliding the Crow card back into the pack and handing it to Carol. 'Your turn!'

Carol silently held the pack of cards in her two hands, closed her eyes then opened them again. She cut the deck and pulled out a card. It was Deer, the deer was a doe, it looked soft and vulnerable, out in the forest by itself. It had a baby beside it, which Marissa thought was very interesting.

'What does a deer mean?' Carol asked.

Marissa flipped through the booklet.

> *When Deer comes to you it is a reminder to connect to your intuition. You can handle this current situation with grace and compassion, trust your instincts. Call on deer to help you become more gentle to yourself and others*

'I guess I have been very hard on myself for being so ill,' Carol said, looking at the card. 'I do like the baby deer. Maybe that's my baby talking to me. Can I take a photograph of it? Maybe by having it in my phone I'll remember to be nicer to myself.'

'Of course!' said Marissa. 'I did that too, the other day when I got Bear and wanted to bring Bear with me.'

'Bear, eh?' said Eli, dipping a biscuit into his tea and then licking off the melting chocolate. 'Which bear? Fozzie Bear? Or Barney? Ha ha!'

Marissa scrunched up her mouth. 'No. Neither of them.'

Carol took her photograph. 'Thanks, and thanks for the tea!'

'You're very welcome.'

Marissa gratefully took the cards back from Eli and Carol and held them for a moment before putting them back in the pack and closing the box.

'They're fun,' Carol said. 'I like them.'

'I do too,' said Marissa, 'Though sometimes I don't really know what they mean, they're very supportive.'

Eli looked at his watch, 'Come on, love, I think we should be heading home. Thanks for the tea Marissa, and for the card. I do like your tree. Maybe we should get one too, honey? What do you think?'

Carol softened. Marissa got the feeling that she had been holding back from Eli on the tree in case it insulted him. He could be just as bad as their parents when it came down to doing new things. 'Yes, I would like that very much, just a small one though, like thc one Marissa has.'

'We can get it tomorrow if you want?'

Marissa got them their coats and walked them the few steps to the front door. Eli went out first. Marissa turned and gave Carol a strong hug.

'Thank you,' Carol said.

'And thank you, too. You're making my family softer and nicer to be around. I really appreciate it,' said Marissa.

It was quiet in the flat when they left. Marissa hadn't pulled a card for herself yet. She decided not to. She changed and got into bed.

She was in her flat, tidying up. Eli had left the place in such a mess. She brought plates and cups from the table to the sink and turned around, only to see more plates and cups on the table. She looked in the sink, the ones she put there were still there, so she brought in the new ones, turned back to the table and yes, again, there were more. Cleaning the room seemed like an impossible task.

She started washing the plates, then the cups, and she'd look into the sink, and more dirty plates and cups appeared. She turned around and saw her room filling up with dirty plates and dirty cups. It seemed to be something out of a movie she saw... But which one? She wanted it to stop, she got very upset, shouted 'No!'

Then suddenly, she was in a field, or was it a meadow? Standing a few feet away was a lone figure with her back to her. She caught her breath, tried to make sense of where she was. The figure turned, it was the medicine woman from the house that night in Peru.

The meadow dissolved and Marissa found herself back in the Medicine Woman's house. There was just the two of them there. 'Come,' beckoned the woman with her hand, and Marissa moved towards her. They sat cross-legged, facing each other at the top of the room, in the same position she sat when she was there several months ago.

'You are starting your training, very good.' she said. Marissa nodded. 'The ancestors are pleased, they say it is about time. I say that you do it in your own time.' She smiled at Marissa. 'Sometime you will need my help. Do not be afraid to call me, I am here. We are all here.'

She gestured behind her and Marissa looked up and saw many women standing behind the Medicine woman. It was as if they were reflected in mirrors, many, many women going back in time over generations and generations... They were not solid and they were not transparent either. Marissa felt a strong emotional connection to all of the women there, and when she looked back at the Medicine Woman, it was as if she was her grandmother or her mother, but yet it was not like that either. She wasn't sure how to explain this.

'Thank you,' Marissa said, with tears in her eyes. The ancestors gradually dissolved away, leaving just the two of them there once more. 'What is your name? What am I to call you?'

The medicine woman smiled, then she dissolved away, too.

Marissa woke up. It was the middle of the night. She got up and poured herself a drink of water, then sat on the sofa. The light from the window shone off of the ornaments on the tree. The angel in particular glinted and drew her attention. She had a lot to think about. *The medicine woman didn't give me her name. How am I supposed to call her if I need her? And why would I need her?* It all felt like it was happening so quickly now. She drank her water and felt a little more at ease. She looked over towards the sink, half expecting to see it filled with dishes, but the dishes were clean and in the draining board, just where she had left them.

+++

Marissa was feeling positive that everything would come together the week before the Galway trip. Even though she didn't find a drum on Saturday, she had finished one of her college assignments and worked out that she could just about fit in 18 sessions in with Olive by June. She was much brighter when she got into work that Monday. Noreen summoned Marissa into her office.

'Close the door behind you, dear,' she said.

Marissa was used to being called into the office. There was often something or other needing doing or sorted out, particularly at this time of year. Marissa hoped Noreen wouldn't dump a pile of work on her lap to all be done at the last minute like she had done the year before.

'Sit,' Noreen said, pointing to the chair on the other side of the desk. Marissa sat, suddenly quivering with nerves. Noreen looked very serious in her lilac suit, her face was deadpanned. *Is this about a Christmas bonus? Or did I do something wrong?*

'Now, woman, you've been here a long time, and I want to know what your intentions are.'

Marissa was totally taken aback. She didn't expect any kind of review, she had been happily surfing away at work, getting all her jobs done, yes, but not adding anything extra in... Noreen went on.

'You've been here for almost three years, and you've been my PA for a year. We both know that you've got more potential than this. It's coming to the end of the year, and I want to chat with you about your future. Your mother would be upset with me if I didn't.' Noreen winked and went on.

'There's a new managerial opening coming up next year. I have my eye on it for you. It's in marketing. I know you don't know much about that but you're very resourceful, and you learn on the hop. And of course, I'd pay for any additional training you may need. It's a great opportunity for career advancement. What do you say?'

Marissa was flummoxed. It really wasn't where she had been putting her energies. She didn't know what to say. But she had to say something. 'Wow, Noreen, that's very kind of you.' She found her footing and continued. 'I've been studying to become a psychotherapist, I've almost finished my diploma, I'll be finished in June, and then I can work towards becoming accredited.'

'Great, well I can shift the managerial position out from February to June, so you can start then, if you need the extra time for exams. You'll never make a career out of therapy, there just isn't any money in it.'

Marissa knew already that therapy didn't pay a lot of money, but it did have the potential to at least cover the bills? *Didn't it? I can't think... I need some time to work this out.* She took a breath. 'Noreen, that's very kind of you, I totally didn't expect this. Can I take some time to think about it?'

'Sure. Take Christmas, and let me know when we start back in the New Year. I'll have to make arrangements, so I'm going to hold you to it. Now, to other matters – Sarah tells me that she's convinced you to go dress shopping with her?'

Marissa was relieved at the change in the direction of the conversation. 'Yes, she has.'

'There's a sale on in my favourite boutique in the Westbury Mall. You should check it out. Why not take an extra hour off for your lunch break and go shopping today? You and Sarah together. Let Sarah know, I'll put it on the roster.'

'Alright, I will. Thanks, Noreen.' Marissa got up to go.

'Just one more thing,' said Noreen, and then she dumped a pile of work on Marissa. 'I need this done before close of business on Friday.'

Back at her desk Marissa sorted the piles of paperwork to try to figure out how she could get it all done. She was determined she was going to Galway, all this work would have to be done by Thursday evening, by hook or by crook. She'd miss the Christmas party if she had to. Sarah came by the desk looking for her

'Noreen told me we get two hours for lunch! Isn't that brilliant! Where do you want to go?'

It felt like a conspiracy between Noreen and Sarah to make sure Marissa missed her Galway trip, looked her best AND showed up at the party. *That's a little bit silly, I'm just overwhelmed.* She knew they were genuinely concerned about her, and she was happy that it didn't upset her as much as it would have done a year ago. Marissa looked at the clock, it was 11:47am. *I'll aim to get the work done, AND go to the party, AND get the train on Friday morning as planned. I can do this!*

She looked at the clock again. 'Can we go at 12:30? It would give me some time to organise this lot.' Marissa nodded down at the work pile on the desk.

'Oh no! She didn't flippin go do that to you again, after last year too?'

Marissa shrugged her shoulders. 'Looks like it, yeah. I'm taking Friday off and I won't be back until we reopen in the New Year. I might need a little help? Either that, or I'll skip the party and work instead...'

'Hey, you can't skip the party, I need you to come. I'm not as busy as I usually am. Fire some of it over to me. I'll give you a hand out.'

'Seriously?'

'Yeah, all in the spirit of Christmas, of course! My best travel buddy, can't let you end up stuck in the office. But you have to promise me something?'

'Ha ha, I can't promise you anything until I know what it is first,' said Marissa, handing Sarah four manila folders stuffed full of paperwork. 'Thanks for this, by the way. I really appreciate it.'

'Sure, no probs. Yeah, promise me you'll at least try on a few dresses that I pick out for you?'

'Okay I can do that.'

Sarah beamed with delight. 'Yay! And one more thing?'

'Go on...'

'One dance with Tim at the Crimbo party?'

Marissa scrunched up her face.

'He's really nice, really he is, and he admitted to me the other day that he fancies you!'

Tim was kind of cute, and she had a feeling that he had been watching her for a while. But that could be pushing things, she wasn't sure if she was ready yet for something like that.

'You didn't join that dating website, go on, it's the least you can do for me...' said Sarah in a pleading voice

'I'll think about it.' she said. One dance with Tim wasn't really a bad payoff if Sarah did manage to get all that work done.

Sarah brightened. 'Great! See you in about half an hour, downstairs.'

The shopping trip *was* fun. They made it back to the office in a little over two hours with two dresses and a pair of shoes for Marissa, and a dress and two skirts and a sparkly silver top for Sarah. The sale in the Westbury did indeed have some interesting pieces, but they were still very highly-priced for a sale, so the girls found some better bargains on Grafton Street. They also picked up some accessories, Sarah got a headband with flowers entwined around it and a small black handbag with Christmas silvery sparkles had caught Marissa's eye. Sarah had insisted that she buy it. Marissa also bought more coloured balls for her little tree, and a small glass ornament. They were very happy with their purchases.

'You look great in the red,' said Sarah. 'Wear that one to the party. Hey. I can do your make-up for you! It's going to be so much fun!'

'Okay. Why not!' Marissa was really getting into the spirit of it, it surprised her that she was so free and easy, and honestly, she hadn't had that much fun going clothes shopping in a long time. The combination of Sarah's sense of humour and the atmosphere of the Christmas shoppers added to Marissa's feeling of lightness. If worse came to worse, she decided she could always come into the office after Galway, before the New Year and finish the paperwork. She was going to Galway, and that was that.

She was almost looking forward to the Christmas party too, though she wasn't sure if it was for the party itself or the break from work that would come afterwards. And Galway, well, she hadn't been in Galway for a very long time, not since she was a child and went with her parents to spend some time in Salthill. She remembered standing on a beach in Clifden in the rain, the powerful waves calling to her, and her father telling her that if she was to walk from there in a straight line, she would end up in America. America seemed so big and far away then, the idea that the sea could bring her there, the same sea that she was looking at right then, was impressive.

Marissa stayed behind that evening as late as she was able to to see how much of the work she could get through herself. There was at least a week's worth, and she only had three days now, even with Sarah's help, and she couldn't really pile any more onto her, or anyone else for that matter. 'Damn it anyway,' she said out loud as she locked up the building and walked home in the dark evening.

She passed by the chipper on her way home, the smell was tempting, and it reminded her of the circumstances around her last visit there. She shuddered. *Funny how the body remembers...*

CHAPTER SIXTEEN

It was the Wednesday before Christmas. The office was buzzing, everyone was excited and looking forward to the party the following night, and to their well-earned, and for some, not so well earned, two weeks off. Most offices closed down for Christmas and the New Year, there were always lots of parties planned and people got a little hyper. Hence it being called the Silly Season.

The atmosphere in the office was verging on silly for sure. Many people wore Santa hats, had flashing Christmas ornaments pinned on their shirts, some were wearing Christmas jumpers. Marissa was getting into the spirit of it, probably for the first time in her life. After working late on Tuesday, and Sarah helping out (much more than she expected), she only had four folders worth of work to go. She went out for lunch with some of the team, and she tried a pumpkin spice latte (never again!).

She was able to get out of the office by 7pm. She still had two work folders to get through the next day if she wanted to go to the party. Marissa got off the bus early and walked through Rathmines. All the shops were open late and there was a festive air about the place. People were smiling and laughing, wrapping paper was on sale and colourful Christmas lights brightened up the street in the faded evening light. Marissa realised she hadn't bought Amanda or Marcus their Chanukah gifts yet, so she found gifts and decided to pay them a visit and drop them in on her way home. She bought flowers for Naomi and books for Helena, Leonard and her Uncle Lou. Chanukah was usually a much more jovial affair in their house than at her parents. She wasn't sure if Helena and Leo would still be there with the children by the time she arrived, but she had a feeling they would be, even though it was late. Helena got the door.

'Hi, Marissa! Lovely to see you – do you want to come in?'

It was always nice to see her cousins and her Aunt and Uncle, she didn't intend to stay for long, but they insisted she join them for dinner as they were just about to sit down. She had nowhere else to be, so she agreed, and there was plenty of food. Naomi laid a place setting for her at the end of the table. The candles in the menorah were practically burned down to nothing.

'Did you get your big present yet, Amanda?' asked Marissa when they had a moment alone.

'Not yet, it's the 8th day soon, so I hope I will get it then – I asked for a bicycle!' Amanda looked at her sideways. 'Are you okay? You look like something's wrong.'

'Yes, love, I'm fine.'

'No, Aunty M, I mean really, are you okay? You seem different – you'd tell me, wouldn't you?'

'Of course, Amanda, yes, I'm really okay. I'm just tired after a long day at work. I've got my work Christmas party tomorrow night, I even bought a new dress for it.'

'What's it like?' Amanda's eyes were wide, 'Are you excited?'

'It's dark red, off the shoulder, backless, strapless and very, very short. I've also got six-inch stiletto heels to go with it!'

Amanda knew when Marissa was pulling her leg. 'No way. That's totally not you.'

Marissa laughed. 'Correct, it's not me. You're good! Okay, my dress is dark red, mid-length, classic lines and I like it. I'll send you a selfie when I put it on if I remember. Okay?'

'Cool. Thanks again for the nail polish set, I love it, especially the glitter – hey, do you want me to do your nails for you?'

'Why not. Thanks! Sarah is going to do my make-up, I never thought of having my nails done to go with it.'

Marissa and her sparkly fingernails left her Uncle Lou's that night fed and watered and happy. After dinner Marissa showed Helena and Leo some of her photos from Peru, she still had them on her phone. It felt so long ago, yet the medicine woman and Ausangate were still close to her heart. Funny how she didn't have any photographs of that night, nothing on record. *Maybe it didn't actually happen at all – was it just in my mind? No, it did happen, it must have happened.* But if the woman came to her in a dream, maybe the whole thing was a dream. *It's amazing how you can fool yourself if you spend enough time trying to.* She remembered the smell of cigarettes in Miguel's car, *that* had to be real. She didn't mention any of this to them, she didn't want to tell them about Galway either. It felt better to keep it to herself, for now anyway. Two days to go.

Thursday eventually dawned with a clear orange sky, the sun was coming up later and later each day as they headed towards the shortest day of the year. Sarah invited Marissa to come back to her place to get dressed up for the party, namely so she could do her make-up and make sure she was wearing that little red dress. Marissa was so focused on finishing Noreen's workload. By some miracle, at 3pm, she closed the last file. With a huge feeling of completion and satisfaction, she brought the whole lot into Noreen's office and left it all on her desk. Marissa felt a great relief not having any work hanging over the Galway trip or over the Christmas break itself. *I'll buy Sarah a drink later to say thank you, I couldn't have done it without her.*

Noreen wasn't in that day, she had taken a personal day, but she'd be at the party later. Her office was empty. Marissa took a moment and closed Noreen's door behind her. She went behind the desk and sat in Noreen's large, fancy black office chair. She swung her weight into the back of it, and it rocked with her. Nobody else had a chair like this, it really was 'The Boss's Chair'. She spun around in it, imagining it was hers, even for a few moments. A large window surrounding Noreen's office with Venetian blinds looked into the open plan office. She regularly opened the blinds to look out at everyone else on the office floor. Marissa didn't dare open them now, just in case anyone saw her, not that they'd mind. *Is this something I really want? To be the boss lady? Upper management? I would need to take up Noreen's offer fast to get on track for it if it is. But is it for me?*

As she asked herself these questions she knew the answer. If she wanted to prove she was serious management material she realised she'd be in work for much longer hours, and she wouldn't have time for clients. Her heart fell. *Well, I don't have many clients right now, but when I'm ready to graduate, I kind of want to have my own private practice.* She imagined renting a room and working for herself as a therapist. It would be nice to have something that she built up from scratch, something that was completely hers. Barbara had been talking about doing this for ages, possibly a few of them getting together and renting a space together, that could really be fun. But only last night Uncle Leo said that a therapist wouldn't make enough money to afford to buy a house in Dublin. He wasn't belittling her, when he asked her how she was getting on in her studies she told him of her plans, his natural response was: 'It's a wonderful thing you are doing, helping other people, but it will not be enough to support you financially'. He seemed so matter of fact about it. And Noreen was too... Were they both right? Her heart didn't want to think so. She swivelled around in Noreen's chair and stood up, shook her body a little. She really would have to take this offer seriously, she really needed to think about what she wanted for her future.

She could see everyone in the office had already started to leave for the pub. *When the cat's away...* The party wasn't until 5.30pm in the hotel across the road. *They'd all be drunk by the time the party starts.* It looked like the party has already started. What was she still doing here? She left Noreen's office, closing the door, got her coat and went to find Sarah.

'Hey. Everyone's already trickling out to the pub. Should we go now too? I left the finished work on Noreen's desk. Thank goodness we got it all done, I owe you for that big time. Are you ready to go?'

'No probs, seriously, girls help girls out. You would do it for me too.' She smiled and raised an eyebrow. 'Now to the real business. Let's get the heck outta here!'

Sarah lived in a flat over a shop just a few streets away. Marissa didn't remember the last time she'd been there, it was possibly a year ago? As they walked, she enjoyed listening to Sarah's chatter. Sarah unlocked her paint speckled door and they went through the narrow corridor and up the stairs into her tiny apartment. It was newer than Marissa's place and much brighter. The landlord had refurbished it two years ago when the new building regulations for apartments came in, because he had to, not because he wanted to. As bright and clean as it was, Marissa much preferred her own much more spacious, unfashionable, old garden flat.

'Come in, come in!' Sarah was smiling, obviously delighted to have a visitor. Her place was spotless, everything was neat and put away, the complete opposite of Marissa's expectations after seeing how messy her side of the room was in Peru.

'I knew you were coming,' she winked, 'so I tidied up a little. Let's have an aperitif and then do make-up and get changed.'

Sarah went into her kitchenette and came out with a bottle of vodka, two glasses and some orange juice. She poured two large ones and gave one to Marissa.

'To happy times!'

'Happy times!' Clink! 'Hey, thanks for being such a good friend, Sarah.'

They drank.

'Hey, It's my pleasure.'

'I know I've been a bit of a drag lately, well, looking back, probably ever since you met me, I've been a moody so and so.' She took another swig from her glass. 'But I feel different now, like something that was stuck is moving, or gone. I feel a lot happier now.'

'Aww, Marissa, I'm glad for you. It's about bloody time, though, but I'm glad for you. And I lurve your sparkly nails!'

'Amanda did them,' said Marissa while Sarah ushered her into the bathroom, there was a vanity mirror and make-up laid out on the counter.

'Well she has good taste. Hmmm, now will you let me do what I want with your face tonight? Proof that I'm such a good friend?'

'Ha ha, okay. Go on then.'

'And I haven't forgotten your promise to dance with Tim.'

'Jeez. He's so tall... Did he really say he fancied me?'

'Ahh yeah, kind of. Yeah. Maybe. Well, he definitely will want to after I finish with you!'

The vodka was beginning to loosen Marissa up. 'Yeah, go on then, do your worst!'

Sarah went to work with her brushes and powders, stopping only to refill both glasses with a second vodka and orange. Marissa was getting a little tipsy as she had worked through lunch and had forgotten to eat.

'Now, take a look – what do you think?'

Well, it still was most definitely Marissa, but she looked different. Older perhaps? She wasn't sure if she liked the deep red lipstick, the blush and the eye shadow was darker than what she was used to too. 'It's nice?'

'Nice? You're gorgeous! Silly girl. I like it, and Tim will love it. Go put on your dress, and I'll do me.'

While Sarah did her own make-up, Marissa carefully took off her clothes so as not to smudge hers, and put the dress on. She stepped into her new shoes, they were a little tight. Sarah walked in, expertly made-up.

'Wow. You look fantastic. Here – hang on.' She went to a small dresser drawer at the top of a cabinet in her room and pulled out the hairband with the flowers entwined in it, and proceeded to place it into Marissa's tangle of dark brown curls.

'Let me... yes, that's it. Perfect. Go on – look in the mirror, I've got a full length behind the wardrobe drawer – yes, that's the one.'

Marissa looked at her reflection in the mirror, it really didn't look like the Marissa she saw in her head. She looked good, the hairband really added to the overall effect, she never would have... *Well, that's the whole point, wasn't it?* She smiled.

'You like?' Sarah was putting on her sparkly top and one of her new skirts.

'Yeah, I like. Wow. Is that really me? Thank you.'

'Almost ready now. Do you want another drink before we go?'

'Ahh, I think two is enough before food, and I didn't have any lunch.'

Sarah was fixing her hair in the mirror. Marissa was suddenly overcome with emotion, she went over to Sarah and gave her a hug.

'You *are* a good friend, Sarah. I think Peru changed my life and I wouldn't have gone if you didn't ask me. Thank you for all this, too.' She spread her arms out and did a twirl.

'Look, you've had a shit few years, but it's over now, it's time to live, to have some fun. To meet a new man, maybe.'

'Actually, I am planning some fun, and I'm doing some new things,' said Marissa. 'I'm going to Galway tomorrow for the Solstice, I'm doing shamanic training. Because of Peru.' She put on a funny voice and said, 'I'm a medicine woman in the making!' She took a bow.

Sarah laughed. 'Well I never. You kept that one a secret from me! You never did tell me where you disappeared to on our last night over there, don't think I didn't notice.' Marissa blushed.

'I went with Miguel, he took me to meet a medicine woman, and she told me that I could be one too. I met my mountain that night, too, the one that was pulling me. It was amazing. I sometimes wonder if I made the whole thing up. But I was really gone that night, wasn't I? So it must have really happened then. I didn't tell anyone yet about the training this weekend, about Galway, only you, you're the only one.'

She hugged Sarah again. 'I guess someone should know what I'm doing in case I end up dead and nobody knows where I am!'

'Oh dear, well yes, I suppose, just as well somebody knows, so. But I think you might be drunk already. Let's get to the party and get some food into ya.'

Without missing a beat, Marissa said, 'Sarah? That Ralph was a bastard. He should have told you he was married or left you alone. Such a mean thing to do. I really, really hope you find someone who treats you properly.'

'Yes, he was a bastard wasn't he. And so do I. Look at us, it's not like me to be the sensible one!! Let's go.'

By the time they got to the hotel Marissa's feet were so sore from her new shoes that she had almost sobered up. The hotel was decked out for Christmas, there was an 8ft tall Christmas tree in the lobby, tinsel and lights wound around the bannisters and the walls, and Christmas music playing in the PA system. There was a sign with several company names listed on it beside the stairs indicating their room for the evening.

'Ooh, we have to share,' said Marissa peering at the sign and wishing she could ditch her shoes already.

'This could be interesting,' Sarah added, raising an eyebrow. 'I wonder if there will be any eligible bachelors.'

They found the room they were meant to be in, and there was nobody at the door to take their names so they just walked in. The room was already full, there was a throng of people at the bar, and at first glance they couldn't see anyone they knew.

'Jeez, we are swamped out of it,' Sarah said. 'How will we ever get served at that bar? And where's our gang? Oh look, there are three tables with our name on it over there!'

Marissa and Sarah found two spaces at one of the tables reserved for their company and sat down. Marissa kicked her shoes off under the table and rubbed her feet together. 'Ahh, that's better. I should have worn tights or something. It hurts!'

'Ah hate that. Lemme get you a drink, hey? What do you want, another vodka?'

'Great, thanks, Sarah, see you in about an hour so!'

'I won't be waiting that long, sure I have my ways.' Sarah smiled and winked at Marissa and went off to fight her way through the crowd.

There were bread rolls and butter on the table. Marissa took one, spread butter onto it and ate it in three bites. She looked around for Sarah, who was almost at the front of the queue at the bar, chatting away to the people around her, looking radiant in her sparkly top. Marissa knew that she wouldn't tell anyone her 'secret'. She really was a good friend.

Marissa decided she had to make an effort and say hello, so she attempted to put her shoes back on (she got them on after two tries – ouch, but it had to be done). She hobbled over to Sarah and was handed another vodka, and Sarah introduced her to three new friends she made at the bar from the other companies. They chatted to them for a while and then found their own people who had indeed been drinking all afternoon, so they were in very jolly Christmas spirits.

Noreen showed up just before dinner was served. Thankfully she sat at the other table so Marissa didn't feel on the spot about the management offer. Not that Noreen would have done that, she was very good about sticking to her word, when she said she'd give her time, she would do it. Marissa waved across the tables to her as she was served a huge plate of turkey and ham, mash potatoes, cabbage and Brussels sprouts. Marissa didn't eat pig, a vestige of being brought up Jewish, so she left the ham and ate most of the rest of it, leaving just a few sprouts on the plate.

There was something comforting about a big plate of Irish hotel-cooked Christmas dinner. The food balanced out the vodka and put Marissa on a more even keel. Her belly was a little swollen now, and heavy, but she was much more relaxed, and she really wasn't worried about impressing anyone so it didn't bother her. The hotel staff were clearing the tables and bringing out plates of Christmas Pudding and traditional Christmas cake, and large steaming pots of tea and coffee. Marissa felt too full to eat anything more. Tim had been sitting across the way from her, they had made small conversation during the dinner which was fine, but after the main course he moved chairs and came and sat down beside her. Marissa withdrew a little, she felt slightly cornered. As he leaned in to make small talk she could feel the anxiety starting to build inside her. He whispered, 'Sarah did a favour for me last week and in exchange, she told me that I had to dance with you, but I have a confession to make. I already have a girlfriend.'

Marissa was suddenly relieved, butterflies immediately breathed out. She relaxed and replied, 'That's cool with me, but it looks like we still have to dance together to appease Sarah. Then we are both off the hook – what do you think?'

Tim looked visibly relieved also, he smiled and nodded his head. The music was a playlist of 1980's songs, infectiously catchy, and after they took away all the plates Marissa felt like taking off her shoes and dancing. Tim was a surprisingly great dancer for someone who looked like they were all arms and legs. Once they had their dance together, making sure that Sarah noticed them, they stayed together in a group of work friends, enjoying the freedom of the music, enjoying not having to impress anyone. Tim winked at Marissa and she laughed. Sarah saw it and was delighted, which made both Tim and Marissa laugh even louder.

Sarah felt her work was done and sought a new partner for herself amongst the other companies there. Marissa switched to drinking water for the rest of the night and she danced until the music ended, at midnight. Some of the others wanted to go on to a club, but she had a train to catch in the morning so she pushed her feet back into the dreaded shoes and managed to grab a taxi home.

She let herself into her apartment, threw the coat on the back of the door and sat on the couch, in her dress, shoes kicked off (never to be worn again) and dirty feet, and she was happy. She was feeling sticky from dancing, her make-up seemed like a coating of paint on her face. She really wanted to get up and wash but it was so peaceful in her flat after the loud music and the banter, and all the drink, she was enjoying the stillness. The moonlight came through her little window over the sink and glinted off the angel ornament on her tree, just as it had done on the previous night. The angel seemed to be looking directly at her, so she looked back directly at it. 'When will I ever meet an angel?' she said out loud, addressing the angel on her tree. She suddenly became formal, stood up, cleared her throat and addressed the angel in her Christmas Tree.

'I'm asking. Please, can I meet an angel?'

In almost the same moment, Marissa felt a sudden whoosh of energy, her knees went weak, she lost her balance and fell backwards into the sofa. She couldn't see a bright light in the room, or a large being, which was what she imagined an angel might look like, but she felt something big, right there, right beside her that definitely wasn't there before.

Marissa wasn't afraid. She took a minute to tune into it so she could feel it better and perhaps understand what was going on. She was definitely sober now. To all intents and purposes, her room was exactly the same, but the energy there felt totally different. Marissa felt strong energies rushing through her body, lifting and moving; it was as if her body switched itself on and came alive. She felt swirling in her stomach, then her heart burst open like a flower blossoming, all of the grief that she didn't know was still in there suddenly flew out of it, leaving her with a great sense of peace. She felt light and heavy at the same time. She was both cold and hot. She closed her eyes and let go of her thoughts so she could really feel it, feel everything. Then softly, gently, she had a sense of something withdrawing from her, pulling back, then leaving altogether. The presence was gone. She opened her eyes and noticed a feather on her left knee, it was only a small one, from one of the cushions perhaps? She picked it up and looked at it.

They say angels leave feathers behind. She shook her head, like a dog shakes its body when it's wet. *Was that an angel? It must have been an angel. It was so big, so powerful, yet so gentle. And the feather – yes, it must be a real, genuine angel!*

Marissa let it sink in, she wasn't able to describe how she felt – she had never felt like this before. She heard a word in her mind, 'elated'. She had never used that word before, but yes, that was the word. Elated. Blissful. She felt herself come back into the room, more present to herself and more present to her body. Energised, she went into the bathroom, ran a hot shower, peeled off her dress, extracted the hairband from her hair, and got in. She washed off the night, washed off her make-up, washed her body and her feet. Warm and dry in fresh pyjamas, she fell into bed. Once she wrapped the covers around herself, she fell asleep straight away.

CHAPTER SEVENTEEN 

Marissa woke up from a deep and nourishing sleep and looked at her clock. She had forgotten to set the alarm, but the time was 7:20am, ten minutes before the time she would have set it for anyway, so she was on time. She was dehydrated from all the vodka, her mouth felt like a forest was growing in there. Even though she had been drinking pints of water, her body wasn't used to that much alcohol. She got up and put the kettle on and fell back into the bed. Tobermory came over and sat on her legs.

'Hello, sweetheart. I'll be away for a few days, I'll miss you.' She stroked his fur and he started to purr. 'Michelle from upstairs will pop in and feed you, you'll be grand.'

Tobermory mewed in response, shook off her hand and jumped off the bed. He padded into the kitchen and sat by the door, wanting to go out. She got up again, opened the door to let him out and made some tea.

Once she felt more awake, Marissa laid out the clothes she wanted to bring to the workshop on the bed. Two pairs of jeans, a jumper, a raincoat, several tops, slippers, underwear, pyjamas, an oversize cardigan and her wash bag. She wasn't sure which would be better, wellingtons or walking boots. It had been dry, so the boots went into the pile. Her feet were still sore from the night before so she found some plasters and heavy socks to keep them protected. Séamus was mysterious about what was planned for the few days away, and she really wasn't sure what to bring. All she did know was that they'd be away for three nights, and they needed to meet at the main street in Clifden later that day, at 2pm. She had to get a train to Galway, then catch a bus that left Galway City Centre at 12:15 to get there, with a little time to spare. Marissa found a wind-up torch that she had been given by her father several years ago when she was going on a camping trip and thought she would bring that with her, just in case.

It's a pity I don't have a drum. I really wanted one. She chose some clothes from the bed to wear, then packed everything else into a small backpack. She watered her plants, locked up her flat, pet Tobermory one more time, then stepped outside. The taxi she had ordered the day before was already there, waiting for her.

There was no traffic. She got out and paid the driver, then the rain started. Marissa found the platform for the 8:55am to Galway and chose a window seat. She put her bag on the shelf above and looked out the window as the train pulled out of the station. She watched the changes in scenery as the train went through Dublin, out to the suburbs and into the country. Raindrops ran down the window pane, slanting down faster as the train gained speed. Marissa started to wish she had brought her wellies instead of the walking boots.

Maybe I can pick up a pair in Galway before I get the bus... I'll probably be the only one there without a drum. The more she thought about it, the more agitated she became. *Why do I let my thoughts get the better of me? And I didn't bring my cards for support, oh dear! I should have brought them, I don't know what I'm going to be getting myself into. This is off to a bad start. I was so sure this was the right thing to do. Maybe I was wrong. Maybe I shouldn't go. I can just take the next train back to Dublin.*

Marissa felt her thoughts twisting around in her mind as if she was binding herself in a straitjacket. She felt tight and trapped and the anxiety rose quickly. She realised she was working herself into a panic attack. *I have to breathe, I have to stop thinking.* But it was too late, it was as if the rollercoaster ride that her mind was bringing her on was going out of control. She wrung her hands together and started to rock in her chair. She felt like she was drowning, like she was losing control. 'Help me,' she said in a small voice inside her mind. It was almost as if her voice was being taken from her, even in her mind.

A large presence swept in and surrounded her, and suddenly she felt her heart lift. *Oh, oh, it's the angel from last night – he heard me, oh my goodness! Thank you! Thank you.*

She felt something unwind in her mind, she felt a snap as if the angel had cut thick ribbons that had been tying her up in knots. She felt herself coming back to herself again.

What the heck was going on? It came on so quickly, she was so grateful for the angelic intervention.

'You called me. I am here.' Marissa heard a voice inside her, it was of a different texture than her own. It seemed to be coming from her left side, her left ear, as if the angel was sitting beside her on the left-hand side.

How do I speak to you? How do I call you? Who are you? I have so many questions. Marissa felt much calmer now. She looked around the train carriage at the people reading their phones, listening to music, some were asleep. And she was talking to an angel. It felt strange but wonderful.

I just call you? Do you have a name? Marissa saw a picture appear in her mind, it was of Michael Landon from *Highway to Heaven*, she loved that TV show, she used to watch it when she was little. *He was an angel – I remember now! Are you called Michael, too?*

She felt a full-body yes, ripples of light and prickles of electricity that made every hair stand on end raced through her body and then it was gone. *Michael. Okay then. Hello Michael, it's nice to meet you. And thanks for coming last night! That was you too, wasn't it?*

Again she felt a 'Yes', but it was a little softer this time.

She didn't want to be pestering an angel, so she just sat for a while, enjoying the feeling of the presence of the angel around her. She wondered if it, if he, had wings, like many of the pictures she had seen of angels. What was an angel anyway? Her breathing had calmed down. The train stopped at Athlone station, 1 hour to Galway central.

'Music'

She was sure she heard that clearly, but what did it mean? She got her phone out of her bag and plugged her headphones into it, but what music was she to choose? This was quite confusing, however, she was relieved she wasn't having a panic attack. *Maybe the music is meant to distract me for the rest of the journey so the anxiety won't come back?* She flipped through her music playlists and found one she liked and pressed play. The rain had stopped, she felt much better, the sense of the angelic being beside her gradually faded as she listened to the music.

An hour passed. The train slowed down as it approached Galway station. Everyone was getting up from their seats and getting their bags down from the shelf. Marissa decided she'd wait until the rush had dissipated. She didn't need any more anxiety just now.

She had about forty minutes before the bus to Clifden was due to leave, so she went for a walk into Eyre Square to see if she could find some Wellington boots. She hefted her backpack over her shoulder, the weight of it was reassuring, somehow grounding. She didn't know where she was going, but she thought she was bound to find a shoe shop somewhere. *Galway is a small enough town, sure I won't get lost.*

She found herself standing in front of a music shop window. There was a wonderful display of various musical instruments, sheets of music and Christmas decorations. Her eye was drawn to the back of the display where she saw some bodhrans. Many of them were beautifully decorated with colourful Celtic knots and designs on them. She peered into the window and realised they would make great Shamanic drums. She entered the shop to be greeted by a pleasant looking, long-haired man, possibly in his late sixties, wearing an Aran jumper and a pair of well-worn jeans.

'Hello there! How can I help you today?'

'I'm looking for a drum. I saw some in the window that looked ideal. Can I see what you have?'

'Certainly. Come this way.' He led her to the back of the shop where there was a large counter. 'Anything in particular?'

'I'm looking for a drum you can hold in your hand and beat, not too big though, but it can be loud, if I need it to be loud. I think I'll know it when I see it. It's for a Shamanic workshop.'

'Ahh, a Shaman's Drum. I don't get asked for many of those, but I do have a few upstairs. I'll get them. I'll be a minute or two.'

Marissa looked at her watch, she didn't have lots of time but she felt the calmness from the train, she wondered if the angel was still with her, would he help her choose her drum? Then she remembered the angel saying 'music' to her – did he mean this? The music shop?

The shop owner came back with a selection of four drums under his arms. 'I've only got these four at the moment. Maybe one of them will be what you're looking for?'

He laid them all down on the countertop. Three of them were painted, one had a Celtic Spiral in black, the largest one had the face of a stag in brown, and the smallest one had a Celtic cross, again in black. Before Marissa could get overwhelmed or agitated about which one to choose, she remembered a scene from *Star Wars*, where Luke was told to 'Use the Force'. She decided to see which drum felt like it was the one for her rather than to think about which drum would be the most suitable.

He pulled out a beater. 'Try them all and see which one you like best.'

She hesitated, then went for the smallest drum, with the spiral on it. She held it in her left hand, took the beater in her right hand and closed her eyes, and banged the beater off the drum. The sound felt tight and high pitched, without any depth to it. She knew right away that wasn't her drum, it didn't sound right to her at all. She put it back down gently and chose another, this one was wider than the first and slightly larger. Marissa did the same thing again, closing her eyes, banging the beater off of the skin of the drum. That sounded better. There was a depth to the sound from it, a resonance. The drum felt solid in her hand.

She did this for all the drums but she kept coming back to the second one with no painting. She tried it again. The tone of the note from the drum when she beat it felt right to her. *Yes. This is the one.*

'I like this one,' she said. 'How much is it?'

'This one is from America – it's buffalo skin. The rest of them are deer skin, interesting that you choose this one.' He showed her the price tag which stretched her budget just a little bit. She knew that she had to have it.

Marissa looked at the drum in more detail. It had the brand name written on it in small writing, it looked well made, thicker than the bodhrans, and not too heavy in her hand. 'Yes, yes, I'll take it. Thanks.'

'This is a very good drum, it won't shrink in the cold, and it will handle a bit of rain, not too much though! And it has its own beater too. I'll have to go find it, give me a few minutes.'

The shop owner took his beater back from Marissa, picked up the other drums and disappeared upstairs.

Marissa held her new drum in her hands. She turned it around and tapped the skin with her fingers. 'Rummadumdum,' it said to her. She smiled. 'Hello to you too,' she said, back to the drum. It felt right.

The man came back with a beater for her, a brown stick with a black cloth head stuffed with soft material. 'I don't have a pouch for the drum, I'm afraid, you'll have to use a bag from the shop.'

'That's fine,' said Marissa as they walked to the front of the shop to the cash register. She handed him her bank card.

The shopkeeper put the sale through. 'That drum has been sitting upstairs for several years. Most people prefer the painted drums.'

Marissa smiled and her heart swelled with excitement as the man found a plastic bag the right shape to fit her drum into. He slid the beater into the back of the drum behind the strings and placed them both carefully into the bag, with little room to spare.

'I think the drum must have been waiting for me. I'm getting less and less surprised at the amazing things that happen when you're on a spiritual journey. Thank you so much for minding it for me, I will take good care of it.' Marissa said, taking the receipt and putting her bank card back into her wallet.

'Be careful what you wish for – you could be asking for trouble!' he said to Marissa and winked at her. 'Use her in good health.'

'I will! Thanks again,' said Marissa, wondering what he meant by that.

Walking back out onto the street, Marissa felt like she had been gone for over an hour but it had only been twenty minutes. It started raining again. She checked the time on her phone and saw a message from Amanda, just saying hello. She texted hello back and a love heart emoji and got a love heart emoji in return. She still had twenty minutes before the bus was due, enough time to find a pair of wellies, perhaps?

She thought she heard someone shouting her name, she turned around, and there was Terry. 'Hey, fancy meeting you here!'

'Hi, Terry!'

'Well, look at that, you bought a drum, yes?'

'Yes! I need wellies now too, then I'm ready for our weekend.'

'Ahh, famous last words being ready, I don't know if any of us are really ready.' Terry winked at her.

Marissa decided that he was okay after all, perhaps he had been messing with her when he said he was sad for her.

'Hey, I've got my car, I'm driving to Clifden. Do you want a lift?'

She thought for a moment. *Why not – amazing things do happen when you're on a spiritual journey... Sure didn't I just say that a moment ago? I have to say yes now.* 'Oh yes, please. That would be fantastic! Can you wait for me to get my wellies first?'

'Sure. I was going to have some food, do you want to join me for lunch? Then we can get your wellies and get on the road.'

'Thank you, that would be great!'

'I know a little café just around the corner.' They walked for a few moments together. 'There it is! Let's go in here, the coffee is great, do you like coffee?'

'I love coffee.'

'So we could be friends then. Good. I'm very fussy about who I am friends with, and they *have* to like coffee!'

Terry led Marissa into a steamy café. They shook the rain off their coats and hung them up on the coat rack by the door. Marissa positioned her backpack on the floor in between the chairs at their table. She sat down, placing the drum bag at her feet between her legs, so she could squeeze her knees together and be reassured by its presence. The waitress brought the menu, they glanced at it quickly and ordered straight away.

'Chips and egg and a Cappuccino for me, please,' said Terry to the waitress.

'Melted cheese on toast and an Americano, please,' said Marissa gratefully.

Terry cocked his head towards Marissa as soon as the waitress had left. 'I'm having a *Shirley Valentine* moment.'

Marissa looked puzzled.

'*Shirley Valentine*? Chips and egg, not eggs and chips... Oh, don't worry, lovey, about what that means, I'm just a little scattered today. I guess I'm nervous about the weekend. I've no idea what Séamus is going to do with us. I only met him once before. How about you?'

'I went to his 'Introduction to Shamanism' day last month, or was it the month before last?' Marissa started counting on her fingers, then gave up. 'I can't remember. It feels so long ago, yet it seems just like yesterday. Time is doing funny things to my head. Anyway, I liked him, I thought he was really interesting.'

'Oh yes, he is very interesting for sure.'

The waitress brought the coffees. Terry went on. 'I just love his hat. I've been watching him on YouTube and reading his writings on his blog for a while now. I saw him at a ceremony at the Mind Body Spirit Fair in the RDS. He opened the fair and gave a talk about Shamanic Journeys. I went up to him afterwards and talked to him for ages. He asked me personally to come to this, I was so surprised. I've not done a workshop with him before. It's exciting! Everyone at the 'getting to know you' afternoon seemed very nice, it could be so fun. Or it could be a disaster. I guess we have to wait and see...'

The waitress brought the food.

'That was quick! If only the Dublin cafés were so quick! Anyway...' Terry dipped a chip into the yolk of his fried egg, 'What brings you to Séamus? Why are you here? What are you looking for? Oh yes, you're the psychologist, aren't you! I've forgotten who everyone is. But I remember you – psychology scares me. Are you going to analyse me?'

Marissa laughed. 'No, it doesn't work like that, anyway, I'm here to learn shamanism, not to work on you or anyone else. Psychotherapy is what I am studying, it's different to psychology. It's more practical, working one to one with people, it's therapeutic, not analytic.' She took a bite of her melted cheese, it was very hot.

'Interesting.' said Terry. 'I'm actually relieved. I don't fancy being analysed. I'm sure there's lots wrong with me that someone else might say that I need to fix. I know my family would love to have me analysed.'

He had almost finished the food on his plate. Marissa wondered how he could talk so much and eat so fast at the same time. She had barely started into hers.

'Take your time, dear, it's fine by me.' Terry sat back in his chair and looked at the people at the other tables. 'Ooh, look at her, over there. I'll bet she's a difficult person to be around.'

Marissa tried to refrain from looking, she focused on eating but managed to stifle a giggle.

'You never said – what do you think about Séamus?'

Marissa wasn't sure yet. She didn't think she wanted to say so early either. 'I like him well enough so far,' she said, hoping that was a neutral enough response. She finished her cheesy toast and drank down her coffee.

'I'm going to reserve judgement for later, or possibly not judge at all.' She looked at the clock on her phone. 'Shall we go? We have to be there for 2, it's nearly 12:30.'

'Oh yes, we should go, we can't be late for our first day.'

They went to the cash desk, Marissa hefted her backpack back over her shoulder and balanced her drum in her arms while she pulled out her wallet to pay. 'Let me get this, as you're going to be driving us both.'

'Why, thank you! If you insist!'

As Marissa paid she asked the woman at the cash desk, 'Where would I get a pair of wellies?'

'There's a shoe shop just up the road from here, and another one in the shopping centre. They both should have wellies, it has been raining a lot these past few weeks. Yes, I think the one up the road did have them in the last time I was there, just the other day.' The woman smiled as she handed Marissa her change.

'That's great, thank you so much.'

Marissa had to take her backpack off again to put on her still-wet coat, then she and Terry went out in the rain. It wasn't as heavy as it had been earlier. Terry led the way, looking in every window commenting on something or other that struck him at the time. They got to the shoe shop and Terry wouldn't go inside. He suggested instead that he'd look after Marissa's bags if she wanted to 'save herself lugging them around', so she took him up on it. She got herself a pair of army green wellies and then he led her to where his car was parked. It was a small blue Toyota, and it looked well used, and well lived-in.

'It's my sister's car, I robbed it on her, I think half of this stuff belongs to her. Here –' He opened the boot but it was packed full of bags of various shapes and sizes, some open and spilling out. 'Oh dear. Never mind! You'll have to put your bags in the back seat.'

He pushed the bags tightly back in under the lid and closed the boot. Marissa opened up the back door then Terry came over and moved a few things around to make some room. *No wonder he feels scattered, it looks like he has the contents of a whole wardrobe in there.*

Terry went to the passenger seat, opened the door, then climbed inside. 'Hang on a tick,' he said, and he threw a few things from the front into the back.

In the meantime, Marissa found some space to squeeze her backpack in behind the passenger seat. She carefully placed her new drum on the back seat beside it. Managing to close the door, she deftly climbed into the passenger seat in the front.

Terry settled himself into the driver's seat. 'Sorted?'

'Yes, thank you. And thanks again for the lift.'

He turned the key and the radio blasted loudly as the car engine thrummed into life. He quickly turned the radio down, looked, then indicated and pulled out of the space. He took the main road out of the city. 'Well, Clifden, here we come!'

The car was nifty and fast, even though it was laden down and felt low to the ground. They made quick time to Clifden, and by the time they parked, they were five minutes early. During the drive, Terry had told Marissa all about his family, his sister, and some funny stories about growing up in Cork. It was still raining but only drizzling lightly.

'Where did he say to meet on Main Street?' asked Terry. 'This street is very long!'

'I have a feeling we'll find it,' said Marissa, 'Let's go outside and look for them.'

They both got out of the car, put their raincoats on and walked towards an obelisk in the middle of a roundabout.

'This isn't the Main Street,' said Terry, looking at his phone at Google Maps.

'Hey, look, there's Liz!' said Marissa, waving. Liz waved back. They both crossed the street to meet her.

'Hi! I thought I was lost,' said Liz, 'I'm so relieved to see you guys! Oh, look – there's Séamus!'

They all turned to see Séamus walking across the road to where they were. With him were Zaad, Stephanie, Jenny and two other people they didn't know. At that moment, the rain eased off and the sun came out, filling the sky with a beautiful light that glinted off the shop windows. A faint rainbow appeared, just at the end of the road. *Magical!*

'Hello, hello, how are yiz! It's great to see yiz all!' Séamus said. He was in an oversize raincoat, his hat kept the rain off his face. 'Are we all here?' he pulled out a list from his inside pocket. 'Stephanie, Zaad, Jenny, Terry, Liz, Marissa, meet Saoirse and Finn. We're all here. Grand stuff.'

They all nodded to each other, saying hello. Zaad held out his hand to Finn, and it was shaken enthusiastically.

'Now, lads, we're not staying in Clifden Town. I know I've been very mysterious. We'll be heading out to a magical place called The Monastery. Off the beaten track a bit, someplace really special, I know you'll love it. It's just down the road from here. It's walled, secluded, private, and there's no shops – and no escape! So yiz'll be trapped with me for the next few days. So you'd better all go shopping now for whatever supplies you'll need. Hands up – who has a car?'

Terry, Steph and Zaad put up their hands. 'And of course there's myself, that's four cars, plenty for us all to squeeze into. Right folks please! The meals will be served to you, there's plenty of tea and coffee and the likes, all included in your stay. But if you need cigarettes or chocolate, biscuits or any other type of snack it's your call, get them or forget them. Get something for the altar too, an offering. I'll leave that up to you. I'll meet you back here in ten minutes. Any questions?'

Liz put up her hand. 'What sort of offering? What should I get?'

'A gift, for the land. Something that can degrade, that's natural. Anyone else? No? Right so, see yiz in a bit.'

Marissa bought chocolate, a packet of digestives, some jelly sweets and a six-pack of *Tayto Cheese and Onion* to cover all the basics. She found fresh flowers for her offering, she hoped they would suffice. She went back to Terry's car but he wasn't there so she leaned back against it to wait. After about five minutes he arrived with Liz, and her bags, and their shopping. *How are we all going to fit inside?* Terry unlocked the car and started rearranging things again. It took a while to organise, but they all eventually managed to squish inside.

Séamus had an old black 1984 BMW which was all the worse for wear, slightly scratched and dented. It seemed to fit his overall style and personality. He got into it with the new people, Saoirse and Finn, waved to them all out the window, then pulled out into the road. The convoy of cars followed his out of the town.

Four cars twisted and turned, following country roads. About fifteen minutes into the drive, Marissa had butterflies. *I thought he said it was just down the road?* She looked at Terry, he was concentrating avidly on keeping up. She turned and looked at Liz who seemed stiff in her body. The three of them were getting more nervous with every twist and turn in the road, not knowing when it would end or where they would end up.

After another ten minutes Terry asked, 'Is he bringing us down the rabbit's hole?' It took a moment for them to get the joke, then Liz and Marissa laughed, but nobody replied.

Séamus made a sharp turn onto a side road which brought them up a sharp, steep hill. It was so steep Terry had to put his car into first gear. There was another, sudden, sharp turn, and the road meandered for a few moments, then, thankfully, they all could see the tall, iron gates. The BMW drove through them and into the estate, and the three cars followed.

Their phones had dropped off the network about a mile earlier. Wherever they were was off the map. Liz had been trying to discern their exact location from landmarks, but they all had quickly given up trying.

'I'm glad we're following him, I'd never have found this place,' said Terry squinting and sitting up taller to better keep his eyes on the road. Marissa was feeling a little more settled, but they continued driving for another half a mile before they could see a large, grey, Edwardian house with a smaller gatehouse beside it.

'That must be it,' said Terry. 'Jeez, it's going to be cold in that place. Glad I brought my fleecy blanket with me.'

'That was a good idea, wish I thought of bringing one,' said Liz.

Séamus parked his car in front of the main house and leaned against it, waiting for them. Terry pulled his car in beside the others.

When Marissa eventually extracted herself from the car she realised how tight her body was. She stretched, leaning backwards, and caught a glance of how tall the house actually was. She straightened up, feeling the presence of the house looming beside her. It seemed very old and felt slightly menacing.

'It's not ornate enough to be Hogwarts,' said Terry quietly to Marissa. 'No gargoyles anyway. I wonder what it's like inside?'

Everyone unloaded their stuff from the cars and brought bags inside the main door. There was a bustling of activity, everyone was pleased to have finally arrived. A list pinned on the noticeboard on the main wall had their names and room allocations.

'Find your room, bring up your bags and come down to the front room in ten minutes.' Séamus pointed to a large black door that was opposite the main stairs.

Marissa stood in the hallway and took a moment to get her bearings. She looked up at the tall ceiling in the hallway, it was very plain, the paint was peeling off. *It could do with redecorating. I think Terry is right, it will be cold in here.* Then she noticed the stairs. She suddenly felt a shock run through her whole body, like electricity. She did a double-take – was it some sort of flashback? *Deja Vu?* No, it wasn't that. It was something, though. She was certain she had seen those stairs before, the way they curved up against the wall, the exact angle of the steps. *In a dream? I don't remember dreaming them. This is so weird.*

The others were already making their way to their bedrooms. Marissa looked at the list, she was sharing with Saoirse in a room on the second floor. She climbed the stairs, found the room and went in. She put her bags on the floor, not wanting to claim a bed without checking first with Saoirse, who she hadn't met yet.

Marissa walked over to the long tall window and pulled back the net curtains so she could see outside. The room faced the back of the house, they were surrounded by forest, there was a small garden beside the house, just grass, it looked more like a field, and then it just seemed to disappear into the trees. Marissa wondered if it was a natural forest or planted, there were young and old trees of mixed varieties. They were very secluded here. *If someone died here, who would find the body?* She felt a shiver ripple through her body. She pulled out her mobile phone from her bag and saw there was very poor phone coverage here, just like in the car, flickering from one to two bars, then to none. But at least there was coverage. It was already getting dark. *Well, tomorrow is the shortest day of the year.* She shivered again, but this time from the cold.

Saoirse came into the room and with her came a light breeze. She was tall, had a slender build and small round Harry Potter style glasses. She had short, light brown straight hair. When she saw Marissa she smiled, she seemed open and approachable. Marissa liked her immediately.

'Hi, I'm Marissa. I didn't pick a bed yet, I wanted to meet you first.'

'Hi. Wow, we really are in the middle of nowhere here.' Saoirse walked over and stood by Marissa, looking out into the forest. She smelled like a familiar floral perfume. 'You can leave the curtains open, I guess, we are so high up, it's not as if anyone is going to look inside. I prefer it brighter.'

Saoirse turned to Marissa and said 'Nice to meet you, Marissa. I missed the 'getting to know you' afternoon, it feels like I'm intruding a little bit.'

'Oh, no, not at all, we haven't really spent time together as a group, just a few hours. I'm sure we'll all catch up with each other pretty quickly once we get into it.'

'You go ahead and choose a bed, I don't mind which one you take.'

'Okay, thanks!' Marissa put her backpack on the bed nearest the window and began to unpack some of her things. She sat down for a moment to get her bearings. There was a sink on the wall opposite the twin single beds with a small mirror above it. *The toilets must be shared, down the hall, what a pain. I'll look later.* She splashed water on her face to wake herself up. Looking around for a towel, she saw two bundles of folded faded cotton towels on a shelf. She reached for one from there. It felt dry and scratchy as she patted her face dry, but it would do. Maybe next time, she would bring her own towel, and a fleece blanket, too. *I should start a list on my phone for next time...* She was tired after the late night, the night before, and the long day of travel. She was glad of her oversize cardigan for wandering down cold corridors in the middle of the night to use the bathroom.

Saoirse put her bag on the other bed and said, 'I'm going to head downstairs and meet the others. See you in a few minutes.' She left the room.

Marissa moved back to her spot by the window, still holding the towel. She suddenly became aware of how much tension she was holding in her body. She slowed down her breathing and brought her awareness into her feet, but it felt like she wasn't really in her body at all. She could be in a dream. There was a quality about everything that seemed, well, otherworldly. She sighed, not really knowing what to do about it, or whether she even should do something about it. It was completely dark outside now, unlike at home in Dublin with the light pollution from the street lamps. Marissa hung the towel on the rail beside the sink, got her cardigan and drum, and went downstairs.

CHAPTER EIGHTEEN

The front room was large. It had a 12ft ceiling and a massive stone fireplace with a Connemara marble hearth. There were a few candles and an ashtray on the mantlepiece, and over it was a large portrait of a man, possibly a landlord from plantation times. The fire was blazing and lit up the room, burning a combination of peat and firewood. It looked welcoming, and it should have been hot, but it wasn't warming the room. The heat seemed to be going right back up the chimney. Old framed paintings of landscapes hung on the white wallpapered walls. The room seemed well used for workshops or community gatherings; it didn't give off the comfortable air of a family home. Three well-worn sofas surrounded the fireplace, each one had a patchwork knitted throw over it, making the room much more colourful and less formal. Terry, Stephanie and Liz were already chatting away on one sofa, Zaad was sitting by himself on the other. Marissa went over and sat down beside him.

'Hi,' she said to him.

He looked up and smiled. 'Hi.'

'How are you doing?'

'I'm a little nervous. Strange house, strange people – oh I don't mean you are strange, I just mean...'

Marissa laughed. 'Yes, I know what you mean. I feel the same. I don't really know anyone here. You could all be murderers! And this seems to be a haunted house... Which movie did we step into?'

Zaad laughed. *He has nice eyes, why am I yammering like a teenager?*

Jenny and a man Marissa didn't know came in, (*That must be Finn?*), found some room and sat down. They chatted to each other, then Séamus made his entrance.

'Well, well, well. Here we all are now! Great to see yiz all! We made it.' He walked around the sofas and stood with his back to the fire. He turned to face it and spent a moment rubbing his legs and sides as if to warm himself up. Rubbing his hands together, he turned back to the group, smiled and began.

'Now. We have a mad-capped, mad-packed few days ahead. We'll be very busy, so you'd better keep your eyes and mind open so you don't miss anything. Welcome to The Monastery. You will get to know this place and these grounds well, for we will be doing most of our workings here.'

He hunkered down, caught the eyes of the group and winked while he whispered, 'It's haunted.' He looked up at the group to get their reaction, which was appropriately freaked out. Marissa felt a shiver go down her spine, then she noticed Zaad looking straight at her with a bewildered look on his face.

Séamus laughed and stood straight and tall again. 'I may be joking, but I'm also serious. Please don't upset the resident Spirits. I will share more about that later.' He rubbed his hands together. 'Now, lads, first the practicalities. Toilets, kitchen and fire escapes. We have them all.'

The group laughed and relaxed a little bit. Just a little.

'I would prefer if you keep your phones in your bedrooms, no photographs on social media, this is a sacred space, on sacred grounds. That's what I mean – so please don't 'check in' on Facebook, tag each other or even say that you are here. We don't need the interference as we have work to do.'

Terry reached for his phone.

'You can delete it later.'

Terry put his phone back into his pocket.

'We'll be having a solstice ceremony tomorrow morning at sunrise which is at 8.34am. And I want you to experience it, so no photographs and no phones there also.'

'Now! I want yiz all to meet Finn and Saoirse,' he nodded to each of them, and they both smiled at the group. 'They'll be joining us for this weekend and then deciding if they wish to continue. As are each of you – free to go, yes, any of ye can drop out at any time, but if you miss a workshop then you can't necessarily re-join us, unless there are extenuating circumstances.'

'Now to more pressing matters. The food is cooked by Mrs Mahon, who lives in the gatehouse. She leaves our meals in the dining hall, it's a serve-yourself affair as we often work past their usual mealtimes. Better yet, we have the place all to ourselves, so it can sit there until we are ready for it. Breakfast is at 7:30, lunch at 12, and dinner is at 6pm, however, *our* session times are not set – each day will be different, so pay attention. That is the shamanic way. Be with what actually is, not what you think it is. Keeps me young. And the meals will wait for us.' He looked at his watch, 'It's almost 6. So let's have dinner, then we start our first official session at 7.30pm sharp. See you back here soon.'

Marissa had been looking at the group as Séamus was talking. Stephanie had her notebook out and seemed to be writing everything down. *He hasn't even started teaching yet?* Finn looked distracted, Zaad beside her seemed very tense, Terry looked like he was at a holiday camp and Liz, Saoirse and Jenny were paying avid attention to every word. *This is the group, they seem a nice bunch of people. I'm sure it will be okay. No murderers here.*

Dinner was still being prepared, so Marissa went up to find the toilets (basic) and shower (very basic) then back to her room. She took a moment and lay down on the bed, shutting her eyes. She was beginning to feel a little dizzy, she wasn't sure why. Perhaps it was dehydration, she had drunk an awful lot more than she was used to last night. Or perhaps it was fear of what was to come.

'Aren't you coming down for dinner? It's practically gone. I saved you a plate, I left it in the kitchen for you.' Saoirse was kneeling down, tapping Marissa on the shoulder.

'Oh! What time is it? I must have fallen asleep – thank you!' Marissa stretched and rubbed her eyes.

'You okay?'

'Yeah, we had our work Christmas Party last night, I guess I was just catching up with myself.'

Saoirse smiled. 'Ahh, that makes sense! I hope it's not too cold. Your dinner, I mean!'

After Marissa quickly wolfed down a plate of almost cold lasagne she brought a cup of tea into the front room where the others had gathered. Séamus was there, sitting by the fire, laughing and joking with the rest of the group. It felt very relaxed, the room had finally warmed up and the fire was burning a warm glow. Séamus had made an altar in the middle of the floor out of a small rug. He had placed a large quartz crystal upon it. Beside it were fresh flowers, similar to those that Marissa had bought in Clifden, a candle, and a rattle. He stood up, placed another log on the fire, then turned to the group to begin the session. The room quietened as he began to speak.

'Let's open sacred space. Everyone stand.'

They stood up, placing notebooks, blankets and cushions down as they turned, with Séamus, to honour and invite the Four Directions to join them in the room. Just as he did in the previous workshop, at each direction he recited a verse to honour that direction. Marissa listened with a wide-open heart, each word he spoke seemed to form a deep connection with her soul. Séamus then invited Mother Earth and Father Sky to hold space for them, to sit and watch over them all for the weekend. He lit the large pillar candle on the altar cloth and sat down.

'We are blessed to begin this work on the Winter Solstice. It is a time of deep reflection, the shortening of the days, going into hibernation, into darkness. The dark time is necessary for growth, it is a gestation. Not to be dreaded or feared, as we can come out the other end of it wiser if we set our intention to do so.' He took a breath and changed his tone of voice.

'We will journey now to find out what it is that we need to know for the coming weekend, and perhaps for the winter months. You've all gone on a journey with me before, but as I said to you in the email, I require a beginner's mind, you must see it all as fresh and new. We begin again. Some of you have drums, some of you don't, you can bring your drum to the solstice ceremony tomorrow at daybreak. For now, just listen to mine, and travel. We will set our intention as a group to journey to the heart of hearts, to the Shamanic Lower World, to ask 'What do I need to know now?' Stay seated, close your eyes, listen and observe, do not interact, do not interfere. And, we fly.

The soft beat of Séamus's drum connected to the rhythms of the heartbeat of the world, lub dub, lub dub, brought them downwards into the luscious forest landscape. Marissa felt herself easily dissolving with his words, shifting out of her mind and into a space of pure light and images, vibration and feeling.

Down through the rock and stone her awareness went, down through the many layers of the Earth's mantle, until she reached the centre of the earth, the Shamanic Lower world. It was cool and crisp, a rainforest with hanging vines, large fronds and lush vegetation. She remembered being here before. A large snake slithered up to her and stared at her for what seemed to be the longest time. It was yellow with a black mottled pattern, it could have been 20ft long for all she knew, yet she wasn't afraid. Eventually, it spoke.

'I am Sachemama, grandchild of Sachamama, the greatest medicine snake of all the worlds. And who are you?'

Marissa bowed. 'I am Marissa, medicine woman in the making.'

The snake laughed, a big, hearty laugh that did not seem to come from such a cold and reptilian body.

'You call yourself a medicine woman? No, you are not that. Not by a long shot. You have much to learn, child. I am more than 500 years old and even I do not call myself a medicine snake, for it is up to the forest dwellers to recognise me and know whether I am of use to them or not.'

'I apologise. I wasn't sure how to introduce myself.'

'Just your name is enough. Marissa. And you learn quickly. Apology accepted. Now, come, child, I have much to show you, and we have very little time. Get up on my back and wrap your hands around my neck, yes, just like that, good. Good.'

Marissa felt the warm, strong body of the snake undulating beneath her as it glided past trees and flowers, vines and fallen boughs of rainforest trees. Even though she had never actually been to a rainforest, she felt like she knew this place well.

The snake moved swiftly. Marissa was not aware of her legs or of her body, and soon she was looking out of the eyes of the snake, as if she had transmogrified into the very snake itself. Her own muscles rippled and pushed as she willed herself forward, she could feel her long reptilian body stretch and contract, large scales protecting the soft parts of her body. She wove from side to side moving swiftly forward, revelling in the feeling of freedom.

She came to a riverbank and slid into it, cutting through the cold water. She had no need to take a breath. Then she came out onto the other side of the river as herself again, the snake beside her, only it was small now, smaller than the length of her arm. The landscape here was different, the air felt different, yet it looked like the forest, only it was not. Something was not the same.

She walked in the same direction she had been going in before. Sachemama twisted herself around her leg, moved across and up her body, settling on her arm, wrapping herself around Marissa like a bracelet. She hissed, the snake seemed to be talking. Marissa raised her wrist up to her ear so she could hear her better.

'We are in a different land now, a different place, but there is learning here for you. I am not as powerful here as I was there, this is the land of humans. Look around you, child, what do you see?'

Marissa looked around. The landscape had changed drastically, the forest had transformed into a library. Once she got her bearings, she realised it was a similar library to the one she liked to go to when she was in college, yet it was different, bigger. Bookshelf after bookshelf stretched back, almost infinitely, she couldn't see where they ended. There were people sitting at tables reading, but she couldn't see their faces. The space seemed dull and grey in comparison to the lush rainforest.

'It's bleak in here,' she whispered to the snake.

'Lifeless, dull, look at their faces, yesss, less hope, hope-less.'

Marissa looked. The people seemed to be, well, almost zombie-like. Nobody seemed happy, nobody was colourful, they turned the pages of their books and were completely oblivious to Marissa and Sachemama.

Marissa went to the bookshelf to look at the books, but the titles of the books were illegible.

'It doesn't matter what they are reading, they get their information from a book, but shamanism cannot be taught this way. You must experience it. Live it, dream it, or awaken to it. Come, there is nothing more to see here. Let's go.'

Marissa left the library through the front door and found herself in a playground. It was bright and sunny, many young children were playing, some with a skipping rope and singing, some jumping hopscotch, others chasing each other and laughing. She realised they were in a schoolyard during lunch break.

'The children, they look so happy. It's beautiful.'

'It's all ahead of them. Some get lost in the system. Remember, they all have the potential for joy. But the system, it will squash you if you do not hold onto your own colourful self.'

The snake unwound itself from her wrist, and as she felt it loosening she bent down and offered it to the ground. Sachemama slithered away into the bushes so Marissa followed her. The deeper she went into the bushes, the larqer the snake became, and then they were back in the tropical forest again. Sachamama looked much more at home here, she grew to her full size, looming tall and intimidating, but Marissa felt only love.

The snake turned to look at her. 'Remember this, dear child, remember me, Marissa, I want to help you. I am here to answer your questions. I am here to help you remember your own true colours.'

The images dissolved away, Marissa could hear Séamus's drum calling her back to the room. She took a while to orient herself. It really felt as if she had gone somewhere very far away.

+++

The next morning they were up and dressed for breakfast at 7:30am. Marissa had tossed and turned all night the night before. The bed was too hard and then too soft, it was too cold and then too hot. She had woken up several times thinking there was someone in the room with her, then she remembered Saoirse was in the bed nearby. Saoirse slept quietly and barely turned in her sleep. When she woke that morning she felt disoriented until she remembered she was in Galway. She sat beside Saoirse as she ate her cornflakes, trying to wake up.

'How did you sleep last night?' she asked Saoirse.

'I heard you tossing and turning, I was awake most of the night.'

'I thought you were sleeping the whole time, I was almost jealous! I think I was awake all night… But I must have slept a little bit as I feel okay this morning. At one point, though, I felt like there was someone in the room with us. I thought it was you, but I'm not so sure now.'

Saoirse rubbed her eyes, upon second look, she did look tired, too. 'That's so weird you say that, I thought there was someone in the room too, but then I thought it was you. Oh dear. I did think at one point that someone was standing at the end of my bed. Now this is really freaking me out. Didn't someone say it was haunted here?'

'Yes,' said Marissa, finishing off her bowl, 'I do believe Séamus said that yesterday before dinner, several times.'

Saoirse shuddered and Marissa felt prickles down her back and along her arms.

'And we have another night here tonight, oh no!'

'Many more nights here if we come back for more trainings here. But I supposed this is the type of thing we need to be able for if we are studying shamanism. The spirit world isn't as far away as we think it is.'

'Perhaps not,' agreed Saoirse. 'But I would rather it stayed out of our bedroom.'

They laughed nervously together.

'Let's go up and get our drums for the ceremony, it's starting very soon. Have you brought an offering?'

'Yes, I have flowers – how about you?'

'I brought some flowers too!'

They both went upstairs and bumped into Terry, Zaad and Finn.

'Hiya! Did the ghost keep you awake too?' asked Terry with a tired smile.

'Oh my God! No way!! What is going on with that?' exclaimed Saoirse.

'I know – mad, isn't it? We will have to ask Séamus what to do. I need my beauty sleep.' Terry winked at Marissa and went into his room, which was right beside theirs. Marissa felt suddenly dislodged from her body as if she wasn't really there at all.

'I guess walls don't stop ghosts,' Saoirse said in a disheartened way as both girls went into their room to find what they needed for the ceremony. Marissa's drum was tucked away under the bed. She put the flowers on the coverlet, took the drum, held it in her hands for a moment, then hugged it to her stomach. 'Hello', she said to it, 'I hope you like being my drum. I hope we have lots of fun together.' She waited a moment, but the drum said nothing, but the feeling of it pressed against her body helped bring her back into it. Marissa found and put on her coat, her alpaca scarf and hat and took it, and her flowers, downstairs.

Everyone was gathering by the main door. 'Ooh, I love your hat! And your scarf too! Where did you get it?' asked Saoirse.

Marissa blushed, though she didn't know why. 'I was just in Peru last October. I got it in the market.'

'Very appropriate choice,' said Terry in an approving tone as he arrived down at the door.

'Where are we supposed to go? It's 8am already, the Sun is beginning to come up.' asked Finn. They could hear drumming outside.

'That must be Séamus,' said Liz. They all ran out the door to follow the sound.

Séamus was around the side of the old Edwardian house standing next to a fire pit made of a circle of big stones with a large space in the middle, which had been set with a bonfire. To one side of the fire pit was an old stone table with legs that looked like the feet of a lion. Upon it sat a large pillar candle, a few stones, some flowers, a bunch of sage and a large feather that looked like it came from a seagull.

Séamus was drumming softly with his eyes closed. The others gathered in a semi-circle around him, listening and waiting for him to finish. He seemed pleased at this. After a time, he stopped drumming, and they all stood for a moment in silence. The early morning bird song became more apparent then, it rose from the bushes and trees around them, enveloping them in a chirping chorus. It felt like nature was taking part in the ceremony, too.

'Hello all. This morning we honour the coming of the light, the lengthening of days, as we move into the time of darkness. We honour the seasons, the flavours of the Mother, the richness of the hibernation as we go within. We are cyclical beings, we are connected to the Earth, to the Sky, the mountains and the Sea. We are not infallible, we are not supreme beings, we are part of the connectedness of all things. We enter the womb to heal, to rejuvenate, to transform, not to die, but to be reborn in the Spring with the return of the light.' Séamus turned and looked at the group. 'I see you brought your drums and rattles. Good. Place your offerings on the table.'

Each of them went to the table and put their offerings upon it: flowers, chocolate, oats, a cigarette, a half-eaten piece of toast. They returned to their places in a circle around the fire pit.

'We give thanks to the Sun, to the Moon, to the sky, to the seasons, to the winds, to the Mother. We are here in service and offer ourselves on the pathway of light. We are grateful for the lengthening of the days. We know that for light to increase we must embrace darkness as balance. We raise our drums to honour each other, to honour the coming of the darkness and all that it is present and alive in this very moment.'

A bird hopped onto the stone table and started investigating the toast. Séamus ignored it and continued.

'Now. I raise my drum, and it shall sing in honour of the dimming light. Let your drums sing alongside mine, and we will find our natural rhythm.'

Séamus began to drum and they followed. With many drums and rattles it seemed chaotic but after a few minutes they seemed to blend and weave their sounds together to make one sound, one drum, one rattle.

Marissa really enjoyed being part of this. She was aware of being in the group, aware of being outside as it was a little chilly, but she didn't mind it. This time she didn't travel or journey anywhere in her mind, she was very much there, feeling the cold, the crunch of sticks and gravel beneath her feet, and wishing she had brought her gloves. She gently hit her new beater off of her new drum, letting her hands do the work. Séamus's eyes remained closed, she watched his beater hit his drum and noticed he was leading them, that his drum held the lead and they followed him beat for beat, she noticed her breath as they went on, the drumbeats two to a breath in, two to a breath out. The drums were breathing, they were breathing the drumming. It was lovely. She felt herself relaxing and connecting to the sound of it, the rhythm of it. Her heart, the drumbeat, her drum, Séamus's drum, it was as if they were all one.

Then she heard someone behind her giggling as a second bird came to squabble with the first one over the remaining bits of toast and oats. The rattling fell out of beat, and then the drumming followed. Séamus continued, but the magic had broken, something wasn't quite the same. When Séamus banged loudly three times, they all stopped at once. They stood in the silence, which seemed even quieter than before, because the drumming had stopped.

Séamus put his beater inside his drum and placed them both on the grass beside his feet. He reached for and lifted up the sage from the table and raised it to the sky. The birds on the table had flown, the flowers, some of the oats and the chocolate, remained. The Sun was rising, the colours stretched across the sky were so beautiful, the oranges and yellows reminding Marissa briefly of the sunset in Miami when she had been on the airport train with Sarah. It was a clear and fresh morning. Marissa was feeling good to be alive. And she was really, really happy with her drum. She held it to her body again, loving the feeling of it.

Séamus held out the feather and sage and turned to the group. 'We will now cleanse and clear our energies to honour the darkness to come, so we enter with only what we need to bring with us. Who will be first? Come now, don't be scared.'

More giggles from the background. Nobody came forward, then Marissa found herself stepping forward, her drum in one hand and beater in the other.

'Marissa, good. Come.' She went to him. 'Turn and face the group, and I will use the feather to clear your aura. It's a shamanic cleansing, I will teach you all how to do this in time.'

Séamus held the sage and the feather in the same hand, and as he ran the sage smoke through her aura, he flicked the feather through Marissa's energy field to follow it. He didn't touch her body at all, keeping several inches from her person he used upwards and downwards flicking motions with his wrist, as if she was dusty and the feather was flicking smoke deeper into her energy field, to clear the dust away. He moved around her, front and back, side and side. Then the top of her head, and then at her feet. It took about two to three minutes, the others waited and watched him at work. When he was satisfied, he put his hands together in prayer position and said, 'Thank you,' to her, and she, still holding her drum, did as best as she could to mimic him, saying, 'Thank you.'

She returned to where she had been standing.

'Who's next?'

Knowing what was in store, the others weren't as hesitant as before. It took a long time for Séamus to get through them all.

'Now all of ye, list in your minds the things yiz are grateful for. Good. And now we will hold a moment of silence in reverence to Great Spirit.'

A few minutes passed. Some of the group were getting antsy. Marissa wasn't happy with the giggling, she suspected it might be Terry, but it was difficult to tell as it was muffled. Séamus seemed oblivious to it.

'Our first session of the day starts in the main room in twenty minutes. See yiz there, bring your drum, the coverlet from your bed and leave your coats and phones upstairs.'

'Can I bring a notebook?' said a new voice, it was Finn.

'Yes, yes, of course. Notebooks and pens are welcome. As are your enthusiasm and your questions. See you inside.'

The fire was lit. Séamus sat on a wooden chair to the left of it, and the others were piled into sofas. Jenny and Liz sat on cushions on the floor with their notebooks and drums beside them. Everyone had a sheen of cold air around them.

'We have a lot to get through this weekend. We'll have three teaching sessions today and one tomorrow morning before we close. Remember the prayer when we opened sacred space last night? To begin our training, we work with the first verse. I'll repeat it for you now.'

Without getting up Séamus closed his eyes for a moment, cleared his throat, and then began:

> *'Great Spirit of the North, we come to you and ask for the strength and power to bear what is cold and harsh in life. We honour our ancestors who have also received the winds that truly can be overwhelming at times. Support us and warm us as we do our work, hold us as we release the patterns that are holding us back and place them into the fire.'*

He sat back a little and shifted his position. After another moment, he spoke again.

'This is the work we will do for the next several months. The work of the North. And fitting that we do this in the winter months. This Winter, we stand in the direction of North. North Facing, to face the cold and harshness of our inner wounding. We face directly into the wind, releasing what is cold and harsh, so we can be warm once more. What do you think it means to be warm? Finn?'

'Not cold?'

'Ha, ha. Good, but not quite. Know that this isn't school, you won't be penalised for a wrong answer. Here, there are no wrong answers, just answers that are either off track or in alignment. So be curious, do not be afraid to ask. And as I may not have *the* answer, I also will not have *your* answer. Perhaps the answer you want lies only within you.'

'There is no one way. I am just a guide, I cannot tell you how to heal your past wounding. But I am here to show you ways to heal, point out objects and directions on the path. To help you blossom and come into your own... But you have to choose to do it, you must choose to grow. And growth is painful. It hurts to transform, think of the caterpillar. But he has no other choice, he must become the butterfly. Complete transformation. Humans, however, have a choice. And many of them choose not to take this path, even when, at times, the path comes to them and hits them in the face. Humans are experts at creating distractions, avoiding things, making excuses. You are the brave ones. This time next year, you will not be the same as you are now. You begin this journey of growth together. And together, you have each other. Fellowship on the path. Makes things a whole lot easier.' Séamus smiled.

'Remember this moment, those of you who are still with me, for I will lose someone. I will also gain someone. Everything changes and grows, or it stagnates and dies. Humans too. You will look back upon this day in future times and realise how far you have come. You will need to be willing to go deep, to look at yourself, to receive criticism and compliments. To meet your demons, the ones within and the ones without. This is not easy work. That is why there are only seven of you here, on this course, even though I have worked with over 200 people this year at the basic level.'

'So back to today. To the work of the North, the first point on our compass. There are many layers in this verse, in the work of the North. Such as 'We honour our ancestors.' How many of you know who your ancestors are? You know your parents, possibly know your grandparents, but what about your great grandparents? Or your great great grandparents? Now is your opportunity to work shamanically, to meet them in the journey and listen to their stories, to honour their suffering and all that they endured so that you could be here, right now, in this moment.'

The group had become quite emotional, tears were forming in Marissa's eyes, she noticed tears were rolling down Stephanie's face too. She used the sleeve of her cardigan to wipe them away.

'And this, the hardest work of all, the work you will keep coming back to time and time again to – 'Hold us as we release the patterns that are holding us back and place them into the fire' – you may never release all of your patterns, you may never even learn what they all are. The work of the North, of this direction, could take you years to complete. Lifetimes. Around and around we go, we go around this work many times if we are devoted, and it will never end, until we die. Are you ready?'

There were enthusiastic yes's and nods around the room.

'Are you really ready to face your darkness? To look at yourself truthfully? To be able to face truth in its purest form? This is the most difficult of all the spiritual work, for it is the true work, not the airy-fairy work, not the love-and-light work. No, this work goes deep, it can hurt, and it starts right here, with you being willing to step up. To be a healer, to help others to heal is all well and good, but listen...'

He paused. Everyone craned in.

'...you cannot be a useful guide, bring anyone else down any road, down any pathway, that you have not already travelled yourself. If you have not truly driven out your own darkness, faced your own monsters, stared at your own demons, then you cannot possibly recognise darkness or hold space in the dark for anyone else. For you in your clarity, your cleanliness, the light that you bring when you have emptied yourself is the space where the healing work happens, and you, standing in truth, in alignment with what is real, are simply a witness. As am I, in your guide. A witness.'

He stood up and placed his hand on his heart and looked at them sincerely.

'And I am truly honoured to be here, to do this for you, with you all. To offer my services. So you can go out into the world as the great healers that you have the capacity to be, and as a group, to spread more light than I ever could on my own.'

He sat down, put his hand in his lap and watched as they absorbed his words.

'Now then. Any questions?'

The room was silent. It felt as if Séamus's words were still vibrating, resonating in the room, echoing off of the walls, the ceiling. There was also a sense of more than just nine of them in the room, it felt like the room was crowded, thronged with people. It felt quite heavy, uncomfortable. When Marissa brought her awareness back to her body she realised that she ached. She suddenly wanted to get up and walk around, open a window or go out the front door for a breath of fresh air, but the fire was heating the room and it wouldn't have been appropriate. She shifted in her place, wriggled around to shake the feeling from her body, it eased slightly, but not completely.

Terry raised his hand. 'Séamus, I'm excited about this, but I'm also a little nervous. I'm glad you said that it's not like school, I never liked school, I didn't fit in there.' Terry's soft lilting voice seemed to cut into the air and broke whatever tension had formed. Marissa felt a little better.

Terry continued, 'I have a question, but it's not about what you were just talking about. Or maybe it is, when you said the Ancestors, it could be ancestral. Anyway. It sounds silly, but I wanted to say it now because I didn't sleep a wink last night. I think there's a ghost in my room – is this place haunted?'

There were sighs and giggles and another release of one of the layers of tension of the room.

'Yeah, Séamus,' piped up Stephanie. 'I had a bad dream last night that someone was sitting on my bed looking at me. I woke up with such a fright I couldn't get back to sleep.'

'Me too!' said Jenny. 'I thought they were in my room too!' She turned to Stephanie. 'Is it the same person? You felt it too? Oh my God, this is so creepy.'

Séamus cleared his throat and looked around the room.

'Well, I can see we are getting into this work faster than I anticipated. Yes, many spirits walk the halls of this old house. The original owners were all murdered in their beds, including their young child, a little girl, whose spirit is often seen in the dining hall. And since then, others have passed away in their sleep, in this very house, too. When you have a large space such as this, with spirits here, others become attracted in by their presence. These have nothing to do with the residents at all. They just like the company.'

Marissa shuddered, Saoirse was suddenly pale and Terry was wide-eyed and sitting up straighter in his chair.

'Some of you probably don't believe in ghosts. I do not call these spirits ghosts because they deserve honour and respect, just as you do. And they are real, they are here, they walk the earth all around us. People don't see them, they ignore them, but on this path, you cannot. This is part of the courage that you will need, these 'otherworldly' beings have always been here. So know that we will not be 'ghostbusting'. These beings have a right to be here, just as we do. However, there are some things that we can do to ensure we live in harmony with Spirit and have a good night's sleep tonight. We will talk about that in the final session of the day. In the meantime, we need to be here, to focus on the work at hand.'

'Remember, shamanism is working with what is real, what you feel, not what you think or know. Just as you did not believe there were presences in your room last night, yet you knew there were, you will be faced with a struggle of what is real versus what your brain tells you is acceptable reality. Everything you think must be questioned, your limiting beliefs emptied out, or you create such great limitations before you even begin. There is so much more to this world, to this existence, than any type of scientific equipment could ever, ever measure. When you feel a chill, is it a spirit passing by? Or is it someone walking on your grave in future times? Or is the window open?'

They all laughed.

'Keeping grounded and centred is vital. Vital. I cannot say this enough. There are layers upon etheric layers that we need to look at. This makes it even more complex. For there is no such thing as time, it's all relative. Your past lives walking into this life – what makes you think past lives happened in the past? Your human brain cannot comprehend the truth that everything is happening all at once. We can only see and understand a logical timeline, so we organise our lives around that. What happened yesterday, what happened last year and what we plan to do tomorrow, is not a straight line.'

'And control – humans crave control over everything – EVERYTHING – our environments, our material possessions, even over other human beings. In truth, we do not control any of it. That saying – God laughs while we are making plans. It is the truth. Only with darkness behind us can we manipulate and live in the illusion of control, but we still do not control, for it is a grand illusion. And the more we are deluded that we are in control, the more control the darkness has over us.'

'So much you need to learn, we need to take it slowly. Let us pause, let us return to this moment, the present moment, the gift that we have to breathe and slow everything down. Slowing down, another vital part of the work. For only when we slow everything down can we see what is in front of us. Now then. We journeyed last night to learn what we need to know now. And let me add that all of these journeys are for you, for I will not ask you what you saw, these journeys – this training, it is your integrity that will bring you through. Like I said, it is not school, there are no exams, but you will be tested, oh yes. You won't see these tests coming, they will sideline you, sometimes confront you, and this is how you learn. For the one that decides if you are ready or not is not I, not you, but Spirit. Welcome to the University of Life, welcome to Earth School.'

Séamus paused to make sure they took it in.

'Today, we will go on three further journeys. This afternoon we will go to the spirit of our drum, so we can feel more connected and in-tune with it. Joke intended.' He waited for the laughter but everyone was still processing what he had been saying, and it took them a few minutes before they nodded and smiled at him.

He continued. 'Tonight, we will go on a journey for another person, so you can experience the magic of bringing back a message that makes no sense to you, but perfect sense to another. And now, staying focussed on the work of the North, we will journey to our ancestors and ask them for their blessing. As I said earlier, I am just a guide, but I do expect everyone here to do the work. So you can repeat any of these journeys in your own time if you do not come back with information this time. Or any of the work we do here, it is up to you to be the adult, to decide if you have understood, have completed it fully, or need to revisit and try again. Know this – you need to go again and again to break through until you get what you intended. If you are not receiving information, then journey to the blocks that you have to listening or receiving. There are multiple layers, as I have said before, and you may need to step back a little before you can move forward.'

Marissa grabbed a cushion and sat on the floor with her drum beside her. She wrapped herself in the blanket in preparation for the journey to the ancestors. To her ancestors. Who was she going to meet? She was excited, she was pleased that she hadn't felt nervous all day, not even at the mention of ghosts or spirits that walked through the building where they were. That surprised her. This felt right and good to her, she knew she was in the place she was meant to be. She was feeling less disassociated now and much more present. Séamus's voice, his words, seemed to open up something inside her. She felt the solid truth behind everything he was saying, and like someone who had been shackled and bound, she felt his words were freeing her. She felt like she could breathe better, allow herself to go from what she knew instead of what her brain told her to believe, which was something she had often struggled with. The idea that this work could help her figure that out, well, that would certainly change everything for her. Yes. She said a big YES to this. *Yes yes yes!!*

Séamus started drumming, not everyone looked like they were ready, but she was. The drumming was becoming very familiar to her, it was comforting, and it was becoming natural to consciously travel. Séamus guided them to the Upper World, using the tree as a portal, or, as he called it, the Axis Mundi.

'You're standing in front of this tree, its branches reach high above your head, they scrape against the sky, the light pouring down as you look up to the highest branch, but you cannot see it. You start to climb. You reach for the first branch and pull yourself upwards. Then the second, and the next, and the next...'

As he drummed, Marissa's awareness faded from his voice and into the image of the tree…

...she was there, really there, she could feel the closeness of the branches, almost smell the dusky moss which covered the trunk. The tree was alive, moving, growing, shifting, creaking, she didn't expect that. Suddenly a door appeared in the trunk of the tree, and it opened. There was a space to climb inside, she went in. It was warm and well lit, there was a spiral staircase winding upwards. She followed it. Around and up, around and up, until she arrived at the top of the tree and exited out onto a wooden platform which was right at the top of the tree.

'A treehouse!' She looked around. Branches wound around and worked their way through the open framework of the platform floor, she could see light coming through the planks, but she wasn't scared, even though there were clouds below and around her, just as they had been in Machu Picchu. She did not feel vertigo here. Above, she could see crisp, beautiful blue sky. She wasn't cold and she wasn't alone, around her flying above the clouds were colourful winged creatures, the light catching at their feathers and scales, their skin and their wings, glistening bokeh sparkles were thrown by the sunlight. There were other beings beside her on the platform, too, though she couldn't really see what or who they were. Some seemed very tall and long, others short and wide.

A large winged creature approached the platform and landed beside her. It was a dragon, and there was plenty of room for it to land without disturbing anyone else. It was a large, white dragon that reminded her of Falcor from one of her favourite childhood movies, The Never Ending Story. *His big face smiled up at her with wide, friendly eyes, and she felt a great love. She moved towards him then stroked the fur on his neck. He shivered with pleasure, then motioned for her to climb onto his back, so she did. She held on to the fur at the base of his neck and felt her legs grabbing him tight as he climbed up into the air.*

They flew far away from the tree very quickly, no clouds were in sight, the air was getting thin and the blue turning to black but she had no trouble breathing. They seemed to be flying up into the stars. Blue sky dissolved into a gradient of black darkness speckled by pinpricks of light, constellations of fire, the light of which was enough for her to see. She felt safe and happy, she trusted the dragon, who seemed to know where he was going.

He approached a star, or was it a planet? As he flew towards it, a whole world appeared around her. There was a grassy mountain top and a bright blue sky with a hint of pink. It seemed just like home, but it wasn't home. There was something different about it that she couldn't put her finger on, it was more translucent, brighter. Her dragon landed on the grass and lay down so she could get off. She did. Marissa thanked him and scratched his ear, he bowed his head to her and then waddled away on short stout legs, to graze.

'Marissa? Marissa? Is that you?' Marissa turned, her heart leapt when she realised it was her Grandmother Lilly, she hadn't seen her in fifteen years. She ran to Lilly and hugged her tightly. She looked up and saw her Grandfather Archie there too, her father's parents.

'Oh, it's so good to see you, Grandmama, Grandpapa!'

'Come, child, let us take some tea together,' said Lilly, holding out her hands.

The three of them were suddenly sitting at a white garden table which was laid out with a very fancy afternoon tea. A three-tiered cake stand was filled with delicate slices of all kinds of marvellous, colourful iced cakes. There were bright coloured plates and a beautiful china teapot set with cups. There seemed to be more people sitting around the table than just the three of them, but Marissa could only see Grandmama Lilly and Grandpapa Archie.

'Tea, my dear?' said Lilly. 'I'll pour.' She lifted the heavy kettle and poured a green steaming hot liquid into the small, flower-patterned cups. ' I'm not really sure about all of this shamanic business. Is it safe?'

'I think so, Grandmama,' Marissa said, suddenly not sure if it was safe or not.

'Hmmm. What about this Séamus fellow, is he safe?'

Marissa laughed. 'So far, yes, he seems quite safe to me.'

'Well, Archie? What do you think?'

'The tea looks quite strong enough my dear, thank you.' said Archie

'No, silly, about the shamanic business.'

'Ahh,' said Archie. 'Well, my father wouldn't have approved, nor his before him. It's most certainly not the way we would have been brought up.' He stirred what seemed like purple sugar into his teacup, it turned his tea bright yellow. ' But this isn't about us, this is about you. Things are changing, things are different now.'

He raised an eyebrow and looked directly at Marissa. ' We would have always gone to the Rabbi first, yet you do not have a Rabbi in your life. We see the world stepping away from religion, we must make space for the new generation to do whatever it is they need to do. Perhaps they will come back to religion, perhaps not. But the world certainly needs more healers, doesn't it, my dear?'

Archie leaned into Lilly and put his arm around her shoulders. They looked much younger than Marissa remembered them. She looked a little closer, they seemed to be in their thirties, possibly around the same age as Marissa herself?

'Yes, dear, healing is always a good thing.' She took Marissa's hands in hers and looked at her earnestly. 'Know this, we are proud of you. We may not understand what you are doing, but we will support you in it. We were much harder on your father than your father is with you, dear. If we could change that, perhaps... But he turned out well, and so did you. Anyway, you have my blessing.' She looked at Archie, who nodded. 'Our blessing.' She let go of her hands.

Archie laughed. 'No, Bernie won't like this. What is unfamiliar can be terrifying. But you leave it with me. I'll see what I can do from here, from behind the scenes, so to speak. A conversation in dreamtime might ease his mind.'

Falcor, as Marissa had decided to call him, approached the table and nudged Marissa gently with his head.

'Looks like you have to go, it's been wonderful to see you, poppet. Next time we can come to visit you a little closer to home!'

Marissa got up from the table, reluctant to go. 'I remember you both so vividly, but you were much older than you seem to be now?'

'Yes, dear, why be old if you don't have to be! Our best years were while we were in our thirties, and we do enjoy appearing at our best. Oh, it is so good to see you!'

They embraced.

Back in the room in Galway, tears were rolling down Marissa's cheeks, she could feel them pooling around her neck.

Falcor made a noise, pulling her back into the journey, so she let go of the physical sensation of wetness and waved to her grandparents, then she climbed onto his back once more. She could hear the drum changing to the callback signal.

Falcor flapped his wings and his body lifted gently up into the sky. He flew up and away from wherever it was that they were, a star, a planet? She didn't know. She was beginning to think she didn't need to know. It was beautiful, and maybe the next time she visited, she would have enough time to try the tea? The planet was small and far away now, Falcor and Marissa were surrounded by starlight. A gradient of blue spilled into the dark, then it was bright again, and then she saw planet Earth. They swooped down and through the atmosphere, there was the forest, the platform, the tree.

Falcor landed gracefully. Marissa disembarked and turned to him and thanked him. He bowed, she hugged him and scratched behind his ears, she couldn't help herself. He wiggled and did a happy dance on his little legs, a little bit like a dog might do. Marissa laughed. Then she left him and walked towards the tree trunk. She opened the door, instead of a spiral staircase, there was a slide.

'Just like the Faraway tree!' *She sat down and carefully positioned herself on the slide, and let go. She slid around and down and around and down, and she came to the bottom of the tree and gracefully stepped off and out from its trunk.*

She wanted more time. The drum had stopped and she knew everyone else in the room had already finished, but she kept her eyes closed, trying to stay with the tree for a little bit longer. She placed her hands on its trunk, breathed with the tree, said hello to it, and a thank you. She felt the branches bow to her, and she felt light in herself.

She opened her eyes. Everyone had gone, she was the only one left in the room. She watched the dying embers of the fire, shook herself off, stood up and placed another log into it to keep it burning for the afternoon session. She went in and joined the others for lunch, unable to speak about what she had just experienced just yet.

CHAPTER NINETEEN

'I'm seeing a lot of images in my journeys from movies and books that I saw or read in my childhood. I saw Falcor in the last journey, for example, and *The Faraway Tree*. Why is that?'

It was the opening discussion for the next session. They had a good lunch and some time to walk in the forest and process their journeys from the previous session.

'Good question Marissa.' Séamus was holding council at the top of the room. 'We sense the energy that we are engaging with, but we cannot understand frequency and vibration in the same way as, say, scientific equipment can give us a reading in watts, volts and amps. So our mind has to do something to convert this energy into something that we recognise. So it looks through the catalogue of our experiences and finds an image that best represents the energy that we meet. You mentioned Falcor, he appears quite often in people's journeys, but only for those who have seen the movie. Others may see the same energy you saw as a big white bird. And again, some would name it an albatross, others a seagull, or others may simply say it's a big white bird because they don't have a name for it. What you see energetically could also be something more nondescript, an abstract shape with a power and essence. But we need to make sense of it, so we attribute the power and essence we perceive to an image that fits, or almost fits, such as Falcor.'

Séamus stretched and disconnected from the group for a moment as if he went somewhere to check something. Then he came back, nodded at Marissa, and faced the group once more. 'This is a great question, Marissa, thanks. It really sets us up for the work that is to come. Form and shape are what we need, as humans, it's what we work with. It helps us make sense of things. It's much harder without form. In-form. Bringing it into form. Information. Form as an image in our minds. But being in form in this reality can have its difficulties too...' He thought for a moment, then picked up the drum and turned it in different angles in his hand.

'Well, look at this drum, for example. It looks like this from the front, round, but from the side, is it a box? You cannot see the whole of the drum depending on the angle that you are looking at. But you all know this is a drum, if you were to see a sliver of it in one of those guessing games, guess the object, you'd probably decide immediately that this is a drum. So your mind fills in the rest and is very eager and happy to do so. The problem arises when your brain fills in the rest before you are certain what that small piece actually is. This is a projection of your wanting it to be a drum, of your need to be right. But you might not be right. It could be a box or something else totally unexpected. And we cannot think of everything. Shamanism is where you don't project a form onto something just because your brain wants it that way. To make it easier and predictable for yourself. No, you can't have easy and predictable here.'

'Being open to what is, instead of what you decided it is, is where the magic happens. And this only comes when you do your inner work so you no longer project YOUR needs onto the energies that come to greet you. You need to be able to empty your mind, absolve yourself from your needs, so you can see a sliver of an image for what it is in that moment without turning it immediately into something that it is not. You need to have the patience and forthrightness to allow it to come into form, by itself, in its own way.'

Some of them were furiously taking notes. Marissa sat and basked in it, taking it all in, soaking it up like a sponge. Stephanie raised her hand, Séamus nodded.

'Is this like the story of the blind men and the elephant?'

Séamus slapped his thigh and stood up in excitement. 'Yes!' He pointed at Stephanie and exclaimed, 'Exactly.' He lowered his hand and walked around the room as he spoke, his enthusiasm was contagious. 'One man felt the hair of the elephant's tail and thought the elephant was completely hairy, another man felt the thinness of the skin on the elephant's ear and thought the animal was a thin, paper-like thing. The third blind man felt only the horn on the feet and thought the beast was, well, you can guess what he thought. The thing is, they were all right, but they were all also wrong.' He sat back down again in his seat.

'The thing is – we can only process what we have already seen, or imagined. It is much more difficult for us to understand something completely new to us. And we are mostly surrounded by close-minded people who will not allow themselves to see what is often right in front of them. Closed minds perpetuate closed minds. It's comfortable to stay small. Going against the grain is very hard. But you're doing it, you're here. You probably always felt like you were different to the others around you. Welcome to the truth of who you are – a creative, imaginative, powerful being who is taking life with both hands and discovering the richness and beauty of everything that is already here. There is no heaven up there, no hell down there, it is all here, all around you right now. Life is what you make it, and with open eyes and open heart, you see so much more.'

He took a drink of water and paused to let them absorb what he just said. After a moment, he started again, but his voice changed, the tone softened.

'There is a myth of invisible ships, back in the time of Captain Cook. The native peoples did not see his ships approaching the shore, but the medicine man did. He ran to the chief and told him there was something big approaching, many big objects coming. He said they needed to prepare their weapons, that he thought they were a threat, but the chief did not believe him. He brought the chief to the beach and pointed in the distance, straight at the ships that were several miles away from shore, but again, the chief did not see them. Several hours later, the ships were closer, and the medicine man brought the chief out again. The chief brought some of his men with him, and still, they didn't see anything. The final time they came the ships were practically upon them, and it was only when they had anchored close to the shore and cast their anchor, and the men from these great ships were in smaller boats making their way to the beach, did they see them. For their minds had no way to make sense of these vast creations as they had never seen ships before. Only when the ships had come to shore, and the people had landed among them that the tribesmen reacted. Whether this myth be real or imaginary, it illustrates my point. You. Must. Get. Your. Head. Out. Of. The. Way. And. Feel.'

The room had darkened significantly while he was speaking. Séamus looked at his watch.

'It's getting late and we have another journey to do. The sun has gone down, and dinner is at 6, so we have an hour. We'll be working until 10pm tonight, but we do need to take our breaks so you can process what you've seen. Our next journey is to the spirit of your drum so you can forge a connection with it, so it works with you on your healing path. You cannot pick up any drum and expect it to work with you, you must ask its permission first. Those of you who do not have a drum, hold up your hands.'

Saoirse and Jenny held up their hands.

'Don't worry, you can journey to the spirit of the drum that is waiting for you. This way you will recognise it when you see it. So all is not lost.'

They seemed relieved. Then Terry put up his hand. 'Séamus, when you say the spirit of your drum, do you mean there is a ghost living in the drum? I'm not sure what you mean, exactly.'

'Thanks, Terry. There is spirit, life-force, in everything. Everything that is in front of you, this table, this chair, the carpet, it is made up of matter in form, in this reality, yes?'

Everyone nodded.

'Just because you can't see it, or don't expect that sofa to get up and walk across the room,' he paused with a raised eyebrow for laughter, 'it doesn't mean there is a deadness there. The cloth that covers the sofa was once a living, breathing thing – cotton on a cotton plant, wool on the back of a sheep, or the skin of a cow. The wood that makes the frame once was a tree. The steel in this candleholder was born from rock and stone, molten lava in the belly of the mother. Even artificial items are manufactured from something, they came from somewhere. The further they are from nature, the harder it is to perceive their life force. The life force in, say, that sofa, is sleeping, dormant. But that sofa has many stories to tell, it can show you where it came from, what it is made of. The cloth can speak to you of the hands that wove it, the wood can tell you of the forest where it came from. Whole buildings speak, have a life force and energy of their own. You have heard of sick buildings? Buildings that have not been tended to, full of stagnant energy needing to be refreshed. Yes, this is all real and all part of the shamanic journey – everything is alive. And once you open your mind, you can sense it. The beauty of it, the harshness of it, the elegance and inelegance. The polarities, the equilibrium. Great question, Terry. Thank you. Anyone else?'

Finn held up his hand. 'Okay, yeah, I get that plants are alive and that their energy could be in a cloth that has been made from them, yes, okay. And wood, yeah, it was a tree once. But how can a rock be alive, or glass? Or metal?'

Séamus shifted in his seat. 'Glass is from rock, melted into a liquid. When you next see a rock, hold it in your hand. It seems to be static, unmoving. But over time, aeons and millennia, it has changed its shape. Even glass is moving all the time. Metal is made of rock too, bits of rock extracted and heated up, mixed together. They were parts of rocks at some point in time.'

'Remember what I said to you earlier? Time isn't what we think it is. In the blink of an eye, *our eyes*, nothing about a rock has changed. But think about how a fly perceives time, it moves so fast because its life is so quick. It sees you coming to swat it before you have even decided you were going to swat it, the fly laughs at your ineptitude because you are so slow and stupid. You move in the slowest of slow-motion, according to a fly's brain. The rock, well, its lifespan is far longer, it changes its shape and form on a much longer timescale. Just because you don't see it moving does not mean it is dead. You can see the glass in very old windows, pooling at the bottom of the window frame, it's thicker there. Connect with the energy of any rock and stone, in fact, do it in the break, get a stone and do a journey into it, notice what it is made of, the shape of it, where did it come from? Is it native to here? The spaces between the atoms, there is movement there, but because your eye cannot see it, is your brain arrogant enough to say that it is not moving?'

Séamus turned to the group. 'Finn has given you all extra work to do! Say thank you to Finn! I will check on you to see if you have done this in your free time.'

There was a scribbling sound of pen scratching on paper. Séamus walked around the room and stopped, and turned to them. 'A rock may be sleeping. But the life force is there, deep within it. Just as you meet people who seem to be asleep or disconnected from this life. They still have the potential to wake up, to open their eyes to what is really here, and not what they are told is here.'

'But it is dangerous to wake these people up too quickly. For something similar to those boats of Captain Cook may be right upon them when they awaken, it can be the stuff of nightmares. Madness. People can go mad completely and lose their orientation, their sensibility, they need time to make sense of things. Some people will never wake up, and it's not your job to wake them, but if they wake by themselves and need your help, then you can step in. Enough! We need to journey. Prepare yourselves.'

Séamus made everyone with a drum place it over their hearts, then the drumming began. *Bang bang. Bang bang. Lub dub. Lub dub. The drum. Heartbeat. Bang bang. Come on. Lub dub. Relax. Bang bang. Lub dub. Bang bang. Primal beat. Slow down. Close your eyes.* The drum was singing. Holding them.

'Bring your awareness down, down, down into your heart. You are standing in your heart. You are small and big at the same time. You are powerful and powerless, you are everything. You are nothing. Your heart is open, it is active, it is shining. Feel the radiance around you as you step into it. Your heart has many colours, many feelings, what are they? Your heart is now connected to the heart of your drum. Your drum is calling to you, beckoning to you, for it has already chosen you, and now you are choosing it. Step from your heart into the heart of your drum. Where did it come from? Where will it bring you? Let go and journey and I will call you back.'

Marissa felt a sliding sensation, she felt disoriented in her body, slipping outwards and onto the skin of her drum. She looked down at her feet and the ground was moving beneath her, first sloping at one angle, then another. She couldn't keep her balance, there was no footing... She was going to fall over but there was nothing to hold onto, she felt nauseous, she wanted to vomit. She held her arms out to try to balance and then realised she was standing on the skin of the drum and it was what was moving, side to side. Suddenly it flipped upwards and she grabbed onto the edge, she was holding on by her fingertips now, the drum was trying to shake her off. This couldn't be right.

'Angel Michael, please help me.' *There was a stillness. The drum righted itself, and she was standing upon it. There was a mist surrounding her, it was dark wherever she was. She noticed a shadow behind her, it felt like her angel, she was instantly at ease.*

Marissa took a moment to calm herself, the feeling of nausea passed. She got down on her hands and knees and caressed the skin of the drum, then it seemed to rip open and she fell, down and down but this time it felt better, she could sense her angel there beside her. She saw the ground coming up to meet her, she righted herself and landed feet first, like a cat. She was in a grassy place with a big wide open sky, there were tall, powerful red mountains in the background, she had never seen mountains like this before in real life, it made her think of images she had seen of Arizona.

She noticed a massive white buffalo chewing the cud beside her. It turned to her, so she went over to it, and then it spoke.

'Ahh, Marissa. Welcome. We make connection. I am the spirit of your drum.'

Marissa remembered the card she had pulled weeks ago, the white bison, she felt a realisation like a starburst opening inside her head.

'Yes, that was me, your card. I knew you were coming. I am here to support you. I am happy to meet you.'

'Why was it so difficult to reach you? I struggled to get here. I am glad you are happy to meet me, but I don't understand why I felt like you wanted to shake me off of you?'

The bison chewed the cud and seemed thoughtful. 'Ahh, yes. Well, I don't want it to be too easy for you. We must see your dedication, your resourcefulness. And a cleansing. The drum was sitting in the shop for a very long time, the dust had infiltrated. Dust has a life force of its own too, it sucks the goodness out. Creates a barrier between you and a thing. You broke through. I am happy to be your drum. It is good to be with you again.'

Marissa was filled with love.

Marissa hugged the drum to her body in gratitude and snapped her out of her journey. She didn't feel the need to get back to the bison, she was happy to doze until Séamus called them all back into the room.

Then she remembered. *The drum said it was good to be with me again. Again? Was this in another life? Another time?* She was loving this, it was like a game of pass the parcel, taking a layer off revealed another layer. But instead of being in a rush to rip them all off to get to the gift in the centre, Marissa felt like the experience of unwrapping the gift was a gift in itself.

Later she sat at the dinner table with Jenny, Stephanie, Saoirse and Terry. They were talking about their journeys, everyone had a totally different experience. Terry was sharing enthusiastically.

'The ancestral journey, that was the best one for me, I loved that one so much. I never met my great grandparents, and all four of them were there.'

'Don't you mean eight of them?' asked Saoirse.

Terry counted on his fingers 'Ohh yes, you're right, four grandparents, eight great grandparents. That's a lot of ancestors! Imagine if only one of those couples didn't meet each other. Then I'd not exist! Wow. I suppose when you even think about just my mother and father, and all those sperms, and eggs... The chances of me existing at all are slim to none.' He took a thoughtful bite of his shepherd's pie. 'Of course, when you look at it spiritually, then the chances of me being here, as me, are much more likely. Less random. The more I do this, the more I believe that nothing is random at all.'

'What do you mean?' asked Stephanie.

'Well, I don't know exactly. If you think there is a grand creator being, like God or something, not that I'm religious at all, but anyway if God wanted me to be here, it wouldn't matter who my parents were, or when they had sex, or which sperm fertilised which egg, I'd be here in some form or other. Ahh, yes, now I see what Séamus meant by form! By George!'

'I think he's got it,' Marissa said to Saoirse and they laughed. But Liz looked none the wiser.

'I'm totally confused now.' She said with a sigh, scraping at a bit of potato with her fork.

'I guess we are all figuring it out,' said Marissa, trying to reassure her. 'Anyway, I was only referring to what he said when he said, 'By George, I think he's got it'. It's from a movie.'

'You're great with the movie references,' said Jenny.

'I do read a lot and watch a lot of movies,' agreed Marissa. 'I never felt like I belonged anywhere growing up. I guess I found comfort in the stories. Some things stay with you, some things don't, depending on your circumstances, I suppose.'

'I suppose.'

There was a pause, then Jenny asked, 'What was your drum journey like? It was so weird for me.'

'I couldn't get into it,' Stephanie said. 'Seamus was banging his drum in the background, yet all I could think about was what was for dinner. I'm not settling into this at all.'

Jenny added, 'I was amazed that even though I don't have a drum, I did go somewhere, I met an antelope or a deer, I'm not sure, it was very deer-like. We had a lovely conversation, it was in a forest. What about you, Marissa? What was your journey like?'

Marissa shifted in her seat. 'Well, it was very uncomfortable to start with. I was in a fog, I couldn't see anything, then I felt like I was falling. I called for my angel. His name is Michael, I only just met him a few days ago.'

'Ooh, you must mean Archangel Michael?' asked Liz. Jenny and Stephanie were now listening intently.

'I don't know about Archangels... What are they? I just know my angel's name is Michael, he told me on the train to Galway.' Marissa blushed a little bit, she wasn't sure how that would go down with the group. But nobody flinched or laughed, in fact, they took the piece of information as if it was a normal thing, like 'she was wearing a yellow hat', 'my angel told me his name on a train.' *I could get to like this. Being able to speak freely in a group is so refreshing.*

Stephanie offered 'Well, angels have a hierarchy, I read all about this, and I've taken three angel workshops. I've met the Archangels Michael, Jophiel, and Ariel. I love the angels so much!' She clasped her hands together. 'But I've never met one on a journey before. I'm excited now! I didn't know that they could mix together, shamanism and angels, I mean! This is great.'

'I've never met an angel before meeting Michael – I mean, Archangel Michael,' Marissa said, correcting herself.

'There are many angels for many things, many jobs, and then there are guardian angels that mind us, one angel per person,' said Stephanie.

'Or more than one,' Jenny added.

'Yes, some people have more than one,' Stephanie agreed. 'And some people have archangels as guardians, too. They may sound grand, the archangels, but they work very hard and often seen by many people. They say the more you call on them, the more powerful they become. So they like you calling on them. You can always call on an archangel for help, or an angel. No matter who you are. Anyway, above the Guardians and the Angels are the Archangels. They're in charge of the Angels. Then above them are the Seraphim, but some of the Archangels are also Seraphim.'

'This sounds very confusing,' said Marissa, trying to keep track.

'Oh yes, I get mixed up all the time', said Stephanie. 'There's also the Cherubim, baby angels... like Cupid.'

'But Cupid is a Greek God, isn't he?' asked Saoirse.

'Oh dear,' said Stephanie, 'I had this all straight in my head before.' She counted off on her fingers 'Angels, Guardian Angels, Archangels, Seraphim, Cherubim, Virtues, Thrones, Dominions, Powers. Yes, that's it, but maybe not in that order, I'm really not sure of the order. Anyway, the Thrones don't work with people, neither do the Dominions or the Virtues. The Virtues work with the Saints, and the Powers are like armies of angels, defending us against evil. I think that's right.'

'Wow, this all seems very complicated, there's so much to learn,' said Marissa, intrigued.

'Yes, totally. Some people say there are twelve archangels, others say there are seventy-two. So I guess nobody really knows. I find it very interesting, though.' Stephanie finished off the food on her plate, put her fork and knife together, then pushed the plate away.

Terry spoke, 'I've never heard of Thrones, Dominions, Powers, I have heard of Virtues, at least I think I have, or maybe it's a virtue, like a value... No, I think that's what it is I was thinking of. Virtuous. The Virtuous Angels, that's a great name for a rock band! I want a tee-shirt that says that. How amazing that would look!'

Finn, Zaad and Liz came over to join them.

'Are angels religious then?' asked Marissa, not wanting to tell anyone about her backgrounzd just yet, but she didn't want to betray her upbringing either by talking to Christian angels. It all felt a little bit strange to her. Her mother would say 'not kosher'. But her angel, Archangel Michael, (yes, that felt right, she felt like she got his nod of approval to that), surly he wasn't bound by religion if he was already there, helping her?

'In Islam,' Zaad said, 'we have angels. They tell us that the angels were created before human beings. I do not know very much about them, I must ask my family. Something finally I can talk to them about!' He laughed, and everyone else joined in. 'Ahh, yes, it is difficult to know what is safe for discussion at home. It's great to be with you and be able to talk about everything so freely. Anyway. If it helps, I know for sure that we have Angel Gabriel in my religion.'

'Archangel Gabriel – yes, I forgot, I've met him too!' said Stephanie, brightening up.

'Are you religious?' Marissa asked Zaad directly.

'Kind of, I'm not sure, really. I go to the temple with my family, it is something that we do together, but I neglect to say my prayers every day. I say them when I remember, but it is difficult at university to stop the lecture and to get out my prayer mat. I prefer to stay in the lecture and not call attention to myself.'

Marissa nodded. 'Same as me, I don't go to synagogue anymore, and I am only going through the motions when I am with my family.' As soon as Marissa said that, she felt her heart leap into her stomach.

'You are Jewish?' Zaad asked curiously, not missing a beat.

So much for trying to hide it. She nodded.

'Wow,' said Terry, 'and there I was thinking we were in little Catholic Ireland, and I was the odd one out, being the Protestant in the group!' He turned to Zaad. 'Of course, and you, too, an odd one. Not Catholic, I mean!' He giggled nervously, hoping that he wasn't insulting anyone. Zaad laughed with him.

'I'm a Buddhist,' said Jenny proudly. 'My parents converted and brought me up as Buddhist. I'm 'the vegetarian' in the group. I'm actually surprised there's only one of us.'

The others stayed silent to think this over.

'I guess we are all black sheep, or "not typical" as we are doing this work,' said Liz. They all agreed. Marissa felt more at ease.

Finn looked at his watch. 'Our next session starts soon, I want to go for a walk before we start. Maybe I'll find a rock and say hello to it,' he rolled his eyes and added, 'Sorry about that, guys.' Everyone laughed.

'I do hope Séamus remembers to help us with our ghost problem,' said Saoirse. 'I really need to get some sleep tonight.'

'Do you believe in ghosts, Saoirse?' asked Terry. 'I'm not so sure they exist at all. In fact, I think Séamus is making the whole thing up just to freak us out.'

Suddenly there was a crash from the back of the room, they all jumped.

'What was that?' Terry asked, suddenly looking nervous.

Finn got up from the table and went to the back of the long hall to look. He called back over to them. 'It looks like a plate fell from the shelf and smashed on the ground. I'll pick it up, no bother.' Finn bent down and started picking up the broken plate.

Saoirse turned to Marissa. 'I hope that was just a plate falling off a shelf...'

'I don't know Saoirse, do you think a ghost, sorry, I mean a spirit, could do something like that?'

'I'm beginning to think anything is possible,' said Saoirse. 'Séamus did say that little girl was seen a lot in this room...'

Everyone suddenly stood up and found an excuse to go outside. Marissa decided to take a walk outside too to clear her head; there was a lot of information swimming around in it, and she needed to shake the spooky feeling and analyse the images of her journeys.

It was pitch black outside. The sun had gone down at 4.15, it was only 6.30, but it was as dark as if it was the middle of the night. *That's what he meant by time being relative, I guess. We are already more than halfway through the workshop. How could it have gone so quickly?* She needed to get her head straight. *I'm not feeling safe here, I'll turn on the torch.* Marissa pulled it out of her pocket, wound it up then turned it on, grateful for her Dad's gift from so many years ago. The torch threw light and shadows onto the branches and tree trunks. *Interesting. Without the light there's no shadow, only darkness.*

Marissa remembered about the rock. She looked around on the grass but didn't see any. Then, out of the corner of her eye she saw a butterfly hovering over one of the bushes. *In December?* It flapped around for a little bit, then it came over to her and settled on her jeans, just below the knee. She didn't move. She waited for a few minutes, and then it flew off again. *Wow, amazing. Butterflies in December. What does that mean? Does it have to mean something at all?*

The grass was a bit wet but it had been dry most of the day so it hadn't turned to mud. She didn't need to wear her wellies after all, yet on reflection, she realised her anxious search for them did bring her to her drum, so perhaps they had already served their purpose. She wondered about the significance of things, the connectedness of them all, and how this gift of hers kept on unwrapping to find more gifts beneath. She switched off her torch and allowed her eyes to get used to the dark. It was so unlike Dublin, she loved it. After a few moments, she could see stars twinkling in an almost black sky. Thick clouds partially blocked her view, as did the tops of the trees. A bird called, the clouds gently passed by and she felt a rustle of wind in the trees and could smell the wet pine needles from the ground. Marissa felt at peace. She said thank you to the trees, to the Earth, to the Sky. She looked up and saw a shooting star. Her heart opened at the sight of it, so much so that it almost hurt. She felt expansive, fully present, safe, at home. *I belong.* She slowly made her way back to the house, enjoying the sensations of belonging. The next session was about to begin.

CHAPTER TWENTY

'Now lads, I'm gonna pair yiz all up and send yiz off to do some work. If you don't have a drum, make sure you're with someone who does.' Séamus's accent was back, thick, fast and heavy. His hair was loose, out of its ponytail, and there was an aura about him as if he was surrounded by light. Marissa had noticed when he was animated and deep in 'teaching mode', it seemed to disappear. The energy in the room was different now. They were all in rapt attention.

'Remember, this is the first time yiz are doing proper healing work, so don't be putting yourself under any pressure to 'get it right'. There is no right or wrong, I've said that before and I'll say it again. It is what it is, and that's the whole point – if you start taking 'what is' and change it into 'what isn't', or 'what you think it is', then it's been tainted. Shamanism is about pureness, just like they say in dream analysis – the first interpretation of the dream, the one that rolls off the tip of your tongue, is the one that is true. Anything beyond that is speculative, perverted. Once your mind gets a hold of something, it twists it around. We want to change how we use our minds, instead of putting things into an empty space, use your brain to make space for things that *are* there, to reveal themselves. Then your brain can help you interpret them. Much better. Your brain isn't comfortable with empty space, that's the learning, like a stage, with a big curtain on it. You and your brain are in the stalls watching for the show. Ye both need to be patient and wait for the curtain to open, to see what shows up. Remember – ye're watching the show, from the stalls, from the best seat in the house. You're not up there on the stage acting, for then you're watching yourself, and what's the point in that?'

He walked around the room, holding his drum.

'Now. Back to our work for tonight. You've heard me drumming for you. Now you'll be drumming for each other.'

The energy in the room lifted with excitement. Everyone's eyes were on Séamus. He went on. 'There are three parts to the sequence of the drumming for a journey. The opening: where the drum grabs hold of you and connects to the heartbeat of the Mother.' He banged his drum in the opening sequence.

'Then, there is the travelling: where the drum holds a space for you to fly. *Lub dub, lub dub, lub dub.*' Again, he demonstrated this on his own drum.

'Lastly, the call-back: where the drum catches a hold of you, wherever you may be, and gently brings you back the way you came.' Once more he demonstrated it. 'This part is important. You need to do it once soft, then again a little less soft, then stronger, then three times strong. Usually, it's the last round that people who journey will hear. But the call-back must be gentle so that unconsciously, then subconsciously, the journier knows that it's time to return. Write it down, if you need to.'

There was a frantic reaching for notebooks and pens and the sound of turning pages and pens scratching. Marissa, on hearing the drumming sequence broken up felt an internal 'click', and then it was already in her. It was a knowing, she had just forgotten, and now she remembered it. It was the strangest feeling, this remembering.

'Good. Now. Everyone will be drumming for someone else, and everyone will be going on a journey for someone else. Interesting, hey? It will be great! So you all need to pay attention. Here are the drumming pieces again, so you are sure of them. First, we open.' He played the opening piece on his drum for three minutes in rounds, making sure they got it. 'Now, the flying part, the holding space.' He played this section for only a minute as they were most familiar with this one. 'The call-back.' He spent longer on this one, as he wanted to make sure they all understood it.

Some people were looking worried at the idea of having to do this themselves, others looked excited. Marissa was holding her drum close in anticipation, looking forward to the experience.

'Now, choose a partner.'

Marissa looked around the room, but before she could even think about who to partner with, Zaad stepped forward. 'I would very much like to be your partner,' he said, 'because I am Muslim, and you are Jewish, I think it would be symbolic and important for us to work together, especially for our first time.'

It felt right to Marissa too, special in fact. She smiled and agreed. They sat together, as everyone shifted places in the room to sit beside their partner. Séamus began again.

'Great stuff. Now lads, what you're going to do is find a quiet space in the house where one of you can lie down and journey, and the other one will drum. The person going on the journey will set their intention for the journey to bring back something for the person who is drumming.'

Terry immediately shot his hand up in the air. 'Something? What kind of thing?'

'Yes, Terry, I was coming to that! These journeys, where are we going? What are we experiencing when we go on a journey? Anyone?'

'Astral travel?' offered Finn.

'Well, sometimes it *could* be astral, but it's not about leaving our body to go to a specific place. It's different. Anyone else?'

There was a hesitancy, then Jenny put her hand up.

'Yes, Jenny?'

'You were saying consciousness and the imagination, something about veils between the worlds, the pathway to your soul. Is that where we go?'

'Exactly. Well done! Yes. We travel into our consciousness, into the subconscious mind, the unconscious mind, the collective consciousness. Into the collective. Anyone tell me what that is?'

Marissa offered, remembering the work she covered in her Transpersonal Therapy training. 'The collective is an idea that comes from Jung's psychological studies, he said that people share the same consciousness which holds ideas, archetypal energies and cultural pain, that we are all connected and we all dip in and out of this consciousness, it can affect us more than we realise.'

'Excellent. You've done some research on this?' Séamus asked, with an eyebrow raised.

'I'm doing a psychotherapy diploma and we covered some of this in our Transpersonal Therapy module.'

'Ahh, yes. Very good. Yes, indeed, that's exactly what it is.' He put the drum down and spun in a circle, then faced the group once more. 'So! In essence, on a journey, we are dipping in and out of the collective consciousness, and in and out of your *own* consciousness, and the consciousness of your client, the person you are working with. You dip into their subconsciousness and bring back something that they recognise but weren't aware of. Or their unconsciousness, bringing back something that they had no idea about. And it may not make any sense to either of you – but both of you need open minds to visit the Theatre of the Soul. The trouble is, when you dip into these pools of consciousness, it is possible that you choose something from your own unconsciousness and bring it back and tell that person that it's theirs. You must be very careful and clear in yourself to be able to tell the difference.' He picked up his drum and banged loudly to emphasise each word: 'Do. Your. Inner. Work.' He put the drum back down again. Everyone was wide-eyed.

'Okay. One more thing we need to be very clear on before we begin. Everyone has a field. I don't mean a grassy field where you can plant potatoes, no. I mean an energy field, a field of consciousness around their body, where their energy flows. Most of you know this, many of you work with this already,' he nodded to Jenny. 'Reiki, for example, works directly with the energy field of your client. Shamanic work does too. But the difference between Reiki and shamanic work is that Reiki is non-intrusive, where Shamanic Healing can be. Intrusive means that something is introduced, something is released, something is altered within the field of energy of your client. We will go into that in more detail later, however, the principles must be laid out from the beginning.'

'You *must* get permission from the person who you are working with before you work with them, as you alter their energy field in some way. It is a violation of ethics and human rights if you do it deliberately without their knowledge. As I've said, we will be spending a lot more time on this in future workshops, and we will be working directly with energy fields the next time we meet. So are ye ready? Able? Willing?'

All of them nodded.

'Great stuff. So here's the intention for this work for now – for the one journeying to travel into the consciousness, or the energy field, of the one drumming. Seek something that they have not been aware of, something they need to know, and bring it back to them. It's not just knowledge you will be seeking, this is where it gets fun. It's energy. Soul essence. See this energy come to you in form. Ahh, now you see, it all comes together, yes?'

'This energy comes in the form of a gift – like a flower, a sword, or a magic wand. You will be gifted an object on your journey for that other person – got it? Good. Hold the form that you see in your mind's eye as precious, and when you come back from the journey, you will be holding this precious energy in your hands. When the drumming stops, the drummer needs to sit in silence, and the journier will gently 'blow' this energy from their hands into the drummer's energy field.'

'Hence your need to ask permission – to travel into their energy field, and then to change something in it. So I expect you to ask them before you begin. Me saying it up here doesn't count. Jenny? Will you come up to the front for a moment?'

Jenny stood up and picked her way around the bodies strewn around her to stand up beside Séamus in front. He clasped his hands together in front of him.

'Now, Jenny, I'm just using you to demonstrate. I'm not actually doing anything in your energy field.'

Jenny nodded.

'So, imagine the gift is inside my hands. Let's say I was given a rose. The energy took the form of a rose in my mind, but it's not in form in this reality, so you cannot see it. But that doesn't mean it isn't there. I am holding the energy in my hands, like this.' He then turned Jenny so that she was facing him and placed his hands level with her stomach. 'I feel that the rose wants to go into Jenny's stomach. But you might feel that your gift for whomever you are working with will want to go somewhere else, the head, the heart, that's all good and okay. So what do we do next?'

He knelt down and placed his hands in proximity to Jenny's stomach without touching her body. Then he brought his lips to his hands and blew, and as he blew he opened his hands, to demonstrate the energy shifting out from him and into Jenny's energy field. He stood once more.

'This is how you give an energetic gift to your client. Let them integrate it for a moment, then you can tell them what you saw on the journey and what the gift was. Your client might guess what it was, based on what they felt when you blew it into their field. However, their brain may interpret the frequency and vibration of that gift in a different way to your brain – just think of a dog – go on, do it now. I can guarantee that each of you has a different breed, colour and size of dog in your mind right now. And if you just felt the energy of 'dog', at least one of you would have seen it as a wolf, or a fox. Anyway. Talk afterwards, share what you saw and what the gift seemed to be, to you. Take the first thing that came into your mind, just as I said above. Don't think too hard about it, and you won't get it wrong. Prepare to be amazed. Now off yiz go, and have fun!! Be back here in about an hour. Feel free to bring a cuppa back with you.'

Marissa and Zaad took their drums, a cushion, and a couple of blankets and left the main room to find somewhere to work where they wouldn't be disturbed by the others. They bumped into Stephanie and Finn, who were already settling into the dining room, so they decided to try upstairs.

'We could go to my room?' suggested Zaad. Marissa nodded, so he led the way. He entered and turned on the light. The room was empty, it was a similar room to the one Marissa shared with Saoirse. It smelled slightly stale, there were three beds, two of them unmade and clothing strewn on the floor. *Looks like Terry's made his bed, but the other's haven't.* Zaad blushed, quickly straightened out the covers on his bed, then put his drum and blanket on top.

'Who will go first for drumming?'

'I don't mind,' said Marissa. 'You choose.'

Zaad thought for a moment. 'I will drum first, and you journey. Would you like to lie down on my bed?'

Marissa shivered. 'I think the floor may be better. Thanks, though,' said Marissa, feeling his bed was a little too intimate. She arranged a blanket on the floor and the cushion as her pillow. Before she lay down she asked, 'As I am journeying for you, do I have your permission to do this work?'

'Ahh yes, good, yes. Yes, of course,' said Zaad, smiling at her.

For a moment Marissa thought she might fall into his beautiful brown eyes – that would be a journey in itself. She pulled herself out of it and replied, 'Good. Thanks. My intention for this journey is to find a gift for you and bring it back.'

Zaad smiled again. Marissa lay down on the blanket on the floor and he helped her cover herself with the other blanket.

He started to drum. It was a hesitant sort of drumming, it did match Séamus's instructions, but it didn't sound the same. Marissa closed her eyes and brought herself down into her body, into her heart, just like she had done before in the other journeys. The drumming changed, it wasn't consistent. When he missed a beat it drew her attention away from what she wanted to do. So she decided to let him drum in the background and to focus on her own heartbeat instead. *Lub dub, lub dub, lub dub.*

She was in the forest. She found her tree. Her heart opened, she was so happy to see the tree that she ran over to it.

'Marissa, my love, it is so good to see you again,' said the tree. As it spoke, its face appeared.

Marissa smiled. 'Beautiful Spirit Tree, I am here for Zaad. I am to take him a gift of energy. Can you help me?'

'Ahh, yes, of course. Come, I will take you to where you need to go.'

A door opened in the tree and there was a staircase going downwards. 'The lower world,' Marissa thought and followed the steps down and down and down.

She came out of the tree and found herself in a desert. It felt like the sun was pounding down on her face, she lifted her hands and saw she was wearing white robes. She looked up and realised she was sitting on a camel.

The camel was walking towards a large white tent, it stopped and sat down, so she dismounted.

The tent was beckoning her to come inside so she entered. It was dark. There was a large table with many objects laid out upon it, cutlery, plates, pitchers and pots, all of them copper, silver or gold. There was a large Arabic man in flowing colourful robes standing beside the table.

'Which one would you like?' he asked her with a smile.

'Which one is for Zaad? I am here for him.'

'Zaad? My Zaad?' the man became suddenly emotional. 'How is he? What is he doing?'

Marissa smiled. 'He is great, he is doing very well. How do you know him?'

'He is my great-grandson, he has never met me, but I know him. Oh yes, I know him. I follow him to school, to college, I am so proud of him. Tell him for me that he does not need to regret anything. That I am happy. Here, you can bring him this.'

From inside his robes he took out a pendant, it was silver, worn, and star-shaped, it almost looked like the Star of David. He offered it to Marissa, she took it in her hands and looked at it more closely, no, it wasn't a Star of David, it had too many points. She realised it was made of two squares instead of two triangles.

'Thank you,' she said, and bowed her head.

'And who are you?' he asked.

'A friend of Zaad's,' she replied.

'It is very nice to meet you. I wish you happiness and joy also. I would like to give something to you, too.' He presented the table and said to her, 'Pick anything that you like.'

Marissa's eye fell over all of the beautiful and not so beautiful objects on the table. Her eyes kept moving back to one of them, it was small, it looked like the lamp from the story of Aladdin.

'Yes, yes, you can have this. Know that there is no genii inside of this lamp, for the genius is in you! My blessing to you, and thank you for visiting.' He picked up the lamp from the table, rubbed it with the side of his arm, nodded and laughed, and then handed it to Marissa.

Marissa bowed in gratitude. She heard the drum changing to the call-back signal, it gave her a shock, it was very loud! Thankfully, Zaad quietened his drumming back down again, and she was able to bring her awareness back to the tent, but it had already dissolved. She was standing in the desert and the camel was gone. She turned to face the direction that she had come from. And there she found the tree waiting for her. She entered the trunk and climbed the staircase, coming up and out into the forest again.

She turned to the tree. 'Thank you so much.'

The tree seemed to bow to her. She looked at her gift and at the gift for Zaad. 'What do I do with my gift? I know I have to give his to him. She placed her lamp at the base of the tree. 'Will you mind this for me?' she asked the tree.

The drumming had stopped. Marissa kept her eyes closed, but she was back in the room now. She couldn't get back into her journey, she didn't know if the tree had said 'Yes'. She slowly stood up from her blankets, keeping her hands clasped, as the energy of the star-shaped pendant was still inside.

Zaad put his drum down and stood in front of her. *Where in his field do you want to go?* Marissa waited for a moment, then blew the energy into Zaad's stomach, just like Séamus had with Jenny. She hoped she got it right.

They just stood there in silence for a few moments.

'I felt that,' Zaad said. 'It was powerful. What was it?'

'It was some sort of pendant, it was in the shape of a star. I got it from your great grandfather. He told me to tell you that he is proud of you. That he's happy, that you do not need to regret anything.'

'Really? Are you sure it was him?' Zaad was rubbing his forehead, he seemed troubled by this instead of pleased.

'I don't know if it was him, it was what I saw. I was in the desert, on a camel. It brought me to a large tent, and I went in. There he was, a tall man in robes, standing beside a table. There were many things on the table, gold, silver, it all seemed beautiful.'

Zaad looked like he was going to fall down. He reached for the bed, steadied himself and then sat down on it.

'I have heard stories about him, my great grandfather. He worked as a trader, he sold objects in the marketplace. It fits. He said, 'No regrets,' really?'

Marissa nodded. 'Yes, he said he followed you to school and to college, that he was very proud of you. He seemed happy to see me too once I told him I was a friend of yours.'

Zaad smiled. 'Yes, you are my friend. What did the star look like? The one that you gave to me, the gift?'

'I can draw it if you want, it might be easier than explaining it.'

Zaad found a notebook and a pen beside his bed and he handed them to Marissa. She could see the notebook had other writing in it, it looked so beautiful, swirls and round symbols.

'Is this Arabic?'

'Yes. We speak it at home. When I write down my thoughts, it is useful because nobody else can read it!'

They both laughed. Marissa drew the star, it was a square, and then another square on top of it, rotated slightly.

'Ahh, yes, I recognise that. It is a symbol of Islam. They use it in the Quran, our religious book. It marks the end of a chapter.'

'Or the beginning of a new chapter perhaps also?' Marissa sat down on the bed beside Zaad.

'Perhaps. Yes, this is a good thing. A new chapter of my life, I can move forward with no regrets. This is very good.' He laughed.

Marissa laughed too. It felt good to laugh. She suddenly became conscious of the others, in case they were in the room next door, she didn't want to disturb them if they were doing their journey work.

'Let me get a drink of water,' she said, 'then I will drum for you.'

'Oh yes, good idea,' said Zaad. 'I will get a drink also.'

They went to the kitchen and filled fresh glasses of water. Marissa felt very comfortable with Zaad.

'I don't want to make this about me, but I am very glad that you recognised the gift, that it made sense to you. It means for me that my journey was real. I've never seen a star like that before. Just thinking about that gives me shivers, this is real. It's really happening!'

'I know, I cannot wait to journey now for you, I wonder what I will see!'

Back in Zaad's bedroom they set themselves up for part two of the work. This time Zaad was on the floor, he didn't want the second blanket over him. Marissa picked up the drum. She started the opening sequence.

Zaad sat up suddenly. 'Oh, I did not ask your permission. Do I have your permission to journey for you? To bring you back a gift and breathe it into your energy field?'

'Yes, of course,' Marissa said and smiled. She started drumming again. She watched him as he closed his eyes, lay back and journied for her. She shifted from the opening sequence to the heartbeat of the world. Remembering how Zaad's inconsistent drumming had pulled her away from her own journey, she focussed on staying with the beat. She felt the beater soft in her hand as she used it, feeling the connection between her and her new friend. She liked that. *My drum is my friend. Yes, this feels good.* After a time, she wondered if she had drummed for long enough. Should she keep going? Should she start the call-back sequence? She didn't know what time it was or how long she had been drumming. She hadn't kept track of it on her phone, she didn't have her phone with her at all that day. She hadn't missed it, either.

She looked at Zaad, his eyes were moving behind closed lids. He seemed to be doing something, so she decided to stay with the beat for now. She closed her eyes too, felt the rhythm, let go of her thoughts, became the drumbeat as well as the drum. She felt like the drum was an extension of her body, she discovered that the rhythm had changed naturally. It was as if the drum started to drum her, instead of the other way around. Then she stopped, waited a beat or two in silence, then drummed out the call-back signal, softly, then louder, then she played the final sequence and stopped.

Zaad still had his eyes closed, although they were not moving as much as before. She waited, and couldn't help but look at his smooth skin, his lips. They looked so soft. *Stop it!* But she had to admit that she did want to run her hands through his long hair. There was a curl of it over his forehead that especially called out to her to be touched. She held herself back, and he opened his eyes and smiled at her. He sat up slowly, hands clasped, then he stood.

She put down her drum and stood in front of him. He raised his hands up to her heart and looked at her expectantly. She nodded then he blew the gift into her heart. It felt cold and then warm. She felt tingles in her chest.

He was standing looking at her, checking to see if she was okay. She didn't know what he had done, but it felt nice, gentle.

'It was a butterfly,' he said to her. 'It was orange with black around its wings and some black and white spots. Does that mean anything to you?'

'Actually, yes, yes it does. I was outside this evening, just after dinner, and a butterfly that looked just like that landed on my leg. I thought it was very strange, as it's so late in the year.'

'Oh. That's beautiful. There was more.'

'Tell me.'

'I was in a jungle, I don't know, I just appeared there. I met a snake, a very big one, it was yellow, with black spots. Lots of black spots in these images for you! The snake was scary but I was not afraid, it seemed to be safe. It winked at me! That is all I remember. I hope it makes sense to you.'

Marissa remembered her journey to Sachemama, the granddaughter of Sachamama. This must be her, appearing to Zaad. 'Yes, I know this snake. She is a guide for me, she says she will help me with my medicine. This is wonderful, Zaad, you met my snake!' She clapped her hands together and spun around the room in joy. *This is so unlike me, what is going on?* Zaad laughed and caught her and held her for a moment, then let her go. Their eyes met, she looked away.

'Thank you,' he said, taking a step away from her.

She smiled. It was okay. 'Let's get some tea and go back to the main room for the last session of the day.'

'Good idea.'

Marissa brought the blankets, cushion and her drum back to the main room. She could hear crying from behind the sofa in the corner and went over to investigate. Terry was comforting Liz, who was crying. She had mascara streaks all down her face.

'Are you okay? What happened?' As she said it she remembered about not asking detective-style questions, the rules of psychotherapy. She reminded herself that she wasn't a psychotherapist here, she was a shamanic practitioner in training. That felt better to her. She focused on Liz.

Terry spoke. 'She's been inconsolable since I gave her the gift. Maybe you can help her with your therapy skills?'

'Only if she wants me to. Do we have time?'

'I don't know.' Terry looked at his watch. 'Not really.'

Zaad appeared with two cups of tea, he gave one to Liz, who took it gratefully. It seemed to help her calm down.

'I'm here if you want to talk about it later,' Marissa said.

'Thank you. Maybe. Thanks.' Liz held the tea and her breathing slowly returned to normal.

'I brought it for you, but it seemed like she needed it more,' Zaad whispered to Marissa.

'Yes, that was a good thing you did. I can get my own cup now. Thank you for thinking of me!'

Tea in hand, Marissa came back from the kitchen and found a seat beside Zaad. The others were all there, some had tea, some did not. Séamus was outside the main house, talking on his phone. They waited for him to come.

He seemed frustrated. He switched off his phone, put it in his pocket and faced the group. Running his fingers through his hair, he shook it back off his face, sat down on his chair and closed his eyes for a moment. Then he cleared his throat and opened his eyes.

'So. How did it go for yiz all? Was it difficult to do? It's late, so we can't stay long talking. I'll only take one of ye to share. Who wants to share?'

Stephanie put up her hand, Séamus nodded, and everyone else seemed relieved, as if they weren't quite ready to talk just yet.

Stephanie spoke. 'I was worried I'd make a mistake. I couldn't see very much on my journey, and the gift I got didn't make any sense to me. Only when I told Finn what I got for him, he knew exactly what it was. It's really helped me have more confidence in myself, I shouldn't worry so much.'

'Finn, what was it like, working with Stephanie?'

'Stephanie brought me back a football, she didn't know the context. When I was about 8 years old, I was on the local football team, the under 11's. I broke my leg during a match and I couldn't play for a while. My leg never healed the same and my mother told me she didn't want me playing football anymore. I had forgotten all about it. Stephanie said she journeyed to a football pitch and there were children playing football, one of them gave her the ball for me. Amazing!'

'What do you think it means?' Séamus asked. The whole room was silent in anticipation.

'Maybe that I got that part of myself back? The part that loved football? Maybe I need to join the local team again. I really loved playing. I'd forgotten how much I loved it.'

'Well done Finn. Yes, that gift, all of the gifts are energetic. Parts of you that were lost somewhere along the way. Or they're parts of your ancestry, your heritage, that were lost along the way. They're healing energies, coming to help you grow and to let go. They're signs that you are on the right path, they're parts of you that want to come home. You've all done good work this weekend. We've gotten through more work than I thought we would.'

'Now it's coming up to bedtime, it's getting late. I haven't forgotten about the Spirits. I will do a clearing ceremony so that we all sleep soundly tonight. Watch and stay silent, observe. I am not teaching you this, perhaps I will another time. Because of the lateness of the hour, this is the best thing to do.'

Séamus took a tea light out from his pocket and asked Jenny for the saucer from under her teacup. He placed the tea light on the saucer and lit it, then he took some sage out from another pocket and lit that too. He waited until the sage was smoking, and then he walked around the room, holding the saucer with the tea light in one hand and the sage in the other, waving the sage around so that the smoke filled the room. Marissa watched his technique, partially amazed that he was doing exactly what she had done in her room in Cabra. She had got it right. She felt really pleased with herself.

Séamus then walked out of the room and went up the stairs, they followed him quietly, and he went into each of their bedrooms and did the same thing. He stood in the landing and crushed the sage on the saucer to put it out and put the saucer with the tea light and sage down on the floor. He positioned his legs wide apart, and he opened out his arms, so he was standing like a jumping jack, then he closed his eyes. He whispered to himself. They couldn't hear what he was saying. Séamus then looked up, with his eyes open, and drew in the air around each of the bedroom doors as if he was painting something onto them. He stopped and stood normally.

'Now, I've sealed your rooms off and I've cleared the building. I asked the spirits to leave yis alone for the night. The best thing ye can do is stay quiet and respectful, and don't break the seal. We had a great day today. Well done. We start tomorrow at 8 for our final session. We finish at noon. The bus to Clifden is at 12.30, but I think some of ye are driving back to Dublin, so perhaps at breakfast, yiz could organise lifts with each other. See yiz in the morning, and sleep well.'

He doffed an imaginary hat to them all, took a slight bow, and went downstairs.

The group stayed in silence, looking at each other for a few moments.

'Well, I hope that worked,' said Stephanie.

'Me too,' said Terry. 'I'm going to get another cuppa. I'm too hyper to go to bed just now.'

They broke up for the night. Marissa decided that bed sounded great. She had the bathroom to herself so she took a lukewarm shower, put on her pyjamas, and climbed into bed. She was exhausted. She dreamed of butterflies.

CHAPTER TWENTY ONE 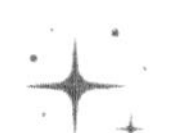

Marissa woke up early, restless, with her mind whirring around in circles. It was still dark outside. *It's the last day of the workshop. I can't believe it, it's going really quickly.* She looked around at Saoirse and saw she was still asleep. Marissa concentrated on her breathing for a while but it didn't help her mind settle, so she decided to get some air. She quietly got washed and dressed. She hefted on her big cardigan, grabbed her torch and crept downstairs.

She pushed at the big heavy front door, it wasn't locked and opened easily. She slipped outside and let it close softly behind her. She walked to the spot where she had met the butterfly the evening before, feeling the soft wind against her cheek. Marissa thought she could hear water nearby, then realised it was the bristling of the wind through the pines. It was still very early, about 5.30am, everyone was still sleeping, and it was too early for the birds. She sighed. Relaxing more deeply, she realised she felt safe here, surrounded by nature. Whatever Séamus did last night to keep the 'ghosts' at bay, seemed to have worked. They would all be grateful for that. Marissa felt like so much had happened in the past two days that she needed some time to clear her head and make sense of it. This had been much more intense than her psychotherapeutic training ever was.

Simply standing outside by herself in the fresh early morning air was helping her to feel more grounded. She needed her mind to stop spinning, she felt anxiety brewing, and she wanted to be clear for the day. She decided to try Séamus's method of the theatre.

She was alone. The theatre looked like it was from The Muppet Show. She sat down on a red velvet chair in the front row. 'Please, can you help me calm my mind? What do I need to do to calm my mind?' *The heavy red velvet curtain opened onto a scene.*

It was a busy office, it looked like her workplace, but it wasn't quite the same. There were many desks, each one filled with paperwork. The paperwork was spilling over and onto the floor. 'Interesting, it's getting very cluttered there. Is this my mind? It certainly feels like it is.' *The desks merged and blended together to make one desk, still, they were all heavily covered in paperwork.* 'I need somewhere to file away all this information.' *A filing cabinet appeared on stage beside the cluttered desk. She got up from her chair in the stalls and climbed three short steps up onto the stage. She approached the desk and the cabinet. As she did this, the theatre around her seemed to disappear.*

Marissa studied the filing system, it seemed archaic, constrictive. 'What if I get a new cabinet? Or a different type of cabinet?' *She had always disliked the old fashioned metal drawer style filing systems, she remembered spending summers working at her uncle's place, shoving invoices into paper files and paper files into cabinets. She shivered at the memory. She tried to imagine this filing cabinet changing into something else, but it wouldn't shift, it was stuck.* 'I'll work around it.' *Marissa imagined a new cabinet appearing beside it, this one was made of dark, red-stained wood with large drawers that had deep carvings on them. The top drawer opened and there was a whole Universe inside. Marissa's heart leapt – star systems with planets whirling in circles around them, and there was a large sun at the centre.* 'Bigger on the inside, like the TARDIS! But if I was to throw my files into that drawer would they be lost forever? I don't think I want to do that.'

Marissa imagined the drawer closing, the Universe now hidden from her sight, she instantly felt much better. 'Imagine being responsible for a whole Universe. No wonder Dr Who gets so stressed out!' *Her current problem had not been solved, there were still masses of paperwork piled up around her, looking for a home. She waited and the next drawer down opened up. Nothing jumped out of it like it had the last time. She cautiously peered into the drawer and inside of it she saw a library, with well-stocked bookshelves. There was nobody inside it reading the books, though. It felt like it was* her *library, but she didn't think she had ever read that many books in her life.*

'What if it was over several lifetimes? Maybe these are all the books I have ever read across all of my lifetimes. That could fit.' *She scanned through the shelving units and discovered some empty shelves.* 'That will do, for now.' *Then she visualised all of the documents and files flying in from the floor and table in her 'office' up and into the second drawer, down into the library and onto the empty shelf. A sign appeared, just like a label in a library, saying 'To be organised'. That felt right, she couldn't just heap the files in a pile, or not categorise them, but she didn't have time to do it now and she needed some free space for today's session.* 'Ha ha, this is hilarious.'

Marissa felt instantly better once the drawer had closed and her 'internal office' felt decluttered. She felt lighter then, she stretched out her arms and dropped the torch on the ground, she hadn't even turned it on. There was light coming from the East, she recognised it as East from Séamus's four directions prayer – *"The sun rises in the East," Sure I learned that at school...* She turned towards it, it was very faint. It was still too early for the sunrise, the moon was in the sky and there were more stars visible here than in her flat in Dublin. She kept her arms out and closed her eyes again, remembering that Séamus did the very same thing last night when he cleared the space of the Spirits.

What exactly did he do? She turned around slowly and lifted her arms higher, feeling the stretch deep into her muscles. She twisted her hips one way, then another, her body felt good, she felt alive, even though it was earlier than she would normally awaken. She opened her eyes again. She felt different, clearer in a good way. In these past few days her anxiety levels had decreased significantly. She liked the group she was with, she felt part of something, accepted, seen. It was different to her counselling class, she thought the people here were more open, more honest. Sure, some of the psychotherapy guys were lovely, they all were lovely, but they kept themselves to themselves. *How could that be? When they become emotional and share their past hurt, even their current hurt, why do these people feel more authentic to me?* She bent down and touched her toes, enjoying the feeling of her spine being lengthened and stretched. She picked up her torch and stood up tall again, then started to walk, to move; she could really feel the ground beneath her feet. She walked a complete circle around the house. When she came back to where she started, she felt like she needed to do it again, so she did it again, and then again once more, making three complete circles clockwise around the big, grey, Edwardian stone house.

Then she suddenly felt hungry so she went inside to the kitchen and made herself some toast and tea. Liz was sitting at the dining table wrapped in a blanket, still in her pyjamas. She was writing in a notebook.

'Hi,' said Marissa. 'You're awake too. Do you want me to make you some tea and toast? I'm getting some for myself.'

Liz seemed groggy. She pulled herself out of her writing. 'Hi. It's early, isn't it? I couldn't sleep anymore. Yes please, toast and tea sounds lovely.' She went back to her writing.

Marissa opened the paper around the new loaf of bread and put four slices into the large toaster. She got two of the least chipped mugs she could find from the cupboard and popped a tea bag into each of them. She switched on the already full kettle and went back to sit by Liz. She didn't say anything. A few moments passed. When the kettle boiled and the toaster popped she went over to get it, then brought everything back to the table with knives, butter, marmalade, and milk. She buttered her toast and started to eat, still not saying anything. Liz put down her pen and closed her notebook.

'Thanks, for not interrupting, I mean. And thanks for the tea and toast.' She picked up the milk then looked around. 'Is there any sugar?'

'Oh! I'll go look.' Marissa got up and went to the cupboard, found an open packet of sugar and brought it back to the table with a spoon. By the time she came back Liz had almost finished the first slice of toast. 'Thanks' she said, stirring two teaspoons of sugar into her tea.

'You were hungry!'

'I suppose I was.'

'How are you doing today? You seemed upset last night when I walked in on you and Terry.'

'Yeah, I was upset. I still am, I guess.'

'Do you want to talk about it? It might help. But only if you want to.'

'Yeah, maybe. You won't tell anyone, will you?'

'No, I won't. I'm training to be a psychotherapist. I totally understand and respect confidentiality.'

'Thanks, yes, I think I should tell someone. I didn't even tell Terry yesterday, that's why he was so worried.' She ate the rest of her toast and drank some tea to wash it down.

Marissa gave her plenty of time. She knew from her training that rushing someone who is upset is a bad thing. Liz seemed to appreciate this and she seemed more relaxed for having the few minutes of silence.

'So Terry went on that journey for me to bring back a gift.'

Marissa nodded.

'He knows nothing about me, right? We never met outside of these sessions with Séamus, so it was really strange. His gift to me was a feather. It was downy, a baby feather, soft and fluffy. That was okay, he blew it into my heart. Then he told me about his journey, that's what made me so upset. He went to a place that looked like the Teletubbies television show, with rainbows, rabbits and birds... One of the Teletubbies was there too, the purple one with the triangle on its head. Tinky Winky, only Terry didn't know his name, just that he was purple. He spoke to Terry, his voice was very high and childish, like a cartoon voice. Terry said it was sweet, he liked it. Anyway. Tinky Winky gave Terry the feather and told him to tell me I have an angel watching over me, that the angel loves me very much and was very happy to have met me.'

Marissa didn't say anything in case there was more. And there was.

Tears started to form in Liz's eyes, after a moment, Liz went on. 'I lost my baby, she died in her sleep. She was only eighteen months old, it was three years ago. The doctors didn't know what happened, I've been blaming myself for it. See, I had been pregnant before, and I had an abortion when I was twenty-two, before I met my husband. I never told him about it. My husband and I, we really wanted a baby, we were trying for a long time before she was conceived. Not getting pregnant, well, I thought I was being punished. I was so happy when Julie came into our lives, she was wonderful. And then, she died, so suddenly. I got angry, upset, and I blamed myself. I started cutting myself, I've been working on that, I've stopped doing that now. But there's a part of me, deep inside, that is still angry at me for having that abortion. I blame myself for our baby's death.'

Liz stopped talking, a tear dripped down her face. Marissa stayed silent.

Liz gathered her thoughts and continued. 'I've separated from my husband now. We couldn't reconcile the loss, it has been such a difficult time. For both of us. We were always fighting and I was so angry at myself, I took it out on him. It's been about six months now and I thought I was getting over it. I really didn't expect this to show up this weekend.' The tears were falling now and Liz's eyes were red. She was looking at Marissa, she needed some validation.

'I don't think you can ever get over something like this. You just get used to living with it. Like a scar, it's always a part of you.' Marissa took a breath. 'It's okay to be upset, it's a natural thing. You got a shock, you weren't expecting this.' Marissa got up and found some kitchen roll and offered it to Liz who used it to blow her nose.

'No, I wasn't expecting this at all. I don't know what I was expecting, actually.' She tucked the used kitchen roll into a small ball and shoved it up inside the sleeve of her pyjama top. 'And you want to know what the weirdest thing is?'

'Go on.'

'I had decorated her room with Teletubbies wallpaper. Julie's room. She loved Tinky Winky best. She had a Tinky Winky teddy that she slept with, she couldn't go to bed without it.' The tears started again, deep sobs, Liz's whole body shook from them.

Marissa sat there with her, not sure if she should hold her hand, or even touch her at all. She did know not to try to get her to stop crying. It was good to cry, to get it out, and knowing that Marissa knew why she was crying made it all the more healing. The sobs eventually lessoned and Liz slowed down her breathing. Marissa got the feeling she needed something to help her to come back into the moment.

'Isn't it amazing that Tinky Winky came to Terry? He must have thought he made the whole thing up. It's kind of funny in a way, he probably thought he would find a wise medicine man, or one of your ancestors. He probably got a shock too!'

Liz calmed down and wiped her eyes with her sleeve. 'Yes, he probably did. He thought he made a mistake, and he still doesn't know why I got so upset. I wasn't able to tell him.'

'Maybe you could tell him now, now that you've told me. It would really boost his confidence to know he actually did get the message right.'

'Yes, I think I could tell him now. Thanks for listening. I don't know why I wasn't able to talk before. To him I mean. He is so nice, I suppose the whole thing really caught me by surprise.'

'Well, I'd be surprised too. It is such a profound connection to your baby, yet only you would understand it. It's beautiful.'

'I wish I could see her again, speak to her, say goodbye properly.'

'Maybe you can. She did have a message for you, so she's still around somewhere. In Spirit, isn't that what Séamus said?'

'Yes, you could be right. She did say through Terry that she loves me very much, and she was happy to have met me.'

'Yes. So she's not gone completely then. Julie, what a beautiful name, she's an angel now, isn't that what Terry said?'

Liz took a few moments to register this. 'Yes, she's an angel now. My Angel Julie. How beautiful.' She smiled and brushed the last few remaining tears away from her face.

'I don't know much about angels, that's Stephanie and Jenny's territory, but I'd like to learn. It must be wonderful to know that your baby is there, looking out for you, as an angel.'

'I never really thought about it like that, I was still focusing on the loss. Maybe this is a new way to connect to her. Maybe I can connect to the first baby too. I always imagined it was a boy. It would be nice to know that he's okay too.'

'Something to think about, maybe for next time?'

'Yes. I've taken up so much of your time, it must be getting late, and I'm not even dressed yet!'

Liz stood up and stretched. She cleared the plates and brought them over to the sink. Marissa brought over the cups. Liz turned to Marissa.

'Can I give you a hug?'

'Yes, I'd like that very much.'

'Thank you.'

Marissa said, 'You know, the more I think about this, the more amazing it is. Tinky Winky, I really do wonder what Terry thought when he met him... It's actually quite funny, poor Terry!'

Liz started to laugh, 'Yes, Terry went to visit the Teletubbies and met Tinky Winky, brought me back a feather and I started to cry, and couldn't speak for the rest of the night. Poor Terry! I wonder what he was thinking about too. I will have to speak to him. And I'd better get dressed. See you in the last session. Thank you again.'

She gave Marissa another hug and went upstairs.

Marissa finished the washing up and put away the dishes, the others were starting to trickle in to get their breakfast, it wasn't quite 7:30am just yet. Terry was one of them. He came straight over to Marissa.

'I saw you were talking to Liz, is she okay? I am really worried about her.'

'Yes, she's okay. She had a lot to process, I think talking to me has helped. You didn't do anything wrong, by the way. She wants to tell you herself so I won't say anything.'

Terry looked visibly relieved 'Oh Jeez, that's a relief. I thought I'd really fecked it all up. Her reaction scared the hell out of me. I had no idea what to do. I was so glad when you and Zaad came in. Hey, what's the story with you two anyway?' He cocked his head to one side, waiting for some gossip.

'Story? There's no story.'

'I will beg to differ, girl, I beg to differ. Just you wait, Terry knows.' He tapped his nose with his index finger twice. 'I can smell these things out a mile away. Ha ha! Do you want some breakfast?'

'I had toast already, thanks.' Marissa didn't want to approach the subject any further, Zaad was in one of those files that she put deeply away in her library in the cabinet. At least she hoped she had put it in there, so why did she suddenly get all nervous and jittery? She wasn't quite ready for this. She needed to focus on the work.

Saoirse came in. 'Oh, there you were, you've been gone for ages, I woke up and you weren't there – are you okay?'

'Yes thanks, I was awake early so I got up and went for a walk. How are you doing? Did you sleep?'

'Like a log! Whatever Séamus did last night with those ghosts, I mean, spirits, really worked. I must ask him about it. It could be handy for the future, you never know.'

After breakfast, everyone settled into the front room for the last session of the weekend. There seemed to be a mixture of excitement and sadness. Marissa certainly didn't want the weekend to come to an end, even though she had a lot to look forward to when she went home. It was nearly Christmas and she didn't have to go back into the office. She was really enjoying the group, getting to know her new friends, and getting to know herself a little better, too. *And it's so magical. Yes, it's totally magical here.*

It was raining. The wind and rain hit off the main window of the room, each heavy drop of rain landing with a thump then trickled down the glass. The hearth held the ashen remains of last night's fire, it wasn't set so they couldn't light it just yet. There was a sharp chill in the room. Some of her friends were wearing woolly hats and scarves. Marissa felt a shiver going down her back, she ran upstairs to get the blanket from her bed and her alpaca scarf. She literally bumped into Zaad in the corridor.

'Oh! Sorry! Hi!' Marissa blushed.

'Hi Marissa! No worries. Hey, did you sleep well?' Zaad smiled, showing his perfect teeth.

'Yes, very well, thanks, though I woke up early. You?'

'I did awaken early also, yes. I was thinking about the work that we did together. I found it very special, you meeting my great grandfather. I would really like to meet him too. Perhaps we could work together again, the next time?' He smiled at her.

Marissa smiled back. 'Yes, I'd like that. Séamus will be starting the session soon, I'm just grabbing my scarf and a blanket – it's cold in the room. Maybe you need yours, too? See you downstairs.'

Zaad smiled and Marissa's heart did a flip. That file on him, where the heck did she put it? She'd have to go looking again.

She came back into the main room to find that Séamus was already there. Zaad followed soon after. Liz had saved her a spot so she squeezed into it, grateful she wasn't squashing in beside Zaad. Séamus cleared his throat.

'Are we all here then? How are yiz all doing? Did yiz sleep?'

There were many nods, 'Good's and 'Yes's'.

'Ahh good. We finish at noon and I have a lot to get through today. So to recap what we've already done, we've gone on a journey to find out what we need to know as we begin our medicine work. We went to the ancestors to get their permission to grow. Some of yiz had really important experiences there, well done. We went on a journey to connect to the drum that we have, or the drum that you're about to have – and yiz'll have that sorted for the next session in the spring, right?'

Finn and Liz nodded their heads.

'Then yiz went on your own journeys for each other last night. I want to hear a little bit more about that. But as you may have noticed, I'm not spending a lot of time listening to all of your experiences. That's because I'm not treating yiz like babies. You're not babies. That means you need to take responsibility for yourselves and ask for extra help if you need it. I don't know yiz need something if yiz don't tell me. Right?'

They all nodded.

'Good. Now. Does anyone have any question or issue that came up from last night that's still weighing on your mind today?'

Terry hesitated, then kept his hand down. Liz softened in the chair beside Marissa, who knew that she would rather not discuss this in front of the group.

Saoirse put her hand up.

'Saoirse. Who were you working with?'

'Jenny.'

'And is she okay with you sharing?'

Saoirse looked at Jenny, who nodded.

'Grand, so. What's the story?'

'This is more about me than about Jenny, actually. She went on a journey for me, and the gift was the stuffed rabbit teddy bear that I had since I was five years old. I lost it when I was about nine. We moved house, and it must have been left behind. I was devastated at the time, but I'd forgotten all about it, it really was a surprise. How did Jenny know about it? She said she wasn't able to remember what she saw on her journey. She was worried she'd got it wrong, but she knew it was a teddy bear-shaped like a rabbit. She even described the ears and the colour.'

Jenny added, 'It was so strange, I didn't know where I was, I couldn't see anything, like I was lost in a fog. I have trouble going on journeys, I guess I didn't do too badly, though, if the rabbit was something special to Saoirse.'

Séamus thought for a moment. 'Remember what a journey is. It's going into the subconscious, the unconscious, the soul and the collective. And remember, the clearer you are as a person, the easier it is to see what is in front of you. We can have difficulty telling objects apart, especially at this early stage, what is yours, what is hers, you know what I mean. But that may not be what happened here. You said that when you lost this rabbit Saoirse, you were devastated, you didn't know where it went. It's possible that Jenny wasn't going to find out where it went to either, so she didn't know where she was when it found her. It found her because it was looking for you, or it wouldn't have shown up for either of you.'

He turned to address the group. 'We don't get all the answers, we get the answers that we need at the time that we need them. And *everything* is significant – whether you see or you don't see. And everything is alive, even teddy bears have energy in them, the energy that we put into them, because we loved them. They are just as alive as the rocks and plants – for the Shaman, everything has a life force. There is a meaning behind everything. This journey Jenny went on is a good example of being blind. She didn't know where she was, what she was receiving or where she was going. You are all blind to each other as you don't really know each other yet. Going in blindfolded, not having expectations, that's very important. If you expected to find a rabbit, or a teddy, then you'd have been making it up in your mind and not really connecting in to the energy. When we know too much, that gets in the way. That's why it's harder to work with people you know, people you love, like family. Going in blind is the best way to work. A teddy bear rabbit is quite a specific thing to find at this stage of your training. Good work Jenny and Saoirse. Anyone else want to share?'

Finn put up his hand. 'I had trouble with my journey for Stephanie. I couldn't settle into it. I found a ruby to bring back to her, but I don't know if I made it up or if it was real. She liked the ruby, but I had no images around it, and neither did she. Maybe it was a bit like Jenny, I'm glad to have heard about her experience, it makes me feel better.'

Séamus replied, 'This is a process. You're not supposed to get in alignment with it right at the beginning, you need to work on it. So don't be too worried, I'm sure that Stephanie got what she needed this weekend, even if you, or she, isn't sure exactly what that is. This isn't work for your brain, it's for your soul. It's energy work. You're probably also tired. Processing everything we are doing here takes up time and space, yet we are only getting started. As time goes on you'll build up your 'shamanic muscles' and be able to handle more and more without your brain saying 'I've had enough, I'm done here', and shutting down on you.'

He stood up with his drum in hand and softly banged it, getting louder and louder until the drum reverberated across the whole room. Marissa felt it echoing through her body. The energy of the room changed, something lifted, it felt like they were all more awake and ready for the next piece of work. The rain continued to lash down outside, it was as if the rain was trying to compete with the drum, but there was no competition. Séamus stopped and waited for a moment or two before putting the drum down. He looked at each one of them in turn. Then he began.

> *'Oh Great Spirit of the North, we come to you and ask for the strength and power to bear what is cold and harsh in life. We honour our ancestors who have also received the winds that truly can be overwhelming at times. Support us and warm us as we do our work, hold us as we release the patterns that are holding us back and place them into the fire.*

'We are still doing the work of the North, and this morning, in our final session of this first training weekend, we are going to look at what you need to let go of, these patterns that are blocking you from seeing the journeys, from seeing the truth, so you can be a clearer channel for the work. Your job is to become the hollow bone, the empty container, so that you can interpret what comes through you in a clean and clear way, rather than projecting your own pain and your own flaws onto the message.'

'So, what are your patterns? How are they blocking you? Do you constantly tell yourself you're a failure? Are you criticising yourself harshly? Are you the writer who refuses to put anything on the page because they just know that it will be terrible? Everyone has something different. Here's the key to the shamanic work we are doing – it is energetic. You probably know exactly what your pattern is. You've probably already tried to shift it, to clear it. But you just keep coming back to it, or it keeps coming back to you, somehow. It's still here. And it will be here with you for a long time to come, but at least after today, you will be able to start working on it in a different way to shift it, so that over time, eventually, it won't stop you from writing that book, or making that speech, or standing up and singing in front of a crowd. Or going on a journey and knowing that you're not making it all up. That's why it's so important to clear this here, in this the first direction of our inner compass. Before we go forward, the work goes deeper, gets more complicated, darker. You need to be on your own side, not afraid to face yourself in the dark. When you are facing other people's darkness, you want to be able to recognise your own.'

Marissa got a shiver down her spine at the thought of facing other people's darkness. An image of Martin came into her mind, a memory of how she felt that time in Cabra when he freaked her out. Yes, that was darkness showing through, his fiery eyes and scary teeth. Maybe this work would help her be stronger and better able to be of use to him. Yes, this felt right. She was going to face her own darkness, it would be okay. She looked around her, Stephanie seemed uneasy, so did Jenny. Marissa wondered if angel work and darkness work went together.

'Now. We are going to do this work using the journey as our guide, and we will be going for another person, not for ourselves. It is often easier to see what is going on for someone else, and this is good practice for you when you will be working with a client. I want yiz to pair up with someone different now. You all give permission to do the work because you are here, yes? But how deep it goes is up to you. Some of this will be strong, some of it not as strong, depending on how determined you are to clear these blocks in you. People get used to their blocks, they wear them as a comfort blanket, it stops them from living up to their true potential. But they weigh you down, dim your light.'

'Now then. You're going to journey to find out the energetic cause of one of the blocks stopping your client from healing. You're not to fix or change anything, you're just on a journey of discovery. So no smashy smashy, just go in, take a look around, and come back. Then tell your client what you saw, no holds barred, just like it was. No brain making stuff up. We are not blind men looking at elephants. We are the shaman who can see the boats, even when the others can not. Now, off yiz go, and come back here when yiz are done for the final Q&A and the closing ceremony.'

Liz caught hold of Marissa's arm. 'Will you be with me?'

'Sure. Did you talk to Terry yet?'

'No, not yet.'

'Are you able to say something to him? I think it would help?'

She shook her head. 'I'd just start crying again – can you say it to him? It's okay for you to say it.'

'Okay, if you're sure. Where do you want us to go to work?'

'I don't know.'

'How about upstairs, my room, if Saoirse isn't there. I'll just grab Terry first in case he is worried about this next journey.' Liz nodded her agreement.

Marissa ran after Terry, who was already on his way into the kitchen.

'Terry, wait! I wanted to talk to you for a moment.'

He turned, looking very serious.

'I heard about Tinky Winky.'

He crumpled. 'I have no idea what that was. It was the last thing I expected to meet. And then Liz, well her crying, she was inconsolable.'

'I just wanted to let you know, what you did, it was a good thing. The message, the gift, it was healing. Liz isn't able to talk about it with you just yet, but she said I could tell you that you did right by her. You're good at this.'

He brightened. 'Really? I was so worried.'

'Yeah, really. I have to go now, but I wanted you to know so you weren't afraid of messing this journey up.'

'Hey, thanks, girl.' He gave her a hug, it felt nice. 'I really appreciate you telling me, especially now. I was feeling sick with nerves about this next one. I feel much better.'

'I'm glad. I was worried you might be. I get anxiety all the time, I know how unpleasant it can be.'

'Friends then for sure. I'm here if you ever need me, ' said Terry with a smile.

Marissa went upstairs. Liz was sitting on Saoirse's bed.

'Are you ready to do this?' asked Marissa, relieved that Terry took himself off the hook.

'Yeah. I haven't got a drum, though.'

'That's okay, You can use mine.' As she said this, Marissa wasn't really sure if she wanted to hand her drum over to Liz, but she knew it was the right thing to do.

'I'm not sure I'm ready for another upset,' said Liz.

'I know. Maybe we should do yours first then, to get it over with.'

'Okay.'

Marissa gave her drum to Liz. She took a breath. *It's okay, it's just for one journey.* She went to her own bed, plumped the pillow and lay down. 'Hey, I might go to sleep here, I think I'll lie on the floor instead.' She spread the blanket on the floor, took her pillow and lay down. It was a little cold, she got up again and put on her hat and got another blanket. She lay down again.

'Okay I'm ready. I'm going to journey for you to find the source of one of the blocks stopping you from healing.'

Marissa closed her eyes, waiting for Liz to start drumming.

She found herself falling, as if she was falling through the floor. It wasn't like the journey to her drum, this was different. It was like she was going down an elevator, down and down and down. Liz had started drumming but it didn't seem to matter, whatever this was, it was pulling her right down, so she let go of her resistance and allowed it.

She landed on a grassy lawn, got up and brushed herself off. She looked around. The grass was perfect, each blade the same size and height. She wondered if it was fake, then she started wondering if she was back in Teletubby land. In the distance she heard a wolf howling, so she walked towards it. As she walked she found herself in a forest, going deeper and deeper in. The sound of the howling kept moving further and further away. She was losing it, so she started running, she felt a sense of urgency, but the branches and trees seemed to get in the way, brushing off her face, rubbing her cheek, trying to trip her up. She pushed them away and kept going, but she seemed to be going around in circles, it was getting frustrating. She couldn't tell which direction the howling was coming from, so she stopped and just stood there.

The wolf was watching her from a distance. It came over to her, it was white and quite young, not scary at all. It cocked its head sideways and looked at her, its blue eyes bright in the dark, then it left. A moment later, all the trees disappeared and she was in a kitchen, with lino on the floor, bright lights and white kitchen cabinets. There was a baby in a high chair and a young girl standing in the middle of the room crying. The girl was wearing a dress, she had long hair and she was holding and rubbing her hand, as if it had just been slapped. There was a man standing over her, shouting at her. The baby seemed oblivious to it all, it was playing with its food, and it threw its beaker onto the floor. This seemed to incense the man, possibly the father of the crying girl, making him scream all the louder.

The scene went silent, as if it was a movie and someone had pressed pause.

Marissa picked her way around the room, weaving around the people there, she wanted to pick up the beaker from the floor but then she remembered she wasn't to interfere. She suddenly heard a word loudly inside her head. FEAR. Then the callback signal brought her back into the room and she was back, as if she had been suddenly kicked out of where she had been.

She sat up and rubbed her eyes. She wanted some water.

'Well? What did you see?' asked Liz impatiently.

Marissa remembered she had a bottle of water beside her bed from the previous night, she found it, opened it and took a swig out of it.

'It happened very quickly, I fell, I was in a field, I think it was artificial, then suddenly I heard a howling, like a wolf, so I followed it into a forest. It seemed like the forest was fighting me. I chased after the wolf but was going around in circles. It was white, the wolf, and young. It came to me once I stopped running. Then I was in a kitchen, a baby in a high chair, a young child crying, her father was shouting, at least I think it was her father. I think he had slapped her hand. The baby dropped the beaker on the floor, then I heard the word fear. That's it.'

'Oh. I wonder if that was me as a little girl. My father did lose his temper a lot, but I don't remember being slapped. And I do have a little sister, but I have an older brother too. Fear. That's interesting. I do feel a lot of fear.'

Marissa thought for a moment. 'The girl had long hair and wore a pretty dress, the kitchen had white cabinets. Does that fit?'

'Maybe. I don't know.'

'I think it's more about the word fear than about the details of the image... Maybe your fear has you feeling lost, like I felt lost in the forest. And your pattern of fear has you going around in circles, running away or towards something. When I stopped running the wolf came to me. And he seemed nice, not scary at all. Maybe you need to stop running and let your fear come to you. Maybe that's how you break the pattern.'

'That's interesting, yes, I do see that I do that. Okay. I'll work with that. Thank you so much.'

She handed the drum to Marissa. 'Can we take a break for a moment? I think I need to get a drink too.'

'Sure.'

Liz left the room. Marissa felt like Liz really hadn't paid attention to her suggestion. She walked around a little to stretch her body out and looked out the window at the rain. *How can I journey to these places and still be here at the same time? And why are there so many images when they didn't all seem to be needed? And where is here, anyway?* Liz came back in, and Marissa brought herself back to the present moment.

'Are you okay on the floor?' asked Marissa, turning to her.

'Yes, it's fine, thanks.'

Liz got on the floor in Marissa's place, smiled and closed her eyes. Marissa sat on the floor beside her and picked up her drum. She took a moment to connect to it, visualising the white buffalo. She felt a smile inside of herself and a calmness that helped her focus on the job at hand. She started drumming the opening sequence, then she went into the middle sequence, heartbeat of the world. She cleared her mind, let her beater do the work, she still felt like she was getting to know her drum, it felt good to hold, she loved the sound of it.

I should practice with it when I'm back home. She went with the flow of the beat while keeping an eye on Liz, who still had her eyes closed. After a few minutes, she started wondering if she should stop, play the callback signal. Liz started moving a little bit, so she took that as a sign and played the callback. She thought it was too short, maybe she stopped too early. She kept drumming a little longer, then she stopped, reached over to place the drum onto her bed. She waited for Liz to come back to her.

'I had the most wonderful journey,' said Liz, eventually sitting up and rubbing her eyes. I met my angel! She's so beautiful.' Liz turned and looked at Marissa. 'Oh no! This was supposed to be for you, wasn't it, to journey into your blocks. Oh no. That's not what happened at all.'

Marissa wasn't sure if she was relieved or disappointed. 'That's okay, Liz, I don't mind. You probably needed it more than I did.'

'I'm so sorry! We can meet up before the next workshop and do this again, I'll be better able to focus on you. Is that okay?'

'Yes, that would be great. Don't worry about it. It probably wasn't supposed to be for me today.'

They went back downstairs, Marissa feeling slightly bereft. Terry and Stephanie were chatting away happily, talking about movies and tarot cards. Marissa didn't want to sit beside Liz just then, she started feeling a little claustrophobic *But no nerves, strange...* She went into the kitchen and got herself a cuppa to make some space between them. Coming back, she could see Liz talking to Stephanie and Terry looking bright and animated. She *was* happy for her, she just wanted some space for herself. She sat on a free sofa and cradled her tea. Jenny and Saoirse came into the room and joined her.

'How are you going?' Jenny asked.

'I'm okay. That was a little strange, but it's okay.'

'Yes, there's been a lot of strange this past few days, but strange in a cool way. I'm really enjoying this. Hey, you said you were interested in angels, there's an angel meditation class on the day after St Stephen's Day in town, do you want to come with me? You live in Dublin, right?'

Marissa perked right up. 'Oh yes, that sounds great, really does. Yes, I'm in Dublin. Thanks for asking me!'

Jenny took her phone out from under her clothes. 'Shh, don't tell Séamus. I know we were supposed to leave them upstairs but I'm addicted to my phone, I feel naked without it. Probably worse than naked. Here put your number in and I can text you or phone you with the details later on.'

Marissa put her phone number into Jenny's notepad app and handed her back the phone. She tucked it back into her clothes.

'Cool. Thanks!'

Everyone had arrived but there was still no sign of Séamus. Marissa wondered where he went to when he wasn't with them. Then the front door opened and he came in, wearing a raincoat and his hat. He had his drum tucked under the coat, he put it down, hung his coat up on the rail, put his hat on top, turned and winked at Marissa.

'You like my hat,' he said to her.

She laughed. 'It's very cool.'

He addressed the group, 'Right, folks, please. Are we all here? We need to close up, finish up and get yiz all home. How was that exercise? Does anyone want to share?'

Terry put his hand up.

'Terry! Go for it.'

'Thanks, Séamus. That was just amazeballs. I mean, wow. Stephanie was great, but hey, I was pure amazing.'

Everyone laughed.

'Okay. Well. I journeyed for her, she said it was okay for me to tell you. I asked to see her blocks, and I saw some Lego blocks at first, I thought that was funny, like a pun on words, blocks, Lego blocks, you know. Anyway, I realised that I was in a child's playroom, but there was no child. I looked around the room, not wanting to disturb anything. There were dolls there, some books, a knitting set of some sort. That was it. I didn't see anything else, and then I came back. But what was amazing was that I described everything to Stephanie, and it was her playroom, even the toys I saw were the ones that she loved the most when she was growing up. But I don't know how that's a block or a pattern for her. I'm excited, though. I thought I wouldn't be any good at this!'

'So you were clear in your intention to see her blocks?'

'Yes.'

'And you didn't just see a child's playroom with toys, you saw her exact childhood playroom?'

'Yes! Yes, I did.'

'So how is a child's playroom a block? This isn't a trick question, Terry, I want you to think about it. Anyone?'

Nobody put up their hands, but Marissa felt she knew the answer. She hesitantly raised her hand.

'Marissa?'

'I'm wondering if the playroom is a safe space where she can hide and regress to a safe space, maybe she doesn't want to grow up. Well, maybe not Stephanie exactly, but some part of her. Or maybe her inner child needs some help.'

'Very good,' said Séamus. 'It could be all of these things. The darkness masquerading as a child's playroom, with delicious toys to entice her, to distract her, all of her childhood favourites. Stephanie, does this fit for you?'

All eyes turned to Stephanie. She was bright red with embarrassment and squirming in her seat.

'Hey, I know this is difficult, that's what I said to you earlier, that's why few people travel on this path. But I know you can do it. Face your darkness, we are all here to support you. But you have to do it, to own it, what is yours, your patterns that keep you from growing up, the patterns of regressing or hiding. Does this resonate?'

Stephanie nodded.

'It probably resonates with most of you in the room, in ways that you don't know just yet. Great work, Terry, and well done, Stephanie. Recognising it is the first step to healing it.'

Stephanie looked like she wanted the sofa to swallow her up.

'Anyone else want to share?'

Zaad put up his hand. Séamus nodded.

'Finn was journeying for me. He said he went to a very small space like he was in prison. There were big iron gates all around him, he said he didn't have very much room to move. Then he saw a way out, it was an illusion, the gates on one side of him were actually not touching, he could walk straight out of them to freedom. I feel trapped all the time, especially when I'm with my family. Perhaps I imagine that they trap me, but I do know in some parts of my life, I certainly am trapped. I didn't feel this way while I am here, this weekend. I want to thank you for that. I don't know what I can do to change this in my real life, I would love to stop feeling this way all the time.'

'Good work, Zaad. It looks like you may have a way out, you just need to see what is real, and what is the illusion. Start from there. Finn, do you have anything you want to add?'

Finn shook his head.

'It's getting on for time. Let's talk about the homework. Homework for you personally, and homework for you to do with someone else. We will meet again in the spring. I will contact you with dates, and it will probably be back here. I'm working out the details.'

'In the meantime, firstly, I want you to use your drum and record for yourself a few drumming tracks. Use the opening sequence, then drum for the heartbeat of the world. Play this middle section for ten minutes for a short journey and again for twenty minutes for a longer journey. End with the callback. So you will have two drumming tracks, a short and a long one. You can make as many of these as you want.

'Secondly, use the tracks to go on three journeys for yourself. Again, you're not to fix or change anything, you're just observing. First journey is to the North direction, to meet a spirit guide. This guide can be one you already know. It can be a power animal, I'll leave it to Spirit to bring to you what you need. Second journey is to your childhood, to a moment in time when you were younger where you were upset with something connected to the block that you discovered today. Imagine that you're right there, in the room with yourself. If you set the intention, you don't need to think too hard about it. Remember, it might not be literally you visiting your inner child, but the energy is the same, it's just how you interpret it. Third journey is to you, in the future. Ask yourself for some advice. That one is a doozy.'

Everyone was writing furiously, Marissa included.

'That's your personal work. You need to document it with the time and date of when you went, what you saw, how you felt, what was good and what was not good. Then send that to me in an email. I will remind you at the end of January.

'You also have client work to do. I want you to work with another person, it is good practice for you. I think use each other for now, and then later in the year, you can find someone outside the group to use as a guinea pig. So think about who that may be. But for now, you'll need to get in touch with each other outside of here, so before we leave, make sure you've got each other's phone numbers. I'll make this one easy as you're still just starting out. Simply repeat the journey for the gift, and ask for a message too. Do this with someone you have *not* worked with here this weekend. You will have to meet up in person to do that. I want this also written down and sent to me with the personal work.'

'Now, does anyone else have any other questions?'

After a minute, while people were finishing up writing, Saoirse put up her hand.

'Séamus, what did you do last night that stopped the spirits from waking us up?'

'Ahh, yes, I was wondering if one of you would ask me that. I did a warding and banishing on your bedrooms. It's not quite the same as the work that we are doing here. You need to have done a lot more work and be much stronger before you can start messing about with that. I'd rather not go into the details of it. Don't worry, it's all ahead of you if you stay the course.'

Saoirse nodded, looking disappointed.

Terry put up his hand. 'So we have to record three drumming tracks, do three journeys for ourselves, and one for someone else?'

'Exactly. Now. Let's close the directions, all except for the North direction, as we are still doing our work in the North. We leave the North open, and it will travel with you, to hold you all and keep you safe as you go deep and cleanse and heal those patterns.'

He stood up and banged his drum, facing East. Everyone put down their notebooks and blankets and stood with him. He recited the prayer East, West and South, some of the group recited it with him as they were getting to know it. He ended in the middle of the room, said thank you to Earth and Sky. He then stood over the altar, drumming over it. Then he stopped, turned to the group and said, 'Thank yiz, thank yiz all. This is great, yiz are all doing great. My door is always open, if yiz need me yiz know where I am. I'll see yiz all next time.'

Marissa felt a push to ask one more thing. 'Séamus? Can you send us a copy of the words of your prayer? I'd love to learn it for next time.'

'Great idea, Marissa, yes, I'll do that. Remind me if I forget. Happy Christmas, everyone! Have a lovely New Year, and I'll see yiz in Feb!'

Marissa gladly accepted Terry's offer of a lift to the train station in Galway. He was travelling to Cork for Christmas, so he couldn't drive her all the way to Dublin. She had her return ticket anyway, and she wanted some space to think, so that was fine by her. They were quiet in the car, it was just the two of them, both of them had a lot to process. Marissa was glad he wasn't as chatty as before, she didn't want him making jokes about Zaad and her. There was no Zaad and her.

As soon as they got off the minor roads and onto the main road, their phones had coverage, and suddenly all the texts and emails came in on both of their phones. It was funny, Marissa had fourteen text messages, Terry had forty-eight, and sixty-three emails.

'You're very popular!' Marissa was happy she wasn't forgotten, although most of the messages were from her mother wondering where she was. *Oy vey*! Michelle had texted too, it looked like Tobermory was fine but missing her – *How does she know?* She also got several texts from Sarah, who asked if she was still hungover from the party, if she survived Galway and could they go out together on New Year's Eve. The party seemed like last year. It felt like she had been away for much longer than three days.

Terry dropped her just outside the train station, it was too busy to park so she hopped out, got her stuff and waved goodbye. She saw Stephanie in the distance also at the train station but Stephanie didn't see her, so she didn't call out. She wanted space on the train journey to think. She had Zaad's number, well, she had everyone's number now, but she had Zaad's number. Should she contact him to do that journey homework? Or should she meet someone else? He did say he wanted to work with her again, but Séamus said to work with someone else. Maybe she would just text to say hello. She was tingly just thinking about it.

She fell asleep on the train. When it pulled into Dublin in the early evening it was dark. She was roused awake by the activity of people getting their bags. Back to reality. There was Christmas music playing in the train station, decorations were up, glistening and blinking in the darkness of the evening. It was nice, but she felt sad that it was over, for now anyway. Marissa felt like she had been to another planet. She put her backpack on her back; she had folded her new (unused) wellies and managed to stuff them inside. *What was all that panic about? I didn't need them after all. I do get myself into a right tizzy at times, over nothing.* Marissa carried the bag with her drum in it and walked home through town slowly, taking in the sights and sounds of Dublin. It felt like she was coming back down to Earth.

CHAPTER TWENTY TWO 

Seven days had passed since the workshop with Séamus but it felt like it had been a month. Marissa enjoyed the time off work, relishing the time on her own to process what had happened for her. She slept, sorted out her 'filing cabinet' and 'library' a little better, and spent some time getting to know her drum. She had even recorded a few drumming tracks, but she didn't go on a journey yet.

Christmas Day was dinner at Eli and Carol's. Carol's parents were on a cruise and Carol wanted to have a turkey dinner, so she invited Marissa and it was just the three of them. Eli had been very relaxed about it, 'allowing' Carol to put up a small tree. Carol's stomach was enlarging as the baby grew, and thankfully, her morning sickness was lessening. She was able to cook and enjoy the food. Marissa brought over some gifts and a box of biscuits, she did all the washing up, it had been a lovely afternoon.

It was St Stephens Day and Marissa hadn't yet heard from Jenny about the angel workshop which was supposed to be the following day. She thought she'd send Jenny a text so she pulled out her phone, waited for a moment, not sure how to phrase it. She eventually typed:

> HI, hope you had a Happy Christmas. Is the angel meditation workshop still going ahead tomorrow? Can you let me know where and when?

After half an hour, there was still no reply. Marissa remembered how Jenny said she didn't go anywhere without her phone, that she was addicted to it. *I hope Jenny's okay, the text does look like it was sent. I guess if I'm meant to go, I'll hear back in time*

Marissa didn't fancy going into town for the sales, there always were too many people on Stephen's day. Instead, she tidied her flat, organised her books and her wardrobe, and put together a bag of things to drop into the charity shop. Looking at her wardrobe she noticed for the first time how few colourful items she owned. *Maybe it's time to buy some new clothes?* Marissa didn't feel like dropping in on her parents and the whole day still stretched ahead of her. She turned the heating on and cuddled up on the sofa with her duvet to watch a movie. Tobermory jumped up beside her and circled once, then settled at her feet. Her phone buzzed a text from Terry. She had it beside her, she picked it up and read it.

Hope u had a lovely Xmas. Fancy being my partner for the journey work? I'll be in Dub week after New Year's, can we meet up?

She perked up and wrote back immediately: Sounds gr8, look forward to it!

Brilliant, drop u a note next week! Enjoy the rest of the hols!

Marissa was beginning to feel a little worried, she had decided she really wanted to go to the angel workshop. She felt anxiety building up in the pit of her stomach and she wasn't engaging with the movie. She stretched and Tobermory jumped down and jumped up into the armchair. Switching off the TV she got her laptop out, and looked up 'Angel workshops in Dublin.' There were at least twenty results, she scanned through most of them but kept coming back to one. 'Reiki Level 1 Workshop.' It wasn't angels, but it was Reiki, and she was interested in learning more about that, too. The workshop was at the end of January. *That's ages away.* She clicked the link and was brought to the page of Dolores Carmody, Reiki Master, Greystones, County Dublin. She checked out Dolores's website. There was a photograph of Dolores on the 'About Dolores' page, it was taken in a garden in front of a rose bush in bloom. Dolores was about sixty, she had nice eyes, grey hair in a bun and was wearing a purple shawl. Marissa looked up her credentials, she was a Reiki Master teacher, Seichem Master teacher, Aura-Soma practitioner and also offered Angel Card readings. *There's a lot of stuff there that I know nothing about.*

Marissa was so engrossed in Dolores's website she didn't hear the text from Jenny coming in. The phone rang and gave her a fright. Jenny was phoning her, she picked it up.

'Hi Marissa, so sorry I didn't remember to send you the information. I was with my family, I didn't see your text until just now. Did you have a nice Christmas?'

'Hi Jenny, that's okay, yes I had a nice break, thanks. I needed it after all the work we did with Séamus!'

'Yes! Me too! I couldn't stop sleeping, and I'm still exhausted! Anyway, about tomorrow, something's come up at home, I'm not able to go now. But you could still go if you wanted to?'

'Sure. Why not?'

'It's in Temple Bar from 10–4, over The Music Shop. You can get a ticket at the door. It's being run by Cheryl Bryant.'

'Thanks! Have you been to a workshop with her before?'

'Actually, no. It was advertised in the Reiki Federation newsletter. She's a member, I'm a member too! But I've never met her.'

'Oh, okay! I'll check it out, thanks.'

'Have you got your partner yet for the client work?'

'Terry just asked me this morning. Have you?'

'No, not yet, looks like I'd better sort it out soon! Talk to you again sometime!'

'Yes, thanks for phoning. Talk soon!' Marissa hung up, slightly relieved knowing the details, but anxiety still thrummed in her stomach at a low-level.

Now she had two teachers to choose from for the new work that she wanted to do. She looked up Cheryl Bryant's website and found it easily. Her photo was on the home page, it was a studio portrait. Cheryl was younger than Dolores, in her late thirties with medium-length, straight brown hair, in a perfect bob. She posed in her photograph with her hands under her chin, she had a beautiful smile and looked like she could be a model. Marissa found the workshop listed on her 'Events' page. She flipped over to Dolores's webpage, her website seemed much more homely. Marissa looked at her credentials again and noticed she was also a Reiki Federation Member. Marissa was a little relieved at that but she didn't know why. *She seems more authentic than Cheryl? But Cheryl's workshop is tomorrow, and I've no plans for tomorrow... Maybe I'll just go along and see. And it's only €30. Sure, what could go wrong?*

The next day was cold and overcast, the city seemed tired after all of the festivities. It was that silent time of days between the joyous celebrations of Christmas, and the coming New Year. There were a few sales on, the shops were open, but there weren't many people about. Marissa walked from her flat to Temple Bar and easily found The Music Shop. She stood outside looking for the door to 'Little Haven' where the workshop was to take place. She saw the sign for it above the main shop sign, over a slim door between buildings. She found a small buzzer and pressed it.

'Hello?' a small voice spoke from the speaker.

'I'm here for the workshop,' replied Marissa.

'Ahh. Good. Come on in.' A buzzer sounded and the door unlocked. Marissa pressed it open and went inside, closing the door behind her. She shivered. *It's as cold in here as it was outside.* There was a narrow corridor with stairs, Marissa walked up two flights and came up and out into a bright reception area. *This feels better.*

The woman standing there looked like she could be an older version of the Cheryl Bryant on the website. Her hair was longer though, straggly and dull. She wore a full length flowing dress and her face, particularly her eyes, looked very tired.

The woman smiled. 'Welcome, my name is Cheryl, and you are?'

'Marissa.'

'Hi Marissa, it's lovely to meet you. I wasn't expecting you. How did you know about today?'

Marissa smiled back. 'Jenny told me about it, and I found your website.'

'Ahh, good. It's always good to know the website is working. I don't know Jenny? Anyway. I'm glad you're here. I'm just waiting for a few more people, then we will start. Can you pay me first?'

'Sure.' Marissa opened her handbag, fished out her wallet, took out the €30, and handed it to Cheryl.

'Thank you.' Cheryl placed her hands in prayer position and did a small bow. Marissa smiled, but inside she began to feel a little bit on edge.

'Please leave your shoes here.' Cheryl gestured to a wooden rack and waited while Marissa took her runners off and placed them on one of the railings. Cheryl then led Marissa down the corridor and into the main room. It was big and bright with wooden floors, it looked like a yoga studio. There were twelve fold-up chairs laid out in a circle but only three women were there.

'Please sit. I'll be in shortly.'

Cheryl left the room. Marissa smiled at the others, chose a chair and hung her coat on the back of it, then sat down. She looked at her phone to check the time. It was 9:55am. She doubted that nine more people would show up in the next five minutes. The others looked at her and smiled. They were sitting together and had been talking, so they seemed to know each other. Her edginess began to turn into a nervousness. She rocked slightly in the chair, looking around her, trying to settle herself.

Why am I feeling anxious? Is it too soon since Séamus's workshop? Maybe if Jenny was here too, it would be better. Well, I'm here now, I should give it a chance. It could be fun. She focused on her breathing until she felt more steady.

A few minutes passed then Cheryl came back into the room. 'It's wonderful to see you all. It looks like it will just be the five of us today. Let's put away some of these chairs.'

They reorganised the circle so that there were only five chairs, and they all sat down. The room felt very empty.

'It must be because it's so close to Christmas. I thought it would be a great time to connect to our angels, well, never mind. We are here now. Sandra, Rebecca and Denise, this is Marissa. We'll have a lovely day, just the four of us.'

It was a very awkward morning. Cheryl was chatting for a long time with Sandra and Rebecca about people they had in common. Denise smiled apologetically at Marissa for most of this conversation. It seemed that Sandra was Rebecca's mother, and they had been to many workshops together before.

Finally, Cheryl began the workshop by saying a prayer. Once that was over, she invited everyone to get a blanket and she pulled out a small CD player and put on some music.

'Now everyone, make yourselves comfortable and close your eyes. Listen to my voice and I will bring you to meet your guardian angel.' She took out a piece of paper and started to read from it. Marissa closed her eyes and tried to relax. The music grated on Marissa's nerves, it wasn't helping. Cheryl's voice was faint, not strong like Séamus's. His voice caught you and brought you with him wherever he was going. Marissa could listen to Séamus forever, but Cheryl was hesitant and stumbled over herself from time to time, even though she was reading the meditations from a page. It was hard to hear her over the music, which reminded Marissa of something they'd play in an elevator, and after a time, she began to be quite agitated. When it was over, she felt very disappointed. She wasn't able to relax and focus on the meditation at all, let alone feel like she was making a connection with her Guardian Angel.

It didn't flow. Marissa walked through town deciding what to have for lunch. *It felt forced, not natural. Will I go back?* She felt sorry for Cheryl only having the four of them turning up, if she was to leave it would be very noticeable. Marissa realised she had tension in her body, it felt better to walk it out. The others had brought packed lunch's in with them and seemed happy to stay in the centre and eat. Marissa said she needed to go out to buy something, and here she was, deciding whether to have fish and chips, a veggie wrap, to go back or forget about the workshop altogether and go to the movies instead.

Movies sound great. If I do a runner it would look very bad, though. Maybe I should go back. She chose the veggie wrap, promising herself she could have the fish and chips for dinner after. That would help her get through the afternoon. *I guess I'm going back then.* She got a packet of Tayto and a lemonade to go with her wrap and reluctantly brought the food back to the yoga centre as it was too cold to sit outside and eat it. It *was* a yoga centre, Marissa had noticed the noticeboard when she left. *Cheryl must be renting it for the workshop, she probably has lost some money on it then. I'm sure it cost a good bit to rent that room.*

She rang the bell and Cheryl let her in. She took her shoes off again and sat with the others as they were chatting and finishing their lunches. *Roads and weather, strange that we have to take our shoes off but we can bring food and drink in here.* Marissa opened her can of lemonade and decided she would practice her counselling techniques for the afternoon as she was still feeling very awkward and uncomfortable.

Person-centred counselling, for the therapist, sometimes involves sitting with resistance and difficult feelings. Marissa remembered her tutor saying 'When you can't escape from something, like being stuck in a traffic jam or in a queue for the doctor's, it is a good opportunity to practice non-judgemental compassion.' When you have no choice but to sit it out, being an observer, rather than waiting, takes the pressure off. When you do this, you remove your expectation that something has to happen to keep you amused. Nothing really happens in a traffic jam or in a queue, and once you no longer need to be fulfilled, it releases you from your expectations and makes life a little easier.

Marissa tried to relax into her non-judgemental practice, nothing was really happening in this workshop, she wasn't learning anything from the teacher, anyway, or so she thought. But she was distracted, agitated, and nervous. It was difficult to stay non-judgemental. *So what is my learning here? Or what were my expectations? I expected that Cheryl would teach me something? Or I expected that I would have a deeply profound experience like the ones I had in Clifden? Let it go, breathe, just be here.*

She noted the sense of disappointment that she still felt as she closed her eyes for another guided mediation with that bloody awful music. *Maybe it's too soon after Séamus. He's really something, that workshop was very powerful. I learnt a lot. I guess I need a really good teacher. Cheryl isn't a good teacher, not for me anyway. No wonder there are only a few of us here. Oh dear that's a judgement, isn't it. I'm not able to sit with this at all. Damn and blast. I need another strategy then – maybe I could go on a journey while she's doing the meditation? Yes, that's a great idea, I'll try that.*

Marissa closed her eyes and tried to travel into her body the way she did when Séamus was drumming in the background, but it just wasn't happening. She opened her eyes, the other women looked blissful. Whatever it was, it was working for them, but not for her. She looked at Cheryl and then suddenly Cheryl looked directly back at her. Marissa felt a sudden flash of heat enter her body and travel down her spine, into her left leg. She shuddered and closed her eyes again. Something felt very strange. Now she *really* wanted to get out of there, and fast.

She used her mindfulness technique try to slow down her breathing, to feel the floor beneath her feet. *No, it's not working.* She started to feel itchy like ants were crawling on her leg and up her body... *What the heck was that heat? Did she do something to me? I have to leave. It feels wrong. As impolite a this is, I really can't stay here. I tried. I tried. I really, really have to leave. That's it.* She opened her eyes, looked at Cheryl and mouthed, 'Thank you.' She quietly got her coat and bag and left the room. Putting on her shoes, she let herself out.

Once she was outside in the fresh air she felt a little better, but she still wasn't right. She couldn't name what it was that was wrong, she was almost on the verge of panicking, it felt much better to be out of that room and away from there. She felt a twinge in her leg but she kept walking, gradually the feeling of ants crawling on her skin dissolved away. After a while she found herself standing outside Easons on O'Connell Street, one of the biggest bookshops in Dublin. She went in and felt overwhelmed for a moment, then she got her bearings. *If I can't meet an angel today at least I can buy a book about them.* She located the Mind Body Spirit section then went there to look for books about angels. She calmed down as she studied the titles on the shelves. 'An Encyclopaedia of Angels' looked good, she picked it up and browsed through it. It seemed to have a lot of general information about angels, gods and goddesses. *More things that I know nothing about!* Marissa brought it to the till, queued up, bought it and went home, forgetting all about the fish and the chips.

She felt dirty and sticky. This wasn't like that time with Martin, this was inside her. Her mind kept going back to that moment where she saw Cheryl looking straight at her, and the flash of heat. *Did she put something into me? Or take something from me? I must be making this all up. I'll be fine. It's all fine.*

Tobermory came over and brushed up against her, mewing. She knelt down and stroked him. He looked at her and seemed to frown. Then he hissed at her and ran away, going straight out the cat-flap in the back door. *Wonder what's up with him?*

An image of Dolores appeared in her mind. Marissa got out her laptop and looked her up again, finding her website easily. Looking at her photograph she felt a little more settled. She wasn't ready for another workshop just now, it wasn't until the end of January anyway. Dolores offered Reiki sessions. *Maybe that would help?* She spontaneously sent an email:

Hi, I'd like to book a Reiki session please. Thanks, Marissa.

She got an out of office email almost immediately. And then, a few minutes later, she got another email.

Hello Marissa, I have a session tomorrow, if you want to come and see me, it's €40 for an hour. I can see you at 3pm, please let me know, and I will give you the directions to my healing room.

Marissa felt relieved and wrote back right away. *Oh yes please! Thank you! See you tomorrow!*

Marissa tossed and turned all night. She saw images of Cheryl staring at her, her face turning into Martin's face, which turned into some sort of Devil face with fire and fangs, then it turned into Zaad smiling at her, and then into James. She woke covered in sweat. Her covers were soaked, and so were her pyjamas. She looked at the time, it was only 4am and she was shaken, frightened even. It felt like there was someone in her bedroom, standing at the end of her bed, staring at her. This was worse than the ghosts in Galway, there, it felt like they didn't wish her any harm. Here, now, it seemed like this energy was malicious, whatever it was, wanted something from her. It was nasty and she suddenly became very scared. *It's like my nightmare spilled out into the room and is right here with me.*

She got up and turned on all the lights, put on her large cardigan, opened the back door and padded outside in bare feet to sit in the night air. It felt better out here. The cool air helped her regulate her temperature and she started to feel more grounded. She dug her feet into the chips of stones from the garden. She really did feel strange, not at all like herself. She was glad she was going to see Dolores tomorrow. She didn't know why, but she felt that Dolores would be able to sort everything out. *This is awful. I need help. Oh, I forgot, I can ask my angel for help. Archangel Michael, please help me. Something is wrong, I think Cheryl did something to my energy, can you fix it?*

She waited. Nothing. She shivered from the cold, then went inside, closing the door behind her, and sat on the sofa, pulling a blanket around herself. *Where is Tobermory? I've not seen him since he ran outside earlier this evening.*

She didn't want to go back to bed, she still felt scared. Out of the corner of her eye she saw her drum, then she remembered how Séamus banged his drum and changed the energy of the room. She reached over to it and picked it up, holding it close to her for a little while. She felt something inside of her ease. She drummed with her fingers, then with the beater, softly to not disturb the people upstairs, but then louder and louder again. Marissa began banging it full-on loud. She stood up and walked into her bedroom and banged her drum very loudly, and started shouting: 'Get out, get out, whatever you are. I don't want you here, you are not welcome here, get out, GET OUT!'

She stopped. It felt better. She put the drum down on her bed. *This is my room, how dare anything come in here without my permission!* She wanted to go back to sleep, but not here. She left the light on and brought her duvet back to the sofa. Sitting up with the duvet over her, she left all the lights on and eventually drifted back to sleep.

When she woke up she was lying down, it was 10am, her phone was ringing on the floor beside her. It was Jenny.

'Hey, how was the workshop? Sorry I didn't make it.'

Marissa couldn't speak about it, not just yet. She couldn't speak about anything at all in fact. *Why did I pick up the phone?* She made an effort to talk.

'Hi Jenny, it wasn't great, to be honest. I didn't like her, Cheryl. I'm not feeling so good, can I call you later?'

'Sure, sorry you're not well, you didn't like her? Wow, okay. Yeah, text me or call later, whenever. Oh, I'm partnering with Zaad for the journey homework, thought you'd want to know. See ya.'

She hung up. *Why would I want to know that? Sure he has to partner with somebody.* Marissa slowly got up and dragged her duvet back into her bedroom. Her body felt heavy and it ached. The light was still on in her room, but it felt like, well, her room. Had she made the whole thing up? She thought she was going crazy. She still felt sticky and dirty, she needed a hot shower, she needed some help... Actually, she didn't know what it was that she needed...

CHAPTER TWENTY THREE 

Marissa couldn't sit still. Even after she showered dressed and ate, Marissa saw images of Cheryl in her head, contorted, nasty and evil images. She had to get away from them. She needed to get out of her flat and into the fresh air. The more she thought about how she was feeling, the more agitated she became. Dolores' healing room was in her house in Greystones and it was going to take a bus and a train to get there. She didn't have the energy to sit still for that long so she ordered a taxi and arrived in Greystones two hours early. She went to the beach for a walk, still trying to figure out what was wrong. Her thoughts were racing a mile a minute, she knew she was distressed, she wasn't able to centre herself or focus on one thing for more than what seemed like a few seconds at a time, so her mindfulness practice was not going to help at all.

She felt her anxiety turning into panic. It was much worse than what she was used to. She had had two panic attacks before, one after another, just after James had left. They were the most unpleasant experiences of her life and the reason why she had to move in with her parents. On top of everything else upsetting her, she became worried that it was going to happen again.

She bent down and picked up a stone from the shore. She felt the sharp corners cutting into the palm of her hand for a moment, it was something solid and real. She threw it into the sea, flinging it out as far as she could. She picked up another, felt it pressed tightly in her hand, then threw that one in, too. It took a few more stones and some very strong throws for her to start feeling less panicked. The salt from the sea and the wind and the cold winter sun painted a picture of an ordinary winter's day. But there didn't seem anything ordinary about what she was experiencing. Marissa imagined she was throwing Cheryl out to sea. If she was metaphorically out to sea, she was definitely struggling to keep her head above water.

She remembered the painting in her room in Cabra, the dark sea, the ship, the storm. It felt kind of like that, only she didn't have a ship, it was just her in the water. She started walking up and down the beach again, getting angry at herself for going to that workshop, getting angry at Cheryl, although she didn't really know if Cheryl had actually done anything to her. Perhaps she needed someone to blame. She could blame herself. *I was greedy, wanting more. I wasn't satisfied with what I already had. Why couldn't I just be with the work I had already done? Either way, it doesn't matter now. I need help, this is happening and this is real and it's awful. I hope Dolores can help me. Why didn't I phone Séamus?*

Now there was an interesting question. She had his number in her phone, why didn't she even think of him? What would it be like to have a session one to one with him? Well, if Dolores didn't work, then she had a plan B. That felt good, at least she had a plan. She decided to stop blaming herself, sure wasn't she only learning this stuff? She was bound to make a mistake somewhere along the line, and maybe in a few days or months, she'd look back at this time and realise she learnt something from this, too.

She was still very early for her appointment for Dolores but she didn't want to go into a café and sit and wait, she felt too agitated. Her phone buzzed a text, it was Dolores:

I can take you now if you're ready.

How did she know? Yes please. I'll be there in a few minutes.

That would never happen with a psychotherapist, they had been taught to be very strict with their boundaries around session times. She was grateful but puzzled. *Well, it's not psychotherapy, but client boundaries would still be very important, for safety reasons at the very least.*

Dolores's healing room was at the back of her home on a quiet estate just off the main road of Greystones village. Google had no trouble finding it. Marissa rang the buzzer at the side gate, just as per Dolores's instructions.

Dolores opened the door, took one look at Marissa and said, 'I had a feeling you were in trouble. Don't you worry, dear, we'll sort this out together. Come on in.'

Dolores led a very grateful Marissa down a path through her garden and into a beautiful wooden conservatory with triple glazing and French doors. It was warm inside. There was a massage table with blankets, two chairs and a table with a small statue of Buddha, some crystals, a jug of water and two glasses upon it. The room smelled wonderful. Marissa wasn't sure if it was lavender or chamomile, but either way, she liked it. There was a cabinet with lots of little bottles of different shapes and colours and two large wall hangings with symbols. Marissa wasn't sure what they were, but she thought she'd seen them somewhere before.

Dolores pulled the blinds down and asked Marissa to sit down on one of the chairs. Dolores sat in the other one, facing her. She looked exactly like her photograph and Marissa felt safe.

'Now, dear, what's going on? How can I help you?' Dolores's smile was so comforting, Marissa immediately burst into tears.

What is going on? This is so strange – not like me at all. Get a hold of yourself, girl.

Dolores gave Marissa some tissues and she took three, blew her nose, wiped her eyes and tried to calm down, but she still felt panicked and agitated. She wanted to shake her body like she was a dog shaking off water. It felt as if it didn't belong to her anymore.

Dolores stood up and moved behind Marissa, placing her two hands on Marissa's shoulders, one on either side. She didn't push down on her, her hands were very gentle and comforting. Marissa felt less squirmy, and then she suddenly felt very tired. She didn't want Dolores to stop. Whatever it was, it seemed to be working.

Dolores stayed there for a few more minutes, then said, 'Let's do some Reiki now. We can talk afterwards. Is that okay?'

Marissa nodded. Dolores helped her take off her coat and shoes, she took her jumper off and left it on the chair. She got up and lay down on the massage table. Dolores put a pillow under her knees and a blanket over her. 'Just breathe,' she said, and Marissa felt calmer than she had done in several days.

Dolores started working. Marissa could not see what she was doing, all she knew was that she was already feeling better. She closed her eyes, she trusted this woman. She knew as soon as she saw her photograph, that she trusted her. She also knew that she had felt something was not right around Cheryl's workshop. *So why did I go to that workshop even when it didn't feel right to me? Why did I ignore my intuition? I must make sure that I always listen to my intuition in the future.*

Marissa felt Dolores's firm hands squeezing her upper arms, then her calves, and her feet. She must have gone to sleep as she didn't remember a thing.

'I'll get you some water and give you a few minutes to yourself. Take your time getting up, you might be a little light-headed.' Dolores poured some water into a glass from the jug on the table, then left the room.

Marissa lay under the blanket for a while, listening to the afternoon bird song, listening to her breath. She was calm again. She was hesitant to move, but she thought she should make an effort as Dolores would be returning soon. She rolled onto one side, then pushed herself to a sitting position. One of her legs slid off the massage table and she sat like that for a few moments, looking around her. She swung her other leg off and dropped her feet to the floor. She padded over to the table, took the glass and drank the water, all of it, it felt good and cold in her mouth. She felt the cold liquid spilling down her throat, her oesophagus and into her stomach. She felt better, yes, she felt like she was back in her body, she felt more present, and it also felt as if an irritant had been removed. There *was* something there, and now it was gone. Yes. It was good, much better. She smiled and relaxed her body, she put on her shoes and jumper and sat down on the chair.

Dolores knocked on the French doors, then opened them and came inside. She smiled at Marissa and sat down in the opposite chair. 'You had quite a time in the wars, I'd imagine. How are you feeling now?'

'Oh, thank you. I'm much better now. I don't know what happened, but whatever you just did really helped.'

'You're very sensitive and intuitive. You picked up some nasty energy from somewhere, is someone angry at you? Do you know where it came from? It was a psychic attack.'

Marissa shivered, hearing the words psychic attack. She had never heard of that before, but it sounded right. She saw Cheryl's face in her mind, laughing at her. She blocked it out.

'Yes, I think I know where it came from. I was at an angel meditation workshop yesterday, I had to leave before it was finished, I didn't feel good. I think it happened there.'

Dolores nodded. 'This type of thing is common, it happens much more often than you'd know. If it was only yesterday then it was very powerful, whatever attached itself to you. And also a sign of how sensitive you must be. Usually it takes much longer to develop, and for a person to notice it. It can be weeks or sometimes months before they realise that something is wrong. Usually, by then, the person thinks they're physically sick or that it's a mental health issue. But it's neither, it's energetic. And they can stay sick for years if they don't sort out the problem at the energetic level. You did the right thing to come to me. Your angels must have given you a nudge.'

'I didn't do Reiki today, it wasn't what you needed. I worked with Seichem, it's also an energy medicine, and it allows me to open your aura and remove energy that doesn't belong there. You could call it psychic surgery. It was straightforward to do, and I'm satisfied that you're clear of it, whatever it was. Your energy told me that you're on a journey, you seem to be in a growth phase?'

Marissa nodded.

'I think as you're so sensitive, you probably will need to learn some form of psychic defence.'

'That sounds interesting, yes I'd like to learn that. Is that Reiki? I saw that you're teaching a workshop in January.'

Dolores poured herself a glass of water and took a sip from it. 'No, it's not Reiki. Reiki is a relatively straightforward healing modality. It's humans that are complicated. Try to get a complicated human being to be in simple flow, to let Reiki flow through them in a pure and uncomplicated way, that's the difficulty! If you'd like to join my Reiki workshop I'd be happy to have you there. It would be a good place for you to start, you need to take one step at a time. Right now, however, you need to take some time to rest and recover from what has just happened.'

'Thank you. When I saw your website I just knew you'd be able to help. I got an out of office email though, you said you were on holidays? How did you know I needed you? And knowing I was here early? How did you know that?'

Dolores laughed. 'I had a feeling you were in need. I occasionally see people during the holidays if they need healing. The people that simply want healing for the sake of it can wait. My door is always open, and you needed it, I could feel it.'

Dolores looked at her clock, it was 4.15pm. Marissa felt she had taken up enough of her time, she had been there nearly two hours. Dolores probably had someone else coming after her. 'Let me pay you?'

'Thank you.' Marissa got €50 out of her wallet and gave it to her. Dolores went looking in a drawer in her cabinet for some change.

'Keep the change, please.'

'No dear, it's €40, I don't need any more than that. I'm happy to be of service, and I am delighted that you are feeling better. I think it's best that we don't talk any more about this for now. Perhaps in the New Year, when you're feeling stronger, you could come back for another session, a follow-up, and we can talk some more.'

Dolores found the €10 note and gave it to Marissa, and sat back down again.

'I've sealed you up with a golden light of protection. If you see it in your mind, imagine that it is solid and protects you completely, as if you're inside a golden egg. Can you do that?'

Marissa imagined a golden egg and herself inside of it. 'Yes, that's good.'

'You work with Archangel Michael. He's with you, he told me that you are doing great, and he's proud of you.'

Marissa felt a strong cold shiver down her back, the one that meant 'yes' to her. She felt really happy, so it *was* Archangel Michael, after all.

'Was there anything else?'

'He said that you can ask him for protection if you are feeling vulnerable, he has a purple-blue cloak that he can put over your shoulders, to cover you up. He's right here, he's smiling. Can you feel him?'

Marissa wasn't sure. She imagined a blue cloak going over a golden egg. She thought that was funny, but she felt a little more secure once she imagined it.

'Thank you. It's very reassuring, what you said, and knowing you're here really helps. I will definitely come back and see you again. Thank you so much!'

Marissa stood to go. Dolores handed her her coat and helped her put it on.

'Get some rest now, and drink lots of water today, it will help your system rebalance. Do you have a bathtub at home?' Marissa nodded her head. 'If you could take a bath with Epsom salts, it will help your body and your energy too. It's a good way to clear your energy, if you can, that is.'

'Thank you so much,' said Marissa, making a mental note to stop by a chemist and get some Epsom salts on the way home. She turned to leave.

Dolores closed her eyes for a moment, then opened them again. 'Wait, one more thing!' She went to her cabinet, opened the drawer, rummaged through it, found a little bottle, and then handed it to Marissa. It was clear plastic with a purple liquid inside of it, its label said 'Saint Germain'.

'Archangel Michael wants me to give you this, it's a gift from me to you. I'll show you what to do with it.'

Dolores took back the bottle and opened it and poured three drops into her left hand. She then asked Marissa for her left hand, and she poured three drops into it as well. She closed the bottle and gave it back to Marissa, who put it into her coat pocket. Dolores rubbed her hands together and held them in front of her face, motioning for Marissa to do the same. As Marissa copied her, she breathed in the smell of the liquid, it was perfumy, nothing she could recognise, but it did have a pleasant smell.

'Now do what I do,' Dolores said, and she held her hands in the air. 'The energy of Saint Germain flows from my left hand, all around the world and into my right hand.' She then waved her hands through her energy field in circular motions. 'This cleanses your aura,' she said.

Marissa copied the hand motions and imagined the energy from her left hand travelling all the way around the world, then back into her right hand. It seemed a little strange, but it was okay. She then waved her hands through her energy field, copying Dolores, and could feel some subtle changes.

'Oh! Is this like sage?'

'Yes, it's a similar idea, but this liquid works with different frequencies and vibrations to those of sage. You can sage yourself and sage the room, but this little bottle is just for you, not for a room. If you wanted to clear a room, you could buy a room spray.'

'Is your aura and your energy field the same thing?'

'Not quite, your energy field is much larger than your aura, your aura surrounds your body, your energy field extends much further than that.'

'Thank you so much.' Marissa turned to go but came back again. 'I have a silly question to ask you.' Marissa blushed, but she really needed to know.

'No question is silly, please, do feel free to ask me anything' Dolores's kind face put Marissa at ease.

'I'm Jewish, but I don't practice my religion. What I mean to say is, I'm not a Christian. I don't know very much at all about angels and saints. It feels strange, but I am very happy you told me that Archangel Michael is with me. Does it matter about religion?'

Dolores smiled. 'No, funnily enough, religion doesn't have to come into spiritual work. But, if you were to look back at the Jewish texts you'd see many angels there, including Archangel Michael. Angels and saints transcend religion when you are doing spiritual work, healing work. They are of the light, and when a person, no matter their background creed or race wants to work in the light, then they come and offer their help.'

'But you must invite them to help you, they will not interfere of their own free will. You can ask Archangel Michael for protection, and you can use the Saint Germain essence as often as you wish. There is plenty of time for you to learn more about all of this. You are tired now, you've had a difficult time. Come and see me in a few weeks, we can talk some more then.'

Marissa suddenly wanted to give Dolores a hug. Dolores gave Marissa a hug. *How did she know?* Marissa thanked her again and left. She walked slowly up the garden path to the gate. It was so good to not be agitated anymore. Dolores's garden was beautiful. She had cut back the roses, a bird feeder hung from one of the trees, the lawn was perfectly manicured and it felt very safe and peaceful there. She opened the gate and walked through it, closing it behind her.

As she walked towards the Greystones DART station she felt like she had been away somewhere and was coming home after a long journey. What a strange experience. She was tired, much more relaxed (thank goodness) and ready for that fish and chips she had promised herself.

When she got home, fish and chips safely tucked away in her stomach and a packet of Epsom salts in her bathroom, she banged her drum again, walking slowly through her flat, asking Archangel Michael to protect her flat, to protect her, and Tobermory. Tobermory seemed to approve, although after a while, he didn't like the noise, so he let himself out into the garden. She followed him out and banged the drum in the garden too, laughing as he tried to get away from her. She didn't care what the neighbours would think. She imagined Archangel Michael put his blue cloak not over just her, but also over Tobermory and an especially large cloak went over her flat. *And the garden too, please, and the neighbour's garden, and the whole street... Oh, where does it end?*

She ran a hot bath for herself. She hadn't had a bath in a very long time, it felt good to sink her tired body into the hot, salty water. Her body let go of another layer of tension. After a good long soak, she got into her pyjamas and tried her Saint Germain essence again, taking her time, running her hands through her whole aura. She felt much better. She didn't feel scared in the flat at all.

She texted Jenny.

> I'm feeling better now, I had a Reiki Session with Dolores, she's really great. I'm happy now, glad you've arranged your homework partner. Talk to you soon.

Jenny wrote back straight away. Dolores Carmody?

Yes

Oh I love Dolores, she's great, she was one of my Reiki teachers. I'm glad you found her! And I'm glad you're feeling better too! Look after yourself, see you in the New Year!

Marissa sent Jenny back a love heart emoji and got a star and a crystal ball emoji back. It was reassuring that she knew Dolores. Marissa finally felt content and safe. She closed her eyes, yes, her apartment was clear and hers again. And she had learnt something from this experience, she couldn't doubt that. It wasn't pleasant, but it was valuable learning all the same. She slept very well that night.

CHAPTER TWENTY FOUR 

It was New Year's Eve and Marissa was invited to a family meal at her parents' house. In the evening she was going to meet Sarah, who had two tickets for a party. They planned to get ready in Sarah's flat and do the same thing they did at Christmas – hit the town together and celebrate.

Marissa had kept Archangel Michael close in her mind for the past few days and she didn't have any recurrence of her agitation or panic. Cheryl's face had stopped appearing in her mind every few minutes. It was still there, in the background, hovering, but it was once every couple of hours now, instead of many times per hour.

Marissa went through her clothes and tried things on to pick an outfit for her night out. She settled on the second dress she bought with Sarah and deliberately chose a pair of flat shoes that she had worn several times before, and her new sparkly bag. She found a pretty cardigan to go over the dress as it was still cold, and of course, her coat. She changed back into her jeans and a jumper then made her way to her parent's house.

'Marissa, come in! Great to see you!' Marissa's mum was looking bright and cheery. A blast of heat hit Marissa as she went into the house.

'Hi Mum, Hi Dad! How are you both doing?'

'Good, good thanks. How are you, love?' replied her dad, coming over for a hug.

They went into the back room together, the table was set for five people. 'Is Eli coming?'

'Yes,' her mum replied, 'and Carol too. I'm so relieved she isn't getting sick anymore. I was very anxious about it.'

Marissa looked at her Dad, who made a face that meant 'don't say anything', so she smiled and didn't say anything.

'Do you need any help with the food?' Marissa asked.

'I think it's all under control. Would you like a drink? I've got wine, soda, cordial?'

'I'm going out with Sarah later, so I think tea is good if that's okay?'

'Course it's okay, love,' said her Dad, putting the kettle on. 'Are you going anywhere nice?'

'She's invited me into town to a party. She went to this place before, last year, and she said it was fun. I thought I'd tag along, I didn't feel like being on my own tonight.'

'I'm very glad you're going out, it's wonderful to see you looking so well and happy,' said Rose, and with a wink she added, 'It's been a long time. Maybe you'll be bringing a boy home to meet us soon.'

The doorbell rang. 'I'll get it.' Marissa said and rushed out of the room. Eli and Carol were standing there with windswept faces.

'Hello guys, you look great. Come on in, Dad and Mum are in great form today, she's already going on about me having a boyfriend.'

'Hi Sis,' said Eli. 'So nothing's changed then?' He gave Marissa a hug.

'Hi Sis!' said Carol with a giggle, and she also gave Marissa a hug. They both laughed.

'Don't mind her,' said Eli as they came into the house. Marissa took their coats and they went into the back room. Carol went straight for the sofa.

'Eli! Carol! Lovely to see you both. Tea? Coffee? Wine? No wine for you, of course, Carol, dear!'

It was a lovely gathering once Marissa composed herself. She was happy that everyone finally was getting on so well. The whole religion thing with the baby seemed to be over, it didn't come up once in conversation. They had lots of other news to catch up on, and the food was delicious – fresh salmon and potatoes.

They had finished dessert, and Marissa's dad was making coffee. The silence was weighing heavily on Marissa. She didn't like keeping secrets from her family at the best of times, and she had a lot to tell them that they didn't know about. *It's not really a secret, but how do I tell them without them being worried? And without the drama for me?*

She wasn't sure how to start or how to even say it. She tested out several opening lines in her mind, but all of them seemed inappropriate. *Should I say: 'I've been doing some spiritual work?' Well, that sounded less scary than mentioning Shamanism, but it would open a whole conversation about spiritual work... What about saying I went to Galway? But why did I go? I really have to say something.* But then her father started the conversation for her.

'So, Marissa, how are you getting on with college? Are you learning anything interesting? You must be looking forward to going back next term, it's your last term, isn't it?'

Suddenly Marissa had an idea. 'Yes, one more term Dad, then I have to do client work, which will take me a while. I also have to do extra-curricular workshops for my personal development hours.' *It's not exactly a lie.*

'Ahh, personal development, I've heard about that. But what is it exactly when it's at home?'

'It's studying something that will help you grow in a personal way. It gives you more depth of character. Like meditation or healing work.' Marissa felt herself speak without blushing. *Yes, this is the right track.*

Then Eli jumped in with a cheeky look on his face. 'Healing work? What's that?'

Don't push it Eli. 'It can be anything,' said Marissa, trying to be diplomatic. 'Anything that helps you grow, that challenges you a bit. I'm always looking for ways to expand my knowledge to help my client work. College recommended a few different workshops and I'm looking at maybe learning about energy medicine, spiritual work or meditation. I might do a mindfulness practitioner course next year.' *Where did that idea spring from? It sounds good, I might actually do that!* 'It's good to have lots to draw from when there's someone in distress in front of you in the room.'

Marissa's mother poured the coffee. 'What kind of spiritual work, darling? And I've never heard of energy medicine, what is that?'

'I'm not sure yet, I have to go find out! I will let you know more when I do.'

They seemed happy at that. Eli gave Marissa a wink, and she kicked him under the table. That was enough family discovery for today.

Marissa arrived at Sarah's flat wearing her chosen outfit and no make-up (as instructed), she was also bearing gifts – a bottle of vodka and a bottle of orange juice. Sarah was delighted and they started into the vodka and orange almost straight away. Sarah insisted on doing Marissa's hair, and she taught Marissa a new way to put make-up on her eyes. Marissa was very relaxed. She was still basking in the relief of managing to tell her family about her extra-curricular studies without actually telling them about her extra-curricular studies (although she still wanted to punch Eli). By the time the girls left Sarah's flat, they were both tipsy, happy and dressed up, ready for a night of dancing and who knows what else.

Marissa felt beautiful, she loved the attention Sarah gave her and was happy that their friendship seemed to be growing stronger. Everything Sarah was saying was funny, and as they walked down Grafton Street in the dark, linking arms just for the fun of it, they looked in the windows of the shops. They stopped outside Brown Thomas and reminisced on their childhood visits to see the Santa windows. Both Marissa and Sarah had similar memories. They wrapped their arms around each other and started to sing 'Mistletoe and Wine', laughing as they got the words wrong. The colours of the lights seemed extra bright for New Year's Eve, people were in a jovial mood, groups of people were stopped on the street chatting excitedly.

'Come on, we need to find the club and get in before the queue is too long,' said Sarah, dragging Marissa by the arm down a side street. The bouncer smiled and let them in, they left their coats in the coatroom, then went up to the bar and ordered Martinis to celebrate the night that was in it. Marissa had never been to this club and she had never had a Martini. Sarah came here all the time, everything seemed second nature to her. And as they sat at a table near the bar, the music played and Marissa let go of her need to prove anything or to be anything other than what she already was. She relaxed, possibly for the first time in a very, very long time. Sarah got up and danced and Marissa stayed watching from the table, just like she did in Peru.

Everything Marissa looked at was beautiful. The people dancing, the people smiling, Sarah… It felt like everyone was in love and she was filled with possibilities for the future, for the year to come, and for the new friends she was making in all of the realms. She got up and danced too, forgetting herself and all her worries.

A few hours later, in the moments just before midnight in the nightclub, a sweaty but happy Marissa looked around her in the dark room dangerously crowded to overfull with people. She couldn't see Sarah anywhere but she wasn't worried. She pulled her phone out of her tiny sparkly handbag and the battery was dead, but even if she could have phoned, Sarah wouldn't have been able to hear her phone ring with the noise of the music.

Marissa got her bearings as the room was very full and it seemed to be spinning. The disco lights made circles on the floors, ceilings and walls. The disco ball threw fragments of light onto the faces of the people dancing in the dark. Marissa suddenly got a flash of anxiety, white hot, up and down her back. Thoughts of being separated, being crushed in the crowd, not finding Sarah again flew through her mind but then she remembered and called out for Archangel Michael. She was not drunk enough to have lost her sensibility, but she seemed slightly blurry, not fully awake, not asleep, but not really in the present moment either.

Marissa calls her angel in her mind and then an angel comes, oh yes, it certainly comes, she can feel every inch of him… He is huge, she feels him more strongly than she has ever felt him before. He wraps his wings around her and sweeps her into a feeling of strong safety, a feeling of pure, unconditional love. Marissa feels like she's falling but she's not, she feels like she's exploding with love, but she isn't. Her heart opens and opens and opens and her energy expands and expands and expands, she feels taller, 6ft tall, 10ft tall. She feels lighter, more expansive than her body, she is almost flying above the crowd, dancing with the disco ball, she is free. But she is in her body, she moves her arm, then the other arm, her leg, then the other leg, then she hears the music once more. She starts to dance, moving to the beat of the music, she sees the people around her also dancing but it is like she is somewhere other than where they are. She is disconnected from them yet she is still above them all looking down, yet she is them, they are her, they are together and they are separate. Some part of Marissa knows that they are not tuning into the same frequency as she, the people there do not feel what she is feeling. She doesn't even need the music to dance, she moves and spins, releases all the tension, all the worry, all the anxiety her body has been holding. There was so, so much tension, she didn't realise she was holding onto so much of it, and there's more and more of it leaving, years and years of pain and fear and anxiety flowing out of her, she gets softer and softer and all the more open and lighter and taller and expansive...

Marissa can feel a river of love, no an ocean of love flowing through her, through her body, lifting her, transporting her to a place of pure love, but at the same time she can see the people dancing around her, she is still right here, in the nightclub. She knows this. Her awareness has expanded and she is tapping into another world that has always been here, just sitting inside the reality that we think is our real world. She, with this connection, in almost ecstatic bliss, her body floating, lifting, a smile so big on her face, it is magical, blissful, this bliss fills her, enthrals her, it escapes words, she has never experienced anything like it, it cannot be described, all that she can do is surrender to it.

And after the party, after the bells have rung in the New Year, after she was grabbed and kissed by a stranger feeling their strong hands around her waist and their hot breath on her cheek, after they let her go, after all the 'Happy New Year's' and the change in tempo of the music, after all the lights went on and the night club spilled its people out onto the streets, Marissa, still minus Sarah, walked home wrapped in the arms of her Angel, each step feeling as if she was floating.

She woke up the next morning in her own bed in her apartment. She didn't remember how she got home, she didn't remember washing off her make-up and putting on her pyjamas. But she must have done, because there she is, clean and changed. Her dress from the night before lies crumpled on the floor, her coat is on the back of the front door. Her body feels, well, better than it's felt in years.

Sinking back into this feeling of bliss, of the delicious slumbering moments before waking up completely, Marissa feels totally relaxed in mind, body and soul, as if she had spent the night with the most miraculous lover who had kissed every inch of her body over and over again. She awoke feeling completely and utterly loved. And she wants more, she wants it again, more than anything else she had ever experienced... She is in love, with love.

CHAPTER TWENTY FIVE 

A week later, Marissa was back at the office. She tried to ease herself back into her routine, but it was difficult after the break away. Classes and sessions were starting back too. She had not felt the feeling of bliss since New Year's Eve and was experiencing a massive anti-climax. It was a terrible low after a high, a tremendous disappointment. She found herself pleading with Archangel Michael to come back to her, standing outside in her garden at midnight in her pyjamas with tears in her eyes and a heavy heart. Her brand new lover had left her. Marissa's body seemed heavier, she became lethargic, angry, she was wondering what happened and was constantly asking for help, wanting to experience the bliss again.

She had felt Archangel Michael since that night, but not strongly. She started wondering if the angel that came to her that night was, in fact, him. That thought worried her, so each time it arose, she pushed it aside. The fact that something so beautiful, so remarkable, existed, elated her. It was a paradox holding such disappointment with such expectation and hope. Why didn't people speak about experiences like this? She spent hours Googling ecstatic experiences, spiritual bliss or transcendence, but all the accounts all seemed to be focussed around taking a substance, or being in deep meditation, or were lectures by spiritual gurus that seemed long, convoluted and definitely not what she was looking for.

Marissa began to doubt that she had the experience at all. Was she just drunk? Or did someone put a drug into one of her drinks at the nightclub? But she had stopped drinking halfway through the night, she didn't even remember having a glass of water. *Or did I do something wrong? How do I get it back? I suppose I couldn't live in a constant state of bliss, but I want to experience it again... What do I need to do to get it back, that feeling, it was so... so... oh I can't put words to it.*

She knew she had to face reality and going back to work was more helpful than she realised. As she went through the workload on her desk, planning her calendar for the week ahead, her urgency dissolved away and was replaced with more practical matters. She had another session scheduled with Martin and she was also concerned about the impending meeting with Noreen. She still hadn't decided whether or not she'd take the management position.

Yet everything in Marissa's world felt different. Everything looked different, this wasn't like coming back from Peru with the colours enhanced, no, this was more like she could see through things, she would focus and unfocus her eyes and wonder if her teacup was really there in front of her or if she just imagined it. *It's like the TV we had at home when I was growing up. Sometimes there would be two channels appearing at once, even when we tuned into the show we wanted, the other one was still there, somewhere in the background.*

Whether the experience had really happened or not (and Marissa was learning how powerful her mind was and how easily it could trick her into believing anything), Marissa *was* a different person and wasn't really sure who she could talk to about it. *Terry? Jenny? I don't know them well enough yet. Zaad? No, definitely not him. Séamus? Dolores? I don't want to bother them about this. Maybe Terry...* She wrote a text to him:

> Hiya, Happy New year. Let's arrange our homework journey night? I had a mad experience over Xmas, I need to talk to someone about it.

She read the text three times, deleted the last sentence, then sent it.

She knew what her dad would say about the job offer: 'It's good money, Noreen's a good, thoughtful woman, dependable. You'd have a job for life. You'd be a fool if you don't take the offer.' She could hear his voice in her mind, she didn't need to hear it for real. If Noreen and Uncle Lou were right, she'd never have enough money if all she did was see psychotherapy clients full time. She would need to have something else to keep her going.

She sat back at her desk with her second cup of tea of the day to find a summons from Noreen in her inbox. Her heart leapt. *Perhaps*

I could ask for more time? No point putting this off. She got a tea for Noreen on the way to her desk and knocked softly on her office door.

'Come in, ahh Marissa, Happy New Year, I trust you had a good break?'

Marissa put both mugs on the table. 'Yes, thank you, it was just what I needed to catch up with myself.'

Noreen looked tired, her face was puffy, but her makeup was immaculate as usual. She was wearing a dark blue skirt and jacket with a crisp white blouse and white glasses frames to set them off. She had a small sliver broach on her jacket lapel, it depicted sparkly angel wings.

'I like your broach,' said Marissa, wondering if this was a sign.

'Thank you! It was a Christmas gift from my husband, he really is an angel. He looks after me very well. Marissa, I'm glad you're here – thanks for the tea – I wanted to thank you for getting all of that work done before the break.'

'I got a little help.'

'Yes, I realise that, and you delivered, which shows good planning and organising skills. Well done. I wanted to talk to you about my proposal. I must apologise. I can see that I took you by surprise, and I'm wondering if perhaps you'd like a little more time to decide?'

Marissa breathed an audible sigh of relief. 'Oh yes, please, that would be wonderful.'

'Okay, good. But I still think you could be doing so much more, as you've just proved to me. So how about I bring it up again in six months and we can discuss it then?'

'Thank you!'

'And in the meantime, I will give you more responsibilities, and I'm making Sarah your assistant. It would do her good to have some direction from you, she does get a little scattered from time to time. And it would do you some good too, to have experience managing someone.'

Marissa didn't know what to say. *How will Sarah react to hear I'm her new manager?*

'So that's sorted. Now, Let's go through your new responsibilities. I want to hand over some accounts to you to run for me, and I need you to take a look at the figures for the Cahill account and to set up the first-quarter projections for the sales team.'

After an hour and a half with Noreen, Marissa sat back at her desk and looked out the window. Her head was spinning once again. Having extra time was a relief, she really had been torn about that. And the work Noreen gave to her really was straightforward. She didn't feel clear on staying or going, but having some extra help would be, well, helpful. But Sarah? Oh dear. All she could do was give it a try.

It was Tuesday. Marissa had made her appointments with Olive and with Mr Blakemore for later in the week and she had college that day after work. Terry was going to be in Dublin that weekend and they had arranged to meet at her place for their journey homework. She was looking forward to it, and to seeing him again. She wasn't sure if she would tell him about the psychic attack or about the angel on the dance floor – *Whatever that was...* Life was certainly much more interesting than before.

Now to tell Sarah. Marissa emailed her with their usual single subject line no body-text email: *Coffee out?* Sarah arrived at her desk in a flash. She wore a big smile on her face, hair scooped into a long ponytail and a well cut, wine coloured skirt and jacket with a pink blouse. She looked good, well-rested after two weeks off. She took one look at Marissa's face and her own face fell.

'What's wrong? What happened?'

Marissa looked around to see if anybody was watching them. Sure I might as well tell her now, better than dragging her outside and keeping her waiting.

'Let's talk in the boardroom, it's empty.'

They both walked the few paces to the boardroom, and Marissa closed the door behind her. 'Please, sit down.' Sarah sat.

'Lookit, I didn't ask for this and I'm not sure that I want it...'

Sarah was getting very impatient. 'What?!' She cocked her head to one side, still concerned, not knowing what to expect.

'Okay. Noreen just made me your manager.'

'What?' She cocked her head to the other side, then righted it again, doing a double-take. 'You're my manager now?' She sounded completely taken aback.

Marissa nodded her head. Sarah's glow faded for a moment as she processed the information. Then she widened her eyes, but she didn't look as bright as before. 'But that's good, isn't it? It means you're moving forward. In your career, I mean.' She smiled, it seemed a little forced.

'Maybe. I'm not sure. I really, really don't want this to affect our friendship. Can you give me some time to figure it out, to get used to it? You might need some time, too.'

'Yes, that sounds like a good idea. Okay.' She seemed more grounded now.

'How about you just keep going as before, finish up what you've been working on, and we can have a proper meeting about it together in a day or two.'

Sarah paused for a moment then asked, 'Does this mean we can't go out for coffee then?'

Marissa smiled, visibly relieved. 'Of course not. Let's go. I'll get my coat.'

That evening Marissa still needed to clear her head so she got off the bus a little earlier than usual and walked to her psychotherapy class. The evenings were still dark, but there was a hint of the days getting longer. That day it was warmer than usual and the trees and flowers showed signs of waking up. *Spring is coming too early, the seasons are changing. I remember last year, spring didn't seem to come in until April. What's going on?*

It was good to be back in college, everyone was in good form. There was lots of laughter and lightness in the canteen as everyone got themselves a pre-class cuppa and caught up over the holidays. Marissa couldn't help but feel like she was holding back – should she say something to them about the shamanic workshop? Why was she making such a big deal out of this? What was she really afraid of? *I guess I'm afraid, not so much about what they might think of me, but perhaps about how I would fit in, ahh yes, that's it. My Achilles heel is belonging, and this is another thing that is 'different' about me, another reason why I wouldn't belong. That explains why I don't want to tell Mum and Dad too, they'd not get it, and they don't understand me anyway.* At her realisation, Marissa suddenly felt much more settled in herself and less defensive. If it was about belonging, well, who did she belong to only to herself? And if she wasn't at ease with herself, then why would anyone else be?

Barbara interrupted her train of thought. 'Remember that thing they told us in class last term, during the Motivational Interviewing module – you know, about habit forming and how we sabotage ourselves?'

There were five of them sitting at the table. Marissa brought her attention back to them all. Barbara was animated; Emmet looked wrecked tired after the break; Yvonne had had her hair done – it was a different colour now and she seemed very happy. Kate and Ronan were listening avidly.

'Ha ha, is this how you tell us you sabotaged yourself over the break with the boxes of biccies and chocolates?' Kate started laughing.

Barbara blushed. 'Actually, yes.'

Kate stopped laughing.

'I couldn't help myself,' Barbara continued, 'and it's not funny. I've been trying to lose weight for over a year now. I thought I'd be able to get a handle on this with the motivational interviewing techniques. I'm so disappointed. I probably put on several pounds over the holidays. They come on easily but not off.'

'I know,' said Kate in an apologetic tone. 'I was laughing near you, not at you. I've the same problem myself. And they would have to leave these lying around here too.' She motioned towards the amply filled plates of bourbon and custard creams on the table.

'Well,' said Emmet, helping himself to three biscuits, 'If you ladies are going to be so worried about a few pounds here and there, I'm wondering if you're actually really worried about it enough to do something about it? Or are you just talking about it? Surely you can just cool it on the snackaroonies for a while?'

Both women glared at Emmet, if looks were laser beams, he would have melted on the spot.

Ronan piped up. 'I was listening to one of those motivational speakers over the break. He was doing a TED talk, he made a really good point about goals and commitment. He basically said that if you're not committed to a goal, then there's a reason why and you need to look at that before you'll get results. He talked about the difference between being interested in doing something and being committed to doing something.'

'Oh, that sounds good – tell us more.' Kate softened and looked at Ronan expectantly.

'Well, I'm not sure if I can remember any more, but you can go look him up yourself, it was on YouTube. I think his name was Scott Taylor.'

'Scott Taylor? I've heard of him,' said Emmet, his mouth full of biscuit, totally oblivious to how the women were feeling. 'He's that guy who does Law of Attraction?'

'I don't know if he does that, but he is a coach. Business coach, I think, large businesses, corporate type stuff. I found him very refreshing. Motivational coaching, or something like that. He's entertaining, a great speaker.'

Yvonne joined in. 'My cousin went to one of his workshops when he came to London a few years ago. He said it was an amazing experience, and his life changed for the better after.'

'It's nearly time for class,' said Kate, looking at the clock on the wall. They all started to clear away the table and get their bags. She added, 'I'll check him out. Scott Taylor. Thanks, Ronan.'

Barbara leaned into Marissa as they walked into the classroom. 'You're very quiet today, did you have a nice break? Is everything okay?'

'Yeah, it was nice, thanks. I'm just working something out. Some stuff came up. It's grand, though.'

They had Ms Greene again for this module, it was Advanced Person-Centred Therapy. Barbara made a point of sitting next to Marissa, she thought it was a nice gesture.

'Happy New Year everyone, it's lovely to see you all again.' Ms Greene was looking splendid in turquoise cords and a matching jacket. Her large red earrings set her outfit off very well. 'This term, we are going to be spending most of the time practising. I know you are all seeing clients or are just about to see clients, so I'm hoping that I'll be able to support you and put some, or all, of your fears at rest. The more effort you put into this module, the more you will get out of it, so don't hold back.'

Marissa felt the butterflies starting up. She really wasn't ready to share her inner thoughts with the group just yet.

'I'm happy for you to experiment with each other and bring in some of the techniques you've learned in the other modules, but we will be making person-centred the focus of our work. We will be together for the next six weeks, and we will have a practical assessment rather than a written one. So yes, that does mean you will be doing a therapy session up in front of the class.'

Ms Greene paused to gauge their reaction, which was suitably terrified. She smiled, which did not put the room at ease. She continued. 'This means all of you will get a chance to be a client and a therapist during these assessments. So it will take a while as there are so many of you, and each session is fifteen minutes long. We may need to schedule some extra classes to get it all done. So be prepared!'

The energy in the room was electric, everyone was anxious at the thoughts of being in front of the group doing a therapy session, on show for all. The thing that Marissa feared most was being the client, even more than being the therapist. She was very happy as the therapist. But then she realised that she'd have time to figure out what issue to work with. But it would have to be a real one and something that she could talk about for fifteen minutes. She wrote a note to herself in her book to remember to prepare for that.

'Now. Let's break up into triads and practice – client, observer and therapist, each of you have twenty minutes as each. I'll call time.'

Marissa looked around for Yvonne or Kate to join herself and Barbara, but they were already paired up with someone else. Kellie came over, 'Can I work with you?'

'Sure,' said Marissa.

'We need someone else...' said Kellie.

Marissa then realised that Barbara had been nabbed by Emmet and suddenly wasn't available.

'Look, there's Linda,' said Kellie. 'Hey Linda, over here!'

They arranged three chairs so that two were facing each other and a third off to one side for the observer. Kellie and Linda weren't a part of Marissa's social group, she didn't know them very well, but that was fine. It was all hands on deck when it came to class, and always good to work with a variety of people. Marissa asked, 'Who wants to go first?'

'Bags me be observer,' said Linda, and she took the observation seat. Kellie looked at Marissa.

'Do you want to be therapist?'

'Sure,' said Marissa. They took their seats.

'So, what would you like to talk about today?' Marissa found her flow.

Kellie took a moment. 'Actually, yes, there is something I'd like to discuss. It happened over the holidays.'

After a very straightforward twenty minute session untangling an argument between Kellie and her father, Kellie seemed very happy and willing to own her part of it. It was time to swap roles. Linda was keen to get working and Kellie had played client and wanted to observe.

'Hello Marissa, what would you like to talk about with me today?'

Marissa, as usual, wasn't ready. She had been thinking more about the assessment than about that evening, she felt on the spot and quite flustered all of a sudden. *Think think think, what issue can I talk about? I don't want to tell them about Eli and Carol, nor about the shamanic work, nor about the angel, or Dolores... I know. I'll talk about work. That's safe!* Marissa hadn't realised that she had been sweating with anxiety. She focused and began, ignoring the drips of sweat that trickled down the backs of her legs.

'Hi Linda, yes, there's a problem I'm having at work that I'm trying to figure out. I was offered a promotion, and being here, doing these classes, I wasn't sure if I could juggle the extra workload. My manager is very understanding and has given me more time to think about it, I think she really wants me to take it. But in the meantime, she's given me more work to do and an assistant to help me. And my assistant is a friend of mine. I don't know how it is going to affect our relationship.'

That's brilliant. It is chewy enough to get us through fifteen minutes at least. I can see already Linda is enjoying this, and I feel safe talking about this. Phew. Off the hook.

CHAPTER TWENTY SIX 

Later that night, back at her flat, Marissa brought a steaming cup of tea outside and sat in her pyjamas in her garden under the night sky. Tobermory wound himself around her ankles and sat beside her. She enjoyed the sense of his presence and could feel the thrum of his purring all the way up her legs. Linda actually offered her some good ideas as to how to manage Sarah. She felt more confident with the task ahead of her. She needed to figure out how to be a client in class without getting so stressed about it. *I need to make a list of issues to bring in with me that will make my life easier.*

She took a sip of tea, it was good to be busy again. She felt more focused than she had done the week before, and much more like herself. She enjoyed the cold air, the hot tea in her mouth, the breeze on her face. Spring was coming. She carried Tobermory inside and plopped him on the bed with her. He curled up on her duvet and purred as she fell asleep.

She woke up from a nightmare in the bed that she had slept in, back at the Monastery in Clifden. She was disoriented. She rubbed her eyes and opened them more fully.

There were several people there in the room with her. One was a little girl who was crying, another was an old man with long white hair. Who were these people? She wasn't afraid of them but she felt pressurised. It seemed like they wanted something from her.

She got out of the bed and noticed that she wore a long white nightdress, unlike anything she owned. She left the room to get away from the people there. The house looked just the same as it did, but it wasn't the same, it seemed more alive. Walking along the corridor she met a man walking in the other direction. He was in his thirties, wearing an old-style suit and holding a briefcase. He saluted her as she went past him, she went down the stairs, her hand on the handrail as she walked. It all seemed very familiar.

She got to the main hall and went into the front room. This room was decorated differently to before, the furniture was more ornate, a card table, leather-covered chairs, a chaise longue. No sofas. The paintings were different too, fresher, brighter. There were fresh flowers on the coffee table. A woman lay on the chaise longue, wailing. Marissa went over and saw that she was covered in blood and wailing. She felt a cold shiver down her back and an urge to get out of the building.

Suddenly she found herself standing outside, at the back of the big house, beside the trees. She was still in the long white nightdress, her bare feet were on wet grass. The trees loomed above her, they felt ominous, almost threatening. They were swaying, but she didn't feel any wind. She turned and looked back at the house, the stone grey building seemed to be swaying, shifting in and out, it was distorted.

She started to panic, she wanted to run but she was glued to the spot. She tried to lift one leg and then the other, but her feet were stuck to the ground. She heard something howling, then through the forest she saw movement, red eyes in the dark peering at her through the trees. First one set, then another, until there were many sets of eyes looking at her. She called out, 'Help me!'

Marissa woke in her bed in her flat in Dublin covered in sweat. Tobermory was nowhere to be seen. She looked at her alarm clock, it was 4.44am and pitch black outside. She sat up in the bed and turned on her reading light. She thought she'd write down what she saw. It felt important, strange, yes, but there was so much information, and it did feel so familiar. Marissa found the notebook she kept by her bed and wrote down descriptions of the girl, the old man, the businessman and the woman covered in blood. Marissa sensed that she was connected to this house. Somehow it felt familiar to her, even though she was sure she had never been there before the workshop. She remembered standing in the hallway looking at the angle of the stairs, it was so familiar the way they wound up to the first floor. She was sure she recognised them from somewhere. *Were they in a movie? Yes that must be it.* It felt creepy nonetheless. Another shiver rippled down her back.

She put down the notebook. She was wide awake now. She lay back down in the bed but she couldn't shift the image of standing there by those trees. *What were those eyes? Were they looking at me or just looking? And why do I feel like I know those people?*

'I'm goin to a gig later,' said Sarah, twirling around in the office. 'What you doin' tonight? You wanna come with me?'

'I'm meeting Joanne for dinner,' said Marissa with a stack of papers in her hand. She was trying to consolidate Sarah's work from before the Christmas break with the work that she was supposed to be doing now. It wasn't adding up. 'Can you explain this, here?' said Marissa, 'and why it doesn't match with this?'

'Ahh come on, leave it till tomorrow... I've a hair appointment at four, and I want to nip out early. Madison are playing in Wheelan's – you sure you don't want to come? Come on, it's gonna be brilliant.'

Marissa sighed. 'Look, Sarah, I'm happy for you to leave at four if you can help me with these figures now, and ask me first, rather than sneak around. Let's start off our work relationship on a good footing? We can be friends outside of work, but we have to be work colleagues when working together.'

'Work, work, work,' said Sarah, disappointedly pulling out her chair and sitting down beside Marissa. 'Does this mean you're not going to be any fun anymore?'

'Maybe not as much fun *in* work, but I'm still fun outside of it.' Marissa used the idea she got from Linda at the practice session, making clear boundaries so Sarah would not take things personally. She didn't know if it would work though, it was hard to do in practice.

'Look, if I finish dinner early I can come meet you and listen to the band. I might even bring Joanne with me. Do you need a ticket to get in?'

Sarah perked up immediately. 'No, it's entry at the door, first-come, first-served – hey, make sure your phone is charged up this time, will you?' She cocked her head to one side and stuck out her tongue. Marissa couldn't help but laugh.

'Okay, yes, that was silly of me. Eli said I probably need to get a new battery or a new phone. I'll look into that too. But we have to learn how to be workmates in work, and mates outside work, okay?'

'Okay, sure. Yeah, I can do that. Now, what was the problem with the figures?'

Marissa looked at the time on her phone, it was 8:30pm. She tucked her napkin under her plate. Over dinner, Joanne talked about the new manager at her husband's workplace and how she thought it would mean he'd finally be home more often and about how her children were doing at school. Afterwards, Joanne had to run away early, her husband was in Dubai and the babysitter couldn't stay later than 9pm. As she sat there thinking about lighting a fire and cuddling up with Tobermory, she felt obligation kick in. She should go to the gig.

Marissa left a tip on the table, got her coat and caught a bus into the city centre. Dublin on a Wednesday night wasn't really a time she'd normally be going out, but Dublin on any night gave her anxiety and she didn't normally go out anyway. She felt disconnected from the pull of the city's energy this time. She wasn't looking for anything, didn't want a man, or to get drunk, or to fill some ache inside. She looked at the people as she walked through the streets to find the pub where Sarah had said she'd be. They either had their heads down looking at phones or their shoes, or they were laughing and joking in groups, with a pint in one hand and a cigarette in the other. *So many people out mid-week...* Since the smoking ban had come in, many pubs had invested in garden heaters, they would put them outside on the street in front if they didn't have a courtyard at the back, so smokers gathered in the chill of the air to partake of their cigarette addiction with pints in hand. Smoke-free zones made the inside of pubs a little more habitable. She got to the venue and there was a queue outside. She texted Sarah as she joined it.

Here, in queue, where r u? She only had to wait a few minutes before her phone buzzed its reply: Inside – yay great see u soon

The room was hot. Marissa took off her coat and texted Sarah again: Where r u? Just as soon as she sent it, she spotted her. Her hair was down, she was in a pink sparkly dress, and she was chatting away to three others in a group at the back of the room. Marissa wove her way through the crowd to join them.

'Hey! Great to see you! This is Richard, Annette and Sandra, we all went to school together!'

Marissa nodded hello. 'I'm gonna get a drink. Does anyone want anything?'

'We're grand thanks, you go ahead.'

Sarah seemed free and easy with Marissa. She was relieved, all of the animosity from earlier that day was gone. Marissa went up to the bar to order a Diet Coke. She thought she'd give the alcohol a miss. The band were setting up on a makeshift stage, testing the sound system ('one two, one two'). Everything seemed to slow down around Marissa. She took her drink and said thanks to the barman and turned, placing her back to the bar, so she could look at the room full of people. *I wonder what they dream about... What they think about... What drives them? Are they satisfied with their lives, or do they want more?*

She cast her eye over the different groups of people, some were dancing, some dressed up, some in jeans, high heels, runners, messy hair, make up. *Everyone wants something else, but we all want the same thing, ultimately. Don't we?* She brought her drink over to Sarah's group.

The music started so it was too loud for talking. The band were quite good, though they were nothing to write home about. Sarah kept looking over to her as if checking her to make sure she was having fun. After the music she stayed for another drink, they talked about roads and weather, then she left, walking home in the crisp night air.

She loved her independence, she loved how she was more confident in herself, she loved what she was doing, as if she was living another life outside this reality. Doing the ordinary things and the extraordinary things. She was trying to find balance with both. She made a mental note to go out with Sarah every once in a while. She did enjoy herself. Her phone buzzed a text, it was from Sarah.

> Hey thanks for coming, I was upset, with the management thing, not that you got promoted and I didn't, more like I thought we wouldn't be friends anymore. Glad that's not the case. See you tomorrow xx

Marissa smiled and texted back. Thanks for asking, friends first, and always xx

That Thursday she started back in Cabra. She hadn't been there in three weeks. Mr Blakemore sent her an email letting her know that he had two new clients for her as well as Martin. Martin was still her last client of the evening. She felt a little anxious thinking about their last session together as she set up the room. She took her little bottle of Saint Germain out of her handbag and rubbed it through her aura like Dolores had shown her. She lit the sage and smudged the room, but she felt something was missing. She had received Séamus's email with the opening space prayer, maybe she would recite that? *It will make the space my own.* She hadn't learnt it off by heart just yet, so she found his email on her phone and read it out, it felt a little silly, though. She didn't know which direction North was, so she opened the compass app, it pointed towards the wall with the painting on it, then it shifted and pointed to the opposite wall, and then it shifted again back to the painting. *What does that mean?*

Marissa opened the four directions deciding the painting must be the North wall. She called in Mother Earth and Father Sky. Finished, she sat in one of the chairs and waited for her first client of the night. It did feel better, even if just a little bit. Within a few minutes the buzzer buzzed and she let her first client in.

Fiachra was quite tall, he had an apologetic sense about him as he stooped over as if to make himself smaller. He was wearing ripped jeans and looked quite dishevelled, his hair hadn't been washed in a while and there was a stain on his jumper. Marissa welcomed him in and invited him to choose a chair. He chose the chair she hadn't been sitting in, so she sat back down into hers.

'Hi, I'm Marissa, you must be Fiachra. Nice to meet you. We have six sessions together, I'm here to help you with whatever you wish. Anything you say in here is confidential, it won't leave this room. Unless I need to bring it to my supervisor or I feel that you are likely to harm yourself or someone else. Now that formal bit is out of the way, what would you like to talk about with me this evening?'

Fiachra shuffled around in his seat. 'Hi Marissa, erm... yea. I'm not happy and my doctor said I should come and talk to someone about it.'

'Okay, great.'

Fiachra flinched.

'Oh, I mean, it's not great that you're unhappy, but it is great that you're here.'

He relaxed.

'So tell me, how long have you felt this way?'

'About two years, I think, since I lost my job. I've not had a job since, and I've stopped looking for one now.'

'I'm sorry to hear that.' Marissa found herself about to ask him what his job was, what his skill set is, what type of job he was looking for then she remembered. *I'm not a job coach, I'm a therapist. Stick to the feelings.*

'How are you feeling about all of this?'

'Yeah, it's been a bit shit, actually. I've stopped caring now. I don't see the point.'

'The point of what?'

'Of looking. Of caring. Of anything.'

He started fiddling with his fingers in agitation. Marissa took a breath.

'Okay, Fiachra. I just want to tell you that I'm not here to help you get a job, I'm not here to get you motivated or to give you a kick and tell you that you should be grateful. No, I'm here to listen to you, to hear your thoughts, for you to tell me your dreams, so I can reflect back to you a source of hope that is deep inside you. It is in there, you've just lost the connection to it.' *That sounded good, I would like to go see someone who said that to me.*

'That sounds good to me.' He smiled and sat back in his chair, crossing his legs.

'Ahh, there's a smile. That's a good start.'

Marissa shook Fiachra's hand at the end of their session and he seemed happy enough to come back the following week. She took a moment in the empty room and felt a kind of a mustiness there. She clapped her hands over the chair where Fiachra had sat, and after three or four claps, it seemed to clear. There was a knock on the door, her next client was here.

'Hi, I'm Cliona, are you Marissa? The woman in reception let me in so I just came up myself.'

'Yes, hi Cliona, I'm Marissa. Nice to meet you. Come in.'

Cliona was in her early twenties and wore fishnet tights and a black leather miniskirt, with black boots up to her knees and a black baggy jumper. Her hair was shaved close on one side and shoulder-length on the other, the long bit was dyed pink with two inches of black roots growing through. She had four earrings in one ear, two in the other and a heavy tattoo that crept out from under her clothing onto her neck. It looked like a Maori symbol, something primal. She reached out her hand out to shake Marissa's and Marissa could see another tattoo on her wrist, which climbed up her arm and back into her clothing.

'You can choose a chair, whichever you like,' said Marissa.

Cliona walked straight over to the painting and looked at it. 'This is some mad fucking painting,' she said. 'It's evil.'

Marissa went over and stood beside her.

'Evil? Why?'

Cliona pointed to the ship. 'Well, look – there's no people on this ship, it's in a mad storm and it's going out to sea. Out of control. Everyone is dead. Mad.'

'I get how you can see that. I never thought of it as evil, though. Interesting how we can see different things in the same image. Is there anything else there you see?'

'Yeah, over there,' she pointed to the lighthouse. 'That's hope, that light. It's too late, though. They're already fuckin' dead.'

Cliona turned back to the room and looked around, then plonked herself into the chair that Fiachra had just been sitting in. She crossed her legs and her arms, looking very defensive. Marissa sat back in the other chair. *I will take my time and breathe, and give her plenty of space to talk about whatever she wants to talk about.*

Marissa began. 'We have six sessions together. Whatever you say here is between you and me, unless I think you're about to harm yourself or someone else, then I will have to report it to my supervisor. What would you like to talk about tonight?'

'Me? Harm someone? No bloody way. I'm the one that was harmed. Fuck that shit. My dad fucked me up. My life is fucked. My boyfriend just left me, and I'm angry. He said I was too angry, that's why he left.' Cliona made a fist with one hand and rubbed it into the palm of her other hand. She continued. 'Yeah, I know I'm angry. Fuck sake, of course I'm angry. I know why I'm angry too. But I'm still angry, and my life is still fucked. So there. What are you going to do about that?'

Marissa took a breath. 'Wow. Okay. Well, honestly it's not up to me to do anything about it. But I would like to help you do something about it.'

Cliona shrugged her shoulders and tightened her body as if getting ready for a fight. 'Like what?' She sat back in her chair, crossing her legs and arms, her lips sealed tightly.

Marissa noticed how defensive Cliona became. If anger was a thing you could throw, Cliona threw all of the anger she carried into the room right there with Marissa. And Marissa guessed she wouldn't want to pick it up again. But why should she? That's why she was here.

'Well,' she began, 'I can listen to you, try to understand what's going on for you, and maybe if you'll let me, I could help you carry your anger in a different way.'

Cliona sat forward again in the chair, curious now. 'Oh? Carry it differently? What does that mean?'

'If your anger was, say, an object, like a stone or a rock, how big would it be?'

'Huge. Bloody massive. Like a mountain.'

Marissa nodded. 'Okay. Let's say you've been carrying this rock around with you for a long time. I just felt like you threw it into the middle of the room just now, but I'm thinking that you've not really shown me how big it actually is. You're hiding the size of this rock from yourself, too, because it's so big it scares you. What do you think of that?'

Cliona took a moment. 'Maybe.'

'Well, what would it be like for you to let me see it with you? Just to see it, you and me, in this room. Nobody else needs to see it. If anything, it might give you some relief to put it down, to not have to carry it for a moment or two. Even just knowing that I know how big it is might help.'

'I don't get it.' She sat back again and scratched her head.

'Well, they say a problem shared is a problem halved. If I was to see how much anger you have, then you know that someone else knows how angry you are. Then you're not doing it on your own anymore.'

'I suppose...'

'Listen, you're here now, and however you're managing to carry everything and live your life, I think you're brilliant.'

Cliona twitched at the compliment but she stayed silent. Marissa went on.

'You're still here, functioning. You showed up tonight carrying all that heavy anger. It hasn't crushed you.'

'Not yet anyway.' Cliona nodded and seemed to soften a little bit. 'But sometimes I do feel wrecked. Maybe that's when it gets too heavy. I can't carry it all the time.'

'I know we've only just met. Perhaps you don't want to show me because you don't know me. That's fine – we have six sessions, so you don't need to show me everything tonight. Do you want to take a week to think about it?'

Cliona laughed. 'Fuck no. Let's do it now. I'm sick of this. How do I do it?'

Marissa thought for a moment. What if they went on a journey to Cliona's anger to see what it was made of? She got an image of a mountain range, not just a single mountain but many mountains. How could she bring shamanism into her session? She knew that this would work, but was there a way to do it without the drum? She was only starting off, but was it worth taking a risk?

'I have an idea, would you be willing to try something new? It's not exactly psychotherapy, but I think it will help.'

'Deadly. Yeah. Let's go for it.'

'Okay. Close your eyes and relax. It's okay, I promise.'

Cliona closed her eyes. Her body didn't soften, but that was okay. Marissa closed her eyes too.

'Now, imagine that you and I are together, travelling, walking on a road. Can you see it?'

'Yeah. We're on a dirt track in the forest.'

'Good. Yes, I see it now too. You and I are climbing up a hill, we are going to meet with your anger, just to see how big it is. How do you feel?'

'Great. I'm ready.'

'We come to the top of the hill, and we see a landscape, something huge, beautiful, a big sky. Like in the middle of America. Lots of space. It's clear and clean. Like a desert. Okay?'

'Yeah. I've got it.'

'Now. Show me how big your anger is. I can see a mountain appearing. It's not a mountain though, it's a big rock, the size of a mountain. Do you see it?'

'Yeah! I do. Hey, wait, there's a smaller one beside it. And another big one. This is great. Okay. What now?'

Marissa wasn't really sure what to do next. She saw the smaller mountain just as Cliona mentioned it, but she hadn't seen the second big one. It was very strange. She thought they should take it slowly. 'Let's wait a moment, relax here, see what shows up next. What else do you see?'

Cliona started to relax a little in her chair, her breathing slowed down. 'I see you, and me, and three mountains, and some boulders, and hey, wait, something else. Some kind of animal.'

'I see one too. It's like a dog, a coyote. He's raggedy and looks a little mischievous. Is that what you see?'

Cliona laughed. 'Yes! He looks like that coyote from the Roadrunner cartoon!'

'Yes! He does. What's he doing here? Oh wait – ha ha, Cliona, he's brought some dynamite with him!'

'Ha, ha, no way! Dude! He's the man!!'

Both of them started laughing.

'I guess he wants to blow up something,' Marissa said. 'What do you think?'

'Yeah! Cool! Let's do it!'

'Okay, let's allow Coyote to place his dynamite into one of the boulders?'

'Hey, he's going for the whole mountain, the big one. Ha ha I hope this works. You know he always forgets something.'

'He's asking you to light the fuse, Cliona. I think he wants *you* to blow it up. Are you okay with that?'

'Yeah. This feels great. I'm gonna do it now. That fuse better light!'

'I see you lighting the fuse, yes it has lit, do we need to step back a bit? Yes. Now, tell me, what do you see next?'

'It just exploded. We blew a hole in the middle of the mountain!'

'Yes. It's like a bite is taken out of it! Brilliant. It's unstable now, it's swaying a little bit. Hold on, it just collapsed on itself. It's still there, but it's smaller. Can you feel it?'

'Yes, I think so.'

'It's a mess here now. I see the Coyote saluted us, and he's gotten into a car and driven off into the sunset. He's funny! We are left with three smaller mountains and a lot of rubble. Do you see it?' Marissa could really see it. *This is great fun!*

Cliona shifted position in her chair. 'I think so. I don't know. But hey, I feel different. My body, it's less tight? Does that make sense? Give me a minute. Yeah, I can see it, it is a mess. Can we get a big vacuum cleaner to clean all this up?'

Marissa laughed. 'That's a great idea. Let's call in a big vacuum cleaner... no wait... I see something else coming. It looks like ants. What do you see?'

'That's so weird, just when you said that I could see them!'

'They're black ants, walking in a train. They're picking up pieces of rubble and going off with it somewhere. Where are they going? Shall we follow them?'

'This is mad. Wow. Yes, let's follow them.' Cliona was really excited and sounded happy.

'We are both following the ants, there are so many of them, each of them is holding a rock that's at least twice their size. We are catching up with the leader. They're going over a sand dune and down a hill to a lake. There's a lake here, in the desert! How cool is that? The ants are dropping the boulders into the lake, and they're fizzing up, then dissolving away. The lake is still clean. Wow, that's amazing.'

'Like bath bombs! Brilliant!' Cliona had a big smile on her face.

'Yes like bath bombs. Let's stay here until they're finished.'

After a moment, Cliona spoke, 'I think that's it?'

Marissa said, 'The lake looks clear, and the ants have gone. Yes?'

'Yes. Let's go back to the mountains again.'

'Yes, okay. We will go back the way we came to the space where the mountains were. How does it look to you now?'

'Much better, more compact.'

'I'm hearing a word – manageable. More manageable. You can manage this better this way. Shall we come back to the room now?'

'Yes! This is great. Thank you!'

Cliona opened her eyes. She looked brighter, her face was fuller, her mouth softer. She had a definite physical shift. Her shoulders were less tense and she was smiling.

'Thank you! I don't know what happened, but I feel a heck of a lot better. That was fun! I was dreading tonight but now I'm looking forward to next week.'

'Me too. Listen Cliona, don't do anything different this week. Just notice what feels different. That's my sense of what you need to do with this. Notice what is different around you, and tell me next week. I'm interested to know if what we just did can help you.'

Cliona stood up and hesitated, then asked, 'Can I give you a hug?'

'Sure,' said Marissa, and she stood and received a hug.

'That feels good! I feel good. Fuckin' amazing. Thank you so much! See you next week.'

Marissa was feeling great. She loved doing this work when it went well, this was why she was here. She felt affirmed in her choice to be a psychotherapist, but wait, was this psychotherapy? *What the heck was it?* She wasn't sure. And there was Martin at the door. He had a present for her.

'Come in Martin, Happy New Year! It's good to see you.'

'It's good to see you too, Marissa. Happy Christmas, I mean Happy New Year. I wanted to get you something, it's something small, I hope you like it.'

As he took off his coat and hung it on the back of the door, Marissa opened up the gift. It was a carving in wood of a bear. She was touched.

'I love it. Thank you so much.' She put the bear down on the table between them, right beside the candle.

Martin sat in his usual seat, the one where Marissa had just been sitting. 'I saw it and knew I had to get it for you. Hey, I know it might have been a little awkward there before Christmas. I do like you Marissa, I don't want to cause any trouble.'

'We'll figure it out together, Martin, as long as we keep talking. So, what would you like to talk about today?'

'I'm not sure really.'

'How was your Christmas?'

'Oh God. It was awful. My mother was in a mood for most of it, she started yelling at me on Christmas Eve, telling me how I'd ruined her life. She was crying and throwing things around. I went into my room and stayed there for most of the night and the next day. I didn't come out until Dad convinced me to.'

'That sounds like it was difficult for you.'

'Ahh, yeah, it's always difficult at home. They don't understand me. Sometimes they're walking around me on tiptoe like they might break me or something. Other times they're angry and yell at me. My older brother even punched me in the stomach once. He said I was a basket case, taking all Mum and Dad's attention away from him. He wanted to do something, I think, we were travelling somewhere, yes that's it, we were going to go on a holiday, and I had an episode and had to be hospitalised. So Mum wouldn't go then, and he had to stay home that summer. So yea, I get it, I know he's pissed at me. I can't help it. I can't control this.'

Martin was looking at Marissa straight in the eye. She shifted in her chair, feeling a discomfort rising up her body. It was too much all of a sudden, all the anger with Cliona and now his upset. She decided to use the egg visualisation that Dolores gave her to protect herself. She imagined herself as impenetrable and strong, a golden egg, no cracks, no weak spots. Impenetrable.

Martin sat back and shifted his focus away.

That was weird. Did he know I just sealed myself up?

'Do you want to talk some more about your family? You don't have to... Whatever you want to talk about is fine with me.'

'Actually, no, I don't want to talk about them. It's nice to be away from them for a bit. They don't like me going out by myself, they're okay with me being here and at my gran's. That's about it, really. It can feel like I'm under house arrest or something.'

'I'd imagine so.'

'So, tell me about yourself, Marissa? What's your family like?' Martin put his hands together in prayer position and had an open face, like he was taking a confession.

'No. I'm your therapist, you're my client. Are you uncomfortable with that?'

He sat back with a disappointed look on his face. He looks like he's five years old and has just been told he can't have any more cake.

'Maybe. Yeah. No. Not you, actually. No, I think it's about me, not about you.'

'Can you tell me more?'

'Well, it's like I don't have anything that's for me, that isn't about my illness. So what else can I talk about? I used to love playing football. I was on a team and everything.' He looked at his stomach and legs. 'I'm so unfit now, I'd not be up for that.'

Marissa had an image of him running through the park in the early morning sunlight. 'Have you ever thought about running?'

'Running? No.'

'Is there a park near where you live?'

'Actually, there is. It's a nice little park. I take the dog there sometimes when it's not raining.'

'I have a feeling,' Marissa said, taking a risk, 'that you'd actually enjoy running, maybe in the park, in the early morning? When nobody is around. What do you think?'

'Maybe.'

'Maybe if you did some running for a few weeks, you'd get your fitness levels back up, and then you could try for football again? I think it would be really good for you to have, as you said it, something for yourself, and this would be time out from your family and from the focus of your mental health.'

'I did read recently that experts say when you're fit, it's easier to manage stress.'

'Maybe it wasn't a coincidence that you read that.'

Martin looked in deep thought. 'I guess on my way home from running, I could call into the coffee shop that I like and get something nice there for myself.'

Marissa smiled. 'Why not? It could become a daily habit for you, and you would have time to think while you're running too. Do you think you'd try it maybe once or twice before we meet next week? You could start with walking if running is too much at first.'

'Don't hold me to it, but I'll certainly think about it. Thanks, Marissa, I think it could be good for me. Hey, I told the management here that I liked working with you. I hope that's okay?'

Marissa smiled. 'Yes, it's very okay. I like working with you too.' *He certainly keeps me on my toes.*

When all the sessions were over, Marissa locked up the room and walked to the bus. *Oh no! I forgot to close the healing space that I opened with the prayer. What do I do?* She had an urge to go back and open up again, but she could see a bus coming around the corner. She was torn for a moment, then decided to get the bus. She was tired.

When she was sitting down and the bus was on the way through town, an image came into her mind. She saw herself back in the room, standing there, saying the closing prayer. *Okay then, I'll try that.* She found Séamus's email, read the closing prayer in her mind and pictured herself in the room as she did it. Something that felt open now felt closed. *Yes, that was good.* She then saw herself opening the window and letting the air in, clearing out the space. *But the window doesn't actually open... Never mind.* She imagined the room with bright sparkly energy, all clean and fresh, ready for the next person to use it.

Then she brought herself back into the present moment, took out her headphones and turned on some music.

CHAPTER TWENTY SEVEN 

Terry's coming today! Oh shit, look at the state of this flat - cat hairs everywhere! 'Tobermory! Where are you? Look what you did! This flat is a disgrace! I can't have a visitor see my place looking like this!' Marissa leapt out of bed and began cleaning her flat from top to bottom. Tobermory looked amused to see her scrubbing and sweeping, dusting and organising. He sat there waving his tail and licking his paws.

'Laugh at me all you want, smelly cat, this has to get done. Anyway, most of this dirt is because of you – shedding your hairs all over my carpet, floor, and everywhere else, thank you very much!'

Tobermory didn't change position, he seemed to be thinking: 'It is right that you clean up after me, for you are my human.'

Marissa glared at him. 'If cats could talk, we probably wouldn't keep them as pets, so it's probably just as well they don't.' Then she smiled to show she didn't mean it. Tobermory said nothing to prove a point, then went out the back door through his cat-flap.

Marissa surveyed her flat. It seemed much cleaner now. The sofa and cushions were plumped up, her drum was out by the fireplace and she had even tidied up her desk. She made the bed with fresh new sheets and pillowcases, and she bleached and cleaned the bathroom. She jumped in the shower to wash the grime off of herself, then got dressed and made herself some toast and tea.

She opened the windows and the fresh cool January air filled the flat. Terry wasn't due for another half an hour or so. She lit her candle and sat cross-legged on the floor beside her coffee table and pulled out her deck of oracle cards from the shelf beneath the glass. She opened them carefully and held the cards in her hands. *Hello my lovely cards, I've not checked in with you in a while. I wonder why. Anyway, I'm here now, I'd like a card for today, please.* She shuffled and cut and took out the top card. 'Swan – Lovers'. *It's certainly not about me and Terry. Ha ha! I remember I got this card before, but I can't remember what it meant if it's not about actual lovers...*

She looked up the booklet again.

> *When you get the Lovers card it could be a sign that a new love is coming into your life, or that you are healing some aspect of the relationship you have with yourself.*

Healing some aspect of the relationship you have with yourself. Hmm. Marissa pulled out her notes from Séamus so she'd be ready for the journey with Terry. The homework was to journey for someone else to retrieve a gift and a message for them. *Oh no! I totally forgot I have to do three journeys myself too. We haven't gotten the dates for the next workshop yet. I suppose I have time. Jeez, I'd better write it in my diary so I remember.*

The doorbell rang. Marissa got up and went to answer it. Terry was there, he was filled with sunbeams and light, he was happy to see her. He looked good and was wearing a white designer tracksuit which looked like it had an oil painting wrapped around it. It was very unusual.

'Hello Marissa, darling, isn't your flat just gorgeous? I love this area, it's so quaint. I brought you something small – well, I thought we could share them, if you make the coffee!' Terry handed Marissa a bag with freshly baked brownies from the bakery down the road.

'These are my favourite! Thank you!', she said, inviting him in.

'Oh how dinky, you've got access to the garden – can I see?'

'Of course! I'll stick the kettle on. Did you bring your drum? I've got mine if you didn't.'

'No dear, I totally forgot mine, I was thinking about something else when I left Bruce's flat this morning, but sure never mind, we can use yours, just as you said. This garden is only gorgeous'. He stepped outside past the garden furniture and straight to Marissa's favourite spot. 'I'd say you do all of your thinking right here, what a beautiful spot!'

Marissa put the kettle on and went outside to join him. 'Ha ha, yes, how did you guess?' She smiled, not feeling intruded upon which would have been her usual reaction. It felt nicely surprising.

'This is exactly where I would do it if I lived here! It's great, a hideaway oasis in the city.'

'Just outside the city, but yes, only about twenty minutes walk to the city centre, and the bus is right outside. I love your tracksuit. It's so unusual! Do you want coffee or tea? I have real coffee?'

'Oh yes, real coffee definitely. I'm not a fan of instant.' He held out his arms and examined them as if to remind himself of what he was wearing. 'This old thing? I suppose so, yes, I've had it for years... I can't remember the name of the designer. Anyway. Mores to the point, tell me about your Christmas, did you have a good break?'

Marissa went back into the kitchen and Terry followed, he sat on Tobermory's armchair as she organised the coffee. *Just as well I hoovered that chair.* Marissa made the coffee in a French press for two and put the brownies onto little side plates.

'Do you have any cream? No? Milk is fine then, just thought I'd ask!'

'No cream, and yes, the Christmas break was interesting. Do you take sugar?' Marissa brought everything to the coffee table. Terry raised an eyebrow.

'No sugar, thanks. Interesting? Do tell!'

'Well, I think I was on a little bit of a buzz after our weekend with Séamus and I ended up going to an angel meditation workshop just after Christmas. Jenny told me about it. Only Jenny didn't show up, and something happened in it that made me, well, it's hard to describe. I wasn't myself. It happened very quickly, as if something jumped out of the teacher and went into me, and made me crazy upset.'

Marissa carefully pushed the plunger down in the French press, then poured the coffee into the mugs.

'Do you have a fork?' asked Terry as he stirred the milk into his coffee.

'Oh yes, of course.' Marissa jumped back up, found two forks, and took out some January strawberries from the fridge. She brought the container over to the table.

'Oh how lovely! Strawberries in January! What is the world coming to? Are they from Egypt?' He looked at the label and confirmed his suspicions. 'Hmm, now there's a place I'd love to go to sometime.'

Terry took a strawberry, cut into his brownie and took a bite of both, swallowed, then sipped the coffee. 'Heavenly. Thank you.'

'Now, girl, I hear you about the energy driving you crazy thing. That exact same thing happened to me a few years ago. This isn't my first time at a workshop, you know.'

'No, I didn't know, I just assumed we were all beginners.'

'Oh no, not at all! Finn has already done the training with Séamus. This is his second time doing it! No, dear, you can't assume anything about anyone! Especially on the spiritual path... Anyway. Let me tell you about what happened to me! I went to an angel workshop over in London, there must have been about 400 people there. I couldn't believe it, I'd never seen so many people in one place for a workshop before. Anyway, there were three teachers, and we did some healing. It was a two-day workshop. I had to place hands, do spiritual healing, on this woman. She was very sad, her husband had died the previous month, and they had lost a baby two years before the workshop. Honestly, she was riddled with grief girl, she shouldn't have been there at all. She hid it well. I can't tell you how much I cried after that weekend, I didn't know what had happened to me. It just wouldn't stop. That's how I found Séamus, actually.'

Terry took another bite. Marissa was listening avidly, waiting for more.

'So yes, I found Séamus and he worked with me, one-to-one. He told me that the grief from this woman had infiltrated my energy field, and some part of me was also grieving at the time, so that made it worse. Well, of course I was, this was around the same time that I came out to my parents, oh what a horrendous time that was. They were furious with me. My Dad still has trouble with me. Anyway. I was upset about my parental reaction, and this woman was so upset, I don't know if I'm an easy target, but Séamus told me her grief spilled into me, and she felt better – oh yes, she felt a lot better for sure. She friended me on Facebook and kept sending me messages. I had to block her, in the end, to get away from her! And it took three sessions with Séamus before I felt better. But it did eventually settle down. What about you? How are you feeling now?'

Looking very concerned, Terry turned to Marissa expectantly. 'You told me you only knew him from the videos?'

'Of course I did. I didn't know you then, I can't disclose everything, and I'm learning how to keep good boundaries. I'm not quite there yet, but I'm doing much better than before. I know you now, so I can tell you more things. But anyway, tell me about you.'

'Oh, that makes sense, yes. Me? I'm okay now, but it *was* terrible, whatever it was that happened to me irritated the hell out of me. I kept seeing the teacher's face in a distorted and scary way. It was like something from a horror movie, only I'm pretty sure it was just in my mind.'

Terry shook his head. 'Oh girl, what do you think they base those movies on in the first place? I can't watch them anymore. It hits too close to home.'

'You're probably right. I was on the verge of having a panic attack it was that bad. I've had panic attacks before, what's almost worse than having one is the fear of having one. I'm so glad that I thought of asking for help. I found a Reiki Master, her name is Dolores, she really calmed me down. I liked her immediately. I only went once, it seemed to be enough. I really want to see her again. I might learn Reiki from her. She has a workshop coming up in about two weeks time... Do you fancy it?'

'Can't. But thanks for asking. I'm up to my eyes in work at the moment, they're sending me to Marrakesh for a photoshoot, getting the summer looks in early. They always have to be at least six months ahead. I think, though, I might just stick with Séamus for now.'

He finished off his brownie and took another sip of coffee. 'Listen, girl, I'm really glad you're okay. This spiritual work, it's not fun and fluff, it's serious. Really serious. I have a friend that got seriously ill after something happened to him at the Dublin Mind Body Spirit Fair. One of those big exhibitions, lots of different people, lots of different things going on, and lots of energies flying around. My friend, well, he had a healing done, and then he had another healing. He liked it so much he did one more. It pushed him over the edge, he ended up in a psychiatric hospital for eight weeks. He had hallucinations and they put him on medicine, and now he has to take it all the time. He's not the same as he used to be.'

He turned and faced Marissa. 'Be careful who you work with and what you get involved with. Take it seriously. Please.'

'I will, I really will, especially after what happened. I didn't know. I suppose there's learning there, but your poor, poor friend. I'm so sorry.'

'Yeah, he was a time bomb I suppose, but he *was* looking for help when this happened, that's the crappy part.' He rubbed his hands together, finished the strawberries and stood up. 'Well now, will we get started on the work? I don't want to rush, and it's so good to see you again, but I have to meet some people for dinner.'

'Sure! No problem.'

Marissa cleared away the mugs and plates and pushed the table back so they had room.

'I was thinking we could lie down here, maybe on the sofa? or on the floor?'

'Sofa is great. Do you want to drum first?'

'Sure,' said Marissa, happy to drum first, wanting to get her head around what Terry had just told her. She supposed she was jumping in too fast with both feet, wanting to learn everything all at once. She reluctantly admitted to herself that it wasn't the best idea she ever had. *I could slow down, but I really want to learn. I am feeling a little overwhelmed. Anyway I need to focus on the drumming now.*

Terry grabbed the throw from the back of the couch, used a cushion for his head, and stretched out on the sofa. Marissa settled on the armchair, on the edge of the seat, holding the drum out in front of her.

'Ready?' Marissa asked.

'Yes! Hang on – what I am journeying for?'

Marissa checked her notes. 'You're to journey for me, to find a gift for me, and a message.'

'Right. Ready.'

Marissa held the beater in her hand and brought her awareness into her heart. She started to drum softly, then as she became more connected, she began the opening sequence. Terry had his eyes closed, his lids were fluttering already. *Wow, that was fast he must really have been ready!* Marissa went into the heartbeat of the world sequence, lub dub lub dub, and as she drummed with each lub dub she felt as if she was returning to herself. She felt more present, heavier in her body. She felt solid. It felt good. *I must do this for myself just to do it, it is very stabilising.*

She looked at Terry. His eyes were settling down more, she didn't think the journey was over yet, so she stayed with the rhythm. Lub dub, lub dub, lub dub. Images of the jungle forest reached out to her, but she pulled back from them and stayed in the room. Then she felt it was time to shift tempo, so she softened her lub dubs and then paused, then she played out the callback signal. Once she had finished, she put the drum up against the side of the armchair and waited for Terry to open his eyes. It took a few minutes. He rubbed his face with his arm and sat up slowly.

'Wow girl, that was powerful. I need a moment.' He stretched and shifted position so that he sat cross-legged on the floor. 'Okay. There was a forest, oh, it was luscious, like a tropical rainforest. And I met a snake. She was big, beautiful, yellow with dark spots, brown, I think.'

Marissa got shivers as he described Sachemama.

'And what else, yes, she told me to follow her, so I did, she brought me to a laboratory in a cave. It was really cool actually, lots of little bottles, it was like chemistry, I did chemistry for my leaving certificate. It looked like you were distilling something.'

Ahh, distillation, that's it! That's like the dream I had ages ago, mixed with the jungle. He's really clear on this, it's a little freaky.

'I felt like there were things there you were working on, and things that I wasn't allowed to see, so I didn't want to push my luck – that's one powerful snake there, I didn't want to cross her! Oh yes, I remember now. She brought me through the cave and we went deeper and deeper in, and right at the centre, there was a fire pit and an old woman. She was sitting there, she was dressed like one of those people you see in South America, all colourful with her robes. She was very pleased to see me. She gave me a snail for you and told me to tell you that there's plenty of time. And that everything is unfolding as it should. Then you brought me back. It was so vivid. I really enjoyed it, I hope this makes sense? Does any of it fit?'

'Oh my God does it fit? It fits exactly. That's my medicine snake and my medicine woman. I've met them both already. The woman I met in real life when I was in Peru! And I dreamt about the science experiment before too. I did chemistry as well, I loved it. Oh, you're so clear, you've made my day with that journey.' Marissa was smiling, her heart had lifted. Terry was also very pleased, his face was bright and beaming with her validation.

She continued. 'Distillation, I had forgotten that's what it was called. Thanks so much for that. Now, don't you have to give me that snail?'

'Oh yes! I forgot. I've got it here in my hands.' Terry said, 'It's for your brain! Ha ha! No surprise there.'

Marissa stood up, and Terry did too. He took a moment and then placed his hands on the back of Marissa's head and then blew the snail into her energy. Marissa didn't think she felt anything change, but she was happy with the symbolism of snail, to slow down. *Yes, I really do need to slow down a little bit.* She decided she needed to put a photo of a snail on her phone as wallpaper.

'Now me! Let's swap around.'

Marissa settled herself on the sofa, pulled the throw up over herself, and nodded to Terry, who was having just too much fun now that he got such clear images.

'Ready?' he asked

'Yes,' she said and closed her eyes. *I hope I can do as well for Terry as he did for me. What if I get it completely wrong? Oh dear. No, I have to stop thinking like this and just let it happen.* Terry began to drum. Marissa relaxed and went with the rhythm.

She was standing on the top of a stony mountain. There were no trees, no grass, it was quite a barren landscape. It was hot, the sun was out, and there was no shade. A large bird circled overhead. She walked, unsure of where she was going, then noticed a tree, so she went towards that. As she approached it, she realised it was dead. The bird landed on its bough. As it came into focus, Marissa could see the bird was a vulture. It started to talk.

'Pieces of eight, pieces of eight,' it said, and turned and looked directly at Marissa. 'You are trespassing. It is not your place, you shouldn't be here. Go now, before we come and get you.'

Marissa's heart leapt, she felt like she had done something wrong. Then the landscape suddenly disappeared, and Marissa found herself at the lake, her lake with the stepping stones and the mountain. 'Ausangate. Hello my lovely mountain.' *Terry was there with her, sitting on a rock in the middle of the lake, kicking his feet. He laughed. He reminded her a little bit of David Bowie, he looked more androgynous here than in real life, and younger. His body was very long, he wasn't standing but he looked like he would be taller than a human would normally be. Marissa thought he looked a little bit like an alien. He pointed to the water beneath.*

Marissa felt a pull to go down. She took a breath, and jumped in, diving down and down into a forest of algae, tall fronds on long, dark green stalks as thick as her arm. She had a mermaid's tail, the water cleared and she swam without needing to breathe. She felt pulled in a direction, down to even deeper water. After a time, lights, underwater lights, and an underwater city appeared. It was like the one she saw before when she was swimming with her serpent. 'Is this my journey, or Terry's?' *She kept with it and went down to the city, following the pull, and she arrived at big city gates. There was a procession there, waiting for her, and she was made welcome, invited inside. It was a palace, there was a giant seahorse inside and he bowed to her, and she bowed back. The seahorse gave her a crown with jewels on it. She thanked him.*

Marissa could sense that Terry had stopped drumming but she hadn't come back yet. She brought her awareness more fully into the journey, and back to the seahorse.

He was yellow and very friendly-looking, he looked closer to a real seahorse than an animated one. She asked him if there was a message for Terry. He nodded. He said, 'He is the prince of all he surveys. He knows this already. Tell him that the King is waiting for his visit.'

Marissa thanked the seahorse, turned and left, threading her arm through the crown as she swam upwards towards the fronds of the algal forest, the light guiding her as she kept swimming to find the top of the water. She came up for a breath, and she wasn't a mermaid anymore.

Terry was there on the rock. 'See ya in a few,' he said, saluted her, then disappeared. Marissa got out of the water and came into her heart and back into the room.

When Marissa came back into the room she looked at Terry, almost surprised to see him looking human. *Well, of course he looks human. What's that about?* She thought for a moment before speaking, deciding not to mention the vulture. It felt like it wasn't for him. The vulture did say she was trespassing, so she figured she had gone to the wrong place. She shook her head to try and shift the feeling of it. She sat up and rubbed her arms to get the blood flow back.

'Well, how was it? What did you see for me?' Terry looked expectantly at her.

'Yeah, sorry. I went far away. You were in the journey, waiting for me, you looked like David Bowie, taller than you are now, tall like an Alien or something.'

'Ha ha! Cool! I love David Bowie. And Aliens are cool too. What else?'

'I dove into the lake and I turned into a mermaid. I went down to a city under the sea. I've seen the city before but I've never been inside it.'

'Oh how lovely! Was it Atlantis?'

'I don't know… What's Atlantis?'

'It's a place that used to exist for real a very long time ago, they basically blew themselves up. Anyway, I've been told I have connections to Atlantis, that's why I was asking. Some people say it's still here, you know, near Barbados somewhere, where those airplanes keep disappearing.'

'Bermuda triangle?' Marissa offered.

'Yes! That's the one. Barbados, Bermuda, one day I'll be able to tell the difference, when I visit that is! Go on, is there more? You were gone for ages.'

'Yes, there's more. I went to Atlantis, or whatever city it was. It looked like a royal palace. I met a seahorse and he gave me a crown for you and told me to tell you the King is waiting for your visit.' Marissa checked once more with herself and decided once more to leave out the part about the vulture, she wasn't quite sure what to do with it but it didn't feel right to tell Terry.

'The King, eh?'

'Oh yes, and the seahorse, he was lovely, big and yellow and so friendly, I wanted to hug him. Anyway, he also told me to tell you that you're the prince of all you survey. I hope this makes sense to you? Does it fit for you?'

Terry thought for a moment. 'Well, I did love the story of the little mermaid when I was a boy. And I did often dream of being a merman, and... wait... the seahorse, he was yellow, I think I've seen him before. Not sure about the King and Prince stuff and a crown as a gift. Hmm. Perhaps I'll find out I'm royalty! Ha ha! Not in this reality anyway, not with my parents! Ha ha, funny. But it's nice. And does confirm my connection to Atlantis. Maybe I should journey there myself. Thanks, Marissa.'

Marissa stood beside Terry and was drawn to put the crown into his stomach. *Funny, you'd imagine a crown would go on his head. Oh well, I will go with the feeling.* She blew it in, and he looked like he got a kick, his whole body shook, and he went weak at the knees. He sat back down on the sofa.

'Jeez, you okay?' Marissa sat beside him. He had gone pale. She held his hand.

'Remember when I told you this stuff was serious?'

She nodded her head.

'Well, that was serious. That crown. Now I get it. I don't know if I can talk about it right now. I need some time. And some sunshine. Thank God I'm going to Marrakesh soon, I love it there. And these dark days, why, it's dark already. Feels like 10, but it's only 4 o'clock! I'd better get my stuff together and go.'

Marissa was concerned. 'Are you sure you're okay? It's fine if you don't want to talk about it, but I'm not happy with you rushing out the door after shaking like that. Please, stay for a few more minutes, so I know you really are okay.'

Terry turned to Marissa. 'I can see that you mean that. Marissa, I'm very glad to have met you. You're a genuine, good person. Thank you.'

'You're welcome. No bother at all, totally selfish really, I would be afraid if you fainted and fell in front of a car later on, I'd blame myself forever.'

Terry laughed.

'Look, it's been an emotional afternoon. Let's have a cup of tea, and then you can go, okay?'

'Great.'

Marissa tidied up the flat after Terry had left and sat down with a fresh cuppa for herself. Camomile this time. Her thoughts drifted back to the vulture. And the swan. And the snail. Lots of animals were showing up for her today. *Wonder what that's about. That vulture, it felt nasty. Giving me a warning, or was it for Terry? Pieces of eight? Wasn't that Pirates? Not a vulture, shouldn't it be a parrot?* Marissa remembered the pirate from the beginning of *SpongeBob*. What other pirates did she know? Not many, bar Captain Hook and Peter Pan. *Hang on, weren't there were mermaids in Peter Pan? And didn't Terry look younger when they were back at the lake? Maybe the vulture was for him after all?*

She picked up her phone to text him, but she changed her mind. He was out for dinner with his modelling friends, and she didn't want to upset him if he wasn't ready to hear about it. He did get emotional. She really liked him. She was glad they were friends. *If it's important then it will show up again. I hope so, anyway.*

She thought she'd try her oracle cards again. She pulled them out from the small shelf under the coffee table and opened them up, held them in her hands, and cut the pack. Swans again. Her heart leapt, she felt like she was missing something. So strange. *Lovers?* She didn't know if she was changing something in her relationship with herself? Maybe that was it. She saw Zaad's face briefly flicker in her mind, it had been a while since she thought about him. She wasn't even sure if she got his face right.

'You think too much,' she said out loud, then looked on the internet to find a picture of a snail. Finding one she liked, a very small colourful snail climbing up a leaf with a raindrop, she made it into her phone wallpaper.

'Slow down, girl. Slow the fuck down.'

CHAPTER TWENTY EIGHT

She got the email from Séamus just as she was leaving for work the following morning.

> *Next workshop weekend Feb 14th, Clifden Monastery 2 nights. Subject: Work of the EAST. Make sure you've sent me your NORTH homework beforehand. Bring Drum, warm clothes and a black stone.*

A black stone? What kind of stone? How big? What is he talking about? Three weeks to wait, three weeks to do her personal journey homework. She didn't know why she had been putting those off. It also meant that she was free the last weekend of January, she could go to Dolores's Reiki 1 weekend. But was it too much? She was feeling confused.

She had her session with Olive at lunchtime. This would be a great topic to discuss with her if she was feeling brave enough. But it would help her sort out her mindset. Yes, that felt difficult, but right.

Olive sat back in her soft chair. She was wearing her green ensemble and her hair was scooped back into a bun. She had pink glasses on today, Marissa thought she looked very elegant.

'So let me get this right. You've been on a shamanic weekend and an angel meditation workshop,' Olive sat forward and raised an eyebrow, 'Thank you for informing me, by the way, although it did take you long enough.' She sat back and her face softened, with a look as if to say she had known this all the time. 'Now you're thinking of doing a Reiki weekend, which, in my humble opinion, is a good idea. But I'm not supposed to tell you that, so you didn't hear it from me.' She crossed her legs. 'You're also keeping up your college classes, seeing clients and you're doing supervision. And your next shamanic weekend is coming up soon? Isn't this rather a lot to take on all at once?'

They had been talking roads and weather for the first fifteen minutes before Marissa felt ready to say what she had wanted to say. She blushed in acquiescence. 'I know, yes. It really does sound like a lot, almost too much, really. I'm not sure if I *should* do the Reiki, but, you really think it's a good idea?' Marissa brightened. 'I really feel like I need to understand energy better. That's why I wanted to tell you – do you think it's too much?'

Olive smiled. 'You're in an expansion phase dear. Yes, I do think Reiki is good as a self-care practice, particularly for psychotherapists. You've got the passion, I can't give you advice, you know that. However, it does seem like you have the capacity for it all at the moment. How do you feel?'

'I think I'd be disappointed if I didn't go to the Reiki workshop. I am kind of looking forward to it already, and I've been to Dolores for a Reiki session. She is lovely, you'd like her. Maybe. Anyway, she has a lot to teach me, there is so much I don't understand.'

'The issue I would imagine you *would* be having if I were you, is getting tangled up in it all. The emphasis in psychotherapy, as you're learning, is on wholeness and integration. However, in my opinion, sometimes you do need to separate things out and keep them separated so you can make sense of them. We can't integrate something if we haven't processed it yet. Throwing everything in together can become one big muddle of a thing. So it's usually better if you separate things out while you're learning. Do you think you can do that?'

Marissa was thoughtful for a moment. The image of her library inside the filing cabinet drawer came into her mind. She'd been to visit it several times since she established it, and it was getting easier for her to access. She peered a little closer into the drawer in her mind's eye, wondering if she could have another filing cabinet in a drawer inside the library itself. That seemed too complicated.

'I suppose it is possible… to break it all up and keep it separate. You're right, I do feel like I can take it on, it's almost as if I'm on some sort of quest. There's a momentum behind me, I have a pushing feeling, like I'm being pushed forward into everything. I can't seem to sit still, I want to learn, I want to know more.' As she spoke, Marissa was almost rocking in her chair, expressing the pushing she was experiencing.

Olive took her time to respond.

'Time in stillness is very important while you're processing brand new information. Stillness means you're not busy thinking or trying to make sense of anything. All of your thoughts, you must push them into the background to sort themselves out. So that you can replenish yourself.' She took her glasses off and cleaned the lenses with a tissue she pulled out from the inside of her sleeve. She put them back on again and spoke in a serious tone. 'In my experience, as long as you take time to absorb and contemplate, if it feels like you need to do it, then you can do it. But to be in balance you would need to make a point of doing that, of being still. It doesn't happen by itself.' Olive raised an eyebrow at Marissa, knowing her weakness at this stage in their relationship. She smiled, and Marissa smiled back.

Olive continued. 'There is probably a reason for this urge, the pushing that you speak of. It could be the right time for you to do this. It's quite interesting. Where is the sensation coming from? In your body, I mean.'

'At first, I thought it was a pulling from my heart, but it's not. I felt a pulling in a journey, once I felt it, I knew what it was. This, it's more of a pushing, from behind my stomach? I feel it in my hips – down my spine too. Kind of like I can't sit down and rest, I need to be doing something. But it's not agitation, it's... motivation?'

Olive laughed. 'Well dear, you might be doing more learning this year than some people do in a lifetime. It certainly sounds like momentum to me, with a lot of enthusiasm behind it. I'd suggest you go with it and keep tabs on how you're feeling. Make sure you're not leading yourself into overwhelm. Write everything down, keep a journal to help you keep track of what's going on. Slow down as much as you can, and I cannot stress enough how important it is to sit in stillness.'

'Thank you. Yes, that's a good idea. I have a journal but I don't write in it very often. I'll make a point of it, and of sitting in stillness, every day from now on.'

'Yes, good,' said Olive with a tone that implied she didn't really believe her. 'I know you will do your best. There is learning too, in that. Now, when you are writing, pay attention to your thoughts, feelings, what's going on around you. If you're stuck you can use that as a writing prompt – 'How do I feel?', 'What do I think?' Even asking yourself, 'What do I know?' can really open up your flow. You can bring your journal into these sessions if you want, or not.' Olive reached for her diary and opened it to a page, had a look, then turned back to Marissa.

'Now dear, it's time to finish for today. Our next session will be a little later than usual, I'm afraid, I've been asked to speak at a conference, so is next Tuesday lunchtime good instead of our usual Wednesday?'

'Yes, that's fine. What's the conference? What are you talking about?'

'It's the annual psychology gathering, my talk is entitled 'Jungian Transpersonal Theory in Modern Day Mindfulness Practice.' It's experimental. A little like your shamanic journeys, dear.'

'That sounds very interesting!' Marissa noted the change of date, then gathered her things and got up to leave.

Olive walked her to the door and looked at Marissa with a glint of something in her eye. 'I'm excited for you, you're in a very interesting time of your life. What you are doing is important – we need people like you to bring psychotherapy into the next phase. I'm very pleased to hear all that you've said today.'

Marissa had never heard Olive say anything like that before. *Is she allowed say that, as my therapist, I mean? But it is nice to hear. She does genuinely seem happy for me.* 'Thank you, Olive. And thanks for your support. See you next time!'

Back at the office, Marissa's afternoon went quickly. She and Sarah were more at ease with each other, 'mates outside of work, workmates in work' seemed to have helped them both come to terms with their new dynamic. Sarah even seemed to be anticipating Marissa's expectation that she would actually do the work she said she would do. She took a coffee break at her desk at 3.30pm and looked up Dolores Carmody's website. The Reiki 1 weekend was still advertised. *I need to be at this, I don't know why, but I really need to go. Alrighty then, it's decided.* She emailed Dolores and asked if there were any spaces left, told her she still felt good after her session and letting her know she'd really like to learn more about Reiki. Once she sent it, she felt confident that she was doing the right thing by signing up.

She had a few minutes spare before her meeting started. She switched off her computer monitor to get in a few moments of stillness. She sat at her desk, placed her two feet on the ground, and tried to clear her mind. She immediately thought about Dolores, remembering the Buddha statue on her desk. That switched to what she'd be making for dinner that night, the shopping list of food that she had to get for herself, and all the homework that she still had to do for Séamus.

It was Thursday, client day. Marissa was lying in bed before needing to get up for work. She had been practising stillness sporadically since seeing Olive the day before but her mind kept wandering into the Reiki workshop, her upcoming client sessions, particularly about Martin. And then she realised she wasn't being still at all. *This stillness thing isn't going to be as easy as I thought it would be.* Marissa sighed and tried again. Using mindfulness as an anchor she focused on her feet on the ground, her legs beneath her, her knees, her hips, the support from the chair... But that wasn't stillness either, it seemed her mind always needed something to do. Then, as if on cue, Tobermory jumped on the bed, demanding her attention. *Every time I almost get there, something always interrupts me.*

She got to Cabra early. She lit the candle and used it to light her sage and smudged the room. She rearranged the chairs, then used her Saint Germaine to cleanse her energy field. She sat down and asked herself how she was feeling, and she had a sense of peace, confidence, and readiness for what the evening was going to bring. She tried once more to still her mind, but just then the buzzer rang. It was Fiachra. She let him in, and he was at her door a few moments later.

'Come on in. It's lovely to see you again.'

Fiachra seemed a little more confident since the previous week. He had washed his hair and was wearing a clean jumper. He looked like he made an effort. *We may be going in the right direction.* He chose a chair and sat down, looking at her expectantly.

'So, Fiachra, tell me, how has your week been?' Marissa sat down opposite him and smiled.

'Hi.' Fiachra shuffled in his chair. 'Yeah. Thanks. It was a bit better than last week, thanks. I was thinking about what you said, about finding the hope that's inside me. I've been so busy feeling bad about not having a job, I guess I lost any sense of hope.'

'I'm glad you're feeling better, even if only a little bit. Even a little bit is something, isn't it?'

'Yeah. I guess so.'

Fiachra stared into space, he didn't seem any more willing to talk than he had been before. Marissa thought she'd try a different tactic while staying with the context of hope.

'I thought I'd ask you a question if that's okay? Can you answer it for me?'

'I'll try.'

'Thanks! Great. I want to know, what does hope mean to you?'

Fiachra shrugged his shoulders and sat back in the chair. Then he sat forward again. 'I guess it is a reason to get out of bed in the morning. Hope means not giving up. Feeling like I will get a job, eventually. Maybe even find a nice girl and get a place of my own. That's what I really want, a family for me.'

He sat back in the chair again. 'I still live at home, with Mum and Dad. It makes me feel bad, like I failed or something. I'm thirty-two already, most of my friends are married, they have houses, babies on the way... I thought I'd be the same as them, but I'm not.' Fiachra started fiddling with his hands, he looked down and began picking at his nails.

Marissa gave him some time to continue the dialogue but it seemed like he had said all he wanted to. *Why is it so difficult to get some people to engage? It's like pulling teeth...* She decided to try again, from another angle.

'Do you remember a time when you felt hopeful?'

Fiachra looked up and into the distance, he seemed thoughtful. 'No. Oh wait, yes. I do. I was young, I must have been around eight. I was looking forward to Christmas. Yeah, I remember now, I really wanted Santa to bring me a computer. I was excited, and so disappointed when I didn't get it. That's when I found out that Santa was my Dad. I think that changed something for me. They hadn't enough money for a computer, rather than say that Santa didn't have it for me, they told me Santa wasn't real.' Fiachra sat up and laughed. He brushed his fringe out of his eyes. 'I got a selection box from him instead – ha ha. I was so upset. I remember I punched my pillow and cried.' He sank down in the chair again. 'I think I lost faith in life. Or interest. Not sure which. And Santa never came again after that.'

Marissa was quiet for a moment. 'Ahh, I can see why you'd lose hope at that. Feeling that there's less magic in the world. Hope and magic are almost the same, do you think?'

'Well it would be magic if I could get a job.' Fiachra smiled. 'And even more magical if I got that house and family – do you know any magicians?' He was laughing again, but it sounded more authentic than before. Marissa laughed too.

'No, the only magicians I know are illusionists. Real magic is different. I think you want a real house, not a cardboard cut-out or a pretend house.'

'I wouldn't mind renting a house, at first. It would be better than staying at my mother's. I met a nice girl a couple of weeks ago and I couldn't bring her back home... I was mortified at the thought of her coming down to breakfast the next morning and what Ma might say.'

Marissa nodded her head. She remembered the first time James stayed over at her place, she was also still living at her parents' house. It was embarrassing, as she had thought her parents were going to be out. She didn't feel a pang when James's face came into her mind, and that in itself was quite pleasant. Her heart seemed fine. *I think something inside me that was gaping open has closed up and is healing. Finally! This is great.* She smiled to herself and then remembered she was still in session with Fiachra. He was looking at the painting of the ship at sea and picking at his nails again. *Oy vey this is such an effort, there must be something I'm missing.*

'Fiachra. I can't magic you a house, and I can't magic you a job either. But I can help you feel more hopeful, and perhaps that will change your energy and help you feel better about yourself. And then when you do go looking for a job, people will feel that off you, that hope, and they'll like it. It could improve your chances. Of getting a job, I mean.'

'Or a girlfriend?'

'Or a girlfriend. Yes, why not? You don't need one to have the other. Tell me about the girl you mentioned.'

They talked for the rest of the session about his friends, the girl, and they made a plan together for him to get in touch with her before he came back to the next session next week.

As Fiachra got his coat to leave, he held out his hand to Marissa. 'Thank you. I didn't know why the doc said I should come talk to someone, but I do feel a lot better after talking to you. Can we shake hands?'

'Sure, and I'm very glad you're feeling better.'

They shook, and Marissa opened the door to let him out. She had 10 minutes free before Cliona was due in. She went down to the kitchen, got herself a glass of water, and stretched out her legs and arms.

Coming back up to the room, she felt a little bit taller. Even though I didn't see any tangible change in Fiachra, it still feels good to know that he felt better after talking to me. I must make sure I have more patience for him for next time. I don't have to push him or change or fix him, I just need to listen to him. Good learning.

Cliona arrived a few minutes late, out of breath, but seemed much happier than she had been on their first session. Her pink hair seemed a little less severe. She was wearing jeans and runners instead of her leather mini skirt and fishnets, and a sweatshirt with a smiley emoji. *What a transformation!* She seemed much more relaxed too.

'Hi!' She took the same seat as she had last week and smiled at Marissa, who took her seat opposite her.

'Hey, thanks so much for last week. It was great! Can we do some more like that?'

Marissa's mind went suddenly blank. *Strange.* 'Hi, Cliona, lovely to see you. You look well. How do you feel? Can you remind me of what we talked about last week?'

'We blew up some rocks, remember? Coyote?' She turned and crossed her legs. 'I feel grand today, heaps better, thanks.'

'Ahh yes, I remember now. Coyote, of course!' The images flooded back to Marissa as if her internal filing system suddenly found the book of Cliona and opened it to the right page. She was back on track again. 'Sure, we can do some more. And I'm glad you're feeling great. I'm also glad you showed up to your session. People don't tend to come when they feel better. But tell me first, how was your week? Was anything different for you?'

'Yeah, it was a fuckin' weird week alright. After I left you I got a text from my ex wanting to meet up with me. So I waited a few days, you know, not to seem too keen or anything, we texted a bit, then I met him. He apologised, said he wanted to try again. I didn't jump right in, but I said I'd think about giving him another chance. He admitted he was afraid of me when I got angry.' She shifted in her seat and faced Marissa directly. 'I want to do more blowing up rocks tonight. I think I would like to try again with him. Maybe he knew I was working on this? What do you think? I don't know. It felt good to see him, and I must say I've not been as angry since we did that thing. Can we do it again?'

'Sure. Let's take a breath and go back a little bit. What was it like for you to hear him say that he was afraid of you?'

Cliona looked less comfortable than before. 'It was strange. Weird, not nice really. I remembered being scared of my dad when he got angry at me. I know what it feels like to be afraid of an angry person. I don't want to be that person.' Cliona shifted around in her seat. 'My boyfriend, my ex, I mean, he's lovely, a soft, gentle person. He's good for me. And he loves Ari. So I want to fix this.'

'That's a big realisation and not an easy one for you. You were afraid of your father's temper, and now your ex-boyfriend admits that he is afraid of yours. So you're owning it and wanting to fix it. That's wonderful and courageous for you to admit it, to yourself and to me. Did you tell him too?'

Cliona laughed. 'No fuckin' way, no I didn't tell him. Not yet anyway. And it's nothing official yet. I want to see if he meant it first, see if he sticks around.'

'How long have you been together?'

'A year and six months. It's been my longest relationship. We met at a festival, we both liked the same bands and kept bumping into each other. He said it was, you know, fate. I didn't know what fate was, so I just went with it, cos I liked him. I do like him. I want it to work out. Ari loves him too, Ariana. She's my girl, she's three now, such a sweetheart. Difficult as fuck sometimes, but you know, kids. Yeah, I hope it works out. So yeah, I want to do some work on myself.'

Marissa took a breath, trying to focus on the issue at hand rather than understand everything all at once. *Stick to the anger, stick to the dad relationship.* 'We might need to talk a little bit about what it was like for you living with your dad. Is that okay?'

'Yeah, I guess so.'

'Is he still around in your life now? '

'Short answer, no. I guess I took Mum's side, and once he was gone, she kind of turned me against him. So I stopped phoning him once I was eighteen. Mum kicked him out when I was sixteen. When he was at home with us, me and my two younger brothers, it was bloody awful. He'd get drunk every weekend, shout and scream at us for any reason he could find. I screamed back at him one night and got a whack across the face. Never tried that again. It was much quieter when he left, but I sometimes think that he left some of his anger behind, in me.'

'Are you angry at him now?'

'Yeah, fuck sake, course I am. How could he think it was alright to treat us that way? And he never helped us out, with money, with anything. I didn't get any texts, not even a card on my birthday, or anything about Ari when she was born. Imagine he's a grandad now and he didn't even bother to... He might as well be dead. So yeah, I am angry at him, very angry.'

Cliona was sitting on the edge of her seat now, her shoulders were tight, she was getting stressed. Marissa wanted to defuse it but wasn't sure how to, but she didn't want to avoid going deeper, either. She wondered where to go with this, to go back further? That would only bring up more anger. Then she had an idea.

'If your dad was here, right now, in the room with us, what would you say to him?'

Cliona jumped as if she got a fright, she looked around seeming worried, and then she relaxed, realising that he wasn't actually there.

'Jesus, don't spring that one on me. You gave me a start.'

'I'm sorry, I didn't know it would upset you that much. It must have been very traumatic living with him.'

'Being in the same flippin room as him was traumatic, jeez. My body reacted to you saying that.'

'It seems like it goes very deep.'

'Yeah it does.' She sighed. 'If I was to see him now, I don't know what I'd say to him, or if I could even talk to him at all. He whacked me more than once you know, my brothers too. I've had bruises that lasted months from his outbursts. He hit Ma one night, right in front of all of us. Gave her a black eye. That was the worst. It wasn't long after that she kicked him out.'

Cliona seemed to calm down talking about this, she wasn't getting emotional or teary-eyed. Marissa decided to leave her the space to continue, rather than get in the way of the flow.

'It was the best thing for all of us, kicking that bastard out of the house. I've been scared, you know, of ending up like her. Like me ma. I don't want to do that, it's not right. Not fair. Shouldn't hit a child. Not ever. Didn't realise that I'd end up like him instead of her.'

Cliona sat back and pressed her knees together, wrapping her hands around them as if she was giving herself a hug.

'This one, my boyfriend, I mean my ex, he's nice. He'd never do that to me. He'd never hit. I like him. I want it to work out. So when can we go visit the coyote?'

Cliona did have great fun smashing and exploding rocks on the visualisation with Marissa. Marissa wasn't sure if she was making it up or if she really had so many things to explode, but Cliona seemed to feel much lighter in herself leaving. *That really was the point, though, for her to feel better. I guess I'll have to wait and see where this goes. As long as Cliona doesn't avoid talking about her dad, and her temper, there is bound to be some improvement. I'll ask Mr Blakemore what he thinks next time I see him.*

As she was thinking, Marissa plumped up the pillows to get ready for Martin's visit. She was never sure what he would bring in with him. Last week went well enough, she remembered, so why did she seem to be anticipating trouble? She sat in the chair that he liked to sit in and looked around the room. What was he thinking when he sat there, looking at her? Was he testing her? Was she coming up to his expectations, or was she a good match for him? She shook her head, trying to get rid of the sense of competition. It made no sense, where was it even coming from? Her buzzer rang and she jumped. She let him in the main door. A few moments later, there was a knock on her door, Marissa got up and let him in.

'Martin, how are you? Come in, take off your coat, have a seat.'

'Hi, Marissa, it's nice to see you again.' Martin took off his big heavy coat, hung it on the back of the door and took his usual seat. Marissa moved to the other chair and sat down. They sat together for a moment not speaking.

'So, how are you?' Marissa looked at Martin expectantly. He seemed like he wasn't really present behind his eyes, preoccupied. Then he snapped back into the room.

'Hi Marissa, sorry, I do that sometimes, it's the medication. It makes me tired.' Martin looked around. 'I've never really looked around this room before, it's quite nice here, except for that painting. What a dark and depressing thing to have in a room where people are trying to feel better.'

Marissa relaxed a little. *Martin's just a person, remember? He's not some evil demon.* She laughed. 'Yes, I know, they really weren't thinking when they hung that in here, were they?'

'Maybe some old lady died and left it to them in her will, and they felt they had to take it because they had nothing else to hang up on the wall?'

Marissa laughed. 'Yeah, maybe. Or maybe the person that used to live here said they could use this room on the condition that the painting stayed up there on the wall.'

Martin laughed too.

'So, Martin, what can I do for you this evening?'

Martin scratched his head. *It's funny how they say in books and cartoons that people scratch their heads while they're thinking, but they actually really do it.*

'I don't know. It's nice to get out of the house, to have somewhere to go. You did tell me last time that I should do that more often, have somewhere to go. We talked about my taking up running again, and maybe football.'

'Yes, I remember, how did that go for you?'

'Well, I was sick last week for a few days, I spent the days in bed, so I didn't go running, but I did go for a walk. That was nice, it was fresh and bright, and I liked being outside by myself. It was nice to get away from the family. I think maybe starting with walking would be better than nothing. Running seems like it would take up too much energy.'

'Something is always better than nothing,' Marissa agreed.

'That's true.' Martin smiled. *He's so ordinary, why am I making such a big thing out of him? Maybe I should confront it, maybe it's me making this up all this time.*

'So,' said Marissa, feeling a little awkward, not really knowing where to go with this. She went out on a limb. 'Have you been seeing things since we last spoke about it? I mean, you saw my bear before, and I will admit that freaked me out a little bit.'

'I'm used to it,' Martin said. 'Hey, look, it's no big deal, don't be getting upset about it.'

'That's easy for you to say... I'm still learning and I don't want to make any mistakes. I certainly don't want to make any mistakes with you.' Marissa looked him in the eye. 'I know you've had a bad track record with counsellors, in that you've not liked them, I mean, and I don't want you to not like me, but it's not about whether you like me or not. I need to feel comfortable with you and you with me, so that it will work. With us, I mean. I want to be useful to you, and I don't want to be afraid of you, of what you are going to see, or say to me.' *Jeez, I wasn't planning to confront him. Oh no, what have I done?*

Martin sat up straighter. He was taking this seriously. 'Thank you for saying that. Nobody has ever confronted this with me before, I'm really grateful to you for saying it. It means we can actually talk about things, instead of me hiding them in case I scare you.'

'Yes, please, that's what I want.'

'That's more useful to me than anything. If I can talk to you about what I see, I could feel like someone understands me. I don't have someone like that in my life. I'm not trying to freak you out, honestly, I'm just talking about how I am.'

'Yes, exactly. I want you to feel like you can tell me anything, but I have to feel like we are on the same page first. We have been dancing around each other a little bit I think, not really sure of each other. So this is good to talk it out and get it straight.'

'So here's me.' She continued, 'I see things too. But not like you – not right in front of me like I see people. I see them in my mind. A little bit like on a cinema screen, only it's inside my head and I'm there, in it, and here too, at the same time. So I don't see an actual bear when Bear comes, but I get a sense that it's a bear, I see an image in my mind of a bear, and I can feel the bear, in my body.' Marissa felt Bear appear as she was speaking about him.

'Yes, there, he's there now, I can see him. He's so big and friendly, he's not going to hurt me. He's glad we're talking like this too.'

Marissa had a cold rush of blood through her entire body as Martin described her bear to her. He sounded almost the same as she had imagined: brown, big belly and huge paws.

'This is unsettling for me, but it's okay,' Marissa said. 'I guess I needed you to know this about me, so we can continue to work with each other.'

Martin smiled. 'So, do you know about the angel?'

'What angel?' Marissa really didn't expect to hear more. The tension in her body was electric.

'The angel that's here with you too,' said Martin

'What? No. I've met Archangel Michael, at least I think I have, I don't know any other angels.'

Martin smiled again. 'I've met Archangel Michael too, and this definitely isn't him. This angel is just as big as he is though, he's standing a little bit further away from you, towards the back of the room. He's very strong. I'm not sure what his name is, I think I've seen him before. I'm not as good with hearing as I am with seeing but I can lipread a little bit, or they can show me a sign or a symbol so I understand it better. Meta something. That's what I'm getting anyway. We could ask him if you want?'

Marissa wanted to calm the excitement that rushed inside her body. *Another angel in the room? Another being wanting to work with me, to teach me, protect me, be with me?* This was super exciting, but she was the therapist and she felt that she was running away with herself. She wanted Martin to tell her more, but that was turning the session into something else entirely. Something about her and not about him. She caught her breath and used all of her will to focus on Martin.

'Thank you so much, Martin, you're very kind to tell me that, but I don't want us to run away from the reason why you're here – it's about you. I'm here to help you, not the other way round. Although it is fun and exciting to hear you confirming what I've been feeling and cannot see, I don't want you to think that I want this from you. Or I'm using you for this. Does this make any sense at all?'

'Of course it does. Marissa, it's going to be okay. I've not felt this free in a long time. Imagine what it's like not being able to talk about what I really see or how I really feel? Everyone that I've tried to do it with before has been so scared, they shut down. I'm not a child, I'm not stupid, I'm thirty-four years old. And sometimes I can't tell the difference between what I see and what others can see, it really depends on how well I am, whether I've taken my medicine or not. I get confused. And then I trip over myself. That's why my mother is scared of me too sometimes, she doesn't trust me at all. She doesn't know if I'm going to be talking to Grandpa in the living room when Grandpa has been dead for fifteen years, it's her father, she gets very scared when I do that. I forget he's dead sometimes, and I talk to her too, like she knows he's there and is joining in the conversation.'

Martin sighed. 'Her answer to everything is medicine, go see the doctor, go get some more medicine. And I don't like that. She treats me like I'm a baby. So I don't talk to her about things much anymore. So this, with you, is amazing. Really amazing, to be able to talk about this without being judged. I know you're not judging me, you feel the bear that I see, so there is something to this. I'm just as excited as you are.'

They smiled at each other.

Martin went on. 'And right now, I see this big and powerful angelic being at the back of the room and he wants me to tell you he's here. And your bear, he's behind you, and the old medicine woman over here,' he pointed to Marissa's right, 'she's smiling and she's wearing lots of necklaces, and the Indian woman, over there,' he pointed to Marissa's left, 'she's with you too. She's been here the whole time. She seems very nice, very patient. I can see that you haven't met her yet, the colours, the connections are not the same between you both as they are for you and the others. The room is full, Marissa, full of these beings that are with you, and you have no idea that they are there. Well, *you* have some idea, but imagine a room full of people who have no clue about this stuff, and they still bring all of their guides and angels and family members who have died with them... It can be tremendously overwhelming for me. You want to know how I am, well, I'm much happier being able to talk about all of this.'

Marissa couldn't fathom what that would be like for Martin. She hadn't gotten past the mention of the Indian woman... *Who was she? Native American Indian? Was it the woman from my dream?* She got a shiver again, a full-body 'Yes' coming through and rocking her to her core. She tried to shove the excitement back but she couldn't help it, she was beginning to be overwhelmed too. *Breathe. In and out. Breathing now, feeling feet on the ground.*

'Look, Marissa, I'm happy to talk about these things, honestly. Maybe I even need to. And just being here with you is helping me, for now.'

Marissa was relieved that Martin seemed much more relaxed with her, and once the session was over, he went to hug her, and she let him. It felt like they had reached a new sort of understanding. He genuinely seemed delighted he could tell her anything.

She stayed back in the room long after he left, sitting in her chair, head spinning, not really sure how she was feeling. By the time he left, he had told her about the Bear, the Angel, her Medicine Woman, the Native American Indian Woman (He had clarified that she was indeed a Native American Indian) and some fairies, a few elves and some sort of tree spirit. He said that the fairies and elves weren't for Marissa, that they lived in the Priory. He had seen them before, they wander about the rooms listening in. He thought that maybe the tree spirit was once a tree growing there and they cut it down and built the building where it used to be, but Marissa thought the tree could be her tree from her journeys, however, she didn't mention that to him. They didn't get a name for the new angel, just Meta something. She thought she'd look it up in her angel book once she got home.

She felt like she needed to do something before she left, to close down the space, like Séamus closed down the space at the workshop. *Yes, that's a good idea, I didn't open the space, though, but I feel like I need to close something down that opened.* Marissa opened her notebook app on her phone, she had copied and pasted the prayer in there. She read it out while staying in the chair as she didn't have the wherewithal to get up and stand to face each direction.

Great Spirit of the North – we thank you for offering us your strength, your power. We honour you, we honour those that came before us and those that will come after us. We release you now, with great gratitude. Ho!

Great Spirit of the East – we thank you for lending us your wings, for showing us the way. We are humbled in your presence, we see how far we have come, but we acknowledge we have much further to travel. We release you now with great gratitude. Ho!

Great Spirit of the South – we thank you for helping us shed our skins and transform into the beings that we are becoming. We endeavour to continue with the process of healing and growth. We release you now with great gratitude. Ho!

Great Spirit of the West – we are humbled to have been in your presence, reminding us to have great appreciation for each moment of every day of our lives. We see life everlasting in everything around us. We release you now with great gratitude. Ho!

She stood up and held her hands out wide as she spoke the last verse.

Oh magical Mother, oh mystical Father, thank you for holding us as we do our healing work. We peel the illusion from our eyes and see the world as it really is, to know and experience the interconnectedness of all things. With majesty and grace we offer ourselves in service, to follow the beauty way, the path of light. And to walk gently upon you and leave no footprints, only light. And so it is.

As she said the final 'And so it is', she felt much better. She also felt a 'yes, it's okay to go now.' She locked up behind her as she was last to leave the building.

Walking to the bus in the dark of night, she imagined a tall angel behind her, the bear beside her and the women to the left and the right of her. *Poor Tobermory will get a fright when I bring everyone back home with me.* She laughed. *He is probably used to them all already anyway. Poor Tobermory, indeed!*

CHAPTER TWENTY NINE

Only Olive knew that she was going to the Reiki Level 1 workshop. Marissa didn't know why, but she wasn't keen to share what she was doing with anybody else. *I don't feel guilty about it, I just don't want to explain myself right now... I guess it's okay to be like this.* She packed a day bag to bring with her: a bottle of water, a jumper and a notebook and pen. 'Wear comfortable clothing' was the only instruction, along with directions to the hotel. The workshop didn't start until 10.30am which was a much more civilised time than for Séamus's weekends, but she wasn't familiar with Greystones, not really, so she left plenty of time to find the hotel.

Marissa felt the cold as she walked to the bus stop. She was glad she had her alpaca hat with her, she put it on over her brown curls, hoping they wouldn't get too flattened. Her scarf still brought her pleasure when she wrapped it around her neck, but the smells of Peru had faded, even though the memories of them had not. The bus came quickly and she wasn't waiting long for the DART, which took her out to Greystones. She looked out the train window, waiting to see the sea as the train went further south. As soon as it came into view, Marissa smiled and her heart opened. Finding the hotel from the DART station was straightforward. She went inside and straight up to reception.

'I'm here for the Reiki workshop with Dolores Carmody. Can you tell me which room it's in?' Marissa smiled at the receptionist. She smiled back and referred to the day's schedule.

'Yes, it's in the Bowman suite, downstairs in the back room. Just follow the signs.'

'Thanks so much!' She walked through the hotel, past the main stairs and behind that, there was another stairway leading down, with a sign saying 'Bowman Suite'. Marissa followed the sign, went past toilets and along a long glass corridor that opened up at the end into a beautiful glass room, with another sign which told her she was in the right place. It looked like an extension of the main building, built relatively recently. It was bright and spacious, with fresh paint and much brighter curtains than the ones she saw in the reception area. The door to the suite was open so she went in. There was a beautiful view of the hotel gardens; a light mist was rising from the grass, the bulbs underneath still dormant, waiting for the days to warm up and lengthen a little more before bursting into bloom.

Dolores stood with a table behind her at the main door. She smiled when she saw Marissa come in and held out her hands to greet her. Dolores wore sky blue trousers, a pink blouse and a soft green, Aran knit cardigan. A turquoise scarf was draped around her neck and she had a massive quartz crystal on a gold chain hanging around her neck. Her hair was loose and she smelled of lemons. Marissa took her hands and smiled in return.

'I'm happy to see you again Marissa! Welcome welcome. Do come in! Take a seat! We will begin once the others are here. Have a workbook, you can leaf through it if you want, but we will be covering most of it during the workshop.'

Marissa entered the room, which also smelt of lemons. There were eight chairs laid out in a circle, five people were already sitting there, two men and three women. Marissa took one of the empty chairs, hung her coat on the back of it and sat down.

The table where Dolores was standing had books, leaflets, crystals, glasses and bottles of water. There was also a bouquet of flowers, and a candle. There were four massage tables towards the back of the room, they all had pillows and blankets laid out upon them. The room was pleasantly warm, which was surprising considering all the glass. *It must be triple glazed, very fancy! Mum would be impressed!* Marissa settled in her seat and smiled in acknowledgement of the other people. They smiled back at her, then she looked down at her feet, still a little too early for introductions, and Marissa didn't feel like initiating anything. *Many new people are coming into my life right now, I'm not sure if I want to get to know any of them. Jeez, Marissa, relax. I'm sure they're all very nice.* A few minutes passed and two more people arrived. Soon all the seats were filled. Dolores came and stood at the top of the room.

'Hello everyone, welcome to my Reiki 1 workshop. I'm so happy to have you all here.'

There was a knock on the door, three more people were outside.

'Oh my goodness, you made it! It's great to see you! Come in, come in.'

There were some spare chairs up against the wall, space was made and more chairs were obtained, and the circle enlarged to accommodate the newcomers.

'Well! I really didn't expect such a large crowd, this is wonderful. It's really good to see you all here.'

Marissa counted the people, there were ten, plus her made eleven. And Dolores herself, making twelve. Everyone seemed older than her shamanic friends – there was only one other person there that was around Marissa's age, or so she thought. And again, they were mostly women, there were four men in the group, one of them reminded her of Ronan from college, he had wild hair, a fuzzy beard and a soft gentle energy about him. She felt safe, they seemed like nice people.

Dolores walked around the group rubbing her hands together as if they were cold. She arrived at the top of the circle and stood behind her chair for a moment, taking things in. Marissa was watching her, wondering what was to come. *What would Martin see in this room?* She looked around, wondering how many beings were actually in there, beings that they couldn't see, that the people in the room had brought with them. Then she remembered about the fairies, elves, and tree spirits. *This room is built in a garden, there must be fairies and other nature spirits in here too... Yet it feels so peaceful and quiet, considering there is so much life in here!*

Dolores sat down, she looked ready to start. 'Let us begin. We are here today to learn about Reiki. By the time we finish tomorrow evening you will all be able to work with Reiki Healing Energy with yourselves, and with your family and friends. And your pets too!' Dolores smiled and her eyes sparkled as she looked across the circle and nodded to one of the women in in the group who sat up straighter, nodded back and smiled.

'Let me be clear. It doesn't matter what religion you are or if you believe in God or not. You can work with Reiki either way. I personally believe in God, and I like to open my workshops with a prayer. Does this bother anyone?'

There were shrugs and shaking of heads, nobody seemed to be upset by this. 'Wonderful. And so I begin.

May the light of God surround us.
May the love of God enfold us.
May the Power of God protect us.
The Presence of God watches over us.
The life of God flows through us.
The joy of God uplifts us.
The beauty of God inspires us.
Wherever we are, God is.
All is well, and so it is.'

'And so it is.' the room echoed back.

Marissa sat there and took it all in, she felt calm and relaxed, she liked the prayer, she didn't think there was anything in it that would upset anyone. *Why did Dolores have to ask first?*

'Now. Does anyone know what Reiki is?' Dolores looked around the room. 'Come on, don't be shy!'

A few hands went up. Dolores nodded towards one woman who was possibly in her sixties. 'It's healing energy,' she offered.

'Yes, Reiki is healing energy, but it's much more than that. Anyone else?'

One of the men's hands went up. 'It's a religion?'

'No, it's not a religion, but it can be a way of life. Reiki has a set of principles for living, just like some religions do, but it doesn't ask you to worship. There is no church to go to, and you are beholden to yourself, not to a priest. Anyone else?'

Another woman put up her hand and seemed sheepish when she asked, 'Is it a massage?'

Dolores laughed. 'You're right to ask me this!' Dolores looked at the group. 'There's no such thing as a silly question, if you feel called to ask a question it might be because someone else needs the answer and may not be brave enough to ask – so ask away! To answer *your* question, I have seen 'Reiki Massages' offered yes, but Reiki isn't a massage. This is a misconception. Sometimes people combine Reiki with massage, however, they are two separate modalities. Does anyone know what a modality is?'

Marissa put up her hand before she could stop herself. 'A modality is a way of working, a framework with its own structure, rules, boundaries.'

'Exactly,' said Dolores. 'Reiki is a modality of healing, with principles for living that you can apply to yourself, or not.' Dolores looked around at everyone and smiled. 'Reiki can change your life, if you let it. Or it can just be something that you do, for healing, for yourself or for others. But it starts with you, you must heal yourself first. That's the hard part.' She winked at the group, and someone else put their hand up.

'How long does it take to become a Reiki Master?'

Dolores answered, 'These are wonderful questions. Thank you. Just as you can take the Reiki principles into your own life as a way of living, you can look at Reiki Master as a certification or an actual way of being. In this world, currently, we live in a consumer culture. Having things and what you do, is more important than who you are. So you can take the three Reiki workshops, one after another, and obtain a certification of Reiki Master in only a few weeks. If that's what you want to do. But it doesn't mean that you hold the energy of a Master of Reiki. That is, in essence, something that can take years. But the whole idea of Reiki Master is a misconception. The Reiki is the master, and we are always of service to it. The true Reiki Master knows this. Being a Reiki Master on paper is another thing altogether.'

'You have a choice. You can proceed with Reiki in your own time, as fast or as slowly as you wish, depending on which path you want to take. It's refreshing to discuss this up-front so early in your training. You will find that I don't hold back when it comes to my opinion. Your choice is personal, you can go on the journey of Reiki, or you can pick up the qualifications you need to say that you're a Reiki Master. It's up to you.'

Dolores let this sink in before she continued. 'Level 1 is for you and for family and friends. If you want to become qualified as a Reiki practitioner, a therapist that offers Reiki treatments, you need to progress to Level 2. You don't need to be a Reiki Master to see paying clients. You will be able to use Reiki with people after this weekend, but not charge for it.'

Someone raised their hand. 'My mother is sick, do I have to wait until Level 2 to be able to give her a Reiki treatment?'

'No,' said Dolores, 'you can give Reiki to your mother after this weekend, most certainly. You won't be charging her, I assume?' There was laughter.

'It's when you want to be a professional healer, that's when you need Level 2. There is also a third workshop that you really should take before you're really ready to see paying clients, it's called 'Reiki Practitioner Level'. It's an Irish Reiki Federation workshop. If you were in America you wouldn't need that, there are alternatives that you may need instead, depending on the rules and regulations of the country that you are in. It's important for you to know what these are, depending on where you are practising, for insurance reasons.'

'Thank you.'

Dolores looked around the group to see if there were any further questions, all eyes were on her. 'I'm sure you're all excited to get started, so let's take more questions later. I'm sure you will have lots of them. We will start with the Reiki attunement. This is where I 'tune' you all in to the energy of Reiki 1.'

'Reiki 1 has its own level of vibration, it's like shining a torch into the night sky. Level 1 is for emotional healing, so some of you may become emotional as you work. It also affects your physical body, so you may use it to ease aches and pains, to help your body come into healthy balance, and to boost your immune system. Reiki 2 amplifies the reiki light within, it's like you upgrade to a stronger torch which also connects you to the ground so you won't fall over, so you can carry the strength of the light. It works on the mental body, helping your mind come into alignment with the work you have done on your emotional body. You also learn how to practice distance Reiki healing, where you work with people who are not in the room with you. Reiki 2 energies affect the body in a different way to Reiki 1, this is why I recommend taking time in between workshops. You need time to come into alignment with each level so that you can embody it.'

One of the women put up her hands 'What about Reiki 3?'

'Yes, I was coming to that,' Dolores said with a smile. 'Reiki 3 energy turns your level 2 torch into a laser beam so you can focus more energy in a much more powerful way. Reiki 3 *is* the Master level. It is very silly to expect you to integrate and embody all of those changes in three weekend workshops. That's why I want you to consider taking Reiki very seriously, and taking it slowly. Some people are happy to stay at Reiki level 1, it's strong enough to bring powerful changes into your life, without having to go any further.'

Dolores got up and walked around the group as she spoke. 'The attunement I will do for you now will take about thirty to forty minutes. We cannot be interrupted, please make sure your phones are off, and if anyone needs to go to the bathroom, now is the time. You will be sitting in your chair during this ceremony. It is a ceremony, it's a beautiful experience. I will come around to each of you in turn and place Reiki symbols into your aura. That's the space around you where your life force energy flows. The Reiki symbols will 'attune' you to Reiki, tune you in, so to speak, so that you can receive it.'

The door to the Bowman suite opened and a male hotel staff member came in. 'Do you need anything, Mrs Carmody?'

'No, thank you, we are fine here.'

'Great. I'll drop up the coffee and tea in about an hour or so.'

'Perfect, thanks.' He left the room.

'Looks like we have an hour, please rearrange your chairs, turn off your phones, go to the bathroom if you need to. We will start the attunements in five minutes.'

Marissa didn't need to go to the bathroom, but she felt like stretching and moving about a bit. She wandered to the end of the room where the massage tables were and went past them to the large windows at the back. She looked out into the hotel gardens, there was a light frost on the grass which was melting as the sun was coming through the clouds. The rose bushes had been cut back, the hedges were perfectly manicured. It was late in the morning for the frost to still be there, but it had been particularly cold that night. It looked beautiful, magical even. She turned to the room and observed the bustle of the people as they readied themselves for what was to come. There were murmurs and excitement, you could almost taste it. Everyone was looking forward to being able to use Reiki and it felt good to be in a room with strangers who were all happy and helpful.

Dolores picked up a Tibetan chime and hit it off of itself. It made a beautiful 'ding' sound which reverberated throughout the room. Everyone settled themselves in their seats. Dolores walked around the group circle again, moving bags out of the way as she needed to be able to stand in front of, and behind, everyone easily for the attunements. She went back to the table with the water and switched on some music. There were a few coughs and some shuffling. 'I will begin now. Please sit in silent meditation as I work, we must respect everyone's process.'

The music was warm, rich, and not unpleasant. Marissa was relieved, especially after the fiasco with Cheryl. She sat and focused on her breath, feeling her feet on the ground. She could sense Dolores working her way around the group. She watched her out of the corner of her eye, she seemed to be writing things in the air, blowing something into someone's forehead, *Just like the gift from the journey!* Dolores went behind each person and did something to the back of the neck, Marissa wasn't sure, then she was whispering to them and placing their hands in different places. She decided to focus on her breath again, she trusted Dolores and she didn't need to know all the answers for now. She'd find out when Dolores came to her.

When Dolores eventually came to Marissa she smiled, and Marissa smiled back. Dolores asked for her hands, she drew something in the air over her heart and her forehead. Marissa felt feint, like a trapdoor opened up in the floor and she was falling down through it, but she knew her body wasn't falling, it was the weirdest thing. She felt cold, then hot, then she started to sweat. She found herself becoming anxious and just at the moment when it became too strong to bear, Dolores went behind her and placed her hands on her shoulders. That gave her an instantaneous calming effect. Dolores stood there for a while chanting something, a prayer perhaps? As she did, Marissa felt like herself again, she felt her stability returning to her. Then Dolores came back to face Marissa and smiled, bringing her hands into prayer position. Marissa did it too, just as she had seen the others doing before her.

Dolores took one of Marissa's hands and placed it on Marissa's upper chest, and placed the other hand beside it. She knelt closer to

Marissa's ear and said, 'You're now connected to the light of Reiki. Allow the energy to flow down from the top of your head, into your throat and heart, then up and over your shoulders, down your arms and out through your hands. Feel the energy coming through your body as you breathe, and allow the energy to enter your body through your hands. Place your hands wherever you feel aches and pains on your body, just don't cross your arms. You can ask me more questions later.' Dolores moved on to the person beside Marissa.

Marissa kept her hands glued to her body in the position that Dolores had put them in. What happened? Well, yeah, besides being attuned to Level 1 Reiki. But the falling sensation? The sweating? The heat? I didn't expect any of that. It was strange. I feel okay now though. Her hands were a little uncomfortable in those positions so she shifted them slightly until she felt more comfortable. She was able to see the garden from where she was sitting, she thought she'd focus on that for a while and try to let her thoughts go. They were becoming too demanding.

Marissa became aware of the music again, it was as if she had disappeared for the time that Dolores was with her. She became more aware of the people around her and the room she was in. *Yes, that's better now.* She relaxed. Her breathing eased back to normal. Then she felt a lightness, a light rushing sensation through her body. *Is that coming from my hands? No, wait, my breath? No, I can't tell.* She felt lifted, lighter. A little lightheaded. The door to the suite suddenly opened and there was a banging and bashing noise as the hotel staff brought a trolley in with tea, coffee and biscuits. Marissa turned to see if Dolores had finished, and she had. She was sitting in circle with the others, her own hands on her own body and eyes closed, just like the rest of them. *Had it been an hour already?* The hotel staff left the room. Dolores waited for another few minutes, then she got up and switched off the music. The room seemed suddenly empty without it.

'Welcome back,' Dolores said. 'Take your time, stretch, walk about, have some tea. We can talk about your experiences as a group afterwards. For now, you can talk amongst yourselves, have a cuppa and bring yourself back into the present moment.'

Marissa dipped into her handbag and fished out her phone to check the time. It had been an hour and a half since they started. It felt like only five minutes, ten at most. Tea sounded like a great idea. She got up and stretched and went to join the queue for tea. Everyone was chattering and excited about their experiences. Marissa wasn't able to talk just yet, she helped herself to a cuppa and two bourbon creams and sat back down in her chair. The woman beside her turned to her and spoke. 'Wasn't that amazing?! I saw flashing lights, all different colours, and I felt like I was being lifted out of my body, I was up above us all looking down. And now I feel so happy! What about you? What was it like for you?'

'I'm not sure yet, I'm still trying to process it. I'm glad it was so good for you. I'm Marissa, by the way.'

'Juliet. Nice to meet you!' Juliet was about fifty years old, wearing jeans and a red cable knit jumper. 'How did you meet Dolores?'

Marissa hesitated before answering. 'I, eh, I went to her for a Reiki session, and I liked her. She suggested I come this weekend. You?'

'Yes, same! I've been a client of hers for a long time. I went because I was so stressed with work, she was able to help me relax. I slept great after the Reiki, so I thought I should learn how to do it myself.'

Dolores came back and sat down, motioning for everyone else to do the same. People made their way back to the circle, some bringing unfinished cups of tea with them as they took their places.

They sat in silence for a moment. 'So how was that for you?' asked Dolores.

'It was powerful.'

'Amazing.'

'I saw lots of colours.'

'I felt like I was flying.'

Everyone had something different. Marissa seemed to be the only one that felt like she was going down through the floor. Nobody was wrong, nobody held anything over anyone else, they were all just sharing their experiences openly. Marissa was struck by the number of different ways that everyone had experienced the attunement. *If someone outside of this group was watching us, it wouldn't have seemed like Dolores was doing anything at all, yet it had such a profound effect on all of us.*

'Welcome to the world of Reiki! You've all now been attuned. I want to make sure that you are confident in tuning in to Reiki before we break for lunch.'

Dolores then showed the group how to connect to the Reiki energy, how to flow it through their bodies and how to give themselves a Reiki treatment, or a self-treatment, as she called it. They got to practice doing it for about 10 minutes and then they broke for lunch.

Marissa was glad of the downtime and went for a walk to clear her head. She got a sandwich and a can from a newsagent and sat on a bench on the seafront, which was only about 10 minutes away from the hotel. She liked Greystones, the beach wasn't too busy, there were some people walking dogs and a few children running around chasing the waves. *I'm now attuned to Reiki. What does it actually mean? Will this change me? I didn't think of that... What should I expect now?* She finished her sandwich and put the wrapping in the litter bin. *I like Dolores, it feels good with her. I'm glad I found her. It's another adventure for me.* She bent down and picked up a stone and studied it, remembering the last time she was there, throwing stones, on the verge of a panic attack. *Oh! I need a black stone for Séamus, don't I! I could get one from here.* She walked up and down the beach, looking for a black stone. She found one she liked, put it in her pocket, said 'Thank you,' to the beach, and then made her way to the hotel.

When she got back to the Bowen Suite, Dolores was showing someone from the group how to use a bottle of Saint Germain. The rest of the people were watching, most of them were back in their seats. Marissa took off her coat and joined them once more. Dolores turned to them all. 'While we're waiting for the others, see if you remember how to connect, and then you can try the self-healing practice again.'

Someone put up their hand. 'How do you decide where to put your hands?'

'We will talk about that in a moment when everyone's back. Don't worry. For now, just put your hands where you feel guided. Some people say their hands move by themselves as if they know where to go. See if you can do that without thinking too much about it.'

Marissa set her intention to connect to Reiki energy, then waited to feel it trickle into the top of her head. She wasn't sure if it did or not, but she kept going with the protocol. *Let it trickle down, then flow into my body, into my heart, up and over my shoulders, down my arms, and out through my hands.* Her hands started tingling, but she didn't feel it flowing down her shoulders and arms. She looked at her hands for a moment, flexing her fingers, as if looking at them would make things clearer, but she was none the wiser. Marissa placed her hands on her lap, palms down, then looked around to see what other people were doing. One woman had her hands on her head. *Why didn't I think of that?* Someone else had their hands on their heart. Marissa moved both hands to the top of her head and sat like that until Dolores started the next part of the workshop.

'And we are back! Well done everyone, you're all doing great. I want to take a few moments to talk to you about healing.'

Marissa sat back in her chair and focused on Dolores's voice.

'Healing is not straightforward. We do not control it, nor do we control Reiki energy. The principle behind healing is this – it's a remembering of who you are, and a letting go of who and what you are not. Letting go can hurt. Some of you,' she looked around the room at the group, 'have been holding onto your pain for as long as you can remember. Pain can define who you are. If this is the case, then when you let go of pain, you may not recognise yourself. It's important for you to realise this, as some will be fighting the healing process. This is normal and natural. If our state of discomfort is familiar to us, a state of vibrant health is not as familiar. We prefer the familiar, even if it is not healthy, and we are naturally afraid of what we do not know or understand.'

There were nods and murmurs of agreement in the room.

Dolores continued, 'Many of you have come to see me for Reiki sessions because of stress. When you're stressed, your body contracts, recoils, tightens up. When you heal, you relax, your body opens up, and the stress leaves. So you're letting go of stress, you're letting go of pain, too. What people don't actually realise is when the body opens up, it releases pain. This creates what is called a 'healing crisis', where people get sick, experience pain as it passes through them to be let go of. It's a purification process, and it can hurt. Nobody tells you that, and if you fight it, you make it worse. So, after today's attunement, some of you might be experiencing a healing crisis. Go gently with yourselves, drink lots of water, visualise the pain, whatever form it appears in, moving through you and being released from you.'

Shit, just what I needed, I hope I don't get sick from this.

'Is it like a detox?' asked one of the participants.

'Yes, very similar. With detox symptoms, too, at times. But the good news is,' Dolores continued, 'that you now are attuned to Reiki. So by doing your self-practice, it can ease the symptoms of this detoxification process. As long as you keep control of your mind, of your thoughts, and don't try to analyse what you are feeling, just allow it to come up and through you. Say goodbye to it and let it leave your system, leave your body, so you can be healthier in body and spirit. The mind will follow – yes, now perhaps you can see why Reiki level 2 is for the mind.'

There was one session left before the day was complete. The group had tried further self-practice, some of the people there were getting impatient to place their hands on someone else and do healing on them, but Dolores wasn't having any of it. 'We will learn that tomorrow, today is for you.'

In between two practice sessions, Dolores gave them a brief history of Reiki. She told them the story of Mr Usui, who created the practice, and Mrs Takata, who brought Reiki to America. 'There are many versions of the story, which ones are true, we don't know. Many people fight to have their version as the correct one, but it doesn't really matter. All we need to know is that Reiki is a beautiful system for healing, and just as we don't need to examine the pain as it leaves through us, we don't need to know the intricacies of the history of Reiki in order for it to be effective.'

They ended the day with the Reiki Principles. 'Some people start their workshops with these principles,' said Dolores, 'But I like to leave them until later in the day, as most people I work with are excited to practice Reiki almost straight away. And the attunement, once it settles, is more like a remembering. We were all able to heal ourselves, and thanks to Mr Usui, we have a system now. Know that healing can come naturally to many people. You might think of someone that you know who has never done healing or trained with a Master but is a natural healer. They just feel good to be around, their energy is good and you always feel better after you leave them. Reiki is a formal, structured way to enhance your energy. Children up to the age of seven are naturally tuned into Reiki energies. No, I don't know why seven, I think it's something to do with the psychology of self-actualisation.'

Marissa was interested to hear a psychological term being used in a Reiki workshop. *These things are interlinked, after all, I wonder why they seem so separate from each other in the trainings...*

'Back to the principles. As I've said earlier, they are not necessary for Reiki, but they are the keys to a spiritual life, which is greatly encouraged. They can unlock a deep peace in you and open up the Reiki channels within you for more powerful healing. Reiki is everywhere, it is pure life force energy, and the purer you are in thought, mind and deed, the larger your capacity for channelling Reiki.'

Someone put up their hand. 'What is a channel?'

'You are, dear.' Dolores said with a smile. 'You are all the channels, and Reiki moves through you and out from you and into the world. The clearer your channel, the purer the quality of Reiki that comes through. That's what makes you a powerful healer, not the certification but the purity of the channel. Now. The principles.'

Some people had been writing down notes all day but this was the first time that Marissa felt the need to get her pen and open her notebook. She wrote 'Reiki 1 workshop' at the top of the page and underlined it.

'Principle 1 – Just for today, I shall not worry.
Principle 2 – Just for today, I will not be angry.
Principle 3 – Earn your living honestly.
Principle 4 – Honour your elders.
Principle 5 – Be grateful to every living thing.'

'So, as you can see, these are ways to live, principles or tenets of being, rather than magical healing instructions. And they are a choice. Mr Usui wanted all Reiki practitioners to choose them as a code of honour, but in reality, it must be up to you. If there are no further questions, I will give you some homework, we will do one more self-healing practice, and we will close the workshop for today.'

Marissa found it easier to connect to the Reiki energies during that last practice of the day. *Maybe I'm already connected, but I'm able to feel them moving through me more clearly now.* She placed her hands on herself on the train back into town. She did Reiki on the bus while going home, and after she let herself in and switched on the heating, she sat on the sofa and continued to practice Reiki. Tobermory jumped onto her lap and started purring. He rubbed his head against her stomach, rolled onto his back and stretched his paws out into the air.

'Hello to you too,' said Marissa, laughing. His purring seemed especially loud. 'You seem very happy to see me, you must be hungry?' Tobermory seemed to take offence at this and jumped off her onto the floor, but he was soon back again, rubbing himself up against her legs and purring loudly once more.

'Well, looks like Reiki will be good for you, too,' said Marissa, realising she was still wearing her coat. She got up and hung it up, fed Tobermory, and put some dinner on for herself. Her homework from Dolores was to practice Reiki for a twenty minute session. She was already looking forward to day two. She put the immersion on for a bath and settled in for the night with her cat, a movie, and a Reiki self-practice session.

CHAPTER THIRTY

The room was dark. Marissa found a lamp and lit it, it took a few moments for her eyes to get used to the glow. She realised she wasn't in a room at all, it was a cave. She walked around to explore. Many books were piled up on shelves that had been cut into the rock. Some of the books were strewn on a table, she went over and leafed through them, there were strange symbols on the pages. She browsed through the books, turning the pages, not really recognising anything. One of the symbols she had seen before, she wasn't sure where. It had spirals and opened outwards, it looked a little bit like music. A particular book seemed to be calling to her, pulling her in, she approached it without thinking. It was a large, heavy, dusty book, as she looked at it, it opened to a page which had a symbol that frightened her. That was unexpected, Marissa's heart jumped at the sight of it, the symbol seemed ominous and threatening but she didn't know why. There was a triangle in the centre, or was it two triangles? And a curve on either side. It beckoned her in closer, into its centre, she was pulled closer towards it. It seemed as though the triangles were moving, the longer she looked at it, the more she felt the symbol come alive, starting to spin. Marissa looked down at her body, there was a light issuing from her heart which moved outwards and into the centre of the symbol on the page – was she feeding it? She felt weak. Now she felt heat coming from the symbol, growing faster and stronger, it became a burning heat, the page started smoking and the symbol was brighter now, red hot and spinning faster. Marissa's heart was beating quickly, she felt weak, was her energy being consumed by this... thing? She started to panic but she couldn't move. The symbol shifted and lifted itself up off of the page and hung suspended in the air, growing larger and larger, hanging there as if it was gathering itself, as if it was about to devour her whole. The book it came out of was on fire.

Marissa woke in a sweat. It took her a moment to realise where she was, the dream had felt so real. She felt a weight pressing down on her chest. The image of the symbol was burned into her memory, she went into the front room, got a pencil and drew it on a blank page in her notebook. Looking at it gave her a full-body shiver, so she changed her mind, scribbled on it, tore the page out, scrunched it up and put it in the bin. She got up and washed her face, hard, as if to try to wash the memory of the image out from behind her eyes. She looked at herself in the mirror to check that she was still herself. It was 3am. She clapped her hands really loudly to clear the energy in the room, she did it without thinking, it was almost automatic. She rummaged through her handbag and found the Saint Germaine, used it to cleanse her energy field, then got back into bed and reconnected to the Reiki light. She wasn't happy, she got up again, went to the bin, tore the paper into shreds and put half into the bottom of the bathroom bin and the other half deep in the kitchen bin. She found her quartz crystal and her drum and brought them to bed with her. She was so tired she fell asleep almost straight away and woke up two hours before her alarm went off, refreshed.

She didn't remember the dream. She wondered why her drum was there bedside her. She got out of bed and shook her covers, the crystal landed in the thick rug by the bed with a thump. *I had my crystal in the bed? This is very odd. I feel a little strange, heavy in my chest a little, but I have no recollection of anything... Oh yes! Reiki today. It's going to be great, I'm a little nervous, though. I remember Olive said anxiety and excitement can feel similar, maybe this is a little bit of both.*

She got up, tidied up her apartment, showered, dressed and ate. Her phone buzzed a text. *Who is texting me so early on a Sunday?* She looked, it was her Mother.

> Nu? When are you coming to visit? We are home today – come for lunch, bring bagels.

Marissa sighed. How could she tell her mother she was busy without telling her what she was doing – ahh yes, she remembered. CPD. Continuous Professional Development.

> Sorry can't today, I'm at a workshop for CPD, won't be finished till 6. Maybe next weekend?

CPD? OK. Call when you can talk. I miss you. Love you.

Love you 2 xx

Marissa got off the DART in Greystones. It was too early to go in so she decided she'd treat herself to a coffee in a nice café before class. She got a table and ordered an Americano and scrolled through her Facebook feed as she waited to be served. Someone had posted an article about empaths called 'Ten signs that you're sensitive to other people's energy.' *Dolores never mentioned any of that psychic stuff she talked about when I met her... She didn't even mention the Saint Germain or any protection, but she showed someone how to use it yesterday. I must ask her about that.* She pulled out her notebook and wrote it down so she'd remember. Writing the words 'Saint Germain' gave her a vague recollection of using the Saint Germaine during the night, but it wasn't clear. The coffee arrived and she dismissed it from her mind. It tasted delicious, she drank and enjoyed it, paid and strolled over to the hotel. There was still about 10 minutes before start time, and when she got into the room there were already a few people there.

Everyone seemed very relaxed. It felt nice, the room was bright, and the sun was shining in through the windows. Marissa found the same seat she was sitting in and left her coat and bag there, then went over to the table and helped herself to a bottle of hotel water. She couldn't help but be drawn into the conversation that was going on beside her.

'Well, I couldn't believe it! She kept phoning and phoning until I had to answer. She was so persistent. Then once I picked up the phone she was yelling, yelling, I tell you. About what? I have no idea! She hung up on me! It was so strange.'

'That is very strange, alright,' a second woman chimed in. 'Here's strange – my son phoned me last night, he hasn't called me in a month! He moved out about a year ago and is in college in London. I had given up trying to phone him, he never wants to talk. He actually picked up the phone and called me! I couldn't believe it. He was really happy to hear my voice, and he said so!'

'What are we talking about?' asked Marissa curiously.

'We all seem to be getting texts and messages from people that we haven't heard from in a long time, asking us how we are. It's so funny, but it's strange too.'

One of the men from the group came over to join the conversation, he was about sixty-five. He looked like a teddy bear that needed someone to mind him. 'My daughter, she drove over to my house last night, she's not done this in over six months. She checked I had the heating working, she did my washing up, and she wants to take me out to dinner tonight. It's lovely, but I never thought that it was anything to do with the Reiki – is this the type of thing you mean?'

Has the Reiki changed something for them already? I did get a text from Mum, but she does text me from time to time. It was strange though that she asked me over today, she normally gives more notice than that. Has the Reiki changed something for me, too?

Dolores came into the room like a breath of summer air on a winter's day. Everyone took their seats but continued to chat amongst themselves. Dolores smiled and sat down at the top of the circle. There was a moment of silence, then the woman who had someone yelling at her asked a question.

'Dolores? Does the Reiki attunement affect our relationships?'

Dolores looked as if she was expecting this question. She smiled and said, 'It can do, yes. You see, when you become attuned to Reiki energies, your personal energy changes. You have what some people call an 'energy signature' like a fingerprint. It's yours and yours alone, it vibrates and resonates with a certain frequency and vibration. The frequency and vibration can shift when you receive an attunement. It also shifts when you're happy or when you're sad, it can be a subtle or strong change, depending on what is going on for you at the time. And people who are connected to you can feel the shift. We are all connected. It's subconscious, they may not even be aware they can feel it, yet they can still react to it. So tell me, what's been going on since our attunement ceremony?'

Everyone who shared, shared again, with Dolores listening this time.

'Yes, this makes sense,' she said. 'Imagine that you are connected to everyone you know in a tangle of little cords, like the threads in a spider web. You see, we make connections to people we meet through energy cords, and the energy cords are thick or thin depending on how much energy is fed into that relationship. For example, the energy cord can be small if we only met the person once, and over time that cord can dissolve to very very tiny, if they're out of our mind, our line of sight, or our awareness. Like someone you met once at a party and talked to for a while, and then you never see again. You're still connected to them, however, but it doesn't have a strong impact on you. With people you care for deeply, it's different, the energy cord between you both grows stronger. The cords between family members, such as a mother and daughter,' she turned to the woman whose mother was yelling at her, 'or between lovers,' she turned to another member of the group, who blushed, 'these cords can become very dense, quite thick and strong. And there's nothing necessarily wrong with it, it's just the way it is. There's a flow of energy between each person, so if the energy of one person changes, it flows through the cord and the other person may feel it. It seems that you all noticed this already just from our Reiki attunement yesterday. Energy is amazing, it never fails to surprise me, even after working with it for all this time. Remember, just because you can't see it doesn't mean it isn't real.'

Suddenly a million questions flooded Marissa's mind. *Can Martin see energy cords? And James – are we still connected by energy cords? Did he feel a change in mine now, because of the Reiki? Will he contact me?* Her heart flipped, thinking about the possibility of a text or a phone call from James... *And Mum, yes, okay, she must have felt something going on with me that was different. Mum worries about me all the time, it makes sense now. And do we make energy cords to our spirit guides? It must be very complicated if we stay connected to everyone we meet, and they are connected to everyone they meet... What about the people we haven't met yet, are we connected to them before we even meet them?* Marissa felt the anxiety welling up as quickly as her questions, she hadn't felt that in a while. She had to stop thinking. She pressed her feet into the carpet in the room and slowed her breath. She had tuned out of Dolores's teachings while she was figuring this all out, she heard Dolores speaking nearby and slowly brought her attention and focus back to Dolores's voice. She was speaking to one of the women in the group.

'I'm sorry you didn't sleep well, it can also be an effect of the attunement – but it will settle down I'm sure, especially today after all the practice we are going to do. I had mentioned you could get detox-like symptoms, it's all perfectly normal. Anyone else feel sick last night? Or sleep really well? Or not sleep at all?'

Marissa was feeling a little calmer now. She didn't contribute, she didn't want to share. *That is a thing that I do, not wanting to share. I wonder if that's a pattern of mine. But I don't think I have to share if I don't want to.*

A couple of the other people from the group wanted to share their stories, which mirrored what had already been said. Then it was time to get to work. Dolores held their attention.

'Today, I'll show you how to give Reiki to another person. I'll teach you the hand positions, and I'll take all of your questions before we finish up this evening. But first I want to talk to you about permission. It's vital that you have someone's permission before you heal them. This means the person you work on must give permission before you place your hands on them. Giving permission for healing to take place is a fundamental part of that person's healing process. When they are aware of the healing, some part of them receives more of it than if they are not aware. Does this make sense?'

Everyone nodded.

'It's especially important to be clear about permission and boundaries by the time you get to Level 2 as you can be working with distance healing, which is not hands-on. It's unethical to heal someone when they are not aware of what you're doing. We'll talk more about that at Level 2 if you decide to join me later on this year or whenever you feel ready to.'

'So to be clear, placing hands on anyone's body obviously needs their permission first. However, you might find that you're with family, and you put your hands on them, if this is something you usually do, and you discover that Reiki naturally flows through you and into them. Holding hands with someone, giving someone a hug, that kind of thing. You can feel the Reiki coming through you and into them without even realising what's happening, especially if they need it, for example, if they're having a bad day and are feeling depleted. It's like physics, the energy will move through you to them, to replenish them. It's not a formal thing, but you do need to notice it if it happens so that you can be clear in your own boundaries and let them know, or switch it off, or simply just be with it. Whatever you feel is appropriate. You can always ask them if they'd like some Reiki.'

Someone put their hand up. 'If it happens naturally, why do I need to ask them?'

Dolores paused for a moment. 'You know, when it comes to your children, you don't need to ask them, you can simply give it freely. But when it comes to adults, for them to respect the Reiki energy, they need to be aware of what is happening so they can value you, your time, and you as the healing channel. We will talk more about value in Reiki level 2, as you're not charging for your time with Level 1. But you need to value yourself from day one, start as you mean to go on. People cannot take it for granted that they'll get Reiki from you whenever they feel they want some. It's important for you to get something in return, so that the Reiki is valued by you and by them. Even if they just make you a cup of tea.'

Dolores stood up and stretched. 'Now for practice. We have four plinths, and there are eleven of you, so that's three groups of three and a two. Don't worry about pairing up, we will have plenty of time to swap around. I need someone to demonstrate on. Amy, would you like to volunteer?' One of the quieter members of the group, in her fifties with short silver hair and glasses smiled and nodded enthusiastically and stood up from her chair.

'Thank you,' said Dolores, smiling. She made her way over to one of the plinths, and everyone got up and followed.

Dolores chose a plinth with plenty of space around it so the group could stand in a circle around her and it. 'Amy, please lie up on the bed here, with your shoes off.' Amy slipped off her shoes, climbed up onto the plinth and lay down on the bed, on top of the blanket.

'You never need to take your clothes off for Reiki. Some people say that it doesn't pass through rubber-soled shoes, but I have never experienced this myself. If you have a broken limb and are in a cast, the Reiki will travel through the cast and into your limb to encourage it to heal. You're not the director of the Reiki, remember that. The Reiki will go to where it is most needed. So you could place hands on someone's head, and the Reiki could be travelling through them and into their feet, because that's where they need it most. We need to let go of our attachment to knowing all the answers, or understanding the details.'

'You should always have a blanket at hand if your client gets cold. You must anticipate this as some people lose heat when they are receiving energy healing. Your client must always be comfortable, so make sure that their head is supported and never block their airways with your hands.' Dolores covered Amy with a blanket.

'And now to start the treatment.' Dolores stood at Amy's head and put her two hands together on the crown of Amy's head. 'This is position one. These positions must also be comfortable for you, as the practitioner, because you might need to stay in them for a while. This one is not so comfortable for me as my wrists are flexed,' She moved her hands so that they still covered the same spot but didn't have to flex her wrists. 'This way is better for me, and Amy gets the Reiki either way. You can get creative and see what positions work best for you.'

Dolores moved and placed her hands over Amy's face, not actually touching her, but just above. ' This is position two,' She placed her hands over the throat, not in a way to strangle, but more to cradle it. 'Here we have position three, a little tricky depending on the angle you are at, again, mind the throat, some people are not comfortable with someone else's hands here, so make sure your client is okay while working here.' Dolores continued to work her way down Amy's body, placing her two hands in various locations and configurations, giving the number of each position and a few variations for each one.

'Don't worry about remembering these exactly, in fact, you don't even need to remember the numbering system either. Unless, of course, you want to be a Reiki teacher!' Everyone laughed. 'If that's the case, I recommend you take the workshops a second time, so you can learn how to teach. Right now, you're the student. Know that Reiki is not strict, and you don't have to do any of the positions in a certain order. However, while you're learning here today I would like you to start at the top of the head, and work your way down the body to the feet, or if there are three of you, one can do that, and the other can start at the feet and work their way up. Place your hands lightly on your client, they don't want to feel your body weight, but they do feel reassured with your presence.'

Everyone was nodding, some of them were scribbling notes, even while standing up, which wasn't an easy thing to do.

'We said a prayer yesterday to open the healing space, do you remember? With a Reiki session it is good to open a space, do the healing work, then close the space around your client. It's good for you too, it's a ritual and will help you disconnect from them afterwards. Every teacher has a different way of teaching Reiki, so be clear, this is my way, and when you're more confident, you will find your own way.'

Dolores showed them how to open a healing space around the client, then she demonstrated once more how to connect to the Reiki energy, flowing it through her body, out from her hands. They all did this with her. Then Dolores placed her hands on the client (Amy), gave her a quick treatment, then closed the healing space. She became very serious.

'This is Reiki. You open, heal, then close. There are no chakras, no colours, no readings of the aura. There is no psychic connection, even though you may pick up information while working on a client, it is NOT part of Reiki. I must stress this. I've had clients come to me who were told damaging things after having Reiki with someone who had little or no duty of care. Something that you say to somebody who is having a Reiki session can make a very strong impression on them, you can plant ideas in their mind that are not true, you can upset them more than you know. You are not training as practitioners right now, remember this is Level 1 Reiki, but you must recognise this from the outset. You cannot, nor should you ever give advice, and if you have information that you feel your client needs to hear, ask yourself three times if they need to hear this. If the answer is still yes, then always preface it with a disclaimer.'

'What do you mean by a disclaimer?' piped up Marissa, who got a surprise at hearing her own voice for the first time that day.

'You can say something like "This information that I have for you isn't Reiki, it came through to me while I was working on you, I don't know if it's important, but I feel like I need to say it to you, I don't even know if I heard it correctly. You can do whatever you want with it – ignore it, take heed of it, it's totally up to you." Now with the disclaimer in place and being clear that it isn't Reiki, I know that many people have had some valuable messages delivered that way to them. But most people just say what they have heard, felt or sensed, without the duty of care. Please know that you must put your client's wellbeing ahead of your need to be right, to be clever or to heal. And above all else, know that you are not the one healing them. The Reiki comes through you, you are the channel for it, and the Reiki does the work. Not you. Okay?'

There seemed to be a group agreement. Marissa thought it was very refreshing to hear the boundaries set out so clearly. It meant they all knew what Reiki was and what it wasn't from the outset. Dolores continued.

'Now. I'd like you all to practise what I just showed you in groups of three, and a two. One person is the client, two people can work on the same person at the same time. Amy, you can be a practitioner now. Perhaps you'd all like to take off your shoes for this?'

Amy got up, and everyone found someone to work with. Marissa was in a group with the man that reminded her of Ronan, and the youngest woman. They went to one of the massage tables.

'Hi, I'm Marissa,' she said, introducing herself to the others.

'I'm Leonora,' said the woman. She had long sleek dark hair, was wearing a short skirt with black tights and a tunic top. She seemed quite nervous 'I'm actually Dolores's niece. It's my first time doing Reiki, so I hope it's okay!'

'Hi, I'm Matt,' said the man with a smile. Matt was rotund, looked to be in his late forties, he had a pleasant, smiling face and an open, friendly way about him. He had bushy fair hair with a tinge of red, a little bit of a beard on his face and wore a lumberjack shirt and jeans. Matt said, 'Who would like to be the client first?'

Marissa was volunteered by Leonora. Shrugging her shoulders, Marissa climbed up on the plinth and lay down, placing her head on the pillow. Leonora offered Marissa a blanket, which she took gratefully and placed over her legs. Matt closed his eyes and rubbed his hands together, he looked like he was started to connect to Reiki.

'We have to open the space,' Leonora whispered to Matt.

'Oh yes, I'd forgotten!'

Marissa closed her eyes and focused on how she was feeling. Her earlier anxiety had gone, she felt relaxed and comfortable. She liked the people here, she felt someone touch her hair very gently, she also felt someone holding her feet. She opened her eyes and saw Matt standing at the foot of the massage table, he was cradling her feet, one in each hand.

'Is this okay?' he asked her.

'Yes, thank you, it's actually quite nice,' Marissa said. She closed her eyes again.

She felt the hands on her body, she tried to tell the difference between Matt and Leonora. Matt seemed much more confident touching her than Leonora was. At one point, they met in the middle, and for some reason, it seemed that there were eight hands on her body at the same time. It was quite disorienting, her head, feet, and middle had hands holding her. She wanted to open her eyes but her eyelids were heavy and she couldn't. She wasn't asleep though, she felt quite floaty. She suddenly smelled lemons and heard whispering, she realised that Dolores had come over to their table.

'Yes, very good, now you need to seal that off, like this, and then you need to bring your client back to the room, back to the moment. Like this.'

Marissa felt different hands on her arms, squeezing them gently, and she felt her legs and feet being held. Dolores said, 'We're finished now, welcome back to the room'. Marissa rubbed her eyes and then opened them. She sat up and felt a little woozy. She was offered a glass of water, which she gratefully accepted. Leonora and Matt were anxious to know how she was.

'I'm good, yes it was good.' They both smiled. 'It seemed like I had eight hands on me at the same time, it was strange for a little bit, I could feel you, but I felt the energies moving too. It was very nice.'

Marissa got down from the table and stretched like a cat. It was her turn to be a practitioner. Leonora got up on the plinth and laid down. 'Can I get a blanket over my legs, please?'

'Sure,' said Marissa, spreading a brown fleece over Leonora's legs and feet. Leonora nodded her thanks and closed her eyes.

'Do you want to open the space?' whispered Matt.

'Can we do it together?'

'Yes, Okay.' They both opened space around Leonora on the plinth, just as Dolores had shown them earlier.

'Do you want to start at the head?' asked Matt, in a whisper again.

'You started at my feet, so you can start at the head this time if you want to?'

Matt smiled. 'Yes, that would be nice, thank you.'

Marissa connected to the Reiki light. It seemed to be getting easier each time she did it. She felt it flow through her body, into her heart, up and over her shoulders, and down her arms. She felt it coming through the palms of her hands, it was warm and tingly and very pleasant. She stood at Leonora's feet and placed one hand on each of them. She stood there, flowing the Reiki in, or at least she thought that was what she was doing. She wondered then was it time to change position. She looked at Matt who nodded his head, and they both shifted to the next logical place on Leonora's body. They worked this way until they met at the middle, Matt on one side of the plinth and Marissa on the other. Marissa placed her hands just over Leonora's stomach, and then Matt placed his hands about three inches above Marissa's hands. *Ahh, maybe that's why I thought there were so many hands on me!* They looked at each other and smiled, then they kept going. Marissa moved towards Leonora's head and Matt towards her feet. When they had finished, Matt nodded again at Marissa, and they both closed the space, just as Dolores had instructed. Then Marissa placed her hands gently on Leonora's arms and gave them a gentle squeeze. She whispered into her ear, 'Hi. We're done now. Welcome back to the room.'

Leonora had fallen asleep. Marissa thought it was funny. She held Leonora's feet firmly, just as Dolores had done for her. It seemed to help. Leonora came back and woke up, then Matt went to get some fresh water for her.

'Hi. How was that?' Marissa asked.

'It was amazing. So powerful. I felt so much energy. I feel really relaxed now. Thank you!'

Matt was back with the water, Leonora sat up and took a drink.

'I need to run to the toilet, can you wait a few minutes?' she asked both Marissa and Matt, who, of course, both said yes. Leonora stood, slipped her shoes back on and went out of the main room towards the bathroom.

'What do you think of Reiki then?' asked Matt with another smile.

'I like it so far,' said Marissa. 'My cat seems to like it too, he went a little crazy when I got home last night. It was funny.'

Matt laughed. 'I like it too. Are you planning to continue to Reiki Master Level?'

Marissa hadn't actually thought about that. 'I'm not sure, I think I'll enjoy it for what it is right now, and if I want more, I can come back and do more.'

'Fair enough. I want to be a Reiki Master, I'm training to be a Tai Chi teacher too. I think both of them go together really well. It's all about energy lines, life-force and flow. I love this stuff!'

Marissa felt warmth coming from Matt as he spoke, he seemed passionate about what he said. She couldn't help but like him.

'That's a lot of learning you're doing at the same time. I've got a lot going on too,' she volunteered, 'I suppose it doesn't rain, but it pours!'

'Yes indeed! What are you studying?'

'Psychotherapy and Shamanism.' Both of Matt's eyebrows raised up in curiosity, and he was just about to ask another question when Leonora came back in.

'Hey, I'm ready, thanks for waiting for me. It's your turn to be the client now.' Leonora nodded to Matt. He mouthed 'later?' at Marissa, who nodded, then hopped up on the plinth. As Marissa and Leonora took their places he said, 'Two women tending to me hand and foot, what dream is this that I am in?' he said.

Marissa giggled. 'Head and foot more like,' she said, and they all cracked up.

Marissa was more at ease during the session with Matt than she had been with Leonora. She placed her hands firmly on him as she worked, not afraid to touch him, and Matt's snores could be heard within five minutes of them starting. *That's so strange, he was wide awake when we started.* His face was soft as he slept, Marissa wondered what he might be dreaming about.

After they finished, Leonora woke Matt up and he apologised for snoring, it was quite funny. The other groups had finished their sessions and were waiting for them to come back to the circle. Dolores invited them all to share their experiences.

'I felt like I had eight hands on my body at the same time,' one of the women in the group said.

'Yes, so did I!' Marissa added.

'Me too, but more than eight, maybe twelve? I don't know. It was very strange.'

Dolores addressed this 'This is commonly reported by people who experience Reiki, even when only one practitioner's working on them. We don't know why it is. My sense is that the Reiki guides come to help during Reiki sessions. You never know, you could have been facilitated by Mrs Takata or Mr Usui themselves!' Dolores cast her eye over the group, they all seemed very impressed.

'We know that there is so much more to Reiki than we will ever understand. We cannot claim to understand it completely. The more you practice Reiki, the more confident you will be. The more work you do on yourselves, the clearer a channel for Reiki you will become. Reiki will flow through you and help you grow, if you want it. So the best advice I can give to you is this – practice, practice, practice.'

The group broke for lunch, the morning had passed by so quickly. Matt found Marissa as she was putting on her coat. 'Want to have lunch with me?' he asked, blushing.

He must be so much older than me, but he's nice, and I do have to eat. Sarah would be proud of me, okay, I'll do it. 'Why not?' she said. He seemed delighted and opened the door for her as they left the room.

'Such a gentleman!' she said to him, laughing.

They found a quiet pub just off the main street and they both ordered soup. Matt also ordered a pint of Guinness. Marissa wasn't sure if that was a good idea but she didn't say anything. She ordered a Diet Coke and sipped it while she waited for the soup.

'So you're studying to be a psychotherapist? And doing Shamanism?' Matt said while waiting for his pint to settle.

'Yes, I am.'

'Wow, that's mad stuff. Wow, cool. Who are you studying with?' He took a sip of his pint, which hadn't settled completely. He put the glass down on the table and wiped off the creamy moustache.

'Séamus O'Driscoll.'

'Yer man with the hat, from YouTube!! I've seen some of his videos, what's he like in real life?'

'He's great, very nice, kind of dramatic in a way, at times. I like him, and I love the work. The next residential is in two weeks in Clifden, in the Monastery.' *Oh no! Was I supposed to keep that a secret? I'm sure Matt won't tell anyone, it feels okay to talk to him about it.*

'I've heard of that place, is it the haunted one? Have you seen any ghosts?'

'Actually, yes, we met a few, I think. Something weird did happen one of the days we were there. One of the guys said there was no such thing as ghosts, I think a ghost got a little angry at that, and a plate seemed to throw itself off the shelf in the kitchen and smashed all over the floor. It gave us all a fright.'

'Wow, I'd have loved to have seen that. Scary stuff!'

The soup was served, Matt looked at his watch and took a big drink from his pint.

'That's a lot of liquid,' said Marissa. 'Are you sure it's okay to drink alcohol during the workshop?'

'Naw, I'm not sure, but I fancied a pint, so I got one.'

They started into the soup. Matt spread a generous amount of butter on the slice of bread and dunked it into the soup, and then took a bite out of it. *He's not delicate or trying to impress me, I like that.*

'So what do you do when you're not in Tai Chi or Reiki class?'

Matt laughed. 'I'm a mechanic. I fix cars. I like it, but I've been doing it since I was seventeen. I dropped out of school, got an apprenticeship with FÁS, and I've been doing it ever since.'

'That's helping people too, in a way, by fixing their car for them.'

'Yeah I guess so. But I wanted to do something more. I've been doing Tai Chi for five years now. I'm working on my teaching cert but I can't see the day where I will feel confident leading a class. I liked the idea that Reiki was only a couple of weekends.'

Marissa took a closer look at Matt. He was much younger than she had thought. How could she have missed it? She needed to know.

'How old are you?'

Matt laughed. 'What a personal question! I'm thirty-eight. Though people think I'm older than I am. Must be all the stress I've had in my life! Or the smoking! But I don't smoke now, I gave it up last year after my dad had a heart attack. He was a smoker too, it scared the shit out of me.'

'Oh, I'm sorry to hear that.'

'Ah, Da, he's grand, he didn't die, they gave him bypass surgery but he couldn't give up the smokes. Even after all that, he's still smoking like a chimney. So I thought I'd better give them up now or I'd be like him, too addicted, not able to give them up at any age.'

Marissa looked at her phone, it was nearly time to go back. She finished off her soup, it was actually quite delicious. Matt finished off his pint and wiped his soup bowl clean with the last of his buttered bread.

'Hang on a mo,' he said to her and disappeared into the bathroom. *What about Zaad?* Marissa hadn't thought about him at all in the last week or two. *Where did that thought come from? Nothing's happened between me and Zaad, or between me and Matt either.* It seemed strange, making more of something than it really was. And if she had a choice between Zaad and Matt, well, there was a tension between her and Zaad that wasn't there with Matt. He was fun, she felt relaxed with him, with Zaad, it seemed very serious. *Sure, I'm not married to anyone, what am I worried about?*

Matt came out of the bathroom.

'I hope you washed your hands,' Marissa said with a cheeky grin.

He looked shocked and then smiled. 'Ha ha,' he said, 'You've a great sense of humour, I like that. Come on, we need to go back to the workshop before Dolores misses us.'

Matt and Marissa walked briskly back to the hotel. Just before they went inside, Matt said, 'Here, give me your phone.' She did. He phoned his phone from hers, it rang once in his pocket, and then he hung up and handed her phone back to her. 'If you ever want to meet me, now you have my number.' He winked at her. They went inside. Marissa found her seat, and Matt found his. She felt her pulse racing. Once Dolores started talking, she calmed down.

'Sometimes when you're working with other people, they release heavy emotional energy as part of their healing process. Sadness, anxiety, guilt, shame, fear, all of these emotions are energies, and they're heavy, which is why we find them unpleasant. Have you ever walked into a room and felt heavy energy?'

Everyone nodded, three conversations started at the same time, and they hushed each other down so they could hear Dolores continue.

'There's a tool that we can use as Reiki practitioners, it's called the Violet Flame. When I attuned you yesterday I also attuned you so you can work with the Violet Flame. The Violet Flame works with Saint Germain.'

At the mention of his name, Marissa sat up taller in her seat.

'Saint Germain and the Violet Flame will help you transform heavy energy. You can't just get rid of it, like throwing it in the bin, it has to go somewhere, so transforming is important. You visualise a violet flame in the room with you, like a little fire, and you can 'send' the heavy energy into it for transformation. When I say send, it's about will. You've heard of willpower? So you use the power of your will to shift the heavy energy from you, and from your client, into the Violet Flame. Here, I'll show you.' Dolores concentrated, then she said, 'I activate the Violet Flame, Saint Germain, Saint Germain, Saint Germain, please activate the Violet Flame.' She brushed her arms as if removing cobwebs from the room and then balled them up and threw the imaginary cobwebs into the imaginary violet flame. 'Thank you for transforming these heavy energies,' she said to the flame. To all intents and purposes, it looked like nothing had happened, or changed. But there was a subtle difference in the feeling of the room.

Dolores got the group to activate a central Violet Flame in the middle of the circle, to brush themselves down, and throw the heavy energies into the centre. Marissa did it and felt again, a subtle difference, it wasn't dramatic, she thought it was a nice idea. *It might come in handy in the room in Cabra.*

After two more hands-on practices on plinths, in different groups, they were sitting back in circle for the closing session.

'We are coming to the end of our weekend. How are you all doing?' Dolores asked. Everyone seemed happy and confident that they knew what Reiki was, how to do a self-practice and how to use it with other people. Marissa reflected on the whole weekend, they certainly had covered a great deal of information. She remembered the question she had written down in her notebook earlier that day about psychic protection, but it didn't seem right to bring that up right now. Maybe she would meet with Dolores for another private session and ask about it there.

'You didn't cover chakras or aura colours, I'm a little disappointed in that.' This from one of the women in the circle.

'I'm sorry you're disappointed,' said Dolores, 'But as I said before, that's not Reiki. It's important for you to realise that Reiki is only one of many energy healing modalities, and you're here to learn Reiki Level 1. If you want to learn about chakras, chakra healing, psychic surgery, you need a different workshop! And yes, I do teach some of these things, I'm also a Seichem Master, which is a different form of energy healing, in Seichem, we work directly with the aura, and we can perform psychic surgery. But you're only beginning, and it's important to keep things simple. You don't need to add anything to Reiki, Reiki in itself is enough, but there is a tendency amongst practitioners to feel that they need more. As long as I've been working with energy, I keep coming back to the simple fundamentals of Reiki. Purification, practice and stillness. If you have these three things, then you've got all you need. Anyone else?'

'Thank you for qualifying that,' said the disappointed woman. 'I suppose I am very keen to learn more.'

'And that is a good thing, go slowly, go deep, and be wise. There is a lot of misinformation out there, jumping in too fast, too deep, too strong can cause difficulties. I've met some of you before, for that very reason.'

Marissa felt herself blushing, and she kept her head down.

'It's all learning, you've done nothing wrong by doing that. Novice enthusiasm is wonderful. It's a pity that not all teachers are pure and clear, however, and you do need to be discerning around who you get involved with.'

It was coming up to time. Dolores invited them to stay 10 minutes later than planned and do one more session of self-practice. The group readily agreed.

As they packed up their things, Marissa went over to thank Dolores.

'Oh my dear, I am so glad you enjoyed it. I know that you will find great benefit from Reiki, I hope you consider doing the self-practice daily. Perhaps by the summer you will be ready for Level 2. Come and see me nearer the time, and we can discuss it?'

'Oh! Yes please. That sounds marvellous! Thank you so much. I had a lovely day.'

'And do come and see me again, in my healing room, if you need to. I'm always happy to help. You have my number.'

'I will. Thanks.'

Matt was hanging around the reception area of the hotel, he looked a little sheepish. Marissa was happy to see him. 'What are you doing later?' he asked, looking down at his feet.

'I've got to go home and look after my cat, but nothing really much after that.'

He brightened up. 'Do you want to go to the movies? With me, I mean?'

Marissa's heart leapt, then she thought for a moment. 'You know what, I really would. But not tonight, I'm too tired. I've got a lot to process from the weekend, yes I know it's far too sensible, isn't it.'

He shrugged his shoulders and cocked his head to one side, raising an eyebrow.

'I've got your number, I'll text you later, we can plan something for next week?' Marissa suggested.

'I don't believe you,' he said to her with a smile, but she could see the disappointment in his eyes. She couldn't decide if he was serious or putting it on. Marissa sighed. She didn't like feeling as if she needed to make this new person feel better. She wanted someone to be carefree and easy, like he seemed to be at lunchtime. She was a therapist for goodness sake, she wanted someone to take care of her, for a change. She decided to try a flirty approach just for fun.

'I guess you'll just have to wait and see then.' she said with an eyebrow raised. 'Now you can walk me to the DART station.'

He perked up and offered his arm, Marissa smiled and took it. They walked towards the station and Matt offered, 'I've got a car, I could drive you wherever you wish to go?'

'Excellent. I'll keep it in mind so for next time!'

CHAPTER THIRTY ONE

It was the Sunday evening after her Reiki workshop and the email from Séamus reminding them to send in the homework notes landed in Marissa's inbox. He had emailed them all in the "To" field, she didn't know if it was deliberate or by accident, but now she had everyone's email address. She scanned through their names, it seemed like forever since she had seen them all. Terry, Saoirse, Finn – he was a strange one, Finn. She wondered why he was on the course and for a second time too, according to Terry... He didn't say much that weekend at all. Zaad, then Jenny, Liz (she shuddered, remembering how she became needy with her on the last day) and Stephanie. It had been a while since she heard from any of them. Well, it seemed so anyway. *And Zaad... interesting how his name comes up tonight after me just meeting Matt...*

After dinner, Marissa sat with the resistance she felt to doing her homework to try to break through it. *If I don't do the journeys, they'll get away from me. I'm tired right now, but I feel good. I could do one journey now, just to get it out of the way. I like the idea of ticking it off my list.* She looked through her phone, found the drumming tracks that she had recorded and then dug out her notebook to look at the topics she needed to journey on. *First journey is to the North direction, to meet a spirit guide and ask them what you need to know now. Yes, I could do this now, it's not too late.*

Tobermory was sleeping on the armchair on top of a purple throw that Carol had given her for Chanukah. His purring vibrations filled the room. *I could almost use those to journey on instead of the drum.* It had been a long day. It felt good to stretch out on the sofa. She lay back, closed her eyes and pressed play on the twenty-minute drumming track.

To the North, to the North. Cold in the North, follow the drumbeats, follow the drum. Marissa felt herself getting smaller and smaller. She brought her awareness into her heart and found a door, then opened it and was outside in the cold, on a mountain range. It reminded her of Mount Everest. She closed the door and started walking against the wind. She trekked up the side of the mountain, the strong wind pushed her back down. It felt like very hard work, but she kept going. She fell down, she picked herself up again and continued. The cold wind in her face bit at her cheeks. Her hair blew around her and blocked her eyes as she pushed forward. There was a tent further up the mountain with a fire and a pot sitting on it, it smelled like stew brewing. A Native American Woman wrapped in furs sat under a canopy in front of the tent, waiting for her. Marissa joined her by the fire.

'Why did you bring me here? So cold,' said the woman.

'Séamus said we needed to journey North, to find our spirit guide.'

'But you had already found me.'

'Yes, I know.' said Marissa, not actually sure if she had found her at all.

'Séamus doesn't know everything, although he thinks he is so clever. Here, sit, drink some soup.'

The woman placed some steaming broth into a bowl and handed it to Marissa. She took it with both hands, blew on it and drank. It was delicious.

'What do you want to talk about?' asked the woman, looking straight at her.

'It is just nice to be here with you,' said Marissa, with the wind whipping around them, it was getting difficult to focus.

'Not so nice here. Do we need to stay in this place?' asked her spirit guide.

'I guess not,' said Marissa, and the scene changed.

They were on an open plain, the fire and the broth were still there, as was the tent, but the sun was shining. The bright colours and open prairies were a stark contrast to the white snow and tall mountains from just a second ago. The woman took off her furs and lay them on the ground beside her. She wore a beautiful sky blue and lemon yellow beaded dress with an open and fluid embroidery, very different in style to the medicine woman from Peru. Her energy was different too, she seemed younger, tight and stiff in herself. 'Much better here,' she said and smiled, showing cracked teeth.

'Where are we?' asked Marissa.

'Navajo land,' she said. 'My homeland.'

'How wonderful!' Marissa finished the soup and handed the bowl back to the woman.

'What can I call you?'

'You can call me Emelda.'

'Emelda. Thank you! It's great to have a name for you.'

'Yes, I always have a name. I am glad you asked me. You can call me anytime. Any time, get it?'

'Yes, thank you so much, I will. But why are you helping me?'

'Is my job, I volunteer. I like you, you've got spunk. The coyote, very clever. I liked it. You will do more. I am interested to find out what. And always here, if you need help.' Marissa sat for a while, wondering what to say next. 'She knew about the coyote? What else does she know about?'

Marissa heard the callback signal, but she didn't go back. She let the drumming track play out and stayed with the image of the open plains and Emelda.

'Good girl. You are learning. Work in your own time, not in other people's time. You will know, your intuition will tell you what to do, who to follow, what song to dance to. Not to someone else's. You have good music inside you.' Emelda tapped on Marissa's heart. It reminded her of Peru when the medicine woman did exactly the same thing.

Marissa remembered the focus of her homework and then asked, 'Is there anything I need to know before I return home?'

Emelda thought for a moment. 'You think too much!!' She pointed to Marissa's head. 'Stop thinking! Only through the silence does the answer come. You will find out when you do this for yourself.'

Marissa found her concentration wavering. She was coming back into her apartment and out of the journey. 'Thank you,' she said to Emelda. But the images were already gone.

It felt like she had really gone somewhere, it took a few moments to feel like she really was back. She hauled herself off the sofa, found her notebook and wrote down what she had experienced. She was pleased, She wrote down Emelda's name and circled it. Emelda. She was Navajo. *That's really good and interesting information.* She realised that she actually heard that in a journey, she got clear information. She *was* happy.

She looked at her phone, it was 10.30pm. She saw Matt's number where he had called her. She added him to her contacts so she'd know it was him if he texted. He was nice, a little unpredictable with his pint... Sarah would call him a diamond in the rough, or maybe just a little bit of rough. She giggled. *Why wait?* She texted him: Hey Matt, this is me, texting you. Night. He texted back almost right away with a thumbs-up emoji. Marissa didn't like that, it felt like a 'yeah yeah' reply. Maybe he wasn't really interested in her after all.

+++

Sarah was in good form at work, she had had a date with a new beau and wanted to tell Marissa all about it. It was funny to watch her trying to stay in professional 'work mode' while bursting to tell her the news. 'It's okay, Sarah, I'm your friend as well as your manager. Let's go for coffee later, and you can tell me everything.' Over coffee, Marissa hinted to Sarah about Matt, but it was very subtle, so subtle that Sarah missed it. *Probably better that way.* Matt hadn't texted her yet, but it had only been a day. Maybe he wanted to keep her keen? She wasn't sure.

After work, back at her flat, Marissa ate a dish of noodles and vegetables, decided to do journey number two, and got her notebook out.

> *Journey 2, Second journey is to your childhood, to a moment in time when you were younger where you were upset with something connected to the block that you discovered today. Imagine that you're right there, in the room with yourself.*

When? What moment? And what block? She had an epiphany – *Was this was why I didn't want to do the homework?* This one seemed too personal, and she didn't have too many traumas that she could think of... but she didn't want to visit anything difficult or uncomfortable. *I really don't fancy doing this. What's the next journey?*

Third journey is to you, in the future. Ask yourself for some advice.

I can do this one, no problem. Maybe I'll skip the second one? Who would know... besides me, that is. I could do it tomorrow but I'm in college tomorrow night, I'll be too tired to do a journey. I'll skip the second one, just pretend that I've done it. Yes, good idea. So I'll go straight to the third one now, and I'm done. That's it!

She got her blanket, set her phone on airplane mode, and set her intention to meet herself in the future. She found the drumming track and pressed play.

She was walking down a white corridor. There were framed photographs on the walls, it was like an exhibit in an art museum. She peered at the photos, not art at all, no, her, Marissa, at various stages of growing up. She glanced at them as she walked past, little Marissa, only three, on her birthday, blowing out candles with her grandparents behind her. Little Marissa at five on the swings in the park. Not so little Marissa at twelve in a party dress going to a friend's bar-mitzvah, Marissa at sixteen during the summer with her father in the Wicklow Mountains. All the photos she remembered from before, the ones that matched her memories. She kept walking.

There was a door at the end of the corridor. Marissa opened it and stepped out into an inner-city park, it looked like it could be anywhere, but she didn't recognise the place. People were walking dogs, sitting chatting, children were running around and laughing, the sun was shining. Marissa found a park bench and sat down. After a while, someone came and sat down beside her. She turned to see who it was, this person was female, but the face wasn't clear. Her essence was familiar.

'Are you me, in the future?' Marissa asked hopefully.

'I am one of many possible you's in the future, depending on what pathways you choose.'

'Oh, okay. Hi. Thanks for coming. I'm to ask you for some advice. Can you tell me something that I need to hear?'

'Yes. A life of truth and authenticity is the most difficult of all, but the most rewarding. Truth on the outside for other people is not enough, you must also be truthful with yourself. If you hide the truth it doesn't go away. Self-deception becomes a weight in your energy field. The more deception you carry, the heavier your energy will be, the less clear a channel you become. If you want to be a true healer, you must always be truthful and always clear your channel. But again, this is your choice.'

'I hear what you are saying. Thank you.' Marissa looked at this woman whose face started shifting and changing, and then she could see herself, her own face, only older. Then she realised that she was deceiving herself by pretending she had completed the second journey. It suddenly didn't feel good inside to know that she had been doing this, she hadn't even realised it. She turned to her future self and said, 'I'll go back and do that second journey now.' Marissa felt instantly better.

'Good. When you keep your integrity high it is seen, and noticed. You are accountable to yourself and to God. You will do well, child, for you are still a child, and always a child of God.'

Marissa stayed on the bench with her future self for a while longer, not speaking. Then she turned to the older version of herself, but she was gone. The images faded, and she walked back towards where the door had been. She stood there for a while to get her bearings before opening the door and going back into the corridor.

The images that were there had disappeared, all but one. She went and peered into it. She was about three years old, crying. There was broken glass on the floor and her parents were screaming. The picture was playing like a movie, she quickly realised that it wasn't a photograph at all, it was a memory, but she couldn't recall the incident. She watched for a while longer then the walls around her seemed to absorb her. She found herself there, in the kitchen, where she grew up, as if she had stepped into the memory. She wasn't solid in it, she was hovering, watching, an observer.

The back door slammed and Uncle Lou came barging in a foul temper. 'Damn and blast it, Bernie, how could this have happened? I trusted you, I knew you'd mess everything up.'

Marissa's father looked weakened and upset. He was wringing his hands together. 'Lou, I know, I'm so sorry, I didn't think...'

'Damn right you didn't think. What will Da say now? What will he do when he finds out you lost the entire business? God damn it, Bernie, I told you, you have to stop gambling.'

Rose picked up little Marissa and was cradling her, trying to get her to stop bawling. Marissa noticed her mother was pregnant, must be with Eli. She carried little Marissa out to the living room.

I'm inside the second journey now and I've gone very far back, I remember there was screaming and shouting at home regularly, but it stopped when I was about seven years old. I don't know what happened, but I'm here, observing. Maybe that's enough.

She watched her mother stroking little Marissa's hair, singing to her to calm her down. The men were still shouting in the back. She walked towards the door but didn't want to go inside.

Get me out of here, now, please. The images dissolved away. Marissa was back in the corridor, and then back in her body, and back in her apartment.

Marissa lay on the couch for a while just thinking about what had happened. She picked up her notebook to try to write it down, but the words didn't come. She got up and made tea and sat in silence for a moment. She started writing her piece for Séamus. She admitted that she had avoided the second journey, she wrote what her future-self told her and what she saw in the images of the past. She felt like there was a piece missing, that incident didn't happen to her, yet it must have affected her in some way, if she was brought back into it. She would have to trust that she'd find out why, if it was important.

She got up to bring the tea things to the sink and switched on her phone. It buzzed a text, it was from Matt. She smiled with pleasure to see his name come up on the phone screen. She read it.

> Hi! I'd like to meet if you're still up for it? Let me know, we can arrange something. xx Matt.

Two kisses? Or is he just signing off? Hmm. Marissa washed and put the tea things away, then sat back on the couch. She texted back: Ok, Friday night?

She saw the message bubble on her iPhone, indicating that he was texting her back. It was nice. Before his answer came in she quickly sent: You do know that it'll be a proper date if it's on a Friday...

The bubble stopped, and then appeared again, and then his text: Okay, I think I can handle it

She replied: Great, cool. smiley emoji.

His reply: I'll look up what movies are on and text you again soon. See ya Friday.

+++

It was Tuesday, work, then college. Marissa felt good that she had finished her journey for Séamus. She paid the deposit for the second workshop and wondered if she'd contact any of the others about travelling to Galway together, then she changed her mind. She liked the solitude of the train journey. Terry would be coming up from Cork anyway, so maybe they'd meet in Galway, but that could be messy. No, she'd leave it to fate, like last time.

In college that evening, they had practice to prepare for end-of-term assessments. Marissa was grouped with Emmet and Yvonne. She decided to talk about being truthful when she was the client. She knew that integrity and honesty was very important to her, particularly after her journey to her future self. It was time to be more open with her classmates. Yvonne was the therapist, and Emmet was observing.

'So, Marissa, what would you like to talk about this week?'

'Hi, Yvonne. I'd like to talk about being truthful. I've been hiding things from my family and friends, and I don't like doing that. I think it's giving me anxiety, I'd rather get it all out into the open.'

Emmet sat up straighter in his chair. Marissa could tell he was dying to know what she was going to say next.

Yvonne jumped straight in. 'Being truthful is good, especially if it's making you anxious when you're not being truthful. Do you feel like you can tell me what it is you've been hiding?'

Marissa was quiet for a moment. Emmet looked like he was going to fall off his chair with the anticipation. For an observer, he certainly is calling a lot of attention to himself. Yvonne glared at him, and he settled back down again.

'I guess I have to tell someone,' Marissa started. 'I'm doing spiritual work. It's not religious, it's spiritual healing work. And I've not told many people because, well, I don't know why. Maybe I'm ashamed to tell them? Maybe I'm afraid of what they might think of me.'

It felt better to say it, to get it out in the open. And put like that, it was truthful and didn't sound as strange as she thought it would.

'Why Marissa, that's great! Spiritual healing work sounds fantastic. Why were you afraid to say it before?' Yvonne seemed relieved.

'Like I said, I've been worried about judgement, particularly from my family. They're very judgemental, and spiritual work isn't something they'd really understand.'

Yvonne nodded her head.

Marissa elaborated, 'I've never felt I belonged. In Dublin, I mean. My background is Jewish, so I've never felt completely accepted. I didn't have many friends but my family and I are very close. Not telling them about this has pushed a wedge between us, and I don't like it.'

Marissa realised as she spoke that she had, in fact, been pushing her family away for the last few months. Perhaps she was the one that pushed a wedge there before they could do it. She hadn't told anyone in her class that she was Jewish before either, it felt like a coming out, she suddenly felt vulnerable.

'What was it like, being Jewish in Dublin? Growing up?' asked Yvonne.

This took Marissa by surprise. 'Actually, Yvonne, that's not what I want to talk about tonight.' *Well done me for closing that down immediately.*

Emmet jumped into action, writing furious notes. Marissa was shaking as she spoke, she felt like her boundary had been crossed. She was regretting sharing this with Yvonne.

Yvonne backtracked. 'Sorry, Marissa, I was curious, that's all, and curiosity doesn't belong in a therapy session. I'll try again. Tell me how you're feeling now.'

'Well, Yvonne, I'm feeling shaken by your intrusive question and a little angry. However, I realise that your curiosity is natural and that this is my issue. I need to work with it without getting upset with you.'

Yvonne relaxed, and Emmet kept writing in his notebook. Both Yvonne and Marissa glared at Emmet, he put his hands up, the notebook fell on the floor.

'What, what? What am I doing wrong?' he asked. Yvonne and Marissa looked at each other and laughed. The tension broken, Emmet picked up his notebook and closed it on his lap, and Yvonne continued the session.

'Your honesty here tonight is inspiring me, Marissa. Really it is. It's brave and difficult to be truthful, and I admire it in you. I wish I could be as truthful. You've given me something to work on too.'

Time was up. Yvonne and Marissa stood up and shook hands.

Emmet said, 'So is it my turn to be therapist?' Both Yvonne and Marissa said, 'No!' at the same time, and laughed again. *Yvonne really didn't mean to upset me, it was mostly me being defensive. Look at me, probably also judging her in thinking that she was judging me. I need to stop doing that.*

Marissa felt a lightbulb go on inside her head, suddenly remembering the work of the North – find the old ingrained patterns and break them. *Aha! Here is my pattern – to hide, to judge, to be defensive. Okay, at least I recognise it now. I'll need some time to work on this, but at least I know what it is. I want to be a clear channel, I want to be a healer, maybe more than anything. This is the only way I can do it.*

Yvonne said, 'I think, Emmet, you're to be the client now, and Marissa will be your therapist – is that okay, Marissa?'

'Nobody is gonna ask me what I want then?' said Emmet.

'No,' said Yvonne.

'Okay then,' said Emmet, smiling, and taking the client's chair.

Marissa smiled back at him and took the therapists chair. Yvonne fished her notebook and a pen out of her handbag and sat in the observer's chair.

Marissa began. 'So, Emmet, how are you tonight?'

'Well, I feel like I'm being picked on, but I can handle it.' He winked at Yvonne, who glared at him again, and then smiled.

'What would you like to talk about tonight?'

Emmet was ready. 'My wife and I are arguing all the time, she's been wrecking my head. I don't know how to get her to listen to me. I don't think anything has happened, she's just irritable all the time, it's like anything I do really annoys her.'

Marissa really had to try to hold back the sarcastic comment that formed almost immediately in her mind. *Part of the fun of therapy with friends, I can see immediately why it wouldn't work. Focus, focus, focus.* She turned to Emmet and to the subject at hand. 'Can you give me an example?'

'Okay. Yesterday I told her I was going to the dry cleaner's and I asked her if she wanted me to take anything of hers. She suddenly, out of nowhere, went on a rant about money, telling me that I was ridiculous taking my clothes to the dry cleaner. She really lost her head.'

Marissa thought for a moment. 'Emmet, are you in trouble for money right now?'

'No, not really. Well, we are stretched, I've got to pay for college on top of everything else, and my wife is at home with the kids, you know, so we haven't got as much money as we used to, before college, I mean.'

'From what you've said, it sounds like your wife could be stressed. Maybe she's worried about money and taking it out on you. What do you think?'

'Well, I just thought she was angry at me, but when you put it like that, it's possible, yes. We are stretched, but we are okay, we haven't been going out as much lately. We like to go out for dinner every couple of weeks, and we haven't done that in a few months.'

Marissa found an angle to work with. 'I'm wondering then, if your wife is missing your attention? That because you're not going out to dinner, she thinks that you can't afford it? You're spending time doing assignments and college work, you're not spending as much time with her. Maybe as well as feeling stressed, she feels like she's not as important to you as she used to be?'

'Jeezus, Marissa, that's brilliant! I didn't see it at all myself. Yeah, I think you're right on the mark there. I guess I could take her out for dinner and spend some time with her, that might help.'

'Yes, I think it would help. She might still be angry at you though, she will want to have her say, maybe you could give her some space to get it out of her system first? Then she'll relax and see you're not going anywhere. That you still love her.'

'I do love her. She's great with the kids, and she's a lovely person, when she's not pissed off at me, that is. I do need to tell her that more often. Thanks, Marissa. This has been very helpful.'

'No problem.'

Marissa got home late after class. She felt like she'd made some real progress personally, as well as in practice, though the session with Emmet felt more like common sense than therapy. Marissa did know that sometimes that was all that was required. *It can be difficult to see what's going on when you're right in the middle of it. I should call Mum.* She actually hadn't replied since her mother's text on Sunday. But it was too late, her mother didn't like to take calls after 10pm. *Tomorrow then.*

It was a fresh night. She made some camomile tea and sat in the garden wrapped in the throw from the sofa. Tobermory ran about at her feet, chasing an imaginary mouse. She looked up at the stars.

I'm here in my favourite spot in all the world, and I've changed. I'm not the same person I was six months ago. She took a drink from her steaming cup. The garden is changing too, the buds are beginning to show, it's early but there is growth just bursting to come through. A little like me. Marissa felt like she wanted to do something to mark the occasion.

She went back inside, leaving Tobermory to play on his own, shut the door and sat down on her sofa. She put down her tea and pulled out her oracle cards from the shelf under the coffee table. She lit a brand new scented candle, as it warmed it filled her room with the smell of honeysuckle. She held the cards in her hand and just sat there, connecting to them. She remembered she didn't do her Reiki practice yet so she connected into the Reiki energy. After a moment she felt it enter the top of her head. It was palpable and fresh, like bubbles, bubbling down her face down her throat, into her heart, up and over her shoulders down her arms, and out through her hands, which still held the oracle cards. *I'm powering up my cards! What a wonderful idea!*

Marissa set her intention to draw one card that would give her a sense of how far she had come. She cut the pack and pulled out the top card. It was new to her, she had not seen this one before. Albatross. The bird looked like a big seagull, it was flying over the sea, its long wings outstretched. She looked up the booklet to find out what it meant.

> *Albatross flies far and free, conserving energy to go the distance. They are strong birds and not afraid of a challenge. When you get this card it means you have also travelled far, but you still have far to go. Albatross doesn't sit still and neither should you. Know that you've got the energies behind you, supporting you, just like the wind under the Albatross' wings.*

That sounded beautiful. She put the cards on the coffee table, sat back into the cushions and placed her hands on her body for self-healing practice. Just then, Tobermory was scratching on the door to come in. She got up and let him in, all the while feeling the Reiki going into her body from her crown. Once she closed and locked the door, she sat back down on the sofa, put a blanket over her legs and continued her self-practice. Tobermory jumped onto her and started rubbing himself all over, purring very loudly. Marissa smiled. *Batshit crazy Reiki cat.* She ignored his affections and kept going, feeling the urge to place her hands on her heart. Then just as quickly as he jumped onto her, he jumped off and went to his favourite spot on the armchair and fell asleep. It was quiet now in her flat, and she was enjoying the stillness. Her mind cleared, all was peaceful for a moment, then a thought suddenly dropped into it: *You should buy yourself some Angel cards*

Wow, I felt that! Marissa tingled with the feeling of receiving the information. Her mind went into a spin and she stopped her Reiki practice and tried to ground herself. Marissa was getting used to these moments of quiet inspiration, but it was difficult to be in stillness long enough to receive the messages with her chattering mind. She would definitely look into getting herself some angel cards soon. It would help her get to know her angels, especially Metatron, the new one. She had looked up his name after Martin had mentioned him, but she really hadn't felt like she connected to him yet. New angel cards sounded like a great idea.

CHAPTER THIRTY TWO

Wednesday was busy with work and a trip to visit her mum and dad for dinner. They were delighted to see Marissa and enthusiastic about her spiritual work. Yet she didn't mention Shamanism, she wasn't quite ready to just yet, but she talked about the healing weekend she spent with Dolores and how she could now do hands-on healing for family and friends. Her mother had hurt her shoulder and asked Marissa if she could try the Reiki, and much to Marissa's delight, she seemed to get some relief after only a few minutes. She mentioned Matt to them as well, in passing, and they were enthusiastic about that too. Marissa wondered if she was making up the whole thing about how they were difficult with change, but she remembered that night with Eli and Carol, where he was drunk and locked himself in his bedroom, she knew that really had happened. Maybe one day she'd figure it out, but for now, it was nice to be able to help her mother get some relief and to know that the Reiki she was doing actually seemed to work.

On Thursday, Marissa had her session with Olive at lunchtime. Olive had been pleased with her when she mentioned the therapy in class the night before. It was getting a little easier to talk about herself now. She made it back on the dot at 2pm and had a thankfully easy afternoon, then she left work earlier than usual as she had supervision. Knowing that Sarah could hold the fort, she felt empowered to organise her day herself without needing Noreen's approval. As long as she got the work done, all was well.

Mr Blakemore's office seemed particularly stuffy that day. Marissa noticed dust particles dancing in the thin sunlight that came in through the large dusty windows. She wondered how much dust she was breathing into her lungs or he into his own. Mr Blakemore was at his desk leafing through a particularly precarious pile of paperwork. He spoke without looking up.

'Hmm… Hello, Marissa. Martin has made a report about you. Sit, sit, I'll be there in a second.'

Marissa fiddled with her hair as she took her usual chair, unsure if the 'Hmm' was a good thing or a bad thing. 'Oh? I hope all is well. I thought we were getting along quite nicely.'

'Actually, I was surprised he reported about you so late. He and I had an arrangement.' Mr Blakemore put the paperwork down. He grabbed an A4 pad and a pen and came over to sit opposite Marissa.

'Martin was to tell me after two sessions if he wanted to change counsellor. After the number of people he had been through, I was expecting that to happen. However…,' he paused, for dramatic effect, 'he likes you.'

Gotcha.

'He has asked if he can extend the sessions with you indefinitely. Because of protocol, I need to confirm this is acceptable to you before I sanction it. Due to the nature of his, predicament, Martin can have as many sessions as he wants, unlike the other clients, who we do need to review after five sessions. Where are you now with, who is it now…'

'Fiachra and Cliona?'

'Ahh, yes, Fiachra and Cliona. How many sessions have you had with each of them? I recall they started together in the New Year.'

'I've seen both of them twice. Tonight will be the third session.'

'Good, good.' He made some notes on the pad, then glanced up at Marissa. 'And how do you feel about continuing with Martin?'

'Good.'

Mr Blakemore smiled. He finished scribbling and put down the pen and paper. 'Good job. Well done. Remember, you can still come to me about anything if you feel you need to.'

'Thank you. I hope I won't need to take you up on it, but I will certainly keep it in mind.'

Fiachra was 10 minutes late and he looked pale and flustered. He sat down in his usual chair. Marissa had taken the extra time to try to still her mind. Olive was still insistent upon it, however, it didn't work very well. She tried her Reiki self-practice instead, which, funnily enough, seemed to help her mind quieten down quite a bit. *Maybe I should start with the self-practice, that could be the way into being still.*

Nonetheless, she was very relaxed when Fiachra came into the room, she sat in silence while he settled down. She felt a pull inside her to put her hands on him. She obviously couldn't do that so she questioned it. *Maybe he needs some Reiki?* She visualised the Reiki coming out of her hands, like the torch that Dolores had mentioned in class, and shining out across the room into Fiachra. But she couldn't visualise it entering him and calming him down, it seemed to, well, fizzle out before it got to him. *Maybe I do need Reiki 2 before I can do that, she said it was stronger... Oh, but I didn't ask his permission either, that could be it too...*Fiachra still hadn't spoken.

'Hello Fiachra, are you okay? You're very pale and quiet tonight.'

He turned and looked at her. He seemed far away, distant. 'Oh, hi Marissa. I think I used all my energy up just coming to see you right now. I'm not having a good day.'

'I'm glad you're here. I won't push you to talk if you don't want to.'

'Thanks. I don't think I want to. Just sitting here is good.'

Marissa sat with Fiachra. The only noise in the room was the ticking of the clock on the coffee table. It was like a metronome, tick-tock, tick-tock. Not quite like the drum, but it kept a nice beat. She adjusted her breathing to breathe in rhythm with it. After about fifteen minutes there seemed to be colour coming back into Fiachra's face. The Reiki energy was still flowing in her body, she was breathing with it, and visualising it flowing into him, too. She thought some of it might have made it, but she wasn't sure. When she saw the colour coming back into his face, she thought maybe that was the case, or perhaps just sitting in silence, without having to do anything might have been enough. It was enough just to be there, for now.

'Thanks, I feel a little better now.'

'I'm glad. It can be tough to try to do more than you are able to.'

'Yeah. I like it here, in this room, with you. You don't make me feel like I have to do anything. That's like having a break. You know

I live with my parents, they're always on at me. Get up Fiachra. Did you apply for a job today, Fiachra? Do the housework, Fiachra.' He shrugged his shoulders. 'It gets to be too much sometimes.'

Marissa stayed quiet to give him the space to clear his head. She felt the Reiki light decreasing inside, replaced with an inner calm. He smiled and looked down at his feet.

'Sorry, Marissa.'

'Hey, there's nothing to be sorry for. I'm here to help you, and if saying nothing is helping, I would rather do that than be part of the problem.'

'I wish my parents understood this.'

'Maybe you can say it to them?'

'I don't know how. They don't listen to me, they never ask me. I think they're tired of me being depressed all the time. It's not my fault, I can't help it. I'm going to the doctor, I'm taking the medication, I feel nothing most of the time. And I don't see the point of anything, it wears me down. Some days I just can't do life.'

'I think you're able to articulate how you feel very well, Fiachra. I hope that you try again with your parents. Have you ever asked them to listen to you?'

'Only when I am ground down to next to nothing, then I scream at them and go into my room. I lock myself in sometimes.'

'What if you tried something different?'

'Like what?'

'Well,' said Marissa, 'like not waiting till you're ground down?' She remembered something from an essay she read in college about couples counselling. 'Why not tell them that you'd like to talk to them about something important, and then ask them when would be a good time to talk, so you can have their full attention. Actually, ask for their full attention, I mean.'

'Oh, you mean like you're doing now, with me?'

Marissa laughed. 'Yes, I'm listening to you with my full attention. Did you know in college it takes at least a year for counsellors to learn how to listen?'

Fiachra laughed. 'That's crazy!'

'I know, isn't it? Well, I've been learning how to listen for nearly two years now, and sometimes it can be hard, even for me. So your parents might not have ever learned how to listen. Be patient with them. It doesn't mean they don't want to listen to you.'

Fiachra seemed to take this in. 'Okay, so I need to tell them I want to talk to them and ask them if they can listen to me without sounding like I'm being rude or something?'

'Exactly. That's why you tell them upfront, and ask to make a time, like an appointment with them, so they're ready and they know what they need to do.'

'That sounds very complicated.'

'I know. And they might not be able to listen to you for very long, it can be difficult to stay focussed.'

'Oh.'

'You might not have enough energy to do this when you're feeling bad, but at least you know it's a possibility. You might try it sometime when you're feeling a little better.'

'When I'm feeling better I don't need to tell them I'm feeling crap, though.'

'Ahh, but you do need to tell them what it is like for you when you do feel crap. It might really help if they understand you better, so they don't nag you when you don't have the energy for it.'

Fiachra sat up a little straighter in the chair and focused on Marissa. 'I think I understand what you're saying to me.'

'Good, I'm glad. Because you are doing the best that you can, you're applying for jobs, and you're doing the housework, and sometimes, I know, getting out of bed is all you can do, but you're doing it.'

'Yeah.'

'Depression is such a difficult thing to live with. I wish I knew how to cure it for you, Fiachra.'

'Jeez, if you could do that, you'd probably make a million.'

After Fiachra left, Marissa needed to clear the energy in the room. She felt she was getting better at it, she clapped her hands, lit her sage stick and was smoking the corners of the room when Cliona rang the buzzer. A few moments later, she came into the room.

'Smells great in here. Are you smoking weed?' Cliona giggled.

'Oh, hi Cliona! No, I'm not smoking weed! I'm clearing the energy of the room so that it's fresh for your session. Can you give me another minute?'

'Sure.'

Cliona seemed pleased. She hung up her bright orange coat and sat in the chair that Marissa had just been sitting in.

Marissa finished up and crushed the smoking sage into the saucer that was now a permanent resident in Room number three. She sat down opposite Cliona, pushed her hair out of her eyes, and began.

'So, how have you been this week? What would you like to talk about this evening?'

Cliona looked at the wall and twirled a strand of freshly dyed pink hair around her finger. She licked her lips and turned to face Marissa.

'This is hard,' she said.

'That's okay. Take your time.'

'I got mad at Brendan. My boyfriend. I mean my ex-boyfriend.' A tear formed in Cliona's eye and rolled down her cheek. 'I thought I'd smashed up all the anger... with Coyote, I mean. But Brendan said that I wasn't holding it together, that he couldn't stand it. He didn't want to be with me. It's not even a week.'

More tears smudged her make-up.

'I'm sorry to hear this,' Marissa said, handing her the box of tissues from the coffee table. 'You had a lot of rocks to smash though, maybe we didn't get them all?'

'Maybe.' Cliona blew her nose. 'It's just so hard. Not being angry, I mean. And now I'm angry at Brendan for not giving me a proper chance.'

Marissa cleared her head and tried to find an angle to approach this. 'Change doesn't happen overnight, you know. It takes time. Do you want to tell me exactly what happened between you and Brendan?'

'Not really. What's the point? He broke up with me again. I flippin' hate him now. What's the point of being here? Of even trying? I might as well just give up. Fuck this for a game of Chess.'

Marissa closed her eyes and saw an image of Cliona laughing. It was definitely her, though her hair was dark brown, shoulder-length, and even. She was outside at a café with a man and a child. Two children. They were under a sunny sky, they looked really happy together.

Weird. But it seemed so real to her, even though it was in her mind, so she thought she could mention it.

'Maybe Brendan isn't the one for you? Or maybe he is. Either way, if you give up on yourself and stop working on this, then you're doing yourself an injustice. I see a happy future for you, with children and a man who loves you.'

'Really? A happy future for me? I don't believe you.'

'Yes, I can see it. You're laughing, you have a little girl, about six years old, and another child, I think maybe a boy, much younger, and there's a man with you. The four of you look so happy together.' *Shit, this isn't psychotherapy. Shit, shit, shit. I have to backtrack this somehow. I'm just imagining the possibilities, it's not to say it is real, but who is to know that it couldn't happen?* 'I just think that you shouldn't let what happens between you and Brendan dictate whether or not you do your personal work.' *Phew!*

'Ahh. I see what you mean.'

'When you get angry, what happens to you?'

Cliona shifted in her chair. The tears had stopped. She closed her eyes to concentrate. 'I don't know, I just seem to lose it, I don't care who is there in front of me, or what's going on, I just have to lash out at someone. Mum kicked me out of her house for it, she said I reminded her too much of Dad. I live with Nan now, and Ariana, my girl. You know, it breaks my heart when I scream at Ari, I never mean it, she's such a good girl. But they don't seem as affected by it as Bren.'

'Maybe you're not really seeing what's going on until you see it through someone else's eyes? From what you've said, you, your mother and your sister grew up with your father, he was angry all the time. And now you live with your Nan and Ariana, so they are conditioned to it. Then Brendan comes along, who isn't used to being surrounded by anger, and he gets hit by flashes of yours. That could be enough to scare him away.'

Cliona squirmed a little. 'Yeah. That makes total sense. Jeezuz poor Ari, she must be conditioned to it too, like I was to Dad. Is it too late for her? I don't want to fuck her up the way Dad did to me. I'd like to do more work with you on my anger. Brendan or no Brendan. I'll do it for Ari. I guess smashing up the rocks was fun, but it's not going to solve how I handle things.'

'I'm sure Ariana will be okay, I can see how much you love her, so she can feel the love from you too. But you're right. Smashing up the rocks was good, but it isn't going to be the answer for everything.'

Cliona nodded.

'So maybe to start with, you need to be able to really look at what you're doing when you get angry, so you can catch it before it happens and change it. Does that sound good?'

Cliona was reluctant. 'Yeah, it does.' She wiped more tears off her face and sighed. There was silence in the room for a few moments while she gathered her thoughts.

'Maybe it's too late for Bren to come back? What do you think? Should I say I'm sorry?'

'That's totally up to you. Does he know you've been coming here?'

'No, I didn't tell him.'

'Well, coming here and talking to me is proof that you really want to change this, and if he knew about it, it might help him give you some more time and space to work on it.'

'You saw me in the future with a man and a child? What did the man look like? Was it Brendan?'

Marissa felt it would be too much information to give her, so she said, 'I didn't see his face. He was taller than you and broad-shouldered. The four of you looked very happy. It's just a feeling that I have, it doesn't mean that it's real. It just means that I know you can do this, Cliona.'

Cliona smiled. 'That must be my Brendan, yeah. That's cool. Marissa, what do we need to do? I really want to sort this out.'

What a night, and it isn't over yet. How do counsellors do this all day? I'm wrecked from it, and I still have one session to go! Marissa felt some Saint Germain would help her focus. She got it out of her bag and rubbed three drops on her hands, held them over her face and breathed in the scent. She waved her hands through her energy field and felt them catching on something around her stomach. She didn't know what it was, but she found herself pulling at invisible threads and pulling them out of herself. She didn't know what to do with them, then she remembered what Dolores had told them in Reiki, about throwing heavy energies into the Violet Flame. She visualised the flame in the room with her and imagined herself throwing the threads, whatever they were, into it. She felt a little better, so she kept doing it for another minute or two until she felt lighter in herself again. Then she remembered what Dolores had said about permission. She never asked Fiachra's permission to give him Reiki, but she didn't actually give him Reiki, she was just sitting in the room with him. *Maybe that's what she meant when she said that Level 2 was more complicated when it came to permission? I still have a lot to learn.*

The buzzer rang. Marissa pressed the button to unlock the door, and she heard Martin's tired steps as he reached her room. She stood at the door, holding it open for him with a smile.

'Hi, Martin, come in! Lovely to see you. How was your week?'

Martin smiled back. He came in, took off his coat and flopped down into his usual chair. 'I had a good week, thank you. I felt much happier because of our session last week. Thank you again for that.'

'That's my job. I'm glad I can help.'

Martin cocked his head to one side and looked at her.

'Is there something wrong?' Marissa asked.

'There's something different about you tonight. You have more lights around you, different colours. It's nice. You've not looked like that before.'

Marissa smiled. 'I was on a Reiki workshop last week and I was attuned to Reiki Level 1.'

'Ahh, that's what it is then,' said Martin. 'Or maybe not. I'm not sure.'

'Okay. I've just been practicing my Reiki in between clients – maybe you can see that?'

'Maybe. Anyway, it doesn't feel bad. It feels kind of nice, actually.'

'Great. But this is your session, we can't lose track of that. What would you like to talk about tonight?'

'I don't know. Nothing has really happened this week. I've just felt better in myself, if you know what I mean.'

'I think so, yes. More solid?'

'Yes, solid, that's it.' He scratched his head. 'You definitely seem different today. It's more than Reiki. It's strange but good. Hey, is there a man interested in you?'

'*What*?!'

'Yeah, that's what it is. Ha!' Martin clapped his hands together. 'You've got a man interested in you.'

Marissa blushed. How could he tell? Was it that obvious? But nobody else had mentioned it... What was he seeing?

'He's nice, this man of yours. He has a soft heart. I like him already. Ha, ha, I can almost see his face.'

'How do you know all of this?'

'His energy is here, in the room with you. It's like a shadow around you. Ooh, he can tell I'm talking about him – he's disappearing now. Ha, ha!'

Marissa shivered. She assumed it was Matt he was talking about, but how could his energy be in the room with her if he wasn't a ghost? *He's not dead?* She tried to refocus.

'Martin, enough about me. Please! You're distracting me. Let's talk about you.'

'Okay, but you haven't bought those angel cards yet, and Meta... Metatron, yes, that's the angel that's with you, Metatron really wants you to get those cards. That's enough messages for today, yes?'

Marissa laughed. 'You're amazing, strange, and very difficult sometimes, Martin. But I'm glad you told Mr Blakemore you wanted to stick with me. We will figure out a way of working.'

Martin winked. 'We will, indeed. I can tell you like me telling you things. I honestly don't mind, Marissa. I think that we are supposed to be talking like this. It helps me, and it's helping you, too.'

After the session, which thankfully didn't get any more challenging than encouraging Martin to make plans to go walking more often, Marissa switched on her phone. There were three text messages from Matt. She laughed to see them coming in one after the other. He must have known he was being talked about, for sure. He was asking about their date. *Tomorrow night! The week flew by.*

She replied: Hi yeah lookin forward 2 it. Where will I meet you?

He wrote back right away. Come to me? Dun Laoghaire? We can walk on the pier and grab some food.

Marissa had a bright idea: Hey, can we go to The Angel Shop? I want to buy a pack of angel cards.

Angel Shop? Where? Didn't know there was one in DL.
I'm defo on for that. Dinner and a movie after?

Perfect. @6?

GR8 See ya tomorrow @6!

Marissa was really looking forward to seeing him now. *Angel cards and Matt! It will be a fun night out. And Galway next weekend – I can bring the cards with me! This is all working out beautifully. Who said it would become muddled up? But I'm glad I have this weekend off, I do need to rest. Oh yes, Olive said that. And I've not been sitting still like she said I should. Oh well. I'll have another go at that later.*

CHAPTER THIRTY THREE 

Marissa woke up on Saturday morning in Matt's bed. She sat up and looked across at him on the blow-up mattress on the floor. He was still sleeping, he had a smile on his face. She felt happy – yes, it did feel nice between them. She had missed the last bus so he did the gentlemanly thing and slept on the floor. Marissa connected to Reiki and began her self-practice. After a few minutes he opened his eyes, saw her sitting up in his bed, and sat up.

'Hi!' He rubbed sleep out of his eyes.

'Hi,' said Marissa. 'How was the floor?'

'Okay. My back is a little stiff, but I managed to sleep. Must have been all those pints!'

'I would have slept there. I did offer.'

'Yes, I know you did, but you're the lady. So it was right for me to have the floor.' He rubbed his head and it made his curly hair stand up on its ends. He looked like a baby mouse rubbing his eyes.

'Can I make tea? I need some to help me wake up before I leave.'

'Sure, go ahead. Help yourself.' Matt lay back on his mattress and closed his eyes again.

Marissa pulled on the outer layer of clothing that she had removed and padded on bare feet into his kitchen which was almost as small as hers. His flat was on the third floor of a terraced house, and the kitchen window overlooked the sea, if you could stretch your eyes that far out over the chimneys.

'Did you find everything you need?' He was up, putting on a fresh shirt and opening the fridge, looking for eggs.

'Tea is good, I'm not really a breakfast person,' said Marissa, switching on the kettle and finding two mugs. 'Do you want some?'

'Instant for me, please.'

Marissa opened the cupboard and chose the least congealed jar of the three instant coffee brands he had, as they were all open. 'Strong or weak?'

'Strong. Thanks. Shit, the milk is off. I can run to the local and get another if you'll hang on a minute?'

'I can take my tea black, it's okay.'

'I can't! I need milk, I won't be long, please, wait?'

'Okay.'

Matt grabbed his wallet and keys and went out the door, then Marissa was alone in his apartment. She took the opportunity to snoop around. It was a one-bed with a living room, tiny kitchenette and a bathroom. He had books on a small shelf in his bedroom, mostly short stories and spiritual themes, and a pile of books on his mantelpiece on acupuncture, human anatomy and healing. There was a stack of DVD's of Tai Chi and Martial Art action movies by the TV, and what she assumed to be a Tai Chi uniform hanging on the wardrobe door. His room reminded her of Eli's when they lived together when Eli was a teenager. *He's just a big kid.* She looked at the photos in various frames on the mantelpiece, a much younger, slimmer Matt with a woman that she assumed was his mother, a family posing together on the beach, a photograph of a dog in the sunshine. He had three coffee table books about race cars, a poster of a Porsche and another of a Ferrari on the wall, both cars were racing red. *Of course, he's a mechanic, I forgot!*

Clothes were strewn around on the floor in all of the rooms, and there was a musty smell, but it wasn't unpleasant. She didn't mind. He let himself in, it really didn't take long for him to get the milk. He also had bread and a packet of chocolate biscuits in his hands.

'Hi again!' he said, a big grin on his face.

'Hi!'

Matt went into the kitchen, put everything on the table and cracked open the milk. He poured a big glug of it into his coffee. 'Do you want me to do yours?'

'No thanks, I've got it.' Marissa poured a dash into her chipped mug and threw the tea bag out into the bin under the sink.

Matt was checking his phone and without looking up he said, 'There's a band playing tonight in town, do you want to come with me?' He turned and looked at Marissa, she could tell from his eyes that he really wanted to spend more time with her.

Marissa really did like him, he was funny and easy to be around, but it seemed too much too fast. She looked closer at Matt. *He is really sweet, he's like an open book though, it's nice to be wanted... I don't know, I need to take it slowly after James.* 'Maybe next time? I'm needing some downtime – it's been a crazy week for me work-wise, and I'm going to Clifden next weekend so this weekend is really my only chance to catch up with myself.'

Matt looked crestfallen.

'Hey, last night was really fun. I had a good time... I like you. We can do it again.'

'Ahh cool. Okay.' He looked a little happier.

'You're very needy, aren't you?' Marissa said in a funny voice, half-serious... *That just slipped out – oh dear...*

Matt looked shocked and then curious, was she making fun of him? He didn't seem sure. 'No,' he said, defensively, 'I just like you and I'm not ashamed to say it. I like you, a lot. I want to see you again.'

'And I want to see you again too. That's settled then!'

He echoed back to her, 'That's settled then. And Miss Marissa, I am not needy, perhaps just smitten.' He blushed.

They finished off their drinks in silence. Matt held his hand out, and Marissa gave him her mug. He rinsed them both out in the sink and left them there.

'So what's in Clifden?' he said, raising an eyebrow.

'Weekend two of my Shamanic Training. I've still got homework to finish, so I'm gonna make a move. Text me later?'

Matt smiled. 'You know where the DART is from here?'

'Google Maps,' she said, pointing at her phone 'Best invention, ever.'

'Second only to the actual smartphone itself,' he suggested.

'Ha ha, okay yeah, maybe. Thanks again, it was fun.'

He helped her put her coat on and showed her to the door.

'Matt?'

'Yes?'

'Why do you have acupuncture and human anatomy books on your shelves? I'm dying to know.'

'Ha ha, doing some snooping around while I was out?'

Now it was Marissa's turn to blush.

'I was studying acupuncture for a while. I never finished it. It was too much with everything else. But I might take it back up again once I finish my teacher training.'

He leaned over and gave her a soft, gentle kiss on her cheek. 'See ya soon,' he whispered, and she left.

As she walked in the crisp fresh Saturday morning air towards the DART she touched her face where his lips had just been. Then she patted her bag, checking that the angel cards were still there. They were. She was looking forward to a shower and a change, and then getting to know her angels.

It took her about an hour to get back to her flat. She threw her clothes into the laundry and took a long, hot shower. As she stood in the hot spray, she wondered if Matt's energy was still around her. The thought made her shiver. She imagined peeling it off of herself and putting it into the Violet Flame. She didn't feel any difference. When she stepped out of the shower, her phone buzzed a text from Matt.

> Did you get home safe? Sure you don't want to meet tonight? Smiley emoji.

She didn't want to reply straight away. *Maybe he felt me removing his energy from mine, that's very interesting...*

She dressed and dried her hair and put the kettle on for another cuppa. She was hungry, so she heated up some leftovers, then when she was finished, she sat down on the sofa with her new angel cards. She carefully peeled the plastic off the box and opened it up. The cards had a smell of newness about them, each one had gold edging, and they were bigger than her oracle cards and more ornate. Marissa spread the whole pack out onto the table, face up. She repeated the names of each angel, 'Jophiel, Azriel, Michael, Haniel, Raphael, Metatron...' *Hi Metatron!* She felt a shiver when she said hi, it felt good. 'Raguel, Zadkiel, Ariel, Uriel, Gabriel, Chamuel.'

So many new names, they're like friends I haven't met yet! 'Raziel, Jeramiel, Sandalphon.' She sat back on the sofa and closed her eyes. *Which one of you was dancing with me on New Year's Eve?* She tried to still her mind, but it was very difficult with so many thoughts rushing around at the same time. It was impossible to pick up on any new information.

Just then, her phone buzzed another text: R u not talking to me? I swear I'm not needy. Crazy-face-emoji.

She laughed. Was in shower, can't make it tonight. How about a pint next week before I go to Clifden?

He sent back a smiley emoji and a thumbs-up: Yeah great, see you then!

She stayed sitting in stillness, imagining herself combing Matt out of her hair and her energy. She felt a little more grounded then, so she brought her awareness back to the cards on the coffee table. There were about four cards per angel, each one had a different one-word message, and there also was a booklet. She looked up Metatron on her laptop to start to get to know him better, and just as she started reading, the doorbell rang.

I can't get a moment's peace today. Marissa hesitated before choosing to leave the cards out on the coffee table. She went to the door, it was Michelle from upstairs.

'Hi Marissa, I'm away tonight and tomorrow night, was just wondering if you'd keep an eye on my place for me while I'm gone?'

Marissa smiled, she felt relieved it was just Michelle, and she meant to ask her about minding Tobermory. 'I wanted to talk to you, too. Come in. Do you have a few minutes? Tea?'

'Sure. Thanks, that would be lovely. Do you have any peppermint?'

Once the kettle was filled and switched on again, Marissa looked through her tea selection to see if she could find some peppermint tea. Michelle wore a tracksuit and had her long hair piled up in a messy ponytail on the top of her head. She was shorter than Marissa, about mid forties, and was a solid, grounded type of person. Marissa could always depend on her to feed Tobermory.

'Oh look, angel cards! I've not seen these in years! Are these new?'

Michelle sat cross-legged on the armchair. 'Is it okay for me to pick them up?'

'Sure. Thanks for asking! I was only taking a look at them, I just got the pack yesterday. I'm still getting familiar with it. Do you know about angel cards?'

'Oh yes, I used to do angel card readings for people. I still use the Tarot quite regularly.'

'Tarot? I've heard of that, but I've never seen them before.'

'Oh, they're great, I love the Tarot, It can be difficult to get started with, but once you figure it out, the cards are an amazing tool.'

The kettle boiled. Marissa got fresh mugs, put tea bags in, and poured. 'I've been meaning to ask you, I'm away next weekend, are you around?'

'Yeah, you want me to watch the kitty cat?'

'Yes please, thank you.' When Marissa turned to bring over the tea, she noticed Tobermory was sitting on Michelle's lap.

'He loves you,' Marissa said, laughing.

'Well, I don't know about that, but he certainly knows that I know where the food is.'

Michelle winked at Tobermory who wagged his tail, then jumped off her lap in a huff.

'Do you want any food?' asked Marissa.

'Thanks, but no, I can't stay long. It's a hen trip away in Amsterdam, the plane leaves in a few hours. My best friend, she's getting married, again! She swears this is her last time. I don't know, he seems nice anyway. It should be a fun few days either way. Thanks for watching my place, you've got the keys?'

Marissa went over to check the hooks behind the door, grabbed Michelle's keys and checked she had the right ones. She showed them to Michelle.

'Yep, that's them, great. And you're away when?'

'Next Friday till Sunday night. I'll leave the food in the usual place.'

'Brilliant. I like how it works, we look after each other.' She turned to look more closely at the cards. 'You know that one of the angels will show up for you more often than the others, depending on what you're going through at the time. Come, have a look.'

Marissa came back down and sat on the sofa, putting her tea down on the coffee table beside Michelle's.

'See, there, Haniel? She was a lifesaver for me about a year ago when I lost my job. I have a big soft spot for her, she's courageous and strong, and I felt her strength in me when I had to tell management that I didn't like the direction they were moving in. I had to put it all on the line, and unfortunately for me, well, I had to leave. I felt like I was able to do it with her having my back.'

Marissa listened, nodding and fingering the cards that Haniel appeared in. She did look strong, she was surrounded by light, mostly red, and she had long flowing hair. On one of the cards she had a sword, the word was 'Justice'. On another card she was carrying a ball of red glowing light, and the word was 'Truth.'

'That's really interesting, I'm feeling right now that Archangel Michael is with me, and I've been getting to know Metatron a little bit. In fact, I was looking him up just when you arrived.'

Michelle took another drink of her tea. 'I love Archangel Michael! He was my first angel too. Hey, it's getting late and I've got to pack, can I take the tea up with me? It's delicious! I'll drop the mug back down to you whenever?'

'Sure! Glad you like it.'

'Talk to you soon!'

She left. The flat seemed quieter without her. Marissa went back to the table, back to the cards. She gathered them all up and felt the weight of the pack in her hands. She shuffled them, trying to mix them up so that the Angels were evenly distributed. She liked the idea of flowing some Reiki through them, so she connected to the Reiki light, and after a moment or two, she felt it coming into her body, then through her and into the cards. Something inside the cards seemed to change, it was very subtle, as if the cards weren't sure of her, and once they got the Reiki, they settled down and accepted her as their owner. *Strange, but nice.* They felt more familiar.

Marissa shuffled the cards, cut the pack, pulled out the first card. *Metatron – Trust.* It felt validating to receive that, she was always delighted with any message she got, especially when it matched what she was thinking. She closed her eyes and tried to connect to Metatron. Her mind started to wander, images came into her mind of Matt, of their night out, then to packing for Clifden – *What will I bring?* Then to Zaad – *I wonder if we'll work together this time* – and then to Sarah and work, then back to Matt. She started to imagine herself kissing him, she had kissed him last night, it was nice, but she wanted to focus on Metatron.

It wasn't working. She opened her eyes. Maybe she'd try again later on. She left Metatron at the top of the pack and put all the cards back into the box. She placed the box beside her Oracle cards. She looked at both boxes hidden under the table. She decided to take them both out and put them on top of the table instead. She didn't have to hide anything anymore. It felt better that way.

On Monday there was a note from Noreen, needing her help organising research for a conference she was presenting at in Cork. She was going to present a paper there and needed some help organising the research. Marissa called Sarah into the boardroom for a meeting. Sarah walked in with coffee and doughnuts.

'For the boss!' she said with a smile as she put them down on the table. Then she looked Marissa up and down. 'Hey, Marissa, you look like you had a good weekend? You're all smiling and glowing and stuff.'

'Yes, I did, thank you.' Marissa chose the strawberry doughnut and bit into it. 'Thanks, it's yummy.'

'Fresh from that guy who's near my flat. So, how did it go with that guy from the Reiki workshop?'

Marissa blushed, 'I had fun. He's really nice. I missed the last DART, so I ended up staying at his place.'

'Ooh! Go, you!' Sarah bit into a chocolate doughnut.

'What about you? What happened with that guy you told me about last week?'

Sarah wiped the chocolate off her face. 'It's more like three different guys! I know yes, it's crazy, isn't it. I wasn't sure about it, but it's so much fun, AND I don't know which one I like best, so I'll just go with it for now!'

Marissa did a double-take.

'Ha, ha! Yeah. Richard, Kevin and Thomas! I decided not to be serious with any of them, and I really am having so much fun, it's much better than being exclusive.'

'I'm afraid to ask, but do they know about each other?'

'Well, Richard knows about Kevin, Thomas knows about Richard *and* Kevin, and Kevin doesn't know anything about Thomas or Richard! It certainly makes my life more interesting!'

'How do you keep track of them all? And what you tell them? And which one is which?!'

Sarah laughed. 'Ha ha, it's a challenge, but sure, what else am I gonna be doing?! Now missus, enough about me. Tell me all about your new beau.'

Just then, Marissa's phone buzzed a text from ... Matt.

'It's him!' said Marissa, blushing. 'I swear he knows when I'm thinking of him or talking about him. He's sent a funny picture, look.'

She showed it to Sarah, and they both laughed.

'He's got a good sense of humour,' said Sarah. 'Can you send it to me? I think Kevin would love it!'

'Sure,' said Marissa.

'And so would Richard! Oh dear! I get them confused a little bit too. But back to you - is it serious, like? Between you and Matt?'

'No, it's too soon for that. He is fun, he's told me that he likes me. And I like him, I feel very relaxed around him. He doesn't play games. At least, I don't think he does. Guess I'll find out as time goes on.'

They had been texting each other all day trying to figure out when would be good to meet up before Marissa left for Clifden. Wednesday was Marissa's only free night that week but that was when Matt had his Tai Chi training. He seemed disappointed, but there didn't seem to be much they could do around it. She figured if it was meant to work out, something would open up. It was later that Monday night when he texted her with another suggestion. Late movie after ur class tmorw? or after mine on Wed?

Marissa knew if she didn't get her sleep she'd not be able to get everything done in time to travel, and she really wouldn't be awake enough for a movie after college.

Let's leave it till I'm back? I'm not in a rush – r u?

There was no reply. She felt a weight around her. *Sadness?* Was she feeling Matt's disappointment? She was only slightly disappointed, so it must have been his? *Can we feel other people's emotions?* She felt an answer come from deep within, 'Yes.' *Fair enough!*

She was at the lake. The water was still, the mountains around it were filled with an immense energy of peace. Marissa was standing on the shore looking outwards towards the stepping stones where she had found herself many times before. There was a whistling of wind above her head. A bird cried out, she looked up and saw its wings, beyond that was a stark blue sky with a single cloud moving across it. The cloud looked like a dragon, but then it shifted into an abstract form.

'You are doing very nicely,' said a voice behind her, giving Marissa a fright. She turned around and saw the medicine woman from Peru wearing her ceremonial outfit, the one she had worn that night outside the city. Marissa had a sudden urge to bow, she did it without thinking and the woman laughed loudly, echoes of laughter bounced off the mountains and back again. The bird circled around them both, then cried out once more.

The medicine woman held out her hand and the bird came and landed on the woman's arm. It was a bird of prey, a large eagle or hawk, Marissa wasn't sure which. The bird and the woman seemed to have an exchange, the bird nodded its head, then flew away.

The medicine woman turned to Marissa and said, 'My medicine is your medicine.'

The Navajo medicine woman, Emelda, appeared and stood beside the woman from Peru. Both women seemed to approve of each other.

'My medicine is also your medicine,' said Emelda.

'You have great lineage through past lives, and ancestors' said the Peruvian medicine woman. 'We want to help you.'

Emelda nodded her agreement. 'You will need our help soon,' she said, looking suddenly very serious. 'Do not meddle with things that are not your business.'

'I agree, no meddling. But you are more powerful than you think,'

said the Peruvian woman, clacking her teeth and nodding.

Marissa had no idea what to say to either of them, she really wanted to know the Peruvian woman's name, but as she began to speak, nothing came out. 'Now is not the time' is what she felt inside. She felt deeply honoured to have this meeting with them both, it all seemed very real to her, she could see every detail, the colours of their cloaks, the lines on their faces, how different they seemed to each other, but how familiar they both felt to her.

'It is good you are talking with angels,' said Emelda. 'Haniel would like to talk to you. Spend time in stillness and listen to her. She has many things to say.' The dream faded.

Marissa woke up groggy. It was only 3am. She turned back into the warm duvet and fell back asleep.

When her alarm went off, Tobermory was sleeping on the pillow beside her head. She sat up in the bed, exhausted.

'Hello, lovely cat,' she said sleepily. 'I don't know where I went last night, but it does feel like I went somewhere. I wish you could have come with me.' She stroked Tobermory's face, and he started purring in his sleep. She gave him a kiss, then got up to get the day started.

While in the shower she felt the weight of a warning in her gut from a distant dream, but she couldn't remember exactly what she had been warned against. She dressed, had breakfast and put her textbook for that night's class into her bag. She cleaned up the flat a little, put fresh litter in Tobermory's tray and changed his water. As she walked to the bus stop she remembered the image of both women looking at each other, and looking at her. *Haniel! That was it, I have to stay away from Haniel. But why?*

CHAPTER THIRTY FOUR 

The day at work seemed to last forever. Marissa was glad to get out and be in the fresh air once it was over. She had some time before she had to go to college to grab her usual sandwich and a drink. It was still early in the year, but the evenings were getting a little longer, the crocuses and daffodils were pushing up from the ground, and that day, the air was crisp and clear. She walked down the canal and breathed deeply, trying to clear the fogginess around her from spending a day inside the office building.

Why was she to stay away from Haniel? And there was another thing, but she couldn't remember. Oh dear. It probably was very important, but she really couldn't remember. *Next time I need to write everything down, even if it is 3am.*

College was buzzing, it was a hive of activity. They were taking the assessments very seriously, people were comparing notes, talking about listening skills, there was a nervous tension in the air. 'Are you ready for the assessment?' asked Kate.

'Why? I thought it wasn't for another few weeks?'

'Did you not get the email? There was an administrative mix-up, and they forgot to schedule one of our modules, so they're moving the assessments to this week, this weekend and next week, so we can start the next module on time.'

Marissa's heart leapt. 'Oh dear, no, I'm not ready. And I can't be assessed this weekend, I'm going to Galway.'

'You'd better tell Ms Greene then, I'm sure she'll understand. They didn't give us much notice.'

Marissa went straight to the classroom to find Ms Greene. She was at her desk with the college secretary, both of them poring over documents. She stood and waited for them to see her.

'Marissa, can I help you?' said Ms Greene.

'Hello, Ms Greene. I'm going away to Galway this weekend, to a workshop. I can't reschedule it, so I won't be able to do the assessment then.'

Ms Greene looked at the worksheet and made a few marks on it with her pen. 'That's fine, Marissa, you can do it tonight. I've swapped you with Mary B.'

Marissa felt a nervous tingle throughout her whole body. 'Erm, great. Thanks!'

'See you shortly. Can you tell the others class is starting 10 minutes earlier than usual?'

Marissa went back to the canteen, her shock must have shown on her face. She went and found her friends sitting together at a table.

'Well?' asked Kate.

'Are you okay, Marissa?' asked Yvonne. Emmet was there too, as was Ronan and Barbara. *Ronan doesn't actually look anything like Matt at all. Matt's much better looking...*

'Eh, yeah, I'm okay, I guess I just got a fright! I'm to be assessed tonight. I can't come in on Saturday.'

'Yeah, me too, I'm to be assessed tonight as well,' Barbara said, shrinking a little bit at the thought of it.

'Hey, I'm sure we will all be okay.' Kate's reassuring tone didn't help very much. 'We've practiced plenty, it's not as if we needed to learn something off by heart like we did at school. As long as we stay calm, listen, reflect and breathe, we will all pass with flying colours.'

She was right, everyone knew she was right, but the tension didn't lift.

'I suppose being assessed is like an exam, and exams are a trigger for many of us,' said Barbara.

'Oh totally,' said Emmet. 'And it's the first formal one. But remember, there's another two over the next couple of terms. So if you fail tonight, it's best out of three! But we won't fail.' They all breathed a sigh of relief. They looked around the canteen, it was busier than usual as the Thursday group were there, too.

'I wonder why they're here?' asked Yvonne.

'Yeah, maybe we are assessing them?' said Emmet with his eyebrows raised.

Marissa said, 'I just remembered, we have to get to class early, we're starting early so we get more time for the assessments.'

The group packed up their bags and made their way out of the canteen, telling people from their class as they passed them by. They took their usual seats in the classroom and waited for Ms Greene to begin. Just then, the door opened, and members from the Thursday group filed in and took the remaining seats. Ms Greene stood up and addressed everyone.

'Welcome to the Thursday group,' she nodded over in their general direction. 'It's funny to see how you all have segregated yourselves! We are all here, the Tuesday and Thursday groups are going to be starting assessments together today. I'm assuming you got the email about the missing module? To speed things up a bit, we will mix both groups together and work both tonight and Thursday evening and through Saturday. You don't need to be here unless you're being assessed, although it would be beneficial for you to see the assessments as there is always learning there. So some of you will be asked to come in on Thursday evening if it suits you and on the weekend. I've spoken to many of you, if you're not able to come on the day that we have assigned to you, please come up to me on the break.'

Ms Greene then read out a list of names and allocations, Marissa was indeed going to be that evening, along with some of the Thursday group and a few of her friends.

'If you have been called for Thursday or Saturday and wish to take the rest of this evening off, that's fine, and I will see you at your allocated time.'

Some of the people in the room packed up their things and left. The room seemed a little quieter once they had gone. Ms Greene asked the rest of them to rearrange the chairs so that there were two chairs up at the front of the classroom, one for the client, one for the counsellor, and the rest of the class were going to be observing. They made sure the observation chairs were far back from the assessment chairs to have plenty of room.

Kellie and Belinda from the Thursday group were called up to start things off. They seemed to be prepared to be first as neither of them hesitated to take their seats.

Marissa tried to settle in her chair and watch but she became agitated, as if an insect had gotten in under her clothing. She practised her mindfulness breathing until they took a break. She grabbed herself a cup of tea and went outside to the fresh air to breathe. She needed to do something to calm herself down as she was going to be assessed in the next round. She found a quiet spot in the garden, away from the smokers and sat on the small garden wall. She closed her eyes and tried to figure out what was irritating her. *I know I can do this, I'm good at this. So I'm not really worried, maybe I'm picking it up from everyone else?*

She got an image in her mind's eye of herself wearing her school uniform but she was covered in briars as if she had walked into a bush. She felt small and the uniform felt big. *I'm regressing because it's a test?* She imagined herself brushing the briars off of her arms, legs and chest, and as she breathed, she grew back to fit the uniform so she wasn't small anymore. *But I'm not a school kid, I'm in college, I'm an adult now.* She imagined that the school uniform was dissolving into the clothes she was wearing just then – black pants, a black and white stripy top and a grey cardigan. As the image in her mind shifted back to who she was now, her agitation seemed to settle down. *Archangel Michael? I know I've not asked you for things lately, I'm sorry. I've been caught up. Please can you come? I need some help – can you put your cloak around me?* She imagined Archangel Michael putting his cloak of protection around her and she felt a subtle shift deep within, and felt more consolidated and centred. *Thank you.* Marissa felt a whoosh of energy through her whole body and the smallest touch of bliss, just like on the dance floor that past New Year's Eve, only subtler, less overwhelming, and it was gone as quickly as it had come. She breathed a sigh of release, feeling little lightheaded, but more confident. She looked at her phone, it was time to go in. She left her mug in the canteen and went back to the classroom to wait until her name was called.

Her client was from the Thursday group and she didn't know her, which suited her perfectly. She was in her mid-fifties with silver hair soft around a pleasant face. She smiled at Marissa as they both took their seats.

'Margaret, Marissa, you have fifteen minutes,' Ms Greene reminded them.

Marissa nodded at her, felt her feet on the ground, took a breath, then began. 'Hi, I'm Marissa. Whatever you say to me is completely confidential. I may need to repeat it to my supervisor, but it will not go further than that. However, I have to let you know that if I feel that you may self-harm, or harm others, I have to report that to the relevant authorities. If that's okay with you, then we can begin.'

Margaret nodded her head.

'Great. We have about fifteen minutes together. What would you like me to help you with tonight?'

Ms Greene was taking notes, and so were some of the people in the room. Marissa was trying to pretend they weren't there, that the only people in the room were herself and Margaret. She imagined an artist with a big eraser rubbed out the room and all the people in it. She and Margaret were then sitting in a blank space, which felt immediately wrong. She replaced the room in her mind with Room Three in Cabra. That felt better. She could relax into it then.

'Hi, Marissa. My mother is very sick, she's dying. I'm feeling overwhelmed. I'm afraid of losing her, but I don't want to be emotional when I'm with her, so I don't upset her. She hasn't long to go now, the doctors say a month or two at most.' Margaret's face became warm with emotion, and tears began to well up.

Marissa sensed that this was real. She sprang into action.

'I'm sorry to hear you're going through such a difficult time. It must be very hard for you to manage your emotions right now.'

'Yes, exactly. Some part of me doesn't want to manage them. I want to scream and shout and cry, but I'm not able to.'

'Knowing that you want to do that is good. Perhaps you could make some space to actually do it?'

'Oh I have, I have, but when I'm in that space, nothing comes out. It's like I go completely dull inside. I'm not running away from how I feel, but when I want to let it out, I freeze up, almost completely.'

Marissa didn't reply so she could give Margaret some space to continue.

'My feelings come out themselves, though, in the most unlikely places. I screamed at my son for no reason the other night, and when I heard the words I was using, I knew it was my grief talking. I cried then, in front of him. He's only fifteen and I didn't want him to see me upset but I wasn't able to hold it back. He seemed to understand, but I felt very embarrassed afterwards.'

The tears were falling now. Marissa reached down to the floor and picked up the tissue box, and offered a tissue to Margaret, who took it gratefully. Then she spoke. 'Emotions aren't something that you can switch on or off, depending on your environment. Making time and space to feel them doesn't mean they are ready for you.'

Margaret nodded and wiped her eyes again.

'I'm wondering whether you've told yourself that it's okay to feel emotional at this difficult time?'

'No, I haven't done that. I didn't know you could do that.'

'Do you agree?'

'Well, yes, I do. Of course I do. Maybe I'm not letting myself feel them when they surface naturally?'

'What do you think?'

Margaret took a moment to think.

'You're probably right, it's never convenient to cry or get upset, and I do try to hold it back.'

'What would it be like for you to allow yourself to cry when you feel like crying?'

Margaret laughed. 'That would depend on where I was and who was with me.'

'You would need to feel safe to let the emotions out.'

'Yes.'

'Where are you when you're feeling emotional?'

'I'm usually with my mother. With her, in the same room. I can see her deteriorating, it's so painful to see. She's not the woman I remember her to be. I don't want to hold that as my image of her, small and shrivelled in the bed, weak and proud, and afraid to die. It's heart-breaking.'

'And when you see her, how do you feel?'

'I feel angry, upset, useless. I can't fix it for her. She is going to die.'

Margaret started to cry properly this time. She took another tissue and blew her nose.

'You feel safe here to feel your emotions?'

Margaret nodded.

'And your emotions are right and proper. There's nothing wrong with them, or with you.'

Margaret nodded again and seemed to be pulling herself together.

'So maybe you need someone to be there for you, while you cry, instead of being alone in an empty room. Your son was there that time you cried. Who could you go to instead of him?'

'My husband. He's distant and doesn't like emotions, but he would be there if I asked him to be.'

Marissa checked the clock on the wall, they had just under six minutes left.

'Could you ask him to hold you, actually hold you, so you can cry?'

'I could try it. It might be nice to do that. Thank you.'

'We have a few minutes left. Would you like to try something with me?'

'Sure'

'It might be difficult for you to do, but it could really help. You described your mother to me, shrivelled in the bed, dying.'

Margaret nodded.

'Can you see her now, in your mind, like that?'

'Yes.'

'That is her, as she is now in this moment, but this isn't who she is. Can you tell the difference?'

'Yes, I think so.'

'With the image you have of her in your mind, can you see her shifting back into her old self, maybe when she was around twenty years old?'

'Why, yes I can. She was so beautiful back then, of course I didn't know her, I was just a baby then.'

Marissa smiled. 'Yes, you were. How about seeing her as you remember her best, when you were a little girl?'

'Ahh, yes,' Margaret's face softened, 'I can see her in the kitchen making school lunches for us, and adding in a piece of cake. She loved to bake for us, she was a great mother.' Colour was coming back into Margaret's face again.

'That's beautiful. Can you see her shifting now into how she looked when she was the same age as you are now?'

'Oh yes. Proud woman she was, very opinionated, but I loved her all the same. I mean, I love her.'

'Yes, I can see that you do. You've done amazing tonight, Margaret. Now let the image dissolve back into your mother now, as she is, small in the bed and sick.'

Margaret took a moment, it was as if the breath caught in her throat, and then she relaxed again. Marissa continued talking.

'See, feel and know, that your mother is all of these women, not just the woman you are caring for today. And her body is not her, it's just one part of her that changes over time. This illness, it's what she is experiencing now, but it is not who she is. She's the mother who is opinionated, the one who loved to bake and sneak pieces of cake into your school lunch.'

Margaret smiled and brightened up. 'Yes, that's clever of you. Yes, it's the truth. That really helps me. More than you know. Thank you – thank you so much.'

'Thank you for sharing with me. We have come to the end of our session now.'

Suddenly there was clapping. Marissa snapped back to the reality of being in the classroom with Margaret, she turned to the others and people were standing up and clapping, even Ms Greene was clapping.

'Well done Marissa, well-handled and what a beautiful visualisation to share with Margaret. You didn't falter for a second with this most important piece of work. That was quite emotional for all of us. Let's take a break.'

Marissa looked around the room again and saw that more than half the people had tears in their eyes, some of them were sniffing into tissues. *They must have done that exercise with their own parents in their minds as I did it with Margaret. Wow.*

Marissa went back to her chair to sit for a moment. Kate came over. 'That was amazing! How did you know to say those things?'

'I don't know, it just kind of happened that way.'

'You sure you didn't rob them from a book?'

Marissa nodded.

'How is anyone going to follow that session now? Really, woman. Such a hard act to follow. You have no clue how good you are at this. I'm stunned. Do you want tea?'

The night passed quickly as it was interesting to observe so many sessions one after another. Most of them were quite ordinary, but everyone she knew held themselves well, and got through it. There were moments where Marissa was almost jumping out of her chair, willing the 'therapist' to say or do something that she would have said or done in that moment, but of course, they never did. They finished up at 11pm, too late for a bus. Emmet offered her a lift which she gratefully accepted. *Just as well I didn't arrange to see Matt now. He'd be a wreck wondering where I was.*

'You know, you were just brilliant,' Emmet said as he turned the engine on and reversed out of his parking space.

'You were pretty good too,' said Marissa, switching on her phone and seeing 10 texts from Matt come in. She smiled, she'd save them to read later.

They drove away from the college and towards Marissa's house. Emmet lived relatively close to her but they never seemed to bump into each other outside of college.

'You know what I thought?' Emmet asked.

'No, tell me,' said Marissa, genuinely curious.

'I thought, after watching everyone tonight... Not me, of course, I exclude myself from this observation completely.'

Marissa laughed

'No, seriously. I thought that you were the only one who wasn't afraid to be with the other person's emotions. You didn't shut them down or change the subject, you gave them space to be with how they were feeling. It was different. You didn't talk, interrupt them. I think it's what we are supposed to do, to feel.'

'Yes, I think so too.' Marissa thought back on the sessions she had seen that night, she only remembered what they didn't do, what she wanted them to do. Maybe if they had done that, they'd have gone deeper into feelings. 'We need to feel, it's why we get stuck, when we don't allow ourselves to feel.'

'How did you get so wise?' asked Emmet. 'It's strange, it's like you've changed, this year, well, in the past few months. You were like us when we all started and now you've pulled out ahead.' Emmet stopped at a traffic light and turned to face her. 'Maybe you're on a different track altogether than we are. I don't know. I couldn't take my eyes off you when you were in that session. I hung on every word you said. It was like watching a movie.'

The lights turned green.

+++

Marissa enjoyed the texts from Matt and even sent back a few to him. She woke up the next morning to a Good morning text, which made her smile. She texted back: And 2 u 2!

She went to work singing a song to herself. She knew she passed her assessment and she was really looking forward to going to Clifden that weekend. *It's a pity Matt has Tai chi tonight, it would be nice to see him again.*

Work was, well, work. She didn't have her Olive session this week, it was going to be every other week for now. And now it was time to go home. Marissa got off the bus a few stops early and went into the supermarket to get some food for dinner. She couldn't decide what to eat, she didn't feel like cooking. Her phone buzzed a text, it was Matt, again. She put her bag down and read: Hey I really want to see you, what about a late dinner after my class pleeeeeeease?? I finish at 9

Feck it, yeah, why not. Where?

Class is in town, can u meet me in Morchello's?

Morchello's, that's fancy! She'd want to be hungry, just as well she hadn't decided what to cook yet. Wow really? she texted back

Yeah, I like it.. see you in there about 9:15? I'll get us a table.

Cool!

Marissa picked up some biscuits and sandwich food and let herself into her apartment. The air inside was stale, she opened all the windows and the back door. Tobermory looked up from his throne on the armchair, saw it was Marissa, then went back to cleaning his paws. 'Hello to you too,' she said. Marissa caught a glimpse of herself in the mirror, she looked tired. She made a sandwich and put on some music, then opened her wardrobe.

'Why are all my clothes black, Tobermory?' she said aloud, pulling out various tops and pants, all old, all mostly black. She found a red top at the back of the wardrobe, she pulled it out, it was a while since she'd worn it. Then she remembered why, it was the night that James left her. She stood, waiting with bated breath for the emotions to start, but they didn't. She felt a noticeable space where they used to be. I don't want to wear this out to see Matt though, it doesn't feel right. She threw the red top into the corner in her room. *I need some new clothes.* She found the dress that Sarah picked for her.

'Well, it *is* Morchello's,' she said, laughing. She imagined Matt's face, his hair, his smell, she imagined kissing him again and her stomach did a flip. She ate the sandwich in little bites and took a shower, dressed and put on some make-up. It was only 7:30. She pulled out a laundry basket and threw a few things into it for the weekend, even though it was very early to be packing. There was her drum, she hadn't held it in a long time, she picked it up and held it to her chest, she tapped its skin with her fingers.

'Hello, you,' she said to it lovingly. The drum seemed to respond to her touch. *I'm just being silly now.* She went into the living room and sat on the sofa. Placing the drum on her lap, she pulled out her pack of angel cards. She held them for a few moments before opening them, then she took out the cards and held them in her warm hands for another few moments.

'How is it going to go tonight with Matt?' she asked, then took a breath and pulled out a card and put it on the table. Haniel – Vision. The image of Haniel was very strong, she was wearing battle armour and holding a strong sword with lots of blue and red light around her. *Haniel, but I was told to stay away from Haniel... And what would vision mean? Is this about me and Matt, or something else?*

She put the card back in the pack and shuffled them, and pulled another card. Haniel – Truth. In this card, Haniel looked a little softer, more open, she had a pleading look in her eyes, as if to say, 'Look at me.'

Marissa shrugged her shoulders and put the card back in the pack, and shuffled again. Tobermory leapt onto the sofa, rubbed his head on her leg then settled down beside her.

'Third time lucky, Tobes,' she said and pulled a third card.

Metatron: Pay Attention.

Marissa got a shiver. Metatron had a cube in one hand, a looking glass in the other and he was sitting surrounded by maps and globes. He seemed to have an eyebrow raised. *I must be imagining that.*

Marissa felt a cold shiver going down her back. She fished out the other two Haniel cards, which she found easily, and put all three together on the table. Vision, Truth, Pay Attention.

'Okay, I'm listening. But I was told to stay away from Haniel...'

She got another shiver.

'*Was* I told to stay away from Haniel?' she asked out loud, and waited for the full-body yes. But it didn't come.

'Is that a 'no' then?'

There it was – very subtle, but a 'yes' all the same.

'So am I to talk to Haniel then?'

The 'yes' was a little stronger.

'Okay, wow. I totally got that wrong then, didn't I?'

This time the yes was much stronger. *Jeez, okay.*

She put the cards away and sat with her drum, trying to make sense of the mixed messages. Her stomach rumbled. She fed Tobermory, put the drum on her bed and got her coat. *Might as well go into town now.*

Dublin City Centre was busy for a Wednesday night. There were many couples about. Marissa went into a café she liked and sat at the table, ordered an Americano and looked up Haniel on her phone. She sometimes felt she could think better when she was surrounded by people.

Haniel is the Angel of Joy, one of the seven Archangels, also known as Anael, and usually appears as female. In Kabballah, Haniel takes care of the seventh sphere, entitled Netzach (translated as Victory). She transported Enoch to Heaven, where he then transformed into Metatron. Haniel is often compared to the Stars and the Moon. She illuminates our soul when we are in the darkness of fear. Call on Haniel to help you move through difficulties and obtain your own victory.

Wow. She's an important one to know. I wonder why I thought I wasn't to contact her.

She read the words again, and the word 'Netzach' caught her eye. *Victory. My middle name is Tory, as in victory...Or so Dad said. This is uncanny.*

Marissa's phone beeped a text: 'I'm here now, are you close by?' It was Matt.

'I'm a few doors down. I'll be right there. Lost track of time.

She paid and left, rushing down the road to Morchello's where Matt was seated and a little sweaty after his class. His face lit up when he saw her. He stood and offered his hand. Not knowing quite what to do, Marissa took it in both of her hands, and they both sat down.

'Wow, you look amazing.'

'Oh, you've not seen me dressed up before! Thank you.'

'You didn't... for me, I mean?'

Marissa smiled. 'Yes, why not? Sure I needed to freshen up after work, and this place is so, well, fancy.'

'I'm, well, I didn't get dressed up, you know, I'm coming straight from class.'

'I know.'

The waiter brought water, bread and menus.

'Cheers,' said Matt, then he got stuck into the bread rolls.

Marissa took a look at what was on offer.

'The spag bol is great here,' Matt said, in between bites of thickly buttered fresh bread.

'I might just go for the soup, I'm not used to eating so late.'

'Ahh, okay. Well, I'm having the spaghetti. It's my favourite.'

'And so I learn something new about you.'

They ordered and the waiter took the menus. Matt was lashing into his second bread roll when Marissa asked, 'Do you know anything about angels?'

He looked thoughtful for a moment. 'Well, a little, maybe. I've read a few books. I took a weekend workshop one time.'

He finished his second roll and the waiter brought the food. 'That was fast, thanks!' Matt took his knife and fork and proceeded to cut up the spaghetti.

Marissa laughed. 'You're not one for protocol,' she said.

'What do you mean?'

'Spoon and fork for spaghetti. You're not meant to cut it up!'

'It's what I've always done.'

Marissa smiled. Her soup was delicious. She took a bread roll from the ever-diminishing number in the basket as Matt hailed the waiter and asked for more bread. 'And butter, too, please.' He turned back to Marissa. 'Why ask about angels? Were you playing with your angel cards?'

Marissa smiled again. 'Yes. But I'm getting mixed messages. At least I think I am. My wires must be crossed somewhere.'

'Hey, why not get a reading done? Like, a professional reading? I know someone. She's really good, my sister went to see her.'

'Oh? That sounds like an interesting idea.' Marissa had never thought of having a reading done. 'Maybe after I come back from Clifden.'

Matt had already almost finished his meal and was mopping up the sauce with yet another roll. 'It will definitely be after Clifden,' he said. 'This woman is booked months in advance, she's that good. But there's no point going to someone who isn't good. Seriously. My sister was very happy with her.'

'Tell me about your sister...'

It was almost 11pm and the streets of Dublin were hitting the night shift. Matt insisted on walking Marissa to the bus stop. 'It's safer for you,' he explained.

When the bus came he was in mid-sentence so he hopped on quickly and was still searching for change as the bus pulled away. With a warm protective feeling, Marissa bipped her Leap card twice on the card reader.

'You're a mad person!' she said, smiling, as she grabbed the handrail and hoisted herself up the narrow staircase to the top of the bus.

'Maybe, or maybe I'm just mad about you...' he replied as he followed her up. Blushing, he sat down beside her in the seat she had chosen at the front of the bus. Marissa pushed herself into him, he pressed back, she stayed there, pressed against his warm body. She could feel the tension between them and was really happy that she didn't have to say goodbye just yet.

'What about your car?' she whispered.

'It's in a lock-up. It'll be fine,' he said, turning towards her. 'I really want to kiss you right now, do you know that?'

'Yes,' she said, melting just a little bit.

They practically fell off the bus when it got to Marissa's stop, and before she could catch her breath, Matt had pushed her up against the wall and was kissing her under the lamplight. He felt warm, heavy, soft, gentle... He smelt of sweat, garlic and sweet apples. His hair was sticking up all over the place and she felt so safe with him, as if she had known him for years. She kissed him back, his lips were soft and salty... They stayed kissing for a long time, exploring, and when they caught their breath, she took his hand and pulled him towards her flat. She put the key in the door and opened it. He stood at the door, waiting for the invitation.

'Do you want to come in?' she asked.

'I thought you'd never ask,' he said, and smiled.

CHAPTER THIRTY FIVE

Matt left at 2am. He had an early start the next day so he got a taxi back to his car. It gave Marissa some space to get her head around their new intimacy. She felt floaty inside, warm and fuzzy. She was glad, in a way, that he hadn't spent the whole night, it was still early stages. *One thing at a time*

She was lazing awake in the bed having woken up at 7. It was almost time to get up for work. Marissa could smell him on the bedclothes, on her body. *He's my first since James.* She found her phone and texted him: Have a good day today, thanks for last night, it was fun. Very fun. She waited for his text back, but there wasn't one. *He must be busy...*

She got into the shower, had a hot one, put on her work clothes and went in. She was still waiting for his text at 11am. *Very unlike him, he's always quick to text me back – was it because we were together? Did he get what he wanted from me? He's not like that, no it's just me making this up...*

Still no text after lunch. Marissa was beginning to get nervous. She had her clients that night over in Cabra, she had to eat but she suddenly had no appetite. She kept remembering the feel of his lips on hers, his hands, how gentle he was, how safe she felt with him... And now, no Matt. It didn't feel right, how could he just ignore her like this? The day seemed to drag on, and then it was time to trek across the city to Cabra.

Marissa had bought some new incense from The Angel Shop and she brought it with her to Room 3. She lit it but it was very smoky and filled the air with a pungent smell. *This really is quite unpleasant.* She tried to put it out but ended up getting ash all over the table. *Dammit.* She was cleaning it up when Fiachra walked in.

'Sorry, am I early? They let me in downstairs so I came up.' He stood at the doorway, not wanting to come in until Marissa invited him. 'Oh, what's that smell?'

'Hi Fiachra, come on in, I was just trying out some incense, it's was terrible! Sorry about the smell. I'd open a window if we had one.'

'That's okay, I actually quite like it.' Fiachra sat down. 'My mother burns that stuff all the time. Sometimes it helps me feel more relaxed.' He smiled at her, took off his coat and sat down in his usual place.

Marissa finished clearing away the mess, put everything into the waste paper basket and sat down. She tucked a stray strand of her hair behind her ear but it popped right out again. She tried to ignore it, and the growing ache in her heart, and she concentrated on focussing on Fiachra.

'What would you like to talk about this evening?' she asked, trying to get comfortable in her chair.

Fiachra seemed much brighter than he had been before, his skin was clearer, his eyes were brighter, he had brushed his hair and was clean-shaven. 'I think I've got an interview for a job,' he said.

That announcement helped Marissa pull herself back into the room. *This is about Fiachra, not about me. I WILL park my stuff outside until later.*

'That's fantastic! Do you want to tell me more about that?'

'Yeah, it's a friend of my mother's husband's business. It's an office job, it's not what I was hoping to do, but it's something, and I'm feeling much happier knowing that he'll be, well, maybe, easier on me, because of Mum and all.'

'And then things will open up more for you – it's easier to get a job when you have a job, isn't it?'

Fiachra sat back in the chair. 'Oh yes, most definitely. I think that's why I've been having such a hard time.'

Marissa nodded her head. She was trying to remember what they had spoken about in the previous session, it had escaped her mind completely. She shifted her weight again in the chair, still trying to get comfortable. Beneath what she hoped appeared to be a calm exterior, anger with Matt was brewing. There was no getting away from it. It was 6pm, and still not a word from him. She was starting to feel abandoned.

'Do you remember the plan that we made two weeks ago?' Fiachra looked at her expectantly.

She had no idea what he was talking about. So much had happened in the past few weeks, it felt more like two months than two weeks.

'Can you remind me?' she said, trying not to sound as though she had indeed, totally forgotten.

'About the girl? That I should get in touch with her?'

Marissa remembered something vaguely about it and nodded.

'Well, I didn't say it last time because I didn't have the guts to do it, but I did it! I called her. She was lovely, and she said she'd meet me. So I have a job interview and a date with Thérèse. Things are really picking up now.'

Marissa smiled, relieved that she could follow the train of conversation even though she wasn't 100% in the room. 'That's wonderful, I'm so glad for you.'

He sat there smiling back at her.

She looked at him. 'You seem much happier now than you were when you first came to see me. How are you doing in general?'

'Pretty good, I'm not as sad as I was. I seem to be making more plans, to do stuff I mean. Like next week, I'm meeting a mate of mine, we're going to see a match together. I'm not really into football, but it could be fun.'

'That's good progress. Speaking of progress, let's do a check-in on where we are together. We have had 3 sessions, this is our 4th, so we have 2 to go. Do you think that would be enough for you for the moment?'

Fiachra looked thoughtful for a moment before answering. 'Erm, yeah, I guess so. Especially if I get that job. I don't know what it is, Marissa, but coming here has really helped me. I supposed maybe just having someone listen to me. I thought a lot about what you said, about how long it can take for someone to learn how to listen. I think that it's given me an idea about my family, like why it's so difficult for them to listen to me. They don't seem interested, but maybe they are really, they just don't know how to do it.'

Marissa thought this was very insightful. She always listened to her clients with a high level of attention, perhaps they were also listening to her.

'That's something that people don't usually realise,' she offered. 'For you to be able to appreciate how difficult it is for someone to listen to you, or to anyone for that matter, without taking it personally, is a very big thing. It will give you more patience for everyone in your life, including yourself! That's really great learning.'

Fiachra looked like he just got an A for his homework, his whole face lit up. Marissa took a proper look at him, his face had colour in it, he was sitting up straighter, and he had made an effort with his clothing.

'Fiachra, when we first met, it was only a month ago, you wore a tracksuit I think? You were pale, unshaven, and you said you felt there was no hope in your life. Now you're sitting here with nice trousers and a clean shirt – did you iron it?'

Fiachra nodded.

Marissa smiled. 'So you've made an effort to look nice, you're talking about a possible new job, a possible date, and you're looking brighter and healthier in yourself. So if you're happy with how things are going, we can finish the six sessions, and then you can come back to Cabra if you need more. However, you may not get me as your counsellor. I just want you to be clear on that.'

Fiachra thought for a moment. 'Yeah, I think that's good. Two more sessions would be great, and maybe by then I'll have a job, so yeah, we can leave it at that.'

As soon as Fiachra left, Marissa got up and stretched, adjusted her clothing and checked her phone. No text. *Is he on Facebook?* She hadn't thought about that. She looked Matt up and couldn't find him, but she found ten other Matts with the same last name from all over the world. It was a little disconcerting.

Time was ticking and Cliona was coming. She tried to breathe out the anxiety, but it was getting more pronounced, and all her mindfulness work didn't seem to make any difference. Then she remembered her Reiki. She sat back in the chair and placed her feet flat on the ground. She connected to the Reiki light and drew the energy down into her body. She flowed it into her heart, up and over her shoulders and down her arms. She didn't feel very much happening so she placed her hands on her stomach and chest, as that's where she felt the most agitation. She started to relax a little bit. *He does like me, he's probably just busy today.*

A few minutes later her buzzer rang, then a moment later there was a knock on the door.

'Come in.'

Cliona came straight in and plonked herself in the chair opposite Marissa. Marissa realised that she hadn't given her a choice of which chair, as she was still sitting in hers. She took her Reiki hands off her own body and looked at Cliona. She seemed very tired, her eyes had dark circles underneath them and her skin was pasty, rough looking. Her hair seemed extra pink, the left side had been freshly shaved and she was back in fishnets and a short skirt.

Cliona crossed her legs, then her arms, then looked at Marissa. A single tear dripped down her face, smudging her make-up. Then she looked down at the floor and started jittering, kicking her top leg up and down.

'Are you okay?' Marissa asked worriedly, forgetting herself.

'Yeah. I mean, no, not really.' Cliona looked up at Marissa. 'Hey, I can tell you anything, right?'

'Yes, of course, and it stays here, between us. I won't tell anyone. I'm here for you.'

'Okay. Great.' Cliona looked at the floor again, then uncrossed her legs and crossed them the other way.

Marissa took a breath and brought her own awareness into her hips, her legs, her feet, and into the floor. She breathed out the residual anxiety that had been in her stomach and felt more grounded, probably for the first time that day.

Cliona seemed to settle a little bit. Marissa waited for her to speak.

'Yeah, well,' she began, 'I got angry again. At Brendan. Jeezus, Marissa, he's so good to me. He came back, we tried again and I lost it. Again. Twice in a row in two weeks. And now I've not heard from him in three days. Three fuckin' very long days. I've texted him tons and tons of times, I've said I'm sorry, I've left voicemails... He's just not responding to anything.' She turned in her chair. 'And you know what the worst bit is? It's me. I know it. It's all my fault. I'm so disappointed in myself. I won't blame him if he has really given up on me this time.'

Marissa took another breath in and out, waiting to see if there was more, but Cliona wanted to see her reaction. Marissa said, 'Well, you can't give up on yourself. And I won't give up on you. This isn't easy work, it really isn't, and it takes a lot of time. But we can do it if you want to. Only if you want to, that is.'

Cliona sat up and brushed her tear-streaked face. 'Yeah I want to. I think my heart is breaking. Brendan, he's such a good guy. You know, I see him with Ariana, she's only three, he's so good with kids, I imagined that we would be together having our own.' She got up, straightened her skirt and flicked her hair back and sat down in the chair again, this time a little bit straighter. She looked Marissa in the eye. 'Right Marissa, what do I have to do? Tell me, and I'll do it.'

Marissa was a little taken aback by the burst of enthusiasm. 'Okay, yes. Well. Where do we start?'

She closed her eyes and felt Cliona's presence much more strongly in the chair and in the room. She could hear Cliona moving about in her chair too. She decided she needed to seek some guidance so she opened her eyes and said, 'Can you give me a moment and I will figure out the best way to move forward with this?'

'Sure.'

'Can you relax in the chair there for a few minutes?'

'Yeah, I'll try. But I'm not so good at relaxing.'

A bell went off for Marissa. *If she can't relax, she's strung up all the time and then lashes out at the people close to her. She needs to learn how to let off steam, how to relax, really relax, so that she's in a better place more of the time.*

Marissa smiled, breathed out, then opened her eyes.

'Cliona, let's start with you learning how to relax. Then we can look at how you experience anger, what it feels like in your body, so you can catch it and diffuse it. You might not recognise it right now, but once you can relax, you will be able to feel it more clearly.'

'And can we blow up some more rocks?' Cliona said, cocking her head to one side and smiling.

'Yes, course we can.'

Cliona was much happier leaving the session than she was when she had arrived. Marissa thought it was interesting that Brendan hadn't spoken or texted her in three days, with her, with Matt, it had only been, well, less than a day. They had said in college that your clients could reflect things back to you that you were going through yourself. It seemed possible. Marissa felt much happier knowing that she did some good work with Cliona, but her heart really hurt, especially after last night.

She had a few minutes before Martin came. She checked her phone once more. Nothing. Her heart sank even lower. She was about to put her phone back into her handbag when it buzzed. Matt!

> Sorry, I overslept, didn't get home till 3.30, didn't want to wake u with a text. I ran out the door at 9.30 and forgot my phone. Must have been cos I had other things on my mind. All. Day. Like you. Can u chat?

A hot flush filled Marissa's whole body, from her feet upwards to her head. She felt a rush of relief pulsing outwards and a release of tension, more tension perhaps than she realised she had been carrying. Her face felt wet, as if she had been crying. She texted back: Got a client now. I'll phone you after?

Martin knocked on the door and she quickly switched off the handset and popped it into her bag, her face still flushed.

'Hi, Martin. Come in.'

Martin came into the room, took one look at Marissa and said with a big grin on his face, 'You *have* got a boyfriend! And that's my chair! Hey, it's okay, I'll take the other one.'

Once again, he gets the upper hand – sometimes it feels more like sparring than therapy. 'Please, you can sit here if you prefer,' said Marissa, getting up.

'No, you're grand – it's interesting to sit here for a change.' Martin hung his coat on the door and sat down, still grinning. 'So, what's his name?'

'Hey, who's the therapist?!' They both laughed, and Marissa softened a little. She decided to disclose to him. 'Yes, I've got a new boyfriend.'

'I knew it. He really likes you, his energy is all over you. Hey, is he the guy who was here the last time? He's much stronger in your aura now.'

Marissa felt tingles up and down her body. She was dying to ask Martin how he knew, what else he could see, but that was being silly and not the purpose of their meetings. She was also trying to catch her breath from Matt's text. She pulled her awareness into herself and into the room as best as she could.

'Let's make this about you, okay? How are you? What's been going on for you this week?' Marissa became firm, well, as firm as possible, considering the circumstances.

As they talked roads and weather, Marissa felt herself calming down. She felt a little exposed, mind you, that Martin could see everything about her was unsettling. But she felt after the last couple of sessions that she could relax a little more around him. But then the session took an unexpected turn.

'Yesterday, I thought I was going to have a psychotic episode. I was getting nervous, so I started that breathing exercise you taught me with the butterflies. Breathe in and breathe out the butterflies. It seemed to help. But I can still feel it, threatening me. It's on the edges, creeping closer, I can feel it coming for me.'

Marissa knew that Martin was more comfortable talking with her now, but here he was heading into unknown territory and she felt the need to be on full alert. She shifted in her chair, placing her two feet on the ground.

'I need to ask you, are you taking your medication?'

'Yes, and I told my mother too. Just in case it came on.'

'Okay. How can I help you with this?' *Maybe it's not as bad as I thought.*

'I don't know. I guess I just thought I should tell you.'

Marissa really didn't know where to go with it. She was always told to bring everything back to feelings so she asked, 'What does it feel like?'

Martin slowed down for a moment and thought about it. 'It's like worms, crawling out of the woodwork, crawling closer and closer to come and get me.' Martin's face became pale and distant. 'The worms, they're so big, they come closer and they grab hold of me, wrapping around my arms, my legs... They want to drag me somewhere away from here.'

Martin's eyes closed, it seemed like he was fading out of the room. His presence was suddenly very weak. 'I don't want to go with them, but I can't stop them taking me, I'm powerless. I leave my body.'

He turned to her and his eyes flickered, then glazed over. He seemed to shrink and collapse into the chair. Then he sat up suddenly, his eyes opened very wide and he stared directly at Marissa with eyes that seemed darker than before. He said in a strong, completely different voice, 'And then I take over.'

Marissa felt prickles all over her body, biting cold fear pressing in all around her, it was as if she was pinned to the chair, she couldn't move. Martin looked like he was 3ft taller, distorted, somehow, yet was still sitting down. He was still staring at her. He smiled, his smile seemed too big for his face, it was malevolent.

He spoke. 'Hello, Marissa. Nice to see you again.'

The voice was definitely not Martin. Sharper, darker, elegant, piercing right through to someplace deep inside of her. Each word was perfectly pronounced, with immaculate intonation.

Marissa was suddenly terrified. She called out the first name that came to her lips – it was an effort to part them, the word escaped almost like a hiss than normal speech. 'Haniel!!!'

Then she felt a blaze of red light, and then softness. Then, nothing. The room seemed to spin for a moment, then echo in its emptiness, compared to how it was just a few seconds ago. Marissa looked at Martin, her hackles were up, ready for a fight, but he was almost asleep, very pale. After a moment, the colour started returning to his face, and he gradually opened his eyes as if waking up from a nap.

'What happened?' he asked.

'I don't know.' Marissa was trembling. 'You were here and then you... well, it seemed like you went away somewhere. But you're back now.' Marissa couldn't, no, she wouldn't tell him about what seemed to come into his body in his place, albeit only for a moment. She wasn't even sure herself of what happened.

Martin rubbed his face and sank into the chair. He was pale again, but it was a different kind of pale, as if pasty from illness. 'That hasn't happened to me in a long time. I thought it was an episode coming on. Sorry, Marissa, if I had known, I wouldn't have come in tonight.'

Marissa was still reverberating with fear, and she felt violated too, by that voice, exposed. It saw her. And then it was gone. Whatever it was that had been there was definitely not there anymore.

She checked with her inner guidance system, her inner compass, and she got an all-clear. She felt a rush of cool air and a slight lifting of the fear from her heart. Her head was swimming with thoughts about what might have happened. Then she got a strong image in her mind of a glass of water.

'Water – Martin – would you like some water?'

He nodded his head. Marissa poured two glasses and they drank them down. She refilled them and they sat in silence. After a few minutes, Marissa felt like she was beginning to catch up with herself, but she knew that she was very shaken.

'Well, I don't know what happened there, but it was like you weren't you, for a moment. But you're here now.'

'Thank you. For calling Haniel, I mean. That was a good idea.'

She still felt the raised hairs on the back of her neck, but she knew in her gut that she, that they, were now safe. 'Yes, thank you, Haniel, for coming when I called. I don't think we have really met properly, Haniel and me. I'm relieved she came so quickly.'

Martin nodded. 'Can I go home now? I'm so tired. I just want to sleep.'

'Yes, of course. We'll call it a night. Look after yourself.'

Marissa helped Martin get his coat and walked him to the door. He left, coat under his arm.

Turning back to the room, Marissa got a cold shudder down her back. She really couldn't explain what had happened. *So much for the sage. What the hell was that? Somehow, something must have gotten inside of Martin. That's what it seemed like. Whatever it was. It was horrible, dark, it... Oh, I don't know. I don't want to think about it right now. It's too terrifying.*

Marissa didn't want to stay in the room any longer. She got her coat and bag, blew out the candle, turned off the light and left.

CHAPTER THIRTY SIX

Matt put three spoons of sugar into a hot cup of tea, stirred it and gave it to Marissa, who was wrapped in a blanket, shaking on the sofa in her apartment. She had called him in a state right after she left the room in Cabra. When she heard his gentle voice she started crying, and then she panicked, so he dropped everything and met her at her apartment. The more Marissa thought about what had happened, the worse it got.

Matt put the tea on the coffee table and sat down beside her putting his strong mechanic's arms around her and they rocked in a hug until she felt better.

'Have some tea, love. It will help, the sugar is good for shock.'

'You called me love,' Marissa said, finally smiling.

'Oh, sorry.'

Marissa smiled wider, 'Hey, I liked it. Thank you.'

Matt smiled and nudged her towards the tea. She picked it up and drank some. He was right, the sweetness revived her, it helped bring her back into her body and stabilise.

Tobermory wasn't sure about Matt, he had stayed away the other night and now he was staring at him from across the room, very suspicious of him.

'I don't think your cat likes me,' said Matt, glancing over at Tobermory.

'He will have to get used to you,' said Marissa. 'Thanks for coming over. I was too scared to be on my own.'

'I could get used to this myself,' said Matt with a grin. Marissa shrugged off the blanket, she was still in her coat underneath.

'Are you getting warmer? That must have been some shock you got.'

The image of Martin's face with his wide eyes and large smile staring right at her was imprinted on her brain as if a branding iron had forged it there. *Or was it Martin? What was it?* She couldn't get it out of her head.

'It wasn't Martin, it was... a thing. Some kind of thing got into his body. I'm not able for this, it's too powerful, too much for me.'

Matt helped Marissa take off her coat. He put his arms around her again and kissed her face. She softened. 'I'm here, I've got you now. You're okay. Maybe we should phone someone about this, but it's too late tonight. I'll stay with you, if you want me to.'

'Yes, please.'

'Have you eaten?'

'I'm not hungry.'

'I'll put something together for us anyway, and if you don't want it, that's okay.'

Matt got up, went to Marissa's tiny kitchen and opened the fridge, then looked through her cupboards to see what was there. Marissa lay back in the chair, feeling the support of the sofa and the comfort of Matt's presence. Tobermory crept over to her and jumped up, and sat in her lap. He started purring right away. The sugar had helped, the weight of the cat on her lap also helped, and Matt making noises in the kitchen lifted her heart. She wasn't alone anymore.

Marissa pulled her mind into the room and focused on what was there. It helped her feel more like herself again, and she was very grateful for Matt, she watched him as he cooked, she didn't mind him going through her cupboards. She closed her eyes and asked Haniel to come and take the image of Martin out of her brain. But nothing shifted. His face was distorting now in her mind, looking like a cartoon Dracula from one of the tv shows she used to watch as a girl. It shifted back into Martin's face, only his eyes were pleading, he wanted her to help him, but she didn't know how. *I'm stronger than this.* Then she heard that voice echoing in her mind, 'Hello, Marissa'. It gave her prickles down her back, but not as bad this time. *Was I just replaying that in my mind, or is it here? No, it's my mind. Playing tricks on me.*

Matt came over with toast, a fried egg and a tomato. 'I hope this is okay.'

'Yes, it's great. Thank you.'

He put it on the coffee table and went back to get his own plate. He sat down beside her. 'Oh, I forgot the cutlery!'

'I'll get it,' said Marissa, gently placing Tobermory onto the sofa as she got up. Her body was stiff and sore. She went over to the drawer and got two knives and two forks, she found the salt and pepper and brought everything over to the table.

Matt had already started into his food. 'Eat something,' he said, with his mouth full.

Marissa looked at this man, so kind, soft, gentle with her, and something inside her melted. Something hard and old, something that felt like it was to be discarded, it was past its time. She felt new growth in her chest, like a bud opening. She looked at Matt as he shovelled egg onto the toast and then into his mouth and she smiled. He was like a big teddy bear, but he was strong, too.

'He said he could see your energy in my aura,' she said.

Matt stopped eating and turned to her. 'Who said?'

'Martin. He could see you in my energy field. '

Matt smiled. 'Well, I guess I could be in there... I'm always thinking about you. But I won't be happy until you've eaten your egg.'

Later that night, curled up in bed together, the curtains left open so that the night sky could throw some light across the duvet, Marissa felt safe. The images were slowly dissolving away, Matt's strong arm was around her, and she knew nothing could hurt her. Not tonight, anyway.

Marissa woke up with a start. 'Oh God, I'm going to Clifden today, and I've not packed or anything!'

Matt was still sleeping beside her. He rolled over and groaned. 'Is it time to get up?'

Marissa looked at her phone, it was 6.30am. 'It's still early. Thank goodness. I've got time to sort myself out.' She lay back down and turned towards him. 'Hey,' she said softly.

He smiled. 'Hey yourself.'

'You're lovely to me. Thank you for looking after me so well.'

'You're lovely too. And you got through the night. And you'll be with people all weekend.' Matt raised himself up using his arms, and he sat up in the bed. 'Listen, I think you're going to the right place, you can talk to Séamus about what happened and get his help, in case it happens again. Not that it will, but you never know.'

Marissa brightened up considerably. 'Yes, you're totally right. I must ask Séamus about this. The timing is good. I'd better get up and get my stuff together.'

'I'd better get up too, I've got to get to work.' Matt got out of bed and came back with his toothbrush.

'Hey! Where did you get that?'

'It was in my coat, you know, just in case!'

They both laughed. Laughing was good, it felt good, like an antidote to the poison of the last eight hours. Marissa got up and stretched, pulled her old rucksack down from the high shelf in the wardrobe and started throwing things into it from the laundry basket.

Matt took a shower and put on the same clothes he was wearing when he arrived. 'I've to get a bus and the DART so I'd better go now, I'll get breakfast on the way to work – text me later? Tell me how you're doing?'

'Yeah. Deffo.'

'Okay. See you soon.'

Matt kissed her softly on the lips, and Marissa let herself feel their connection, the new bond between them. He then let himself out of her flat, which suddenly seemed much quieter without him.

Marissa went to the back door and opened it to let the air inside. Tobermory went straight outside. She followed him and cleared away, then sat in her favourite spot. Everything seemed so ordinary, as if nothing at all had happened. The tree was still there, the flowers were budding up, the air was fresh, birds were singing and the sun was rising. It could be any ordinary day. She stayed outside for a few minutes in silence. The world was turning, the spider was building a cobweb in the bush in front of her. Everything in the garden was alive, moving, shifting, whether she was in it or not. She imagined her worries dissolving, it felt good. She felt a strong presence beside her. She asked herself if it was Archangel Michael. She heard a voice in her mind, 'It will be okay.'

'Thank you,' she replied. She saw Archangel Michael nodding to her in her mind, then backing away and disappearing.

'Haniel? Can I talk to you?'

There was a softness there that wasn't there before. A kindness and a gentleness, feminine, but strong.

'Hi. It's me, Marissa. But you know that already,' she giggled. 'What a day, what a thing to happen. What was that? What happened? Is Martin okay?'

Marissa heard the question come out of her mouth before she could realise, and she felt a 'Yes' echo throughout her body. But she got a sense that it was more complicated than that. A feeling of 'All in good time' reverberated throughout her body. 'Leave it now. Go to your workshop.'

Yes, I should leave it for now, but it's hard.

Marissa made it onto the 11.25am train as planned. She had gone into work for a couple of hours, bringing her packed rucksack and her drum, and she even remembered her black stone from Greystones, too. The drum received a few raised eyebrows but she didn't care. Sarah said she was good to hold the fort for the afternoon, Marissa knew that she'd be cutting off early, either with Thomas, Kevin or Richard, as Noreen was in Switzerland. Possibly even at lunchtime. But sure, that's the joy of being an employee, and she would have probably done it too if she wasn't a manager now.

Marissa felt her eyelids closing as she rocked to the rhythm of the train. She was still tired, even though Matt had stayed with her, she hadn't slept well. Aside from all of the excitement of the night before, she wasn't used to sleeping with another person. Matt was like a rock when he slept, he hardly moved at all, which made it easier, but he did snore, just a little bit. It was strange to have another person there beside her through the night, strange in a nice way. She leant her head against the train window and felt the humming of the engines as the train took her through the countryside and out into the heart of Ireland.

The train was pulling into Tullamore when her phone buzzed a text from Terry.

> Hello Missus, what time do u arrive in Galway? I'm heading there from Cork now, been driving 2 hours should be there in an hour. Want a lift?'

She brightened up. 'Yes please, I'm at Tullamore, my train gets in @ 1:45'

'U will b there b4 me. Call u when I arrive. Can't wait 2 c u.'

'Yay!'

Marissa had been dozing. When the train pulled into the station she grabbed her rucksack and drum, and got out onto the platform. Just then, her phone rang.

'Terry! Would you believe it? I'm just out of the train now!'

'Ha! I'm right here – look outside, I'm waving at you!'

She turned to the main road and saw Terry, phone in one hand, with the other in the air waving at her madly!

She waved back and hung up the phone, picked up her gear and went outside. Terry seemed very happy to see her and he hugged her tightly. They put her rucksack in the boot. He was wearing tight white leather pants and a sky-blue tee shirt with a matching white leather jacket. His bleached blonde hair had been freshly cut and he had a quiff of a fringe that fell over his pale blue eyes. His car was much tidier. 'I was expecting company this time!' he said laughing. 'Want to get a coffee first? I need a break from driving.'

'Oh yes, please, and I need to get a few supplies for the weekend now that I know what we're up against!'

'And so it is!'

In the car on the way to Clifden, Marissa wanted to tell Terry everything about the night in Cabra with Martin but something held her back. She thought she should talk to Séamus first. Thankfully the images of Martin's face had faded right down, and anyway, all Terry wanted to hear about was Matt.

'So, have you slept together yet?'

'You have a one-track mind!' Marissa said, laughing.

Terry winked. 'Maybe, maybe not. But what's poor old Zaad going to do now that you've got a boyfriend?'

Marissa had totally forgotten about Zaad. 'I don't know,' she said. 'Was there anything there between us really? Just insinuation and a little bit of tension... Anyway, I can't bring a nice Muslim boy home to my Jewish mother. She'd probably have a heart attack!'

Terry thought this was hilarious. 'Yeah! Maybe you should do it anyway, just for a laugh – or you could take me home with you, a gay Protestant from Cork. Which would be worse?'

They both laughed. Marissa felt happy. 'Well, my brother would be encouraging me to bring you back with me, in fact, he'd want to be there when I did it! But really, I've not told them about Matt yet, I'm not ready to. It's still too new.'

'Where did you meet him?'

'At a Reiki workshop – hey, I'm Reiki Level 1 now!'

Terry bowed his head towards Marissa as he held onto the steering wheel. 'It's an honour to meet you, Ms Reiki Level 1.'

As they pulled into Clifden Town, Terry said, 'Let's have a blast this weekend, yes? No drama.'

'And no Teletubbies!' Marissa added.

Terry shivered. 'Ooh, I'd forgotten about that. Yeah, I do declare this a Tellytubby-free zone.'

'Do we meet the others here, or do we continue on to the Monastery?' Marissa asked.

'I'm not sure. I need some petrol anyway. I'd like to have a full tank in case I need to make a quick getaway.' Terry winked. 'So let's find a petrol station and we can text or phone the others.'

They pulled into a local station that still had old fashioned gas pumps. Terry hopped out and popped the petrol cap, then hooked up the petrol pump. Marissa leafed through her wallet and pulled out some money. 'Here, let me pay.'

'Ahh no, sure, I've been driving all the way up from Cork. And I want to fill the tank.'

'Half then?'

'Okay, half. Thanks. But I get to drive you back to Galway, and that's included in your half.'

Marissa gave Terry a €50 note and then scrolled through her phone's contact list to find Jenny's number.

Just as she was about to call her, Saoirse texted: Hey! I think we drove past u, r u with Terry? I saw his car on the road!

Marissa texted back: Yeah, getting petrol now. See you there?

Yeah! Can't wait.

'Terry? Saoirse just passed us out on the road. She's going straight to the Monastery. We can just keep going so.'

'Great stuff,' said Terry, coming back after paying with two ice creams. He handed the change and an ice cream to Marissa.

'Ooh, Magnum, my favourite! How did you know?'

'Who doesn't like a Magnum? I got some Tayto's too, in the boot, they were sorely lacking last time.'

'Indeed they were!'

They got back into the car. Terry reset the GPS to the Monastery.

'I wonder will the GPS be able to take us all the way there, after the last time... Sure, we will see...' He started the car. 'So, who really annoys you in our group?' Terry asked as he pulled out onto the road.

Marissa hadn't expected that question. 'Wow, you know, if I decide that now, then they will probably annoy me even more than they did! Anyway, maybe everyone is different this weekend, I know I am. I've changed, it's only been a month or two, but it feels like it's been a year since we met the last time.'

Terry scratched his head. 'Marissa, you're so much nicer than me. Really, I've been hoping that something's happened to Liz, and she won't turn up. That's so mean, isn't it?'

He cocked his head to one side, and for a moment reminded Marissa of a puppy dog wanting to play. She laughed.

'Mean? I don't know, maybe. Or maybe it's self-preservation. Liz does take a lot out of a person. I felt very tired after working with her the last time. I would prefer not to. But maybe if we know that she does it, we could protect ourselves from it.'

Terry thought for a moment. 'But what do we do about it if we know she does it?'

Marissa pulled out her phone. There was a text from Matt, but she went straight to her web browser. 'Hang on, I'll see if there's anything online that could help.'

She looked up 'protection from people who drain your energy', and got an article called *Do you know an Energy Vampire?*

'Hey Terry, do we know any energy vampires?'

'Yes, that sounds like Liz, alright. What does the article say?'

'Maybe she isn't doing it on purpose?' Marissa read the whole article aloud, then came back to the one piece of practical advice. 'So we need to imagine a shield around us, and we are tight inside, and they cannot get into it. Do you want to try that?'

Terry was just steering off the main track and onto the smaller roads that lead to the Monastery. Marissa got a thrill of excitement as she felt they were getting closer.

'Yes, okay, let's try that. It could work, it's worth a shot.'

Marissa flicked over to read Matt's text. Hi love, r u ok? Just checking in.

Her heart flipped when she read 'Hi love'. She read it again, and once more, before she wrote back: Hi love, yes I'm good, I'm in the car with Terry we r almost there. I'm looking forward 2 the workshop. Call u later.

She looked at the text for a moment before sending it, feeling more warmth at her words saying 'Hi love'. She had never sent a text with that in it before. She pressed send. He texted her back right away with a big smiling emoji.

'Are you sending sexy texts to Matt?' asked Terry with a grin as he manoeuvred the car on a tricky turn.

'Ha ha, you and your dirty mind, no. Not sexy. Just nice. Nice texts. It feels nice.'

Terry smiled. 'Nice is good. I wish I had someone I could send nice texts to.'

'You're single?'

The car turned into the drive and started climbing up the big hill to approach the main house. It didn't seem to take as long this time, maybe because they knew where they would end up. The GPS managed to keep them on track, it must have downloaded the map. Marissa noticed how it was much greener this time. February, the trees were waking up, it was still early in the season, but there seemed to be more life around them.

'Could you not tell? Yes, single man, me, for a very long time now. I had a bust-up with my last boyfriend a year or so ago, so didn't want to get serious about anyone. But you never know. You can't trust a model – they look gorgeous and all, but they never text you afterwards. But now that Zaad's available...'

Marissa giggled. The big house came into view. In the light, Marissa and Terry could see it properly this time and in more detail. It was grey stone and there were gargoyles on the corners of the roof, although they couldn't make out what type of gargoyle. Two big planters were placed on either side of the front door with purple and pink flowers in them, crocuses and daffodils were starting to come up in straight lines at the edges of the lawn. There were a couple of cars there already, Marissa wasn't sure who owned which one, but Séamus's car wasn't there.

'He loves to make an entrance,' she said to Terry.

'Who? The big man?' said Terry as he parked in beside a blue Fiat.

'Yeah, that suits him. The big man. Séamus.'

Terry turned to face her. 'Honestly, he loves an audience, he's a bit of a showman. But I like what he has to say. And, he's good. But I'm taking it all with a big pinch of salt.'

They got out of the car and stretched. Saoirse saw them from the window of the main room and waved madly, then came running outside.

'Hi, guys! Hey, can you believe we are here again already? Great to see you!'

Saoirse was wearing jeans, wedge shoes, *Not the most practical shoes for here...* and a fluffy pink jumper. She ran over to Marissa and gave her a hug. She smelled like rosewater, her long hair was tied back in a bun and she had different glasses on this time, they had pink frames and made her look like a librarian. 'Can we share a room again?'

'Sure,' said Marissa, relieved to be on familiar territory. 'Love the rigout!'

Saoirse did a twirl.

'Maybe we can get the same room?' asked Marissa hopefully.

'I've already got it! Yay! Same bed okay? Do you need help with your bag?'

'No hug for me?' Terry asked.

Saoirse laughed. 'Of course, a hug for you!' she went over and hugged Terry.

It felt good to be back.

CHAPTER THIRTY SEVEN

'She admitted that she was terrified, she didn't like me doing it, she wanted me to stop. She actually made it sound like a threat!'

The 'Clifden gang' sat at a table in the kitchen with tea and biscuits, catching up on all the news. Terry declined to crack open the Tayto just yet ('I'm saving it for when we really need it.'). Finn was talking about his relationship with his sister, which had gotten into difficulties since he admitted he was doing shamanic work. 'I mean, come on already, just because you're terrified of something doesn't mean we have to not do it to keep you happy.'

Jenny thoughtfully dunked a biscuit into her tea and then said, 'Well, not everyone understands shamanism, there are many myths there, like Séamus said, and many people tend to run away from what they're afraid of.' She managed to get the biscuit into her mouth just before it turned into mush. She looked much older than Marissa had thought she was at first, Marissa could see several silver 'wisdom strands' glistening in amongst her brown curly hair.

Marissa chimed in, 'That's true, Finn, there's usually resistance to new things. I know my family always show resistance as a knee-jerk reaction before they even really listen to what is going on. Maybe she just needs some time to get used to the idea. And as you can show her you're not gone or radically different, she might settle down with it.'

'It's funny,' continued Finn 'because this is my second time doing the workshop with Séamus, I've been doing this for years already. The only difference now is my being able to tell them.'

The group nodded, taking it in, not wanting to pry into the 'why' in case it upset him further.

'I've not told my family yet, and I probably never will.' Stephanie helped herself to another biscuit. She was wearing a long lavender fringed tunic with sparkles woven into it, it was beautiful, and Marissa couldn't keep her eyes off it. 'You like my tunic?' she asked, smiling and turning to Marissa with arms outspread so she could see it better.

'Oh, yes, it's wonderful.'

'Thank you! I bought it in the market, in the city centre in Galway. You should go there sometime, they have some beautiful things.'

Zaad came into the kitchen. 'Hello everyone, it's good to be back here again.'

Marissa heard his voice before she saw him and she checked in with herself before turning around to take a look. *Yes, he did have a beautiful smile and very white teeth.* He was wearing a white shirt with a brown waistcoat and dark jeans, with runners.

'Hi, Zaad!' said Terry. 'Great to see you! Do you want some tea?'

'That would be good, thank you. It was a very long drive.' Zaad sat down opposite Marissa. Terry winked at Marissa and got up to get another cup from the shelf at the back of the room.

'How was your Christmas and New Year?' asked Saoirse.

'We don't celebrate those things in my house,' said Zaad, thanking Terry as he poured himself some tea from the teapot, 'but I had a lovely time, and I am very well, thanks for asking.' He smiled and looked directly at Marissa.

She smiled back. He's nice, but I'm not feeling there's anything special about him, or between us. That's a relief.

'Who are we missing?' asked Terry, looking around at the group. 'Besides Séamus, that is!'

'Liz isn't here yet,' said Stephanie, 'She texted me to say she couldn't get a half-day from work, but she'd be here this evening.'

'I thought she worked for herself?' said Jenny

'Sometimes you have to take the clients when they appear,' Stephanie said.

'What do you actually do, Stephanie?' asked Jenny. 'I mean, in your job.'

Stephanie laughed. Her laugh was warm and bubbly. 'I ask myself that often also. I am in a big financial company, we provide insurance to the banks. It's difficult sometimes in there, the energies can be very bad. But the money is very good. I think that's why I'm here – this work will help me be at work without taking on the bad energies there.'

'I work in an office too,' said Marissa. 'I was promoted just after Christmas. I have an assistant now, I'm a manager. But I don't know if I want to stay. I much prefer being a therapist.'

'I thought you were a psychotherapist already?' asked Jenny.

'I'm training to be one, yes. I've got a year to go, and then I'll have my diploma. It's a long road to becoming qualified.' added Marissa.

Jenny nodded.

'Hmm, interesting,' said Stephanie. 'I think I wouldn't like to be a private therapist, I will do therapy only on myself! But I want to learn about the magic that is here. I am fascinated with the things we cannot see.'

Finn looked at his watch. 'Hey, guys, I think we start soon. Has anyone seen an agenda for the weekend?'

Terry emptied his mug and started collecting everyone else's empties. Marissa followed suit and gathered up the kettle and some of the biscuit plates.

'Not sure,' Saoirse said, 'He left one up in the main hall last time, I could go have a look.' She ran out to look and Marissa admired how well she ran in high heel wedge shoes. The others helped clear the table and wash the cutlery.

Saoirse ran back in. 'Yeah, he's here, the fire's lit, and we start in ten minutes. And we have to bring our drums with us. See you there! Yay! Here we go!' She ran back out again.

They sat around the fire in the main room with their drums beside them. Liz was there too, looking a little flustered. She had a drum with her this time, as did Jenny. So everyone, and all the drums, were present and accounted for. Except for 'The Big Man'. He was still missing, and it was getting dark outside.

Marissa leaned into Saoirse and whispered, 'I feel like a little child waiting for Daddy to come home.' Saoirse giggled.

Stephanie was on the other side of Marissa and had overheard. She whispered back, 'Yes, I do too. I think he does this on purpose.'

Suddenly the door opened and there he was. He was wearing a Native American Indian style tunic, his trademark hat, a pair of tight brown trousers and cowboy boots. His drum was in a cloth bag which was slung over his shoulder, and his hair was tied back into a ponytail that hung down to the middle of his back. He had a small beard this time, he reminded Marissa of a lone cowboy from the movies she and Eli used to watch when they were little.

'Well hello there! How are yiz all doing?' Séamus cocked his head to one side and added, 'Did yiz miss me?'

Everyone laughed, Finn whooped for joy, and everyone clapped. He came in, bowed gracefully then hung his hat on the coatrack and put his drum case down by the fireplace. He stood at the top of the room and took a good long look at everyone. Then he started laughing, a big deep belly laugh which went on for what seemed like ages. The others looked at each other, wondering what was so funny. Finn started laughing too, and then Stephanie joined in, her belly laugh was warm and friendly, then everyone else couldn't help but laugh too.

'Good clearing, good clearing,' said Séamus, once the room had settled down. 'Now, to matters more serious. We have a lot of work to do this weekend. A *lot* of work. It's great to be back, eh? Let's open sacred space together before we begin. Have you learned the prayer?'

The group stood and opened space. Marissa was still unsure of the whole prayer, but she followed through with the others as they stood to attention in each direction, copying Séamus's rhythm when he drummed. When they had finished the ritual, they sat back down in their places again. The energy of the room felt crystal clear. They all looked expectantly at Séamus, who sat down in his usual chair at the top of the room.

'I got the homework, some very interesting journeys, yes. Some seemed ordinary, some of ye felt let down by that.' He scanned the room, then said, 'Yiz will learn in time. Don't be thinking ordinary is bad – no, indeed, for ordinary isn't always what it seems. Take it at face value, then ask for the hidden learning underneath.'

'Unfortunately, or fortunately, depending on your take on it, we have a very busy weekend ahead. Last time we met, we worked on recognising and releasing old patterns, and we asked for permission from our ancestors to step into our power. Many of yiz did great work since then, well done all. Now it's time to move on to the next direction but have no fear, the work of the North will always continue. We shed in layers, we are not logical beings, so don't be surprised if more ancestral work comes into play this weekend even though it's not our main focus. We just spoke the opening prayer, but you won't mind if I repeat the second stanza, for this is the work we are about to do.'

Séamus stood up and closed his eyes, he went very soft in his body and spoke, almost at a whisper. Everyone had to crane in to hear him.

Great Spirit of the East, direction of birth, of the sunrise,
of hope and faith. We turn to you to help us fly above our
problems, to bring in light to the darkest places, to show
us the direction of the next mountain we need to climb.
Support us and lighten our way as we choose to walk on this
pathway of healing, so we may rise to be the best we can be.

When he finished, he lifted his arms up to the sky as if to embrace the sun, and then the moon. Then he opened his eyes and sat down.

'The pathway of healing. Yiz are already doing the healing work, but yiz have the capacity to become healers, some of ye will be great healers.'

Marissa couldn't help but feel him looking at her when he said this, she felt it like a laser beam across the room, even though he didn't appear to be looking at her at all.

'This weekend we start the healing techniques. I'll tell ye more about energy and the energy field, and we'll have a fire ceremony tomorrow night at dusk. Lots to look forward to. Firstly, before we go into it, I want to know how yiz are all doing. So I brought my trusty friend with me.' Séamus pulled out the talking stick from behind the chair. There was a groan from the audience.

'Now, don't be shy' said Séamus 'So tell us how you got on with the work since we saw you last, and how you are feeling now – any questions or issues you might have that we need to clear relating to the work we have done, before starting something new. Everyone has a turn.' He reached across to the nearest person to him in the group, Liz, who got up and took the stick, then sat down again.

'Hello, Séamus,' she started. 'Hello everyone! I'm glad I didn't miss the evening session, I just got here on time.' Liz's short blonde hair was growing out of its pixie cut, thick curls were pushed out of her face with an Alice band. She looked tired but happy, and a lot brighter than she had been previously. Liz looked around the room. 'It's great to see you all again. I had a good break, I had no trouble doing the homework, but I did find that I had difficulty with the journey itself. I just wonder sometimes if it's real or if I'm making it all up myself in my head. I'd love it if you could answer that for me, Séamus.'

Liz offered the stick to Finn who was next in line. Finn looked at Séamus to see if he would answer, but Séamus gestured to Finn to start talking, so he did.

'Erm, hi. Yeah. I fell out with my sister over the holidays. I was just telling the group. She's afraid of shamanism, I really regret telling her about it now. I feel like it's my job to make her feel better. Anyway. Besides that, the break was good, I had a laugh with Saoirse doing the homework and...' Finn suddenly turned red, the colour crept down from his cheeks to his neck, 'I, erm, I got to know my drum better. I mean, there was one night where I just couldn't put it away, so I took it to bed with me. I don't know why, I just felt like I needed to.' Terry and some of the others sniggered but stopped quickly when Finn glared at them. Séamus nodded, so Finn handed the talking stick to Stephanie.

Stephanie took a moment and cleared her throat. 'I must admit,' she said, putting one hand on her chest as she spoke, 'I had nightmares after our weekend here. I saw ghosts in my dreams, I think they were the ones from here. A little girl, and a woman covered in blood. I'm a little nervous about what might happen tonight. I thought they actually came to visit me, it was so real.'

Marissa felt prickles down her back as Stephanie spoke. She vaguely remembered her dream of the ghosts, too. Interesting that she wasn't the only one.

'Other than that, which was *really* creepy, Séamus,' she said, looking at Séamus for some sort of approval. He nodded his head. 'Yeah, the journey work was beautiful, I met my grandmother in it, and she held me. I cried for a long time. It was really, really lovely. I am so grateful to have been able to meet her again. So bring it on, this weekend, but not the ghosts.'

This time everyone laughed without feeling like they needed to hide it. Stephanie laughed too, then handed the talking stick to Saoirse, who stood up to take it. She smoothed her clothes, adjusted her glasses and then sat down again on the edge of her seat with the stick in her left hand.

'I had the most magical Christmas ever,' she said, looking around to gauge the reactions, 'I felt like I was visited by angels. And strange things were happening all around me. My best friend's dog, I dreamed that it would be hit by a car, but it would be okay, and then a week later, it happened. I was surprised, but also wasn't surprised, it's very difficult to explain. I had to do the journey work a few times, I kept falling asleep to the drumming track that I made, so it took a few attempts to do the three journeys. And I had great fun working with Finn, we had a good laugh together.'

She handed the talking stick to Marissa, who felt butterflies in her stomach just before she took it. Marissa cleared her throat. She felt like there was a spotlight on her, like her every move was being watched.

'Hi, Séamus. I've been seeing clients for my psychotherapy degree and I took a Reiki level 1 course since I've been here last time. I noticed I was putting off doing the journeys, so I really had to make an effort to do them. Once I did, I realised I was avoiding looking at myself at a deeper level. I'm not afraid to do that now. I've noticed a change in me, particularly when I am around my psychotherapy college friends because they don't seem to be changing, well, not as quickly as I am. One of them even said as much to me. Anyway. I'm grateful to be going deeper. For me, this is the most important work, the work of discovering who I really am.'

Marissa was surprised to hear herself say this, but it rang true for her at a very deep level. She noticed Séamus nodding. Marissa handed the talking stick to Terry. As soon as he took it, the butterflies abated and she felt the spotlight, whatever that was, diminish.

Terry was full of bubbles and enthusiasm. 'Well, I just had so much fun with Marissa when we did our work together, I had a great Christmas, and I love love love coming here and being with everyone.' Terry smiled, and his face was alight, he looked beautiful, Marissa could see why he was a model. 'Anyway, I don't really have much to say, which isn't like me at all. I'm just happy to be here. And I brought Tayto for later, enough to share!'

Terry handed the talking stick to Jenny and took a bow, with lots of smiles in support from his new friends.

'I had a strange experience during one of my homework journeys,' Jenny started. 'I went on the journey to meet my spirit guide. It felt like there was a huge wall in the way, in between me and the guide. I couldn't hear anything they were saying to me. I'll never forget this because suddenly I felt a presence nearby. In the journey, I mean. It was something dark, nasty. Like it didn't belong there, like it was trying to break in. I got so scared, Séamus, that I woke up out of it and didn't want to go back on a journey for a few weeks afterwards. What was that? What happened?'

Séamus shifted in his chair, then asked, 'What did it feel like to you?'

Jenny sat back, pushed her hair away from her face and took a breath. 'Really, really nasty. Not creepy nasty, but darker, almost evil. That kind of feeling where your hairs stand up on the back of your neck.'

Marissa couldn't help but remember what happened in Cabra with Martin when she felt the same way. It was only the night before. *Not exactly the same thing though, this was real, in the room with me, Jenny's was in her journey.* Then she remembered Cheryl. She had almost completely forgotten about her. She felt a flash of fear ringing through her whole body. Images of Martin's face and Cheryl's suddenly appeared behind her eyes, distorted, conjoined, they were laughing at her. It was like a cartoon, disjointed faces surrounded by darkness and fire. *Now I'm making this up.* She used all of her willpower to push the images out of her mind and bring herself back to the present moment. She focused on the chair, the fireplace, on Saoirse's bright pink jumper, Terry's feet, Séamus's drum bag. They faded, and she felt more present, but the feeling of them lingered on the edges of her awareness.

'Interesting,' said Séamus. 'But you managed to go on the third journey a few weeks later?'

'Yes,' said Jenny. 'I wasn't interrupted again, if you could call it an interruption. I'm not sure what you could call it. Anyway, I wanted to share it with the group – did it happen to anyone else?'

She looked around the room. Marissa started to speak, but then she suddenly felt as if a hand was clasped around her mouth. She felt gagged. Her throat seemed to shrink and tighten and her feet felt like lead on the floor. Her arms got very heavy, as if in a dream where she couldn't move or walk. She broke out in a cold sweat, and her heart started racing.

'That's all I want to say, really,' said Jenny, handing the talking stick over to Zaad, who was the last one to speak. As soon as Zaad started speaking, Marissa felt as if the hand lifted, she felt released. *What the hell was that?* She was shivering.

Saoirse could feel her shivering and leaned in. 'Are you okay?'

Marissa nodded. Marissa was more determined than ever now to tell Séamus everything.

'I wasn't able to tell anyone what I was doing,' Zaad was saying. 'I don't know if I like keeping it a secret from my family, but I believe it's the only way for now. And I'm very happy to be here.'

Zaad finished his piece and handed the talking stick back to Séamus.

Séamus held the talking stick and looked at the group. 'You've come a long way, my friends. It amazes me each time I run an apprenticeship, it's as if everything speeds up. Each group receives their learning faster than the previous one. We need to make the space to process what is coming up for all of you. I don't want to move too quickly.'

He scratched his head and took a breath. 'I'm feeling that we need to park some of what I had planned to do tonight for a while and take a detour. I'm sure you'll all be happy with what I've got in mind. But we will start with Liz's good and valid question, as I want to answer that now, first. She asked: 'How do you know if it's you making things up in your head, or if the journey is real?''

He nodded over to Jenny, who smiled back at him.

'So, how do you know if your journey is real, or if you're making it up?'

As Séamus answered Jenny's question, Marissa felt like she was thawing, like ice in her blood was melting. She felt better, softer, more contained. It was going to be okay.

'Now lads, let's take a break and get a quick cuppa, and come back here in fifteen.'

Everyone got up to go, but Marissa hung back. Séamus stood at the fireplace, looking into the fire. The colours of the flames were reflected in his face and on his tunic. When the room was empty, and it was just the two of them, Marissa approached him. He turned to her and smiled.

'Something happened to me, Séamus, I need to tell you, I couldn't speak about it earlier. I don't know why, I just wasn't able to… Well, what happened scared the life out of me.' She felt small, once more like a child going to Daddy for help.

'Come here, gentle Marissa,' he said, and opened his arms. She fell into them and started shaking, he held her strongly and she started to cry. She didn't realise she was still holding so much tension in her body from the fright she had gotten. He was patient with her and waited until she calmed down. He invited her to sit beside him on the sofa and he handed her a tissue, which she gratefully received. She blew her nose and dabbed the tears from her eyes.

'Tell me,' he whispered to her.

Marissa felt safe, properly safe, for the first time since Cabra. 'Just there, what Jenny said. I wanted to share, just now, but I wasn't able to speak. It was like I was being gagged. I saw a hand over my mouth. I felt paralysed, like I was in a dream. Is this real? It's so scary…'

'There's more, isn't there?' Séamus asked, turning to face her with a serious look.

'Yes, there's more. I think it started before Christmas. I have a client, I do volunteer psychotherapy sessions. Anyway, my client, he can see things. He's been diagnosed with schizophrenia and bipolar disorder.' Séamus nodded his head, she continued. 'He seemed to, well, disappear the last time I saw him. Right there, in the chair, in front of me. And then something seemed to, well, come into his body instead of him, like it was taking him over. I don't know if I'm describing this right.'

'Don't worry about that, just get it out there.'

Marissa smiled and blushed and looked at her feet. 'Okay, well, it seemed as if a dark energy stepped into his body, Martin's – *Shit, I didn't mean to say his name, oh well* – 'my client, I mean, he changed. Like it was still his body, but it belonged to someone else, something else. This thing, it looked straight at me, and then it spoke to me. He, it, said 'Hello' to me. It sent chills down my back. It was horrible.'

Marissa wasn't able to look at Séamus while she was telling him this, but it didn't seem as horrible once it was out there as it had actually been when she experienced it. Nor as strange.

'Anyway, I called on Archangel Haniel, and as soon as I did that, the energy, whatever it was, left. Almost right away. And then Martin came back, like he woke up from a bad dream, only it was real.'

Some of the others had started trickling back into the room, they saw Marissa and Séamus talking, and they held back to give them space.

'We need to talk some more about this, but I need to ask you one thing before we start back with the group – did it, this entity, mention you by name?'

'Yes.'

CHAPTER THIRTY EIGHT 

Séamus extended the break and told Marissa to get a cup of tea as he needed to think. Terry came to find her.

'Hey girl! What's going on? Are you okay?'

Marissa smiled and put three spoons of sugar into her tea and stirred it like Matt had done. She held the mug in her hands and relished the feel of the warmth going into her body. 'Yeah, something happened to me over the break, it scared me, and I wanted to tell Séamus about it. It didn't feel right to tell anyone else first.'

Terry looked snubbed, like a child who was told they were a second-best friend, not the best friend. 'But I thought we were friends? You can tell me anything!'

'Oh, of course we're friends, Terry! It's not like that at all. Honestly, I was too afraid to talk about this with anyone else, in case it happened again. Hey, don't take it personally.'

Terry turned his back to her and lifted his nose up into the air. 'Well, Miss Marissa, if you're going to be so snobby, I'll just have to go find someone else to play with.' Then he turned around and giggled, then saw that she was genuinely upset. 'Hey, it's cool. Are you really okay? He looked like he was about to make a move on you.'

'Who?'

'Séamus, silly girl. Séamus has the hots for you.'

Marissa shuddered. 'I doubt that very much.' she said.

'Well, I'd keep an eye on him if I were you. Poor Matt doesn't know what he got himself into with you at all!'

'Matt! Oh my gosh, I meant to text him! I'll see you back in the main room soon.' Marissa hugged Terry.

'Seriously, girl, you can tell me anything, I'm here for you.'

'Thanks. I hear you.'

Marissa left her half-drunk cup of sugary tea on the table and ran up the three flights of stairs to her room. Her bag was open, half-unpacked on the bed, clothes strewn everywhere. She rooted through her things to find her phone. There were three missed calls and four texts from Matt. She didn't have time to phone him back, so instead she texted:

Hey, love. Sorry. Been caught up in class. I'm ok. I just told S, he is thinking about what to do. I'm relieved. Thanks 4 the calls & stuff. I'll phone u before bed? I'll text first. xx

She waited until the text had sent, which took a long time as she had to walk around the room to find a spot with coverage, but it sent. She put the phone by her bedside locker, got a cardigan and went back downstairs. The group was there, they were about to begin. Everyone looked at Marissa as she came in and she smiled at them. They were turning into a lovely group of friends. She felt their concern and their questioning and was grateful for it.

Séamus was once again at the helm, and once Marissa was seated, he began in a serious tone.

'In light of what we discussed earlier, we'll begin this weekend looking at protection. Some people say you don't need protection as everything comes from Spirit. While at some level this is true, at another level, they are completely wrong, and totally crazy if they think dark energy won't hurt them. There is dark energy out there, it is real, and it will creep in any chance it gets. Especially if it thinks that there are weaknesses and vulnerabilities to be exploited. In you, that is.'

Everyone was rapt with attention.

'These entities feed off of fear. And in this world, where everything we do is so often from a place of fear, there is plenty of food for the dark energies to feast on. Yiz are here to grow spiritually, to become healers, not fodder for the darkness. I usually don't cover protection so early on in the apprenticeship, however, I believe that sticking to protocol is not always best. That's a good lesson for yiz all, too, when you have a client, and you're looking at protocol and not at them, you're no longer serving them, you're serving your own ego, out of fear. It also means that you've disconnected from your client and you're unable to see what's right in front of you, needing to be healed. Not everyone is the same, and the same method does not work for everyone. You need to be flexible, alert, and very aware of yourself. "Know thyself" is the best protection that you can have, from anything.'

There were lots of nods as he paused to let the information sink in.

'This links back to what I said when I answered Jenny's question earlier – What you think and what you know, and what you think you know, verses what is actually there in front of you can be the same, totally, yes. But sometimes it's not, and you need to step out of the way, release your own expectations and do your inner work to become the clearer channel so that you are not judging, not attached to the outcome and not wanting to be right or have the upper hand. And if you're that stubborn, refusing to really look at the other person, or the situation, or the room that you're in, then you're not healing anything. You are coming from fear, or worse, from pride.'

'And now for the practicalities. First, I will seal the room and the building. This is similar to what I did last time we were here, only I never explained what I was doing. The fact I needed to do it in December should have indicated something was off to me... Never take anything for granted. It doesn't matter how experienced you are, there's always learning to do, always keep alert and on your toes.'

He proceeded to explain warding and sealing, explained that these were techniques stemming from Hermeticism and what would be considered witchcraft, yet they are actually shamanic, and very useful. Séamus got everyone to practice the symbology until they were confident with it. He then asked them to go up to their bedrooms and seal them in the same way he had just shown them and then come back down.

It was dark now, coming up to 8pm and they still had not had dinner. Marissa's stomach was rumbling as she and Saoirse looked down at their notes, then drew the symbols on the walls, ceiling and floor, and called in the white light of protection.

'I hope we get some food soon,' said Saoirse as they went back to the main room. 'I'm gonna faint, I didn't have lunch!'

'Yes, I heard that!' said Séamus, 'We are running behind, and the kitchens I'm sure are not happy with me so let's break for dinner, and come back at 9pm for one more lesson before bed.'

Everyone was chattering at the table, wanting to know what Marissa had said to Séamus. Terry stepped in as her knight in shining armour. 'Sometimes you just can't talk about it,' he said, helping himself to more mash potatoes. 'Leave the poor girl alone, she'll tell us in her own time.' He poured heaps of gravy on top of the potato. 'Mmm, I love mash and gravy. We'll be well protected tonight lads, no worries about those ghosties coming to scare us in the middle of the night this time.'

'I hope so,' said Jenny with a shudder. 'I feel a lot safer now anyway, now that I know how to seal the room off. I want to do it to my house too, I'll do it as soon as I get home.'

Everyone had second helpings, and then a wave of tiredness fell over the group.

'I'm going to take a walk outside to wake up before the last session,' said Finn. 'Anyone want to join me?'

'Yeah, great idea!!'

They all went together, walking twice around the building then splitting off into smaller groups chatting and catching up with each other. Marissa found herself beside Jenny.

'It feels better now, like we can properly start the work of the weekend. I think we needed to do all of that pre-emptive work.' said Jenny

'Yes, totally agree,' said Marissa as she walked on the crunchy gravel.

'I had quite a scare in my journey, but if you couldn't tell the group about what happened to you, you must have had a worse one than I did.'

'Yeah, it was terrifying, actually. I'm still not settled after it, and hearing you speak about what happened to you brought it up again. So I'm glad I'm here. It feels like I'm in the right place.'

'Séamus has his head screwed on. Not like some of them out there. Hey, how did you get on with Dolores? Now there's a lady who knows her stuff.'

Marissa smiled. 'Dolores. I love her. She's fabulous, and her workshop was great. I think the Reiki helped me get over the fright. I'm doing it every day, pretty much.'

'That's great, I love Reiki too. I must remember to do it on myself more often.'

They circled twice more and filed back into the building. Some of the group went to the bathroom to freshen up before the final session of the day.

The fire had fresh logs placed in it and was blazing hot. Marissa sat down beside Terry. 'Thanks for earlier, I'm glad we are friends. I'd tell you if I was able to, I just wasn't able to talk about it.' Terry leaned in and put his arm around Marissa, and gave her a squeeze.

'Look girl, I know. I was only messing with you earlier. Well, not really, you're canny you are, you know things. I want us to be good friends, not just surface friends, but real ones who can depend on each other. I'm a bit afraid of that, actually. I've been let down before. I guess I was just protecting myself.'

'Good friends sounds wonderful to me,' said Marissa. 'The secret to a good relationship is to always be talking to each other. So let's keep talking, and you'll know quickly enough if there's anything to worry about. Which there isn't.' She smiled at Terry, and he relaxed. He took his arm back and she leaned into him and pushed him a little, he pushed back and smiled.

'Right there folks, let's get started. I don't want to rush this part, and I know it's late, and you have full bellies and are sleepy. It's been a long day. But we are running behind. However, it felt right to do what we did, and I feel stronger and more confident starting into this section of work now.'

Everyone held consensus with nods and open body language. Notebooks and pens were at the ready.

'We are going to look at body mapping. This is where you map your client's energy field onto yourself so that you can feel what they are feeling. You need to set clear boundaries around this to ensure you don't take on their illness or pain as your own. You're just dipping into their field, exploring what is going on for them, and then disconnecting. The reason why we do this is twofold. People often are in pain for such a long time that they stop feeling it, and don't actually know where the source of it is. But also, people tell themselves a story around their pain, and that is most likely what they will tell you. You, as the shaman, cannot collude with their story. You must discover what is going on for yourself.' He let this sink in before continuing.

'It's easier to do body mapping when you have no expectations and no story. I know yiz are getting to know one another, but you've obviously not been telling each other which knee is sore or who has a bad shoulder. Tonight is the night to find out all of these intimate details.' Séamus winked.

'It will take time to learn how to do this well but we have time, and it's easier to do it than to explain it. Pick someone you don't know well, and find some space to work, and this is what I want you to do.'

After Séamus gave them a more detailed explanation, Marissa and Finn pared up. Everyone was working in the main room, there was a lot of laughter and banter going on. Séamus left the room to give them space to work. They had one hour. Marissa grabbed a blanket from her bed, and so did Finn. They laid them together on the floor where they could sit opposite one another. The pair had their notebooks open on the floor close by, and they kept looking at the instructions, trying to make sense of them.

'So, you put your foot into my foot, but it's your energetic foot and not your actual foot?' asked Finn.

'Yes, I think that's what he said…' said Marissa, leafing back a few pages in her notebook. 'Or was it the other way around?' She brought her attention back to Finn. 'Okay, I think I can do this. Can I try mapping your energy field first?'

Finn nodded.

Marissa looked at Finn's body. She looked at her own body. He was so much taller and bigger than her, it seemed a challenge to map all of him onto her little body. But she would try. She closed her eyes and felt her life force energy running through her body. She visualised herself as glowing, luminous, and then opened her eyes again, holding onto the vision.

'What do you feel?' asked Finn, smiling shyly.

'I've not done it yet!' said Marissa, laughing. 'Ok. Here goes. Finn, do I have your permission to map your energy body onto mine?'

'Yes,' said Finn with a grin.

Marissa imagined that her shape changed to mirror Finns, but she didn't feel anything change. Then she imagined that Finn's luminous energy body lifted off of him and sat itself onto her, like she was wearing a layer of his energy. Something felt a little different, so she closed her eyes and brought her awareness deeper into her own body. She noticed an ache in her left side that wasn't her usual ache. 'Do you have an ache in your left side?' she asked.

'No,' said Finn.

'Oh, I must be doing it wrong,' said Marissa.

'But I do have an ache in my right side, I get a stitch there from time to time.'

'Oh. Maybe we flipped around, so your left is my right, and your right is my left?'

Marissa felt a full-body 'yes'. She had not felt that sensation for several days and relief that she could still feel it flooded through her. Her whole body relaxed, and she lost the sensation of Finn.

'Are you okay?' Finn asked, 'Something happened to you, you've changed.'

'Are you mapping me?' asked Marissa with a grin.

'Yeah, I got a little bored waiting for you, so I tried it while you were mapping me. It was really cool. What just happened?'

Marissa laughed. 'Ha, ha, I guess we can say goodbye to privacy! But if you're mapping me while I'm mapping you, then are we mapping ourselves onto each other?'

'Now I'm totally confused! Ha ha! This is fun!'

It was time to finish up for the night. Everyone had had fun with the exercise, not everyone had success, but it was a great way to end a long day. Séamus bid them all a good night's sleep, reminded them of the fire ceremony taking place the following night, and asked them to report back in the main room for 9am. Marissa got a big hug from Terry as he went upstairs.

I hope it's not too late to talk to Matt. Marissa found her phone on her bed where she had left it. There was no reply to her previous text. She texted him to see if he was still awake. She sat on the side of the bed waiting for his text back, it was almost 11pm so he could be sleeping. She didn't get a message back right away, so she reluctantly got changed and brushed her teeth at the sink in their room, and climbed into bed. Her phone buzzed just before she closed her eyes.

Glad ur havin fun. Sleep well x

She smiled, turned off the phone and set her alarm for 8am.

+++

The next morning they spent most of the first session practising body mapping. There was a sombre atmosphere, everyone was taking the work seriously, and nobody had mentioned the events of the night before, but all of them had slept.

After the tea break Séamus started into the next part of their learning. 'Now, I'd like a volunteer, please – Stephanie, that's great. Come on up here to the front.'

Everyone moved over so Stephanie could pick her way up to Séamus. The fire had not been lit, it was set for later, the sun was out and shone into the room. There was a chill in the air, everyone had jumpers on, and a few of them had wrapped blankets around themselves. Stephanie was still wearing her sparkly fringed tunic, it was becoming her trademark.

Séamus held his hand out and she took it, turned and faced the others, and bowed.

'We are going to run energy up and down the body, it loosens up any lodged stagnant energy. Stephanie, do I have your permission to work with you? Good. Now, can you turn around please and face the window?'

She did. Séamus placed one hand at the back of her head and the other hand at the base of her spine.

'You can see that I've got one hand on the top, and the other hand at the bottom of Stephanie's spine.' Stephanie did a wiggle and everyone laughed. 'Yes, yes. We all have a natural flow of life force energy running up and down our spine, which changes depending on our metabolism, emotional state, etc. What I'm going to do is charge up Stephanie's spine so that the energy runs a little faster. Using my will, and my attention, I visualise the energy running from one hand to the other, and back again. It speeds things up a little bit when it comes to shifting blocked energies and the like. This is a basic manoeuvre that you will need as a shamanic practitioner. Here, I'm influencing Stephanie's natural energy field, I'm not adding anything in or taking anything away. But she needs to stop wiggling! Now, watch.'

Séamus proceeded to run the energy up and down Stephanie's spine. Stephanie started wiggling again. 'I swear I couldn't help it that time!'

Terry put his hand up.

'Yes?'

'What exactly are you doing, to run the energy, I mean? It just looks like you're holding your hands there.'

Séamus took his hands away from Stephanie and rubbed them together. 'When I do this, my hands get hot, yes?'

'Yes,' said Terry.

'So I can imagine my hands are hot, pulsing, the energy flowing faster. It follows my will, my intention, my own energy, and then Stephanie's energy follows mine.' He put his hands back where they were, one on the back of her head, and one at the base of her spine.

She started wiggling again, and she giggled. 'Séamus, I swear, I am not doing this on purpose!' He laughed too and took his hands away and sent her back to her seat.

'Ok, gang, off yiz go and try it. Then I want you to go for a walk on the grounds and pick up two stones from the environs that call to you, stones that want to work with you. Get the black stone you brought for the next session to go with them, as you'll need it. I've got a visitor coming this afternoon, after lunch. You'll like her. Brigid. She'll have some medicine cloths for you to choose from, for your medicine bag. We have one more thing to do before we break for lunch, so come back here in about fifteen minutes, please.'

Terry leaned into Marissa, 'Sometimes I have no idea what he is talking about.' He shrugged his shoulders.

'Come on, I'll ask my guides, we can figure it out together,' said Marissa, grabbing her notebook and her coat. They headed out of the main room and into the dining hall. 'Why don't you sit here, and I'll try to run energy up and down your spine?'

'Okay,' Terry replied. 'I'd much rather be sitting down anyway. Shall we get tea? We have fifteen minutes!'

'Why not.' Marissa put the kettle on, then came back to where Terry was sitting. She placed one hand on the back of his neck, then hunkered down and placed the other hand on the base of his spine. 'Do you feel anything?' she asked after a few moments.

'Just your hot breath on the top of my head,' said Terry, nonchalant.

'Okay.' Marissa closed her eyes and imagined a hot poker in between her hands, with the energy moving up and down. It took all of her focus and concentration to get the image right. Then she imagined it moving into Terry's body.

'Ouch!' said Terry, jumping up and shaking himself. 'What the heck was that?'

'Too hot?' asked Marissa.

'Jeezus. I've no idea what you did, but it was most unpleasant. I'm up now, I'll get the tea sorted.' He went to the cupboard, got two mugs and two teabags, and poured the water from the kettle. He returned and gave one of the mugs to Marissa, who stirred it and put milk in from a jug on the main table. The milk curdled as soon as it hit the tea.

'Oh shite. I'll have to dump this one out, don't use the milk, I'll dump that too.'

'Yeah, you probably cooked it when you cooked my spine,' said Terry, laughing. 'It actually wasn't that hot, I don't know what it was, it could have been an electric shock. Should we try again?'

'Yes, we need to try it again for sure. Hang on a mo.' Marissa dumped the milk and tea and got herself a fresh cuppa. She brought new milk over from the fridge and poured a dollop into Terry's mug.

'Cheers.'

They clinked mugs. 'Okay, one more try then.' Marissa hunkered down again and put one hand on the base of Terry's skull and the other hand down at the base of his spine. She closed her eyes, feeling the strain of her muscles as she tried to relax in this unusual position. She imagined her hands getting warm, glowing softly. She then imagined the soft glow moving into Terry's spine, rushing down to the base of his spine, and then rushing up again.

'There, I think that's it – are you okay?'

'Hmm? I can't feel anything. But I do feel very relaxed. My turn now?'

'Yes, ok, let's swap places.'

Marissa stood up and stretched, then sat down and took a gulp of her tea (hot hot), and then Terry tried to run the energy on her spine. 'Honestly, Terry, I don't feel anything.'

'Well, neither did I, in all fairness.'

He sat down beside her and they took another drink of tea.

'We had better go out and get those stones,' he added. 'I wonder what they're for. I have my black stone here in my pocket.' He tapped his front trouser pocket. 'The workshop this time doesn't feel the same at all as the first time, does it?'

The gravel was crunching underfoot, and all of the others were sifting through handfuls of gravel and dust for stones to bring back to class. Marissa went up to Saoirse. 'Did you run the energy okay?' she asked.

'I tried to,' said Saoirse, not taking her eyes off the ground 'I don't know if I did it right through.'

'No, neither do I,' said Marissa, trying to see what it was that Saoirse was looking at. 'You'll never find a stone in that gravel. Come on, let's go around the back of the house to where all the trees are.'

'Yes, that's a great idea.'

Marissa and Saoirse moved to the back of the house, Terry skipped along to keep up with them. They looked at the grassy mounds and boggy forest floor, and Marissa spotted a white pebble. She quickly pocketed it and noticed that Terry and Saoirse were having much more luck than she was. She wandered a little bit away from them and saw another stone which could also be suitable, but she wasn't very happy with the shape of it. She put it in her pocket anyway. Terry was waving a large stick in the air and pretending he was fighting a ghost.

'Back away, I tell you, we have wards up you know. Mwhahahaha! They will fry you dead if you come too close to them,' he said. Saoirse laughed, but Marissa thought that he was pushing things a little bit. *Has he really met a spirit, has he?* Then she saw a dark stone that looked a little bit like a cube. *That will do me.* She threw the second stone out, picked up this new one, then shouted back to the others, 'I'm going back into the house.'

'Have you got your stones?'

'Yes, I've got two, I'll get my black one from upstairs. See you inside.'

Marissa climbed the stairs and entered her bedroom. After she pulled her black stone out from the bottom of the rucksack, she checked her phone. There was a text from Matt.

Just saying hi, hope you're having fun.

Marissa felt suddenly more stable, more present. She didn't know that she had been flighty. She sent one back: It's good, different 2 b4. A lot of new material. Not sure I'm getting it.

She put the phone away, and then heard it vibrate, so she pulled it out again, he had replied: Got to start somewhere! Going out with my mates, talk later x

Downstairs, the only seat that was left was beside Zaad. Marissa squeezed in and took the three stones out from her pocket to study them. Terry had brought back one the size of a boulder, he had washed it off in the kitchen and it was still dripping water onto the floor.

'Great, yiz are all back,' said Séamus, who had been waiting for them. 'An announcement before we begin this session. A graduate of mine, Brigid, will be bringing traditional Irish tweeds and knits that you can use to make your medicine bag. That's what the stones are for. Once you work with them, they become your medicine stones. I will explain more about that in a minute.'

'Over the course of the next few workshops we will be adding to our medicine stones, you can also add in other significant items. Your medicine bag will support you in the shamanic healing work that you will be doing with me, and hopefully long after you've finished working with me. Think of it as an altar to your medicine, to what you have to offer. A portable altar that grows more powerful with use. So choose well, choose a cloth that calls to you. And you don't need to pick one from Brigid today, you have plenty of time to get another cloth. Choose something traditional that speaks to your heart.'

'So now for the work. You all have three stones, yes? Good. Stones are great sponges, they will soak up energies, so you can use them to absorb heavy energies that you are having trouble shifting.' He got up and started walking around the room.

'You started the work with recognising and releasing patterns, this weekend is about ramping up the healing process. So these stones are going to help you with the old, stagnant energies that you're still holding onto, that are keeping you connected to the patterns.'

'Here's what we will be doing next. Running energy,' he raised an eyebrow at the group, who responded in kind. 'Opening an energy centre and releasing old stagnant energy into the stone, thereby creating our medicine stones, then closing the energy centre again. We place our medicine stones into a medicine bag, which I will then need you to bring to every workshop from now on. I will now show you the next stage of the process.'

Stephanie volunteered again. This time, Séamus had her lie down on the floor on a rug in front of the group. He reminded them how to run energy, and then he showed them how to open an energy centre (chakra) so that it releases heavy energy into the stone, (he called it Huacha [hoo-cha]), and then how to close up the energy centre and close off the healing.

'Have you got that?' he asked. Some of them were still scribbling furiously into their notebooks. He repeated the instructions twice more. People were still writing when he had finished, including Marissa.

Jenny put up her hand. 'Which chakra are we working with?' she asked.

'The second one, Sacral. Stick with that one for the moment – you can, of course, do this technique on all seven chakras. But for the purposes of today, we will start here.'

Jenny nodded her head.

Zaad put his hand up, squashing Marissa into Liz, who was sharing the sofa with her. 'I am sorry, but you all seem to know what a chakra is, however, I have not come across it before. Can you explain it to me?'

'Yes, of course.' said Séamus. 'Our physical bodies have seven main energy centres, called chakras. These were first mapped by the Indian culture. We have many more energy centres than that, some people say fourteen, others say forty-seven. We will never know how many. The more we learn about the vast metaphysical field, the more we realise that we do not know. Remember, Humans are changing too, all the time, and so is our energy body. But we still work with the main seven chakras, which are mapped on the torso, from your root, here,' Séamus pointed between his legs 'to the crown, up here,' he pointed to the top of his head.

'You can feel them once you start working with energy. They spin, like pinwheels, taking in energy from their surroundings and releasing it again. It's our connection to the world, it's our life force energy moving through us. And sometimes they become blocked. This exercise teaches a technique for unblocking the chakra, there are many more techniques, from many other types of healing modalities. This is the one that we work with here. Ok?'

Zaad had a big smile and was sitting straight in his seat. 'Yes, thank you. I understand now.'

'Great. We will put all the pieces together after lunch into a formal client protocol. For now I want you to get the partner you were with last night for the body mapping and practice this section of the work. Run the energy, place the black stone on the body, open the chakra, purge the huacha, close the chakra, close the healing. That's all, don't worry about going deep, you're just going through the motions here. We will go deeper later today. So off yiz go and practice this technique, using your black stones only, and I'll come around and help and answer any questions you might have.'

Finn nodded at Marissa who smiled, and everybody got to work.

CHAPTER THIRTY NINE

Marissa and Finn had fun working through the technique together to get it straight in their minds. Over lunch, Terry reconsidered his boulder and found a much smaller stone in its place. 'I don't think I'd appreciate having that stone on my stomach,' he said to nobody in particular.

Brigid was setting up her wares in the main room. One of the house staff had brought in a collapsible table from the dining hall, and Brigid was laying out some beautiful tweeds, woollen cloths and woven textiles. There was quite a selection, from traditional family patterns to plain tweeds, tartans, and some modern mystical patterns, too. She also had leather straps and small metal ornaments in the shape of various animals. After eating, people were wandering in to take a look. Jenny and Liz were hanging around, touching and eyeing all that Brigid had on offer. Brigid seemed well used to this and was telling them about the history of some of the cloths.

'This one is from the family Maguire, it dates back to the times of The High Kings. This one here I particularly love.' She reached into her brown carry bag and fished out a most unusual cloth, it was dark blue with golden stars and a moon, 'Inspired by the night sky.' Liz was still fingering the Maguire tweed, turning it around in her fingers. 'How much is this one?' she asked.

'That's €35.' Liz nodded, and Brigid placed the dark blue cloth on the table with the others. Curiosity got the better of Marissa and she went over to join them. As she cast her eye over the various patterns, nothing in particular jumped out at her. She moved over to the small wooden and metal ornaments and immediately picked up a sterling silver bear. Marissa held it up and turned it around in her hand, looking at the detail of his paws and claws, the hairs on his back, and his kind eyes. *Hello Bear. It feels like it has been a very long time since we connected. I think you need to be in my medicine bag. And I'd rather have you help me do my work than the lovely bear Martin gave me.* At that thought, Marissa felt a shiver go down her back. She turned to Brigid and asked, 'How much is the bear?'

'€20.'

'Thanks.' Marissa held onto the bear, she wasn't able to put it down.

'When you buy a cloth for your Mála you will also get the leather thong,' said Brigid.

'What's a Mála?' asked Liz, she had found another cloth, this one was a tartan print in black, red and cream, and she was holding that one up to the light from the window.

'Some people call the medicine bag a Mála, it's the Irish word for bag.' said Brigid. 'But Séamus calls it a Mesa, which is what the Peruvian Shamans call them.' Marissa's heart leapt when she heard Brigid say 'Peruvian', it was as if there were invisible threads in the core of her body that connected her directly to Peru.

Most of the others were at the table now, it was becoming quite crowded. Liz and Jenny had chosen their cloths, Terry found a silver hawk in the miniatures, and he was deciding between a green striped cloth or a more bohemian-looking black cloth printed with an image of the sun. Marissa wanted to choose something that felt right to her as it was going to be her medicine. As she went through Brigid's offerings on the table, she wasn't certain that any of them fit for her. Zaad wanted something traditional from his own culture so he decided he would get his mother to make him something, without telling her why, of course. In the meantime, he was going to use a tee-shirt that he brought with him.

Finn pulled a pale blue cloth out from his back pocket. It had a pattern of the sea printed onto it in silver threads, it was beautiful, looked well worn and wasn't like anything Brigid had on her table. 'I still love this, thanks,' he said to Brigid, who smiled.

'Ahh yes, I remember those, they sold out so quickly.'

Finn smiled back.

'I'm sorry that I don't have any more of them in stock. But I do have some lovely new ones.'

'Which one do you like?' Finn asked, turning to Saoirse.

'I'm not sure,' Saoirse giggled, she already had pulled out three different cloths.

Finn grabbed one of them from her and held it to the light, pointing out the pattern in it, Saoirse seemed very interested in what he had to say. They were leaning into each other.

Are you sure you have a girlfriend, Finn? Marissa couldn't help but notice the two of them flirting. And then she saw it. A cloth, her cloth, it was sticking out of the brown bag under the table. Brigid hadn't laid it out yet. She went up to Brigid and asked if she could see it.

'Yes, of course.' Brigid pulled up the bag and took out the cloth. She opened it up on the table on top of all the others. It looked like something from the market in Cusco, it was Peruvian, mostly black, with criss-cross patterns of pink, red and yellow through it, triangles and stripes in green and blue. Marissa picked it up and held it to her face, she caught a feint smell and was immediately transported back to Cusco. She was back in the market, the hot, dusty streets, Miguel's car. Her heart opened and she felt a river of love flowing through her. It was quite powerful, it almost made her dizzy. When she tried to put the cloth down on the table her hand wouldn't let go of it, just the way it wouldn't let go of the bear.

'I'll take this one, please,' she said, 'and the bear too, please.'

Brigid looked at the cloth she had chosen and her face changed from happy to serious. 'Oh, this one isn't for sale,' said Brigid, holding out her hand to take it back. 'It's a personal cloth, I got it from a friend who was just in Peru. Sorry, it wasn't meant to be in with the others.'

Marissa's heart sank, she was having a lot of trouble handing it back. She still held the cloth and Brigid noticed her disappointment as she eventually, reluctantly, handed it over. Brigid said, 'Hang on, I think I have another one. Maybe you'll like this one too.'

Brigid rooted around in her bag and pulled another cloth out from the bottom. It was similar in colour but the texture was thinner and it seemed like a looser weave. She handed it to Marissa but it didn't have the same effect on her. The threads were lighter, not as substantial. *Not as powerful? I don't know what it is...* Brigid could tell straight away that she didn't like it as much. Then Brigid's face changed back to soft and warm again.

'The other cloth, the one you liked, what is it that you like so much about it?' Brigid was serious once more, but this felt different, more like a test than an accusation.

'I don't know. Can I see it again?'

Brigid handed it back to Marissa who immediately felt relieved at the touch of the cloth in her hands again. She took a moment before answering. 'It feels like an old friend that I have not seen in a very long time.'

Brigid said, 'Yes, I understand. I can see that you've made a sudden strong attachment to this cloth, but I can also feel that this cloth wants to be with you. Things happen in mysterious ways, and I would be doing both you and the cloth a disservice if I was to take it back. Look, this one is much more expensive than the others, as I said, I wasn't going to sell it. However, I cannot get in the way of Spirit, so I will offer it to you for €100.'

Marissa was filled with a mixture of excitement and relief. Money wasn't an issue, she still had money from Uncle Lou, and of course, she had some savings, too. She knew she had to have it, some things were more important than the price tag. 'Yes please! Are you sure?' Marissa could feel her eyes welling up with joy, unbidden, as if they were acting independently of her mind. She had no choice but to go with it.

Brigid looked Marissa up and down, ignoring the frenzy that was going on at the table from the others. She closed her eyes. She nodded her head and opened her eyes again.

'You have some powerful guides,' she said to Marissa. 'They obviously really want you to have this cloth. Yes, I will sell it to you, and the bear, and a leather thong for tying it all together. I'll give it all to you for €111.'

Marissa felt her heart lift, and she had a surge of energy rush through her. 'Thank you,' she said. 'I've got some cash upstairs, I'll go get it.'

'I take cards too, and PayPal, so there's no rush. You can pay what you have and send me the rest later.'

Everyone had found something on Brigid's table, Zaad was the only one without a cloth but he got himself a miniature owl and a leather to tie his future cloth. Terry loved the moon and stars print that he finally decided upon. Saoirse had one similar but almost opposite, it was a sky and sun print.

Marissa spread her cloth out on her lap and was fingering and stroking the intricate patterns and weave. She held it up to her face again and sniffed deeply and was rewarded with a smell of Palos Santos, the wood that they burn in Peru. Brigid also had some on her table, she bought a small bag of it, too. She felt like some part of her that was missing had come home, it was difficult to explain, but it felt very good.

Séamus came into the room and went up to Brigit and chatted with her for a moment, then he introduced Brigid officially to the group. 'I can see yiz have already met!' She was greeted with laughter. 'Brigid was a student of mine and a graduate of the medicine wheel.' Brigid took a bow and everyone laughed. Saoirse and Terry clapped their hands. Brigid smiled, and Séamus went on.

'She will now show yiz how to fold the cloth and wrap it with the leather so yiz can make your medicine bag.'

Brigid gathered a leather thong, one of the cloths, and a few of the statues in her hands, and they all sat around the fireplace in the places where they had been earlier that morning, with Brigid up top where Séamus usually sat.

'Hello!' she said, a little breathless. 'I'm not great at the demos, but I am so happy that you all seem to have found something that you love. This is how you fold the cloth.'

She proceeded to show them how to do it, using the miniatures as stand-ins for medicine stones. Everyone copied her, and soon they all had bundles on their knees. Even Zaad's bundled tee shirt didn't look too terrible. Liz took photos of each stage of the folding so she didn't forget and promised to send them on to the group. Séamus thanked Brigid and took the helm again.

'Well done, lads, I knew you'd enjoy meeting Brigid. Give her a round of applause!'

Everyone clapped and Brigid took another bow, and went back to her table and began packing up her things.

'Now, lads, it's time to get back to work. We are going in deep, so listen carefully, as what I want you to do will take us into the rest of the day, and tonight.'

'Get a partner and find a space to work. It will be almost a full energy healing session. Start by choosing who is going to be the client and who will be the practitioner. And then you'll take it from the top, including opening a healing space by saying the prayer that you've learnt. You can smudge the space too, if you want. Then set an intention for the healing – ask your client what they'd like to let go of. Get them to feel in their body where they are holding the energy of the thing they want to let go of. Then do the energy mapping to verify their intentions, let your client lie down and begin the healing work.'

Zaad leaned into Marissa, who was squashed beside him on the sofa and said in a quiet voice, 'Marissa? I would very much like to work with you. Is that okay?'

Marissa nodded and said, 'Sure, why not.'

Séamus was still giving instructions. 'Run energy through their spine to kickstart their releasing process. Open up the sacral chakra and place one of their stones (not yours but theirs) onto their chakra, unwind it like you've been practising. Continue to run the energy for a few minutes, then leave the chakra open. Now, remember how you went on a journey for an energetic gift for your client? Well, you're going to do that at this point in the healing. Once you have it, remove the stone, and blow in the energetic gift, then close up the chakra, and seal in their energy. Then take a break, your client will need some time to recover from this, so get a cuppa and some food as there won't be a formal sit-down for dinner. Then swap so that the client becomes the therapist and do it all again. Clear?'

'No, can you say it again, please?' asked Terry, who hadn't been writing much in his notebook that day until now. He was rushing to keep up.

'Yes, I can say it again. I want to make sure yiz are all clear on what yiz need to do. It's the biggest healing we have done so far.'

Questions went on for another 15 minutes or so. 'Don't forget it's our fire ceremony tonight, and that must go ahead as planned. Yes, I'm aware we're running behind schedule, but that was inevitable. Fire ceremony is at 9pm, meet me at the front steps and bring your drums.

If you've not finished the work I've set for you here, you can get up earlier tomorrow and do it. Clear?'

Marissa looked at her watch. It was coming up to 3pm, which gave them 5 hours to get the work done. She had been listening avidly and felt like she knew what to do, so there should be plenty of time. She hugged her new medicine bag to her chest, it was strange, as if she already knew what to do before he had given them the instructions. Between the familiarity of her new cloth and the instructions for the healing, she felt like she was coming home to some part of her that she never knew existed. She was excited. Zaad looked up at her expectantly. 'Shall we work in my room?' he asked.

'Sure,' said Marissa. 'Let's get some water to bring with us, we have a long afternoon ahead.'

Zaad and Marissa climbed up the two flights of stairs and went down the corridor together. There was lots of activity going on around them, the others were enthusiastic but nervous. Marissa could feel the tension in the air as everyone gathered together the things they needed for the healing work. They got to Zaad's room (he ran in first to check it was tidy enough for a guest), and a minute later, he invited her in.

'Can I open the window?' asked Marisa, finding the room a little stale.

'I'll do it,' said Zaad, going to the window and opening it up. A fresh breeze poured into the room, there was a chill in the air, and Marissa shivered. Zaad straightened the covers on his bed and arranged his medicine bundle, his drum, and two pieces of Palos Santos he'd bought from Brigid. 'Do you have matches?' he asked.

'Yes,' said Marissa, 'but they're in my room. I'll go get them and come back.'

Zaad nodded.

She didn't want to leave her medicine bundle so she took it with her. She wanted to check her phone, too, to see if Matt had texted. She hadn't heard from him all day and being in proximity to Zaad made her want to connect to Matt. She knew Saoirse and Stephanie were working in her room, so she knocked before entering in case they had begun their session.

'Hey,' said Saoirse, gesturing that it was okay for her to come in. 'What a lot we have to do. I don't know if I'll be able to remember it all.'

'Yeah, I know,' said Marissa. 'I guess it's our first time doing the entire protocol so we can only do our best.' She went to her bed and rooted through her backpack, looking for the matches. She found her phone and put it in her pocket without looking at it, deciding that she'd feel happier keeping it with her for the afternoon.

'Have fun, ladies,' she said and left them to it.

In the corridor she pulled out her phone and checked it. Matt hadn't texted her since the night before, but she only had one bar of coverage. She felt an urge to text him anyway so she opened up the messages and typed: I miss you. Then she thought better of it and deleted it. *Too needy, and I thought he was bad!* She was hesitant to send anything at all, but she really wanted to, so she imagined herself sending that message instead. Then she visualised him receiving it and writing back to her: Miss you, too. She put the phone back in her pocket, feeling a little better, and went into Zaad's room.

Zaad was waiting for her. He was in the exact same position as he was when she had left the room. He smiled, and his white teeth glistened against his sallow skin. 'Do you want to be the client first? Or shall I? I don't mind. Whichever you prefer.'

Marissa was filled with readiness to be the healer, so she took him up on his offer. 'Please, can you be the client first? And I was thinking, to save time if we open sacred space in here together, we don't need to open it twice. We can keep it open until we are finished later tonight. And then we can close it together, too.'

Zaad nodded his head. 'Yes, that's a good idea. Okay, I'll be the client first. I am in your hands, Marissa, I hope you take good care of me.' Marissa wasn't sure if he was messing with her or if he was serious, and then he cocked his head sideways, and they both laughed. There was a slight tension between them, but Marissa felt like she had Matt in her pocket, well, in her phone anyway, which was still in her pocket.

'Let's start with the prayer, then? Which way is North?'

They figured it out with the compass on Marissa's phone, she then put the phone on silent and left it on Zaad's bed. They opened directions, working from memory was difficult but between them they managed to get the gist of it anyway. They both felt that the energy in the room still needed a little work so they lit both pieces of Zaad's Palos Santos and went around smoking the corners of the room and the boys' bags on the floor.

As Marissa worked the smoke over Terry's bed she couldn't help but smile, thinking about how their friendship was blossoming. She got an image in her mind of a little blonde boy running around outside in a garden in the sun. He was wearing blue shorts and no tee-shirt, there was an inflatable swimming pool and he was yelping with delight, jumping in and out of it and splashing around. She smiled, wondering if she was imagining what Terry must have been like when he was little, or just what his personality seemed like to her right now. She crushed the Palos Santos out on the side of the sink and went back to Zaad's bed.

'That is a very good idea! I'll do that too,' he said and crushed his out on the sink also. Then he ran the water and washed away the smoky stain on the ceramic as best as he could.

Marissa stepped into practitioner mode. It was a similar feeling to when she did it in her psychotherapy group, a feeling of professionalism took over, a duty of care, a sense of being responsible for the other. She began

'Okay, Zaad, I am your shamanic practitioner today. Welcome to our session. Please let me know how you're feeling, if you're unhappy with anything that I'm doing, or if something comes up for you that you want to talk about with me. I'm a beginner at this, so I might be going too fast or too slow, so please also tell me if you're uncomfortable or if something I do annoys you.'

Zaad thought about this and agreed. 'Okay, Marissa, I will.'

'What would you like to work with today?'

Zaad was silent for a moment. 'I'm not sure. I have no real pressing issue, I'm just happy to be here.'

Marissa suddenly had a thought. 'I remember yesterday you said that you couldn't tell your family about coming here and about doing this work. What about doing a healing around that? To find out why you have difficulty speaking about what you want?'

Zaad laughed. 'I have difficulty because they do not hear me. I believe that it's because they don't want to hear me. My culture is dogmatic, they're fixed in their ways, and they ignore things that don't fit into their idea of the way life should be. I always knew, growing up in Ireland, that I would be different to them, I didn't think that I would be so different. But this work, it makes me feel more confident. So yes, Marissa, you are right. If I am confident here, with you, then I want to be confident also at home, with them.'

Marissa nodded her head. 'I understand. It's funny, my issue with my family seems to be exactly the same as yours. We are Jewish, I no longer practice my religion, and my family have accepted that. In fact, they don't really practice it either. But like yours, they don't like new things. They are very stuck in their ways, they love tradition, and they fight against anything that threatens it. So I think we're very similar.'

Zaad's eyes were wide. 'You're Jewish and I'm Muslim!' he started to laugh. 'Yet we are similar, indeed! Isn't it strange, we would be told that we should be enemies! But instead, we're making friends, and I think together we should do this work, the same work, for each other.' He nodded his head in affirmation. 'Then it's very significant that we work together, and very interesting too, that we have the exact same issue.' He was smiling now. 'Marissa, I believe that it's God's will that I meet you here and that we are doing this today. I give thanks to God for showing me this sign that all is good. I was worried that he would not like me doing this, but I feel stronger now in my heart that this is a good thing. A very good thing.'

Marissa smiled, then put a blanket down on the floor and got Zaad to sit opposite her for the body mapping. It was still difficult to know if she was doing it right, Finn had been messing about most of the time during their practice sessions. She softened her eyes, relaxed her belly and imagined that Zaad's energy was like a coat that he took off of himself and draped over her. She sat in the 'coat' of his essence and allowed it to permeate her body. She felt nothing different at first, and then gradually she felt a tightness in her right shoulder. 'Do you have tightness in your right shoulder?' she asked.

'Oh yes, for many years, an injury when I was playing football at school.'

Marissa smiled. She felt into her body to see what other unfamiliar pain she could pick up. She felt a tightness in her chest. She moved her hand to it. 'And here?' she asked, pointing to her hand.

'Yes, at this moment I'm feeling a little nervous, so yes, I feel it in my chest, exactly there.'

Marissa was delighted she got it right, she felt almost elated, and then suddenly the 'coat' of energy seemed to disappear. 'Perhaps I just disconnected from you! But that was good, thank you for sharing that with me.'

She got Zaad to lie down but before she began to work on his energy she felt she needed to do something else. 'Breathe and relax your body, I need to call on my guides to come and help me,' she said.

'That isn't in the instructions,' he said.

'Yes, I know, but it feels like the right thing to do, I feel like I need to. So bear with me.'

'No problem. Take your time.'

Marissa sat crossed-legged beside where Zaad was lying. She closed her eyes. She had her drum nearby, she drew it to her and tapped it softly, lub dub, lub dub, lub dub.

She felt her body soften and suddenly she was in a forest. There was a campfire, and around it were her two Medicine women, one from Peru and the other from North America. Bear was also there, and so were Archangel Haniel and Archangel Michael. At least she thought that's who they were. They all seemed very happy to see her, the women clapped at her arrival and came over to greet her. They hugged her strongly and she softened and received the healing hug.

'We're so glad you came to visit us. You did the right thing, well done. We are always with you, you are going on a great adventure. By calling out to us now, you passed a test. We are so proud of you.'

Marissa was beaming, she was so happy to see them, and their joy was contagious. Bear growled and danced behind the three women, and the angels stood watching and smiling.

'Now go. The boy is waiting for you. You're doing great, keep on going.'

Marissa opened her eyes. Zaad seemed to have fallen asleep. She remembered she had to start by running energy through his spine, so she got onto her knees and put the drum down beside her. She placed one hand over his forehead and the other over his stomach, where his sacral chakra would be. She shifted herself until she felt more comfortable, and then she visualised the energy getting warmer and running up and down his spine between her hands. She had an urge to connect to Reiki, so she took a moment and closed her eyes, visualised the Reiki light above her, coming down through her, into her heart, up and over her shoulders and out through her hands. Zaad's body twitched but he didn't wake up, when she looked at his face, she realised he really had gone to sleep.

She ran energy for a moment or two longer and then realised that she didn't ask Zaad which medicine stone he wanted to use. His bundle was still wrapped in the thong up on the bed. *Oh dear, I don't want to wake him up. But I probably should. What do I do?* She sat back and squatted on her heels while making up her mind.

Zaad opened one eyelid, 'Are you okay, Marissa?' he asked.

'Oh you're awake! Great. I thought you were sleeping.'

'Yes, I think I did fall asleep there.'

'I didn't ask you, which medicine stone do you want me to use?'

Zaad sat up, 'Ah yes, we forgot that.' Marissa stood up and got Zaad's tee-shirt bundle, and gave it to him. He opened it, looked at the three stones inside and chose a little brown one. 'Here, this one.' He handed it to Marissa.

'Thank you!' she said, placing the tee-shirt, thong, owl and other two stones back up on the bed. She returned to him, he was lying down again.

'Where is your sacral chakra?' she asked, not sure if she had indeed found it.

'I'm not sure, on my stomach I think? These chakras are a very new idea for me.'

'Okay, don't worry, I'll find it. You rest again.'

Marissa looked at Zaad's body for a moment, she saw a stain on the long-sleeved blue top he was wearing, noticed he had tears in his black jeans, and that his runners were quite old. He was wearing a belt with a silver buckle on it that had a zig-zag design. His stomach was flat, she lifted her hand two inches above it, palm down and fingers splayed outwards so she could sense his energy. She lifted her hand up and down and felt heat coming from his body about an inch above it. She moved her hand forwards and backwards and found there were a few spots that were hotter than the others. She wondered if they were the chakras. She went inwards and asked her medicine women, who both nodded. She opened her eyes but didn't focus, instead, she let her hand guide her to his sacral chakra, which was just below his belly button, or so she thought. She placed the stone there, it wobbled a little bit, but it seemed to stay put.

'Okay, Zaad, I'm going to open your chakra now, like Séamus showed us how to. I'd like you to breathe into your stomach so that you can help me do it. We are going to release the energy that you're carrying around not being able to be confident and speak out at home.'

Zaad nodded his head.

The process lasted about 15 minutes. Marissa could feel the difference in the heat coming from Zaad's body as the energy was released. It took a while for it to start, and after 10 minutes or so, he started to shiver so she got another blanket off one of the beds and put it onto him, lifting the stone off his stomach and placing it back onto the chakra over the blanket.

'Thank you, that feels better,' he said.

'I must go on a journey now for you,' she said, 'Just rest there and close your eyes, you can sleep. I'll journey, get your energetic gift, give it to you, then close off your chakra. You don't need to do anything more. We can talk about it afterwards.'

He closed his eyes, and soon it seemed like he was sleeping again. Marissa drew her drum close to her again. Just the touch of it helped her relax to go on a journey for Zaad. She didn't even need to tap it this time. She softened her body, closed her eyes, and she was back in the forest.

There was her wonderful friend, the medicine tree. He was looking at her with a big smile, so happy to see her. She curtsied to the tree, and he laughed, and she wanted to give him a hug but she felt she needed to ask first. She got the sense that he would love that, so she embraced the tree and stayed there for a moment or two, just feeling the joy of the closeness of their connection. She took a step back.

'I am here for a gift for Zaad, for something that will help him be more confident to speak out at home.'

'Yes, we were expecting you. Come in,' said the tree, and a door in the tree trunk opened, beckoning her to enter.

She stepped inside and through the tree, then found herself in a desert land, she looked at her feet and saw she was standing on sand which had been rippled by the wind. It seemed similar to the place she went to the last time she journied for Zaad. The memories of that journey rippled through her body, but there was something different about this place. She looked up and saw there was a sand dune right in front of her. It seemed to beckon to her, and she started to climb it. She was about halfway up the dune when a small, bright green lizard ran past her foot. She followed it to the edge of the dune and down the other side. There was shade, and a canopy, and what seemed to be a small oasis with a palm tree and a body of water. She felt the pull to go there so she followed her instinct downwards.

Under a white canopy beside the water, a man sat drinking tea from a very elegant tea set that was rimmed in gold and patterned with yellow and pink flowers. He turned to her and said, 'You are here for Zaad! At last.' He smiled. He wore full white and black robes which blew around him as if there was wind, but there was no wind.

'Yes, I am here for Zaad, for a gift, for his self-confidence.'

'Yes. We were expecting you a long time ago. We wondered why you had not come until now.' He said this in a disparaging tone.

Marissa was wondering who the 'we' referred to. She turned and saw a golden snake, it was about 6ft long and coming over towards her. It was very feminine in its appearance, she was slightly mottled on closer look, with green eyes and a small pink forked tongue. She came over and seemed to be sniffing Marissa with her tongue. Marissa wasn't afraid.

'Hello,' she said to the snake.

'Hello,' the snake said back to her.

'I'm here for a gift, for Zaad.'

'Yesss, I understand. I am the gift, I have been waiting for him for a long time.'

Marissa looked at the snake. 'Are you a guide for him?'

The man laughed, a loud, bellowing laugh which didn't sound very friendly. Marissa wasn't sure if she liked this person or not.

'Yess,' said the snake, 'I am the medicine of his ancestors. He has been avoiding me for a long time. He will not be able to be confident until he can look me in the eye.'

'Ahh. It is an honour to meet you, medicine snake.' Marissa bowed, and the snake appreciated her respectfulness. 'How do I bring you back with me to him?' Marissa asked.

'I will come to him in a dream, three times. Tell him thiss. He must engage with me and not run away. If he speaks to me in any of the dreams, then I will give him the gift he is looking for.'

The snake rose up to meet Marissa's eye and opened up its hood. It looked like a golden cobra and was quite intimidating. Marissa felt afraid for a moment but she called on the strength of Bear, and she felt him flow into her body, even though he did not appear.

'You are a strong one,' said the snake, backing down. 'Good. Say hello to Sachemama for me when you see her next time. She is my cousin. We are all related here.' The golden snake pulled back, laughed, then coiled into a ball, found its own tail, placed it into its own mouth, and disappeared.

'She's some snake, that one,' said the man, laughing again.

Marissa didn't like him at all now. She looked at him, wondering why.

'I sense some hostility in you,' he said. 'Come, there is nothing to be afraid of.'

Marissa wondered if it was an aspect of her Jewish side having a fear of this Arab or if he was, in fact, a sinister being.

'In the spirit of reconciliation, I have a gift for you, Marissa.'

From a pocket in his robe the Arab took out a white powdery square. 'It is Turkish delight, very delicious. Sweet. For there to be sweetness between us. Here, eat.'

Marissa couldn't help but recall the Narnia stories and wondered if she would be entranced as Edmond was by the Ice Queen. The Arab handed her the Turkish delight, she took it and held it in her hand. She asked her inner knowing if it was safe to eat, but she wasn't sure if she got a yes or not, so she didn't. The Arab laughed at her.

'Very good, very good, you are a difficult customer. Come come, that wasn't the gift, that was just for the sweet taste of life. Perhaps one day you will be ready for it.'

The man put his hand in his pocket and pulled out a small crystal. It was cut like the double-terminated quartz that Matt had bought for himself in The Angel Shop, only this one was clearer. He lifted it up so the sunlight poured through it and made a rainbow. Then he handed it to Marissa. 'Beautiful lady, and you do not know it. This is for you, for clarity and purpose in your healing. From us. Spirit of reconciliation. We know you are going to do amazing things, and we want to be your allies. Come to us if you need our help.'

Again she was wondering who the 'us' were. He lifted a curtain behind him, and behind it she could see many people all sitting there, an enraptured audience watching the interaction between them. She smiled. She felt no animosity from any of them. They were like a family, but somebody else's family. It reminded her of the first time she met James's family at a party they were having. Lots of new people, different energy, all welcoming but all strangers at the same time. Marissa acknowledged this new connection, she placed her hands together in prayer position. The others did the same. The Arabic man lowered the curtain again.

'See? We will not bite you. We are the same, even though we may smell different, look different, we are just like you. And we want the same thing. Ahh, you thought we were upset with you! No, no, no. Not you at all, no. This boy, this Zaad, he has been reluctant to answer his calling since he was very small. But he is here now, and that is good. Now, it is time for you to go back to him.'

He led Marissa out of the tent and brought her back up the dune. She waved goodbye to him and climbed back up until she reached the top. The door that the tree had created for her was still open, it looked like a Salvador Dali painting – the blue sky, the sand and bright sun, and a door open on the horizon, with the greenery of the forest beckoning through it. Marissa took a moment to absorb the scene, it was vibrant and alive. She knew who she was, she felt the crystal in her hand and it was good. She went through the door, it closed behind her, and she stepped out from the tree.

She turned to her beloved tree and saw his big loving face smiling at her. She was filled with love for him and embraced him again. 'Thank you, my friend,' she said.

'Thank you also. This thing that you do today will have a ripple effect, it is healing the collective. We are so pleased. If this was the only thing you were to ever do, it would be enough. But you will do more. So much more.'

Marissa felt her awareness returning to her physical body in the room beside Zaad's sleeping body. Her body was stiff and sore, she didn't know how long she had been sitting there. She remembered the crystal and looked at her hand, but of course, it wasn't there. She visualised the energy of the crystal dissolving into her own body. She then reached over to Zaad's sacral chakra and closed and sealed it. She drew more Reiki into her body and filled his body with it, and then smoothed and closed off the healing like she did in Dolores's class.

She stood up and stretched, her legs were stiff, and she had pins and needles in her right foot. She visualised golden Reiki light covering Zaad and sealing him in so that he was contained and safe. She rubbed her arms and walked around the room a little bit until the feeling came back in her foot. She checked her phone. It was nearly 6. Where had the time gone?

Zaad was moving on the floor, he was waking up. The stone rolled off his stomach, Marissa went to retrieve it, but when she went to pick it up she felt that it wasn't hers to touch. She left it there for him to get for himself. Zaad rolled onto his side and pushed himself to sitting, and rubbed his eyes.

'Oh dear, I really did fall asleep. What happened? Is it over?'

'Hello there! Would you like some water?'

'Yes, please.'

Marissa brought over the glasses that they had gotten, but the water felt flat or dead or something, it didn't feel good to her.

'I don't like this water.' She poured it out down the sink and filled the glasses from the taps. 'I'm sure it's drinkable,' she said, handing one to him.

Terry came into the room. 'I'd not be so sure, sometimes the water here can be bad. Hey, wait, I have a new bottle under my bed.' Terry reached under the bed and pulled out a bottle. Marissa dumped the glasses and allowed Terry to fill them. She gave a glass to Zaad.

'You guys still working?' Terry asked.

'Yeah. Just finished the first session. I didn't realise this would take so long.'

'Me neither, we just finished the first session too. I got cold, I came back for my jumper. Glad I didn't interrupt you. I'll leave you to it,' he said, nodding over at Zaad, 'and we can catch up in the dining hall during the break.'

Terry left, and Zaad drank the water in one gulp.

'What did you find for me?' he asked. He was slightly pale, he had pushed the blanket onto the floor and was holding his medicine stone.

Marissa took the blanket and wrapped it around him like a shawl, he nodded to her and said, 'Thank you, yes, I'm still cold.'

'It was very strange, I didn't get a gift for you at all. Instead, I met your medicine guide.'

Zaad's eyes widened, and his face lit up. 'I have a medicine guide? Tell me!' he sat up taller, excited, wanting to know more.

'Yes, you do,' said Marissa, smiling. 'She is beautiful, a golden snake with green eyes. She laughed at me! She told me that you have to speak to her when she comes to you in a dream, not to run away from her anymore.'

Zaad scratched his head. Marissa thought it was cute and funny that he did that. 'I run away from her? I'm not scared of a snake!'

'She is a big snake, as big as me,' said Marissa.

'Ahh. Maybe then I would be scared of her,' he said, standing up and stretching and sitting back down again. He seemed lost in thought for a moment. 'Yes, okay, it makes sense now. I did dream of a giant snake, it gave me a fright, I woke from it afraid. Okay, I will try not to do that next time.'

Marissa told him about the tree, the desert, and the Arab too. 'And the snake will give you the gift once you speak to her. She said she will come three times, so I guess that gives you three chances.'

He nodded, taking it in. 'I see this healing, it's not always instant. Thank you, Marissa. But I do feel different. I feel like I am taller now. And I will talk to the snake.' He picked up his medicine stone and stood up.

'Look!' he said in amazement, holding out the stone to her. 'The colour, it's changed, it's darker now, look!'

Marissa took a look at the stone. She hadn't been that familiar with it to begin with, but there was something about it that definitely looked different, it was darker and there was a white spot that might not have been there before.

'Perhaps the energy you released while I worked on you changed the stone? Ahh, okay, now I understand. It's your medicine Zaad, this whole journey, the healing today for you, is all about your medicine. You made a medicine stone, and I met your medicine snake. You are a medicine man, Zaad, you can embrace it now. You can be who you are no matter what your family think of you. This is your natural calling. The man I met on the journey for you told me that. He was pleased to see me, he said that our connection is good and important, I suppose for both the Jewish people and the Muslims.'

Zaad's face beamed into a beautiful smile, he lit up the room with it. Marissa felt warm inside and pleased the healing seemed to go so well.

'Thank you, Marissa, this is a very special day for me, and I am honoured to share it with you. I can't wait to do the healing for you and return this blessing you have given to me.'

'We should go down and get some food first though, I'm a little hungry. It's late, and we have so much to do before the fire ceremony!'

'Yes, let's do that.'

CHAPTER FORTY

The kitchen was quiet as everyone else was still working. The house staff had laid out a cold buffet with soup on the stove that could be heated up as needed, and a large platter full of sandwiches. Marissa and Zaad helped themselves, and Marissa put the kettle on for tea.

They sat together at one of the long tables and tucked into the food, not really speaking. Marissa was getting a little shifty, she kind of hoped that someone else would join them. They finished the soup, Marissa made the tea and started into her sandwiches. 'How are we doing for time?'

Zaad finished off his food and looked at his watch. 'It's nearly 7.30pm.'

'That gives us an hour and a half before the fire ceremony. I wonder what a fire ceremony is? I've never been to one, have you?'

'We have many fires at home, but always in the fireplace!' Zaad said, laughing. 'I am sure it will be very interesting. Are you finished? Shall we go back upstairs?'

Marissa nodded her head. They brought their plates over to the sink, tidied up a little, then headed back to Zaad's room.

Marissa was feeling a little nervous, but as soon as they settled into the room, Zaad stepped into the role of healer. His face changed; he had said earlier that he felt taller, but in that moment, he seemed taller.

'I will close my eyes for a moment and see if I can meet with my new friend, the medicine snake. And then I will be your medicine man.' He meant it, there was no hint of fun or joking here, and suddenly Marissa felt safe with him.

He opened his eyes, took one look at the messed up cover on the floor and started rearranging everything. He gestured towards the newly folded duvet. 'Please, sit.'

Marissa sat and he sat opposite her. He looked at her with soft brown eyes, they seemed sharper but slightly out of focus. There was a hint of the wisdom brimming up within him as he began the session.

'Now, what would you like me to help you with?' he asked, in a softer, warmer voice than he had used before.

Marissa's mind went blank. *Oh no. I'm here again. It feels just like being a client in college. I don't know what I should let go of, or work with.* She looked at Zaad's warm smiling face and she softened, and then she spoke. The words seemed to come out of her mouth of their own accord.

'My fiancée left me right before our wedding, it was almost 4 years ago.' Marissa was surprised that she started talking about this. *This isn't what I planned to talk about! What about feeling free to be myself at home? I guess I could just go with it and see where this will bring me...* She hesitated but kept on going. 'I was very upset, I had a breakdown and had to move back home with my parents. I was about to start a master's degree but I dropped out of college, and, well, didn't do anything much for about 6 months. I had a lot of anxiety during that time, and I still have it in my body, even now. I would like very much to take it out so I can truly move on with my life.'

Zaad nodded, not seeming to mind the change of direction. 'Any boyfriend now?' he asked, cocking his head to one side, but it was more of a medicinal question than a curious one.

'I'm seeing someone, yes, but it's only new, we have just dated a few times.'

He nodded. It felt good to Marissa to get everything out into the open.

He continued, 'And the anxiety, what does it feel like?'

'Well, I am not feeling it right now, but I was a few minutes ago. It comes and goes, it can be very strong sometimes, and can take me by surprise.'

Zaad closed his eyes. 'May I map your energy now, please, Marissa?'

'Yes.'

There were a few moments where Zaad was tuning into her. He shivered then, his whole body spasmed and released quickly, he opened his eyes and looked at her, this time with sadness in his eyes. He looked emotional.

'Marissa, this man who left you, he broke your heart?'

Marissa sighed. 'Yes. He really did. And I think he broke my self-confidence, too. We, I, had made so many plans for us. Then all of that was gone. I didn't know who I was for a very long time. I think I'm only beginning to learn who I am without him.'

Zaad nodded his head. 'Today, I will work on your heart. It is still aching and afraid of being abandoned. I think that you'll never have a serious relationship again until you heal your heart. Don't be afraid to let somebody new in who could love you the way you deserve. Relationships are messy! You will always make mistakes, and this is okay, this is how we learn.'

Zaad was looking directly at her, so sincerely, with love in his eyes. Marissa felt something snap in her chest, right across her heart. It was like a rope breaking, her chest filled with air and her heart swelled. She took in a breath, and it didn't hurt. In fact, it was as if she could finally breathe freely for the first time in a very long time. She hadn't realised that she had been unable to breathe properly, it felt expansive. She softened her shoulders and stretched her arms out, and then placed them back at her sides. *Yes, Zaad said it exactly, I haven't wanted to date or to meet someone new. Matt has managed to burrow himself into my life. I haven't really let him into my heart, not yet anyway. He's lovely company, but is he the man that Zaad spoke of? The one who could love me the way I deserve?*

Zaad broke the train of her thoughts when he got out his notebook and leafed through his notes. He looked up at her and blushed, then said, 'I want to be sure I do this all in the right order.' Smiling, he put the notebook down then said, 'Now, choose your medicine stone.'

Marissa brought her awareness back into the room. 'Oh, yes, of course.' She sat up on her knees and found her medicine bundle from her belongings on Zaad's bed. She unwrapped her bundle, the two stones she had chosen from outside held no importance to her, they were just stones she had picked up randomly. But the black stone she picked up on the beach at Greystone's held more significance. Even though she had used it with Finn earlier, it didn't seem to hold any power, not like Zaad's medicine stone did. She picked it up and held it, and decided she wanted to use it. She gave it to Zaad.

Zaad turned the stone around in his hand and looked thoughtful. 'I have a problem with this work Marissa. We will work on your heart, but the notes say to work on your sacral chakra. What do you think we should do?'

Marissa thought for a moment. 'I suppose we could stick to the notes. I did lose my self-confidence and self-worth, that could be from the stomach area?'

Zaad got up and fished his phone out of his pocket. 'I can look it up on the internet. There's no signal here, hang on.' He went over to the window, 'It's a little better over here.'

He typed in his phone and while she was waiting, Marissa closed her eyes and brought her awareness into her body. She went into her heart and asked her heart if it wanted to be the focus of the work. She didn't get an answer. She brought her awareness lower into her stomach and asked if her stomach should be the focus of the work, but it felt wrong, it felt secondary to the heart work.

She opened her eyes. 'Zaad, I'm happy for you to work on my heart.'

Zaad was at the window shaking his phone, 'The internet keeps dropping off, I didn't get any information.' He turned towards her, 'Are you sure? I can do heart or stomach, it's up to you.'

'Heart please, I want to move on with my life,' said Marissa. Zaad came back to where she was sitting, he reached onto his bed and took his drum out.

'Okay, we'll work on your heart. Lie down, do you want a pillow?'

'Oh! Yes, please.'

Marissa made herself comfortable on the floor and Zaad started to drum. Marissa placed the black stone onto her heart. She closed her eyes and relaxed her body. She did feel safe. She imagined she was floating on a river, a white mist surrounded her; the river was flat and gentle and carried her downstream. Rushes were blowing in the breeze, the sky was cloudy and she let the beating of Zaad's drum relax her even further. Her heart felt softer, wider, bigger. It was a lovely feeling. She drifted off.

After a time, Zaad stopped drumming. She could feel him moving about close by, it was a little distracting. She tried to bring herself back to the images of the river, but it had faded. Zaad brushed against her arm as he worked, bringing her awareness back into the room more strongly. She lay there with her eyes closed softly, feeling her body against the ground, waiting for her next instruction.

'Take a few deep breaths now,' he said softly, 'in, out.'

She breathed in and out, and in, and out.

'Good, I'm nearly finished now.' Zaad knelt over her and blew into her heart, Marissa jumped. Her heart felt heavier all of a sudden, different, more weighty, solid. She opened her eyes and saw Zaad closing the chakra and balancing her other chakras the way that they were shown in class earlier. He smiled at her.

'Are you alright?'

'Yes, thank you. I felt that going in, whatever it was.'

Zaad nodded and kept working. When he was finished, he sat down again at her feet and drummed a little bit more. Then he put down the drum.

'You are healed now,' he said, 'The medicine woman told me to say that to you. She said that when we believe we're sick when we're well, it makes us sick. Believing that we are well is a difficult thing to do, but we all need to do it.' He smiled. 'I liked her, she was funny.'

Marissa stretched and sat up. She rubbed her face. 'You met my medicine woman? Which one?'

Zaad looked puzzled. 'There are more than one? This woman, she was very, very old, she wore a funny hat and a black cloak.'

'Ahh. My lady from Peru.'

'She was very wise, her heart glowed, and she was beautiful. She gave me a flower, a rose, for you. For your heart, that is what I blew into it.' Zaad scratched his head. 'She said she would see me again soon.' He smiled at her. 'Perhaps she is my medicine woman too!' Then he laughed. Marissa laughed with him, noticing how freely her breath was coming in and out of her lungs as she laughed and how much more relaxed she felt. She suddenly remembered the medicine stone. She felt about on the floor for it and found a small shard of it by her hand. She got up on her knees and looked for the rest of it, finding it in several pieces.

'Look Zaad! My medicine stone, it's broken!'

'Oh my goodness, yes! It has. I wonder what that means?'

'My heart feels so much better, so different.' Marissa looked at the pieces of stone in her hand, there was one that was bigger than the others, she turned it around in her hand. 'Oh my God. Zaad. Look.'

She held the stone out in her hand, he peered at it. 'HA!' he said, slapping his thigh. 'Well I never. I never saw anything like this! It is a miracle!'

Marissa laughed. 'I don't know about that, but it certainly is a sign that I will never forget.' She held the stone up to the window, the moonlight was shining in, the sun had set a long time ago. She rolled the new heart-shaped medicine stone between her index finger and thumb. 'Thank you.' She closed her eyes and called on her Peruvian Medicine Woman. She saw her in her mind's eye making the prayer position, she whispered, 'Thank you,' to her, too. *My heart is now healed. Well, it is, according to Zaad and my medicine woman. It certainly feels stronger, but it had only been a few minutes since the healing. I wonder if it will last?*

'What colour was the rose, Zaad? she asked.

'It was pink. And would you believe it's now 8:45? We have 15 minutes before the fire ceremony. I am sure you would like to wash up first? You've been crying.'

Marissa touched her cheek, it was indeed wet. She hadn't even realised.

'Yes, thank you. And thank you so much for the healing.'

She attempted to fold the stone back into her medicine bundle, but she forgot the way to bundle it so instead, she rolled it like she used to roll her swimming gear into her towel for school, stood up and put it on the bed. Then she put her arms around Zaad and hugged him hard. He smelled of musk and amber and something else she couldn't quite place her finger on. She pulled away to see his face at first puzzled, and then soft and smiling at her.

'Let us close this healing space now?' suggested Zaad.

'Oh yes! Of course, we need to do that. Well done for remembering!' Zaad blushed.

When they had finished Marissa said 'See you downstairs at the fire,' then she picked up her medicine bundle and ran out of the room.

There was lots of excitement downstairs. Marissa had washed her face and put on a jumper and coat, her alpaca scarf and hat, and had her drum and beater in her hands. She had given up trying to fold the medicine bundle and she carried her heart-shaped medicine stone in the pocket of her jeans.

It was dark outside, and difficult to see who was who. Séamus was standing around the back of the big stone house with Brigid, who had stayed on. There were two others there she didn't recognise, a man and a woman, and of course, the rest of her group. There was a large bonfire set in the fire pit, it was about 8 ft tall. Séamus was struggling with matches as the wind was quite strong and every time he seemed to light a match the wind blew it out. Terry was hopping from one foot to the other from the cold. He waved at Marissa from the other side of the bonfire, he was laughing and joking with Saoirse and Finn. Brigid finally offered Séamus a rolled-up newspaper and he managed to get that alight, and then he used it to light the bonfire. Once the fire started to take, he pulled out his drum and banged it three times very loudly to get the group's attention.

'How are yiz all doing? That was a big piece of work we did today. I will hear all about it tomorrow. Tonight, we celebrate. Gather a piece of wood from the forest floor and bring it back here, and we will hold ceremony.'

Everyone broke out and went over towards the trees. They seemed less ominous this evening, almost friendly and supportive. Marissa bent down beneath the branches and found a nice, thick stick on the ground, about the length of her forearm. She brought it back to the bonfire, which was beginning to burn nicely.

'Now. Yiz all did some good work today, but yiz all haven't released everything around that work. Scan your body, feel where you're still holding it, then use your intention and blow it out of your body and into the stick. Then when I call you to, in a short while, you can burn the stick on the fire and watch the colours as it lights up in flames.'

Marissa took a moment to tune into her body, her heart felt full. She suddenly wanted to see where Zaad was and realised he was right beside her, wearing a dark blue coat. It was difficult to see him as the night was so dark. He looked for her at the same time then turned and smiled at her, brushing his arm off her body as he lifted his stick to blow into it. She lifted hers and did the same thing. She felt a subtle shift and was filled with a sense of deep peacefulness.

Séamus's drumbeats were getting louder. He motioned to the others to get out their drums and beat them too. Marissa put her stick into her pocket, lifted her drum and beater and started drumming. Lub dub, lub dub, lub dub... *But no, this isn't the same beat, it isn't the heartbeat of the world. What is it?* The drumming was different, louder, she stopped thinking about it and let her beater show her what to do.

They were drumming in synchrony, the flames were licking the sides of the bonfire, rising high up into the sky where the stars were glistening and the sky was a big cosy fleece blanket that kept you warm on a freezing winter night. The group were warming up, the drumming was carrying the group, the smoke filtered over and above everyone and the heat and light dominated the space. They were moving, someone had started to sway, and soon the group were on one foot than the other, then they were moving in a circle around the flames, laughing, drumming, the reflection of the flames licking oranges and reds onto each other's faces, their cheeks hot from the fire. Marissa's hand was getting tired now, her arm too, but she ignored the feeling, when she focused on the beating she didn't notice it so much. She felt very present, and very happy.

Séamus beat his drum very loud, it sounded like the callback signal and everyone knew to stop. Everyone stopped moving too, and all that could be heard was the crackling of the sticks in the fire and the breeze against the trees. They stood like this for a moment or two, and then he spoke.

'Great Mother Earth, thank you for holding us so sweetly, for taking away our pain and embracing us like the mother we never had. We welcome you to our fire ceremony, and in honour of you, we beat our drum.' He beat his drum, everyone joined in, and there was an echo across the circle, and then it stopped and there was silence again.

'Great Father Sky, thank you for shining down upon us, for watching all that we do and who we are becoming. We welcome you to our fire ceremony, and in honour of you, we stamp our feet.' Everyone started stamping their feet, and then, once more, there was silence.

'We come to the fire to purify ourselves. That which we cannot transform can be transmuted by the heat of this beautiful flame. Thank you, Great Spirit of the Fire, for being here to heal us and show us the beauty way. We honour you by shouting into the wind.' He then made a noise, like a wolf's howl, which was gleefully echoed by everyone in the group.

When the noise had died down, Séamus spoke again.

'And now, we, your humble children, offer to the fire our pain, the pain of our childhoods, the pain of loneliness, the pain that comes with being alive in this world. We are of service to you, Great Spirit, and we endeavour to play our part, to do our work and to help others that wish to also honour you.' Séamus held his drum and beater with one hand and with the other, he took out a stick from the inside of his coat and held it up to the sky, then down to the earth. Then he stepped forward, closer to the fire, and he blew into the stick, and placed it into the fire. He scooped some of the smoke and the heat from the fire onto himself as if he was washing himself in it. When he was finished he took a step back, and, putting the beater back into his right hand, began to beat the drum softly. He spoke again.

'I invite you all, one at a time, to step forward and place your stick into the fire and use the heat of the fire to purify your energy field. One at a time, as you feel called.'

He continued to drum softly, the others didn't join in. Nobody moved. He beat the drum for a few minutes, and still, nobody moved. Terry was the first to step forward, he was across the way from Marissa and she could see his face through the flames. He looked serious and contemplative, he blew into his stick, which was quite small, and then placed it into the fire deftly, so as not to burn his fingers. He then mimicked Séamus by 'scooping' some of the heat and flame into his energy field. He closed his eyes and stood there for a minute or two, then he opened his eyes and stepped back into the main circle.

Zaad and Finn stepped forward next, and at the same time, but Finn took a step back and let Zaad have his turn first. Each of them blew into their sticks, placed their sticks into the bonfire, and then stayed for a few minutes, washing themselves with its heat, before stepping back. *How do I know when I've been called?* Then Stephanie took her turn, then Brigid.

Marissa felt as if someone pushed her from behind, she stepped forward, and it was her turn. She felt the hot flames licking up the bonfire, she wondered if her hair would be singed. She pulled her stick out from her pocket and blew more emotional pain into it, from a deeper part of herself. She closed her eyes and held the stick for a few moments, and then blew again, she was truly ready to let go of James, all the pain that he had brought to her, she didn't want to waste any more of her life dwelling upon it. She blew from her liver and her kidneys, she blew from her intestines and her stomach. She blew from her womb, and in that blowing, her eyes filled with tears at the loss of the children she imagined they would have together. She blew again, for the boy and the girl that would never be. She blew in once more, this time more gently for her heart, it was healing and she could feel it, and she resolved to never, ever, stop herself from feeling love because this one man, this one person, thought she was too much for him. She *was* too much for him, too bright, too strong… And he was afraid of her. And that was okay. She understood it now, he wasn't the one for her, she would find someone who would be her equal. Or perhaps he would find her. She blew into the stick one more time, and then put it into the fire.

She didn't feel rushed by anyone in the circle, it was as if they had all dissolved away and it was just her and the fire. She looked into the fire more deeply and imagined she saw lots of tiny dragons within it, and tribal peoples celebrating with fires of their own. She felt like she was looking into the fire and seeing all of the fire ceremonies, going back in time, the very first fire ceremony, all the way up to this one, right here. She felt a sudden joy, and she yelped and howled into the starry sky. It was echoed back by the group, her joy reflected in their howls, she did it again, and they did it again, and she felt free. She scooped some of the heat from the fire and washed herself, her aura, her energy field. She then said thank you to the fire, and bowed, and, for a moment, it felt like the fire bowed back to her. Then she stepped back to her place in the circle. The ceremony continued.

Marissa felt a little chilly back in her place, it was almost as if she had acclimatised to the heat of the flame and she suddenly missed it, even though it was only a few feet away from her. The rest of the group took their turn, none of them taking as long as she did. When they were all done Séamus changed the beat of the drum and encouraged everyone to join in, which they did. Then they all started howling again, and laughing, and dancing, and singing, and they stayed there, in that sacred timeless space, until the fire died down into itself and turned to ash.

CHAPTER FORTY ONE

At breakfast the following morning, Séamus beckoned to Marissa to come and sit with him. He didn't usually eat with them so it was unusual to see him there. She brought her porridge and tea and sat opposite him, wondering what it was about.

'Marissa, I haven't forgotten what you told me on Friday,' he said in a low tone of voice so the others wouldn't hear. He looked very serious. 'I'm concerned, but not worried. I'm going to give the others some work to do this morning so I can spend an hour or so with you.'

Marissa nodded her head. She suddenly didn't feel like eating. She had forgotten all about the dark energy, she was still revelling in the beauty of the fire from the night before. She felt good, her heart was full, and she had slept well. Séamus seemed to be calling the fear back in again, she wasn't sure if it was a good thing. *But what if it comes back when I go back home, maybe it's better to sort this out now, even though I don't feel like I want to.*

Séamus called a few of the others over to sit with him too. Terry's appearance was like a breath of fresh air. He brought a pot of honey to the table and offered it to Marissa for her porridge. She dipped a teaspoon into it and lifted it out, swirling the dense, sticky threads of golden honey around and around before bringing it to her bowl. She watched the honey as it oozed from the spoon onto the top of her cooling porridge as she wrestled with herself, wondering what Séamus had in mind.

'So,' said Séamus to the group, 'What did you think of the fire last night?'

'It was amazing, Séamus,' said Terry as he buttered his toast. He looked up and added, 'If all I had come for this weekend was the fire ceremony, it would have been worth it just for that. It was so powerful.'

Marissa dipped her honey-glazed spoon into her porridge and scooped some onto it. She took it out and looked at it for a moment, there was far too much honey for a mouthful, but she really should eat something. She put it in her mouth and relished the sweetness on her tongue, the warmth from the oats was comforting. She took another spoon.

'But the work we did yesterday was powerful too,' Terry continued, stirring milk into his tea. *He is always busy doing something.*

Séamus sat back in his chair, listening and observing, but a part of him seemed to be preoccupied with something else. *What is he going to do when we're alone?*

Marissa managed to eat half her usual amount of porridge in twice the time it normally took her. She really couldn't stomach any more. Liz and Stephanie had joined their table, but she couldn't tune into what they were talking about. It was as if some sort of fog had surrounded her, making everything outside of it fuzzy, out of focus. She put down the spoon and cradled her tea with her two hands but it had gone cold. She tried to snap herself out of it but found herself feeling incredibly heavy, and suddenly very, very tired.

'Do you want more tea, Marissa?' asked Terry.

'What? Oh. Yes. Yes, please, this one has gone cold.'

'I'll stick the kettle on again,' he said, turning maternal, and stood up, taking her mug and his over to the tea and coffee area. Finn and Saoirse were sitting together at another table, deep in conversation. Brigid and the others from the fire ceremony were not there. Marissa tried to wake up and clear her head but all she wanted to do was fold her arms in front of her and lay her head down on them, on the table, like she used to do in primary school.

Séamus's chair screeched on the floor as he pulled it back. He stood up and brought his breakfast plates to the sink to wash them. As soon as he left, Marissa felt the heaviness of the fog lifting. Terry came back with fresh tea and she felt herself waking up a little more. After the first few sips she felt more present.

'I don't know what just happened,' she leant into Terry as she spoke, 'I was wide awake before I sat down beside Séamus. He wants to do some work with me, just the two of us, this morning. I'm not sure how I feel about it.'

Terry listened attentively. 'I think you should do it. He's a great healer, he's obviously got something he wants to share with you. You can tell me all about it afterwards.' They sat with tea for a few minutes more. Within their silence grew a tension. Terry shrugged his shoulders, giggled, then asked, 'Why is this all always so serious?' He stood up and brushed his fringe out of his eyes. 'I'm done with breakfast. See you in the main room later.'

Marissa nodded. Finn and Saoirse were gathering up their things to go in while Liz, Jenny, Stephanie, and Zaad were still deep in conversation. She gathered up her breakfast things and went to the sink, scraping the rest of her porridge into the bin.

The main room was cold. Séamus was waiting for them all to arrive, pacing back and forth. He looked like he was trying to work something out. Marissa sat on the sofa she liked best, grabbed a faded yellow cushion and hugged it to herself. She had left her medicine bundle, which was more like a roll, upstairs on her bed. She was feeling heavy and slow again, and ridiculously tired. When everyone else was seated Séamus sat and faced the group.

'So, yiz had your first fire ceremony last night! How did you like it?'

'Oh! It was brilliant,' said Liz. 'It wasn't my first, actually, but it was the most powerful one I've been to.'

'It was very powerful, yes,' added Stephanie. 'I *really* enjoyed it. Thank you.'

'Yeah, thank you, Séamus,' said Terry. 'The drumming was amazing. We went to another dimension!'

'Ahh yiz did for sure, yiz went to another dimension. Hah! That's it exactly. And how did yiz go with the work I set yesterday? Did yiz get it all done? Anyone want to share?'

They spent a good half-hour talking about their experiences from the day before. Everyone had a profound experience of some sort. While they were talking, Marissa's concentration was fading in and out. She gave in to it and closed her eyes, and travelled inwards.

Marissa was at the lake. It was daytime. She felt heavy here, too, like she had been dragged backwards through a mountain of sludge. She raised her arms and looked at them, they were covered in something heavy and muddy, she decided to go into the water and wash it all off. She stood at the water's edge then felt like she needed to ask permission before getting in. She didn't want to pollute the lake with this sludge if it was the wrong thing to do.

There was a rushing noise as the sea serpent rose up from the depths of the lake, it seemed quite far away. It looked at her and saw her predicament then swam towards her until it was almost right beside her. Marissa wasn't scared, it was so close, for the first time she could see each scale on the sea serpent's neck – each one well defined with a dark blue edging, the scales themselves almost translucent, shimmering in shades of green and turquoise under the sunlight. The sea serpent opened its mouth and she felt its hot breath spewing forth. A thick, yellow, acrid liquid shot out of its mouth and splashed all over Marissa.

'It's spitting on me!' The thick yellow liquid, as well as the heavy mud, weighed her body down even further. She felt a tingling along her arms and up and down her spine. The spittle was moving, as she watched it, it circled and scrubbed, working on the heavy muddy substance that had been weighing her down, dissolving it away. The serpent nodded at her and looked at the water. She could now enter.

She walked into the lake and as soon as the waters touched her, she felt relief. Everything fizzled away and was transformed. Her body on the sofa in Clifden relaxed, and here, by the lakeside, she felt lighter. She sank her whole body into the water until she was totally submerged and clean. She sank in deeper and felt protected, held, and a huge sense of peace. She opened her eyes, she could breathe under here, she had gills in her neck and she wasn't afraid. She felt something in the room pulling her back so she allowed the images to dissolve, and she came back into the room.

Marissa opened her eyes and for the first time since breakfast, she felt clear. Séamus was chatting with Jenny and he suddenly turned and looked at Marissa. His eyes widened for a moment, then he turned away and continued his conversation. Marissa wasn't sure what was going on but she thought she felt his approval. *Or is he surprised with me? Was this some kind of test?* Séamus finished talking with Jenny and then turned to address the group.

'Now, lads. We finish today at three, so yiz have time to scarper home for the Sunday night's roast dinner. Work smart, as it's already ten o'clock. Jenny, Stephanie and Finn, yiz are to work together.' They nodded.

'Saoirse, you're with Terry, Liz, you're with Zaad. In the case of the three, yiz will figure it out. Do another medicine stone healing and be back here by noon.' They all looked at Marissa and back to Séamus, but he said nothing. 'Off yiz go now, you've a lot of work to do.'

As usual, Terry was the first one to move. He nodded to Marissa, crossed his fingers and held them behind his back so she could see them as he as he left the room. The others followed him out the door to get their medicine things and do the work that Séamus had prescribed.

Marissa stayed, hugging the pale yellow pillow tightly to her chest. It was just the two of them now. She felt waves of anxiety coming in but she pressed herself into the sofa to steady herself. *Medicine women, please come and support me, Haniel? Can you come in too? And beautiful Bear, please come and support me. I don't know what Séamus is going to do with me and I feel I need your help.*

Séamus came over and nodded approvingly. 'Ahh, you brought your guides with you. Good. Now, this demon of yours, I hope he isn't going to give us too much trouble.'

'Demon?'

'You know exactly what I'm talking about.' Séamus sat on the sofa beside her. 'You have some powerful allies, Marissa, I can sense it from ya. Which is a good thing, a very good thing. I want to make sure that you're properly protected. I can't have ya running around all over town being plagued and perplexed by some demon fella tryin to have his way with ya.' Séamus laughed.

Demon? Oh my God. Marissa got a cold shiver down her spine. She tried to hide it but her body shivered involuntarily. She knew it felt right, that's exactly what it was, but she also felt vulnerable and exposed in front of Séamus.

'That's right, girl, I can see right into you, and this demon fella, he can see you too. It's important we sort this – especially as he knows your name. You've got a strength in you, you have lots to learn, but you're strong. With focus and determination, you will overcome it.'

Marissa turned her body so she was facing him, it helped if she could see him. Séamus looked at her with an open face, he held no animosity towards her, he seemed soft, gentle, understanding. She wondered why she felt on guard. *Am I just being silly? He doesn't want to hurt me.* She relaxed a little.

'Good. Now. I need to think. I didn't get an answer directly, I want to know what it is we need to know now, so that you will be safe.'

He closed his eyes and started to hum a tune, his fingers tapped it out on his leg, as if he was tapping on his drum. Marissa didn't move a muscle, she stayed very still. He seemed to be going on a journey.

One of the kitchen staff came in to set the fire for later. She was a slim, young girl with brown hair scraped back in a pony tail. She bustled around, sweeping out the old ashes and rolling up bits of newspaper and firelighters. The acrid chemical smell of the firelighter filled the room briefly. Séamus still had his eyes closed. The girl left quietly so as to not disturb them. Marissa's eyes started flickering and her body started swaying to the humming, she couldn't help herself, but she held her focus in the room and kept her eyes on Séamus.

After a few more minutes, Séamus opened his eyes.

'You have been seen, but he cannot find a way inside, so you are not as vulnerable as he expected. He's not happy about that. You did some good healing work this weekend, that should keep you safe for a while. And the warding I taught you, very important. Don't forget it. However, there's something that we're missing, something you need... I can't seem to put my finger on it. So it won't be today. But I know it will come to me, and as soon as it does, I'll contact you.'

He closed his eyes again as if in deep thought, then he opened his eyes and snapped back into the room. 'I'll do some work on you now, if you'll let me?'

Marissa really didn't want him to but she found herself nodding her head. Séamus stood up and said, 'Good. Now, lie down on the sofa, right here. There, that's it.'

Marissa lay down, putting the yellow pillow under her head. Séamus got one of the throws and put it over her, she felt safer feeling the weight of it. He lifted his rattle out from his duffle bag and started rattling. She closed her eyes. After a moment or two she could smell sage burning, she tried to relax her body a little more but she felt anxiety building up again. Séamus put his hand on the top of her head and Marissa had a full-body shiver. As she shook, in her mind's eye, her whole body turned into a snake, from her head to her feet.

Wriggling on the sofa, she called out to Archangel Michael in her mind. She felt his strong, soothing presence stepping in, and she stopped shaking. At the same time, Séamus pulled back from her suddenly, as if he received an electric shock. After a moment, he started rattling again but Marissa kept her eyes open this time. She wasn't enjoying this healing, she wanted it to stop now. He kept going, however, and she began to get very uncomfortable and agitated.

What should I do? Do I tell him to stop? Or is he actually helping me and I just don't like how this is feeling? Stop now, Stop now, Please stop. Archangel Michael, please help me? What should I do? She felt a 'No' all through her body. She took that as a sign that she had to stop the healing. But the heaviness was back, it felt like someone, or something, had placed its large foot on her chest, she couldn't move, couldn't breathe. She opened her eyes. Séamus was at the other end of the sofa. *It wasn't him. What was it?* She tried to speak but she couldn't. And then, just as quickly as it arrived, the pressing feeling was released, and she could breathe again.

Séamus stopped rattling and turned to her. 'How are you doing?'

Marissa pulled herself up and rubbed her eyes, and her head. She felt strange, still wobbly, she didn't know what had happened to her, at all.

'I… I don't know,' she said. 'What was that? That healing you did for me?'

'Ahh. It was to help empower you, to keep you strong, to fortify the weakness in your energy field.'

Every fibre of her being told her that this was not the case. But was she right? Or was her teacher, Séamus, right? *How do I know what's right?*

She decided she needed to leave. She couldn't spend a moment longer in the room alone with him. 'I have to go to the toilet,' she heard herself saying. 'Is it okay if I go now?'

He came over to her and smiled. 'Of course. I've finished now, anyway, and there's nothing more I can do today. I hope this helps. That fecker knew your name, I don't like that one bit. What I did for you, it should keep him away for the moment. And I will be in touch, I promise.'

Marissa was conflicted. 'What did you do?'

Séamus cocked his head to one side. 'Well, when you come back to me and do the Advanced Medicine Training, I'll be able to show you how to do it. But for now, all you need to know is that you're safe. I'm glad we had this time together. And I'm very glad you told me what happened. You're an amazing lady Marissa, and you're a fabulous healer. You're on the right path, I know you're going to be spectacular.'

Marissa blushed, she really didn't know what to say in answer to that. She took the cover off and felt the cold chill of the room press itself into her body. She stood up, thanked him and went upstairs directly to her room. He seemed surprised that she ran off, he looked like he wanted more acknowledgement, more thanks, perhaps even a hug.

When she got to her bedroom she went straight to the sink and looked at her face in the mirror. She didn't have to go to the bathroom, she just needed to get away from him, from that room. *What did he do to me?* Her face looked the same, she peered into the mirror, closer, yes it *was* her.

She sat on her bed and spoke out loud. 'Archangel Michael? Are you there? I know you're there. What did he do to me? He said it was a healing, but I'm not sure. I have to give him the benefit of the doubt, sure why would he want to hurt me? I must be going crazy to be thinking this way. I'll put it out of my mind now and go join the others.'

She found her phone and saw that it was almost noon. She texted Matt: I miss you, home tonight, can't wait to see you xx'

She lay down on her bed and fell into a deep sleep.

The next thing she knew, Saoirse was shaking her gently. 'Are you okay Marissa?'

Everything blurred into focus. 'Yes, yes I'm ok. I must have fallen asleep. I was so tired. What time is it?'

'We were wondering why you didn't come down for lunch. I came up to find you. There's still time, do you want some food?'

Marissa was suddenly ravenous and awake. 'Thank you, yes, I do.'

She got up slowly, went to the sink again, washed her face and brushed back her hair.

'What happened? We were all wondering – you were alone with Séamus, are you okay?'

Marissa smiled. 'Yes, I'm okay, he wanted to talk to me about what I said on Friday evening, about the dark energy.' Something in her couldn't bring herself to say the word demon. 'I guess he was checking me to make sure I was safe, he said he was fortifying my vulnerabilities, whatever that means.'

'Okay, great, glad you're okay. Come on, it's shepherd's pie, you don't want Finn to finish it all!'

The two girls went down to the dining room. Marissa helped herself to a large plate of shepherd's pie and joined the others.

'So? How did you get on?' asked Terry from across the table. He examined her with his eyes and she could feel his concern.

'I'm okay, though I don't really know what happened,' said Marissa, between mouthfuls. 'He said he was helping me get stronger. I went upstairs after and just fell asleep on the bed.'

'You must have needed it,' said Jenny. 'Sometimes I get so tired after a healing. Séamus is the best healer. I've been to see him three times already, he's such an amazing person. He told me I was fabulous! And that I'd be a spectacular healer one day.' She giggled with delight.

Marissa felt a flash of something inside of her when Jenny said that. She didn't want to let her know that he told her the exact same thing. *This gets curiouser and curiouser.*

They finished up their meals and went upstairs to pack away their things. They needed to vacate the rooms so the house staff could turn them around for the next set of visitors. Marissa checked her phone and saw a text from Matt.

> Thanks love, can't wait 2 see u but can't tonight, I've a family thing. C u Monday? Dinner & movie @ mine?

Marissa's heart fell. She wanted to throw her arms around Matt as soon as she could and hold him tight. She realised she was beginning to anchor into him, even though Zaad had said perhaps he wasn't the one for her. Or was he the one for her? She wasn't sure of anything anymore. Either way, she was disappointed she wasn't going to see him tonight, and that was a good thing, wasn't it?

The group assembled downstairs in the main hall. The room was still a little chilly, but they would only be there another hour or so. Séamus looked authoritative as he stood at the top of the room, holding court.

'Now. Yiz have all done great work, amazing work from what you've told me. This weekend was a big weekend, putting together many pieces. Well done, all of you. Yiz are really on the path now.' He kicked his heels together and did a little jump as he shouted out 'yee-haw!' and they all laughed. He laughed too, and Marissa laughed.

He winked at Marissa and she suddenly felt that all was clear between them, she didn't owe him anything. Perhaps it was all really okay, she was just a little paranoid. They laughed together and it felt good. She must have been going crazy earlier, it did feel good, it felt right and proper, and all *was* well. She relaxed. Her stomach was full, the food was good, she loved her new friends, and she would see Matt tomorrow. The group were still laughing together and it seemed to clear some tension. She looked at them all and felt nothing but love, even for Séamus.

'Right, folks, please,' he said, calling them all back to order. 'I cannot let yiz go without setting some homework.'

There was a groan from the group and then more laughter. 'Take out your notebooks, yiz will need to write this down. We begin with the third verse of our medicine prayer.' Séamus recited:

> *Great Spirit of the South, spirit of growth and compassion,*
> *fertility and warmth. We come to you to you to support*
> *us as we shed our skins and leave the old controlling ways*
> *behind. Unwind from us what is no longer needed and*
> *teach us the way of compassion and beauty, so we can walk*
> *softly and leave no footprints.*

'Now. I expect yiz all to know this prayer by heart, the whole thing, next time we meet in six weeks' time. Six weeks brings us to the end of March. We will do the work of shedding our skin in earnest, but we have already begun it.'

'Yiz have done the work of two medicine stones this weekend, I want yiz to organise to meet each other and do the final medicine stone, preferably with someone you haven't worked with before.' He looked over at Marissa 'Marissa, you will need to catch up, so you'll need to do two stones during this time.'

Marissa nodded.

'For the next time we meet, I want you to bring three more stones with you, three stones that mean something to you, nice bright colourful ones. We will work with them together in the next workshop.'

Séamus looked at the group. 'Your medicine bundles are a disgrace,' he said, laughing. 'I need to teach you how to fold them, again. Everyone get your bundles out and open them up. Yiz can video me, and I'll do a demo.'

Because they had packed and brought their stuff downstairs to free up the rooms, most of them had their phones handier than they had their medicine bundles. Terry and Jenny went up to the top of the room and videoed Séamus from the top, while the rest of them did it from their seats. They all promised to send the videos to each other. Everyone found, re-folded and tied up their bundles and Séamus inspected them all, he opened and re-folded a few of them, once he was happy they all sat down again.

'Now. There's more work yiz need to do before next time. I want an essay on what it means to be a shaman. In your own words. Personal, like. I don't want research or quoting from books. I want to know what it means to be one, and what it means to you. How are you going to live up to your own expectations of yourself? And how are you going to walk in the world? And what do you need to shed from yourself in order to do this? Got it?'

'One last thing – The process we did here this weekend, I want you to do with three people that are not in this group. Guinea pigs, so to speak. Without the medicine stone part. So you're gonna set intention with them to release emotional pain, ask them what they want to release first, do a body mapping, clear their chakras, close the chakras and balance them, then fill them with light and seal up the energy field. And I want it all written up. You must send me three client session reports and your essay. I'll send you a reminder as I want the work at least two weeks before our next meeting.'

Everyone was writing furiously. It seemed like too much to do.

'So yiz are all confident you have the process of the healing work? Go to friends or family for this, and yiz are not qualified to charge anyone. Make sure yiz open a healing space, do the work to the best of your ability, and don't forget to close the space when you're done. Very important. Any questions?'

For the first time since they all got together, there were no questions.

'Good. Let's close this healing space now, together.'

In Terry's car on the way to Galway, Marissa played back the events of that morning in her mind. Terry kept his eyes on the road, it was quite windy and rainy and difficult to see. She was comfortable enough in his company to not feel like she had to fill the silence between them, and he hadn't brought up the healing, which suited her just fine. The weekend seemed to come to a close very rapidly. Marissa felt like there was something unfinished about it, perhaps it was because she didn't complete the work that the others had done to get their second medicine stone. They had all hugged each other goodbye and promised to meet up as a group over the next few weeks. Marissa appreciated the contact. When Finn had held her strongly, it seemed to bring her back to earth a little more.

As they drove into Galway town, Terry pulled the car over into the bus lane and turned on his hazard lights. He turned to her. 'Are you sure you're okay?' he asked with concern in his voice. Marissa smiled. Her heart softened again towards him.

'It's been an emotional weekend, but yeah, I'm okay. Thanks, Terry.'

Terry turned back to the steering wheel and indicated, then he pulled back out into the traffic. When they got to the train station, Terry pulled into the set-down area. He got out and opened the boot, Marissa took out her backpack and her drum. He gave her a hug. 'What time is your train?'

'I think there's one in 20 minutes. I'll be fine. Hey, thanks for the lift.'

'I'm so glad I met you,' he said, giving her a strong hug.

'Me too. Send me that video of Séamus?'

'I'll do it when I get Wi-Fi at home.'

'Thanks. Drive safe.' As an afterthought, Marissa added, 'Hey Terry?'

'Yeah?'

'Will you come visit me? I mean, not to do the homework, but just to visit? You can stay over in my place if you like. My sofa is very comfortable, so I've been told.'

Terry smiled. 'I would love that. Yes, defo.'

CHAPTER FORTY TWO

The train ride home was uneventful. Marissa put on her headphones and listened to music while doodling in her notebook. She was trying to start the essay but she wasn't able to focus. She just thought about seeing Matt and Tobermory and how good a hot Epsom salt bath would feel when she got home. She realised she hadn't heard from her parents at all that weekend so she sent them a text saying she had been away on a personal development weekend and she'd pop in to see them during the week. Her Dad sent her a thumbs up emoji, which wasn't like him. *Maybe he's been hanging out with Amanda?*

She let herself into her apartment a few hours later, dumped her backpack on the floor and put her drum away. She turned on the immersion for her bath and stuck on the kettle. Michelle had taken good care of Tobermory, his litter tray was fresh, she found him sleeping on the bed. He jumped up in fright to see her, arched his back and started meowing at her as if she was a stranger.

'Hey lovely cat, it's only me, it's okay.'

Marissa reached out to pet him, but he jumped away from her and ran to the back door, scratching it and mewing to get out. She went over and opened it and he shot out into the garden and was gone. *Very weird.* She unlocked the cat-flap for him for when he was ready to come back.

Marissa gathered some things in the kitchen to make a pasta dinner, and she organised her clothes for work for the following day. *I was away for a weekend and it felt like 2 weeks, and now I'm back to mundane reality.*

After her dinner, she ran the bath and got in. It felt good. She soaked in the tub for a long time, allowing the salts to get deep inside her muscles and bones. Tobermory still hadn't returned, but she wasn't worried. *Possibly Michelle had been too afraid to let him out, and now he's stir crazy. He'd be back in his own time.*

She got out of the bath and rubbed herself dry, and checked her phone once more. Matt hadn't texted. *Ahh, yes, he's at a family thing.* She did miss him. She put on her pyjamas, hung up her wet towel, locked the back door and switched off the lights. She set her alarm and got into bed, it felt good to lie down, she was exhausted. It was 10pm already. *Where did the day go?* She slept.

She was waiting in a hallway beside an office, she had an appointment. She was in a university? There were cobblestones on the ground, the hallway was part of an atrium. She had seen this place somewhere before on television, or she had been here before, it felt familiar. She kicked her legs like a child as she sat in the incredibly large chair, waiting to be summoned. Her white socks were pulled up to her knees and she wore black patent shoes, a green and black chequered skirt and a white shirt. 'Am I wearing a school uniform?'

A clipboard and two textbooks rested in her lap, but she couldn't read the subject of the textbooks. They felt heavy, like the chemistry ones from school. 'That's it, I must be at school, but it's not any school I've been to in this lifetime.'

A door opened and a young man came out of the office with his head down, he was crying. As he walked past, Marissa saw that he had a small red tail swinging from his behind, it ended in a forked point, like a devils tail. She got a fright and looked again, but it was gone.

Her name was called and she climbed down from the chair. She stood at the door of the office, it was dark wood with a smoky glass window which had writing on it. 'No, that's not writing...' She looked at it again. It was a symbol made of triangles and circles... It seemed familiar, but Marissa wasn't sure. She peered closer at it, it started to spin very slowly of its own accord. It was drawing her in.

'Come in, come in,' beckoned a smooth voice, thick, like honey, snapping her out of a trance. She pulled herself away from the symbol, opened the door and entered the room.

In front of the desk stood a man in his forties. He was sharply dressed in a well-cut, expensive-looking, dark blue suit. His face was beautiful, clean-shaven, he looked like a movie star but Marissa wasn't sure which one. She was sure she had seen him before somewhere. He had short, light brown hair, blue eyes, and his smile was, well, hypnotising. He offered her a chair and she sat down without thinking. He walked around the desk and sat in the chair opposite her.

'So here we are, together at last,' said the man, peering at Marissa from across the table.

'Yes,' replied Marissa, wondering how she knew him. She couldn't take her eyes off of him, he was magnetic, drawing her in. She found herself wanting to touch him, stroke his cheek, press herself against him. She caught this and wondered why? This wasn't like her at all.

'Now I know where you live, and how to find you,' he said, leaning in towards her.

Marissa was still gazing at his face, it started to change, becoming darker, rippling somehow, his eyes were changing too, there was a fire burning within. Suddenly she recognised those eyes... A flash of terror and panic struck her but once again, she couldn't move.

'Yes, you remember me now. Good. I couldn't keep away from you for very long,' he said and started to laugh. His laugh echoed loudly around her, his face distorted and his eyes turned into pure fire, strong fire burning deeply and she could feel how powerful he was.

'What do you want from me?' whispered Marissa, trying to get up to leave but finding herself trapped in the chair, paralysed, unable to release herself.

'Why, your allegiance of course,' he said, still laughing, his mouth wide open, the flames now burning through his throat as well, his face shimmering, his head enlarging and reaching over to her across the table as if he was about to consume her...

Marissa pulled herself out of the dream with all of her might, she had to get out of there. She awoke breathless in her bed, shaking and covered in sweat. It was pitch dark in her room, she had trouble waking up, she felt caught halfway between the dream reality and this reality. She tried to pull herself more into the room but her bedroom didn't feel right. *Am I still dreaming?*

She felt a strong presence there, right there, in the room with her. Was there someone standing at the bottom of her bed, looking at her? She was terrified now, her heart was beating very fast, she went to reach for the light, but it was too far away. She felt that crushing sensation on her chest again, holding her down. She was pinned, totally at his mercy. She heard his voice inside her head.

'Yes, Marissa. I know your name. I know where you live. And how to find you. I can come and get you, any time I want.' He started to laugh again.

Marissa wanted to scream but her voice was gone. The pressing on her chest stopped for a moment, she moved quickly, managed to find the light switch and turned it on. The room was empty, but his presence, the feeling of him, remained.

Read more about Marissa in
Inner Compass. Book 2 – Transformation.

ALSO BY ABBY WYNNE

BOOKS

The Inner Compass Trilogy
The One Day at a Time Diary
Planting the Seeds
Heal your Inner Wounds
How to Be Well
The Book of Healing Affirmations
Energy Healing Made Easy
A–Z of Spiritual Colouring Affirmations
Spiritual Tips for Enlightenment
Energy Healing for Everyone

SELF-PACED HEALING PROGRAMMES

Heal your Inner Child
Heal your Inner Teenager
Creating Good, Strong, Energetic Boundaries
5 Days to Raise your Vibration
Rise Above Anxiety and Fear
High Frequency Lightworker Healing Intensive
How to Be Well Part 1 (based on the book How to Be Well)
The Anxiety Playbook
Programmes are added on a regular basis.
Visit www.abbysonlineacademy.com to find out more.

ABOUT THE AUTHOR

Abby Wynne is a bestselling author and healer living in Ireland. She blends Shamanism, Psychotherapy and Energy Healing to create a unique way of working which she shares with the world through her many offerings. You can join Abby for a live or self-paced healing programme, take part in one of her live group monthly healing sessions, or join her healing circle. Visit her websites www.abby-wynne.com and www.abbysonlineacademy.com

Printed in Great Britain
by Amazon